PENGUIN CLASSICS

THE DEVIL AND DANIEL WEBSTER
AND OTHER WRITINGS

Stephen Vincent Benét was born in Bethlehem, Pennsylvania, in 1898 into a military family. As a result he moved around the United States during his early life, absorbing the culture and geography of such diverse places as Watervliet, New York, Benicia, California, and Augusta, Georgia. These, as well as his immense propensity for reading and his father's avid interest in literature, turned him at an early age into a writer. By his first year as a student at Yale University he had a volume of poetry published, and his work continued to appear at frequent intervals from then on until his death in 1943.

His first great success came in 1928 with the publication of *John Brown's Body*, a long narrative poem about the Civil War, for which he was awarded his first Pulitzer Prize in 1929. He would be posthumously awarded a second in 1944 for another long narrative, *Western Star*. If ever there has been an American man of letters, Benét was one, publishing numerous volumes of poetry, novels, screenplays, radio dramas, literary criticism, and short stories, of which "The Devil and Daniel Webster" is probably the most famous. His early death was partly caused by his overwork writing propaganda for the Allied cause during World War II. Benét was a remarkable stylist whose work goes far beyond the merely popular as it captures much of the culture and customs of the United States.

Townsend Ludington is Boshamer Distinguished Professor of English and American Studies at the University of North Carolina at Chapel Hill, where he directs the American Studies Curriculum. He has edited *The Fourteenth Chronicle: Letters and Diaries of John Dos Passos* and has written biographies of Dos Passos and the American artist Marsden Hartley, in addition to numerous other pieces about American writers and their culture.

Stephen Vincent Benét

THE DEVIL AND DANIEL WEBSTER

AND OTHER WRITINGS

Stephen Vincent Benét

EDITED WITH AN INTRODUCTION
BY TOWNSEND LUDINGTON

PENGUIN BOOKS

PENGUIN BOOKS
Published by the Penguin Group
Penguin Putnam Inc., 375 Hudson Street,
New York, New York 10014, U.S.A.
Penguin Books Ltd, 27 Wrights Lane, London W8 5TZ, England
Penguin Books Australia Ltd, Ringwood, Victoria, Australia
Penguin Books Canada Ltd, 10 Alcorn Avenue,
Toronto, Ontario, Canada M4V 3B2
Penguin Books (N.Z.) Ltd, 182–190 Wairau Road,
Auckland 10, New Zealand

Penguin Books Ltd, Registered Offices:
Harmondsworth, Middlesex, England

First published in Penguin Books 1999

1 3 5 7 9 10 8 6 4 2

LIBRARY OF CONGRESS CATALOGING IN PUBLICATION DATA
Benet, Stephen Vincent, 1898–1943.
The devil and Daniel Webster and other writings / Stephen
Vincent Benet; edited with an introduction by
Townsend Ludington.
p. cm.—(Penguin classics)
Includes bibliographical references.
ISBN 0 14 04.3740 1
I. Ludington, Townsend, 1936– II. Title. III. Title: Devil and
Daniel Webster IV. Series.
PS3503.E5325 A6 1999
818'.5209—dc21   99–29999

Printed in the United States of America
Set in Stemple Garamond

CONTENTS

INTRODUCTION

I

In an introduction to *John Brown's Body*, Stephen Vincent Benét's long narrative poem about the Civil War, the noted American historian Douglas Southhall Freeman declared that "No American poem of this century aroused enthusiasm to the same pitch among readers so diverse in their interest. There was pride in Benét's achievement and, for some, like pride in the discovery that the nation's history contained a chapter that had exalted, gripping epic quality." Published in 1949, Freeman's appraisal conveyed the high regard Americans have had for Benét, not only for the long narrative published in 1928 but for much of his other work that includes poetry, short fiction, novels, screenplays, and radio dramas. He was thought to be every bit the equal of Ernest Hemingway and F. Scott Fitzgerald as a writer—some would have said their superior. Before Benét died in March 1943 of a massive heart attack at the age of forty-four, he had earned a Guggenheim fellowship, been elected to the prestigious American Academy of Arts and Letters, served on numerous committees having to do with arts and letters, and won the first of two Pulitzer Prizes in 1929 for *John Brown's Body*. The second Pulitzer Prize was posthumously awarded in 1944 for another narrative poem, *Western Star*, published in July 1943. When he died, Franklin Roosevelt asserted that "The world of letters has lost one of its most commanding figures." The following year a Liberty ship was named in his honor. In 1998 the U.S. Postal Service issued a commemorative stamp to mark the centennial of his birth. Much lauded during his lifetime, Benét's works have a permanent place in the American literary canon, even if they have never fitted into a high modernist mold.

Not long before he died he wrote the poem "Little Testament," which begins, "I have lived. I have thought and labored, I have loved and possessed my love." It concludes, "Now the mind rusts into madness, the horses run without bit, the paltry body is nothing but mechanics of bone and skin." His love was Rosemary Carr, whom he adored practically from the moment he met her in Paris in November 1920. They were married a year later and until his death exhibited a remarkable devotion to each other: "This nothing spoke for its kin and loved one woman completely," he wrote in "Little Testament." "This is the end of Everything for me—More than for him—for he will live in his writing. Oh my darling. I cannot face it," she wrote in his diary the day he died. She lived for two decades more and had a considerable literary reputation of her own, but the void she felt that day was never filled by anyone else.

His mind did not "rust into madness" nor did "the horses run without bit," but he had every right to think so. He was plagued throughout his life with rheumatoid arthritis so severe that in later life, his "paltry body" was bent like that of a much older man. However tough and disciplined his mind, his body betrayed him and drove him down repeatedly. Fatigue from his work on behalf of the United States Office of War Information during the early stages of World War II played a considerable part in his death; he simply could not maintain the pace of writing he set for himself to support America's efforts in the war.

During his life Benét was a happy man, although he knew physical and emotional pain. He had a wry sense of humor that helped him to withstand most of the darkest moments, and he was loving and kind because he knew great love and kindness from others. Edward Weismiller, a poet who in 1936 won the annual poetry prize awarded by the Yale Series of Younger Poets, which Benét edited from 1933 until his death, recalled him as,

> a round man, with round glasses on a round face with round cheeks. He smoked nonstop, without ever taking his cigarette out of his mouth. The cigarettes were held precisely at the center of his pursed lips and bobbed as Benét spoke around them, the ash dribbling down the vest of his three piece suit. He smiled a lot, and it seemed to me that everything he said in his kind way was incredibly wise.

It is little wonder that Rosemary Carr, who was working in Paris for the *Chicago Tribune* when they met in November 1920, soon fell in love with him, although the day after she met him she wrote her mother about Benét, "a poet, real genius, it seems. You should see him! Plain, large, bites his finger nails, but is too smart for words." He smiled a lot from the first and conveyed his love for her through his talents as a poet. He peppered her with notes almost daily and bemoaned even the shortest separation: "you have no idea what silly things may happen to me from not seeing you for 2 1/2 days," he wrote to her on February 19, 1921. They had lunch together the next day, apparently, then perhaps again on the twenty-second, but by the twenty-fourth he was missing her terribly and wrote again, sending a poem as well. Three days later Rosemary wrote her mother, sending her "Steve's poems about me." "Steve," she explained, "simply writes poetry about what is nearest to him—and we have seen a lot of each other this winter and are the best of friends." To say the least; they became engaged less than a month later. "He is an extremely charming person in lots of way[s]," she added, "as sweet in nature as he is unattractive outwardly." She enclosed seven poems that she had carefully copied, including "Difference," "A Nonsense Song," and "To Rosemary, On the Methods by Which She Might Become an Angel."

He understood himself well and had the good fortune to be genuinely modest. When John Farrar, his close friend and the publisher of *John Brown's Body*, cabled him in March 1928 about returning to the United States in conjunction with the appearance of the volume, Benét immediately wrote back to thank him for the proposal but declined, saying:

> I don't think my physical presence in America would do any good. There are some people whose personalities can arouse interest in their work. I am not one of them. My work is the best of me, and I would rather lie behind it, as perdu as possible. And experience has taught me that this is the best course I can follow. Writing should speak for itself—if it cannot, it is lost. And as for me—I am not even a foreign author. I do not speak Czechoslovakian, I never was bitten by a lion or caught a strange species of tortoise while flying over the North Pole. . . . You can't do much to me except to raise the remark "I didn't know he'd been away."

II

A quick glance at the requests received each year by Brandt and Brandt, the agents for Benét's literary estate, seeking permission to republish one or another of his works should disabuse anyone of the idea that Benét is a forgotten writer, an author of period pieces which have little place as serious works in an era of high modernism. Excerpts from *John Brown's Body*; short stories such as "The Devil and Daniel Webster" and others in the mode of folk tales and legends; poems such as "The Ballad of William Sycamore" or "American Names"; any number of the poems in *A Book of Americans*; and poems such as "Litany for Dictatorships" and his "Nightmare" pieces are consistently reprinted, proof of the interest in the variety of tone and subject matter of Benét's Americana. *A Book of Ameri-*

cans may be lighthearted, but not so the pieces he wrote from the mid-1930s on as he watched dictatorships prosper in Europe and elsewhere.

Benét's work is unusually public; it is wide-ranging, popular, and topical without being superficial. A patriotic New Deal liberal who fervently supported Franklin Roosevelt, Benét could write a poem about the presidential election of 1940 and at about the same time write in an elegiac tone about freedom: "If this should change, remember the tree and the brook,/ The long day's summer, the voices clever and kind,/ The true verse that burned on the page of the book,/ The true love, body and mind. . . . These things were freedom. That is why they were good./ Remember that." In the poem, "If This Should Change," published in *The New Yorker* in June 1941, Benét with quick, broad strokes gathered an array of images—"Huge flowing Mississippi, under full moon,/ The giant landscape where the rivers crawl/ And the shabby apartment and the last year's tune . . ."—which are part of what we know to be freedom. The poem is direct and exhortatory, having an immediacy which gives it power.

That Benét wrote such poetry was no accident. He and his two older siblings, the writers Laura and William Rose Benét, benefitted from their parents' love of literature. James Walker Benét, their father, was a career army ordnance officer as interested in prose and poetry as in his profession. After Stephen's birth, Colonel Benét was in charge of one or another government arsenal, in which capacity he and his family moved from Bethlehem, Pennsylvania, to Buffalo and then to Watervliet, New York, to Benicia, California, and to Augusta, Georgia, by the time Stephen entered Yale University in September 1915.

His brother William recounted that Stephen's love of literature began unusually early: his mother discovered him as a small child reading to a mouse in the nursery. The book he held was upside down; he had not yet learned to read; and the mouse was dead, caught in a trap. The scene was promising. He was a frail boy, having rheumatoid arthritis from childhood and suffering also from the effects of scarlet fever. As a result, William noted, Stephen "did not go in very heavily for games, and began to lead an interior life of the mind. At the same time, his taste in books was catholic enough." His older brother recalled Stephen's fascination with the *Peck's Bad Boy* stories and other boys' books, the romances of Alexandre Dumas, *Men of Iron* by Howard Pyle, and the prose and poetry of William Morris. Their father enjoyed reciting poetry—both good and bad—and encouraged

Stephen to read in "Rebellion [Civil War] Records" and *Battles and Leaders of the Civil War.* In "The Most Unforgettable Character I've Met" Stephen recounted that his father:

> taught me a great many things. For one thing, by example, precept and demonstration, taught me most of what I know about the actual techniques of English verse. He could do so because he knew it—and I do not mean by that he had a gentlemanly acquaintance with the better-known poems of Tennyson and Browning. He knew it from Chaucer to Mary Anne O'Byrne, the Washerwoman poet of Watervliet, N.Y. and his knowledge was extensive and catholic. He introduced us to Beddoes and Stephen Crane, to the early poems of Robinson and the ballads of Father Prout. He could write any fixed form of verse with deftness, precision and tang. And if you came to him with a lame rhyme, a limping meter, an inchoate idea, he could show you, with the precision of a surgeon, just what was wrong.

If ever literature was a family affair, this was an example *par excellence.* The Benéts encouraged each other and delighted in each other's work. In "Know All By These Presents," William wrote out elaborately,

> That this is the early poetic work of Stephen Vincent Benét, prepared for the press by his brother William this four[teenth] day of February nineteen fifteen.
>
> That at least four of these poems are not unworthy to be included in any book of poems he shall hereafter publish.

William then listed four poems and noted others which also had merit. Stephen would have to guard against "being spoiled by too easy successes or the praises of his admiring family." William closed with a flourish:

> AND HEREUNTO WE SET OUR HAND AND SEAL THIS DAY THE FOURTEENTH OF FEBRUARY NINETEEN FIFTEEN, IN THE YEAR OF THE GREAT WAR, THE GREAT EARTHQUAKE, AND THE EFFLORESCENCE OF A GREAT POET.

He and their parents signed the good-humored document. In December 1915 Stephen's first book, *Five Men and Pompey*, was published and included one of the poems William had praised, "The Last Banquet." Stephen wrote the other four in the volume in Augusta, Georgia, during the summer before he first went to Yale.

Given all this, it is easy to understand how Benét could be a modernist in his themes, as in the "Nightmare" poems, but not modernist as are Ezra Pound and T. S. Eliot, two poets whose hermetic work differs dramatically from Benét's in language, tone, form, and imagery. Pound and Eliot were rebelling against almost everything American: their families, their education, American literature—or as they saw it, the lack thereof—and the country's materialism. Benét despised none of these things, although he was deeply disturbed by America's excessive materialism, and they became grist for his literary mill.

He was no journeyman writer; rather he was transitional. His well-shaped short stories usually have a climax and resolution, and his poetry reflects, though hardly exclusively, the influence of nineteenth-century poets such as Tennyson, Browning, and his father's and his favorite, William Morris. He was brilliant, a prodigy whose work began appearing early in his life and continued to be published abundantly thereafter. In 1913 he won a three-dollar prize for his poem "The Regret of Dives," published in *St. Nicholas*. After the appearance of *Five Men and Pompey* in 1915, his work appeared regularly in magazines such as *Century, New Republic, Seven Arts,* and the *Yale Literary Magazine,* and by 1918 he had enough poems for the Yale University Press to issue a collection entitled *Young Adventure*. While the poems are not revolutionary in style, they display his technical capabilities and literary imagination, as in "The General Public." Two years later Henry Holt and Company published *Heavens and Earth: A Book of Poems*. These were for the most part written in 1918 and 1919 and ranged well beyond the work appearing in *Young Adventure*. No "Campus Sonnets" in the later volume; instead it contained "The First Vision of Helen [of Troy]," narratives about "Chariots and Horsemen," poems about "The Tall Town"—New York City—and "The Kingdom of the Mad," and short insights into human character and the contemporary scene such as "Portrait of Young Love."

It is significant that the Yale Press volume included an introduction by Professor Chauncey Brewster Tinker, a well-known teacher and literary scholar at Yale. He was not an ardent admirer of "the New," and in his introduction—which at Benét's request made no specific reference to his work—Tinker spoke of passing "from the smooth-flowing imitations of Tennyson and Swinburne . . . into a false freedom that had at its heart a repudiation of all laws and standards. We may hope," he continued,

that the eager search for novelty of form and subject may have its influence in releasing us from our old bondage to the commonplace and
in broadening the scope of poetry; but we cannot blind ourselves to
the fact that it has at the same time completed that estrangement between the poet and the general public which has been developing for
half a century.

It is a strange, seemingly embittered introduction, but telling in that
Tinker found in Benét's poems something of what he sought in "the
rebirth of poetry."

Tinker's distanced endorsement points to the problems with the
poems for some critics. The work is not complex as is the metaphys-
ical poetry which Eliot admired. The critic John Chamberlain had an
intriguing explanation for why Benét's work is the way it is. Review-
ing *Western Star* in *Harper's* shortly after Benét's death, he wrote:

Steve Benét went to Yale when Dos Passos and Cummings were at
Harvard. I think the choice of college had something to do with his
approach to poetry. Yale has never had a conscious literary tradition.
When it fosters a talent, it does so in high innocence. And the talent itself takes on some of the overtones of that innocent mood. The point
to be made here is that Steve Benét, in his plastic period, felt no pressure upon him to be anything in particular. There were no "aesthetes"
around him. In a campus atmosphere of what has been aptly satirized
as "muscular Christianity," he could be a simple poet following his
own bent. Both those who were muscular and those who were exces-
sively Christian left him alone.

Being left alone, he responded by developing his own essentially
hopeful personality. He wrote a couple of "lost generation" novels—
The Beginning of Wisdom and *Young People's Pride.* But they were
like good coarse bread when stacked up against the spiced cake of
F. Scott Fitzgerald.

Seventeen years after Chamberlain's assessment, a self-appointed
priest of High Culture, Dwight Macdonald, felt compelled to denigrate *John Brown's Body* as an outstanding example of what Macdonald termed "Midcult." The "art" of "Midcult," in his opinion,
was distinct from "Masscult," what is now termed "popular culture,"
but is art *manque* in that it fails to meet the standards of High Culture (for which read Modernism). He called Benét's long narrative an
"orgy of Americana, much admired in its day and still widely used in
the schools as combining History and Literature." Macdonald could

even admire the Invocation, but then the trouble began for him as Benét echoed Eliot, Homer, Kipling, and others. Benét was "a master of the built-in reaction," his work so unsubtle as always "to identify the emotion he wants to arouse" and never to leave his readers "puzzled by the unexpected." Macdonald was in a high dudgeon against "Midcult" and in the same essay attacked Hemingway's novel *The Old Man and the Sea*, Thornton Wilder's play *Our Town*, and Archibald MacLeish's verse drama *J. B.* For Macdonald work had to be difficult to be true Art; anything smacking of "Midcult" or "Masscult" simply could not meet the requirements.

More recently Judith Moffett, a scholar of Benét and also a creative writer, published an appreciation of Benét's work, in particular, *John Brown's Body*. "His affinities as a person and a poet," she declared, "were to the nineteenth century; and the defining conflict for Benét was not the Great War, in which he had played no part, but the Civil War, which engaged his family and his imagination from childhood." The early result was popular success; "ordinary Americans took him to their hearts, and the feeling was mutual." But his fame "proved to be not much more lasting" than the money he earned from *John Brown's Body* and lost in the Great Depression. Why did he develop "into a popular poet but not an enduringly important one"? Moffett supposed that "Benét was rewarded while still a schoolboy for writing stuff that was extraordinarily good *for a schoolboy*, and at college, where he edited *The Yale Literary Review*, he was the best and most prolific poet on campus." Reflecting Dwight Macdonald's dismissal of the popular, she believed that "there was no incentive to aspire for something higher," and as a kind of proof of this she noted "how lightly the poet had revised his lines."

Moffett misremembered the Benét material in the archives of Yale's Beinecke Library. From start to finish, writing for Benét was a laborious process, beginning, as in the cases of *John Brown's Body* and *Western Star*, with numerous notebooks crammed with jottings from the reading he had done. For *Western Star* as published in 1943, there are thirteen notebooks which are carefully identified according to their content. The first is marked:

> Western Star
> Book Two
> Kentucky
> Notebook One

There is also a series of notebooks marked "Western Star Extra Notes," the first of which begins:

> Western Star—Book Two
> Kentucky
> ⌐ Ky by N. S. Shaler ⌐
> Ky owes to Va. most of her founding
>
> Notable emigration of Scotch after 1745—
> Several 1000 in Va. Many Calvinists

and goes on in that vein, Benét hurriedly scratching notes as he read widely. Next came a myriad number of lines written on yellow foolscap, then more finished copy often subject to the editorial criticisms of his agent Carl Brandt, or of editors of the magazines to which Brandt sent Benét's work.

The point is not that he was a better writer than Moffett seemed to think because he was less facile than she recalled him being; it is that his demise as an author deemed to be of the first rank resulted from shifts in literary and cultural tastes. High modernism came to the fore in the 1930s and has remained the dominant mode of serious expression ever since, but Benét's work drew on other sources. Then, too, he became an exuberant New Deal liberal and enthusiastically endorsed Franklin Delano Roosevelt and his policies in peace and war, while from early in the 1950s at least until the 1980s, the intelligentsia—the tastemakers for serious art of every sort—were frequently at odds with government. World War II, which ended in 1945, was "the last good war," as Studs Terkel noted.

I strongly suspect that had he lived, Benét would frequently have stood with the generations weaned on the Cold War, McCarthyism, the Korean War, the Vietnam War, the struggles for civil rights and women's rights—the list goes on. He did not survive, however, and remains locked in a position that seemed to the next generations to be out of step with their stances. His liberalism was not theirs. No matter, for him it was a badge of honor: "If you're a liberal," he wrote a friend in 1940, "that means you're always out on a limb. It isn't very comfortable, on the limb, but then God never intended liberals to be comfortable. If he had, he'd have made them conservatives. Or radicals."

III

John Chamberlain called Benét's first two novels "good coarse bread" and did not mention his three later volumes. Judith Moffett lumped them together as "urgently forgettable" and asserted that "Benét himself despised them." How forgettable they are is a matter for each reader to decide; Benét did not hate them, however. He considered himself first and foremost a poet, but he also understood that one rarely survived on poetry alone, and so he mastered the art of the short story and, to a degree, that of the novel. His first, *The Beginning of Wisdom*, remains significant because it captures something of the flavor of Yale College life in the period immediately preceding World War I and because parts of it are substantially autobiographical. The wisdom that its hero Philip Selaby acquires, if sometimes expressed in overwritten fashion, is far more than sophomoric. At the end of the novel Benét wrote about Selaby:

> He thought of the Heaven of childhood, when tinsel is as solid as steel in gods and toy swords, that kind, small place somewhere on top of the sky. That Heaven and all its saints had fallen to pieces when he first discovered cruelty that was both causeless and unpunished—it had been replaced in a measure by living, in a measure by the crude atheism of twenty that thinks it wickedly fine to defy the lightnings that never descend. Then had come Milly, and after the loss of her, much irony, a working-doctrine of irony that healed as it seared the mind with its freezing wit. Now even irony would not answer completely any more, in face of Sylvia and the vast unreasonableness of life.

Of the other novels, *James Shore's Daughter* is the best, a brief, intense portrait of Violet Shore, the daughter of an entrepreneur who exemplifies that nineteenth-century American phenomenon. Instead of marrying for love, Violet chooses a life that enables her to hold onto her father's great wealth. Garry Grant, the narrator and the man she loves, is a charming person with a fine artistic sense but not someone who could enhance the riches to which she was accustomed. The novel is a measured criticism of American materialism in the spirit of Willa Cather's 1925 novel *The Professor's House*, which Benét was well aware of when he was writing *James Shore's Daughter.* He remarked to Carl Brandt in the summer of 1932 that he was working on a short novel that "will certainly run 30,000 words, maybe 40,000. If I could, I'd get it about the size of Willa Cather's 'The Professor's House' "—and get it to be about the same themes of commercialism and the loss of older values, he might have added.

To assert that he was primarily a poet is in no way to denigrate his talent as a writer of prose. Some of his short stories are superb, going far beyond what one might today think of as the pat *Saturday Evening Post* variety. The magazine during Benét's lifetime was one of the chief venues for short fiction—and it paid better than most of the others. The writer John Marquand asserted that Benét "was the only one of us who could write a story for the *Saturday Evening Post* and make it read like literature." Marquand's judgment was a bit severe—Fitzgerald was also around—but it is telling. Benét's skills grew remarkably during his career so that he moved beyond the neatly shaped tale to ones envincing ambiguity, open-endedness, and deeply serious themes—the qualities one finds in the work of a John Cheever, Raymond Carver, or Alice Munro and not in the sentimental stories of a writer such as O. Henry from an earlier period.

Benét understood about shifts in taste, although he did not live to see his writing go out of fashion. In a lecture entitled "Some Contemporary Aspects of Literature" given late in his life, he discussed the great changes occurring in literature during the 1920s and 1930s, a period he recognized might be split into sections such as "the Jazz Age—the Age of Disillusion—the Age of Pound and Eliot and Joyce—and so on." But literature "never fits very neatly into categories or ages," he observed. Writers work even when what they do does not fit "the mood and fashion of the time." The 1920s and 1930s were a "a time of wide, diverse, and unceasing experiment," he recognized. This did not just happen; it came about from "a wish on the part of many writers to start telling the truth." That meant "enlarging the range of prose fiction so that it could deal with all sides of life—to bring back live words into poetry—[and] to bring back to the theatre something more than drawing-room comedy or the set 'problem-play' where a wise old friend of the family explained everything nicely in the last act."

If we do not generally think of Benét as a champion of the new, it is because of the style of much of his prose and poetry and because we do not think of his popular work with radio as innovative. At the time it was, and his uses of native idioms on occasion were as well. Benét understood and championed the new against the "singular deadness [that] afflicted all branches of American letters." What was missing was "the saltiness, the vigor and the native energy that had given American letters its real character—the huge laughter mixed with as huge a bitterness of Mark Twain—the great voice of Whitman. . . . It was a period of the polite, the academic, and the small." Young writers found "a jungle full of interesting and terrifying animals" beyond the walls of genteel Victorian estates, and in that jungle were "not only whole sections of human experience but whole regions and classes in this country unrepresented in letters." The response to this new America, Benét went on, was not "a self-conscious movement." Rather, "it happened spontaneously and the writers came from all over. No three writers," he noted, "could be more different than E. E. Cummings, F. Scott Fitzgerald and Sherwood Anderson. Yet each, in his best work, was trying to say something true and to break new ground."

Benét was in a particularly advantageous position to champion a new generation of writers. Because of the remarkable success of *John Brown's Body* he was elected to the prestigious National Institute of Arts and Letters in 1929 when he was only thirty-one. Nine years later he was elected to the American Academy of Arts and Letters, a group of fifty eminences from among the two hundred and fifty person National Institute. Charles Fenton, Benét's biographer, remarked that "A young man like Benét, decent, gregarious, well bred, conventionally anxious to please his elders, might have been expected to slide gradually into a dulled acceptance of the prevailing Institute mores," but this was not the case. As a member of the Institute and then the Academy, he was able to achieve recognition for new blood such as Archibald MacLeish, Carl Sandburg, Ellen Glasgow, and Walter Lippmann, despite the opposition of an old guard lodged intellectually in an earlier age. "Arrived hour late at the Institute," he noted in November 1933 in his diary, "where stuffed imbecile R. [obert] U. [nderwood] Johnson & other incompetent old men try as usual to elect mediocrities and suppress ability."

Benét worked tirelessly for the Institute, believing—correctly at the time—that it was the only organization in America which could help writers as a group. He served as chairman of the nominating committee for the Department of Literature, in which capacity he was instrumental in securing the elections of Thomas Wolfe, John Dos Passos, Stuart Chase, Ezra Pound, Joseph Wood Krutch, Charles Beard, William Faulkner, and John Steinbeck as well as others. After his election to the Academy, he and others succeeded in wresting control from a distinctly old guard led by the crusty Victorian academic Nicholas Murray Butler. "Academy trying to put things over," he wrote in his diary in October 1939, and he saw it as "all due to the personal pique of Nicholas Murray Butler. Disgraceful exhibition of old-man pettiness." "Had he lived longer," Fenton concluded his detailed discussion of Benét's involvement with the Institute and the Academy, "Benét would have become president of the organization" which he helped mold into one that aided writers with grants and awards rather than being an inward-turning bastion for self-congratulation and substantial cronyism.

As his lecture about "Some Contemporary Aspects of Literature" makes clear, his understanding of twentieth-century American literature was broad-ranging and open-minded—the traits of the man himself. He assessed what the new generation of writers had:

in prose, the tool of realism, not a new tool but new in its application to certain sections of the American scene. They were shortly to implement this with other techniques, some of them borrowed from or influenced by the newer developments in psychology—particularly the stream-of-consciousness method. They had in poetry, the medium of free verse, and from Laforgue and some of the symbolists through Eliot, still another method—the method which in Eliot really culminated with "The Wasteland." They had the new experiments in the theatre—the breaking of the "well-made" play as they had in the short story, the breaking of the "well-made" story with a punch in the end. . . .

An age of disillusion? If you like to call it that, but an age of continuous discovery and invention as well. The disillusion was there and increased. Realism pushed further and further into the jungle and found stranger and stranger beasts. Chester Gillette [the name of the actual person on whom Clyde Griffiths was modeled] of "An American Tragedy" is hardly an admirable character but he seems like a paragon of virtue compared with the appalling Flem Snopes of Mr. Faulkner's "The Hamlet." Gopher Prairie is a mean little town, but an Athens to Tobacco Road. The poetry that began by being interested in disillusion ended by being disillusioned with disillusion itself. Mr. Prufrock at least thought he could have been a pair of ragged claws scuttling along the floors of silent seas. He could, even in disillusion, wear white flannel trousers and walk upon the beach. But the hollow men had neither thought, dream nor action. They did not even have white flannel trousers. "Shape without form, shade without color, Paralyzed force, gesture without motion." You know how that fine and terrifying poem goes to the final "This is the way the world ends, Not with a bang but a whimper". . . .

Some of the fertile ground of the past twenty years is exhausted. I doubt, for instance, if you can push lingual experiment very much farther than it is pushed in "Finnegan's Wake"—and while some may steal from that very extraordinary book, very few will be able to imitate it. . . .

There are, I think, certain signs of what may develop. It is interesting to see Hemingway, after reducing character to the simplest and most individualistic terms in the Harry Morgan of "To Have and Have Not," then have that character find out that "No one man can go alone" and go on to the Robert Jordan of "For Whom the Bell Tolls" and the theme of that book so clearly stated in John Donne's great words. It is interesting to find the Thomas Wolfe of his last book, "You Can't Go Home Again," at last, if only partially coming to a resolution of the love for America, hate of many of its aspects and terror at its loneliness that runs through so much of his work. It is extremely interesting to find Mr. T. S. Eliot, under the stress of war—or perhaps because of that stress—producing in "East Coker," "Burnt Norton," and "The Dry Salvages" three of his finest pieces of work.

As if his committee work for the Institute and later the Academy were not sufficient, Benét in 1933 accepted an offer from the Yale University Press to serve as editor of its Yale Series of Younger Poets, which each year since 1919 had published what its editor judged to be the best volumes of poetry from those submitted. By 1933 the Press published the single best volume. Until Benét's tenure, the yearly number of submissions had been small and their quality generally modest. He was soon to change that; as George Bradley, a poet published in the Series in 1986, wrote in a superb introduction to *The Yale Younger Poets Anthology*, Benét "found the series a publisher's hobby given over to inconsequential work, and he left it the most prominent venue for new poets in the country." Bradley observed that previously the series had consisted of "faint imitations of standard styles. . . . By contrast, the work Benét ushered into print was usually up-to-the-minute in both manner and content." It was no accident; Benét knew what he wanted and, as his lecture on "Some Contemporary Aspects of Literature" indicates, he had a wide-ranging knowledge of and appreciation for contemporary literature.

As soon as he was appointed editor, he worked with Eugene Davidson of the Press to alter the format of the volumes, and in Benét's typically generous, energetic way, he wrote many of his literary contacts to solicit submissions. The results were impressive. In 1934, for instance, the Press received manuscripts from James Agee, who won the prize that year, and also from Muriel Rukeyser, May Sarton, and Lincoln Kirstein. Benét's generosity extended beyond his artistic openness. He insisted that one hundred dollars of his two hundred fifty dollar fee be given to the winning poet, something that until them had never been done. And his diligence brought in many more manuscripts: in 1935 he read seventy-three submissions, the

Press having sorted out approximately that many more as not worthy of consideration. In addition to the manuscripts received through the Press, Benét dealt with any number of other queries, submissions, and the like in connection with the Series, and he remained kind and fair always. He described it to one aspiring poet, noting that "As for kinds of verse—no particular kind of verse is preferable. All I'm interested in is good work of any kind." Nine months later he wrote the poet again: "Thank you for sending me a copy of 'Mushrooms.' I should not advise, at present, your submitting your verse to the Yale Series of Younger Poets. Perhaps in a year or so." Many another editor would not have been so circumspect.

"Mushrooms" was one of the manuscripts in 1935 that did not excite him, nor apparently, did any of the others, so he tracked down Rukeyser's manuscript from the previous year and published it as the 1935 winner. Her volume, *Theory of Flight*, was the first "to exert significant influence on a subsequent generation of writers," Bradley noted, adding that while Benét "could appreciate poetry that espoused art for art's sake . . . his own taste ran to verse that was willing to dirty its hands with the number-four gravel of this world." In the politicized, Depression-era 1930s, his taste matched that of the reading public: five of the ten volumes he selected during his decade as editor had multiple printings and "sold in the thousands. . . . [His] final selection would sell over five thousand copies, making its author Yale's best-selling poet for two decades." The book was Margaret Walker's *For My People*, which Benét championed and had published in 1942 after she had submitted it repeatedly.

Whatever earlier successes Benét had achieved with the poetry collections *Young Adventure* and *Heavens and Earth* and the novels *The Beginning of Wisdom*, *Young People's Pride*, and *Jean Huguenot*, his great breakthrough as a writer came with the publication of *John Brown's Body* in 1928. He and his wife Rosemary had managed to return to Paris in 1926 with the aid of a Guggenheim fellowship, which eventually was extended for six months beyond its original year. Having settled on his topic, he labored hard over the long narrative, not at all sure that he could come close to his goal, an epic about America.

He struggled with its form, deciding on "a prologue, eight books or sections, and an epilogue," as he wrote in his "Preliminary Report" to the Guggenheim Foundation. The action, he noted, was "continuous," and while it did not "follow history in the strict sense," it was "a poem, an attempt at an interpretation, not a history or a recital of events." While he was trying to keep "the epic quality," he intended to give them an immediacy unlike what one found in histories.

When John Farrar responded enthusiastically to the completed manuscript Benét sent in December 1927, he answered,

> I am very glad indeed that you think so well of [*John Brown's Body*]—needless to say—and particularly glad if it seemed to you to be whole. You lose the feel of the whole, working on a thing that size for so long, and can see nothing but the parts. But I tried to put America in it—at least some of the America I knew. If I did so, some of it should stand till a better man comes along. I feel rather curiously about it myself. I think my best work so far, perhaps, is in it and yet it is more detached from me than anything I have done. It seemed to me that a thing of that sort ought to be tried. A poet of greater faculties would have avoided my failures in it and my superficialities—and there are many of both—but what I have done, I have done to the extent of such capacities as I have. At least I hope it has in it some of the landscapes, the sights, the sounds [and] the people which are American. I tried to put them there. I am tired—not of criticism of America, for no country can be healthy without self-criticism—but of the small railers, the conventional rebels. We also have a heritage—and not all of it is wooden money.

John Farrar sent galleys of *John Brown's Body* to E. A. Robinson, who found parts of it fine, but demurred from complete praise, declaring that "parts of it are as bad as possible." He altered the word "bad" to "mistaken," and Benét responded that the comment was "very Robinsonian." Benét might have worked longer at the poem, he acknowledged, but that would not have served him well. He had done his "damnest" to make it flow, and ten years of work would not have removed the "prosier passages." He observed, "The fault there is not only in me but in the nature of both subject and medium." He was sure that he "could do no better, given such brains as I had. Now it is out of me and I am anxious to do something different and more disciplined."

Regardless of its faults, the long narrative poem was an instant and immense success, being picked up by the Book of the Month Club, which printed a large edition. When Benét heard about it, he was ecstatic: "65,000! My God! What a lot of books! In fact it's still pretty hard for me to realize it." His fame was assured, and from that moment until his death he was one of America's most widely known figures, whose talents were in constant demand. Why was—and is—

John Brown's Body popular? The reasons are many, no doubt, but chief among them is the subject: the Civil War. Benét attempted to and in large measure succeeded in presenting the reader with a panoramic vision of the war from both the southern and northern points of view, although ultimately he sympathized with the northern, Unionist position.

In a lecture he gave well after the publication of the poem, he spoke of having gone to school in Georgia and being told that "the South was entirely and absolutely right," and he pored through books and old volumes of *Century* magazine which carried a series called "Battles and Leaders of the Civil War." He developed a vested interest in the America he read about, so that "when I came to write the poem, the choice of the Civil War seemed inevitable. For it marked a turning point in our national history. Two systems of life had grown up side by side. . . ." His sources were wide and added a kind of authority to what he wrote: "I drew, of course, upon various histories and biographies, upon the official records and papers, and particularly upon letters, diaries, and reminiscences of the period." Since the publication of *John Brown's Body*, a massive literature about the Civil War has developed, but in 1928 there was little that achieved the scope of his work.

The long narrative poem was popular then as it has not been more recently, and Robinson, Edgar Lee Masters, and any number of other poets had success with it. In prose, writers were striving to write "The Great American Novel," and a good example of this effort is John Dos Passos's trilogy *U. S. A.*, which he began at almost exactly the same moment Benét began his epic on an American theme. In the mid-1920s American writers sought more than before to define the nation; the search would become even more intense in the next years during the Great Depression.

Then, too, *John Brown's Body* appealed to readers because of its ease of style. In his "Preliminary Report" about the work in 1927, he told of employing "various meters and verse-forms in the writing and us[ing] various devices of interlude and change of pace in an attempt to keep the thing from growing monotonous." Still, the thing had "a foundation or backbone of rather rough blank verse combined with a dactyllic or anapestic pentameter-form that takes the chief load and binds the whole project together." In an interview in 1933 Benét acknowledged writing in "various meters varying from a rather loose form of free verse and certain passages of rhythmic prose to a few incidental lyrics written in the strict and traditional pattern." He intended, he stated, to adapt the meter to the characters and situations. He spoke of inventing "a kind of rough form [of blank verse] that had a very decided beat that would carry certain names that I wanted to use that seemed more in key with the classic [forms of verse]." He cited as an example the opening of Book Three:

> By Pittsburg Landing, the turbid Tennessee
> Sucks against black, soaked spiles with soil-colored waters.
> That country is huge and disorderly, even now.

He also cited the example of "American Names," one of his best known poems, although there the meter is tighter than in the case above, while the rhyme is absolutely regular. The first stanza reads,

> I have fallen in love with American names,
> The sharp names that never get fat,
> The snakeskin-titles of mining-claims,
> The plumed war-bonnet of Medicine Hat,
> Tuscon and Deadwood and Lost Mule Flat.

His use of a kind of vernacular—both in language and imagery—has a popular appeal, something noticeable in his shorter poems as well as in the long narratives. "Born in the mountains, lonesome-born,/ Raised runnin' ragged thu' the cockleburrs and corn," goes a couplet in "The Mountain Whippoorwill," and one stanza of "The Ballad of William Sycamore" reads,

> The cabin logs, with the bark still rough,
> And my mother who laughed at trifles,
> And the tall, lank visitors, brown as snuff,
> With their long, straight squirrel-rifles.

The poem swings along, direct and clear, the themes very American ones of freedom, courage, independence, and admiration for the man at one with the land—"Go play with the towns you have built of blocks," the last stanza asserts, "The towns where you would have bound me!/ I sleep in my earth like a tired fox,/ And my buffalo have found me." And let us not forget the last line of "American Names": "Bury my heart at Wounded Knee." The true liberal Benét was no thoughtless celebrant of American expansionism and oppression; few Anglo-Saxon writers of his era wrote more compassionately about the plight of minorities.

Much the same thing can be said about his short stories; they are direct and clear, and in such well-known favorites as "The Devil and Daniel Webster" they celebrate American themes and legendary characters—in this case the famous politician and orator. Stories such as those listed in this volume under the heading of "The American Scene" are less celebratory, more likely to be wryly presented vignettes, often poignant, about contemporary life and about people who sadly lacked insight into themselves. More and more in the 1930s Benét wrote the latter sort as he observed the effects of the Great Depression and as he experienced the malaise that could be a part of urban life. And as he watched dictatorships engulf Europe, he turned to writing that was meant to warn his audience about them.

Earlier, in the wake of his first great success, he worked in Hollywood with D. W. Griffith on the production of what was to be an epic film about Abraham Lincoln. If anything contributed to his wry sense of things, it was this experience. While he admired Griffith, like many another writer who on the basis of new fame did a Hollywood stint, Benét came to despise the machinations of the film industry. When he first arrived there in December 1929, he was amused by what he told Rosemary was a "madhouse." "Hollywood," he wrote her, "is one loud, struggling Mainstreet, low-roofed, mainly unskyscrapered town that struggles along for twenty-five miles or so, full of stop & go lights, automobiles, palm-trees, Spanishy—& God knows what all houses—orange-drink stands with real orange juice—studios—movie-theatres—everything but bookstores." Little seemed to be going on at his particular studio, and in all he was not entirely clear why he was being employed, but the money was good.

A month later he was fit to be tied and told Carl Brandt that if he were ever signed up again for a twelve-week contract with the film industry, "there is going to be a good deal of blood flowing around the Brandt office." He declared that "of all the Christbitten places and business[es] on the two hemispheres this one is the last curly kink on the pig's tail. And that's without prejudice to D. W. Griffith. I like him and think he's good. But, Jesus, the movies!" The people who swirled around the industry made him want to vomit, and while he had worked in advertising, "nowhere have I seen such shining waste, stupidity and conceit as in the business and managing end of this industry. Whoopee!" he added, making light of his thorough disgruntlement. Since he had arrived, he had written four versions of *Abraham Lincoln*, at least one of which he thought was good. "That, of course, is out," he noted. "Seven people, including myself, are now working in conferences on a 5th one which promises hopefully to be the worst yet. If I don't get out of here soon I am going crazy." By the middle of February 1930 he was back in New York, delighted to have left Hollywood behind, that "indescribable place," as he told an editor of the *Yale Review* who wanted him to do a piece about films.

As the Depression deepened in the early 1930s and politics took on an immense seriousness, Benét responded with a new depth in his writing. To see this, one has only to compare short stories from the 1920s such as "The Sobbin' Women" (published in 1926 and the basis for the immensely successful film *Seven Brides for Seven Brothers*) with later tales which focus on the pathos of character—"Among Those Present" (1938) and "The Three Fates" (1941)—and tales which attack totalitarianism—"The Blood of the Martyrs" (1936), "By the Waters of Babylon" (1937), and "Into Egypt" (1939). In poetry the same holds true: compare the poems in this volume's section "Youth and Love"—all written in the 1920s—with those in the section "For You Who Are to Come." He formed fiercely liberal convictions; yet, whatever he thought about the shortcomings of capitalism, he questioned the efficacy of Communism. "I'm not very sold on Marxism as a doctrine—they have built it into too cast-iron a theory and life seems to take pleasure in fooling cast-iron theories," he told his friend, the poet Paul Engle.

The inevitable result was his increasing concern to awaken Americans to the dangers facing them. Speeches and radio scripts as well as his more artful work poured out; their toll was his health. He worked on *Western Star* whenever he could, but before his death had accomplished only two books, the second of which was published shortly after his death. He had himself removed Book I from publication, and putting forth what he had written—far less than his intention for the narrative—suggests that he sensed how fragile he was in 1943.

When he died, the encomiums poured in. One of the most moving tributes to Benét came from the writer Pauli Murray, who much later for her family memoir, *Proud Shoes*, would borrow from a line of his about Paul Engle: "Here is somebody walking in America in proud shoes." In a letter to Rosemary she declared:

You cannot help but know there are thousands of lovers of literature today who feel a sense of personal loss with you, particularly those hundreds of struggling young students for whom Stephen Vincent Benét was an inspiration and a guide. His willingness to give personal attention to their needs, to offer words of encouragement, to read through their "stuff" and to write long letters of criticism and suggestion—all these brought him close to us. I am one of these.

One consoling thought occurs to those of us who have lost him. He has scattered fragments of his spirit among us, and many poets, writers and students will continue to be faithful to the great drama of American literature to which he gave himself. Many a younger poet will ply himself the harder that a master's work might go on. Benét is not dead—for the epitaph which he wrote for John Brown might well be his own, and the banner flung back for some of us to carry forward—

> *"And, if the heart within your breast must burst*
> *Like a cracked crucible and pour its steel*
> *White-hot before the white heat of the wheel,*
> *Strive to recast once more*
> *That attar of the ore*
> *In the strong mold of pain*
> *Till it is whole again, . . . "*

And for us darker folk, particularly has he given a hope that cannot die:

> *"Oh, blackskinned epic, epic with the black spear,*
> *I cannot sing you, having too white a heart,*
> *And yet, some day, a poet will rise to sing you*
> *And sing you with such truth and mellowness, . . .*
> *That you will be a match for any song*
> *Sung by old, populous nations of the past,*
> *And stand like hills against the American sky,*
> *And lay your black spear down by Roland's horn. . . . "*

Like ourselves, I know that in your grief such thoughts as these will come to you bringing fortitude and the strength to go on. Forgive the fumbling thing I'm trying to say and try to understand.

"This flesh was seeded from no foreign grain," Benét had declared in the Invocation to his most famous work. He spent a lifetime probing, rebuking, but always ultimately honoring his chosen land and its people. He had hoped to be buried in Arlington National Cemetery, but because he had never been on active military service, his wish was denied. He was buried in the old cemetery in the New England fishing village of Stonington, Connecticut, where in 1941 he and Rosemary had purchased a house that had belonged to an American sea captain and later, to the family of a famous American expatriate, the painter James Abbott McNeill Whistler.

ACKNOWLEDGMENTS

I am grateful to Michael Millman, my editor at Penguin Putnam, for his willingness to undertake this project. Charles Schlessiger offered keen advice as always. Thomas Benét, the son of Stephen Vincent Benét, offered every possible sort of help and in the process became a good friend. In the last stages of preparing this selection Sarah Reuning helped with some important research. Benét's three staunchest supporters, Joan Campion, Tanja Howard, and Patricia McAndrew, have done a remarkable amount to stimulate interest in Benét's work; I thank them for that.

Anyone working on Benét must use the splendid resources of the Beinecke Rare Book and Manuscript Library at Yale University. I am deeply indebted to Patricia Willis, Curator of American Literature, and to all the other members of the staff at the Beinecke who made my research there as a Donald C. Gallup Fellow thoroughly rewarding.

SUGGESTIONS FOR FURTHER READING

"As We Remember Him." Fourteen contemporaries recall Benét, *Saturday Review of Literature,* 26 (March 27, 1943), 7–11.

Benét, Laura. *When William Rose, Stephen Vincent and I Were Young.* (Dodd, Mead, 1976).

Benét, William Rose. "My Brother Steve," *Saturday Review of Literature,* 24 (November 15, 1941), 3–4, 22–26.

Bradley, George, ed. *The Yale Younger Poets Anthology* (Yale University Press, 1998).

Chamberlain, John. "The New Books," *Harper's,* 187 (Oct. 1943). Among the front advertisement pages.

Fenton, Charles. *Stephen Vincent Benét: The Life and Times of an American Man of Letters, 1898–1943* (Yale University Press, 1958).

———, ed. *Selected Letters of Stephen Vincent Benét* (Yale University Press, 1960).

Freeman, Douglas Southhall. Introduction to *John Brown's Body: A Poem by Stephen Vincent Benét* (The Heritage Press, 1949).

Macdonald, Dwight. *Against the American Grain* (Random House, 1960).

MacLeish, Archibald. Introduction to *John Brown's Body* (Holt, Rinehart and Winston, 1980).

Maddocks, Gladys Louise. "Stephen Vincent Benét: A Bibliography." *Bulletin of Bibliography and Dramatic Index,* 20 (September 1951; April 1952), Part I, pp. 142–146; Part II, pp. 158–160.

Moffett, Judith. "Stephen Vincent Benét: An Appreciation on the Centenary of His Birth," *American Poet* (Fall 1998), 30–33.

Stephen Vincent Benét Papers, Beinecke Rare Book and Manuscript Library, Yale University.

Richardson, Robert. "Epic on an American Theme: A Study of *John Brown's Body,*" Unpublished Dissertation, Harvard University, 1961.

Stroud, Parry. *Stephen Vincent Benét* (Twayne, 1962).

WORKS BY STEPHEN VINCENT BENÉT

America. New York: Farrar and Rinehart, Inc., 1944.

Ballads and Poems, 1915–1930. Garden City, N.Y.: Doubleday, Doran and Co., Inc., 1931.

Ballad of the Duke's Mercy. New York: House of Books, 1939.

The Ballad of William Sycamore. New York: Brick Row Book Shop, 1923.

The Beginning of Wisdom. New York: Henry Holt and Co., 1921.

A Book of Americans. (Written in collaboration with Rosemary Carr Benét.) New York: Farrar and Rinehart, Inc., 1933.

Burning City. New York: Farrar and Rinehart, Inc., 1936.

A Child Is Born: A Modern Drama of the Nativity. Boston: W. H. Baker, 1942.

Dear Adolf. New York: Farrar and Rinehart, Inc., 1942.

The Devil and Daniel Webster. Weston, Vt.: Countryman Press, 1937.

The Devil and Daniel Webster. (One-act play.) New York: Dramatists Play Service, 1939. (The motion picture version, *All That Money Can Buy,* has been collected in John Gassner's *Twenty Best Film Plays,* New York: Crown Publishers, 1943.)

The Devil and Daniel Webster. (Libretto.) New York: Farrar and Rinehart, Inc., 1939.

The Drug Shop; or, Endymion in Edmonstown. (Privately printed.) New Haven, Connecticut: Brick Row Book Shop, 1917.

Five Men and Pompey: a Series of Dramatic Portraits. Boston: Four Seas Co., 1915.

The Headless Horseman. (Libretto.) Boston: Schirmer Co., 1927.

Heavens and Earth. New York: Henry Holt and Co., 1920.

James Shore's Daughter. Garden City, N.Y.: Doubleday, Doran and Co., Inc., 1934.

Jean Huguenot. New York: Henry Holt and Co., 1923.

John Brown's Body. Garden City, N.Y.: Doubleday, Doran and Co., 1928.

John Brown's Body. Twenty-first edition, edited and annotated by Mabel A. Bessey, with an introductory essay, "The Coming of the American Civil War," by Bert James Loewenberg. New York: Rinehart and Co., Inc., 1941.

Johnny Pye and the Fool-Killer. Weston, Vt.: Countryman Press, 1938.

King David. New York: Farrar, Strauss and Co., 1946.

The Last Circle. New York: Farrar, Strauss and Co., 1946.

Listen to the People. New York: Council for Democracy, 1941.

Nightmare at Noon. New York: Farrar and Rinehart, Inc., 1940.

Selected Works of Stephen Vincent Benét. 2 vols. Introduction by Basil Davenport. (Name of editor is not given.) New York: Rinehart and Co., Inc., 1942.

Spanish Bayonet. New York: George H. Doran Co., 1926.

Stephen Vincent Benét, Selected Poetry and Prose. Edited with an introduction by Basil Davenport. New York: Rinehart and Co., Inc., 1942. (This paperback edition is considerably less extensive than the hardback edition listed above but contains a few poems and short stories not in the other selection.)

Tales Before Midnight. New York: Farrar and Rinehart, Inc., 1939.

Thirteen O'Clock. New York: Farrar and Rinehart, Inc., 1937.

Tiger Joy. New York: George H. Doran Co., 1925.

Twenty-Five Short Stories. Garden City, N.Y.: Sun Dial Press, 1943.

We Stand United, and Other Radio Scripts. New York: Farrar and Rinehart, Inc., 1945.

Western Star. New York: Farrar and Rinehart, Inc., 1943.

Young Adventure. New Haven, Conn.: Yale University Press, 1918.

Young People's Pride. New York: Henry Holt and Co., 1922.

A NOTE ABOUT THE SELECTIONS

The short stories and poems have generally been organized according to topic (the stories: History and the Supernatural, The American Scene, Politics and Prophecies; the poems: Americans, Youth and Love, Meditations and Complaints). The ordering follows closely that used in the two-volume *Selected Works of Stephen Vincent Benét* (New York: Farrar and Rinehart, 1942).

Benét published practically everything he wrote, most often in a periodical and then in collections of his work. In the case of the short stories, first publication of almost all of them is listed in Gladys Louise Maddocks, "Stephen Vincent Benét: A Bibliography," *Bulletin of Bibliography and Dramatic Index* (September 1951; April 1952), Part I, pp. 142–146; Part II, pp. 158–160. This bibliography does not list the places or dates of publication of the poems. A reader desiring those dates can refer to the copyright pages of *Selected Works, Volume One: Poetry*, or to those of any other collection in which the poems appear.

LITTLE TESTAMENT

I have lived. I have thought and labored, I have loved
    and possessed my love
To the uttermost inch of flesh, till the deep voice cried in
    us both.
I have not cut my coat according to the color of the
    cloth.
When the world passed by me in the street, it could have
    fist or my glove.

My people were soldiers for the most part—they had
    Spain and Ireland in their shroud;
I was a coward and afraid, yet I have not shamed them, I
    think.
I have not refused the drink when there might be venom
    in the drink.
I have written the verse for my pleasure, not for praise or
    money or the crowd.

Loving two countries well, sweet France, like a well-
    sunned pear,
And this red, hard apple, America, tart-flavored, tasting
    of the wild,
I can lie at ease in either, yet may the child of my child
Run the heaps of gold leaves in the Fall, see the red leaf
    hanging in blue air.

With the five dull tools of the senses, I have seen great
    Jupiter enskied,
Tasted the buds of spruce, the buds by the lakeside in the
    Spring,
Smelt woodsmoke and snow unfallen, heard the gold
    horns answer to the string
And touched the entire earth, on the mountain, naked as
    a bride.

I have been a traitor and loyal, a fool and the enemy of
    fools;
Certain friends I would not betray. I have worn ragged
    overcoats for pride.
I shall keep the delusions of my soul a secret until I have
    died,
Because of a stubborn nothing that would not answer to
    the rules.

So it is. So be it with me. I make my mark and depart.
Children of children of my children, you will yet have a
    stinging in your blood,
A dark cell, a hidden laughter, an eye seeing bad and
    good
That chooses one mask in public but a different image in
    the heart.

Now the mind rusts into madness, the horses run with-
    out bit,
The paltry body is nothing but mechanics of bone and
    skin.
Nevertheless I have spoken. This nothing spoke for its
    kin
And loved one woman completely. Let her remember it.

STORIES

HISTORY AND THE SUPERNATURAL

Jacob and the Indians

It goes back to the early days—may God profit all who lived then—and the ancestors.

Well, America, you understand, in those days was different. It was a nice place, but you wouldn't believe it if you saw it today. Without busses, without trains, without states, without Presidents, nothing!

With nothing but colonists and Indians and wild woods all over the country and wild animals to live in the wild woods. Imagine such a place! In these days, you children don't even think about it; you read about it in the schoolbooks, but what is that? And I put in a call to my daughter, in California, and in three minutes I am saying "Hello, Rosie," and there it is Rosie and she is telling me about the weather, as if I wanted to know! But things were not always that way. I remember my own days, and they were different. And in the times of my grandfather's grandfather, they were different still. Listen to the story.

My grandfather's grandfather was Jacob Stein, and he came from Rettelsheim, in Germany. To Philadelphia he came, an orphan in a sailing ship, but not a common man. He had learning—he had been to the *chedar*—he could have been a scholar among the scholars. Well, that is the way things happen in this bad world. There was a plague and a new grand duke—things are always so. He would say little of it afterward—they had left his teeth in his mouth, but he would say little of it. He did not have to say—we are children of the Dispersion—we know a black day when it comes.

Yet imagine—a young man with fine dreams and learning, a scholar with a pale face and narrow shoulders, set down in those early days in such a new country. Well, he must work, and he did. It was very fine, his learning, but it did not fill his mouth. He must carry a pack on his back and go from door to door with it. That was no disgrace; it was so that many began. But it was not expounding the Law, and at first he was very homesick. He would sit in his room at night, with the one candle, and read the preacher Koheleth, till the bitterness of the preacher rose in his mouth. Myself, I am sure that Koheleth was a great preacher, but if he had had a good wife he would have been a more cheerful man. They had too many wives in those old days—it confused them. But Jacob was young.

As for the new country where he had come, it was to him a place of exile, large and frightening. He was glad to be out of the ship, but, at first, that was all. And when he saw his first real Indian in the street—well, that was a day! But the Indian, a tame one, bought a ribbon from him by signs, and after that he felt better. Nevertheless, it seemed to him at times that the straps of the pack cut into his very soul, and he longed for the smell of the *chedar* and the quiet streets of Rettelsheim and the good smoked goose-breast pious housewives keep for the scholar. But there is no going back—there is never any going back.

All the same, he was a polite young man, and a hardworking. And soon he had a stroke of luck—or at first it seemed so. It was from Simon Ettelsohn that he got the trinkets for his pack, and one day he found Simon Ettelsohn arguing a point of the Law with a friend, for Simon was a pious man and well thought of in the Congregation Mikveh Israel. Our grandfather's grandfather stood by very modestly at first—he had come to replenish his pack and Simon was his employer. But finally his heart moved within him, for both men were wrong, and he spoke and told them where they erred. For half an hour he spoke, with his pack still upon his shoulders, and never has a text been expounded with more complexity, not even by the great Reb Samuel. Till, in the end, Simon Ettelsohn threw up his hands and called him a young David and a candle of learning. Also, he allowed him a more profitable route of trade. But, best of all, he invited young Jacob to his house, and there Jacob ate well for the first time since he had come to Philadelphia. Also he laid eyes upon Miriam Ettelsohn for the first time, and she was Simon's youngest daughter and a rose of Sharon.

After that, things went better for Jacob, for the protection of the strong is like a rock and a well. But yet things did not go altogether as he wished. For, at first, Simon Ettelsohn made much of him, and there was stuffed fish and raisin wine for the young scholar, though he was a peddler. But there is a look in a man's eyes that says "H'm? Son-in-law?" and that look Jacob did not see. He was modest—he did not expect to win the maiden overnight, though he longed for her. But gradually it was borne in upon him what he was in the Ettelsohn house—a young scholar to be shown before Simon's friends, but a scholar whose learning did not fill his mouth. He did not blame Simon for it, but it was not what he had intended. He began to wonder if he would ever get on in the world at all, and that is not good for any man.

Nevertheless, he could have borne it, and the aches and pains of his love, had it not been for Meyer Kappelhuist. Now, there was a pushing man! I speak no ill of anyone, not even of your Aunt Cora, and she can keep the De Groot silver if she finds it in her heart to do so; who lies down in the straw with a dog, gets up with fleas. But this Meyer Kappelhuist! A big, red-faced fellow from Holland with shoulders the size of a barn door and red hair on the backs of his hands. A big mouth for eating and drinking and telling schnorrer stories—and he talked about the Kappelhuists, in Holland, till you'd think they were made of gold. The crane says, "I am really a peacock—at least on my mother's side." And yet, a thriving man—that could not be denied. He had started with a pack, like our grandfather's grandfather, and now he was trading with the Indians and making money hand over fist. It seemed to Jacob that he could never go to the Ettelsohn house without meeting Meyer and hearing about those Indians. And it dried the words in Jacob's mouth and made his heart burn.

For, no sooner would our grandfather's grandfather begin to expound a text or a proverb, than he would see Meyer Kappelhuist looking at the maiden. And when Jacob had finished his expounding, and there should have been a silence, Meyer Kappelhuist would take it upon himself to thank him, but always in a tone that said: "The Law is the Law and the Prophets are the Prophets, but prime beaver is also prime beaver, my little scholar!" It took the pleasure from Jacob's learning and the joy of the maiden from his heart. Then he would sit silent and burning, while Meyer told a great tale of Indians, slapping his hands on his knees. And in the end he was always careful to ask Jacob how many needles and pins he had sold that day; and when Jacob told him, he would smile and say very smoothly that all things had small beginnings, till the maiden herself could not keep from a little smile. Then, desperately, Jacob would rack his brains for more interesting matter. He would tell of the wars of the Maccabees and the glory of the Temple. But even as he told them, he felt they were far away. Whereas Meyer and his accursed Indians were there, and the maiden's eyes shone at his words.

Finally he took his courage in both hands and went to Simon Ettelsohn. It took much for him to do it, for he had not been brought up to strive with men, but with words. But it seemed to him now that everywhere he went he heard of nothing but Meyer Kappelhuist and his trading with the Indians, till he thought it would drive him mad. So he went to Simon Ettelsohn in his shop.

"I am weary of this narrow trading in pins and needles," he said, without more words.

Simon Ettelsohn looked at him keenly; for while he was an ambitious man, he was kindly as well.

"*Nu*," he said. "A nice little trade you have and the people like you. I myself started in with less. What would you have more?"

"I would have much more," said our grandfather's grandfather stiffly. "I would have a wife and a home in this new country. But how shall I keep a wife? On needles and pins?"

"*Nu*, it has been done," said Simon Ettelsohn, smiling a little. "You are a good boy, Jacob, and we take an interest in you. Now, if it is a question of marriage, there are many worthy maidens. Asher Levy, the baker, has a daughter. It is true that she squints a little, but her heart is of gold." He folded his hands and smiled.

"It is not of Asher Levy's daughter I am thinking," said Jacob, taken aback. Simon Ettelsohn nodded his head and his face grew grave.

"*Nu*, Jacob," he said. "I see what is in your heart. Well, you are a good boy, Jacob, and a fine scholar. And if it were in the old country, I am not saying. But here, I have one daughter married to a Seixas and one to a Da Silva. You must see that makes a difference." And he smiled the smile of a man well pleased with his world.

"And if I were such a one as Meyer Kappelhuist?" said Jacob bitterly.

"Now—well, that is a little different," said Simon Ettelsohn sensibly. "For Meyer trades with the Indians. It is true, he is a little rough. But he will die a rich man."

"I will trade with the Indians too," said Jacob, and trembled.

Simon Ettelsohn looked at him as if he had gone out of his mind. He looked at his narrow shoulders and his scholar's hands.

"Now, Jacob," he said soothingly, "do not be foolish. A scholar you are, and learned, not an Indian trader. Perhaps in a store you would do better. I can speak to Aaron Copras. And sooner or later we will find you a nice maiden. But to trade with Indians—well, that takes a different sort of man. Leave that to Meyer Kappelhuist."

"And your daughter, that rose of Sharon? Shall I leave her, too, to Meyer Kappelhuist?" cried Jacob.

Simon Ettelsohn looked uncomfortable.

"*Nu*, Jacob," he said. "Well, it is not settled, of course. But—"

"I will go forth against him as David went against Goliath," said our grandfather's grandfather wildly. "I will go forth into the wilderness. And God should judge the better man!"

Then he flung his pack on the floor and strode from the shop. Simon Ettelsohn called out after him, but he did not stop for that. Nor was it in his heart to go and seek the maiden. Instead, when he was in the street, he counted the money he had. It was not much. He had meant to buy his trading goods on credit from Simon Ettelsohn, but now he could not do that. He stood in the sunlit street of Philadelphia, like a man bereft of hope.

Nevertheless, he was stubborn—though how stubborn he did not yet know. And though he was bereft of hope, he found his feet taking him to the house of Raphael Sanchez.

Now, Raphael Sanchez could have bought and sold Simon Ettelsohn twice over. An arrogant old man he was, with fierce black eyes and a beard that was whiter than snow. He lived apart, in his big house with his granddaughter, and men said he was very learned, but also very disdainful, and that to him a Jew was not a Jew who did not come of the pure sephardic strain.

Jacob had seen him, in the Congregation Mikveh Israel, and to Jacob he had looked like an eagle, and fierce as an eagle. Yet now, in his need, he found himself knocking at that man's door.

It was Raphael Sanchez himself who opened. "And what is for sale today, peddler?" he said, looking scornfully at Jacob's jacket where the pack straps had worn it.

"A scholar of the Law is for sale," said Jacob in his bitterness, and he did not speak in the tongue he had learned in this country, but in Hebrew.

The old man stared at him a moment.

"Now am I rebuked," he said. "For you have the tongue. Enter, my guest," and Jacob touched the scroll by the doorpost and went in.

They shared the noon meal at Raphael Sanchez's table. It was made of dark, glowing mahogany, and the light sank into it as sunlight sinks into a pool. There were many precious things in that room, but Jacob had no eyes for them. When the meal was over and the blessing said, he opened his heart and spoke, and Raphael Sanchez listened, stroking his beard with one hand. When the young man had finished, he spoke.

"So, Scholar," he said, though mildly, "you have crossed an ocean that you might live and not die, and yet all you see is a girl's face."

"Did not Jacob serve seven years for Rachel?" said our grandfather's grandfather.

"Twice seven, Scholar," said Raphael Sanchez dryly, "but that was in the blessed days." He stroked his beard again. "Do you know why I came to this country?" he said.

"No," said Jacob Stein.

"It was not for the trading," said Raphael Sanchez. "My house has lent money to kings. A little fish, a few furs—what are they to my house? No, it was for the promise—the promise of Penn—that this land should be an habitation and a refuge, not only for the Gentiles. Well, we know Christian promises. But so far, it has been kept. Are you spat upon in the street here, Scholar of the Law?"

"No," said Jacob. "They call me Jew, now and then. But the Friends, though Gentile, are kind."

"It is not so in all countries," said Raphael Sanchez, with a terrible smile.

"No," said Jacob quietly, "it is not."

The old man nodded. "Yes, one does not forget that," he said. "The spittle wipes off the cloth, but one does not forget. One does not forget the persecutor or the persecuted. That is why they think me mad, in the Congregation Mikveh Israel, when I speak what is in my mind. For, look you"—and he pulled a map from a drawer—"here is what we know of these colonies, and here and here our people make a new beginning, in another air. But here is New France—see it?—and down the great river come the French traders and their Indians."

"Well?" said Jacob in puzzlement.

"Well?" said Raphael Sanchez. "Are you blind? I do not trust the King of France—the king before him drove out the Huguenots, and who knows what he may do? And if they hold the great rivers against us, we shall never go westward."

"We?" said Jacob in bewilderment.

"We," said Raphael Sanchez. He struck his hand on the map. "Oh, they cannot see it in Europe—not even their lords in parliament and their ministers of state," he said. "They think this is a mine, to be worked as the Spaniards worked Potosi, but it is not a mine. It is something beginning to live, and it is faceless and nameless yet. But it is our lot to be part of it—remember that in the wilderness, my young scholar of the Law. You think you are going there for a girl's face, and that is well enough. But you may find something there you did not expect to find."

He paused and his eyes had a different look.

"You see, it is the trader first," he said. "Always the trader, before the settled man. The Gentiles will forget that, and some of our own folk too. But one pays for the land of Canaan; one pays in blood and sweat."

Then he told Jacob what he would do for him and dismissed him, and Jacob went home to his room with his head buzzing strangely. For at times it seemed to him that the Congregation Mikveh Israel was right in thinking Raphael Sanchez half mad. And at other times it seemed to him that the old man's words were a veil, and behind them moved and stirred some huge and unguessed shape. But chiefly he thought of the rosy cheeks of Miriam Ettelsohn.

It was with the Scotchman, McCampbell, that Jacob made his first trading journey. A strange man was McCampbell, with grim features and cold blue eyes, but strong and kindly, though silent, except when he talked of the Ten Lost Tribes of Israel. For it was his contention that they were the Indians beyond the Western Mountains, and on this subject he would talk endlessly.

Indeed, they had much profitable conversation, McCampbell quoting the doctrines of a rabbi called John Calvin, and our grandfather's grandfather replying with Talmud and Torah till McCampbell would almost weep that such a honey-mouthed scholar should be destined to eternal damnation. Yet he did not treat our grandfather's grandfather as one destined to eternal damnation, but as a man, and he, too, spoke of cities of refuge as a man speaks of realities, for his people had also been persecuted.

First they left the city behind them, and then the outlying towns and, soon enough, they were in the wildnerness. It was very strange to Jacob Stein. At first he would wake at night and lie awake listening, while his heart pounded, and each rustle in the forest was the step of a wild Indian, and each screech of an owl in the forest the whoop before the attack. But gradually this passed. He began to notice how silently the big man, McCampbell, moved in the woods; he began to imitate him. He began to learn many things that even a scholar of the Law, for all his wisdom, does not know—the girthing of a packsaddle and the making of fires, the look of dawn in the forest and the look of evening. It was all very new to him, and sometimes he thought he would die of it; for his flesh weakened. Yet always he kept on.

When he saw his first Indians—in the woods, not in the town—his knees knocked together. They were there as he had dreamt of them in dreams, and he thought of the spirit, Iggereth-beth-Mathlan, and her seventy-eight dancing demons, for they were painted and in skins. But he could not let his knees knock together, before heathens and a

Gentile, and the first fear passed. Then he found they were grave men, very ceremonious and silent at first, and then when the silence had been broken, full of curiosity. They knew McCampbell, but him they did not know, and they discussed him and his garments with the frankness of children, till Jacob felt naked before them, and yet not afraid. One of them pointed to the bag that hung at Jacob's neck—the bag in which, for safety's sake, he carried his phylactery—then McCampbell said something and the brown hand dropped quickly, but there was a buzz of talk.

Later on, McCampbell explained to him that they, too, wore little bags of deerskin and inside them sacred objects—and they thought, seeing his, that he must be a person of some note. It made him wonder. It made him wonder more to eat deer meat with them, by a fire.

It was a green world and a dark one that he had fallen in—dark with the shadow of the forest, green with its green. Through it ran trails and paths that were not yet roads or highways—that did not have the dust and smell of the cities of men, but another scent, another look. These paths Jacob noted carefully, making a map, for that was one of the instructions of Raphael Sanchez. It seemed a great labor and difficult and for no purpose; yet, as he had promised, so he did. And as they sank deeper and deeper into the depths of the forest, and he saw pleasant streams and wide glades, untenanted but by the deer, strange thoughts came over him. It seemed to him that the Germany he had left was very small and crowded together; it seemed to him that he had not known there was so much width to the world.

Now and then he would dream back—dream back to the quiet fields around Rettelsheim and the red-brick houses of Philadelphia, to the stuffed fish and the raisin wine, the chanting in the *chedar* and the white twisted loaves of calm Sabbath, under the white cloth. They would seem very close for the moment, then they would seem very far away. He was eating deer's meat in a forest and sleeping beside embers in the open night. It was so that Israel must have slept in the wilderness. He had not thought of it as so, but it was so.

Now and then he would look at his hands—they seemed tougher and very brown, as if they did not belong to him any more. Now and then he would catch a glimpse of his own face, as he drank at a stream. He had a beard, but it was not the beard of a scholar—it was wild and black. Moreover, he was dressed in skins, now; it seemed strange to be dressed in skins at first, and then not strange.

Now all this time, when he went to sleep at night, he would think of Miriam Ettelsohn. But, queerly enough, the harder he tried to summon up her face in his thoughts, the vaguer it became.

He lost track of time—there was only his map and the trading and the journey. Now it seemed to him that they should surely turn back, for their packs were full. He spoke of it to McCampbell, but McCampbell shook his head. There was a light in the Scotchman's eyes now—a light that seemed strange to our grandfather's grandfather—and he would pray long at night, sometimes too loudly. So they came to the banks of the great river, brown and great, and saw it, and the country beyond it, like a view across Jordan. There was no end to that country—it stretched to the limits of the sky and Jacob saw it with his eyes. He was almost afraid at first, and then he was not afraid.

It was there that the strong man, McCampbell, fell sick, and there that he died and was buried. Jacob buried him on a bluff overlooking the river and faced the grave to the west. In his death sickness, McCampbell raved of the Ten Lost Tribes again and swore they were just across the river and he would go to them. It took all Jacob's strength to hold him—if it had been at the beginning of the journey, he would not have had the strength. Then he turned back, for he, too, had seen a Promised Land, not for his seed only, but for nations yet to come.

Nevertheless, he was taken by the Shawnees, in a season of bitter cold, with his last horse dead. At first, when misfortune began to fall upon him, he had wept for the loss of the horses and the good beaver. But, when the Shawnees took him, he no longer wept; for it seemed to him that he was no longer himself, but a man he did not know.

He was not concerned when they tied him to the stake and piled the wood around him, for it seemed to him still that it must be happening to another man. Nevertheless he prayed, as was fitting, chanting loudly; for Zion in the wilderness he prayed. He could smell the smell of the *chedar* and hear the voices that he knew—Reb Moses and Reb Nathan, and through them the curious voice of Raphael Sanchez, speaking in riddles. Then the smoke took him and he coughed. His throat was hot. He called for drink, and though they could not understand his words, all men know the sign of thirst, and they brought him a bowl filled. He put it to his lips eagerly and drank, but the stuff in the bowl was scorching hot and burned his mouth. Very angry then was our grandfather's grandfather, and without so much as a cry he took the bowl in both hands and flung it straight in the face of the man who had brought it, scalding him. Then there was a cry and a murmur from the Shawnees and, after some moments, he felt himself unbound and knew that he lived.

It was flinging the bowl at the man while yet he stood at the stake that saved him, for there is an etiquette about such matters. One does not burn a madman, among the Indians; and to the Shawnees, Jacob's flinging the bowl proved that he was mad, for a sane man would not have done so. Or so it was explained to him later, though he was never quite sure that they had not been playing cat-and-mouse with him, to test him. Also they were much concerned by his chanting his death song in an unknown tongue and by the phylactery that he had taken from its bag and bound upon brow and arm for his death hour, for these they thought strong medicine and uncertain. But in any case they released him, though they would not give him back his beaver, and that winter he passed in the lodges of the Shawnees, treated sometimes like a servant and sometimes like a guest, but always on the edge of peril. For he was strange to them, and they could not quite make up their minds about him, though the man with the scalded face had his own opinion, as Jacob could see.

Yet when the winter was milder and the hunting better than it had been in some seasons, it was he who got the credit of it, and the holy phylactery also; and by the end of the winter he was talking to them of trade, though diffidently at first. Ah, our grandfather's grandfather, *selig*, what woes he had! And yet it was not all woe, for he learned much woodcraft from the Shawnees and began to speak in their tongue.

Yet he did not trust them entirely; and when spring came and he could travel, he escaped. He was no longer a scholar then, but a hunter. He tried to think what day it was by the calendar, but he could only remember the Bee Moon and the Berry Moon. Yet when he thought of a feast he tried to keep it, and always he prayed for Zion. But when he thought of Zion, it was not as he had thought of it before—a white city set on a hill—but a great and open landscape, ready for nations. He could not have said why his thought had changed, but it had.

I shall not tell all, for who knows all? I shall not tell of the trading post he found deserted and the hundred and forty French louis in the dead man's money belt. I shall not tell of the half-grown boy, McGillvray, that he found on the fringes of settlement—the boy who was to be his partner in the days to come—and how they traded again with the Shawnees and got much beaver. Only this remains to be told, for this is true.

It was a long time since he had even thought of Meyer Kappelhuist—the big pushing man with red hairs on the backs of his hands. But now they were turning back toward Philadelphia, he and McGillvray, their packhorses and their beaver; and as the paths began to grow familiar, old thoughts came into his mind. Moreover, he would hear now and then, in the outposts of the wilderness, of a red-haired trader. So when he met the man himself, not thirty miles from Lancaster, he was not surprised.

Now, Meyer Kappelhuist had always seemed a big man to our grandfather's grandfather. But he did not seem such a big man, met in the wilderness by chance, and at that Jacob was amazed. Yet the greater surprise was Meyer Kappelhuist's, for he stared at our grandfather's grandfather long and puzzledly before he cried out, "But it's the little scholar!" and clapped his hand on his knee. Then they greeted each other civilly and Meyer Kappelhuist drank liquor because of the meeting, but Jacob drank nothing. For, all the time, they were talking, he could see Meyer Kappelhuist's eyes fixed greedily upon his packs of beaver, and he did not like that. Nor did he like the looks of the three tame Indians who traveled with Meyer Kappelhuist and, though he was a man of peace, he kept his hand on his arms, and the boy, McGillvray, did the same.

Meyer Kappelhuist was anxious that they should travel on together, but Jacob refused, for, as I say, he did not like the look in the red-haired man's eyes. So he said he was taking another road and left it at that.

"And the news you have of Simon Ettelsohn and his family—it is good, no doubt, for I know you are close to them," said Jacob, before they parted.

"Close to them?" said Meyer Kappelhuist, and he looked black as thunder. Then he laughed a forced laugh. "Oh, I see them no more," he said. "The old rascal has promised his daughter to a cousin of the Seixas, a greeny, just come over, but rich, they say. But to tell you the truth, I think we are well out of it, Scholar—she was always a little too skinny for my taste," and he laughed coarsely.

"She was a rose of Sharon and a lily of the valley," said Jacob respectfully, and yet not with the pang he would have expected at such news, though it made him more determined than ever not to travel with Meyer Kappelhuist. And with that they parted and Meyer Kappelhuist went his way. Then Jacob took a fork in the trail that McGillvray knew of and that was as well for him. For when he got to Lancaster, there was news of the killing of a trader by the Indians who traveled with him; and when Jacob asked for details, they showed him something dried on a willow hoop. Jacob looked at the thing and saw the hairs upon it were red.

"Sculped all right, but we got it back," said the frontiersman, with satisfaction. "The red devil had it on him when we caught him.

Should have buried it, too, I guess, but we'd buried him already and it didn't seem feasible. Thought I might take it to Philadelphy, some-time—might make an impression on the governor. Say, if you're go-ing there, you might—after all, that's where he come from. Be a sort of memento to his folks."

"And it might have been mine, if I had traveled with him," said Ja-cob. He stared at the thing again, and his heart rose against touching it. Yet it was well the city people should know what happened to men in the wilderness, and the price of blood. "Yes, I will take it," he said.

Jacob stood before the door of Raphael Sanchez, in Philadelphia. He knocked at the door with his knuckles, and the old man himself peered out at him.

"And what is your business with me, Frontiersman?" said the old man, peering.

"The price of blood for a country," said Jacob Stein. He did not raise his voice, but there was a note in it that had not been there when he first knocked at Raphael Sanchez's door.

The old man stared at him soberly. "Enter, my son," he said at last, and Jacob touched the scroll by the doorpost and went in.

He walked through the halls as a man walks in a dream. At last he was sitting by the dark mahogany table. There was nothing changed in the room—he wondered greatly that nothing in it had changed.

"And what have you seen, my son?" said Raphael Sanchez.

"I have seen the land of Canaan, flowing with milk and honey," said Jacob, Scholar of the Law. "I have brought back grapes from Eshcol, and other things that are terrible to behold," he cried, and even as he cried he felt the sob rise in his throat. He choked it down. "Also there are eighteen packs of prime beaver at the warehouse and a boy named McGillvray, a Gentile, but very trusty," he said. "The beaver is very good and the boy under my protection. And McCampbell died by the great river, but he had seen the land and I think he rests well. The map is not made as I would have it, but it shows new things. And we must trade with the Shawnees. There are three posts to be established—I have marked them on the map—and later, more. And beyond the great river there is country that stretches to the end of the world. That is where my friend McCampbell lies, with his face turned west. But what is the use of talking? You would not understand."

He put his head on his arms, for the room was too quiet and peaceful, and he was very tired. Raphael Sanchez moved around the table and touched him on the shoulder.

"Did I not say, my son, that there was more than a girl's face to be found in the wilderness?" he said.

"A girl's face?" said Jacob. "Why, she is to be married and, I hope, will be happy, for she was a rose of Sharon. But what are girls' faces beside this?" and he flung something on the table. It rattled dryly on the table, like a cast snakeskin, but the hairs upon it were red.

"It was Meyer Kappelhuist," said Jacob childishly, "and he was a strong man. And I am not strong, but a scholar. But I have seen what I have seen. And we must say Kaddish for him."

"Yes, yes," said Raphael Sanchez. "It will be done. I will see to it."

"But you do not understand," said Jacob. "I have eaten deer's meat in the wilderness and forgotten the month and the year. I have been a servant to the heathen and held the scalp of my enemy in my hand. I will never be the same man."

"Oh, you will be the same," said Sanchez. "And no worse a scholar, perhaps. But this is a new country."

"It must be for all," said Jacob. "For my friend McCampbell died also, and he was a Gentile."

"Let us hope," said Raphael Sanchez and touched him again upon the shoulder. Then Jacob lifted his head and he saw that the light had declined and the evening was upon him. And even as he looked, Raphael Sanchez's granddaughter came in to light the candles for Sabbath. And Jacob looked upon her, and she was a dove, with dove's eyes.

The Devil and Daniel Webster

It's a story they tell in the border country, where Massachusetts joins Vermont and New Hampshire.

Yes, Dan'l Webster's dead—or, at least, they buried him. But every time there's a thunderstorm around Marshfield, they say you can hear his rolling voice in the hollows of the sky. And they say that if you go to his grave and speak loud and clear, "Dan'l Webster—Dan'l Webster!" the ground'll begin to shiver and the trees begin to shake. And after a while you'll hear a deep voice saying, "Neighbor, how stands the Union?" Then you better answer the Union stands as she stood, rock-bottomed and copper-sheathed, one and indivisible, or he's liable to rear right out of the ground. At least, that's what I was told when I was a youngster.

You see, for a while, he was the biggest man in the country. He never got to be President, but he was the biggest man. There were thousands that trusted in him right next to God Almighty, and they told stories about him that were like the stories of patriarchs and such. They said, when he stood up to speak, stars and stripes came right out in the sky, and once he spoke against a river and made it sink into the ground. They said, when he walked the woods with his fishing rod, Killall, the trout would jump out of the streams right into his pockets, for they knew it was no use putting up a fight against him; and, when he argued a case, he could turn on the harps of the blessed and the shaking of the earth underground. That was the kind of man he was, and his big farm up at Marshfield was suitable to him. The chickens he raised were all white meat down through the drumsticks, the cows were tended like children, and the big ram he called Goliath had horns with a curl like a morning-glory vine and could butt through an iron door. But Dan'l wasn't one of your gentlemen farmers; he knew all the ways of the land, and he'd be up by candlelight to see that the chores got done. A man with a mouth like a mastiff, a brow like a mountain and eyes like burning anthracite—that was Dan'l Webster in his prime. And the biggest case he argued never got written down in the books, for he argued it against the devil, nip and tuck and no holds barred. And this is the way I used to hear it told.

There was a man named Jabez Stone, lived at Cross Corners, New Hampshire. He wasn't a bad man to start with, but he was an unlucky man. If he planted corn, he got borers; if he planted potatoes, he got blight. He had good-enough land, but it didn't prosper him; he had a decent wife and children, but the more children he had, the less there was to feed them. If stones cropped up in his neighbor's field, boulders boiled up in his; if he had a horse with the spavins, he'd trade it for one with the staggers and give something extra. There's some folks bound to be like that, apparently. But one day Jabez Stone got sick of the whole business.

He'd been plowing that morning and he'd just broke the plowshare on a rock that he could have sworn hadn't been there yesterday. And, as he stood looking at the plowshare, the off horse began to cough—that ropy kind of cough that means sickness and horse doctors. There were two children down with the measles, his wife was ailing, and he had a whitlow on his thumb. It was about the last straw for Jabez Stone. "I vow," he said, and he looked around him kind of desperate—"I vow it's enough to make a man want to sell his soul to the devil! And I would, too, for two cents!"

Then he felt a kind of queerness come over him at having said what he'd said; though, naturally, being a New Hampshireman, he wouldn't take it back. But, all the same, when it got to be evening and, as far as he could see, no notice had been taken, he felt relieved in his mind, for he was a religious man. But notice is always taken, sooner or later, just like the Good Book says. And, sure enough, next day, about suppertime, a soft-spoken, dark-dressed stranger drove up in a handsome buggy and asked for Jabez Stone.

Well, Jabez told his family it was a lawyer, come to see him about a legacy. But he knew who it was. He didn't like the looks of the stranger, nor the way he smiled with his teeth. They were white teeth, and plentiful—some say they were filed to a point, but I wouldn't vouch for that. And he didn't like it when the dog took one look at the stranger and ran away howling, with his tail between his legs. But having passed his word, more or less, he stuck to it, and they went out behind the barn and made their bargain. Jabez Stone had to prick his finger to sign, and the stranger lent him a silver pin. The wound healed clean, but it left a little white scar.

After that, all of a sudden, things began to pick up and prosper for Jabez Stone. His cows got fat and his horses sleek, his crops were the envy of the neighborhood, and lightning might strike all over the valley, but it wouldn't strike his barn. Pretty soon, he was one of the prosperous people of the county; they asked him to stand for selectman, and he stood for it; there began to be talk of running him for state senate. All in all, you might say the Stone family was as happy and contented as cats in a dairy. And so they were, except for Jabez Stone.

He'd been contented enough, the first few years. It's a great thing when bad luck turns; it drives most other things out of your head. True, every now and then, especially in rainy weather, the little white scar on his finger would give him a twinge. And once a year, punctual as clockwork, the stranger with the handsome buggy would come driving by. But the sixth year, the stranger lighted, and, after that, his peace was over for Jabez Stone.

The stranger came up through the lower field, switching his boots with a cane—they were handsome black boots, but Jabez Stone never liked the look of them, particularly the toes. And, after he'd passed the time of day, he said, "Well, Mr. Stone, you're a hummer! It's a very pretty property you've got here, Mr. Stone."

"Well, some might favor it and others might not," said Jabez Stone, for he was a New Hampshireman.

"Oh, no need to decry your industry!" said the stranger, very easy, showing his teeth in a smile. "After all, we know what's been done, and it's been according to contract and specifications. So when—ahem—the mortgage falls due next year, you shouldn't have any regrets."

"Speaking of that mortgage, mister," said Jabez Stone, and he looked around for help to the earth and the sky, "I'm beginning to have one or two doubts about it."

"Doubts?" said the stranger, not quite so pleasantly.

"Why, yes," said Jabez Stone. "This being the U.S.A. and me always having been a religious man." He cleared his throat and got bolder. "Yes, sir," he said, "I'm beginning to have considerable doubts as to that mortgage holding in court."

"There's courts and courts," said the stranger, clicking his teeth. "Still, we might as well have a look at the original document." And he hauled out a big black pocketbook, full of papers. "Sherwin, Slater, Stevens, Stone," he muttered. "I, Jabez Stone, for a term of seven years—— Oh, it's quite in order, I think."

But Jabez Stone wasn't listening, for he saw something else flutter out of the black pocketbook. It was something that looked like a moth, but it wasn't a moth. And as Jabez Stone stared at it, it seemed to speak to him in a small sort of piping voice, terrible small and thin, but terrible human. "Neighbor Stone!" it squeaked. "Neighbor Stone! Help me! For God's sake, help me!"

But before Jabez Stone could stir hand or foot, the stranger whipped out a big bandanna handkerchief, caught the creature in it, just like a butterfly, and started tying up the ends of the bandanna.

"Sorry for the interruption," he said. "As I was saying——"

But Jabez Stone was shaking all over like a scared horse.

"That's Miser Stevens' voice!" he said, in a croak. "And you've got him in your handkerchief!"

The stranger looked a little embarrassed.

"Yes, I really should have transferred him to the collecting box," he said with a simper, "but there were some rather unusual specimens there and I didn't want them crowded. Well, well, these little contretemps will occur."

"I don't know what you mean by contertan," said Jabez Stone, "but that was Miser Stevens' voice! And he ain't dead! You can't tell me he is! He was just as spry and mean as a woodchuck, Tuesday!"

"In the midst of life—" said the stranger, kind of pious. "Listen!" Then a bell began to toll in the valley and Jabez Stone listened, with the sweat running down his face. For he knew it was tolled for Miser Stevens and that he was dead.

"These long-standing accounts," said the stranger with a sigh; "one really hates to close them. But business is business."

He still had the bandanna in his hand, and Jabez Stone felt sick as he saw the cloth struggle and flutter.

"Are they all as small as that?" he asked hoarsely.

"Small?" said the stranger. "Oh, I see what you mean. Why, they vary." He measured Jabez Stone with his eyes, and his teeth showed. "Don't worry, Mr. Stone," he said. "You'll go with a very good grade. I wouldn't trust you outside the collecting box. Now, a man like Dan'l Webster, of course—well, we'd have to build a special box for him, and even at that, I imagine the wing spread would astonish you. But, in your case, as I was saying——"

"Put that handkerchief away!" said Jabez Stone, and he began to beg and to pray. But the best he could get at the end was a three years' extension, with conditions.

But till you make a bargain like that, you've got no idea of how fast four years can run. By the last months of those years, Jabez Stone's known all over the state and there's talk of running him for governor—and it's dust and ashes in his mouth. For every day, when he gets up, he thinks, "There's one more night gone," and every night when he lies down, he thinks of the black pocketbook and the soul of Miser Stevens, and it makes him sick at heart. Till, finally, he can't bear it any longer, and, in the last days of the last year, he hitches up his horse and drives off to seek Dan'l Webster. For Dan'l was born in New Hampshire, only a few miles from Cross Corners, and it's well known that he has a particular soft spot for old neighbors.

It was early in the morning when he got to Marshfield, but Dan'l was up already, talking Latin to the farm hands and wrestling with the ram, Goliath, and trying out a new trotter and working up speeches to make against John C. Calhoun. But when he heard a New Hampshireman had come to see him, he dropped everything else he was doing, for that was Dan'l's way. He gave Jabez Stone a breakfast that five men couldn't eat, went into the living history of every man and woman in Cross Corners, and finally asked him how he could serve him.

Jabez Stone allowed that it was a kind of mortgage case.

"Well, I haven't pleaded a mortgage case in a long time, and I don't generally plead now, except before the Supreme Court," said Dan'l, "but if I can, I'll help you."

"Then I've got hope for the first time in ten years," said Jabez Stone, and told him the details.

Dan'l walked up and down as he listened, hands behind his back, now and then asking a question, now and then plunging his eyes at the floor, as if they'd bore through it like gimlets. When Jabez Stone had finished, Dan'l puffed out his cheeks and blew. Then he turned to Jabez Stone and a smile broke over his face like the sunrise over Monadnock.

"You've certainly given yourself the devil's own row to hoe, Neighbor Stone," he said, "but I'll take your case."

"You'll take it?" said Jabez Stone, hardly daring to believe.

"Yes," said Dan'l Webster. "I've got about seventy-five other things to do and the Missouri Compromise to straighten out, but I'll take your case. For if two New Hampshiremen aren't a match for the devil, we might as well give the country back to the Indians."

Then he shook Jabez Stone by the hand and said, "Did you come down here in a hurry?"

"Well, I admit I made time," said Jabez Stone.

"You'll go back faster," said Dan'l Webster, and he told 'em to hitch up Constitution and Constellation to the carriage. They were matched grays with one white forefoot, and they stepped like greased lightning.

Well, I won't describe how excited and pleased the whole Stone family was to have the great Dan'l Webster for a guest, when they finally got there. Jabez Stone had lost his hat on the way, blown off when they overtook a wind, but he didn't take much account of that. But after supper he sent the family off to bed, for he had most particular business with Mr. Webster. Mrs. Stone wanted them to sit in the front parlor, but Dan'l Webster knew front parlors and said he preferred the kitchen. So it was there they sat, waiting for the stranger, with a jug on the table between them and a bright fire on the hearth—the stranger being scheduled to show up on the stroke of midnight, according to specifications.

Well, most men wouldn't have asked for better company than Dan'l Webster and a jug. But with every tick of the clock Jabez Stone got sadder and sadder. His eyes roved round, and though he sampled the jug you could see he couldn't taste it. Finally, on the stroke of 11:30 he reached over and grabbed Dan'l Webster by the arm.

"Mr. Webster, Mr. Webster!" he said, and his voice was shaking with fear and a desperate courage. "For God's sake, Mr. Webster, harness your horses and get away from this place while you can!"

"You've brought me a long way, neighbor, to tell me you don't like my company," said Dan'l Webster, quite peaceable, pulling at the jug.

"Miserable wretch that I am!" groaned Jabez Stone. "I've brought you a devilish way, and now I see my folly. Let him take me if he wills. I don't hanker after it, I must say, but I can stand it. But you're the Union's stay and New Hampshire's pride! He mustn't get you, Mr. Webster! He mustn't get you!"

Dan'l Webster looked at the distracted man, all gray and shaking in the firelight, and laid a hand on his shoulder.

"I'm obliged to you, Neighbor Stone," he said gently. "It's kindly thought of. But there's a jug on the table and a case in hand. And I never left a jug or a case half finished in my life."

And just at that moment there was a sharp rap on the door.

"Ah," said Dan'l Webster, very coolly, "I thought your clock was a trifle slow, Neighbor Stone." He stepped to the door and opened it. "Come in!" he said.

The stranger came in—very dark and tall he looked in the firelight. He was carrying a box under his arm—a black, japanned box with little air holes in the lid. At the sight of the box, Jabez Stone gave a low cry and shrank into a corner of the room.

"Mr. Webster, I presume," said the stranger, very polite, but with his eyes glowing like a fox's deep in the woods.

"Attorney of record for Jabez Stone," said Dan'l Webster, but his eyes were glowing too. "Might I ask your name?"

"I've gone by a good many," said the stranger carelessly. "Perhaps Scratch will do for the evening. I'm often called that in these regions."

Then he sat down at the table and poured himself a drink from the jug. The liquor was cold in the jug, but it came steaming into the glass.

"And now," said the stranger, smiling and showing his teeth, "I shall call upon you, as a law-abiding citizen, to assist me in taking possession of my property."

Well, with that the argument began—and it went hot and heavy. At first, Jabez Stone had a flicker of hope, but when he saw Dan'l Webster being forced back at point after point, he just scrunched in his corner, with his eyes on that japanned box. For there wasn't any doubt as to the deed or the signature—that was the worst of it. Dan'l Webster twisted and turned and thumped his fist on the table, but he couldn't get away from that. He offered to compromise the case; the stranger wouldn't hear of it. He pointed out the property had increased in value, and state senators ought to be worth more; the stranger stuck to the letter of the law. He was a great lawyer, Dan'l Webster, but we know who's the King of Lawyers, as the Good Book tells us, and it seemed as if, for the first time, Dan'l Webster had met his match.

Finally, the stranger yawned a little. "Your spirited efforts on behalf of your client do you credit, Mr. Webster," he said, "but if you have no more arguments to adduce, I'm rather pressed for time"—and Jabez Stone shuddered.

Dan'l Webster's brow looked dark as a thundercloud.

"Pressed or not, you shall not have this man!" he thundered. "Mr. Stone is an American citizen, and no American citizen may be forced into the service of a foreign prince. We fought England for that in '12 and we'll fight all hell for it again!"

"Foreign?" said the stranger. "And who calls me a foreigner?"

"Well, I never yet heard of the dev—of your claiming American citizenship," said Dan'l Webster with surprise.

"And who with better right?" said the stranger, with one of his terrible smiles. "When the first wrong was done to the first Indian, I was there. When the first slaver put out for the Congo, I stood on her deck. Am I not in your books and stories and beliefs, from the first settlements on? Am I not spoken of, still, in every church in New England? 'Tis true the North claims me for a Southerner and the South for a Northerner, but I am neither. I am merely an honest American like yourself—and of the best descent—for, to tell the truth, Mr. Webster, though I don't like to boast of it, my name is older in this country than yours."

"Aha!" said Dan'l Webster, with the veins standing out in his forehead. "Then I stand on the Constitution! I demand a trial for my client!"

"The case is hardly one for an ordinary court," said the stranger, his eyes flickering. "And, indeed, the lateness of the hour——"

"Let it be any court you choose, so it is an American judge and an American jury!" said Dan'l Webster in his pride. "Let it be the quick or the dead; I'll abide the issue!"

"You have said it," said the stranger, and pointed his finger at the door. And with that, and all of a sudden, there was a rushing of wind outside and a noise of footsteps. They came, clear and distinct, through the night. And yet, they were not like the footsteps of living men.

"In God's name, who comes by so late?" cried Jabez Stone, in an ague of fear.

"The jury Mr. Webster demands," said the stranger, sipping at his boiling glass. "You must pardon the rough appearance of one or two; they will have come a long way."

And with that the fire burned blue and the door blew open and twelve men entered, one by one.

If Jabez Stone had been sick with terror before, he was blind with terror now. For there was Walter Butler, the loyalist, who spread fire and horror through the Mohawk Valley in the times of the Revolution; and there was Simon Girty, the renegade, who saw white men burned at the stake and whooped with the Indians to see them burn. His eyes were green, like a catamount's, and the stains on his hunting shirt did not come from the blood of the deer. King Philip was there, wild and proud as he had been in life, with the great gash in his head that gave him his death wound, and cruel Governor Dale, who broke men on the wheel. There was Morton of Merry Mount, who so vexed the Plymouth Colony, with his flushed, loose, handsome face and his hate of the godly. There was Teach, the bloody pirate, with his black beard curling on his breast. The Reverend John Smeet, with his strangler's hands and his Geneva gown, walked as daintily as he had to the gallows. The red print of the rope was still around his neck, but he carried a perfumed handkerchief in one hand. One and all, they came into the room with the fires of hell still upon them, and the stranger named their names and their deeds as they came, till the tale of twelve was told. Yet the stranger had told the truth—they had all played a part in America.

"Are you satisfied with the jury, Mr. Webster?" said the stranger mockingly, when they had taken their places.

The sweat stood upon Dan'l Webster's brow, but his voice was clear.

"Quite satisfied," he said. "Though I miss General Arnold from the company."

"Benedict Arnold is engaged upon other business," said the stranger, with a glower. "Ah, you asked for a justice, I believe."

He pointed his finger once more, and a tall man, soberly clad in Puritan garb, with the burning gaze of the fanatic, stalked into the room and took his judge's place.

"Justice Hathorne is a jurist of experience," said the stranger. "He presided at certain witch trials once held in Salem. There were others who repented of the business later, but not he."

"Repent of such notable wonders and undertakings?" said the stern old justice. "Nay, hang them—hang them all!" And he muttered to himself in a way that struck ice into the soul of Jabez Stone.

Then the trial began, and, as you might expect, it didn't look anyways good for the defense. And Jabez Stone didn't make much of a witness in his own behalf. He took one look at Simon Girty and screeched, and they had to put him back in his corner in a kind of swoon.

It didn't halt the trial, though; the trial went on, as trials do. Dan'l Webster had faced some hard juries and hanging judges in his time, but this was the hardest he'd ever faced, and he knew it. They sat there with a kind of glitter in their eyes, and the stranger's smooth voice went on and on. Every time he'd raise an objection, it'd be "Objection sustained," but whenever Dan'l objected, it'd be "Objection denied." Well, you couldn't expect fair play from a fellow like this Mr. Scratch.

It got to Dan'l in the end, and he began to heat, like iron in the forge. When he got up to speak he was going to flay that stranger with every trick known to the law, and the judge and jury too. He didn't care if it was contempt of court or what would happen to him for it. He didn't care any more what happened to Jabez Stone. He just got madder and madder, thinking of what he'd say. And yet, curiously enough, the more he thought about it, the less he was able to arrange his speech in his mind.

Till, finally, it was time for him to get up on his feet, and he did so, all ready to bust out with lightnings and denunciations. But before he started he looked over the judge and jury for a moment, such being his custom. And he noticed the glitter in their eyes was twice as strong as before, and they all leaned forward. Like hounds just before they get the fox, they looked, and the blue mist of evil in the room thickened as he watched them. Then he saw what he'd been about to do, and he wiped his forehead, as a man might who's just escaped falling into a pit in the dark.

For it was him they'd come for, not only Jabez Stone. He read it in the glitter of their eyes and in the way the stranger hid his mouth with one hand. And if he fought them with their own weapons, he'd fall into their power; he knew that, though he couldn't have told you how. It was his own anger and horror that burned in their eyes; and he'd have to wipe that out or the case was lost. He stood there for a moment, his black eyes burning like anthracite. And then he began to speak.

He started off in a low voice, though you could hear every word. They say he could call on the harps of the blessed when he chose. And this was just as simple and easy as a man could talk. But he didn't start out by condemning or reviling. He was talking about the things that make a country a country, and a man a man.

And he began with the simple things that everybody's known and felt—the freshness of a fine morning when you're young, and the taste of food when you're hungry, and the new day that's every day when you're a child. He took them up and he turned them in his hands. They were good things for any man. But without freedom, they sickened. And when he talked of those enslaved, and the sorrows of slavery, his voice got like a big bell. He talked of the early days of America and the men who had made those days. It wasn't a spread-eagle speech, but he made you see it. He admitted all the wrong that had ever been done. But he showed how, out of the wrong and the right, the suffering and the starvations, something new had come. And everybody had played a part in it, even the traitors.

Then he turned to Jabez Stone and showed him as he was—an ordinary man who'd had hard luck and wanted to change it. And, because he'd wanted to change it, now he was going to be punished for all eternity. And yet there was good in Jabez Stone, and he showed that good. He was hard and mean, in some ways, but he was a man. There was sadness in being a man, but it was a proud thing too. And he showed what the pride of it was till you couldn't help feeling it. Yes, even in hell, if a man was a man, you'd know it. And he wasn't pleading for any one person any more, though his voice rang like an organ. He was telling the story and the failures and the endless journey of mankind. They got tricked and trapped and bamboozled, but it was a great journey. And no demon that was ever foaled could know the inwardness of it—it took a man to do that.

The fire began to die on the hearth and the wind before morning to blow. The light was getting gray in the room when Dan'l Webster finished. And his words came back at the end to New Hampshire ground, and the one spot of land that each man loves and clings to. He painted a picture of that, and to each one of that jury he spoke of things long forgotten. For his voice could search the heart, and that was his gift and his strength. And to one, his voice was like the forest and its secrecy, and to another like the sea and the storms of the sea; and one heard the cry of his lost nation in it, and another saw a little harmless scene he hadn't remembered for years. But each saw something. And when Dan'l Webster finished he didn't know whether or not he'd saved Jabez Stone. But he knew he'd done a miracle. For the glitter was gone from the eyes of judge and jury, and, for the moment, they were men again, and knew they were men.

"The defense rests," said Dan'l Webster, and stood there like a mountain. His ears were still ringing with his speech, and he didn't hear anything else till he heard Judge Hathorne say, "The jury will retire to consider its verdict."

Walter Butler rose in his place and his face had a dark, gay pride on it.

"The jury has considered its verdict," he said, and looked the stranger full in the eye. "We find for the defendant, Jabez Stone."

With that, the smile left the stranger's face, but Walter Butler did not flinch.

"Perhaps 'tis not strictly in accordance with the evidence," he said, "but even the damned may salute the eloquence of Mr. Webster."

With that, the long crow of a rooster split the gray morning sky, and judge and jury were gone from the room like a puff of smoke and as if they had never been there. The stranger turned to Dan'l Webster, smiling wryly.

"Major Butler was always a bold man," he said. "I had not thought him quite so bold. Nevertheless, my congratulations, as between two gentlemen."

"I'll have that paper first, if you please," said Dan'l Webster, and he took it and tore it into four pieces. It was queerly warm to the touch. "And now," he said, "I'll have you!" and his hand came down like a bear trap on the stranger's arm. For he knew that once you bested anybody like Mr. Scratch in a fair fight, his power on you was gone. And he could see that Mr. Scratch knew it too.

The stranger twisted and wriggled, but he couldn't get out of that grip. "Come, come, Mr. Webster," he said, smiling palely. "This sort of thing is ridic—ouch!—is ridiculous. If you're worried about the costs of the case, naturally, I'd be glad to pay——"

"And so you shall!" said Dan'l Webster, shaking him till his teeth rattled. "For you'll sit right down at that table and draw up a document, promising never to bother Jabez Stone nor his heirs or assigns nor any other New Hampshireman till doomsday! For any hades we want to raise in this state, we can raise ourselves, without assistance from strangers."

"Ouch!" said the stranger. "Ouch! Well, they never did run very big to the barrel, but—ouch!—I agree!"

So he sat down and drew up the document. But Dan'l Webster kept his hand on his coat collar all the time.

"And, now, may I go?" said the stranger, quite humble, when Dan'l'd seen the document was in proper and legal form.

"Go?" said Dan'l, giving him another shake. "I'm still trying to figure out what I'll do with you. For you've settled the costs of the case, but you haven't settled with me. I think I'll take you back to Marshfield," he said, kind of reflective. "I've got a ram there named Goliath that can butt through an iron door. I'd kind of like to turn you loose in his field and see what he'd do."

Well, with that the stranger began to beg and to plead. And he begged and he pled so humble that finally Dan'l, who was naturally kindhearted, agreed to let him go. The stranger seemed terrible grateful for that and said, just to show they were friends, he'd tell Dan'l's fortune before leaving. So Dan'l agreed to that, though he didn't take much stock in fortune-tellers ordinarily. But, naturally, the stranger was a little different.

Well, he pried and he peered at the lines in Dan'l's hands. And he told him one thing and another that was quite remarkable. But they were all in the past.

"Yes, all that's true, and it happened," said Dan'l Webster. "But what's to come in the future?"

The stranger grinned, kind of happily, and shook his head.

"The future's not as you think it," he said. "It's dark. You have a great ambition, Mr. Webster."

"I have," said Dan'l firmly, for everybody knew he wanted to be President.

"It seems almost within your grasp," said the stranger, "but you will not attain it. Lesser men will be made President and you will be passed over."

"And, if I am, I'll still be Daniel Webster," said Dan'l. "Say on."

"You have two strong sons," said the stranger, shaking his head. "You look to found a line. But each will die in war and neither reach greatness."

"Live or die, they are still my sons," said Dan'l Webster. "Say on."

"You have made great speeches," said the stranger. "You will make more."

"Ah," said Dan'l Webster.

"But the last great speech you make will turn many of your own against you," said the stranger. "They will call you Ichabod; they will call you by other names. Even in New England, some will say you have turned your coat and sold your country, and their voices will be loud against you till you die."

"So it is an honest speech, it does not matter what men say," said Dan'l Webster. Then he looked at the stranger and their glances locked.

"One question," he said. "I have fought for the Union all my life. Will I see that fight won against those who would tear it apart?"

"Not while you live," said the stranger, grimly, "but it will be won. And after you are dead, there are thousands who will fight for your cause, because of words that you spoke."

"Why, then, you long-barreled, slab-sided, lantern-jawed, fortune-telling note shaver!" said Dan'l Webster, with a great roar of laughter, "be off with you to your own place before I put my mark on you! For, by the thirteen original colonies, I'd go to the Pit itself to save the Union!"

And with that he drew back his foot for a kick that would have stunned a horse. It was only the tip of his shoe that caught the stranger, but he went flying out of the door with his collecting box under his arm.

"And now," said Dan'l Webster, seeing Jabez Stone beginning to rouse from his swoon, "let's see what's left in the jug, for it's dry work talking all night. I hope there's pie for breakfast, Neighbor Stone."

But they say that whenever the devil comes near Marshfield, even now, he gives it a wide berth. And he hasn't been seen in the state of New Hampshire from that day to this. I'm not talking about Massachusetts or Vermont.

The Sobbin' Women

They came over the Pass one day in one big wagon—all ten of them—man and woman and hired girl and seven big boy children, from the nine-year-old who walked by the team to the baby in arms. Or so the story runs—it was in the early days of settlement and the town had never heard of the Sobbin' Women then. But it opened its eyes one day, and there were the Pontipees.

They were there but they didn't stay long—just time enough to buy meal and get a new shoe for the lead horse. You couldn't call them unsociable, exactly—they seemed to be sociable enough among themselves. But you could tell, somehow, from the look of them, that they weren't going to settle on ground other people had cleared. They were all high-colored and dark-haired—handsome with a wilderness handsomeness—and when you got them all together, they looked more like a tribe or a nation than an ordinary family. I don't know how they gave folks that feeling, but they did. Yes, even the baby, when the town women tried to handle him. He was a fine, healthy baby, but they said it was like trying to pet a young raccoon.

Well, that was all there was to it, at the start. They paid for what they bought in good money and drove on up into Sobbin' Women Valley—only it wasn't called Sobbin' Women Valley then. And pretty soon, there was smoke from a chimney there that hadn't been there before. But you know what town gossip is when it gets started. The Pontipees were willing enough to let other folks alone—in fact, that was what they wanted. But, because it was what they wanted, the town couldn't see why they wanted it. Towns get that way, sometimes.

So, it was mostly cross questions and crooked answers when the Pontipees came into town, to trade off their pelts and such and buy at the store. There wasn't much actual trouble—not after two loafers at the tavern made fun of Pa Pontipee's fur cap and Pa Pontipee stretched them both before you could say "Jack Robinson." But there wasn't a neighborly feeling—yes, you could say that. The women would tell their children about the terrible Pontipees and the men would wag their heads. And when they came in to church—

which they did once a year—there'd be a sort of rustle in the congregation, though they always took a back pew and listened perfectly respectful. But the minister never seemed to be able to preach as good a sermon as usual that Sunday—and naturally, he blamed the Pontipees for that. Till finally, they got to be a sort of legend in the community—the wild folks who lived up the valley like bears in the woods—and, indeed, some said they turned into bears in the winter time, which just shows you what people will say. And, though the boys were well set up, they might as well have been deaf-mutes for all the notice the town-girls took of them—except to squeak and run to the other side of the road when the Pontipees came marching along.

While, as for the Pontipees—nobody knew what they made of it all, for they weren't much on talking. If one of them said "It's a fine day" and another admitted it was, that was conversation that would last them a long while. Besides, they had work enough and to spare, in their own valley, to keep them busy; and, if Ma Pontipee would have liked more society, she never let on. She did her duty by the boys and tried to give them some manners, in spite of their backwoods raising; and that was enough for any woman to do.

But things never stand still in this world, and soon enough, the boys weren't boys any more, they were men. And when the fall of a tree took Pa Pontipee, his wife didn't linger long after him. There was a terrible fuss about the funerals too—for the Pontipee boys got the minister, but they wouldn't let the burials take place in town. They said Pa and Ma wouldn't feel comfortable, all crowded up among strangers in the churchyard, so they laid them to rest in the Valley where they'd lived, and the town found that queerer than ever. But there's worse places to lie than looking out over the fields you've cleared.

After that, though, the town thought some of the boys, at least, would move in from the Valley and get more sociable. They figured they'd have to—they figured with their Pa and Ma gone, the boys would fight amongst themselves—they figured a dozen things. But none of the things they figured happened at all. The Pontipee boys stayed out in the Valley, and when they came to the town, they walked through it as proud as Lucifer, and when they came to the church, they put just the same money in the collection-plate they had when Ma and Pa Pontipee were alive. Some thought it was because they were stupid to count, but I don't think it was that.

They went on just the same, as I say, but things didn't go quite the same for them. For one thing, the hired girl couldn't keep the place the way Ma Pontipee kept it. And besides, she was getting old herself. Well, pretty soon, she up and died. They gave her as good a funeral as they knew how—she'd always been part of the family. But, after that, though the farm went ahead as well as ever, things in the house began to go from bad to worse.

Menlike, they didn't notice what was wrong at first, except there was a lot of dust around and things didn't get put away. But, after each one of them had tried a week of cooking for the others and all the others had cursed out the one who was cooking something proper, they decided something had to be done about it. It took them a long time to decide that—they were slow thinkers as well as slow talkers, the Pontipees. But, when they decided about a thing, it got done.

"The flapjacks are greasy again," said Harry Pontipee, one evening—Harry was the oldest. "You know what we've got to get, brothers? We've got to get a woman to take care of this place. I can lay a tree within two inches of where I want it to fall. I can shoot the eye out of a grey squirrel in a treetop. I can do all a man should do. But I can't cook and make it taste human."

"You're right, brother," said Hob Pontipee—Hob was the youngest. "I can tan deerskin better than an Injun squaw. I can wrastle underholt and overholt and throw any man in this county. I can play on a boxwood fiddle—but I can't sweep dust so it stays swept. It takes a woman to do that, for there seems to be a trick about it. We've got to get a woman."

Then they all joined in saying what they could do—and it was plenty—but they couldn't cook and they couldn't dust and they couldn't make a house comfortable because that was woman's business, and there seemed to be a trick about it. So they had to get a woman to keep house for them. But where were they going to get her?

"We could get a hired girl, maybe," said Hosea Pontipee—the middle one—but, even as he spoke, there wasn't much hope in his voice.

"That hired girl we had was the last one left in the East," said Harry Pontipee. "Some may have growed up, since her time, but I don't want to go back across the Pass on the chance of an out-and-out miracle."

"Well then," said Hob Pontipee, practical, "there's just one thing to do. One of us has to get married. And I think it ought to be Harry—he's the eldest."

Well, that remark nearly caused a break-up in the family. Harry kicked like a cow in fly-time at the bare idea of getting married, and tried to put it on to Halbert who was next in line. And Halbert passed it on to Harvey, but Harvey said women was snares and delusions, or so he'd heard, and he wouldn't have a strange woman around him for a brand-new plow.

So it went on down to Hob and he wouldn't hear of it—and it wasn't till a couple of chairs had been broken and Hob had a black eye that the ruckus quieted at all. But, gradually, they came to see that one of 'em would have to get married, as a matter of family duty, or they'd all be eating spoiled flapjacks for the rest of their lives. Only then the question came up as to who it was to be, and that started a bigger disturbance than ever.

Finally, they agreed that the only fair way was drawing straws. So Hob held the straws and they drew—and sure enough, Harry got the long one. Sick enough he looked about it—but there it was. The others started congratulating him and making jokes—especially Hob.

"You'll have to slick up, tomorrow," said Hob, glad it wasn't him. "You'll have to cut your hair and brush your clothes and act pretty, if you're going to be a bridegroom!"

Next morning they got him down and cut his hair and put bear's grease on it and dressed him up in the best clothes they had and sent him into town to look for a wife.

It was all right when he started out from the Valley. He even took a look at himself in a spring and was kind of surprised at the young man who looked back at him. But the nearer he got to town, the queerer and tremblier he felt, and the less able to go about doing what he'd promised.

He tried to remember how it had been when his Pa and Ma had been courting. But, naturally, as he hadn't been born then, he didn't know. Then he tried to think of various girls in the village, but the more he thought of them, the more they mixed in his mind—till, finally, all he could think of was a high, wild bank of rhododendron flowers that mixed and shimmered and laughed at you the closer you came to it.

"Oh, Lordy! It's a heavy responsibility to lay on a man!" he said and mopped his forehead with his sleeve.

Finally, however, he made up his mind. "I'll ask the first woman I see, pretty or ugly!" he said to himself, with the perspiration fairly rolling down his face, though it was a cold March day. And he gave his horse a kick.

But, when he got into town, the first woman he saw was the storekeeper's wife. The second he saw was a little girl in a pinafore—and the third was the minister's daughter. He was all set up to speak to her—but she squeaked and ran to the other side of the street as soon as she saw him and left him standing there with his hat in his hand. That sort of took the courage out of him.

"By the whiskers of Moses!" he said to himself, "this marryin' job is a harder job than I bargained for, I guess I'll go over to the tavern and get me a drink—maybe that will put some ideas in my head."

It was there he saw her—feeding the chickens out in the poultry-yard. Her name was Milly and she was a bound girl as they had in those days. Next door to a slave she was, for all she'd come of good stock and had some education. She was young and thin, with a sharp little thoughtful face and ragged clothes, but she walked as straight as an Indian as she went about the yard. Harry Pontipee couldn't have said if she were pretty or plain, but, as he watched her through the window, feeding the chickens, something seemed to tell him that he might have better luck with her than he'd had with the others.

Well, he drank his drink and went out.

"Hello, girl," he said, in one of those big voices men use when they're pretending not to be embarrassed.

She looked up at him straight. "Hello, backwoodsman!" she said, friendly enough. She didn't look a bit scared of him and that put him off.

"It's a nice morning," said Harry, louder, trying to lead up to his point.

"It is for some," said the girl, perfectly polite but going on feeding the chickens.

Harry swallowed hard at that. "It'd be a nice morning to get married, they tell me," he said, with the perspiration breaking out all over him again. He'd meant to say something else, but when it came to the point, he couldn't.

Well, she didn't say anything to that so he had to start all over again.

"My name's Harry Pontipee," he said. "I've got a good farm up the Valley."

"Have you?" said the girl.

"Yes," he said. "It's a right good farm. And some folks seem to think I'd make a good husband."

"Do they?" said the girl. I guess she was smiling by now but Harry couldn't see it—she had her head turned.

"Yes they do," said Harry, kind of desperate, his voice getting louder and louder. "What do you think about it?"

"I couldn't tell on such short acquaintance," said the girl.

"Will you marry me and find out?" said Harry, in a perfect bellow, shaking all over.

"Yes, I will, if you don't ask me quite so loud," she said, very prim—and even Harry could see she was smiling now.

Well, they made a queer pair when they went up to the minister—the girl still in her chicken-feed clothes, for she didn't have any others, and Harry in his backwoods finery. He'd had to buy out her time from the innkeeper for twelve beaver pelts and a hunting knife.

But when the wedding service was over, "Well, we're married," said Harry, with great relief, "And now we'll be going home."

"Oh, no we won't," said she "We're going to the store first and buy me some cloth for a decent dress—for landless I may be and dowryless I may be, but I'm a married woman now, and what's fit for a chicken-girl isn't fit for a married woman."

In a sort of daze, he saw her lay out the price of twelve more beaver pelts in cloth and woman's fixings, and beat down the store-keeper on the price, too.

He only asked her a question about one thing—a little pair of slippers she bought. They were fancy slippers, with embroidery on them. "I thought you had a pair of shoes," he said. She turned to him, with a cocky sort of look on her face. "Silly," she said. "How could anyone tell your wife had pretty feet in the shoes I had?"

Well, he thought that over, and, after a while, something in the way she said it and the cocky look on her face made him feel pleased, and he began to laugh. He wasn't used to laughing in front of a girl, but he could see it might have its points.

Then they rode back to the Valley, her riding pillion, with her bundles in the saddlebags. And all the way back, she was trying him and testing him and trying to find out, by one little remark or another, just what kind of a man he was. She was a spunky little girl, and she had more education than she let on. And long ago, she'd made up her mind to get out of being a bound girl the first way that offered. But, all the same, marrying Harry Pontipee was a leap in the dark.

But the more she tried and tested Harry, the better bargain she seemed to think she'd made. And that took courage to admit—for the way was a wild one and a lonesome, and, naturally, she'd heard stories of Pontipee Valley. She couldn't quite believe they lived with bears, up there, but she didn't know.

And finally, they came to the house, and there were dark things moving outside it. "Bears!" thought Milly, kind of hopeless, and her heart went into her throat, but she didn't let on.

"W-what's that, Harry dear?" she said, holding on tight.

"Oh, that's just my brothers," said Harry, kind of careless, and with that those six hungry six-footers moved into the light.

"Oh!" said Milly, "you didn't tell me you had six brothers." But her voice wasn't reproachful, just sort of soft and quiet.

"I guess it was the wedding kind of knocked it out of my mind," said Harry. "But, there—you'll see enough of 'em anyhow, because we all live together."

"Oh," said Milly again, kind of soft. "I see." And the brothers came up, one by one, and shook hands. They'd intended to cut quite a few jokes on Harry if he did come home with a wife, but, somehow, when they looked at Milly, they forgot about that.

Well, they brought her into the house. It was a handsome house, for the times, with genuine window-glass. But Milly rubbed her finger along a window sill and saw it come off black and then she wrote her name in the dust on the mantelpiece.

"What a lovely big house!" she said, coughing a little with the dust she'd raised.

"It's mebbe a little dusty now," said Harry. "But now you're here——"

"Yes," said Milly and passed on to the kitchen. Well, the kitchen was certainly a sight. But Milly didn't seem to notice.

Presently, "What a great big jar of flapjack batter!" she said. "And what a big tub of salt pork!"

"That's for tonight," said Harry. "Me and my brothers is hearty eaters. We haven't been eating so well since we had to cook for ourselves, but now you're here——"

"Yes," said Milly and passed on to the laundry. The laundry was half full of huckaback shirts and such that needed washing—piles and piles of them.

"What a lot of wash!" said Milly.

"That's so," said Harry, kind of pleased. "Me and my brothers is kind of hard on our clothes—all seven of us—so there's lots of washing and mending, but now you're here——"

"Yes," said Milly, swallowing a little. "And now all you men clear out of my kitchen while I get supper. Clear out!" she said, smiling at them, though she didn't feel much like smiling.

I don't know what she said to herself when they'd left her alone. I know what a man would have said and I guess she said that, too. I know she thought at least once of the money in her stocking and how far it was back to town. And then her eye happened to fall on that great big jar of flapjack batter—and, all of a sudden the whole thing struck her as funny, and she laughed till she cried.

But then she found a clean handkerchief and blew her nose and straightened her hair and set about her work.

Those boys hadn't had a supper like that in months and they treated it respectful. And Milly didn't say a word to them about manners then, though, later on, she said plenty. She just sat and watched them, with a curious light in her eyes.

When it was over finally, and they were stuffed, "Mrs. Harry," said Howard. "You're a wonder, Mrs. Harry!" and "You're sure a wonder, Mrs. Harry!" chorused all the rest of them, down to Hob. She could see they meant it, too.

"Thanks," she said, very polite and gracious. "Thank you, Howard, and you, Hosea, and all my brothers."

At the end of three months, there wasn't one of those boys that wouldn't have laid down his life for Milly, and, as for Harry, he just worshipped the ground she walked on. With all that work to do, naturally, she got thinner and thinner and peakeder and peakeder, but she didn't complain. She knew what she wanted and how she was going to get it—and she waited her chance.

Finally Harry noticed how thin she was getting and he spoke to her about it.

"Can't you ever sit down and rest, Milly?" he said one day, watching her fly around the kitchen, doing six things at once.

But she just laughed at him and said, "I'm cooking for you and your six brothers, and that makes work, you know."

Well, he thought that over, inside him, but he didn't say anything, then. But he came up to her in the laundry another time, and when she was dusting the house another time—she was looking peakeder each day—and asked her if she couldn't rest a spell. The last time, he brought his fist down on the table with a bang.

"This has got to stop!" he said. "Me and my six brothers is wearing you to skin and bone with our victuals and our shirts and the dust we track in the house, and I won't have it no more! It's got to stop!"

"Well, Harry," she said, sort of quiet, "if it's got to stop, it's got to—and pretty soon, Harry. Because, I'm expecting, and a woman that's expecting can't work like a woman in her usual health."

Well, after he got his sense back, after hearing that, he called the whole family into consultation that evening and put it to them plain. They'd do anything for Milly by then.

She led the conversation where she wanted it to go, though she didn't seem to, and finally they decided it was up to Halbert, the second oldest, to get married, so his wife could take some of the work off Milly's hands. So next day, Halbert spruced up and went to town to look for a wife. But when he came home, he was alone and all dejected.

"They won't have me," he said, very mournful. "They won't none of 'em have me—and I asked fourteen of 'em."

"Why, what's the matter?" said Milly.

"Well," said Halbert, "it seems they've heard about the seven of us and the lot of victuals we eat and the wash and all—and they say only a fool would marry into a family like that and they don't see how you stand it, Milly."

"Oh, that's what they say, is it?" said Milly, with her eyes as bright as candles. "Well, your turn next, Harvey."

So Harvey tried it and Hosea tried it and all of them tried it. But none of them had any luck. And then, finally, Milly let loose at them, good and proper.

"You great big lumps of men!" she said, with the cocky look on her face. "There's more ways of killing a cat than choking it with cream. If they won't marry you after you've asked 'em—why don't you marry 'em first and ask 'em afterwards?"

"But how can we do that?" said Harvey, who was the stupidest.

"Well," said Milly—and here's where her education came in that I've made such a point of—"I read in a history book once about a bunch of people called Romans who were just in your fix." And she went on to tell them about the Romans—how they were settled in a country that was unfriendly to them, just like the Pontipees, and how they all needed wives, just like the Pontipees, and how, when they couldn't get them in the ordinary way from the other people of the country who were called the Sobbin's or the Sabbin's or some such name, they raided the Sobbin' town one night and carried off a lot of the Sobbin' women and married them.

"And, if you can't do as well for yourselves as a lot of old dead Romans," she ended, "you're no brothers of mine and you can cook your own suppers the rest of your lives."

They all sat around dumbfounded for a while. Finally Hob spoke up.

"That sounds all right, in history," he said, "but this is different. Supposing these women just cry and pine away when we've carried them off—supposing that?"

"Listen to me," said Milly. "I know what I'm talking about. Every one of those girls is crazy to get married—and there's not half enough men in town to go round. They think a lot of you boys, too, for I've heard them talk about you; but they're scared of your being backwoodsmen, and scared of the work, and each one is scared of being the first to leave the others. I'll answer for them, once you've married them. Is there anybody around here who can marry people, except the regular minister?"

"There's a sort of hedge-parson just come to town," said Hob. "I reckon he can tie a knot as tight as any preacher in the county."

"All right," said Milly. "That settles it."

It was the evening of the big sociable that it happened. They held it once a year, around Thanksgiving time, and those who had rifles and weapons left them at the door. The Pontipee boys had never attended before—so there was a good deal of stir when they marched in, all seven of them, with Milly in the middle. The brothers were shaved and clean and dressed up spick and span and Milly never looked better, in a dress she'd made out of store cloth and her embroidered slippers.

There was quite a bit of giggling from the town girls, as the Pontipees entered, and a buzz around the hall, but then the fiddler struck up and people began to dance and play games and enjoy themselves, and pretty soon they forgot the Pontipees were there at all, except that the Pontipee boys acted very polite to everybody—Milly'd taught 'em that—and, I guess, before the evening was over some of the town girls were wondering why they'd turned down boys like that just because they lived in the backwoods.

But they didn't get much chance to think about it, at that. Because, just as they were all going to sit down to supper—"Ready, boys?" called Milly, in a voice that cut through all the talk and commotion. Everybody turned to look at her. And then there was a gasp and a cry, for "Ready!" chorused the six bachelor Pontipees; and suddenly, each one had one hand on a rifle and the other holding a girl, while Harry and Milly trained a couple more rifles on the rest of the community to keep them quiet. It happened so sudden, half the folks didn't even know it was happening—till the Pontipee boys had their girls outside in the street, and the big doors locked and bolted behind them.

Then there was Cain to raise for fair in the meeting-hall, and people started to beat and kick at the doors—but they built solid, in those days. There wasn't any use in trying to shoot the locks off, because the Pontipee boys had tied up the guard over the weapons and dumped him and them outside in a shed.

It wasn't till pretty near dawn that the doors gave way—and when they did, the townspeople took one look outside and groaned. For it was snowing, lickety split, till you couldn't see your hand before your face—and when it snows, in our part of the country, it certainly snows. The blizzard didn't let up for four days, either, and by that time, the pass through the hills to Pontipee Valley was blocked solid, and nothing to do but wait for Spring and the thaw.

And, meanwhile, Milly had her work cut out for her. It wasn't an easy job, convoying three sleigh-loads full of hysterics all that long, cold ride. But she let them hysteric away, and, by the time they got to the Pontipee house, the stolen brides were so tuckered out that they'd quieted down a good deal.

Still, at first, they swore they wouldn't take bite or sup till they were restored to their grieving families. But Milly had some tea ready for them, in a jiffy—and a woman will usually take tea, no matter how mad she is. Well, Milly let them get warm and a little cozy, and then, when they were on their second cups, she made her little speech.

"Ladies," she said, "this affair makes me mighty sad—to see fine girls like you stole away by a lot of uncouth backwoodsmen. And I'd never have lent a hand to it if I'd known the truth of the matter. But, you and me, we'll turn the tables on them yet. You can't get back to your families till the blizzard lets up, but, while you've got to stay here, I'll see you're treated respectful. And just to prove that"—and she took a bunch of keys from her pocket—"I'll lock this house up tight, with us inside it; and, as for those backwoods Pontipees, they can sleep and eat in the stable with the livestock. That'll teach them they can't fool us!"

Well, that little speech—and the tea—cheered the girls up quite a bit. And by the time Milly showed them to their rooms—nice-looking rooms, too—and let them bolt themselves in, they were pretty well convinced that Milly was their friend.

So a week or so went by like that—the girls keeping house for themselves and never seeing hide nor hair of a Pontipee.

At first, it was a regular picnic for the girls. They allowed as how they'd always wanted to live without any men around, and, now they were, it was even better than they'd thought. And Milly agreed with them as hard as she could agree. She made them little speeches about the worthlessness of men in general and husbands in particular that would have raised the hair off any man's head. And, at first, the other girls listened to her and chimed in, and then they listened, but you could see they were being polite. And, by the end of the week, it was awful hard for her to get a real audience.

So, when she began to catch them looking out of windows when they should have been dusting, and peeking from behind curtains to try and get a sight of the terrible Pontipees, she knew it was time for the next step. For things got duller and duller in the house and little spats and quarrels began to break out among the girls. So, one afternoon, she suggested, tactfully, just to break the monotomy, that they all go up and rummage in the garret.

They rummaged around and had quite a bit of fun, until finally the minister's daughter opened a long box and gave a little squeal of joy.

"What a lovely wedding-dress—whose was it?" she said, and pulled out the long white veil and the dress itself, while the rest stood round and admired.

"Oh, shucks, that's just an old wedding-dress those backwoodsmen made me make when they thought you were going to marry 'em," said Milly, in a very disgusted voice. "Put it back!" But the girls weren't paying attention.

"Will it fit me, I wonder?" said the minister's daughter.

"It's bad luck, trying on wedding-dresses, if you're not going to have a wedding!" said Milly. "Let's go downstairs and have tea." But the minister's daughter was stepping out of her regular clothes already. The other girls helped fix her up—and then they oh-ed and ah-ed, for, I must say, she made a handsome-looking bride.

"That Pontipee boy named Hob's got curly hair," said the minister's daughter, trailing out her veil. "I always did have a liking for curly hair."

"Hob's not nearly as good-looking as Halbert," said the lawyer's niece, quite violent, and another one said, "Handsome is as handsome does—the one they call Harvey isn't so handsome, maybe, but he certainly has nice eyes."

"There's something about a man around the house that brisks things up remarkable," said a fourth one. "Not that I want to get married, but Howard's a nice name, even if Pontipee is hitched to it and——"

"Girls, girls—are you crazy, girls?" said Milly, shocked and horrified. But the minute she started to reprove them, they all turned on her, most ungratefully, and there was a regular revolt. So, at last, she had to give in and admit that there were five more wedding-dresses in the garret—and that if anybody was thinking of getting married, there just happened to be a hedge-parson, spending the winter with the Pontipees. But one thing she was firm about.

"Get married if you like," she said. "I can't stop you. But I'm responsible for you to your families—and, after the ceremony's ended, your husbands go back to the stable and stay there, till I know your families approve of them." She looked very fierce about it, and she made them promise. The hedge-parson married them all—all six in their wedding dresses—and then the boys went back to the stable. And, at dinner that night, the minister's daughter burst out crying.

"I hate men just as much as ever!" she wailed. "But it's terrible to be lawful married to a man you can't even see, except now and then out of a window!"

So Milly saw she had to make some new rules and she did. Three afternoons a week the boys were allowed to call on their new wives, and once in a while, for a great treat, they could stay to supper. But, always with Milly to chaperon.

Well, at first, the husbands and wives were mighty stiff and formal with each other, but, gradually, they got better and better acquainted. Till, pretty soon, the minister's daughter was letting Hob hold her hand, when she thought Milly wasn't looking, and the lawyer's niece was asking permission to sew a button on Halbert's coat—and there was a general atmosphere of courting around the Pontipee place that'd make an old bachelor sick.

Milly took it all in but she never stopped chaperoning.

Well, finally, it was one day along in January. Milly woke up in the morning—and she knew she was near her time. But, first thing in the morning, as always, she reached underneath her pillow for her keys and then she smiled. For somebody must have stolen them while she was sleeping—and when she got up, and went to the window in her wrapper, the door of the house was wide open. And there was Hob and his wife, helping each other shovel snow from the doorstep, and Halbert and his wife were throwing snowballs at Harvey and his, and Howard was kissing the doctor's eldest behind the kitchen door. "Praise be!" said Milly. "I can have my baby in peace"—and she went down to congratulate them all.

Only then, there were the families and the relatives still to fix. But Milly had a plan for that—she had plans for everything. When they stole the girls away, they left a letter she drew up, signed by all the boys and expressing all the honorable intentions you could put a name to. But she was afraid that wouldn't cool down the townspeople much, even when they thought it over, and it didn't.

One day when the first thaws had come and Milly's baby was about six weeks old, Hob came running in from his lookout post.

"They're coming, Milly!" he said. "The whole dum town! They've got rifles and scythes and ropes and they look mighty wild and bloodthirsty! What'll we do?"

"Do?" said Milly, perfectly calm. "You get the boys together and keep out of sight—and tell the girls to come here. For it's women's work, now, that'll save us, if anything will."

When she got the girls together, she gave them their orders. I guess they were a bit white-faced, but they obeyed. Then she looked out of the window—and there was the town, marching up the road, slow and steady. She'd have liked it better if they'd shouted or cried, but they didn't shout nor cry. The minister was in the lead, with his lips shut, and a six foot rifle in his hand, and his face like an iron mask.

She saw them come up to the gate of the Pontipee place. The gate was wide open and nobody there to hinder. She could see them take that in—and the little waver in the crowd. Because that made them feel queer.

Then they caught themselves and came tramping along toward the house, the minister still in the lead. Milly caught her breath, for they still looked awful mad. She knew what they'd expect when they got near the house—every window barred and every door bolted and red-hot bullets spitting through the loop-holes in the walls.

But the windows were open—you could see white curtains in them; there were plants on some of the sills. The door of the house stood ajar and Milly's cat was asleep on the doorstone, there in the sun.

They stood outside that door for quite a little bit, just milling around and staring. It was very quiet; they could hear their own breath and their own hearts knock. Finally the minister brushed his face, as if he were brushing a cobweb away from it, and he gripped his gun and went up on the porch and knocked at the open door. He'd intended to stomp up those steps like a charge of cavalry, but he walked soft, instead. He couldn't have told you why.

He knocked once and he knocked again and then Milly was standing in the doors, with her baby in her arms.

Somebody at the back of the crowd dropped the scythe he was carrying, and another one coughed in his hand.

"You're just in time to christen my child, your reverence," said Milly. "Have you brought that rifle to help you christen my child?"

The minister's eyes dropped, after a minute, and he lowered his rifle but he still held it in the crook of his arm.

"Your child?" he said, and his voice was as low as Milly's, but there was a fierceness in it. "What about my child?"

"Listen" said Milly, raising her hand, and the whole crowd fell dead still. Then from somewhere in the house came the hum of a spinning-wheel, low and steady, and a woman's voice, humming with the wheel.

"That's your child you hear, your reverence," said Milly. "Does she sound hurt, your reverence, or does she sound content?"

The minister hesitated for a moment and the crowd fell dead still again. Then they all heard the hum of the wheel and the hum of the woman's voice, humming back and forth to each other, as they did their work in the world.

"She sounds content—heaven help me!" said the minister, and a twist went over his face. But then there was a sudden outburst of cries and questions from the others. "My child, what about my child?" "Where's Mary?" "Is Susy safe?"

"Listen!" said Milly again, and they all fell silent once more. And, from somewhere, there came the splash of a churn and the voice of a woman talking to the butter to make it come; and the rattling of pans in a kitchen and a woman singing at her work; and the slap of clothes on a laundry board and the little clatter a woman makes setting table.

"There's your children," said Milly. "Hear 'em? Don't they sound all right? And—dinner will be ready in about half an hour—and you're all staying, I hope."

Then the daughters came out and their folks rushed to them; and, after all the crying and conniptions were over, Milly introduced the parents to their sons-in-law.

Freedom's a Hard-Bought Thing

A long time ago, in times gone by, in slavery times, there was a man named Cue. I want you to think about him. I've got a reason.

He got born like the cotton in the boll or the rabbit in the pea patch. There wasn't any fine doings when he got born, but his mammy was glad to have him. Yes. He didn't get born in the Big House, or the overseer's house, or any place where the bearing was easy or the work light. No, Lord. He came out of his mammy in a field hand's cabin one sharp winter, and about the first thing he remembered was his mammy's face and the taste of a piece of bacon rind and the light and shine of the pitch-pine fire up the chimney. Well, now, he got born and there he was.

His daddy worked in the fields and his mammy worked in the fields when she wasn't bearing. They were slaves; they chopped the cotton and hoed the corn. They heard the horn blow before the light came and the horn blow that meant the day's work was done. His daddy was a strong man—strong in his back and his arms. The white folks called him Cuffee. His mammy was a good woman, yes, Lord. The white folks called her Sarah, and she was gentle with her hands and gentle with her voice. She had a voice like the river going by in the night, and at night when she wasn't too tired she'd sing songs to little Cue. Some had foreign words in them—African words. She couldn't remember what some of them meant, but they'd come to her down out of time.

Now, how am I going to describe and explain about that time when that time's gone? The white folks lived in the Big House and they had many to tend on them. Old Marster, he lived there like Pharaoh and Solomon, mighty splendid and fine. He had his flocks and his herds, his butler and his baker; his fields ran from the river to the woods and back again. He'd ride around the fields each day on his big horse, Black Billy, just like thunder and lightning, and evenings he'd sit at his table and drink his wine. Man, that was a sight to see, with all the silver knives and the silver forks, the glass decanters, and the gentlemen and ladies from all over. It was a sight to see. When Cue was young, it seemed to him that Old Marster must own the whole world, right up to the edge of the sky. You can't blame him for thinking that.

There were things that changed on the plantation, but it didn't change. There were bad times and good times. There was the time young Marse Edward got bit by the snake, and the time Big Rambo ran away and they caught him with the dogs and brought him back. There was a swivel-eyed overseer that beat folks too much, and then there was Mr. Wade, and he wasn't so bad. There was hog-killing time and Christmas and springtime and summertime. Cue didn't wonder about it or why things happened that way; he didn't expect it to be different. A bee in a hive don't ask you how there come to be a hive in the beginning. Cue grew up strong; he grew up smart with his hands. They put him in the blacksmith shop to help Daddy Jake; he didn't like it, at first, because Daddy Jake was mighty cross-tempered. Then he got to like the work; he learned to forge iron and shape it; he learned to shoe a horse and tire a wagon wheel, and everything a blacksmith does. One time they let him shoe Black Billy, and he shod him light and tight and Old Marster praised him in front of Mr. Wade. He was strong; he was black as night; he was proud of his back and his arms.

Now, he might have stayed that way—yes, he might. He heard freedom talk, now and then, but he didn't pay much mind to it. He wasn't a talker or a preacher; he was Cue and he worked in the blacksmith shop. He didn't want to be a field hand, but he didn't want to be a house servant either. He'd rather be Cue than poor white trash or owned by poor white trash. That's the way he felt; I'm obliged to tell the truth about that way.

Then there was a sickness came and his mammy and his daddy died of it. Old Miss got the doctor for them, but they died just the same. After that, Cue felt lonesome.

He felt lonesome and troubled in his mind. He'd seen his daddy and his mammy put in the ground and new slaves come to take their cabin. He didn't repine about that, because he knew things had to be that way. But when he went to bed at night, in the loft over the blacksmith shop, he'd keep thinking about his mammy and his daddy—how strong his daddy was and the songs that his mammy sang. They'd worked all their lives and had children, though he was the only one left, but the only place of their own they had was the place in the burying ground. And yet they'd been good and faithful servants, because Old Marster said so, with his hat off, when he buried them. The Big House stayed, and the cotton and the corn, but

Cue's mammy and daddy were gone like last year's crop. It made Cue wonder and trouble.

He began to take notice of things he'd never noticed. When the horn blew in the morning for the hands to go to the fields, he'd wonder who started blowing that horn, in the first place. It wasn't like thunder and lightning; somebody had started it. When he heard Old Marster say, when he was talking to a friend, "This damned epidemic! It's cost me eight prime field hands and the best-trained butler in the state. I'd rather have lost the Flyaway colt than Old Isaac," Cue put that down in his mind and pondered it. Old Marster didn't mean it mean, and he'd sat up with Old Isaac all night before he died. But Isaac and Cue and the Flyaway colt, they all belonged to Old Marster and he owned them, hide and hair. He owned them, like money in his pockets. Well, Cue had known that all his life, but because he was troubled now, it gave him a queer feeling.

Well, now, he was shoeing a horse for young Marster Shepley one day, and he shod it light and tight. And when he was through, he made a stirrup for young Marster Shepley, and young Marster Shepley mounted and threw him a silver bit, with a laughing word. That shouldn't have bothered Cue, because gentlemen sometimes did that. And Old Marster wasn't mean; he didn't object. But all night Cue kept feeling the print of young Marster Shepley's heel in his hands. And yet he liked young Marster Shepley. He couldn't explain it at all.

Finally, Cue decided he must be conjured. He didn't know who had done it or why they'd done it. But he knew what he had to do. He had to go see Aunt Rachel.

Aunt Rachel was an old, old woman, and she lived in a cabin by herself, with her granddaughter, Sukey. She'd seen Old Marster's father and his father, and the tale went she'd seen George Washington with his hair all white, and General Lafayette in his gold-plated suit of clothes that the King of France gave him to fight in. Some folks said she was a conjure and some folks said she wasn't, but everybody on the plantation treated her mighty respectful, because, if she put her eye on you, she mightn't take it off. Well, his mammy had been friends with Aunt Rachel, so Cue went to see her.

She was sitting alone in her cabin by the low light of a fire. There was a pot on the fire, and now and then you could hear it bubble and chunk, like a bullfrog chunking in the swamp, but that was the only sound. Cue made his obleegances to her and asked her about the misery in her back. Then he gave her a chicken he happened to bring along. It was a black rooster, and she seemed pleased to get it. She took it in her thin black hands and it fluttered and clucked a minute.

So she drew a chalk line from its beak along a board, and then it stayed still and frozen. Well, Cue had seen that trick done before. But it was different, seeing it done in Aunt Rachel's cabin, with the big pot chunking on the fire. It made him feel uneasy and he jingled the bit in his pocket for company.

After a while, the old woman spoke. "Well, Son Cue," said she, "that's a fine young rooster you've brought me. What else did you bring me, Son Cue?"

"I brought you trouble," said Cue, in a husky voice, because that was all he could think of to say.

She nodded her head as if she'd expected that. "They mostly brings me trouble," she said. "They mostly brings trouble to Aunt Rachel. What kind of trouble, Son Cue? Man trouble or woman trouble?"

"It's my trouble," said Cue, and he told her the best way he could. When he'd finished, the pot on the fire gave a bubble and a croak, and the old woman took a long spoon and stirred it.

"Well, Son Cue, son of Cuffee, son of Shango," she said, "you've got a big trouble, for sure."

"Is it going to kill me dead?" said Cue.

"I can't tell you right about that," said Aunt Rachel. "I could give you lies and prescriptions. Maybe I would, to some folks. But your Granddaddy Shango was a powerful man. It took three men to put the irons on him, and I saw the irons break his heart. I won't lie to you, Son Cue. You've got a sickness."

"Is it a bad sickness?" said Cue.

"It's a sickness in your blood," said Aunt Rachel. "It's a sickness in your liver and your veins. Your daddy never had it that I knows of—he took after his mammy's side. But his daddy was a Corromantee, and they is bold and free, and you takes after him. It's the freedom sickness, Son Cue."

"The freedom sickness?" said Cue.

"The freedom sickness," said the old woman, and her little eyes glittered like sparks. "Some they break and some they tame down," she said, "and some is neither to be tamed or broken. Don't I know the signs and the sorrow—me, that come through the middle passage on the slavery ship and seen my folks scattered like sand? Ain't I seen it coming, Lord—O Lord, ain't I seen it coming?"

"What's coming?" said Cue.

"A darkness in the sky and a cloud with a sword in it," said the old woman, stirring the pot, "because they hold our people and they hold our people."

Cue began to tremble. "I don't want to get whipped," he said. "I never been whipped—not hard."

"They whipped your Granddaddy Shango till the blood ran twinkling down his back," said the old woman, "but some you can't break or tame."

"I don't want to be chased by dogs," said Cue. "I don't want to hear the dogs belling and the paterollers after me."

The old woman stirred the pot.

"Old Marster, he's a good marster," said Cue. "I don't want to do him no harm. I don't want no trouble or projecting to get me into trouble."

The old woman stirred the pot and stirred the pot.

"O God, I want to be free," said Cue. "I just ache and hone to be free. How I going to be free, Aunt Rachel?"

"There's a road that runs underground," said the old woman. "I never seen it, but I knows of it. There's a railroad train that runs, sparking and snorting, underground through the earth. At least that's what they tell me. But I wouldn't know for sure," and she looked at Cue.

Cue looked back at her bold enough, for he'd heard about the Underground Railroad himself—just mentions and whispers. But he knew there wasn't any use asking the old woman what she wouldn't tell.

"How I going to find that road, Aunt Rachel?" he said.

"You look at the rabbit in the brier and you see what he do," said the old woman. "You look at the owl in the woods and you see what he do. You look at the star in the sky and you see what she do. Then you come back and talk to me. Now I'm going to eat, because I'm hungry."

That was all the words she'd say to him that night; but when Cue went back to his loft, her words kept boiling around in his mind. All night he could hear that train of railroad cars, snorting and sparking underground through the earth. So, next morning, he ran away.

He didn't run far or fast. How could he? He'd never been more than twenty miles from the plantation in his life; he didn't know the roads or the ways. He ran off before the horn, and Mr. Wade caught him before sundown. Now, wasn't he a stupid man, that Cue?

When they brought him back, Mr. Wade let him off light, because he was a good boy and never run away before. All the same, he got ten, and ten laid over the ten. Yellow Joe, the head driver, laid them on. The first time the whip cut into him, it was just like a fire on

Cue's skin, and he didn't see how he could stand it. Then he got to a place where he could.

After it was over, Aunt Rachel crope up to his loft and had her granddaughter, Sukey, put salve on his back. Sukey, she was sixteen, and golden-skinned and pretty as a peach on a peach tree. She worked in the Big House and he never expected her to do a thing like that.

"I'm mighty obliged," he said, though he kept thinking it was Aunt Rachel got him into trouble and he didn't feel as obliged as he might.

"Is that all you've got to say to me, Son Cue?" said Aunt Rachel, looking down at him. "I told you to watch three things. Did you watch them?"

"No'm," said Cue. "I run off in the woods just like I was a wild turkey. I won't never do that no more."

"You're right, Son Cue," said the old woman. "Freedom's a hard-bought thing. So, now you've been whipped, I reckon you'll give it up."

"I been whipped," said Cue, "but there's a road running underground. You told me so. I been whipped, but I ain't beaten."

"Now you're learning a thing to remember," said Aunt Rachel, and went away. But Sukey stayed behind for a while and cooked Cue's supper. He never expected her to do a thing like that, but he liked it when she did.

When his back got healed, they put him with the field gang for a while. But then there was blacksmith work that needed to be done and they put him back in the blacksmith shop. And things went on for a long time just the way they had before. But there was a difference in Cue. It was like he'd lived up till now with his ears and his eyes sealed over. And now he began to open his eyes and his ears.

He looked at the rabbit in the brier and he saw it could hide. He looked at the owl in the woods and he saw it went soft through the night. He looked at the star in the sky and he saw she pointed north. Then he began to figure.

He couldn't figure things fast, so he had to figure things slow. He figure the owl and the rabbit got wisdom the white folks don't know about. But he figure the white folks got wisdom he don't know about. They got reading and writing wisdom, and it seem mighty powerful. He ask Aunt Rachel if that's so, and she say it's so.

That's how come he learned to read and write. He ain't supposed to. But Sukey, she learned some of that wisdom, along with the young misses, and she teach him out of a little book she tote from the

Big House. The little book, it's all about bats and rats and cats, and Cue figure whoever wrote it must be sort of touched in the head not to write about things folks would want to know, instead of all those trifling animals. But he put himself to it and he learn. It almost bust his head, but he learn. It's a proud day for him when he write his name, "Cue," in the dust with the end of a stick and Sukey tell him that's right.

Now he began to hear the first rumblings of that train running underground—that train that's the Underground Railroad. Oh, children, remember the names of Levi Coffin and John Hansen! Remember the Quaker saints that hid the fugitive! Remember the names of all those that helped set our people free!

There's a word dropped here and a word dropped there and a word that's passed around. Nobody know where the word come from or where it goes, but it's there. There's many a word spoken in the quarters that the Big House never hears about. There's a heap said in front of the fire that never flies up the chimney. There's a name you tell to the grapevine that the grapevine don't tell back.

There was a white man, one day, came by, selling maps and pictures. The quality folks, they looked at his maps and pictures and he talked with them mighty pleasant and respectful. But while Cue was tightening a bolt on his wagon, he dropped a word and a word. The word he said made that underground train come nearer.

Cue meet that man one night, all alone, in the woods. He's a quiet man with a thin face. He hold his life in his hands every day he walk about, but he don't make nothing of that. Cue's seen bold folks and bodacious folks, but it's the first time he's seen a man bold that way. It makes him proud to be a man. The man ask Cue questions and Cue give him answers. While he's seeing that man, Cue don't just think about himself any more. He think about all his people that's in trouble.

The man say something to him; he say, "No man own the earth. It's too big for one man." He say, "No man own another man; that's too big a thing too." Cue think about those words and ponder them. But when he gets back to his loft, the courage drains out of him and he sits on his straw tick, staring at the wall. That's the time the darkness comes to him and the shadow falls on him.

He aches and he hones for freedom, but he aches and he hones for Sukey too. And Long Ti's cabin is empty, and it's a good cabin. All he's got to do is to go to Old Marster and take Sukey with him. Old Marster don't approve to mix the field hand with the house servant, but Cue's different; Cue's a blacksmith. He can see the way Sukey would look, coming back to her in the evening. He can see the way she'd be in the morning before the horn. He can see all that. It ain't freedom, but it's what he's used to. And the other way's long and hard and lonesome and strange.

"O Lord, why you put this burden on a man like me?" say Cue. Then he listen a long time for the Lord to tell him, and it seem to him, at last, that he get an answer. The answer ain't in any words, but it's a feeling in his heart.

So when the time come and the plan ripe and they get to the boat on the river and they see there's one too many for the boat, Cue know the answer. He don't have to hear the quiet white man say, "There's one too many for the boat." He just pitch Sukey into it before he can think too hard. He don't say a word or a groan. He know it's that way and there's bound to be a reason for it. He stand on the bank in the dark and see the boat pull away, like Israel's children. Then he hear the shouts and the shot. He know what he's bound to do then, and the reason for it. He know it's the paterollers, and he show himself. When he get back to the plantation, he's worn and tired. But the paterollers, they've chased him, instead of the boat.

He creep by Aunt Rachel's cabin and he see the fire at her window. So he scratch at the door and go in. And there she is, sitting by the fire, all hunched up and little.

"You looks poorly, Son Cue," she say, when he come in, though she don't take her eye off the pot.

"I'm poorly, Aunt Rachel," he say. "I'm sick and sorry and distressed."

"What's the mud on your jeans, Son Cue?" she say, and the pot, it bubble and croak.

"That's the mud of the swamp where I hid from the paterollers," he say.

"What's the hole in your leg, Son Cue?" she say, and the pot, it croak and bubble.

"That's the hole from the shot they shot at me," say Cue. "The blood most nearly dried, but it make me lame. But Israel's children, they's safe."

"They's across the river?" say the old woman.

"They's across the river," say Cue. "They ain't room for no more in the boat. But Sukey, she's across."

"And what will you do now, Son Cue?" say the old woman. "For that was your chance and your time, and you give it up for another. And tomorrow morning, Mr. Wade, he'll see that hole in your leg and he'll ask questions. It's a heavy burden you've laid on yourself, Son Cue."

"It's a heavy burden," say Cue, "and I wish I was shut of it. I never asked to take no such burden. But freedom's a hard-bought thing."

The old woman stand up sudden, and for once she look straight and tall. "Now bless the Lord!" she say. "Bless the Lord and praise him! I come with my mammy in the slavery ship—I come through the middle passage. There ain't many that remember that, these days, or care about it. There ain't many that remember the red flag that witched us on board or how we used to be free. Many thousands gone, and the thousands of many thousands that lived and died in slavery. But I remember. I remember them all. Then they took me into the Big House—me that was a Mandingo and a witch woman—and the way I live in the Big House, that's between me and my Lord. If I done wrong, I done paid for it—I paid for it with weeping and sorrow. That's before Old Miss' time and I help raise up Old Miss. They sell my daughter to the South and my son to the West, but I raise up Old Miss and tend on her. I ain't going to repine of that. I count the hairs on Old Miss' head when she's young, and she turn to me, weak and helpless. And for that there'll be a kindness between me and the Big House—a kindness that folks with remember. But my children's children shall be free."

"You do this to me," say Cue, and he look at her, and he look dangerous. "You do this to me, old woman," he say, and his breath come harsh in his throat, and his hands twitch.

"Yes," she say, and look him straight in the eyes. "I do to you what I never even do for my own. I do it for your Granddaddy Shango, that never turn to me in the light of the fire. He turn to that soft Eboe woman, and I have to see it. He roar like a lion in the chains, and I have to see that. So, when you come, I try you and I test you, to see if you fit to follow after him. And because you fit to follow after him, I put freedom in your heart, Son Cue."

"I never going to be free," say Cue, and look at his hands. "I done broke all the rules. They bound to sell me now."

"You'll be sold and sold again," say the old woman. "You'll know the chains and the whip. I can't help that. You'll suffer for your people and with your people. But while one man's got freedom in his heart, his children bound to know the tale."

She put the lid on the pot and it stop bubbling.

"Now I come to the end of my road," she say, "but the tale don't stop there. The tale go backward to Africa and it go forward, like clouds and fire. It go, laughing and grieving forever, through the earth and the air and the waters—my people's tale."

Then she drop her hands in her lap and Cue creep out of the cabin. He know then he's bound to be a witness, and it make him feel cold and hot. He know then he's bound to be a witness and tell that tale. O Lord, it's hard to be a witness, and Cue know that. But it help him in the days to come.

Now, when he get sold, that's when Cue feel the iron in his heart. Before that, and all his life, he despise bad servants and bad marsters. He live where the marster's good; he don't take much mind of other places. He's a slave, but he's Cue, the blacksmith, and Old Marster and Old Miss, they tend to him. Now he know the iron in his heart and what it's like to be a slave.

He know that on the rice fields in the hot sun. He know that, working all day for a handful of corn. He know the bad marsters and the cruel overseers. He know the bite of the whip and the gall of the iron on the ankle. Yes, Lord, he know tribulation. He know his own tribulation and the tribulation of his people. But all the time, some-how, he keep freedom in his heart. Freedom mighty hard to root out when it's in the heart.

He don't know the day or the year, and he forget, half the time, there ever was a gal named Sukey. All he don't forget is the noise of the train in his ears, the train snorting and sparking underground. He think about it at nights till he dream it carry him away. Then he wake up with the horn. He feel ready to die then, but he don't die. He live through the whip and the chain; he live through the iron and the fire. And finally he get away.

When he get away, he ain't like the Cue he used to be—not even back at Old Marster's place. He hide in the woods like a rabbit; he slip through the night like an owl. He go cold and hungry, but the star keep shining over him and he keep his eyes on the star. They set the dogs after him and he hear the dogs belling and yipping through the woods.

He's scared when he hear the dogs, but he ain't scared like he used to be. He ain't more scared than any man. He kill the big dog in the clear-ing—the big dog with the big voice—and he do it with his naked hands. He cross water three times after that to kill the scent, and he go on.

He got nothing to help him—no, Lord—but he got a star. The star shine in the sky and the star shine—the star point north with its shin-ing. You put that star in the sky, O Lord; you put it for the prisoned and the humble. You put it there—you ain't never going to blink it out.

He hungry and he eat green corn and cowpeas. He thirsty and he drink swamp water. One time he lie two days in the swamp, too puny to get up on his feet, and he know they hunting around him. He think that's the end of Cue. But after two days he lift his head and his hand. He kill a snake with a stone, and after he's cut out the poison bag, he eat the snake to strengthen him, and go on.

He don't know what the day is when he come to the wide, cold river. The river yellow and foaming, and Cue can't swim. But he hide like a crawdad on the bank; he make himself a little raft with two logs. He know this time's the last time and he's obliged to drown. But he put out on the raft and it drift him to the freedom side. He mighty weak by then.

He mighty weak, but he careful. He know tales of Billy Shea, the slave catcher; he remember those tales. He slide into the town by night, like a shadow, like a ghost. He beg broken victuals at a door; the woman give them to him, but she look at him suspicious. He make up a tale to tell her, but he don't think she believe the tale. In the gutter he find a newspaper; he pick it up and look at the notices. There's a notice about a runaway man named Cue. He look at it and it make the heart beat in his breast.

He patient; he mighty careful. He leave that town behind. He got the name of another town, Cincinnati, and a man's name in that town. He don't know where it is; he have to ask his way, but he do it mighty careful. One time he ask a yellow man directions; he don't like the look on the yellow man's face. He remember Aunt Rachel; he tell the yellow man he conjure his liver out if the yellow man tell him wrong. Then the yellow man scared and tell him right. He don't hurt the yellow man; he don't blame him for not wanting trouble. But he make the yellow man change pants with him, because his pants mighty ragged.

He patient; he very careful. When he get to the place he been told about, he look all about that place. It's a big house; it don't look right. He creep around to the back—he creep and he crawl. He look in a window; he see white folks eating their supper. They just look like any white folks. He expect them to look different. He feel mighty bad. All the same, he rap at the window the way he been told. They don't nobody pay attention and he just about to go away. Then the white man get up from the table and open the back door a crack. Cue breathe in the darkness.

"God bless the stranger the Lord sends us," say the white man in a low, clear voice, and Cue run to him and stumble, and the white man catch him. He look up and it's a white man, but he ain't like thunder and lightning.

He take Cue and wash his wounds and bind them up. He feed him and hide him under the floor of the house. He ask him his name and where he's from. Then he send him on. O Lord, remember thy tried servant, Asaph Brown! Remember his name!

They send him from there in a wagon, and he's hidden in the straw at the bottom. They send him from the next place in a closed cart with six others, and they can't say a word all night. One time a toll-keeper ask them what's in the wagon, and the driver say, "Southern calico," and the tollkeeper laugh. Cue always recollect that.

One time they get to big water—so big it look like the ocean. They cross that water in a boat; they get to the other side. When they get to the other side, they sing and pray, and white folks look on, curious. But Cue don't even feel happy; he just feel he want to sleep.

He sleep like he never sleep before—not for days and years. When he wake up, he wonder; he hardly recollect where he is. He lying in the loft of a barn. Ain't nobody around him. He get up and go out in the air. It's a fine sunny day.

He get up and go out. He say to himself, *I'm free,* but it don't take hold yet. He say to himself, *This is Canada and I'm free,* but it don't take hold. Then he start to walk down the street.

The first white man he meet on the street, he scrunch up in himself and start to run across the street. But the white man don't pay him any mind. Then he know.

He say to himself in his mind, *I'm free. My name's Cue—John H. Cue. I got a strong back and strong arms. I got freedom in my heart. I got a first name and a last name and a middle name. I never had them all before.*

He say to himself, *My name's Cue—John H. Cue. I got a name and a tale to tell. I got a hammer to swing. I got a tale to tell my people. I got recollection. I call my first son "John Freedom Cue." I call my first daughter "Come-Out-of-the-Lion's-Mouth."*

Then he walk down the street, and he pass a blacksmith shop. The blacksmith, he's an old man and he lift the hammer heavy. Cue look in that shop and smile.

He pass on; he go his way. And soon enough he see a girl like a peach tree—a girl named Sukey—walking free down the street.

The Die-Hard

Where was a town called Shady, Georgia, and a time that's gone, and a boy named Jimmy Williams who was curious about things. Just a few years before the turn of the century it was, and that seems far away now. But Jimmy Williams was living in it, and it didn't seem far away to him.

It was a small town, Shady, and sleepy, though it had two trains a day and they were putting through a new spur to Vickery Junction.

They'd dedicated the War Memorial in the Square, but, on market days, you'd still see oxcarts on Main Street. And once, when Jimmy Williams was five, there'd been a light fall of snow and the whole town had dropped its business and gone out to see it. He could still remember the feel of the snow in his hands, for it was the only snow he'd ever touched or seen.

He was a bright boy—maybe a little too bright for his age. He'd think about a thing till it seemed real to him—and that's a dangerous gift. His father was the town doctor, and his father would try to show him the difference, but Doctor Williams was a right busy man. And the other Williams children were a good deal younger and his mother was busy with them. So Jimmy had more time to himself than most boys—and youth's a dreamy time.

I reckon it was that got him interested in Old Man Cappalow, in the first place. Every town has its legends and characters, and Old Man Cappalow was one of Shady's. He lived out of town, on the old Vincey place, all alone except for a light-colored Negro named Sam that he'd brought from Virginia with him; and the local Negroes wouldn't pass along that road at night. That was partly because of Sam, who was supposed to be a conjur, but mostly on account of Old Man Cappalow. He'd come in the troubled times, right after the end of the war, and ever since then he'd kept himself to himself. Except that once a month he went down to the bank and drew money that came in a letter from Virginia. But how he spent it, nobody knew. Except that he had a treasure—every boy in Shady knew that.

Now and then, a gang of them would get bold and they'd rattle sticks along the sides of his fence and yell, "Old Man Cappalow! Where's your money?" But then the light-colored Negro, Sam, would come out on the porch and look at them, and they'd run away. They didn't want to be conjured, and you couldn't be sure. But on the way home, they'd speculate and wonder about the treasure, and each time they speculated and wondered, it got bigger to them.

Some said it was the last treasure of the Confederacy, saved right up to the end to build a new *Alabama*, and that Old Man Cappalow had sneaked it out of Richmond when the city fell and kept it for himself; only now he didn't dare spend it, for the mark of Cain was on every piece. And some said it came from the sea islands, where the pirates had left it, protected by h'ants and devils, and Old Man Cappalow had had to fight devils for it six days and six nights before he could take it away. And if you looked inside his shirt, you could see the long white marks where the devils had clawed him. Well, sir, some said one thing and some said another. But they all agreed it was there, and it got to be a byword among the boys of the town.

It used to bother Jimmy Williams tremendously. Because he knew his father worked hard, and yet sometimes he'd only get fifty cents a visit, and often enough he'd get nothing. And he knew his mother worked hard, and that most folks in Shady weren't rich. And yet, all the time, there was that treasure, sitting out at Old Man Cappalow's. He didn't mean to steal it exactly. I don't know just what he did intend to do about it. But the idea of it bothered him and stayed at the back of his mind. Till, finally, one summer when he was turned thirteen, he started making expeditions to the Cappalow place.

He'd go in the cool of the morning or the cool of the afternoon, and sometimes he'd be fighting Indians and Yankees on the way, because he was still a boy, and sometimes he was thinking what he'd be when he grew up, for he was starting to be a man. But he never told the other boys what he was doing—and that was the mixture of both. He'd slip from the road, out of sight of the house, and go along by the fence. Then he'd lie down in the grass and the weeds, and look at the house.

It had been quite a fine place once, but now the porch was sagging and there were mended places in the roof and paper pasted over broken windowpanes. But that didn't mean much to Jimmy Williams; he was used to houses looking like that. There was a garden patch at the side, neat and well-kept, and sometimes he'd see the Negro, Sam, there, working. But what he looked at mostly was the side porch. For Old Man Cappalow would be sitting there.

He sat there, cool and icy-looking, in his white linen suit, on his cane chair, and now and then he'd have a leather-bound book in his hand, though he didn't often read it. He didn't move much, but he sat straight, his hands on his knees and his black eyes alive. There was something about his eyes that reminded Jimmy Williams of the windows of the house. They weren't blind, indeed they were bright, but there was something living behind them that wasn't usual. You didn't expect them to be so black, with his white hair. Jimmy Williams had seen a governor once, on Memorial Day, but the governor didn't look half as fine. This man was like a man made of ice—ice in the heat of the South. You could see he was old, but you couldn't tell how old, or whether he'd ever die.

Once in a great while he'd come out and shoot at a mark. The mark was a kind of metal shield, nailed up on a post, and it had been painted once, but the paint had worn away. He'd hold the pistol very steady, and the bullets would go "whang, whang" on the metal, very loud in the stillness. Jimmy Williams would watch him and wonder if that was the way he'd fought with his devils, and speculate about all kinds of things.

All the same, he was only a boy, and though it was fun and scary, to get so near Old Man Cappalow without being seen, and he'd have a grand tale to tell the others, if he ever decided to tell it, he didn't see any devils or any treasure. And probably he'd have given the whole business up in the end, boylike, if something hadn't happened.

He was lying in the weeds by the fence, one warm afternoon, and, boylike, he fell asleep. And he was just in the middle of a dream where Old Man Cappalow was promising him a million dollars if he'd go to the devil to get it, when he was wakened by a rustle in the weeds and a voice that said, "White boy."

Jimmy Williams rolled over and froze. For there, just half a dozen steps away from him, was the light-colored Negro, Sam, in his blue jeans, the way he worked in the garden patch, but looking like the butler at the club for all that.

I reckon if Jimmy Williams had been on his feet, he'd have run. But he wasn't on his feet. And he told himself he didn't mean to run, though his heart began to pound.

"White boy," said the light-colored Negro, "Marse John see you from up at the house. He send you his obleegances and say will you step that way." He spoke in a light, sweet voice, and there wasn't a thing in his manners you could have objected to. But just for a minute, Jimmy Williams wondered if he was being conjured. And then he didn't care. Because he was going to do what no boy in Shady had ever done. He was going to walk into Old Man Cappalow's house and not be scared. He wasn't going to be scared, though his heart kept pounding.

He scrambled to his feet and followed the line of the fence till he got to the driveway, the light-colored Negro just a little behind him. And when they got near the porch, Jimmy Williams stopped and took a leaf and wiped off his shoes, though he couldn't have told you why. The Negro stood watching while he did it, perfectly at ease. Jimmy Williams could see that the Negro thought better of him for wiping off his shoes, but not much. And that made him mad, and he wanted to say, "I'm no white trash. My father's a doctor," but he knew better than to say it. He just wiped his shoes and the Negro stood and waited. Then the Negro took him around to the side porch, and there was Old Man Cappalow, sitting in his cane chair.

"White boy here, Marse John," said the Negro in his low, sweet voice.

The old man lifted his head, and his black eyes looked at Jimmy Williams. It was a long stare and it went to Jimmy Williams' backbone.

"Sit down, boy," he said, at last, and his voice was friendly enough, but Jimmy Williams obeyed it. "You can go along, Sam," he said, and Jimmy Williams sat on the edge of a cane chair and tried to feel comfortable. He didn't do very well at it, but he tried.

"What's your name, boy?" said the old man, after a while.

"Jimmy Williams, sir," said Jimmy Williams. "I mean James Williams, Junior, sir."

"Williams," said the old man, and his black eyes glowed. "There was a Colonel Williams with the Sixty-fifth Virginia—or was it the Sixty-third? He came from Fairfax County and was quite of my opinion that we should have kept to primogeniture, in spite of Thomas Jefferson. But I doubt if you are kin."

"No, sir," said Jimmy Williams. "I mean, Father was with the Ninth Georgia. And he was a private. They were aiming to make him a corporal, he says, but they never got around to it. But he fit—he fought lots of Yankees. He fit tons of 'em. And I've seen his uniform. But now he's a doctor instead."

The old man seemed to look a little queer at that. "A doctor?" he said. "Well, some very reputable gentlemen have practiced medicine. There need be no loss of standing."

"Yes, sir," said Jimmy Williams. Then he couldn't keep it back any longer: "Please, sir, were you ever clawed by the devil?" he said.

"Ha-hrrm!" said the old man, looking startled. "You're a queer boy. And suppose I told you I had been?"

"I'd believe you," said Jimmy Williams, and the old man laughed. He did it as if he wasn't used to it, but he did it.

"Clawed by the devil!" he said. "Ha-hrrm! You're a bold boy. I didn't know, they grew them nowadays. I'm surprised." But he didn't look angry, as Jimmy Williams had expected him to.

"Well," said Jimmy Williams, "if you had been, I thought maybe you'd tell me about it. I'd be right interested. Or maybe let me see the clawmarks. I mean, if they're there."

"I can't show you those," said the old man, "though they're deep and wide." And he stared fiercely at Jimmy Williams. "But you weren't afraid to come here and you wiped your shoes when you came. So I'll show you something else." He rose and was tall. "Come into the house," he said.

So Jimmy Williams got up and went into the house with him. It was a big, cool, dim room they went into, and Jimmy Williams didn't see much at first. But then his eyes began to get used to the dimness.

Well, there were plenty of houses in Shady where the rooms were cool and dim and the sword hung over the mantelpiece and the furniture was worn and old. It wasn't that made the difference. But stepping into this house was somehow like stepping back into the past, though Jimmy Williams couldn't have put it that way. He just knew it was full of beautiful things and grand things that didn't quite fit it, and yet all belonged together. And they knew they were grand and stately, and yet there was dust in the air and a shadow on the wall. It was peaceful enough and handsome enough, yet it didn't make Jimmy Williams feel comfortable, though he couldn't have told you why.

"Well," said the old man, moving about among shadows, "how do you like it, Mr. Williams?"

"It's—I never saw anything like it," said Jimmy Williams.

The old man seemed pleased. "Touch the things, boy," he said. "Touch the things. They don't mind being touched."

So Jimmy Williams went around the room, staring at the miniatures and the pictures, and picking up one thing or another and putting it down. He was very careful and he didn't break anything. And there were some wonderful things. There was a game of chess on a table—carved-ivory pieces—a game that people had started, but hadn't finished. He didn't touch those, though he wanted to, because he felt the people might not like it when they came back to finish their game. And yet, at the same time, he felt that if they ever did come back, they'd be dead, and that made him feel queerer. There were silver-mounted pistols, long-barreled, on a desk by a big silver inkwell; there was a quill pen made of a heron's feather, and a silver sandbox beside it—there were all sorts of curious and interesting things. Finally Jimmy Williams stopped in front of a big, tall clock.

"I'm sorry, sir," he said, "but I don't think that's the right time."

"Oh, yes, it is," said the old man. "It's always the right time."

"Yes, sir," said Jimmy Williams, "but it isn't running."

"Of course not," said the old man. "They say you can't put the clock back, but you can. I've put it back and I mean to keep it back. The others can do as they please. I warned them—I warned them in 1850, when they accepted the Compromise. I warned them there could be no compromise. Well, they would not be warned."

"Was that bad of them, sir?" asked Jimmy Williams.

"It was misguided of them," said the old man. "Misguided of them all." He seemed to be talking more to himself than to Jimmy, but Jimmy Williams couldn't help listening. "There can be no compromise with one's class or one's breeding or one's sentiments," the old man said. "Afterwards—well, there were gentlemen I knew who went to Guatemala or elsewhere. I do not blame them for it. But mine is another course." He paused and glanced at the clock. Then he spoke in a different voice. "I beg your pardon," he said. "I fear I was growing heated. You will excuse me. I generally take some refreshment around this time in the afternoon. Perhaps you will join me, Mr. Williams?"

It didn't seem to Jimmy Williams as if the silver hand bell in the old man's hand had even stopped ringing before the Negro, Sam, came in with a tray. He had a queer kind of old-fashioned long coat on now, and a queer old-fashioned cravat, but his pants were the pants of his blue jeans. Jimmy Williams noticed that, but Old Man Cappalow didn't seem to notice.

"Yes," he said, "there are many traitors. Men I held in the greatest esteem have betrayed their class and their system. They have accepted ruin and domination in the name of advancement. But we will not speak of them now." He took the frosted silver cup from the tray and motioned to Jimmy Williams that the small fluted glass was for him. "I shall ask you to rise, Mr. Williams," he said. "We shall drink a toast." He paused for a moment, standing straight. "To the Confederate States of America and damnation to all her enemies!" he said.

Jimmy Williams drank. He'd never drunk any wine before, except blackberry cordial, and this wine seemed to him powerfully thin and sour. But he felt grown up as he drank it, and that was a fine feeling.

"Every night of my life," said the old man, "I drink that toast. And usually I drink it alone. But I am glad of your company, Mr. Williams."

"Yes, sir," said Jimmy Williams, but all the same, he felt queer. For drinking the toast, somehow, had been very solemn, almost like being in church. But in church you didn't exactly pray for other people's damnation, though the preacher might get right excited over sin.

Well, then the two of them sat down again, and Old Man Cappalow began to talk of the great plantation days and the world as it used to be. Of course, Jimmy Williams had heard plenty of talk of that sort. But this was different. For the old man talked of those days as if they were still going on, not as if they were past. And as he talked, the whole room seemed to join in, with a thousand, sighing, small voices, stately and clear, till Jimmy Williams didn't know whether he was on his head or his heels and it seemed quite natural to him to look at the fresh, crisp Richmond newspaper on the desk and see it was dated "June 14, 1859" instead of "June 14, 1897." Well, maybe it was the wine, though he'd only had a thimbleful. But when Jimmy Williams went out into the sun again, he felt changed, and excited too. For he knew about Old Man Cappalow now, and he was just about the grandest person in the world.

The Negro went a little behind him, all the way to the gate, on soft feet. When they got there, the Negro opened the gate and spoke.

"Young marster," he said, "I don't know why Marse John took in his head to ask you up to the house. But we lives private, me and Marse John. We lives very private." There was a curious pleading in his voice.

"I don't tell tales," said Jimmy Williams, and kicked at the fence.

"Yes, sir," said the Negro, and he seemed relieved. "I knew you one of the right ones. I knew that. But we'se living very private till the big folks come back. We don't want no tales spread before. And then we'se going back to Otranto, the way we should."

"I know about Otranto. He told me," said Jimmy Williams, catching his breath.

"Otranto Marse John's plantation in Verginny," said the Negro, as if he hadn't heard. "He owns the river and the valley, the streams and the hills. We got four hundred field hands at Otranto and stables for sixty horses. But we can't go back there till the big folks come back. Marse John say so, and he always speak the truth. But they's goin' to come back, a-shootin' and pirootin', they pistols at they sides. And every day I irons his Richmond paper for him and he reads about the old times. We got boxes and boxes of papers down in the cellar." He paused. "And if he say the old days come back, it bound to be so," he said. Again his voice held that curious pleading, "You remember, young master," he said. "You remember, white boy."

"I told you I didn't tell tales," said Jimmy Williams. But after that, things were different for him. Because there's one thing about a boy that age that most grown people forget. A boy that age can keep a secret in a way that's perfectly astonishing. And he can go through queer hells and heavens you'll never hear a word about, not even if you got him or bore him.

It was that way with Jimmy Williams; it mightn't have been for another boy. It began like a game, and then it stopped being a game. For, of course, he went back to Old Man Cappalow's. And the Negro, Sam, would show him up to the house and he'd sit in the dim room with the old man and drink the toast in the wine. And it wasn't Old Man Cappalow any more; it was Col. John Leonidas Cappalow, who'd raised and equipped his own regiment and never surrendered. Only, when the time was ripe, he was going back to Otranto, and the old days would bloom again, and Jimmy Williams would be part of them.

When he shut his eyes at night, he could see Otranto and its porches, above the rolling river, great and stately; he could hear the sixty horses stamping in their stalls. He could see the pretty girls, in their wide skirts, coming down the glassy, proud staircases; he could see the fine, handsome gentlemen who ruled the earth and the richness of it without a thought of care. It was all like a storybook to Jimmy Williams—a storybook come true. And more than anything he'd ever wanted in his life, he wanted to be part of it.

The only thing was, it was hard to fit the people he really knew into the story. Now and then Colonel Cappalow would ask him gravely if he knew anyone else in Shady who was worthy of being trusted with the secret. Well, there were plenty of boys like Bob Miller and Tommy Vine, but somehow you couldn't see them in the dim room. They'd fit in, all right, when the great days came back—they'd have to—but meanwhile—well, they might just take it for a tale. And then there was Carrie, the cook. She'd have to be a slave again, of course, and though Jimmy Williams didn't imagine that she'd mind, now and then he had just a suspicion that she might. He didn't ask her about it, but he had the suspicion.

It was even hard to fit Jimmy's father in, with his little black bag and his rumpled clothes and his laugh. Jimmy couldn't quite see his father going up the front steps of Otranto—not because he wasn't a gentleman or grand enough, but because it just didn't happen to be his kind of place. And then, his father didn't really hate anybody, as far as Jimmy knew. But you had to hate people a good deal, if you wanted to follow Colonel Cappalow. You had to shoot at the mark and feel you were really shooting the enemy's colors down. You had to believe that even people like General Lee had been wrong, because they hadn't held out in the mountains and fought till everybody died. Well, it was hard to believe a wrong thing of General Lee, and Jimmy Williams didn't quite manage it. He was willing to hate the Yankees and the Republicans—hate them hot and hard—but there weren't any of them in Shady. Well, come to think of it, there was Mr. Rosen, at the dry-goods store, and Mr. Ailey, at the mill. They didn't look very terrible and he was used to them, but he tried to hate them all he could. He got hold of the Rosen boy one day and rocked him home, but the Rosen boy cried, and Jimmy felt mean about it. But if he'd ever seen a real live Republican, with horns and a tail, he'd have done him a mortal injury—he felt sure he would.

And so the summer passed, and by the end of the summer Jimmy didn't feel quite sure which was real—the times now or the times Colonel Cappalow talked about. For he'd dream about Otranto at night and think of it during the day. He'd ride back there on a black horse, at Colonel Cappalow's left, and his saber would be long and shining. But if there was a change in him, there was a change in Colonel Cappalow too. He was a lot more excitable than he used to be, and when he talked to Jimmy sometimes, he'd call him by other names, and when he shot at the mark with the enemy's colors on it, his eyes would blaze. So by that, and by the news he read out of the old papers, Jimmy suddenly got to know that the time was near at hand. They had the treasure all waiting, and soon they'd be ready to rise. And Colonel Cappalow filled out Jimmy Williams' commission as captain in the army of the New Confederate States of America and presented it to him, with a speech. Jimmy Williams felt very proud of that commission, and hid it under a loose brick in his fireplace chimney, where it would be safe.

Well, then it came to the plans, and when Jimmy Williams first heard about them, he felt a little surprised. There were maps spread all over the big desk in the dim room now, and Colonel Cappalow moved pins and showed Jimmy strategy. And that was very exciting, and like a game. But first of all, they'd have to give a signal and strike a blow. You had to do that first, and then the country would rise. Well, Jimmy Williams could see the reason in that.

They were going into Shady and capture the post office first, and then the railroad station and, after that, they'd dynamite the railroad bridge to stop the trains, and Colonel Cappalow would read a proclamation from the steps of the courthouse. The only part Jimmy Williams didn't like about it was killing the postmaster and the station agent, in case they resisted. Jimmy Williams felt pretty sure they would resist, particularly the station agent, who was a mean customer. And, somehow, killing people you knew wasn't quite like killing Yankees and Republicans. The thought of it shook something in Jimmy's mind and made it waver. But after that they'd march on Washington, and everything would be all right.

All the same, he'd sworn his oath and he was a commissioned officer in the army of the New Confederate States. So, when Colonel Cappalow gave him the pistol that morning, with the bullets and the powder, and explained how he was to keep watch at the door of the post office and shoot to kill if he had to, Jimmy said, "I shall execute the order, sir," the way he'd been taught. After that, they'd go for the station agent and he'd have a chance for a lot more shooting. And it was all going to be for noon the next day.

Somehow, Jimmy Williams couldn't quite believe it was going to be for noon the next day, even when he was loading the pistol in the woodshed of the Williams house, late that afternoon. And yet he saw, with a kind of horrible distinctness, that it was going to be. It might sound crazy to some, but not to him—Colonel Cappalow was a sure shot; he'd seen him shoot at the mark. He could see him shooting, now, and he wondered if a bullet went "whang" when it hit a man. And, just as he was fumbling with the bullets, the woodshed door opened suddenly and there was his father.

Well, naturally, Jimmy dropped the pistol and jumped. The pistol didn't explode, for he'd forgotten it needed a cap. But with that moment something seemed to break inside Jimmy Williams. For it was the first time he'd really been afraid and ashamed in front of his father, and now he was ashamed and afraid. And then it was like waking up out of an illness, for his father saw his white face and said, "What's the matter, son?" and the words began to come out of his mouth.

"Take it easy, son," said his father, but Jimmy couldn't take it easy. He told all about Otranto and Old Man Cappalow and hating the Yankees and killing the postmaster, all jumbled up and higgledy-piggledy. But Doctor Williams made sense of it. At first he smiled a little as he listened, but after a while he stopped smiling, and there was anger in his face. And when Jimmy was quite through, "Well, son," he said, "I reckon we've let you run wild. But I never thought . . ." He asked Jimmy a few quick questions, mostly about the dynamite, and he seemed relieved when Jimmy told him they were going to get it from the men who were blasting for the new spur track.

"And now, son," he said, "when did you say this massacre was going to start?"

"Twelve o'clock at the post office," said Jimmy. "But we weren't going to massacre. It was just the folks that resisted—"

Doctor Williams made a sound in his throat. "Well," he said, "you and I are going to take a ride in the country, Jimmy. No, we won't tell your mother, I think."

It was the last time Jimmy Williams went out to Old Man Cappalow's, and he remembered that. His father didn't say a word all the way, but once he felt in his back pocket for something he'd taken out of the drawer of his desk, and Jimmy remembered that too.

When they drove up in front of the house, his father gave the reins to Jimmy. "Stay in the buggy, Jimmy," he said. "I'll settle this."

Then he got out of the buggy, a little awkwardly, for he was a heavy man, and Jimmy heard his feet scrunch on the gravel. Jimmy knew again, as he saw him go up the steps, that he wouldn't have fitted in Otranto, and somehow he was glad.

The Negro, Sam, opened the door.

"Tell Colonel Cappalow Doctor Williams wishes to speak with him," said Jimmy's father, and Jimmy could see that his father's neck was red.

"Colonel Cappalow not receivin'," said Sam, in his light sweet voice, but Jimmy's father spoke again.

"Tell Colonel Cappalow," he said. He didn't raise his voice, but there was something in it that Jimmy had never heard in that voice before. Sam looked for a moment and went inside the house.

Then Colonel Cappalow came to the door himself. There was red from the evening sun on his white suit and his white hair, and he looked tall and proud. He looked first at Jimmy's father and then at Jimmy. And his voice said, quite coldly, and reasonably and clearly, "Traitor! All traitors!"

"You'll oblige me by leaving the boy out of it," said Jimmy's father heavily. "This is 1897, sir, not 1860," and for a moment there was something light and heady and dangerous in the air between them. Jimmy knew what his father had in his pocket then, and he sat stiff in the buggy and prayed for time to change and things to go away.

Then Colonel Cappalow put his hand to his forehead. "I beg your pardon, sir," he said, in an altered voice. "You mentioned a date?"

"I said it was 1897," said Doctor Williams, standing square and stocky, "I said Marse Robert's dead—God bless him!—and Jefferson Davis too. And before he died, Marse Robert said we ought to be at peace. The ladies can keep up the war as long as they see fit—that's their privilege. But men ought to act like men."

He stared for a moment at the high-chinned, sculptural face.

"Why, damn your soul!" he said, and it was less an oath than a prayer. "I was with the Ninth Georgia; I went through three campaigns. We fought till the day of Appomattox and it was we-uns' fight." Something rough and from the past had slipped back into his speech—something, too, that Jimmy Williams had never heard in it before. "We didn't own niggers or plantations—the men I fought with. But when it was over, we reckoned it was over and we'd build up the land. Well, we've had a hard time to do it, but we're hoeing corn. We've got something better to do than fill up a boy with a lot of magnolious notions and aim to shoot up a postmaster because there's a Republican President. My God," he said, and again it was less an oath than a prayer, "it was bad enough getting licked when you thought you couldn't be—but when I look at you—well, hate stinks when it's kept too long in the barrel, no matter how you dress it up and talk fine about it. I'm warning you. You keep your hands off my boy. Now, that's enough."

"Traitors," said the old man vaguely, "all traitors." Then a change came over his face and he stumbled forward as if he had stumbled over a stone. The Negro and the white man both sprang to him, but it was the Negro who caught him and lowered him to the ground. Then Jimmy Williams heard his father calling for his black bag, and his limbs were able to move again.

Doctor Williams came out of the bedroom, drying his hands on a towel. His eyes fell upon Jimmy Williams, crouched in front of the chessboard.

"He's all right, son," he said. "At least—he's not all right. But he wasn't in pain."

Jimmy Williams shivered a little. "I heard him talking," he said difficulty. "I heard him calling people things."

"Yes," said his father. "Well, you mustn't think too much of that. You see, a man—" He stopped and began again, "Well, I've no doubt he was considerable of a man once. Only—well, there's a Frenchman calls it a fixed idea. You let it get a hold of you . . . and the way he was brought up. He got it in his head, you see—he couldn't stand it that he might have been wrong about anything. And the hate—well, it's not for a man. Not when it's like that. Now, where's that Nigra?"

Jimmy Williams shivered again; he did not want Sam back in the room. But when Sam came, he heard the Negro answer, politely.

"H'm," said Doctor Williams. "Twice before. He should have had medical attention."

"Marse John don't believe in doctors," said the low, sweet voice.

"He wouldn't," said Doctor Williams briefly. "Well, I'll take the boy home now. But I'll have to come back. I'm coroner for this county. You understand about that?"

"Yes, sir," said the low, sweet voice, "I understand about that." Then the Negro looked at the doctor. "Marse Williams," he said, "I wouldn't have let him do it. He thought he was bound to. But I wouldn't have let him do it."

"Well," said the doctor. He thought, and again said, "Well." Then he said, "Are there any relatives?"

"I take him back to Otranto," said the Negro. "It belongs to another gentleman now, but Marse John got a right to lie there. That's Verginny law, he told me."

"So it is," said the doctor. "I'd forgotten that."

"He don't want no relatives," said the Negro. "He got nephews and nieces and all sorts of kin. But they went against him and he cut them right out of his mind. He don't want no relatives." He paused. "He cut everything out of his mind but the old days," he said. "He start doing it right after the war. That's why we come here. He don't want no part nor portion of the present days. And they send him money from Verginny, but he only spend it the one way—except when we buy this place." He smiled as if at a secret.

"But how?" said the doctor, staring at furniture and pictures.

"Jus' one muleload from Otranto," said the Negro, softly. "And I'd like to see anybody cross Marse John in the old days." He coughed. "They's just one thing, Marse Williams," he said, in his suave voice. "I ain't skeered of sittin' up with Marse John. I always been with him. But it's the money."

"What money?" said Doctor Williams. "Well, that will go through the courts—"

"No, sir," said the Negro patiently. "I mean Marse John's special money that he spend the other money for. He got close to a millyum dollars in that blind closet under the stairs. And nobody dare come for it, as long as he's strong and spry. But now I don't know. I don't know."

"Well," said Doctor Williams, receiving the incredible fact, "I suppose we'd better see."

It was as the Negro had said—a blind closet under the stairs, opened by an elementary sliding catch.

"There's the millyum dollars," said the Negro as the door swung back. He held the cheap glass lamp high—the wide roomy closet was piled from floor to ceiling with stacks of printed paper.

"H'm," said Doctor Williams. "Yes, I thought so. . . . Have you ever seen a million dollars, son?"

"No, sir," said Jimmy Williams.

"Well, take a look," said his father. He slipped a note from a packet, and held it under the lamp.

"It says 'One Thousand Dollars,' " said Jimmy Williams. "Oh!"

"Yes," said his father gently. "And it also says 'Confederate States of America.' . . . You don't need to worry, Sam. The money's perfectly safe. Nobody will come for it. Except, maybe, museums."

"Yes, Marse Williams," said Sam unquestioningly, accepting the white man's word, now he had seen and judged the white man. He shut the closet.

On his way out, the doctor paused for a moment and looked at the Negro. He might have been thinking aloud—it seemed that way to Jimmy Williams.

"And why did you do it?" he said. "Well, that's something we'll never know. And what are you going to do, once you've taken him back to Otranto?"

"I got my arrangements, thank you, sir," said the Negro.

"I haven't a doubt of it," said Jimmy Williams' father. "But I wish I knew what they were."

"I got my arrangements, gentlemen," the Negro repeated, in his low, sweet voice. Then they left him, holding the lamp, with his tall shadow behind him.

"Maybe I oughtn't to have left him," said Jimmy Williams' father, after a while, as the buggy jogged along. "He's perfectly capable of setting fire to the place and burning it up as a sort of a funeral pyre. And maybe that wouldn't be a bad thing," he added, after a pause. Then he said, "Did you notice the chessmen? I wonder who played that game. It was stopped in the middle." Then, after a while, he said, "I remember the smell of the burning woods in the Wilderness. And I remember Reconstruction. But Marse Robert was right, all the same. You can't go back to the past. And hate's the most expensive commodity in the world. It's never been anything else, and I've seen a lot of it. We've got to realize that—got too much of it, still, as a nation."

But Jimmy Williams was hardly listening. He was thinking it was good to be alone with his father in a buggy at night and good they didn't have to live in Otranto after all.

The Minister's Books

When young Hugh McRidden was called to the old brick church at Titusville in the closing years of the past century, he felt that strong, slow leap of the heart which comes to all ambitious young men, no matter what their profession, who see their ambitions in a fair way of being fulfilled. Born in one of those small communities in the West Virginia mountains where the Scotch-Irish speech still lingers almost unaffected by Time, he could hardly remember the day when the ministry had not seemed to him the first of callings—and the hopes that had been placed in him made him eager beyond most young men. Tall, lean, and darkly handsome, he carried a fire within him— it had made him the marked man of his time at the seminary—and there was something very appealing about the grave earnestness of his voice. "All fire and bone and sinew," thought the leading elder, John Waynfleet, as he talked to him. "And those gray-blue eyes would face the Devil himself. We've made a good choice, I think—I like spirit in man or minister. Though no doubt he'll give us something of a shaking up—and all the better. Dear old McCullough was a saint but he let us get rather sleepy, in Titusville. I shan't take my mid-sermon nap as easily under this young man."

He chuckled a little internally—the older elders might say what they liked but he held them in the hollow of his hand and knew it— for thirty years he had been an unobtrusively important figure in the councils of the Church. Moderators might come and go, but John Waynfleet remained a pillar—and he felt drawn to this young man. "He'll go far," he thought. "We must find a suitable wife for him. I'm glad he didn't go into the mission-field—he has the spirit for it but we need such men at home."

And indeed, for a time, it seemed as if all John Waynfleet's prophecies were in excellent train for fulfillment. Titusville was an old town, rather proud of itself and its red-brick pavements, its quiet, long-settled wealth, and its fine Pennsylvania cooking. But religiously, as John Waynfleet said, it had grown a little sleepy—and the new broom swept clean. Not only did it do so, but people liked the sweeping, which is a different matter. Dr. McCullough had been a saint and a tradition—but Dr. McCullough, toward the end, had

grown very old. The young people came to church now with a willingness they had not shown in Dr. McCullough's time—the sick and
the poor were visited with energy—the young girls, seeing the grave,
youthful face in the pulpit and hearing the rich voice, musical and
sincere, had the thoughts of young girls but with them a sense of the
Spirit they could not have explained. All in all, the town was happy
in its new minister.

As for Hugh McRidden, he did not think of himself as happy, for
that was not what he sought for in life, but he found his days busy
and new. More comfortable, also, than he had yet been—for Titusville was proud of its manse and kept it well. He need no longer
deny himself the books he coveted—indeed, he had been able to take
over all Dr. McCullough's library as well as most of his furniture at a
ridiculously low valuation. John Waynfleet was responsible for that,
as he was for Mrs. Breek, Hugh McRidden's housekeeper, though
Hugh McRidden did not know it. Mrs. Breek had only one eye but
she was an admirable cook, and while Hugh McRidden seldom noticed what he ate, he was better nourished than he had been in years.
It did not spoil his ascetic look, though now and then it gave him
nightmares.

Church and manse were alike to his mind, the townspeople very
friendly though a little foreign in their ways. And yet, sometimes, he
felt homesick for the West Virginia mountains in spite of it all, and
that puzzled him. The Cumberland hills in the distance were softer
and rounder—they were fair in their blue haze, yet he found himself
wishing for sharper, clearer outlines, he did not know why. He knew
as well as any man that his work was succeeding. And yet, when
the first few months had passed, he still did not feel really at home
in the town, and there was not the satisfaction in these things that
there should be—the satisfaction of work well done. Sometimes he
thought, a trifle wearily, that the people of Titusville, despite their
civil manners, were like their hills—rounded and soft—yes, terribly
soft like their copious feather beds. At first he put it down to his being a stranger, but the feeling increased instead of diminishing. Yes,
there was a feather-beddiness about Titusville and its inhabitants.
You could kick and punch them into any state you liked—but the
feathers would rustle back into place as soon as you shook out the
bed again. There was something almost stifling in so much comfort
and quiet. Then he would think, remorsefully, that he was doing the
godly wrong, and humble himself. And yet he was not overworking,
as far as he knew. It was a queer state for a minister to be in.

He summoned his strength and preached a terrifying sermon on the secret sins of the heart. It created a sensation—and those whom he thought he had lashed in it came up to him afterwards and shook him by the hand. He reproved John Waynfleet sharply for unbecoming language at a meeting of elders—a bold thing to do, but John Waynfleet took it like a lamb and asked him to supper. There was nothing he could do that was not acceptable—and that in a small, self-centered community. And yet the higher he rose in their estimation, the less he joyed in his charge.

Sometimes he put the state of his mind down to the reading he did late into the night and resolved to give it up. And yet it was hard to give up—he had always been starved for books, and Dr. McCullough's library, while not very modern, was a curiously fascinating one. He would not mean to read, and then he would find himself by his study fire, bright and cheerful, with a book in his hand. He was familiar, of course, with the early persecutions of the Church in Scotland; the thing ran in his blood, and sanctified John McRidden had been shot before his own plow-stilts by no less a person than bloody Claverhouse himself. Yet, in these old calfbound books, with their quaint type and browning paper, the scenes and personages of that persecution became singularly alive. They came out of the past as if to a hoarse skirl of pipes—he could see the blood on the heather and hear the wailing of the women. He told himself that profitable and searching examples might be drawn from this early church-history— yet that was not the reason he kept on reading.

There were other volumes too, and odder ones—old tomes on witches and witchcraft, from Glanvil to Mather. They were foxed and the bindings worn. Many of them bore a quaint bookplate—a crowded little woodcut of a number of persons in Puritan costume gathered together for prayer or conventicle in an open glade in the forest; below the scene was the motto, "Seek it and ye shall find"; and in one corner the initials of the artist or owner which seemed to be "J. v. C." These had been well read in their time, though not by Dr. McCullough, for the occasional notes in spidery brown ink on the margins were not in his hand.

Hugh McRidden felt a trifle contemptuous of his predecessor— obviously he had bought or inherited the library of some elder divine, set it up on the bookshelves of the manse, and paid little subsequent attention to it, for the books were not in good condition. Such things were done, as he knew—there were booksellers who made a specialty of fitting out clerical libraries. But he was a lover of books, and it went against his heart to see them neglected or misused. He repaired a few of the oldest—he was clever with his hands—and gave Mrs. Breek special instructions about dusting in the study. She did not seem to take very kindly to the idea—and, indeed, during the first few days of her ministrations, there was an odd smell in the study whenever he entered—a smell of dust and crumbled leather and something else that he could not quite identify, though it reminded him a trifle of churchyard yew. But it was not an unpleasant smell and he soon became used to it, though he found, after that, that it was hard to keep flowers in the room for longer than a day.

When the winter came, Hugh McRidden noticed a further change. It was not a hard winter—in fact sometimes the lax air made Hugh McRidden long desperately for the clean cold of his mountains. But a green Christmas makes a fat graveyard—and time after time, young McRidden was summoned to some old man or old woman's bedside to put heart into them for the last journey. That is part of any minister's duty, and he did it well—yet, though death is the joy of the Christian, it has its ugly aspects, and the faces and words of the dying come back to one's mind. Had he done all that he could for them—had he guided them as he should toward effectual grace? Here and there, there was one who would look at him in a daze—he could not rouse that one to a pressing sense of God's wrath and love—or so it seemed to him, and he reproached himself for it. One even, a stubborn old woman, turned her face to the wall when he began to pray, and said in a sort of whimper, "I'm wishing it was Dr. McCullough praying for me—there's a darkness about you, young minister." Hugh McRidden knew that such talk should not hurt him, yet it did.

What hurt him more was the growing feeling that, in some inexplicable way, he was losing his grip on his parish. It was the weather of course and the epidemic—if epidemic it were—it was hard to rouse enthusiasm when people felt sickly. Yet his Bible class waned, and there was coughing during his sermons. He felt anew as if he were fighting some invisible adversary. He had meant to make Titusville a burning and shining example, yet, when he looked around it, he seemed to have changed it but little. He took his difficulties to John Waynfleet and got what was meant to be comfort but did not console him. "An old town—settled ways—a sickly winter—he was doing as well as man might—the parish believed in him—"

It was a hard thing for Hugh McRidden to say but he said it.

"Tell me, Elder Waynfleet," he said, earnestly, "do I seem changed to you at all?"

"Changed?" said Mr. Waynfleet, slightly puzzled.

"At times I seem changed to myself," said Hugh McRidden, staring broodingly at the fire. "At times I feel as if what that old woman said were true, that there is a darkness about me. It is not pleasing."

Mr. Waynfleet took a look at his face, and exerted himself, as he could upon occasion. He made the young man stay to supper and gave him much sound, sensible talk. He did not speak of a wife, though he longed to—but he spoke of the advantages of horse-exercise and the dangers of over-study. He agreed that Dr. McCullough had been little of a reader and must have purchased his library in a lot from some enterprising bookseller, remarking that some of the volumes McRidden described were odd ones for a minister's shelves. But when McRidden began to talk of the early martyrdoms of the church, and the struggles of the saints against the Accuser of the Brethren, he fell silent and watched his companion keenly. At the end he put in some gentle, sensible words on the general subject of superstition—oddly enough, there had been quite a deal of witch-lore in Pennsylvania, and ignorant farmers still painted certain signs and marks on their barns against the hex. "But I never saw a witch could so much as sour a cream-pan—though I've met some queer cases in my legal experience," he ended with cheerful scorn.

He spoke with authority, but when Hugh McRidden took his leave, he looked after him thoughtfully. "All fire and bone and sinew," he muttered. "But that's the difficulty—and a Scotch-Irishman too. I wish I had a niece unmarried—'tis not good for man or minister to live alone. I thought he was a liberal, too, but, by my faith, when he talked of the martyrs, his eyes burned like a Covenanter's. And, as for the Accuser of the Brethren—he might have wrestled with him, hand to hand." He shivered a little and stared about the room. "Now where have I heard of a bookplate like the one he speaks of? There was some story or other—I wish I could remember it. I must do more for the lad."

It would have been better for all concerned had Mr. Waynfleet been able to carry out his resolution. But the following day he sickened, and, while the case was not grave, his doctor ordered him off for change of air as soon as he was able to travel. Like most men, he was deeply concerned with his convalescence, and he and Hugh McRidden parted as elder and minister with no further chance of intimate talk.

That was a pity indeed, for the very night after he had talked with Mr. Waynfleet, the desire to be at his reading again came upon Hugh McRidden with redoubled force. For a while he strove against it consciously—perhaps Mr. Waynfleet was right and he was neglecting his health for his researches. He would walk in the garden till he tired himself and go to bed early. But, when he pulled back the curtain, a chilly rain was falling and the garden looked glum and dismal. He could not stumble around it in the dark, and the study, with its fire, would be so snug and bright. He liked it better than any room in the house—he could smell its queer smell of leather and dust already. Even as he stood, irresolute, a gust of wind snatched the window shut, and he felt a weight lifted from his mind. He turned down the corridor.

The smell was unusually strong as he entered the study. For a moment he thought of ringing for Mrs. Breek and reproving her for neglecting her duties; then he let it go. He rather liked the smell, and the fire was laid—a good thing, for he felt chill. He lit the fire and pulled up his chair before it. Once or twice, while he watched the flames catch, he looked over his shoulder. Then the fire began to crackle merrily. There was a small brown book on the table beside him—he could not remember taking it from the shelves, yet he must have done so, for Mrs. Breek never touched the books except to dust them. He did not intend to read this evening—he would meditate over his sermon. Yet the only texts that came to him were fearful and gloomy ones: he needed distraction. He opened the small book idly, glanced at its curious title page, and began to read.

Some two hours later he was roused from his fierce concentration of reading by a loud and brawling voice outside. He shook his head impatiently and tried to resume his book, but the song was too loud. It was punctuated by heavy, wavering steps—he could hear them splashing in the puddles of the street. "Oh I'm a snolleygoster and we'll all jine the Union!" sang the raucous voice. "The Union forever, hurrah, boys, hurrah!" Hugh McRidden put down his book angrily. He knew well enough who it was—drunken Danny Murphy who lived in the shanty behind the grogshop at the end of town. He had been a good carpenter once and a Civil War hero—now his pension went to the grogshop and he was the town's disgrace. The young town bucks would amuse themselves by getting him drunk and mocking his windy stories, but the older men still had him play the fife on Memorial Days, for they remembered the Sergeant Murphy of Antietam. As for Hugh McRidden, he had seen him in the gutters, snoring like a beast, and his thoughts of him were not kindly.

"I'm a snolleygoster—" roared the voice. The wavering steps began to come up the path. "Intolerable," thought Hugh McRidden and went to the door.

The man was actually mounting the steps of the manse when Hugh McRidden flung the door open. For a moment they stared at each other in the sudden gush of light. The veined and bulbous nose, the slack mouth, the unhallowed white hair—oh yes, it was Danny Murphy, his clothes dripping with rain.

"Bejasus, if I haven't come to the minister's!" said Danny Murphy, in a stupefied voice. "Now why did I do that? I'm a snolleygoster if I know!"

Then a gleam of wheedling intelligence lighted the broken face for a moment.

"Ah, minister dear," said Danny Murphy, in a practiced whine, "sure it's a poor man I am, and neither bite nor sup in my mouth the livelong day, and the shanty destroyed with rain. It was only a dry place to sleep I was searching—and a cup of hot soup maybe—and to dry my clothes, if your reverence'd be so kind—"

"You're drunk, Daniel Murphy," said Hugh McRidden distastefully. "Why do you come here? Be off before I call a constable."

"Sure, ye wouldn't turn an old man out in the rain—and you a minister?" said Danny Murphy, advancing.

"You are not of my congregation nor my belief," said Hugh McRidden, biting his lips. "There is no place for you here."

"Oh, it's that way is it?" said Danny Murphy, smitten with a sudden truculence. He advanced another step—his hot breath stank in Hugh McRidden's face. "Not a piece of bread in charity—and ye call yourself a man of the church. But I'll tell you what sort of minister ye are—and the black curse of Clare upon it! I'll tell you—"

Then he stared at Hugh McRidden, and beyond him, and the color left his face completely and in a moment. For an instant Hugh McRidden thought the man had died on his feet and stepped forward to catch him as he fell. But Danny Murphy backed away instead, and there was naked fear in his eyes.

"I beg pardon, your reverence," he muttered. "I'll not do it again, your reverence. I did not mean to disturb your reverence—nor your friends—"

"My friends, fool?" said Hugh McRidden, sharply, but Danny Murphy did not answer the question. He backed down the steps, mumbling that he humbly begged all their pardons, and at the bottom turned with a hunted look, and fairly took to his heels. Hugh McRidden watched him run—he ran swiftly for a drunken man and yet with a strained anguish of body as if he feared hands on his shoulder. "The wicked flee when no man pursueth," murmured Hugh McRidden, approvingly. As he shut the door, he heard a shout in which only the word "minister" stood out clearly. Later on, he thought it had been "I wish you luck of your friends, minister," or, "Keep your friends from me, minister," but which he could not be sure.

Nevertheless, when Danny Murphy came to him the following morning, wan and tremulous with sobriety, to offer his apologies, he accepted them. Indeed, though the man was not of his congregation, he even went so far as to spare him a five-minute discourse on the deep damnation of his drunken ways—a discourse to which Murphy listened with a white-faced, strained attention. Now and then his eyes strayed uneasily over Hugh McRidden's shoulder, but he kept perfectly still. Next day the word went through town that Danny Murphy had taken the pledge for the new minister—and Hugh McRidden won added glory. But by that time, Hugh McRidden was past caring.

He was past caring because he had read the book. It was a manuscript volume, bound like certain old diaries and written throughout in the spidery copper-plate hand with which Hugh McRidden was already familiar. It called itself soberly, *An Examen Into The Powers Of The Invisible World*, and it bore the familiar bookplate—but, as Hugh McRidden read it, the words seemed to enter his veins. The style was entirely lucid and reasonable—he could bring no arguments against it, though he tried. After he had finished it in the early morning, he felt entirely composed and better than he had in many days. So that was the way things were—it only remained to prove them. He must go and look at a barn or two in the country when he had the opportunity, and talk to some of the farmers—he knew what the signs and the marks meant now.

Nevertheless, such things are not borne without revulsion, and the next day he found himself praying alone in his church—praying like a frightened child till the tears ran out of his eyes. But that evening he went to his study again and looked at the bookplate under a strong reading glass. It was as he had thought—the figures were gathered together in the grove but for no innocent or Christian purpose. Under the glass, the faces were extraordinarily lifelike and vivid. As he gazed at them, they seemed to move a little. Then he knew that he was lost and opened the book anew.

The second attack of the epidemic was sharper than the first—it even attained notice in the Philadelphia newspapers. They spoke of the heroic work of the local pastor; and indeed, throughout those weeks, Hugh McRidden was indefatigable. After the two doctors were stricken, he was the prop of the town and he seemed to need neither rest nor food. Wherever he went among the sickbeds, a white-faced and silent Danny Murphy followed him, performing the most menial offices with competence and care. They exchanged few words, but there seemed a strong bond between them—nor was it the least of the miracle that Danny did not touch a drop during all that time. "No, I'll not be offending the minister or his friends," he would say uneasily to the proffered glass, and whatever was made of it, men knew it was Hugh McRidden's work. He slept in the stable of the manse now, much to the disgust of Mrs. Breek—though she had to admit that he was quiet enough except for the crying at night, and then a word from the minister would always quiet him.

The epidemic waned at last; oddly enough, with only two deaths, and those long-expected. The town began to think of testimonials, and Mr. Waynfleet, at the Springs, began to think of coming home. The minister himself looked haggard and worn, as was to be expected, but he preached as powerfully as ever and with a strange fervor that moved his sparse congregation to their marrowbones. So must some of the martyrs of the Covenant have preached among the mists and the curlews—the men who knew sin like an enemy in their own hearts.

Then he would go back to his study, and his lamp burned late there. There were other books beside the *Examen*—soon he knew them by heart. The first steps in the knowledge were easy—after that they grew more taxing on the strength. He felt a certain contempt for the broomstick-rides and hexings of tradition—he had saved the child at death's door, though they had not asked him in whose name. There must be a price paid for it, of course. Well, let there be a price. He began to understand the fearful joy of the warlocks, who let themselves be put to the question and burned to ashes rather than abandon their power and their sin. Between good and evil there was a deep gulf fixed; there was a fearsome joy in crossing to the other side.

Yet let it be said to his credit that remorse walked with him often, and sometimes at night he would wring his hands in pain. And when the Spring began to come, sweet and daunting, the first breaths of air from the garden were almost more than he could bear. And yet, with the coming of the Spring, he knew something else must come.

He fought against the knowledge stubbornly—but one may not stand still in these matters. The shadow in the depths of the grove within the bookplate was darker and more tangible each time he viewed it—soon enough he would see the face. When the sun was hot, in May, there would be the meeting of the coven—he did not know where or when, but doubtless he would be shown. But first there must be a sacrifice. And that sacrifice would be the man, Daniel Murphy. Hugh McRidden knew it well enough, in spite of his prayers and tears.

On the whole, it speaks well enough for the remnants of his character that it was this soul and no other that he selected. By any rule of life, Danny Murphy was a scoundrel and a wastrel. He had been scared into righteousness for a moment, but, left to himself, he would sink to the gutter again. The world would be well rid of him indeed; and yet it was a fearful thing to contemplate. But there were things more fearful still, and they were becoming impatient—he knew it by the look of the books. It was the last night of April that he called Dan into his study, having sent Mrs. Breek away.

There were glasses and a decanter on the table, and the fire was very bright and clear on the hearth. The old man's eyes looked longingly at the decanter.

"Come in, Dan, and sit down," said Hugh McRidden with cheerful heartiness. "There's something I want to say to you."

"Your lordship—your reverence, I mean—won't be entertaining your friends tonight?" said the old man, timidly. "Faith, I wouldn't want to disturb them."

"Nonsense, Dan," said McRidden, still cheerfully though with altered color. "Besides, what other friends have I but you?"

"Oh, your reverence has many in the town," said Danny Murphy. "Well—thank you," and he sat down on the edge of a chair. He wetted his lips a little, staring at the liquor and the glasses.

"Yes, Dan," said Hugh McRidden, and his eyes were dark. "It's for you. You've served me well through this epidemic—and I've kept you rather strictly. Now you shall have your reward."

Some time later, Hugh McRidden wiped the sweat from his brow with a handkerchief. He felt soiled and sick at heart. The old man was snoring in his chair now—he would not wake for hours, even at the prick of a knife. But it had been a lengthy business, sitting there and watching a man grow maudlin. Danny had been, by turns, boisterous, bellicose and pathetic—he had told the interminable tale of his bravery at Antietam and wept dishonorable tears for his lost youth. Yes, it had been like watching a soul take on corruption—a soul with not one white spot left upon it—a soul where no grace might grow. Hugh McRidden thought of his own soul and shivered, but it was too late to turn back, now.

He made his preparations—they took time, and a glass of the liquor in the decanter would have steadied his nerves, but he did not take it. He was about to commit a mortal sin but he would not break his rule. When all was ready, he stood and listened. The house was entirely quiet, the smell in the study had never been so strong. He picked up the long knife and looked at the sharp blade. It would all be over in a moment, he knew just where to strike. Then at last he would see the countenance of the shadow in the grove, not as in a picture but face to face. He wondered, idly, just how and when it would appear. Dark and comely, with the beauty of a ruined angel, or hideous yet compelling? It was hard to say.

He picked up the knife with a firm hand and stood in front of his victim. The old man's head had rolled to one side—that made it easier. Now it rolled back again. The eyes opened and stared Hugh McRidden full in the face. There was no recognition in the eyes, but they were full of a lost and hopeless wonder. Somewhere in the wreck of that body, the soul sat prisoner and wondered at being so bound. It could no longer master the body, yet it suffered and endured with an unbearable patience. They were the eyes of a lost dog or a beaten child. Then the lids closed over them again.

Hugh McRidden heard his knife drop to the floor. Then he sank into a chair and covered his face with his hands. He could hear the old man's breathing—it had a quiet sound. After a while, he knew what he must do.

He wondered at his own steadiness as he got the ladder and fixed the rope to the beam of the ceiling. Perhaps this was what they had meant after all, but he did not care very much. It, too, was mortal sin, but the better way. Only he must be quick—he knew that he must be quick. Yes, there was a knocking at the front door, he could hear it echo. But he would be off before they came—it would anger them, doubtless. Only he must fix the rope first—there must be no mistake about the rope—and his hands were so clumsy.

"Forgive me, a sinner," he said, and adjusted the noose. The touch of the hemp at his throat was rough and clinging. He could hear someone calling his name in an agitated voice—had it come to that, already? He shut his eyes, his lips moved once more soundlessly. Then the study door was flung open, and John Waynfleet burst into the room.

"Thank God!" said John Waynfleet, catching him in his arms. "Thank God, I have come in time!"

"You have come too late. I have met the Accuser of the Brethren and I am his. And yet I meant to hang myself at the end," said the miserable young man, and burst into tears.

When the noose had been taken from his neck, John Waynfleet got him upstairs to bed. He was very biddable but started at any slight sound, and it was some time before he sank into a heavy sleep. Then John Waynfleet returned to the study, the key of the minister's bedroom in his pocket. As he opened the study door, he felt dizzy for a moment. "Pah!" he said, half-aloud. "What has happened to the place? It smells like a fox's earth." He began to throw up the windows—that helped a little, though his spirits felt uncommonly depressed. He picked up the knife from the floor and shook his head at it. For an instant the thought came to him, queerly, how well and easily the haft would fit in his hand—then he caught himself, sternly. "So that's the way of it," he said, and broke the knife, carefully, on the stones of the hearth.

When he had done so, he felt relieved and would have said a prayer, had he been able to think of a fit one. Then his eyes fell upon a small brown book upon the table. He picked it up, his spirits sinking as he did so, and began to examine the bookplate with the minister's reading-glass.

When he put the reading-glass down, his face was very white and grave. His hands beat at the air for a moment. "Yes, this is bad work," he said. But John Waynfleet had never lacked courage and he did not do so now. "Lord, lift this burden from thy servant!" he cried, in a strong voice and, catching up the book again in a pair of iron tongs, thrust it deep into the heart of the fire.

There was flame and a roaring noise—and yet to John Waynfleet, when he remembered it, it always seemed more like a flame of shadow than a flame of fire. Certainly there was darkness about it—a darkness that pressed upon the eyeballs. It only lasted for a moment, but, when it was done, John Waynfleet felt himself panting as if he had run a race. There had been something like the tones of a voice as well—but that he never cared to remember. When he looked once more, the book was red ash, and the room much clearer.

"And now, I suppose," thought John Waynfleet with resignation, "I must get this drunken reprobate of a Danny Murphy back to his kennel before he wakens. Well, well, it has been a strange night. Yet it was Danny who wrote the letter that brought me back here—that may be accounted to him for righteousness—though I could not make head or tail of what he said except that the minister ailed. I must never tell McRidden that—it would break him. Best get the lad to my house."

He did so, but when the minister was well enough to sit up, Waynfleet found himself obliged to answer questions, much against his will.

"Yes," he said. "My dear fellow, you are quite sure you are strong enough? Well—the books belonged to a man named Jacobus van Clootz. It was quite a famous case at the time—I have looked it up since—though I do not advise you to read the testimony. Oh yes, he was accused of sorcery and witchcraft—but he disappeared rather strangely during the trial and the body was never found. Before that he had made some sort of incoherent statement that his soul lay in his books, and woe be to them that meddled with it—the usual rant. I am telling you this just to show you there is not a word of truth in such tales. His effects were sold at auction. I can only suppose that some cheap-jack bookseller bought them and, finding them hard to dispose of, let them molder in his cellar for years before he finally foisted them off on Dr. McCullough. McCullough must have had them some forty years—I must say I am very much surprised at him."

"Forty years!" said Hugh McRidden, with a bleak look. "And they were with me but a few months—and yet—"

"You must not take it like that," said John Waynfleet heartily, and clapped him on the shoulder. "Even supposing there could be a grain of sense in such moonshine—and as Christians we must disbelieve it—well, well, there are men who can walk through pestilence untouched. My father told me of such, in the days of the yellow fever. And others no less honest and honorable, who—ahem—are not so fortunate. Besides, as you know, McCullough was nothing of a reader. I doubt if he so much as took down a volume from one year's end to another. He was a man of great simplicity of soul. And as for the books themselves—well they're burned now, every one of them. I saw to that myself. Indeed, when you return to the manse, you will find it has quite a different atmosphere about it."

"I shall not return to the manse," said Hugh McRidden slowly, shaking his head. "I have been greatly ambitious since my youth, Mr. Waynfleet—the core of the matter lies there, you see. Had I thought more of God and less of my own ambition, I would not be as you see me. Now I think I must spend the rest of my life in rooting that ambition out."

"My dear man!" said Mr. Waynfleet—"I assure you—the best medical opinion—a breakdown from overwork that might happen to anyone—you are young and able—I'll not hear a word against you—"

"It is not that, though I thank you," said Hugh McRidden. "What manner of man was this Jacobus van Clootz—an old man, with a barren face, rather pockmarked, and singular, searching eyes?"

"Why, he is so described in the records," said John Waynfleet, uncomfortably. "But—"

"You see," said Hugh McRidden. "No, Elder Waynfleet, it is useless. I hope and believe in God's providence, even for the worst of sinners—but my road lies straight before me, and it is not the road I once thought of."

So it came about that the young and beloved minister left Titusville, after so short a stay. At the farewell service, his words were few and simple, yet there was a gentleness in them that moved his congregation as no other words of his had done. Later on, they heard from time to time of his work among the obscurer missions—and every word was of praise. The last letter John Waynfleet had from him was dated two weeks before the Army of the East overran and burned his outpost mission, and it contained the sentence: "My dear friend, I think and trust that my penance is at last worked out, for I see the old man no longer. Wish me joy." And when John Waynfleet, later, read the accounts of that heroic martyrdom, he knew it was with joy and faith that Hugh McRidden had gone to his doom. He muttered a text about another joy promised in the Scriptures, and felt the tears come to his eyes, for he was a very old man.

There have been three ministers in Titusville since—good men, all of them; but Hugh McRidden is a legend. There will never be another like him, say the ladies who were girls in his time—and they used to point to Danny Murphy for a proof. But Danny has some years gone the way of reformed characters and no longer sits in the back pew of the old brick church, attentive and doglike, an example to all the churchgoing. He sleeps well, no doubt, in the churchyard—but no sweeter than Hugh McRidden in the foreign soil that gave him at last the release and peace for which his spirit craved so long.

O'Halloran's Luck

They were strong men built the Big Road, in the early days of America, and it was the Irish did it.

My grandfather, Tim O'Halloran, was a young man then, and wild. He could swing a pick all day and dance all night, if there was a fiddler handy; and if there was a girl to be pleased he pleased her, for he had the tongue and the eye. Likewise, if there was a man to be stretched, he could stretch him with the one blow.

I saw him later on in years when he was thin and white-headed, but in his youth he was not so. A thin, white-headed man would have had little chance, and they driving the Road to the West. It was two-fisted men cleared the plains and bored through the mountains. They came in the thousands to do it from every county in Ireland; and now the names are not known. But it's over their graves you pass, when you ride in the Pullmans. And Tim O'Halloran was one of them, six feet high and solid as the Rock of Cashel when he stripped to the skin.

He needed to be all of that, for it was not easy labor. 'Twas a time of great booms and expansions in the railroad line, and they drove the tracks north and south, east and west, as if the devil was driving behind. For this they must have the boys with shovel and pick, and every immigrant ship from Ireland was crowded with bold young men. They left famine and England's rule behind them—and it was the thought of many they'd pick up gold for the asking in the free States of America, though it's little gold that most of them ever saw. They found themselves up to their necks in the water of the canals, and burnt black by the suns of the prairie—and that was a great surprise to them. They saw their sisters and their mothers made servants that had not been servants in Ireland, and that was a strange change too. Eh, the death and the broken hopes it takes to make a country! But those with the heart and the tongue kept the tongue and the heart.

Tim O'Halloran came from Clonmelly, and he was the fool of the family and the one who listened to tales. His brother Ignatius went for a priest and his brother James for a sailor, but they knew he could not do those things. He was strong and biddable and he had the

O'Halloran tongue; but there came a time of famine, when the younger mouths cried for bread and there was little room in the nest. He was not entirely wishful to emigrate, and yet, when he thought of it, he was wishful. 'Tis often enough that way, with a younger son. Perhaps he was the more wishful because of Kitty Malone.

'Tis a quiet place, Clonmelly, and she'd been the light of it to him. But now the Malones had gone to the States of America—and it was well known that Kitty had a position there the like of which was not to be found in all Dublin Castle. They called her a hired girl, to be sure, but did not she eat from gold plates, like all the citizens of America? And when she stirred her tea, was not the spoon made of gold? Tim O'Halloran thought of this, and of the chances and adventures that a bold young man might find, and at last he went to the boat. There were many from Clonmelly on that boat, but he kept himself to himself and dreamed his own dreams.

The more disillusion it was to him, when the boat landed him in Boston and he found Kitty Malone there, scrubbing the stairs of an American house with a pail and brush by her side. But that did not matter, after the first, for her cheeks still had the rose in them and she looked at him in the same way. 'Tis true there was an Orangeman courting her—conductor he was on the horsecars, and Tim did not like that. But after Tim had seen her, he felt himself the equal of giants; and when the call came for strong men to work in the wilds of the West, he was one of the first to offer. They broke a sixpence between them before he left—it was an English sixpence, but that did not matter greatly to them. And Tim O'Halloran was going to make his fortune, and Kitty Malone to wait for him, though her family liked the Orangeman best.

Still and all, it was cruel work in the West, as such work must be, and Tim O'Halloran was young. He liked the strength and the wildness of it—he'd drink with the thirstiest and fight with the wildest— and that he knew how to do. It was all meat and drink to him—the bare tracks pushing ahead across the bare prairie and the fussy cough of the wood-burning locomotives and the cold blind eyes of a murdered man, looking up at the prairie stars. And then there was the cholera and the malaria—and the strong man you'd worked on the grade beside, all of a sudden gripping his belly with the fear of death on his face and his shovel falling to the ground.

Next day he would not be there and they'd scratch a name from the pay roll. Tim O'Halloran saw it all.

He saw it all and it changed his boyhood and hardened it. But, for all that, there were times when the black fit came upon him, as it does to the Irish, and he knew he was alone in a strange land. Well, that's a hard hour to get through, and he was young. There were times when he'd have given all the gold of the Americas for a smell of Clonmelly air or a glimpse of Clonmelly sky. Then he'd drink or dance or fight or put a black word on the foreman, just to take the aching out of his mind. It did not help him with his work and it wasted his pay; but it was stronger than he, and not even the thought of Kitty Malone could stop it. 'Tis like that, sometimes.

Well, it happened one night he was coming back from the place where they sold the potheen, and perhaps he'd had a trifle more of it than was advisable. Yet he had not drunk it for that, but to keep the queer thoughts from his mind. And yet, the more that he drank, the queerer were the thoughts in his head. For he kept thinking of the Luck of the O'Hallorans and the tales his grandda had told about it in the old country—the tales about pookas and banshees and leprechauns with long white beards.

"And that's a queer thing to be thinking and myself at labor with a shovel on the open prairies of America," he said to himself. "Sure, creatures like that might live and thrive in the old country—and I'd be the last to deny it—but 'tis obvious they could not live here. The first sight of Western America would scare them into conniptions. And as for the Luck of the O'Hallorans, 'tis little good I've had of it, and me not even able to rise to foreman and marry Kitty Malone. They called me the fool of the family in Clonmelly, and I misdoubt but they were right. Tim O'Halloran, you're a worthless man, for all your strong back and arms." It was with such black, bitter thoughts as these that he went striding over the prairie. And it was just then that he heard the cry in the grass.

'Twas a strange little piping cry, and only the half of it human. But Tim O'Halloran ran to it, for in truth he was spoiling for a fight. "Now this will be a beautiful young lady," he said to himself as he ran, "and I will save her from robbers; and her father, the rich man, will ask me—but, wirra, 'tis not her I wish to marry, 'tis Kitty Malone. Well, he'll set me up in business, out of friendship and gratitude, and then I will send for Kitty—"

But by then he was out of breath, and by the time he had reached the place where the cry came from he could see that it was not so. It was only a pair of young wolf cubs, and they chasing something small and helpless and playing with it as a cat plays with a mouse. Where the wolf cub is the old wolves are not far, but Tim O'Halloran felt as bold as a lion. "Be off with you!" he cried and he threw a stick and a stone. They ran away into the night, and he could hear them howling—a lonesome sound. But he knew the camp was near, so he paid small attention to that but looked for the thing they'd been chasing.

It scuttled in the grass but he could not see it. Then he stopped down and picked something up, and when he had it in his hand he stared at it unbelieving. For it was a tiny shoe, no bigger than a child's. And more than that, it was not the kind of shoe that is made in America. Tim O'Halloran stared and stared at it—and at the silver buckle upon it—and still he could not believe.

"If I'd found this in the old country," he said to himself, half aloud, "I'd have sworn that it was a leprechaun's and looked for the pot of gold. But here, there's no chance of that—"

"I'll trouble you for the shoe," said a small voice close by his feet.

Tim O'Halloran stared round him wildly. "By the piper that played before Moses!" he said. "Am I drunk beyond comprehension? Or am I mad? For I thought that I heard a voice."

"So you did, silly man," said the voice again, but irritated, "and I'll trouble you for my shoe, for it's cold in the dewy grass."

"Honey," said Tim O'Halloran, beginning to believe his ears, "honey dear, if you'll but show yourself—"

"I'll do that and gladly," said the voice; and with that the grasses parted, and a little old man with a long white beard stepped out. He was perhaps the size of a well-grown child, as O'Halloran could see clearly by the moonlight on the prairie; moreover, he was dressed in the clothes of antiquity, and he carried cobbler's tools in the belt at his side.

"By faith and belief, but it *is* a leprechaun!" cried O'Halloran, and with that he made a grab for the apparition. For you must know, in case you've been ill brought up, that a leprechaun is a sort of cobbler fairy and each one knows the whereabouts of a pot of gold. Or it's so they say in the old country. For they say you can tell a leprechaun by his long white beard and his cobbler's tools; and once you have the possession of him, he must tell you where his gold is hid.

The little old man skipped out of reach as nimbly as a cricket. "Is this Clonmelly courtesy?" he said with a shake in his voice, and Tim O'Halloran felt ashamed.

"Sure, I didn't mean to hurt your worship at all," he said, "but if you're what you seem to be, well, then, there's the little matter of a pot of gold—"

"Pot of gold!" said the leprechaun, and his voice was hollow and full of scorn. "And would I be here today if I had that same? Sure, it all went to pay my sea passage, as you might expect."

"Well," said Tim O'Halloran, scratching his head, for that

sounded reasonable enough, "that may be so or again it may not be so. But—"

"Oh, 'tis bitter hard," said the leprechaun, and his voice was weeping, "to come to the waste, wild prairies all alone, just for the love of Clonmelly folk—and then to be disbelieved by the first that speaks to me! If it had been an Ulsterman now, I might have expected it. But the O'Hallorans wear the green."

"So they do," said Tim O'Halloran, "and it shall not be said of an O'Halloran that he denied succor to the friendless. I'll not touch you."

"Do you swear it?" said the leprechaun.

"I swear it," said Tim O'Halloran.

"Then I'll just creep under your coat," said the leprechaun, "for I'm near destroyed by the chills and damps of the prairie. Oh, this weary emigrating!" he said, with a sigh like a furnace. " 'Tis not what it's cracked up to be."

Tim O'Halloran took off his own coat and wrapped it around him. Then he could see him closer—and it could not be denied that the leprechaun was a pathetic sight. He'd a queer little boyish face, under the long white beard, but his clothes were all torn and ragged and his cheeks looked hollow with hunger.

"Cheer up!" said Tim O'Halloran and patted him on the back. "It's a bad day that beats the Irish. But tell me first how you came here—for that still sticks in my throat."

"And would I be staying behind with half Clonmelly on the water?" said the leprechaun stoutly. "By the bones of Finn, what sort of a man do you think I am?"

"That's well said," said Tim O'Halloran. "And yet I never heard of the Good People emigrating before."

"True for you," said the leprechaun. "The climate here's not good for most of us and that's a fact. There's a boggart or so that came over with the English, but then the Puritan ministers got after them and they had to take to the woods. And I had a word or two, on my way West, with a banshee that lives by Lake Superior—a decent woman she was, but you could see she'd come down in the world. For even the bits of children wouldn't believe in her; and when she let out a screech, sure they thought it was a steamboat. I misdoubt she's died since then—she was not in good health when I left her.

"And as for the native spirits—well, you can say what you like, but they're not very comfortable people. I was captive to some of them a week and they treated me well enough, but they whooped and danced too much for a quiet man, and I did not like the long, sharp knives on them. Oh, I've had the adventures on my way here," he said, "but they're over now, praises be, for I've found a protector at last," and he snuggled closer under O'Halloran's coat.

"Well," said O'Halloran, somewhat taken aback, "I did not think this would be the way of it when I found O'Halloran's Luck that I'd dreamed of so long. For, first I save your life from the wolves; and now, it seems, I must be protecting you further. But in the tales it's always the other way round."

"And is the company and conversation of an ancient and experienced creature like myself nothing to you?" said the leprechaun fiercely. "Me that had my own castle at Clonmelly and saw O'Sheen in his pride? Then St. Patrick came—wirra, wirra!—and there was an end to it all. For some of us—the Old Folk of Ireland—he baptized, and some of us he chained with the demons of hell. But I was Lazy Brian, betwixt and between, and all I wanted was peace and a quiet life. So he changed me to what you see—me that had six tall harpers to harp me awake in the morning—and laid a doom upon me for being betwixt and between. I'm to serve Clonmelly folk and follow them wherever they go till I serve the servants of servants in a land at the world's end. And then, perhaps, I'll be given a Christian soul and can follow my own inclinations."

"Serve the servants of servants?" said O'Halloran. "Well, that's a hard riddle to read."

"It is that," said the leprechaun, "for I never once met the servant of a servant in Clonmelly, all the time I've been looking. I doubt but that was in St. Patrick's mind."

"If it's criticizing the good saint you are, I'll leave you here on the prairie," said Tim O'Halloran.

"I'm not criticizing him," said the leprechaun with a sigh, "but I wish he'd been less hasty. Or more specific. And now, what do we do?"

"Well," said O'Halloran, and he sighed, too, " 'tis a great responsibility, and one I never thought to shoulder. But since you've asked for help, you must have it. Only there's just this to be said. There's little money in my pocket."

"Sure, 'tis not for your money I've come to you," said the leprechaun joyously. "And I'll stick closer than a brother."

"I've no doubt of that," said O'Halloran with a wry laugh. "Well, clothes and food I can get for you—but if you stick with me, you must work as well. And perhaps the best way would be for you to be my young nephew, Rory, run away from home to work on the railroad."

"And how would I be your young nephew, Rory, and me with a long white beard?"

"Well," said Tim O'Halloran with a grin, "as it happens, I've got a razor in my pocket."

And with that you should have heard the leprechaun. He stamped and he swore and he pled—but it was no use at all. If he was to follow Tim O'Halloran, he must do it on Tim O'Halloran's terms and no two ways about it. So O'Halloran shaved him at last, by the light of the moon, to the leprechaun's great horror, and when he got him back to the construction camp and fitted him out in some old duds of his own—well, it wasn't exactly a boy he looked, but it was more like a boy than anything else. Tim took him up to the foreman the next day and got him signed on for a water boy, and it was a beautiful tale he told the foreman. As well, too, that he had the O'Halloran tongue to tell it with, for when the foreman first looked at young Rory you could see him gulp like a man that's seen a ghost.

"And now what do we do?" said the leprechaun to Tim when the interview was over.

"Why, you work," said Tim with a great laugh, "and Sundays you wash your shirt."

"Thank you for nothing," said the leprechaun with an angry gleam in his eye. "It was not for that I came here from Clonmelly."

"Oh, we've all come here for great fortune," said Tim, "but it's hard to find that same. Would you rather be with the wolves?"

"Oh, no," said the leprechaun.

"Then drill, ye tarrier, drill!" said Tim O'Halloran and shouldered his shovel, while the leprechaun trailed behind.

At the end of the day the leprechaun came to him.

"I've never done mortal work before," he said, "and there's no bone in my body that's not a pain and an anguish to me."

"You'll feel better after supper," said O'Halloran. "And the night's made for sleep."

"But where will I sleep?" said the leprechaun.

"In the half of my blanket," said Tim, "for are you not young Rory, my nephew?"

It was not what he could have wished, but he saw he could do no otherwise. Once you start a tale, you must play up to the tale.

But that was only the beginning, as Tim O'Halloran soon found out. For Tim O'Halloran had tasted many things before, but not responsibility, and now responsibility was like a bit in his mouth. It was not so bad the first week, while the leprechaun was still ailing. But when, what with the food and the exercise, he began to recover his strength, 'twas a wonder Tim O'Halloran's hair did not turn gray overnight. He was not a bad creature, the leprechaun, but he had all the natural mischief of a boy of twelve and, added to that, the craft and knowledge of generations.

There was the three pipes and the pound of shag the leprechaun stole from McGinnis—and the dead frog he slipped in the foreman's tea—and the bottle of potheen he got hold of one night when Tim had to hold his head in a bucket of water to sober him up. A fortunate thing it was that St. Patrick had left him no great powers, but at that he had enough to put the jumping rheumatism on Shaun Kelly for two days—and it wasn't till Tim threatened to deny him the use of his razor entirely that he took off the spell.

That brought Rory to terms, for by now he'd come to take a queer pleasure in playing the part of a boy and he did not wish to have it altered.

Well, things went on like this for some time, and Tim O'Halloran's savings grew; for whenever the drink was running he took no part in it, for fear of mislaying his wits when it came to deal with young Rory. And as it was with the drink, so was it with other things—till Tim O'Halloran began to be known as a steady man. And then, as it happened one morning, Tim O'Halloran woke up early. The leprechaun had finished his shaving and was sitting cross-legged, chuckling to himself.

"And what's your source of amusement so early in the day?" said Tim sleepily.

"Oh," said the leprechaun, "I'm just thinking of the rare hard work we'll have when the line's ten miles farther on."

"And why should it be harder there than it is here?" said Tim.

"Oh, nothing," said the leprechaun, "but those fools of surveyors have laid out the line where there's hidden springs of water. And when we start digging, there'll be the devil to pay."

"Do you know that for a fact?" said Tim.

"And why wouldn't I know it?" said the leprechaun. "Me that can hear the waters run underground."

"Then what should we do?" said Tim.

"Shift the line half a mile to the west and you'd have a firm roadbed," said the leprechaun.

Tim O'Halloran said no more at the time. But for all that, he managed to get to the assistant engineer in charge of construction at the noon hour. He could not have done it before, but now he was known as a steady man. Nor did he tell where he got the information—he put it on having seen a similar thing in Clonmelly.

Well, the engineer listened to him and had a test made—and sure enough, they struck the hidden spring. "That's clever work, O'Halloran," said the engineer. "You've saved us time and money. And now how would you like to be foreman of a gang?"

"I'd like it well," said Tim O'Halloran.

"Then you boss Gang Five from this day forward," said the engineer. "And I'll keep my eye on you. I like a man that uses his head."

"Can my nephew come with me," said Tim, "for, 'troth, he's my responsibility?"

"He can," said the engineer, who had children of his own.

So Tim got promoted and the leprechaun along with him. And the first day on the new work, young Rory stole the gold watch from the engineer's pocket, because he liked the tick of it, and Tim had to threaten him with fire and sword before he'd put it back.

Well, things went on like this for another while, till finally Tim woke up early on another morning and heard the leprechaun laughing.

"And what are you laughing at?" he said.

"Oh, the more I see of mortal work, the less reason there is to it," said the leprechaun. "For I've been watching the way they get the rails up to us on the line. And they do it thus and so. But if they did it so and thus, they could do it in half the time with half the work."

"Is that so indeed?" said Tim O'Halloran, and he made him explain it clearly. Then, after he'd swallowed his breakfast, he was off to his friend the engineer.

"That's a clever idea, O'Halloran," said the engineer. "We'll try it." And a week after that, Tim O'Halloran found himself with a hundred men under him and more responsibility than he'd ever had in his life. But it seemed little to him beside the responsibility of the leprechaun, and now the engineer began to lend him books to study and he studied them at nights while the leprechaun snored in its blanket.

A man could rise rapidly in those days—and it was then Tim O'Halloran got the start that was to carry him far. But he did not know he was getting it, for his heart was near broken at the time over Kitty Malone. She'd written him a letter or two when he first came West, but now there were no more of them and at last he got a word from her family telling him he should not be disturbing Kitty with letters from a laboring man. That was bitter for Tim O'Halloran, and he'd think about Kitty and the Orangeman in the watches of the night and groan. And then, one morning, he woke up after such a night and heard the leprechaun laughing.

"And what are you laughing at now?" he said sourly. "For my heart's near burst with its pain."

"I'm laughing at a man that would let a cold letter keep him from his love, and him with pay in his pocket and the contract ending the first," said the leprechaun.

Tim O'Halloran struck one hand in the palm of the other.

"By the piper, but you've the right of it, you queer little creature!" he said. " 'Tis back to Boston we go when this job's over."

It was laborer Tim O'Halloran that had come to the West, but it was Railroadman Tim O'Halloran that rode back East in the cars like a gentleman, with a free pass in his pocket and the promise of a job on the railroad that was fitting a married man. The leprechaun, I may say, gave some trouble in the cars, more particularly when he bit a fat woman that called him a dear little boy; but what with giving him peanuts all the way, Tim O'Halloran managed to keep him fairly quieted.

When they got to Boston he fitted them both out in new clothes from top to toe. Then he gave the leprechaun some money and told him to amuse himself for an hour or so while he went to see Kitty Malone.

He walked into the Malones' flat as bold as brass, and there sure enough, in the front room, were Kitty Malone and the Orangeman. He was trying to squeeze her hand, and she refusing, and it made Tim O'Halloran's blood boil to see that. But when Kitty saw Tim O'Halloran she let out a scream.

"Oh, Tim!" she said. "Tim! And they told me you were dead in the plains of the West!"

"And a great pity that he was not," said the Orangeman, blowing out his chest with the brass buttons on it, "but a bad penny always turns up."

"Bad penny is it, you brass-buttoned son of iniquity," said Tim O'Halloran. "I have but the one question to put you. Will you stand or will you run?"

"I'll stand as we stood at Boyne Water," said the Orangeman, grinning ugly. "And whose backs did we see that day?"

"Oh, is that the tune?" said Tim O'Halloran. "Well, I'll give you a tune to match it. Who fears to speak of Ninety-Eight?"

With that he was through the Orangeman's guard and stretched him at the one blow, to the great consternation of the Malones. The old woman started to screech and Pat Malone to talk of policemen, but Tim O'Halloran silenced the both of them.

"Would you be giving your daughter to an Orangeman that works on the horsecars, when she might be marrying a future railroad president?" he said. And with that he pulled his savings out of his pocket and the letter that promised the job for a married man. That quieted the Malones a little and, once they got a good look at Tim O'Halloran, they began to change their tune. So, after they'd got the Orangeman out of the house—and he did not go willing, but he went as a whipped man must—Tim O'Halloran recounted all of his adventures.

The tale did not lose in the telling, though he did not speak of the leprechaun, for he thought that had better be left to a later day; and at the end Pat Malone was offering him a cigar. "But I find none upon me," said he with a wink at Tim, "so I'll just run down to the corner."

"And I'll go with you," said Kitty's mother, "for if Mr. O'Halloran stays to supper—and he's welcome—there's a bit of shopping to be done."

So the old folks left Tim O'Halloran and his Kitty alone. But just as they were in the middle of their planning and contriving for the future, there came a knock on the door.

"What's that?" said Kitty, but Tim O'Halloran knew well enough and his heart sank within him. He opened the door—and sure enough, it was the leprechaun.

"Well, Uncle Tim," said the creature, grinning, "I'm here."

Tim O'Halloran took a look at him as if he saw him for the first time. He was dressed in new clothes, to be sure, but there was soot on his face and his collar had thumbmarks on it already. But that wasn't what made the difference. New clothes or old, if you looked at him for the first time, you could see he was an unchancy thing, and not like Christian souls.

"Kitty," he said, "Kitty darlint, I had not told you. But this is my young nephew, Rory, that lives with me."

Well, Kitty welcomed the boy with her prettiest manners, though Tim O'Halloran could see her giving him a side look now and then. All the same, she gave him a slice of cake, and he tore it apart with his fingers; but in the middle of it he pointed to Kitty Malone.

"Have you made up your mind to marry my Uncle Tim?" he said. "Faith, you'd better, for he's a grand catch."

"Hold your tongue, young Rory," said Tim O'Halloran angrily, and Kitty blushed red. But then she took the next words out of his mouth.

"Let the gossoon be, Tim O'Halloran," she said bravely. "Why shouldn't he speak his mind? Yes, Roryeen—it's I that will be your aunt in the days to come—and a proud woman too."

"Well, that's good," said the leprechaun, cramming the last of the cake in his mouth, "for I'm thinking you'll make a good home for us, once you're used to my ways."

"Is that to be the way of it, Tim?" said Kitty Malone very quietly, but Tim O'Halloran looked at her and knew what was in her mind. And he had the greatest impulse in the world to deny the leprechaun and send him about his business. And yet, when he thought of it, he knew that he could not do it, not even if it meant the losing of Kitty Malone.

"I'm afraid that must be the way of it, Kitty," he said with a groan.

"Then I honor you for it," said Kitty, with her eyes like stars. She went up to the leprechaun and took his hard little hand. "Will you live with us, young Rory?" she said. "For we'd be glad to have you."

"Thank you kindly, Kitty Malone—O'Halloran to be," said the leprechaun. "And you're lucky, Tim O'Halloran—lucky yourself and lucky in your wife. For if you had denied me then, your luck would have left you—and if she had denied me then, 'twould be but half luck for you both. But now the luck will stick to you the rest of your lives. And I'm wanting another piece of cake," said he.

"Well, it's a queer lad you are," said Kitty Malone, but she went for the cake. The leprechaun swung his legs and looked at Tim O'Halloran. "I wonder what keeps my hands off you," said the latter with a groan.

"Fie!" said the leprechaun, grinning, "and would you be lifting the hand to your one nephew? But tell me one thing, Tim O'Halloran, was this wife you're to take ever in domestic service?"

"And what if she was?" said Tim O'Halloran, firing up. "Who thinks the worse of her for that?"

"Not I," said the leprechaun, "for I've learned about mortal labor since I came to this country—and it's an honest thing. But tell me one thing more. Do you mean to serve this wife of yours and honor her through the days of your wedded life?"

"Such is my intention," said Tim, "though what business it is of—"

"Never mind," said the leprechaun. "Your shoelace is undone, bold man. Command me to tie it up."

"Tie up my shoe, you black-hearted, villainous little anatomy!" thundered Tim O'Halloran, and the leprechaun did so. Then he jumped to his feet and skipped about the room.

"Free! Free!" he piped. "Free at last! For I've served the servants of servants and the doom has no power on me longer. Free, Tim O'Halloran! O'Halloran's Luck is free!"

Tim O'Halloran stared at him, dumb; and even as he stared, the creature seemed to change. He was small, to be sure, and boyish—but you could see the unchancy look leave him and the Christian soul come into his eyes. That was a queer thing to be seen, and a great one too.

"Well," said Tim O'Halloran in a sober voice, "I'm glad for you, Rory. For now you'll be going back to Clonmelly, no doubt—and faith, you've earned the right."

The leprechaun shook his head.

"Clonmelly's a fine, quiet place," said he, "but this country's bolder. I misdoubt it's something in the air—you will not have noticed it, but I've grown two inches and a half since first I met you, and I feel myself growing still. No, it's off to the mines of the West I am, to follow my natural vocation—for they say there are mines out there you could mislay all Dublin Castle in—and wouldn't I like to try! But speaking of that, Tim O'Halloran," he said, "I was not quite honest with you about the pot of gold. You'll find your share behind the door when I've gone. And now good day and long life to you!"

"But, man dear," said Tim O'Halloran, " 'tis not good-by!" For it was then he realized the affection that was in him for the queer little creature.

"No, 'tis not good-by," said the leprechaun. "When you christen your first son, I'll be at his cradle, though you may not see me—and so with your sons' sons and their sons, for O'Halloran's luck's just begun. But we'll part for the present now. For now I'm a Christian soul, I've work to do in the world."

"Wait a minute," said Tim O'Halloran. "For you would not know, no doubt, and you such a new soul. And no doubt you'll be seeing the priest—but a layman can do it in an emergency and I think this is one. I dare not have you leave me—and you not even baptized."

And with that he made the sign of the cross and baptized the leprechaun. He named him Rory Patrick.

" 'Tis not done with all the formalities," he said at the end, "but I'll defend the intention."

"I'm grateful to you," said the leprechaun. "And if there was a debt to be paid, you've paid it back and more."

And with that he was gone somehow, and Tim O'Halloran was alone in the room. He rubbed his eyes. But there was a little sack behind the door, where the leprechaun had left it—and Kitty was coming in with a slice of cake on a plate.

THE AMERICAN SCENE

A Death in the Country

After the years, Tom Carroll was going back to Waynesville—to stand by a kinswoman's grave, in the country of his youth. The names of the small, familiar stations were knots on a thread that led back into the darkness of childhood. He was glad Claire had not come. She hated death and memories. She hated cramped, local trains that smelled of green plush and cinders. Most of all she would hate Waynesville, even in mid-September and the grave light of afternoon.

Well, he wasn't looking forward to a pleasant time. He felt fagged and on edge already. There was work for the active partner of Norman, Buckstone, and Carroll in his brief-case, but he could not get down to the work. Instead he remembered, from childhood, the smell of dyed cloth and poignant, oppressive flowers, the black wisp tied on the knocker, the people coming to the door. The house was full of a menace—full of a secret—there were incomprehensible phrases, said in a murmur, and a man in black gloves who came, and a strangeness behind a shut door. Run out and play, run out and play; but there was no right way to play any more—even out in the yard you could smell the sweet, overpowering flowers—even out in the street you could see the people coming and coming, making that little pause as they saw the black wisp. Beautiful, they said, she looks beautiful; but the glimpse of the face was not mother, only somebody coldly asleep. Our sister has gone to dear Jesus . . . we shall meet on that beautiful shore . . . but the man spoke words, and the harsh box sank into the hole, and from it nothing arose, not even a white thing, not even silver vapor; the clay at the sides of the hole was too yellow and thick and cold. He's too young to realize, said a great many voices—but for months nothing was right. The world had stopped being solid, and people's smiles were different, and mother was Jesus's sister, and they gave her clothes away. Then, after a long time, the place was green again and looked just like the other graves, and the knife in your pocket was a comfort, going out there Sundays in the street car.

Barbarous. And tomorrow would be barbarous, as well. The family met only at funerals and weddings, now; and there had been more funerals than weddings for the past ten years. The big Christmas tree was gone from the house on Hessian Street—the majestic tree whose five-pointed, sparkling star had scratched against the ceiling of heaven in the back parlor, spreading wide its green boughs to shelter all generations and tribes of the Pyes and Merritts and Chipmans, their wives and their children, their menservants and their maidservants, their Noah's arks and cigar-cases and bottles of *eau-de-cologne*. The huge tablecloth of Thanksgiving lay folded away at the bottom of a chest—the tables now were too small. There would never be another turkey, with a breast like a mountainside, to fall into endless slices under the shining magic of Uncle Melrose's knife. Aunt Louise and Aunt Emmy had been the last of Hessian Street and, after tomorrow, there would only be Aunt Emmy and the ghosts.

The faces around the table had been masterful and full of life. They had been grown-up and permanent—one could not imagine them young or growing old. Together, they made a nation; they were the earth. If one took the trains of the morning, even as far as Bradensburg, lo, Uncle Melrose was there, at his desk with the little brass postage-scale on top of it, as it had been from the first. If one walked out to Mount Pleasant through the buckeye fall, at the end there was the white gate of Cousin Edna and the iron nigger boy with the rainstreaked face, holding out his black hand stiffly for the buckboards that drove no more. There were princes and dominations and thrones and powers; but what were these beside Aunt Emmy and Cousin Millie, beside the everlasting forms of Mrs. Bache and Mr. Beaver, of the ladies at the Women's Exchange and the man who lighted the gas street-lamps with a long brass spike? Then, suddenly, the earth had begun to crumble. A wind blew, a bell sounded, and they were dispersed. There were shrunken old people, timorous and pettish, and a small heart-stifling town. These and the grown-up children, more strange than strangers. But Hessian Street was over—the great tree was down.

"And Uncle Melrose was a pompous old windbag," thought Tom Carroll. "And yet, if he were alive, I'd be calling him 'Sir.' Oh, Claire's right—the jungle's the jungle—she's saner than I am, always."

It was one of the many maxims Claire found in books. The family was the jungle that you grew up in and, if you did not, somehow, break through to light and air of your own when you were young, you died, quickly or slowly but surely, stifled out, choked down by the overpowering closeness of your own kin. Tom Carroll knew this much—that New York, after Waynesville, had been like passing from the large, squabbling, overheated room of Christmas afternoon into the anonymous peace of a bare and windy street. He had been lonely, often—he had missed Hessian Street and them all. But, oh the end-less, intricate, unimportant diplomacy—the feuds and the makings-up—the inflexible machine of the Family, crushing all independence. Not again, not ever again! And yet, here he was, on the train.

Well, nobody could say that he shirked it. He would have to take charge when he got there, like it or not. It wouldn't be easy, straight-ening everything out—he'd rather handle the Corlis case any day—but he'd done it in other emergencies and he supposed he could do it again. After all, who else was there? Jerry Pye? His mouth narrowed, thinking of Jerry.

The conductor bawled the names of familiar stations, the long au-tumnal twilight began beyond the window. If only things could go smoothly just this once! But something always cropped up—some-thing always had to be smoothed over and explained. *Morton Center, Morton Center!* If Aunt Louise had left no will—and she very prob-ably hadn't—there'd be the dickens of a time, securing the estate to Aunt Emmy. But it must be done—he'd ride roughshod over Jerry Pye if necessary. *Brandy Hill! Brandy Hill!* . . . If only nobody would tell him to be sure and notice Mrs. Bache! He could easily fix a pension for Aunt Emmy, but how to do it best? She'd have to leave Hessian Street, of course. Even cutting the old house into apartments hadn't really solved the problem. She could get a small, comfortable, modern flat over in the new section. The silver candlesticks were the only things Claire would have liked, but they would go to Jerry be-cause Jerry had always failed.

Waynesville, next stop! The flowers had been wired from New York. *Waynesville!* We're coming in. There's an A. & P. on Main Street, and Ellerman's Bazaar is gone. *Waynesville!* . . . And God bless Uncle Melrose and Aunt Louise and Aunt Emmy and all my dear relations and friends and Spot and make me a good boy and not afraid of the dark. *Waynesville!*

Right down the middle of Main Street the train clanged till it stopped in front of the bald, new station. Tom Carroll sighed. It was as he had prophesied. Jerry Pye was there to meet him.

He got off the train, and the cousins shook hands.

"Have a good trip, Tom?"

"Not bad. Real fall weather, isn't it?"

"Yes, it's a real fall. You took the limited as far as Bradensburg, I suppose?"

"Yes, that seemed the quickest thing for me to do."

"They say she's quite a train," said Jerry Pye. "I was on her once—three years ago, you know. Well, I thought, here's where the old man blows himself for once. Minnie would hardly believe me when I told her. 'Jerry Pye!' she said, 'I don't know what's come over you. You never take me on any limiteds!' 'Well,' I said, 'maybe it is extra-fare, but I just decided the old man could blow himself for once!' Well, you should have seen her expression! Though I guess it wouldn't mean much to you, at that. I guess extra-fare trains don't mean much in people's lives when they come from New York."

"I could have taken a slower train," said Tom Carroll, carefully, "but it wouldn't have saved any time."

This remark seemed to amuse Jerry Pye intensely. His thin, sallow face—the face of a dyspeptic fox—gloated with mirth for an instant. Then he sobered himself, abruptly and pointedly.

"You always were a case, Tom," he said, "always. But this is a sad occasion."

"I didn't mean to be funny," said Tom Carroll. "Had I better get a taxi or is that your car?"

"Oh, we've got the family mistake—a dollar down and a dollar whenever they catch you!" Jerry Pye grinned and sobered himself again with the automatism of a mechanical figure. "I drove up in her night before last," he said, pointedly, as they got in. "Evans is a good man and all that, but he's apt to figure a little close on the cars; and as long as ours is dark blue, it'll look perfectly dignified."

"I telegraphed Aunt Emmy," said Tom Carroll and stopped. There was no possible use in trying to explain oneself to Jerry Pye.

"Yes, indeed," said Jerry, instantly. "Aunt Emmy appreciated it very much. Very much indeed. 'Tom's always very busy,' I told her. 'But don't you worry, Aunt Emmy. Tom may be a big man now, but his heart's in the right place. He'll be here.'"

"I told her," said Tom Carroll, distinctly and in spite of himself, "that in case anything of the sort came up, she had only to—"

"Oh," said Jerry, brightly, "we all knew that. We all knew you couldn't be expected to send one of your big cars all the way from New York to Waynesville. How's Claire?"

"Claire was very sorry indeed not to be able to come," said Tom, his hands gripping his knees. "We have one car," he said.

"That's just what I said," said Jerry Pye triumphantly. "I told Aunt Emmy—'you couldn't expect Tom to take the car away from Claire—she'll need it when he's away, shopping and seeing her friends—and naturally she hardly knew Aunt Louise. You wait and see. She'll send handsome flowers,' I said."

"Oh, God, make me a good boy!" prayed Tom Carroll, internally. "It can't last more than ten minutes. Ten minutes isn't really long." He braced himself. "How is Aunt Emmy?" he said.

Their speed instantly dropped to a respectful twenty miles an hour.

"She's wonderful," said Jerry Pye. "Simply wonderful. Of course, Minnie's been a great help to her and then, the end was very peaceful. Just seemed to breathe away." His voice had an obvious relish. "One minute she was there—as bright as a button, considering everything—and the next minute—" He shook his head.

"I'm glad," said Tom Carroll. "I mean——"

"Oh, we wouldn't have wanted her to suffer," said Jerry Pye in a shocked voice, as if he were denying some uncouth suggestion of Tom's. "No, sir, we wouldn't have wanted that. Now when Minnie's mother passed over—I don't know whether I ever told you the whole story, Tom—but from the Friday before—"

He continued, but had only come to the personal idiosyncrasies of the first night nurse when they turned into Hessian Street.

They got out of the car. Jerry Pye was mopping his forehead, though the day was chill. Yes, there was the black wisp on the knocker. But there was a row of bell-pushes where the old name-plate had been. The bricks in the sidewalk were rose-red and old and worn—the long block of quiet houses kept its faded dignity, in spite of a sign, "Pappas' Smoke Shop," a sign, "The Hessian Sergeant—Tea and Antiques." The linden trees had not perished, though their shade was thin.

"If this were a city," thought Tom Carroll, "people would have found out by now that it was quaint and painted the doors green and had studio-parties. Well, anyhow, that hasn't happened."

"Everyone's been very respectful," said Jerry Pye, nodding at the black wisp. "I mean, some people might be touchy when everybody has to use the same front-door. But Mr. Rodman came to me himself—they're the second-floor back. Just leave your bag in the car, Tom. It won't be in the way. I think Minnie's seen us—we figured out if you came today this ought to be the train."

Tom Carroll did not repeat that he had telegraphed or that there was only one afternoon train to Waynesville. He kissed his cousin-in-law's flustered check and was kissed by her in return. Minnie was always flustered; she had been a plump, flustered robin of a girl at her wedding; she was unaltered now save for the dust of gray in her abundant, unbecoming hair; they had never exchanged three words, except on family matters; and yet, they always kissed. He wondered if Minnie, too, ever found this circumstance strange. He should not wonder, of course, especially now.

"How's Aunt Emmy?" said Jerry Pye, in the anxious tones of one just returned from a long absence. "There isn't any change?"

"No, dear," said Minnie, solemnly, "she's just the same. She's wonderful. Mrs. Robinson and Mrs. Bache are with her, now. Remember—we must all be very nice to Mrs. Bache, Cousin Tom."

"I did put a tick-tack on her window, once," said Tom Carroll, reflectively. "But I haven't done that for a long time. Not for thirty years."

Minnie, the robin, was shocked for a moment, but brightened.

"That's right," she said. "We must all keep up for Aunt Emmy. Now, if you'll just go in—" She stood aside.

The spare, small, hawk-nosed figure rose from the stiff-backed chair as Tom Carroll entered. "Good evening, Thomas. I am glad you are here," said the unfaltering voice. "I think you know my good neighbors, Mrs. Bache and Mrs. Robinson."

Tom Carroll took the thin, dry, forceful hands. By God, she is wonderful, he thought, in spite of their saying it—it's taken me years to unlearn what she taught me, but she's remarkable. Why don't they let her alone? *Aunt Emmy, Aunt Emmy, you have grown so small! You rapped on my chapped knuckles with a steel thimble when I was cold; you ran me through and through like the emery-bag in your workbox with your sharp and piercing eyes; you let me see that you thought my father a rascal; you made me lie and cheat because of the terror of your name—and now you have grown small and fragile and an old woman, and there is not even injustice left in Hessian Street.*

The moment passed. Tom Carroll found himself mechanically answering Mrs. Bache's questions while his eyes roved about the room. The conch-shell was still on the mantelpiece, but one of the blue vases was gone. This was the front-parlor—the room of reward and punishment, of visitors and chill, the grandest room in the world—this room with the shabby carpet and the huge forbidding pieces of black walnut that never could have come in through a mortal door. What could you do with it all, what could you do? What could be done with a conch-shell and an iron oak-leaf and a set of yellowed pictures for a broken stereopticon? It was incredible that civilized people should ever have cherished such things. It was incredible that he had ever put the conch-shell to his ear and held his breath with wonder, hearing the sea.

"It was just like another home to the Major and myself. Always," said Mrs. Bache. "I can hear your dear grandmother now, before the

Major was taken, when he had his trouble. 'Alice, my child, you're young,' she said. 'But, young or old, we all have to bear our cross. The Major is a good man—he'll always be welcome in Hessian Street.' The Major never forgot it. He was very badly treated but he never forgot a kindness. And now, Emmy and I are the last—Emmy and I are the last."

She fumbled for her handkerchief in her vast lap.

"There, there, Mrs. Bache," said Tom Carroll, inadequately, "Grandmother must have been a wonderful woman."

"You never even saw her," said Mrs. Bache, viciously, "Tom Carroll saw to that. Oh, why couldn't it have been me, instead of Louise?" she said. "I've been ready to go so long!"

Tom Carroll's face felt stiff, but he found the handkerchief. After a moment Mrs. Bache arose, enormously yet with a curious dignity.

"Come, Sarah," she said to the dim figure in black that was Mrs. Robinson. "It's time for us to go. I've been making a fool of myself. Good-by, Emma. Frank will take us to the church tomorrow. Try to get some rest."

Minnie was whispering to him that Mrs. Bache was very much broken and that Cousin Tom must not mind. Tom Carroll whispered back at appropriate intervals. He did not mind Mrs. Bache. But there was always so much whispering, and it hurt one's head.

Now they were all standing in the narrow hall, and the others were looking at him.

"We can just slip in for a minute before anyone else comes," whispered Minnie, "I know Cousin Tom would rather—"

"Of course," said Tom Carroll. "Thank you, Cousin Minnie." He must have been working too hard, he thought—perhaps he and Claire could go off for a trip together when he got back. Because, after all, it was Aunt Louise who was dead. He knew that perfectly well. And yet, until Minnie had spoken, he hadn't been thinking about her at all.

The statue lay on the walnut bed in the partitioned room that had once been part of the back parlor. Over the head of the bed was a cross of dry, brittle palm-leaves tied with a purple ribbon, and a church-calendar. Against the opposite wall was the highboy that he remembered, with the small china slipper upon it, and above it the ageless engraving of the great Newfoundland dog, head lifted, lying upon the stone blocks of an English quay. "A Member of the Royal Humane Society." There were brown spots on the margin of the engraving now, Tom Carroll noticed. The window was a little open, but everywhere were the massed, triumphant flowers.

A white, transparent veil lay on the face of the statue. The features showed dimly through it, as if Aunt Louise lay in a block of ice. Tom Carroll felt cold. Now Aunt Emmy, putting Minnie aside, went slowly to lift the veil.

Tom Carroll, waking at three o'clock in the morning in his room at the Penniquit House, knew instantly what was in store for him. He might lie on the hillocks of his bed as long as he liked but he would not be allowed to sleep any more.

"You're acting like somebody on the edge of a first-class nervous breakdown," he told himself sternly. "And yet, you haven't been working so hard."

The last year hadn't been easy, but no year was. When times were good, you worked hard to take advantage of them. And when they were bad, you naturally had to work. That was how you got to be somebody, in a city. It was something Waynesville could never understand.

He thought of their life in the city—his and Claire's—for solace. It was cool and glittering and civilized as a cube of bright steel and glass. He thought of the light, pleasant furniture in the apartment, the clean, bright colors, the crisp sunlight on stone and metal, the bright, clean, modern, expensive school where a doctor looked down the boys' throats every morning and they had special blocks of wood to hammer nails in, since apartments were hardly the places to hammer nails. He thought of his office and the things on his desk and the crowded elevators of morning and night. He thought of the crammed red moving vans of October and the spring that bloomed before April in the flowershops and the clever men, putting in the new telephones. He thought of night beside Claire, hearing the dim roar of the city till at last the uneasy lights of the sky were quieted in the breathing-space before dawn.

It was she who had really held their life to its pattern. She had not let them be trapped; she had kept them free as air from the first day. There had been times when he had weakened—he admitted it—but she had kept her level head and never given in.

It had been that way about the old farmhouse in Connecticut and the cooperative apartment in town. He had wanted to buy them both, at different times. It was the Waynesville coming out in him, he supposed. But she had demurred.

"Oh, Tom, let's not tie ourselves up yet!" she had said. "Yes, I know it does seem silly just going on paying rent and having nothing to show for it but a leak in the washstand. But the minute you buy places to live in, they start to own you. You aren't free. You aren't young. You're always worrying. Don't talk to me about just playing with a few acres, not really farming. That was the way Grandfather started. Oh, Tom, don't you see—we're so *right* the way we are! Now, let's go over it sensibly, figures and all."

And she had been right. The old farmhouse, with its lilac hedge, now stood twenty feet away from a four-lane road; the cooperative apartment had failed and crippled its owner-tenants. She had been precisely right. She almost always was.

She had been entirely and unsentimentally right about her mother's coming to live with them for six months out of the year, when that had seemed unescapable.

"It's darling of you, Tom, but, dear old man, it never would work in the world. We've got to be modern and intelligent about the important things. Mother had me, and I'm devoted to her; but, when we're together for more than a week we get on each other's nerves like the very devil. It'll actually be a help to Hattie to have her for the winters—Hattie's always having a fearful time with the children. And we can have her for a long visit in the summer, and in between she can take the trips she's always wanted to take with that terrible Mrs. Tweed. Of course, I don't mean we ought to leave the whole financial end to Hattie and Joe. I'll insist on our doing our share. But I do think people ought to have *some* independence even when they are old and not just be shipped around from one relative to another like parcels, the way they did with Aunt Vi! It's more than sweet of you, Tom, darling. But you see how it is."

Tom Carroll had seen, with some relief, that they were not likely to have Mrs. Fanshawe as a permanent addition to their household, and he had acquiesced. Not that he disliked Mrs. Fanshawe. He got on very well with the rather nervous little lady—which was strange, considering how unlike she was to Claire. It struck him at times that Mrs. Fanshawe, from what he knew of her, had never been a remarkably independent person, and that to begin one's complete independence at the age of sixty-seven might be something of a task. But Claire must know her mother better than he did.

She did get on Claire's nerves and she did spoil the children—he could see that plainly enough. But, then, her visits were seldom very long. Claire would hardly have time to decline three or four invitations because mother was with them for a quiet little time before something would happen to call Mrs. Fanshawe away. And yet she seemed to like his calling her Mother May and pretending he was jealous of Hattie and Joe for stealing away his best girl. She'd laugh her brisk, nervous laugh and say he'd better look out or sometime she'd take him at his word and stay forever. And Claire would be saying, patiently, "Now, mother, are you sure that you have your ticket? And Tom will get you some magazines to read on the train." Afterwards Claire would say, "Oh, Tom, how can you? But she adores it!" and he would mumble something and feel rather pleased. Then Claire would kiss him and go to the telephone.

Only one of the visits had been in the least unfortunate. Claire had been tired that evening, and it was a pity that the conversation had happened to run on the future of the children. "But, of course, you and Tom are planning to make a real home for them sometime?" Mrs. Fanshawe had said. Well, naturally, she could hardly be expected to understand the way he and Claire happened to feel about "homes" in the Waynesville sense. And it had all come right the following morning—had not Mrs. Fanshawe nervously stayed an extra two days in proof? But the evening had carried him back to the hurt feelings of Hessian Street. Tom Carroll was glad there had been another visit before Mrs. Fanshawe died.

She had died in the waiting room of the Auburndale Station, on her way back to Hattie's, after a pleasant month with her old friend, Mrs. Tweed. Even so, she had been considerate; for the station agent knew her and got hold of the Morrises at once—there had been some mix-up about her telegram. Later, they had found out that she had known about her heart trouble for some time.

He had expected to take Claire on to the funeral, but Claire had been adamant. "I will not have you do it, Tom. It'll be bad enough by myself. But I will not have you mixed up in it—it isn't fair. We can have bad memories separately, but I won't have us have them together." She had grown almost hysterical about it—Claire! And so she had gone alone.

He had been very much worried till she returned, with a white changed face that refused to give any details of those three days. "Don't ask me, Tom. I've told you everything I can—oh, yes, everybody was kind and they had her hymns . . . but, oh Tom, it's so terrible. Terrible. The most barbarous, the most humiliating custom I know! I'll tell you this right now, I'm not going to wear mourning. I don't believe in it and I won't submit to it. All the black dresses—mother didn't really like black. Oh, Tom, Tom, when I die don't dare wear mourning for me!"

He had got her to bed and quieted at last. But she had not been herself—the true Claire—for months afterward, though, as soon as she could, she had taken up the strands of their life again and woven the pattern even more deftly and swiftly, as if each new thread were precious and each second not to be recalled.

Naturally, then, it was only right for him to come to this death in his own country alone. Any other course would have been a monstrous selfishness. And yet he wished that he could go to sleep.

Perhaps, if he thought once more of that shining cube of steel and glass that was their planned security, sleep would come. Even death in New York was different and impersonal. Except for the very mighty, it was an anonymous affair. The man in 10B died and, the next fall, they redecorated the apartment for other tenants. In a month or so even the doorman had forgotten; the newsdealer wrote another name on the morning papers. A name dropped out of the 'phone book . . . you had moved again, with October . . . moved to another city—the city at the sprawling edge of town where lie the streets and avenues of the numberless, quickly buried dead. There, too, you would be part of the crowd, and your neighbors would be strangers, as it had been in life. Your dwelling would be well kept-up, for that was written in the contract. No ghosts could ever arise from that suburban earth. For this, John Merritt and Samuel Pye had built a house in the wilderness to be a shelter and a refuge for them and their seed to the generations of generations. It was just.

Something cracked in the shining cube of glass and steel. The girders crunched on one another, wrenching apart; the glass tumbled into nothingness, falling a long way. There was nothing left but the perplexed, forgotten spirit, roused out of long sleep at last to strive, unprepared, against its immortal adversary.

Claire was all right, but she was afraid of death. He was all right, but he was afraid of death. The clever people they knew were entirely right, but most of them were deadly afraid of death.

If the life they led was rich—if it was the good life—why were they so afraid? It was not because they so joyed in all things under the sun that it was bitter to leave them. That was mortal and understandable, that had always been. But this was a blinder fear.

It had not been in sorrow or remorse that Claire had grieved for her mother. She had grieved the most because she had been afraid. And that made Claire a monster, which she was not. But there was something in it, all the same. He could admit it in her because he could admit it in himself. He lay sleepless, dreading the morrow. And yet he was not a coward so far as he knew.

They had won, but where was the victory? They had escaped from Waynesville and Hessian Street, from Fanshawe and Pye and Merritt, but where was the escape? If they were afraid in these years, how were they to deal with the years to come? Tom Carroll heard the clock in the courthouse strike five strokes. And then, when it seemed to him he could never sleep again, he fell asleep.

They drove at the slow pace down Hessian Street into Main, through the bright, morning sunlight. Tom Carroll felt ashamed of the dreams and waking of the night. He had never felt more solid and confident and assured than he did now, sitting beside Aunt Emmy, his tact and his shoulder ready for her the moment the inevitable breakdown came. Thank God! Jerry Pye was driving his own car. Jerry muddled things so. As for what was to come, that would merely be pathetic—the few old people painfully come together to mourn not only one of their own but a glory that had departed, the Waynesville of their youth. He hoped Aunt Emmy would not notice how few they were. But she, too, was old; and the old lived in the past. She could people the empty pews with the faces that once had been there. It was better so. The lords of Hessian and Bounty Streets had ruled the town with a high hand, even as they sank into poverty, but that was ended. You had only to look along Main to see the new names on the shopfronts. They knew not Hessian Street, these Caprellos and Szukalskis, but they thrived and inherited the land. Even Waynesville was growing up—there was little charm left in it, but it was alive. And here was the old brick church of the memories.

He helped Aunt Emmy expertly from the car, but she would not take his arm. Well, he respected her courage. He stood tactfully to shield her from the sight of the coffin, just being lifted down from that other, windowless car. But before he knew it Jerry Pye was beside them.

"Aunt Emmy," said Jerry Pye incredibly, "did Aunt Louise really want old Zenas to be one of the coffin-bearers? Because he's there now, and it'll be too late unless somebody tells him . . ."

He actually made a gesture with his hand. Tom Carroll would have been glad to strangle his cousin. But miraculously Aunt Emmy did not break.

She even walked past Tom Carroll to look deliberately at the six black-suited Negroes who now had their burden ready to carry into the church. Tom Carroll looked as well. They were none of them under forty, and their faces were grave and sober, but there was something ceremonial in their attitude that struck Tom Carroll strangely. They were sad but they were not constrained—they were doing something they felt to be right and they did it naturally and with ceremony. They would remember the ceremony always when the sadness had passed.

"Zenas, Joram, Joseph, William, Henry, Devout," said Aunt Emmy, in a half-whisper. "Yes, that's right. That's right. Zenas should be there. Louise would have missed Zenas. No, Tommy, we will let them pass, please."

When the coffin had passed, to the sway of the easy shoulders, they followed it in. It was the beginning of Tom Carroll's astonishment. The astonishment did not lessen when he found the church half full, and not only with the old.

He had always thought of Aunt Louise as Aunt Emmy's shadow—in his boyhood as someone always hurried but vaguely sweet whose peppermint-drops took away the taste of Aunt Emmy's wrath; in his manhood as a responsibility at the back of his mind. But the minister was a young man, and neither Pye nor Merritt, and he spoke of the Louise Pye, whose singlehanded effort had turned the ramshackle old School For The Instruction Of Freed Negroes into an institution model for its time, in terms that assumed his hearers knew and appreciated the difficulties of that task.

Phrases came to Tom Carroll's ears. They were the conventional phrases of oratory, yet the speaker meant them. "Unsparing of time or labor." "The rare gift of personality." "The quiet achievement of many years." "We can say today, in all truth, a light has gone from among us. . . ." But this was Aunt Louise!

And after the service, and on the way to the grave, and after the service there, the astonishment continued. He was by Aunt Emmy's side, and the people spoke to him. Nearly everyone who spoke to him knew his name. They did not find it odd or kind or a favor that he should be there—he was Julia Merritt's son, who was working in New York. You didn't hear as much about him as you did about Jerry Pye, but it was natural that he should return. Not only Mrs. Bache was under the impression that he had come principally to hear the reading of Aunt Louise's will. They did not think ill of him for it, merely prudent. He could explain nothing, even if he had wished to. There was nothing to explain.

He could not count the number of times he was told that the cross of yellow roses was beautiful—did they know by telepathy that it was from him and Claire? He had thought it garish and out of place beside the other flowers, the late asters and first chrysanthemums, the zinnias and snapdragons, the bronzes and reds and golds of the country fall. But that he could not say.

The Negroes who had borne the coffin knew him. They spoke to him gravely in their rich voices when all was done. Aunt Emmy had a curious phrase for each of them. "Thank you, Devout. Thank you, Joram, Miss Louise will be pleased." It would seem macabre, telling it to Claire. It was not; it was only simple. But that she would not believe.

He remembered, as if in a dream, his plans for succor and comfort when Aunt Emmy should collapse. But it was he who felt physically exhausted when they got back to the house.

This, too, was the moment that he had dreaded the most. Last night he had been able to have dinner at the hotel, but this time there was no escaping the cold meal laid in the basement dining room, the haunted and undue fragrance of flowers that had filled the house for a while. But, when the food was in front of him he was hungry and ate. They all ate, even Aunt Emmy. Minnie did what waiting was necessary and did it, for once, without fluster. Jerry Pye seemed tired and subdued. Once Tom Carroll caught himself feeling sorry for him, once he tried to help him out in a story that was meant to be cheerful and fell flat.

"You know," said Minnie, in a flat voice, pouring coffee, "it seems as if Aunt Louise hadn't gone away so far as before it happened."

Tom Carroll knew what she meant. He felt it too—that presence of the dead, but not grimly nor as a ghost. The presence was as real as the October sky, and as removed from flesh. It did not have to mean that all tired souls were immortal—it had its own peace.

After the meal was over, Tom Carroll walked in the back yard and smoked with Jerry Pye. Now and then he remembered from childhood the fear that had walked there with him, with the scent of the overpowering flowers. But, search as he would, he could not find that fear. The few flowers left in the beds were bronze and scentless; there was no fear where they bloomed.

It was time to go in for the reading of Aunt Louise's will. Tom Carroll listened obediently. He did not even mention the names of Norman, Buckstone, and Carroll. Once, when Mr. Dabney, the lawyer, looked at him and said, "You are a member of the New York Bar, I believe, Mr. Carroll?" he felt surprised at being able to say "yes."

It was a long and personal will made up of many small bequests. He could see Aunt Louise going through her innumerable boxes, trying hard to be fair.

"To my nephew, Thomas Carroll, and his wife, Claire Fanshawe Carroll, the pair of silver candlesticks belonging to my dear Father."

Tom Carroll felt the slow red creeping into his face.

They shook hands with Mr. Dabney. They spoke of what was to be done. Tom Caroll did not proffer assistance. There was no need.

Jerry Pye was offering him a lift as far as Bradensburg—Minnie would be staying with Aunt Emmy for the next week or so, but be must get back to work. But Tom Carroll thought he had better wait till the morning.

"Well, I guess you'll be more comfortable here at that," said Jerry Pye. "I'll have to hit her up if I want to get home before 3 G.M. So long, Tom. You see Minnie doesn't step out with a handsomer fellow now the old man's away. And take care of the Pye candlesticks—at that, I guess they'll look better in your place than they would in ours. Our kids might use 'em for baseball bats. Say, give my best to Claire."

He was gone. "Now, Tommy," said Aunt Emmy in her tired, indomitable voice, "you go back to the hotel and get a rest—you look tuckered out. Nelly Jervis is coming in here to get the supper. Half-past six."

They were sitting in the front parlor again that evening, he and she. It wasn't late, but Minnie had been sent to bed, unwilling. She wouldn't close an eye, she said; but they knew she was already asleep.

"It's queer what a good nurse Minnie is," said Aunt Emmy reflectively. "Seems as if it was the only thing that ever got her shut of her fussiness—taking care of sick people. You'd think she'd drop crumbs in the bed, but she never does. I don't know what we'd have done without her. Well, she's a right to be tired."

"How about you, Aunt Emmy?"

"Oh," said Aunt Emmy, "they used to say there'd be some people the Fool Killer would still be looking for on Judgment Day. I guess I'm one of them. Of course I'm tired, Tommy. When I'm tired enough, I'll tell you and go to bed."

"Look here, Aunt Emmy," said Tom Carroll, "if there's anything I can do——"

"And what could you do, Tommy?"

"Well, wouldn't you like a car?" he said, awkwardly, "or somebody to stay with you—or another place. They say those apartments over by the——"

"I was born here," said Aunt Emmy, with a snap of her lips, "and now Louise has gone, I've got just enough money to die here. It isn't the same, but I'm suited. And, of all the horrors of age, deliver me from a paid companion. If I need anything like that I'll get Susan

Bache to move in here. She's a fool and she's a tattler," said Aunt Emmy, clearly, "but I'm used to her. And Minnie'll come up, every now and then. Don't worry about me, Tom Carroll. We've all of us been on your back long enough."

"On my back?" said Tom Carroll, astounded.

"Well, I'd like to know where else it was," said Aunt Emmy. "You got Louise's money back from that rascal that bamboozled her, and I know twice you pulled Jerry Pye out of the mudhole, and then there was Cousin Edna all those years. Not to speak of what you did for Melrose. Melrose was my own brother, but he ought to have been ashamed of himself, the way he hindered you. Oh, don't you worry about Waynesville, Tommy—you've no call. You did right to get out when you did and as you did, and Waynesville knows it, too. Not that Waynesville would ever admit George Washington was any great shakes, once he'd moved away. But you wait till you die, Tom Carroll"—and she actually chuckled—"and you see what the *Waynesville Blade* says about her distinguished son. They told Louise for twenty years she was crazy, teaching Negroes to read and write. But they've got two columns about her this evening and an editorial. I've cut it out and I'm going to paste it under her picture. Louise was always the loving one, and I never grudge her that. But I did grudge her forgiving where I didn't see cause to forgive. But that's all done." She rustled the paper in her lap.

"How are your boys, Tommy?" she said. "They look smart enough in their pictures."

"We think they are," said Tom Carroll. "I hope you're right."

"They ought to be," said Aunt Emmy. "The Fanshawes never lacked smartness, whatever else they lacked, and your father was a bright man. Well, I've seen Jeremiah's and Minnie's. Boy and girl. Don't laugh at me, because it doesn't seem possible, but Jeremiah makes a good father. I never could get on with children—you ought to know that if anyone does—but I think they'll amount to something. Well, it's time the family was getting some sense again."

"Aunt Emmy!" said Tom Carroll, protestingly.

"Was this a happy house?" said Aunt Emmy, fiercely. "For me it was—yes—because I grew up in it. And I always had Louise and I don't regret anything. But was it happy for your mother and you? You know it wasn't, and a good thing your father took her out of it, adventurer or no adventurer, and a bad thing she had to come back. Well, we did our duty according to our lights. But that wasn't enough. There's no real reason, you know, why families have to get that way, except they seem to. But they will get to thinking they're

God Almighty, and, after a while, that gets taken notice of. I'll say this—it wasn't the money with us. We held up our heads with it or without it. But maybe we held them too stiff."

She sank into a brooding silence. Behind her in the corner the vague shadows of innumerable Pyes and Merritts seemed to gather and mingle and wait. After a while she roused herself.

"Where are you going to live, Tommy?" she said.

"I've been thinking about a place in the country sometime," said Tom Carroll. "If Waynesville were a little different——"

Aunt Emmy shook her head.

"You couldn't come back here, Tommy," she said. "It's finished here. And that's just as well. But, if you're going to build your own house, you'd better do it soon. You won't be happy without it— you've got too much Merritt in you. The Merritts made their own places. It was the Pyes that sat on the eggs till finally they tried to hatch chickens out of a doorknob, because it was easier than looking for a new roost. But you haven't much Pye. All the same, you won't be contented till you've got some roots put down. The Fanshawes, they could live in a wagon and like it, but the Bouverins were like the Merritts—when they'd rambled enough, they cleared ground. And Claire looks a lot more Bouverin than Fanshawe to me, whether she likes it or not."

"I didn't know you knew Claire's family," said Tom Carroll.

"She probably wouldn't tell you," said Aunt Emmy. "Well, that's natural enough. Good Goshen! I remember Claire Fanshawe, a peaked little slip of a child, at Anna Bouverin's funeral, just before they left Bradensburg. The coffin was still open, and some ignoramus or other thought it would be fitting for all the grandchildren to come and kiss their grandma good-by. Mind you, after they'd said good-by to her once already, before she died. I could have told them better, little as I know children. Well, it didn't make much difference to Hattie; she always had the nerves of an ox. But Claire was just over typhoid and after they made her do it she had what *I'd* call a shaking chill, in a grown person. And *yet,* they made her get up and recite the Twenty-Third Psalm in front of everybody—just because she was smart for her age, and a little child shall lead them. Her mother didn't stop them—too proud of her knowing it, I guess. But that was the Fanshawe of it—they had to play-act whatever happened."

Tom Carroll had his head in his hands.

"She never told me," he said. "She never told me at all."

"No?" said Aunt Emmy, looking at him sharply. "Well, she was young and maybe she forgot it. I imagine Hattie did."

"Claire never has," said Tom Carroll.

"Well," said Aunt Emmy, "I'll tell you something, Tommy. When you get to my age you've seen life and death. And there's just one thing about death, once you start running away from the thought of it, it runs after you. Till finally you're scared even to talk about it and, even if your best friend dies, you'll forget him as quick as you can because the thought's always waiting. But once you can make yourself turn around and look at it—it's different. Oh, you can't help the grief. But you can get a child so it isn't afraid of the dark—though if you scared it first it'll take a longer while."

"Tell me," said Tom Carroll in a low voice, "were there—very sweet flowers—when my mother died?"

"It was just before Easter," said Aunt Emmy softly. "You could smell the flowers all through the house. But we didn't have any play-acting," she added, quickly. "Not with you. Melrose had that bee in his bonnet, but Louise put her foot down. But it's hard to explain to a child."

"It's hard to explain anyway," said Tom Carroll.

"That's true," said Aunt Emmy. "It's a queer thing," she said. "I never smell lilac without thinking of Lucy Marshall. She was a friend of mine, and then we fell out, and when we were young we used to play by a lilac bush in her yard. It used to trouble me for a long time before I put the two things together. But the pain went out of it then."

"Yes. The pain goes out when you know," said Tom Carroll. "It's not knowing that makes you afraid."

"If Hattie was closer to her, she could do it," said Aunt Emmy. "But the way things are——"

"It'll have to be me," said Tom Carroll, "And I don't know how."

"Well, you're fond of her," said Aunt Emmy. "They say that helps." She rose. "I'll give you the candlesticks in the morning, Tom."

"Can't I leave them with you, Aunt Emmy?"

"What's the use?" said Aunt Emmy practically. "To tell you the truth, Tommy, I'd got right tired of shining them. Besides, they'll look well in your house, when you get your house."

Blossom and Fruit

When the spring was in its mid-term and the apple trees entirely white they would walk down by the river talking as they went, their voices hardly distinguishable from the voices of birds or waters. Their love had begun with the winter; they were both in their first youth. Those who watched them made various prophecies—none of which was fulfilled—laughed, criticized, or were sentimental according to the turn of their minds. But these two were ignorant of the watching and, if they had heard the prophecies, they would hardly have understood them.

Between them and the world was a wall of glass—between them and time was a wall of glass—they were not conscious of being either young or old. The weather passed over them as over a field or a stream—it was there but they took no account of it. There was love and being alive, there was the beating of the heart, apart or together. This had been, this would be, this was—it was impossible to conceive of a world created otherwise. He knew the shape of her face, in dreams and out of them; she could shut her eyes, alone, and feel his hands on her shoulders. So it went, so they spoke and answered, so they walked by the river. Later on, once or twice, they tried to remember what they had said—a great deal of nonsense?—but the words were already gone. They could hear the river running; he could remember a skein of hair; she, a blue shirt open at the throat and an eager face. Then, after a while, these two were not often remembered.

All this had been a number of years ago. But now that the old man had returned at last to the place where he had been born he would often go down to the river-field. Sometimes a servant or a grandchild would carry the light camp chair and the old brown traveling-rug; more often he would go alone. He was still strong—he liked to do for himself; there was no use telling him he'd catch his death walking through the wet grass, it only set him in his ways.

When at last he had reached his goal—a certain ancient apple tree whose limbs were entirely crooked with bearing—he would set the chair under it, sit down, wrap his legs in the rug, and remain there till he was summoned to come in. He was alone but not lonely; if anyone passed by he would talk; if no one passed he was content to be silent. There was almost always a book in his lap, but he very seldom read it; his own life, after all, was the book that suited him best, it did not grow dull with rereading. There is little to add, he thought, little to add; but he was not sorry. The text remained; it was a long text, and many things that had seemed insignificant and obscure in the living took on sudden clarities and significances, now he remembered.

Yes, he thought, that is how most people live their actual lives—skimming it through, in a hurry to get to the end and find out who got married and who got rich. Well, that's something that can't be helped. But when you know the end you can turn back and try to find out the story. Only most people don't want to, he thought, and smiled. Looks too queer to suit them—reading your own book backwards. But it's a great pleasure to me. He relaxed, let his hands lie idle in his lap, let the pictures drift before his eyes.

The picture of the boy and girl by the river. He could stand off from it now and regard it, without sorrow or longing; no ghost cried in his flesh because of it, though it was a part of that flesh and with that flesh would die. And yet, for a moment, he had almost been in the old mood again, recovered the old ecstasy. Whatever love was, he had been in love at that time. But what was love?

They met by stealth because of reasons no longer important; it lasted through all of one long dry summer in the small town that later became a city. Outside, the street baked, the white dust blew up and down, but it was fresh and pleasant in the house.

She was a dark-haired woman, a widow, some years older than he—he was a young man in a tall collar, his face not yet lined or marked but his body set in the pattern which it would keep. Her name was Stella. She had a cool voice, sang sometimes; they talked a great deal. They made a number of plans which were not accomplished—they were hotly in love.

He remembered being with her one evening toward the end of summer, in the trivial room. On the table was a bowl of winesaps—he had been teasing her about them—she said she liked the unripened color best. They talked a little more, then she grew silent; her face, turned toward his, was white in the dusk.

That autumn an accident took him away from the town. When he came back, a year later, she had moved to another state. Later he heard that she had married again, and the name of the man. A great while later he read of her death.

The old man's rug had slipped from his knees; he gathered it up again and tucked it around him. He could not quite get back into the man who had loved and been loved by Stella, but he could not escape him, either. He saw that youth and the boy who had walked by the river. Each had a woman by his side, each stared at the other hostilely, each, pointing to his own companion, said, "This is love." He smiled a trifle dubiously at their frowning faces—both were so certain—and yet he included them both. Which was right, which wrong? He puzzled over the question but could come to no decision. And if neither were right—or both—why then, what was love?

You certainly strike some queer things when you read the book backwards, he thought. I guess I'd better call it a day and quit. But, even as he thought so, another picture arose.

They had been married for a little more than two years, their first child was eight months old. He was a man in his thirties, doing well, already a leader in the affairs of the growing town. She was five years younger, tall for a woman; she had high color in those days. They had known comparatively little of each other before their marriage—indeed, had not been very deeply in love; but living together had changed them.

He came back to the house on Pine Street—told the news of his day, heard about the neighbors, the errands, the child. After dinner they sat in the living room, he smoked and read the newspaper, she had sewing in her lap. They talked to each other in snatches; when their eyes met, something went, something came. At ten o'clock she went upstairs to feed the child; he followed some time later. The child was back in its crib again; they both looked at her a moment—sleep already lay upon her like a visible weight—how deeply, how swiftly she sank towards sleep! They went out, shut the door very softly, stood for a moment in the hallway, and embraced. Then the woman released herself.

"I'm going to bed now, Will," she said. "Be sure and turn out the lights when you come up."

"I won't be long," he said. "It's been a long day."

He stretched his arms, looking at her. She smiled deeply, turned away. The door of their room shut behind her.

When he had extinguished the lights and locked the doors he went up to the long garret that stretched the whole length of the house. They had had the house only two years, but the garret had already accumulated its collection of odds and ends; there were various discarded or crippled objects that would never be used again, that would stay here till the family moved, till someone died. But what he had come to see was a line of apples mellowing on a long shelf, in the dusty darkness. They had been sent in from the farm—you could smell their faint, unmistakable fragrance from the doorway. He took one up, turned it over in his hand, felt its weight and texture, firm and smooth and cool. You couldn't get a better eating apple than that, and this was the right place for them to mellow.

Mary's face came before him looking at him in the hallway; the thought of it was like the deep stroke of a knife that left, as it struck, no pain. Yes, he thought, I'm alive—we're pretty fond of each other. Some impulse made him put down the apple and push up the little skylight of the garret to let the air blow in on his face. It was a clean cold—it was autumn; it made the blood run in him to feel it. He stood there for several minutes, drinking in cold autumn, thinking about his wife. Then at last he shut the skylight and went downstairs to their room.

A third couple had joined the others under the tree, a third image asserted itself, by every settled line in its body, the possessor not only of a woman but of a particular and unmistakable knowledge. The old man observed one and all, without envy but curiously. If they could only get to talking with one another, he thought, why then, maybe, we'd know something. But they could not do it—it was not in the cards. All each could do was to make an affirmation, "This is love."

The figures vanished, he was awake again. When you were old you slept lightly but more often, and these dreams came. Mary had been dead ten years; their children were men and women. He had always expected Mary to outlive him, but things had not happened so. She would have been a great comfort. Yet when he thought of her dead, though his grief was real, it came to him from a distance. He and she were nearer together than he and grief. And yet if he met her again it would be strange.

The flower came out on the branch, the fruit budded and grew. At last it fell or was picked, and the thing started over again. You could figure out every process of growth and decline, but that did not get you any nearer the secret. Only, he'd like to know.

He turned his eyes toward the house—somebody coming for him. His eyes were still better for far-away things than near, and he made out the figure quite plainly. It was the girl who had married his grand-nephew, Robert. She called him "Father Hancock" or "Gramp" like the rest of them, but still, she was different from the rest.

For a moment her name escaped him. Then he had it. Jenny. A

dark-haired girl, pleasant spoken, with a good free walk to her—girls stepped out freer, on the whole, than they had in his day. As for cutting their hair and the rest of it—well, why shouldn't they? It was only the kind of people who wrote to newspapers who made a fuss about such things. And they always had to make a fuss about something. He chuckled deeply, wondering what a newspaper would make of it if a highly respected old citizen wrote and asked them what was love. "Crazy old fool—ought to be in an asylum." Well, maybe at that, they'd be right.

He watched the girl coming on as he would have watched a rabbit run through the grass or a cloud march along the sky. There was something in her walk that matched both rabbit and cloud—something light and free and unbroken. But there was something else in her walk as well.

"Lunch, Father Hancock!" she called while she was still some yards away. "Snapper beans and black-cherry pie!"

"Well, I'm hungry," said the old man. "You know me, Jenny—never lost appetite yet. But you can have my slice of the pie; you've got younger teeth than mine."

"Stop playing you're a centenarian. Father Hancock," said the girl. "I've seen you with Aunt Maria's pies before."

"I might take a smidgin', at that," said the old man reflectively, "just to taste. But you can have all I don't eat, Jenny—and that's a fair offer."

"It's too fair," said the girl. "I'd eat you out of house and home today." She stretched her arms toward the sky. "Gee, I feel hungry!" she said.

"It's right you should," said the old man, placidly. "And don't be ashamed of your dinner either. Eat solid and keep your strength up."

"Do I look as if I needed to keep my strength up?" she said with a laugh.

"No. But it's early to tell," said the old man, gradually disentangling himself from his coverings. He stood up, declining her offered hand. "Thank you, my dear," he said. "I never expected to see my own great-grandnephew. But don't be thinking of that. It'll be your baby, boy or girl, and that's what's important."

The girl's hand went slowly to her throat while color rose in her face. Then she laughed.

"Father Hancock!" she said. "You—you darned old wizard! Why Robert doesn't know about it yet and——"

"He wouldn't," said the old man briefly. "Kind of inexperienced at that age. But you can't fool me, my dear. I've seen too much and too many."

She looked at him with trouble in her eyes.

"Well, as long as you know . . ." she said. "But you won't let on to the rest of them . . . of course I'll tell Robert soon, but——"

"I know," said the old man. "They carry on. Never could see so much sense in all that carrying on, but relations do. And being the first great-grandchild. No, I won't tell 'em. And I'll be as surprised as Punch when they finally tell me."

"You're a good egg," said the girl gratefully. "Thanks ever so much. I don't mind your knowing."

They stood for a moment in silence, his hand on her shoulder. The girl shivered suddenly.

"Tell me, Father Hancock," she said suddenly, in a muffled voice, not looking at him, "is it going to be pretty bad?"

"No, child, it won't be so bad." She said nothing, but he could feel the tenseness in her body relax.

"It'll be for around November, I expect?" he said and went on without waiting for her reply. "Well, that's a good time, Jenny. You take our old cat, Marcella—she generally has her second lot of kittens around in October or November. And those kittens, they do right well."

"Father Hancock! You're a positive disgrace!" So she said, but he knew from the tone of her voice that she was not angry with him and once more, as they went together towards the house, he felt the stroke of youth upon him, watching her walk so well.

About the middle of summer, when the green of the fields had turned to yellow and brown, Will Hancock's old friend John Sturgis drove over one day to visit him.

A son and a granddaughter accompanied John Sturgis, as well as two other vaguer female relatives whom the young people called indiscriminately "Cousin" and "Aunt"; and for a while the big porch of the Hancock house knew the bustle of tribal ceremony. Everyone was a little anxious, everyone was a little voluble; this was neither a funeral nor a wedding but, as an occasion, it ranked with those occasions, and in the heart of every Hancock and Sturgis present was a small individual grain of gratitude and pride at being there to witness the actual meeting of two such perishable old men.

The relatives possessed the old men and displayed them. The old men sat quietly, their tanned hands resting on their knees. They knew they were being possessed, but they too felt pride and pleasure. It was, after all, remarkable that they should be here. The young people didn't know how remarkable it was.

Finally, however, Will Hancock rose.

"Come along down-cellar, John," he said gruffly, "Got something to show you."

It was the familiar opening of an immemorial gambit. And it brought the expected reply.

"Now, father," said Will Hancock's eldest daughter, "if you'll only wait a minute, Maria will be out with the lemonade, and I had her bake some brownies."

"Lemonade!" said Will Hancock and sniffed. "Hold your tongue, Mary," he said gently. "I'm going to give John Sturgis something good for what ails him."

As he led the way down-cellar he smiled to himself. They would be still protesting, back on the porch. They would be saying that cellars were damp and old men delicate, that cider turned into acid, and that at their age you'd think they'd have more sense. But there would be no real heart in the protestations. And if the ceremonial visit to the cellar had been omitted there would have been disappointment. Because then their old men would not have been quite so remarkable, after all.

They passed through the dairy-cellar, with its big tin milk-pans, and into the cider-cellar. It was cool there but with a sweet-smelling coolness; there was no scent of damp or mold. Three barrels of cider stood in a row against the wall; on the floor was a yellow patch of light. Will Hancock took a tin cup from a shelf and silently tapped the farthest barrel. The liquid ran in the cup. It was old cider, yellow as wheat-straw, and when he raised it toward his nostrils the soul of the bruised apple came to him.

"Take a seat, John," he said, passing over the full cup. His friend thanked him and sank into the one disreputable armchair. Will Hancock filled another cup and sat down upon the middle barrel.

"Well, here's to crime, John!" he said. It was the time-honored phrase.

"Mud in your eye!" said John Sturgis fiercely. He sipped the cider.

"Ah!" he said, "tastes better every year, Will."

"She ought to, John. She's goin' along with us."

They both sat silent for a time, sipping appreciatively, their worn eyes staring at each other, taking each other in. Each time they met again now was a mutual triumph for both; they looked forward to each time and back upon it, but they had known each other so long that speech had become only a minor necessity between them.

"Well," said John Sturgis at last, when the cups had been refilled, "I hear you got some more expectations in your family, Will. That's fine."

"That's what they tell me," said Will Hancock. "She's a nice girl, Jenny."

"Yes, she's a nice girl," said John Sturgis indifferently. "It'll be some news for Molly when I get home. She'll be right interested. She was hopin' we might beat you to it, with young Jack and his wife. But no signs yet."

He shook his head and a shadow passed over his face.

"Well, I don't know that you set so much store by it," said Will Hancock consolingly, "though it's interesting."

"Oh, they'll have a piece in the paper," said John Sturgis with a trace of bitterness. "Four generations. Even if it isn't a great-grandchild, so to speak. I know 'em." He took a larger sip of cider.

"That won't do me a speck of good when I get home," he confided. "And Molly, she'll think I was crazy. But what's the use of livin' if you've got to live so tetchy all the time?"

"I never saw you looking better, John," said Will Hancock, heartily. "Never did."

"I'm spry enough most days," admitted John Sturgis. "And as for you, you look like a four-year-old. But it's the winter——"

He left the sentence uncompleted, and both fell silent for a moment, thinking of the coming winter. Winter, the foe of old men.

At last John Sturgis leaned forward. His cheeks had a ghost of color in them now, his eyes an unexpected brightness.

"Tell me, Will." he said, eagerly, "you and me—we've seen a good deal in our time. Well, tell me this—just how do you figure it all out?"

Will Hancock could not pretend to misunderstand the question. Nor could he deny his friend the courtesy of a reply.

"I haven't a notion," he said at last slowly and gravely. "I've thought about it, Lord knows—but I haven't a notion, John."

The other sank back into his chair, disappointedly.

"Well now, that's too bad," he grumbled, "for I've been thinkin' about it. Seems to me as if I didn't do much else *but* think most of the time. But you're the educated one; and if you haven't a notion—well——"

His eyes stared into space, without fear or anger, but soberly. Will Hancock tried to think of some way to help his friend.

He saw again before him those three figures under the apple tree, each a part of himself, each with a woman beside it, each saying, "This is love." Now, as he fell into reverie, a fourth couple joined them—an old man, still erect, and a girl who still walked with a light step though her body was heavy now.

He stared at these last visitors incredulously at first, and then with a little smile. Nearly every day of the summer Jenny had come to call him when he sat under his tree. He could see her looking across the gulf that separated them—and finding things not so bad as she had thought they might be. Why, I might have been an old tree myself, he thought. Or an old rock you went out to when you wanted to be alone.

There had been her relatives and his. There had been all the women. But it was to him that she had come. To the others he was and would be "Father Hancock" and their own remarkable old man. But Jenny was not really one of his own; and because of that she had from him a certain calming wisdom that he did not know he possessed.

He heard an insect cry in the deep grass and smelled the smell of the hay, the smell of summer days. Love? It was not love, of course, nor could be, by any stretch of language. To her it had been summer and an old tree; and to him, he knew what it had been. He was fond of her, naturally, but that was not the answer. It was not she who had moved him. But for an instant, on the cords of the defeated flesh, he had heard a note struck clearly, the vibration of a single and silver wire. As he thought of this, the wire vibrated anew, the imperishable accent rang. Then it was mute—it would not be struck again.

"I tried to figure it out the other day," he said to John Sturgis, "what love was, first. But——"

Then he stopped. It was useless. John Sturgis was his old friend, but there was no way to tell John Sturgis the thoughts in his mind.

"It's funny your sayin' that," said John Sturgis reflectively. "You know I came back to the house the other day, and there was Molly asleep in the chair. I was scared for a minute but then I saw she was sleeping. Only she didn't wake up right away—I guess I came in light. Well, I stood there looking at her. You came to our golden wedding, Will; but her cheeks were pink and she looked so pretty in her sleep. I just went over and kissed her, like an old fool. Now what makes a man act like that?"

He paused for a moment.

"It's so blame' hard to figure out," he said. "When you're young you've got the strength but you haven't got the time. And when you're old you've got time enough, but I'm always goin' to sleep."

He drained the last drop in his cup and rose.

"Well, Sam'll be lookin' for me," he said. "It was good cider."

As they passed through the dairy a black, whiskered face appeared at the small barred window and vanished guiltily at the sound of Will Hancock's voice.

"That old cat's always trying to get in to the milk." he said. "She ought to take shame on her, all the kittens she's had. But I guess this'll be her last litter, this fall. She's getting on."

The tribal ceremonies of departure were drawing toward a close. Will Hancock shook John Sturgis' hand.

"Come over again, John, and bring along Molly next time," he said. "There's always a drop in the barrel."

"And it's a prize drop," said John Sturgis. "Thank you, Will. But I don't figure on gettin' over again this summer. Next spring, maybe."

"Sure," said Will. But between them both, as they knew, lay the shadow of the cold months, the shadow to be lived through. Will Hancock watched his friend being helped into the car, watched the car drive away. "John's beginning to go," he thought with acceptance. "And that's probably just what John's telling Sam about me."

He turned back toward his family. He was tired, but he could not give in. The family clustered about him, talking and questioning. John's visit had made him, for the moment, an even more remarkable old man than ever; and he must play his role for the rest of them, worthily, now John had gone. So he played it, and they saw no difference. But he kept wondering what day the winter would set in.

The first gales of autumn had come and passed; when Will Hancock got up in the morning he saw white rime on the ground. It had melted away by eleven, but next morning it was back again. At last, when he walked down to his apple tree he walked under bare boughs.

That night he went early to his room, but before he got in bed he stood for a while at the window, looking at the sky. It was a winter sky, the stars were hard in it. Yet the day had been mild enough. Jenny wanted her child born in the Indian Summer. Perhaps she would still have her wish.

He slept more lightly than ever these nights—the first thing roused him. So when the noises began in the house he was awake at once. But he lay there for some time, dreamily, not even looking at his watch. The footsteps went up and down stairs, and he listened to them; a voice said something sharply and was hushed; somebody was trying to telephone. He knew them all, those sounds of whispering haste that wake up a house at night.

Yes, he thought, all the same it's hard on the women. Or the men too, for that matter. But sooner or later, the doctor would come and take from his small black bag the miraculous doll wrapped up in the single cabbage leaf. He himself had once been such a doll, though he couldn't remember it. Now they would not want him out there, but he would go all the same.

He rose, put on his dressing-gown, and tiptoed down the long corridor. He heard a shrill whisper in his ear. "*Father! Are you crazy? Go back to bed!*" But he shook his head at the whisper and went on. At the head of the stairs he met his grandnephew, Robert. There was sweat on the boy's face and he breathed as if he had been running. They looked at each other a moment, with sympathy but without understanding.

"How is she?" said Will Hancock.

"All right, thanks, Gramp," said the boy in a grateful voice as he kept fumbling in his dressing-gown pocket for a cigarette that was not there. "The doctor's coming over but we—we don't think it's the real thing yet."

Someone called to the boy, and he disappeared again. The corridor abruptly seemed very full of Will Hancock's family. They were clustering around him, buzzing reassuringly, but he paid little attention.

Suddenly, from behind a closed door, he heard Jenny's voice, clear and amused. "Why how perfectly sweet of Father Hancock, Bob! But I'm sorry they woke him—and all for a false alarm."

The reassuring buzzes around him recommenced. He shook them off impatiently and walked back toward his room. But when he was hidden from the others he gave a single guilty look behind him and made for the back stairs. They won't follow me, he thought; got too much to talk about.

He switched on the light in the cider-cellar, drawing his dressing-gown closer about him. It was cold in the cellar now and it would be colder still. But cider was always cider, and he felt thirsty.

He drank the yellow liquid reflectively, swinging his heels against the side of the barrel. Upstairs they would still be whispering and consulting. And maybe the doctor would come with his black bag after all, and to-morrow there would be a piece in the paper to make John Sturgis jealous. But there wasn't anything he could do about it.

No, even for Jenny, there was nothing more he could do. She had taken his wisdom, such as it was, and used it. And he was glad of that. But now he knew from the light tone of her voice that she was beyond such wisdom as he had. The wire had ceased its vibration, the leaves of the tree were shed, like dry wisdom on the ground. Well, she was a nice girl and Robert a decent boy. They would have other children doubtless, and those children children in their turn.

He heard a low sound from the other corner of the cellar and went over to see what had made it. Then he whistled. "Well, old lady," he said, "you certainly don't waste your time." It was the old black house-cat who had stared through the dairy window at himself and John Sturgis. Already she was licking the third of her new kittens while the two first-born nuzzled at her, squeaking from time to time.

He bent over and stroked her head. She looked at him troubledly. "It's all right," he said reassuringly. "They've forgotten about us both—and no wonder. But I'll stick around."

He refilled his cup and sat down upon the barrel, swinging his heels. There was nothing here that he could do, either—cats were wiser than humans in such matters. But, nevertheless, he would stay.

As the cider sank in the cup and he grew colder he fell into a waking dream. Now and then he went over to stroke the cat, but he did it automatically. He was here, in a bare old, cellar, drinking cider which would doubtless disagree with him, and in all probability catching his death of cold. And upstairs, perhaps, were life and death and the doctor—new life fighting to come into the world and death waiting a chance to seize it as it came, as death always did. Moreover, these lives and deaths were his lives and deaths, after a fashion, for he was part of their chain. But, for the moment, he was disconnected from them. He was beyond life and death.

He saw again, in front of him, the three couples of his first dream—and himself and Jenny—himself giving Jenny, unconsciously, the wisdom he did not know. "This is love—this is love—this is love—" and so it was, each phase of it, for each man there spoke the truth of his own heart. Then he looked at the apple tree and saw that it was in flower, but fruit hung on it as well, green fruit and ripe, and even as he looked a wind was blowing the last leaves from the bare bough.

He shivered a little, he was very cold. He put his cup back on the shelf and went over for a last look at the old cat. The travail was over—she lay on her side, beset by the new-born. There was green, inexplicable light in her eyes as he stooped over her, and when he patted her head she stretched one paw out over her kittens like an arm.

He rose stiffly and left her, turning out the light. As he went up the stairs, "Adorable life," he thought, "I know you. I know you were given only to be given away."

The house was silent again, as he tiptoed back to his room. His vigil had been unsuspected, his watch quite useless; and yet he had kept a vigil and a watch. To-morrow might have been too late for it—even now he trembled with cold. Yet, when he stood before the window, he looked long at the winter sky. The stars were still hard points of light, and he would not see them soft again, but earth would continue to turn around, in spite of all these things.

Among Those Present

My dear, I'm exhausted. They just wouldn't leave El Morocco, and then we went on to hear that girl sing those songs. Irish ballads, you know, and she's really a Brazilian—it gives them a quality you simply wouldn't believe. And the wonderful thing is, she learned them from a phonograph record. She can't speak a word of English otherwise. So she just sings them over and over, and everybody cheers. But everybody. Ted said he'd always been against inventing the phonograph, and now he was sure of it—but that's just the way he talks.

Well, if I do say it myself, it was rather an amusing crowd. Larry Dunn, you know—the Dunns are stuffy rich, but Larry's a darling—he does candid-camera studies that are just as good as Werbe's and you'd never know he was rich at all, except, as Ted says, when it comes to not reaching for the check. And the Necropuloffs—Russians, my dear, and so brave! Their father was actually eaten by wolves or something and they know the most ghastly stories about Stalin. And Mike Glatto—he's movies—All-American Productions—and rather unbrushed, in a way, but quite fascinating—and the Jenkinses, of course—and Jane Pierce, who does the cocktail column for *Sport and Society*. Oh, yes, and the little Lindsay girl that Ted knows—but she didn't come on to the other place. She couldn't—she works or something—so Ted dropped her and met us afterward.

Just as well, in a way. She didn't really quite fit in and she lives in some unheard-of place like Riverside Drive—Ted was hours finding us. But the rest of it—well, they're just the sort of people you can only find in New York.

I suppose it was my fault, staying quite so late. Ted growled a bit, coming home—said, wouldn't it be cheaper in the end, if we rented the house and lived in the checkroom at the Stork Club. But I think that was the guinea hen we had for dinner—guinea hen always disagrees with him, but there's a new way of basting it with brandy that Jane Pierce taught me and I couldn't resist it. And, to be utterly frank, my dear, I needed something. A little revelry. You see, I'd been to the Coles' that afternoon. And that was grim.

Oh, just a rather grim party. Hordes of people and warm Martinis.

They usually give such good parties too. No, it wasn't seeing Bob and the bride—Lucille Cole phoned me they'd probably be there. And we're utterly friendly, of course—I always ask him how his work's going. I think you have to be civilized about these things. You don't scream and faint any more when you meet your ex-husband. And I'm hardly Alice Ben Bolt. But I did feel a little hurt that he hadn't told me. After all, it's still a surprise to pick up the paper and see that your former helpmeet has married somebody you've never even heard of. And in Florida, of all places! Of course, he's been painting down there. But I did send him a telegram when I married Ted.

Funny, too, I always imagined he'd pick somebody rather maternal. A nice widow or one of those hearty, earthy girls with rather flat feet. Painters are so apt. But this. . . .

Oh, that fresh, untouched type, my dear, if you happen to like it. A brave little profile, you know—a gallant little figure in sports clothes. And, I'm afraid, dancing curls. Just another Joan of Arc. They seem to produce them, nowadays. Only, I fail to see why they call her "little." She'd be quite as tall as I am if she wore heels.

No, but really an infant. Really. Twenty-one. And—oh, yes—they're going to live in the country. They were rapt about it. In fact, they've got their eye on a farmhouse. I suppose she'll raise chickens. Or doves. She's the type for doves. And Bob will turn the old stable into a studio, and they'll do it all themselves and take photographs too. It's too grim to think about, really. And she'll greet him with a flushed, happy face, when he comes home from his work, and cook little meals. Only they say she has money—so it'll probably be two very good maids. Till the children come, of course, and they have to build on the wing. . . . No, not yet, but they certainly will. Dozens of them—all Joans of Arc.

I think I'll have another cocktail, my dear, I'm a little tired. . . .

Ted? No, he was spared, though I'm sure the bride would have liked him. . . . Oh, he's very well. He liked you, my dear, by the way. . . . No, really—no, I could see. And next time it must just be ourselves and we'll have a good long talk about the old days. Ted's so funny. He's always insisted that there never could be such a place as Little Prairie. So I was delighted when you phoned. I said, "It's little Kitty Harris—the child with the bang that used to have a crush on me in school. And she's here in New York with her husband—and, my dear, they'll be babes in the wood and we must rescue them." So, you see.

Now, tell me again just what your husband does. . . . Oh, research.

That's always so intelligent. And that rather lean-jawed look—very attractive, my dear. Oh, you'll have no difficulty at all. But you must begin as you mean to go on—that's the important thing. And anything I can do—well, just treat me as a mother confessor. After all, I was a mouse myself when I first came to New York—but a mouse!

The one thing is, it's so easy to get tangled up with a lot of stodgy, unimportant people. And no husband is a help about that. Why, if Ted had his way, we'd do nothing but give dinners for his partners and his Harvard classmates—not to speak of the family. And Bob was just the same about painters. He thought putting on a dress shirt meant prostituting your art. While, as a matter of fact, it's just as easy to meet the amusing people as the dull ones. All you need is the tiniest start, and perhaps a wee bit of guidance. After that, as I've often said, it just rolls like a snowball. Ted says they'll come anywhere for free liquor. Isn't it wicked of him? Well, of course, you can hardly give a party on Aunt Emma's dandelion wine. But that's only a part of it; it needs a certain sense. Take our little party last night—well, perhaps I am supposed to have a gift for that sort of thing, but it was so simple, really. And Paul Necropuloff said it reminded him of his Great-Uncle Feodor's *dacha* in the Caucasus and nearly cried. . . .

Oh, you'll have a wonderful time. You don't really live till you're here, my dear—I assure you. I sound positively dewy-eyed, don't I? But there you are. I always knew it was going to be my town, and you'll feel the same way. Little Kitty Harris! And you'd sit reading "The Five Little Peppers" while we big girls played jacks on the porch—I can see it all so plainly. I must get some jacks; I believe they still have them in stores. We'll have a party and play them; it'll be a furor. We introduced parcheesi, you know, while I was still married to Bob, and people played it for months. . . .

Well, of course, my dear, you've kept up so much more. I do think it's so brave of you. It sometimes seems to me as if I could never have lived there at all. And Mother will send me long clippings about Hick's Garage being torn down and Willy Snamm being made head teller at the Drovers' National—as if I remembered people named Willy Snamm! . . . Oh, my dear. I'm so sorry. I didn't realize that he married your cousin. But it is a quaint name. And four children— darling, how forthright of them! That's wonderful. I suppose if I'd stayed in Little Prairie, I'd have four children myself. . . . No, we haven't. . . . Somehow, one keeps putting it off.

But when I think of what we've both escaped—at least now you're here, too, my dear—it seems absolutely providential. I so well remember our first winter—Bob's and mine. And how discouraged he got. His work wasn't going well, though he was quite sweet about it, and he kept saying he'd like to feel the earth under his feet again. They will say the weirdest things. And I must say that, now and then, I felt pretty discouraged myself. Sometimes, when Bob was out, I'd take a bus uptown and then walk past the old Waldorf-Astoria and wonder if I'd ever know the people who went there. The Waldorf! Imagine! And I had to look up the Ritz in the telephone book to find out where it was. Why, we didn't even know a speak-easy, except the Italian place on Charlton Street, with the dollar dinner and the menu in purple ink. And then, that spring, I got my job on *Modes and Manners*. And we met the Halleys and things really began.

Though, as a matter of fact, it was Ben Christian who first took us to the Charlton Street place. . . . Oh, yes, my dear, very well. He used to sleep on our couch when they'd evict him. He was writing *Bitter Harvest* then, and I must say he'd read it aloud at the drop of a hat. Well, I did make a few suggestions—the women were simply impossible, and he knew it. Rather sensitive and sweet in those days, with untamed hair and a thin face—well, his face is still thin. He used to call me "The Kid from Little Prairie" and say we made him believe in marriage or something. And we'd sit around in the Charlton Street place and he and Bob would talk for hours. I still remember that awful wine. There were moth balls in it, I'm sure. But we thought it was wonderful.

Well, of course, that sort of thing is all very nice when you're new. Very picturesque and all that, when you're looking back—though the ravioli always tasted of thumbs. And Ben used the place in *Bitter Harvest,* so that was all right. In fact, it got to be quite celebrated and people would come from uptown. Ben was rather rude about that— he'd call them "slummers" and say they came to watch the quaint animals perform. Of course, I'd know now that it was just an inferiority complex, because he was born on Hester Street himself—but I was a child in those days. I hadn't even read Jung.

He wasn't rude to the Halleys, exactly, but he was—well, suspicious. And the worst of it was, he made Bob suspicious too. I had quite a time getting him over that. And, really, I can't imagine why. Because, after all—and in spite of everything that's happened—the Halleys were our kind. But he used to say that the worst thing about the arts was the people who thought you could collect them like Pekingese. I'm sure I don't know what he meant by it. It must have been just a psychosis. Like washing your hands too much.

Now, I must say, I have an instinct about those things. I don't claim any credit for it; it's just in you or it's not. And I knew, when we first saw the Halleys, they were people we ought to know. It was weird, my dear—just like a premonition. Though I don't suppose I'd think that Miriam was quite so distinguished now. She's gone off terribly, recently. And one does get tired of Halstead's imitations. He's been doing them so long. Well, I suppose you'd have to do something if you were married to Miriam.

But they were the first real New Yorkers we really knew. I don't mean people like Ben Christian, who happened to be born here, but people that counted. They took us to our first first-night, and I'll never forget it. And Miriam wore her long gold earrings and they knew the star. But, my dear, the struggle I had to get Bob into a dinner coat! I finally just had to show him that it was an investment, as, of course, it is. And even then, he would call it a tuxedo. But the Halleys just laughed and thought it was quaint and American.

They'd have asked Ben Christian, too, if they'd thought he'd come. They were always very nice about Ben, and Miriam bought dozens of copies of *Bitter Harvest* after the reviews came out. But he simply couldn't understand them—it was a blind spot. He kept on saying they were slummers and that he'd respect Halstead a lot more if he spent his money on a racing stable instead of backing bad plays and collecting worse pictures, just to please Miriam. Because, he said, there are certain people who are born to own racing stables. And there's one thing about being a horse—now and then you get a chance to kick somebody like Halstead square in the slats.

Which I think was very unfair, when Halstead had got Bob three game rooms to decorate and Miriam had started him on book jackets. Of course, it wasn't Bob's real work, but it meant he was beginning to be known. And they'd have done just as much for Ben, if he'd let them. I used to tell him so. But he'd just grin at me and say, "Don't be fooled, kid. I know those helping hands. Remember Little Prairie!" Well, it didn't mean much, in the first place, and finally, he got to saying it all the time. And I do think that's boring.

I'm certainly the last person in the world to come between a husband and his friends. I've always been very careful about that, with both Bob and Ted. But there does come a point—you'll see. And the first big party we gave in the old studio. . . . Oh, Christian came, my dear, if you can call it coming. We were blessed with his physical presence. But he wouldn't even drink—just sat in a corner and glared. As if he wanted to get away, but didn't quite know how. And for no reason.

Of course, I didn't know as much about parties as I do now, but

still it was fun. And Bob almost sold a water color because of it. I'm
sure the woman would have bought it if she'd ever seen it again.

Well, we patched things up afterward, but they never were quite
the same. I think it really hurt Bob—and I certainly tried to make it
up to him. I even thought we might have a baby, just to take his mind
off things; though where we'd have put it, I don't know. But then,
thank heaven, Ben fell in love with a girl and moved to Brooklyn—
and, my dear, the relief! She was years older than either of us and
wore embroidered smocks—and even Bob saw there was simply no
use going on.

And by that time the Charlton Street place had put in a garden and
waiters, so it wasn't fun any more. There were too many people who
went there, and you'd be bothered. So we took our courage in both
hands and moved uptown. Beekman Place—it hadn't really begun
then. Bob never liked the light quite as well, but it looked much more
like a studio when I'd fixed it up, and, after all, when you're doing
game rooms, you have to do them on the spot.

And then the rush began. There's nothing like it—we simply went
everywhere. Of course, I'd be a little more selective now. But I remember Halstead saying to me, "Well, little one, you two have certainly taken the town," and Halstead never exaggerates. And Bob's
first show went over with a bang—they even ran a photograph of
him in *Vanity Fair*. I don't know why he wasn't more pleased with it;
he may have thought the pastel sketches were hasty, but everybody
else thought they were divine.

Well, of course, if one critic calls your work "superficial," that's
the one review you read. You ought to be glad that your husband's a
scientist.

Naturally, it was prohibition then—it sounds quite prehistoric,
doesn't it? But New York's always the same. We went to 42 long before it was 42. And the most amusing people were around—it's really
sad to think back. That's the one sad thing about the city—the people
who drop out. Of course, there are always new ones, but it isn't quite
the same. Well, the Reeces, for instance—they were darlings, and had
a perfect doll's house of a place. But then they started having children
and now they're living in Jersey, of all places, and one never sees
them any more. And Allan Lark is permanently in Hollywood
and they say he drinks terribly. And Ethel Shand—my dear, you
wouldn't remember her, but she made a great hit in "Welcome,
Folks," and then she just dropped out of sight. The last I heard, she
was doing some ghastly sort of work for a Middle Western radio sta-

tion and she'd lost her looks completely. Oh, it's a casualty list. I think of it every time I go into Tony's.

One must just keep the chin up, that's all. And I've always tried. Even when Bob began drinking—and I've never quite understood that. My dear, I'm not a prude, but I can take it or leave it alone. And, as a matter of fact, it has very little effect on me. It never has. You wouldn't know I'd had a cocktail before I came here, would you? While Bob has always had a weak head. I suppose it's his shyness, partly. He needs just about two drinks to get over it and be amusing and affable. But after that you have to call in the marines.

And I certainly never tried to stop him or play the injured wife. I don't believe in that. But I did think it was a pity he should spoil things when we were having such a nice time and meeting all the right people—and I suppose he saw it. Men are so sensitive. And if I could take a cocktail or two without making a spectacle of myself, I don't see why he should feel he had to do the same. As I said, once or twice, we could just admit we were different and let it go at that. But that only seemed to make him worse. Ted says it would, but then Ted hardly knows Bob at all. And when I asked Ted what the real reason was—because men stick together so—he only said, "Well, perhaps he felt it deadened the pain." Which doesn't make sense, my dear.

Anyhow, I noticed he was just drinking milk at the Coles'. The bride, I suppose. But it's just as artificial, I always think.

I remember one enormous party at the Nesbitts'—well, I saw how things were going and I felt simply desperate—the Nesbitts are so important. And I just couldn't get to Bob. So I was perfectly frantic—and then I looked across the room, and there was Ben Christian! In a white tie and tails, my dear—imagine! Well, he'd had his second big success. Well, any port in a storm, so I went over. And he was really quite friendly. He grinned and said, "Hello, kid! Remember Little Prairie!" And I said, "Well, how do you like it?" looking at his tie. And he grinned again and said, "It's the biggest, shiniest merry-go-round in the world. That's all right. But, gosh, what funny people they get on the horses!"

Then he asked after Bob, and I said, "He's over there," and he looked, and the queerest expression came over his face. "Why, he's tight!" he said.

"Are you telling me?" I said.

"I wouldn't have believed it," he said. "But why? Oh, well. We'd better take him home."

"If you only would," I said. "He's got his keys and the light turns on by the door. And, of course, I want to pay for the taxi."

He looked at me again, with that funny expression. "No, thanks," he said. "I can manage. Well, so long, Little Prairie!"

That's the way he is, you know—abrupt. And he did take Bob home, and everything was all right when I came in. I've always been very grateful. Of course, I meant to thank Ben when he came back to the party himself, but he didn't come back. And when I tried to phone, next day, they said at his publisher's that he'd left for the Coast.

Well, of course, that was just one time, but there were others. Really, dear, I don't know how I stood it. I couldn't have, except for my friends. They were wonderful. And most of them understood so perfectly—though I must say, I always said, "You mustn't take sides. And just treat Bob as you always have. We can't all of us succeed." I've always been like that; I try to see both sides. Though I must say it did hurt me a little, about the Halleys.

It may be very provincial of me, but I don't quite see what business it was of theirs. Though, of course. I appreciated their loyalty to Bob. I suppose that was why they did it. But, really, to hear them talk, you'd have thought I'd Led Him to the Bottle. Well, dear, you can see for yourself. And about children making a difference—why, it was pre-Victorian! When I'd told Bob in the beginning that I didn't mean to tie him down, like so many wives.

Then, finally, Halstead started on the Perils of the Big City and What New York Does to People, and it was a little too dreary. And as far as Ted was concerned—why, I'd barely met him then—though, of course, I knew who he was. But I never dreamt. Oh, well, I suppose they meant it for the best. But it rather hurt me. They didn't even offer me a cocktail—I had to stop by at Tony's afterward. And there was Bob, with the Russian friend. So that was that.

All the same, I really hated breaking up the apartment. Those things are a trifle grim. Especially when they look at you in that blond, rather appealing way. You just have to be quite sensible and talk about the furniture. Remember that, my dear. Not that I wouldn't have been glad to let Bob have it. But he meant to go South anyway—he told me so. . . .

Reno? Well, dear, it isn't New York, but it isn't bad. I met some very interesting people and let my hair grow out. That was really for Ted, and I hope he appreciated it. Of course, I never thought, at the time, we'd be anything more than very good friends. Why, he'd been a bachelor for years! But it must have been—well, predestined, for he's often said it was quite as much of a surprise to him. Don't you think that's rather sweet?

I remember how dazed he was when we drove down to City Hall for the license. . . . Oh, after I'd got back, of course—almost six months. And he hadn't even brought a ring, poor lamb; we had to stop at a jewelry store on the way. Men are such babies, aren't they, about practical things? Well, it seemed to me there was absolutely no use in putting it off, when he was supposed to go to California for the firm. He might have been out there for months, and that would have been trying for both of us. Especially as people were beginning to talk a little. You know how they are. Well, someone has to make the decisions. And, as it turned out, the business wasn't so important after all and we had a whole heavenly month at Santa Barbara. But we were glad to get back. After all, there's no place like New York.

It was quite a change, of course, but, if there's one thing I do know, it's how to make adjustments. Of course, it's rather a distinguished family, really. My dear, I should be honored, I hope you know. And a divorced woman too. Why, the family halls on the Hudson rocked to their foundations. At least, I suppose they did. But there's only Brother Eugene in New York, thank goodness. Not to speak of Sister Claudia—that's his wife. And there, my dear, is a woman. . . . Oh, you know. On the boards of schools and things, and takes an intelligent interest in politics—too tiring. And just a simple string of real pearls—the kind that look false. I asked her once if she knew the Stork Club—just to make conversation—and she said, "Was it anything like the Metropolitan?" Well, at least I've rescued Ted from people like that.

But I do what I can, and we have them at least twice a winter. I think that's only fair. When I go to see Ted's mother, I always wear my hair over my ears and knot it in the back. And we always spend two weeks with her in the summer. And that works out quite nicely—I've a definite plan for it. I just consider it a rest cure—shorts and lying around in the sun. The food's good, too—that's one comfor—and Madeira, if you like Madeira. I'm afraid Grimes—he's the butler and positively antediluvian—was rather shocked by my shorts, at first. But he's got over that.

And Ted really has a wonderful sense of humor about it all. Because I remember asking him—oh, just amusingly—if I wasn't a little of a surprise. Though, heaven knows, I do everything I can. And he looked at me in that quizzical way he has, and said, "Well, Great-Uncle Marshall married a lady called Toots Latour, and the family stood that for fourteen years. So I guess they can stand you, darling." Wasn't it quaint of him? I simply screamed. So, now and then, I call myself the Skeleton in the Closet and he always laughs.

I asked him what happened to Toots Latour—well, the poor thing finally died and Great-Uncle Marshall married again—oh, very respectably, this time! Of course, they didn't have divorces in those days. But such interesting things happen in old families. Ted's got quite interested in the family history recently—he even found a miniature of Great-Uncle Marshall, and he's got it in his study, over his desk. He says he feels it ought to be there. Touching of him, isn't it? I asked him if he couldn't find one of Toots Latour, too, but he said he really didn't think it was necessary. . . .

Yes, I think we've adjusted very well. Of course, there's always a certain amount of weeding out to do—you'll start with a clean slate and that's such a comfort. But when Ted's partners come to dinner, I just jolly them along and pretend they're gay and amusing, even when they aren't. I feel it's the least I can do. And Judge Willoughby—he's the senior partner—and, my dear, a real old buck, with a darling little beard. I always have a wonderful time with him. Well, his wife's one of those iron-gray women with nutcracker faces, so you can hardly blame him. I do think there's so much a woman can do for her husband, if she tries. And that's the real criticism I make of women like Mrs. Willoughby. You can see that she's never tried at all. Ted says that's because she's never had to, but I can hardly agree. And, as for distinction—my dear. I don't care if she does know that stodgy set in London. We're Americans over here, I should hope, not title hunters. Why, Paul Necropuloff hardly uses his title at all—and he's really a prince!

Of course, it's meant giving up my own work. But I was willing to make the sacrifice—I told Ted so. Though I've been wondering about it just a little bit, of late. After all, we've been married almost six years—quite an age. But then, the magazines have changed so. And people are quite different, somehow, when you ask them about real jobs. I wouldn't want a full-time one, of course, with my responsibilities. But take somebody like Dorothy Thompson. She doesn't run a column every day. And after all, what did she do but live in Germany? I'm sure I've done more interesting things than that.

Naturally, I know what Ted's family would expect. But I think rather definitely not. After all, there are plenty of grandchildren, with Claudia and Eugene. It isn't that I'm afraid in the least. But one has to look at it from a sensible point of view. Even if some people do, at all ages. And as a matter of fact, Ted hasn't even brought up the subject in a long time.

And then—well, you're lucky, my dear. After all, you are quite an infant. . . . Well, that's sweet of you, but I know. There seem to be so many of them about, nowadays. Not that it really makes any difference what age you are. But I noticed the other day how gray Miriam Halley is getting. Of course, she's years older than I am, but it gave me a turn.

Then, they're so exclusive, too, the young. One just has to grab, I suppose, and I do hate grabbing. I leave that to people like the Ingram woman. But that's what I mean. She's supposed to write, I believe, and it does make things easier. And really, one should do something. It gets to be three o'clock in the afternoon so soon.

My dear, I'll tell you a secret. I've been thinking about a novel. Or even reminiscences—they're doing them earlier now. And I haven't told a soul about it—well, of course, I mentioned it to Ted—and then, Ben Christian. I thought he'd be interested and I hadn't seen him in ages. . . .

Well, he's rather hard to get nowadays, my dear—especially since they talked about him for the Nobel prize. But we got him. Just a quiet little party.

I kept it down to twelve for dinner; though, of course, people swarmed in afterward.

Well, he's improved in some ways. His dress collars fit him, for one thing. But of course one never gets a chance to really talk at a dinner party. And then he had to leave early. Just when Marcus Leigh was doing his divinely naughty songs.

So, I just called him up the next day—and, my dear, the to-do! You'd think the man was royalty. But he finally said he was free from four to five, if I cared to run in. My dear, it's the dreariest hotel and the dingiest little cocktail bar. I can't imagine why he stays there.

He's abrupt, you know—very abrupt. The same old Ben. The first thing he said was, "I like that husband of yours. Nice guy." Well, that was pleasant of him, of course. But when I started asking his advice about writing, he hardly seemed to be listening.

Finally he said to me, "Well, Myra, you know how it is. The people who are going to write novels, write them. And the ones who want to be writers just talk about it. But I'll give you a note to my agent—he's got good nerves. By the way, have you written any of it yet?"

"Well, not exactly," I said. I'm always honest.

"I thought so," he said. "And what's it going to be about, if I may ask?"

"Why, New York, of course," I said, and he just looked at me. He has the queerest way of looking at you sometimes.

"New York?" he said. "Why not Little Prairie? You knew something, then."

"Oh, Ben—do we have to be tiresome?" I said—for, really, that old joke!

"I'm not tiresome," he said. "Just surprised. After all, I was born here. And I don't pretend to know all of it. But you—"

"What do they know of England that only England know?" I said.

"Well," he said, "you do know one thing if you're born on Hester Street. You know it's more than forty restaurants, five night clubs and a hospital."

And then he went on and talked the queerest stuff. All about little people living in the Bronx and butchers in the market, and Wall Street and corporation lawyers and the men who dig the new subways. And how it was fifty cities and you never got to the end of them, and how a man could spend his whole life looking, and still not know it all. I suppose it'll all be in his next book—it sounded like that.

"But you know it!" he said. "You know it!" and he sounded quite angry. "Forty restaurants, five night clubs and a hospital! You know it all! Well, I only hope you write the book! Can I lend you a map of the city? No, it wouldn't do any good."

Well, of course, there's no use arguing with a man in his condition, so I just thanked him for his interest, and let it go at that. He looked at me again.

"Look here, Myra. I'm going to talk to you," he said. And then he said, "No. What's the use? It's got into the bloodstream."

"I don't know what you mean," I said.

"Oh, nothing," he said. "I was just thinking aloud. Because they come every year, I suppose—ten thousand of them—the kids with a little talent and a lot of youth. And they end up thinking it's wonderful to hear a Class B heel sing dirty little songs. Or some of them. Oh, well."

"I'm glad you're so appreciative of my friends," I said.

"Oh, forget it," he said. "I was just remembering things—it's a bad practice. But remember what I said about that husband of yours. He's a nice guy, but he looks as if he might have brains. And sometimes, you know, you can make the dose too strong."

Well, that was cryptic, I suppose—poor dear Ben, he always loved to make those mysterious remarks. But, all the same, he gave me the note to his agent. So, if I burst into print, my dear, you musn't be surprised. The only thing is, I haven't quite decided just what publisher to have. I was going to start in yesterday and rough out an out-line. But, of course, one must find the time. And then, seeing Bob and the bride—well, it does give one something of a shock.

So it was such a relief—just sitting and visiting with little Kitty Harris, and hearing all about your plans. You can't imagine. . . . Well, my dear, just the barest touch and then I must fly. Your husband will think me very naughty, but I did want you to see the place. It's rather a favorite *boîte* of ours, and everybody comes here, but everybody! Bob might even bring the bride here—though, really, she might as well go to the Grand Central. They have milk bars there.

And we'll see each other very soon, shan't we? I've so enjoyed chatting about the old days. And the least little thing you want advice on—I'm right on the end of the phone. We're having a party tomor-row night, but you wouldn't be interested. Just dullish people—Har-vard classmates and such—but I thought this would be a good time to work some of them off. I rather wish I'd thought of you before, though—you might have helped me out with the little Lindsay. She's rather a firm-faced child. She'll fit in all right with Ted's friends—af-ter all, they like them young. And I needed an extra woman. But I can't think how Ted happened to think of her—he doesn't often make suggestions. And we'd just had her too. But he happened to be looking at the miniature of Great-Uncle Marshall, and out it came.

A Life at Angelo's

I don't know why everybody keeps on going to Angelo's. The drinks aren't any better—in fact, they're a little worse, if anything—and the dinner never was much. I'm getting so I can hardly look a sardine in the eye any more.

Of course it's a quiet place, and they don't let in many college boys. It's generally just the old crowd from five o'clock on. Oh, people come and go naturally—the way they do in New York. If they didn't, I don't suppose Angelo could keep on running. But what I mean is, you can drop in almost any time after curfew and find somebody you know to have a quick one or a couple of quick ones with. And then, if that's your weakness, you can stay and get dinner; though I wish they'd try another brand of sardines.

Suppose everyone stopped coming, all at once? Or suppose the place closed? I don't like to think about that. I suppose it's bound to happen, sooner or later, when Angelo's made his pile—they always go back to Italy. Then there'll be all the trouble and bother of finding another place; and the crowd won't be the same. You can't keep a crowd together, once you move the place, in New York. It seems pretty safe, though, at the moment, I'm glad to say. There's never been any real trouble, you see; no one ever gets shot at Angelo's and when the visiting firemen get too noisy, Rocco just eases them out. Rocco's the little one with the grin, and he doesn't look strong, but how he can ease a fellow out when it's necessary! He did it to me only once, and I've never held it against him. That was just after Evie and I had broken up.

No, I don't think there's any need to worry for a while yet. And when there is, I'm sure Angelo will tell me about it far enough ahead so I can make my arrangements. After all, I'm one of his oldest customers. I don't go back to the Twelfth Street place, the way Mr. Forman does, but seven years is a long time in this man's town. They're easing Mr. Forman out at 11:30 these days. It used to be all hours when I first knew him, but a man can't expect to drink like that at his age and not show it in the whites of the eyes. That's another thing I have against all this changing around. You get started going from one place to another and buying taxis and going in for general snake dancing; and before you know where you are you're on a party, and the whole next day is bad. Well, now, if you work at all, you can't afford to have the week days go bad on you. I'm not talking of Saturday night—there's a law about that. And of course those impromptu harvest homes are a lot of fun when you're young and new to the town. But when you've had a little sense knocked into you you're a fool if you don't run on schedule. Isn't that so?

Now, at Angelo's, you always know where you are. A couple of quick ones or so before dinner, and the red at dinner—or the white, if you're dining with a girl. Then a little touch after the coffee and a couple of long ones and a nightcap, and home at twelve by the old college clock. And all the time you're talking with somebody you know—about their wives, or their husbands, or religion, or the market, or what's new in the crowd—just rational conversation and maybe a little quiet singing, like "Work is the Curse of the Drinking Classes." Sometimes Mr. Forman sits down and tells one of his long stories, but generally he'd rather stand at the bar. And sometimes the whole crowd clicks, and sometimes it doesn't, and sometimes that Page girl gets started on her imitations.

But anyway, it's something you're used to, and you're doing it again, and it's warm, and you know the people, and you don't have to go home. And Angelo's there, getting a little fatter and sleeker every year, and with a little bigger white edge around his waistcoat. Now and then he'll set up some *strega* for you, if he's feeling right. I don't like *strega* myself, but it would hurt his feelings to refuse. And then, in summer, there's the little back garden, and the fat cat that always had kittens, and the pink shades on the lamps. Rocco will be telling you the fish is ver' fine—and you know it isn't, but who cares?—and you can sit and watch the lights in the skyscrapers and hear the roar of the town, going by outside. You don't have to think at all. It's restful that way.

I can remember when I used to think a lot. And wonder about the people who came to places like Angelo's, and who they were, and why they came, and what they did with the rest of their time. I used to make up stories about them, going back to the apartment with Evie, and we'd both get excited over them; and forget to turn off at ou own corner, we were talking so hard. That was when everybody we met was brand-new and bound to be interesting, and it was fun going to shows together in the gallery and having pancakes afterward at Childs'. I was always going to write some of those stories down, and she helped me make notes of them. I found the start of the one about Mr. Forman the other day. Well, what was the percentage in keeping it? I've seen a good deal of this writing racket since; and I ought to know what will sell and what won't. And anyhow, I'd just made him an old soak, and he's really a pretty interesting man.

Besides, that's something you get over. Wondering, I mean. Once you're on a normal schedule, you don't have time. I used to think it was funny—meeting people the way you do and having them tell you all sorts of inside things, the way it happens, and yet not really knowing them or tying them up with anything outside. But that's stopped bothering me. You just have to let them come and go, or it breaks the charm.

Going home to dinner with Jim Hewitt was what cured me, finally. I never met a fellow I liked better at Angelo's and we told our real names. So, when he suggested breaking the family bread one evening, I took him up. Good Lord, he lived at Scarsdale and they had three children! The baby was sounding off like a police siren as we came in, and we had one round of weak orange blossoms before the fodder. Mrs. Hewitt liked orange blossoms. Then, afterward, we sat around and played three-handed bridge and Mrs. Hewitt and Jim discussed the squeak in the car. I couldn't have stayed all night; I'd have had the mimies. Jim was sort of ritzy for a while after that, but he got all right again, finally. I guess they must have hitched up the sled dogs and moved north to White Plains or something, for I haven't seen him in I don't now how long.

Of course, now and then something comes along that you have to take notice of. People get married or divorced, and Angelo will always open a bottle of champagne, no matter which it is, if they're really old customers. I remember the party the crowd of us gave to cheer up Helen Ashland when she heard about Jake's remarriage. She certainly took it like a sport—we were thinking up funny telegrams to send the bridal couple all evening. I don't believe she really had hysterics either. That was just Bing Otis' idea. And she couldn't have meant it when she said she hated us—she'd always been the life of the crowd. Anyhow, I think she got married again last year—somebody was broadcasting about it. If she ever comes back to Angelo's, I'll have to get the low-down.

That's another thing about the crowd—the way they stick together when anything happens. I'll never forget the night Ted Harrison went out. Of course, he'd been going into reverse for quite a while, and whenever he got particularly sunk, he'd talk about doing a one-way jump through a window; but we knew Ted and just kidded him along. So when he did do it, after all, it was mean. Anyhow, he had the sense not to stage his act at Angelo's.

We went to the service afterward—those of us that could. That's what I mean by all of us sticking together. It was one of those gray winter days, and cold. There was a little boy, and he was crying. I don't see why they brought him there. I didn't know Ted had a boy. I know the rest of Ted's family sort of upstaged us. But we felt we ought to be there; though it was funny how little you could remember about Ted except parties. Well, there isn't much to those services, the way I look at it. But then we went back to Angelo's and he was fine.

Evie never took to Angelo's somehow, even at first. She felt she had to like the dinner, because it was cheap, but the atmosphere of the place never really appealed to her. She liked going to places where there was music or where somebody famous might be sitting at the next table. Of course, it was generally an out-of-town buyer or a cloak model, really, but she got just as big a kick out of pretending. We used to have dinner home a lot, too, that first year. It's wonderful how much food you can get for the money, living like that. Though, of course, it's really cheaper for me to eat at Angelo's, now I'm alone.

I've thought sometimes of getting a regular maid or one of those Japs who just come in and get dinner and clear away. There'd be money enough, for Evie never would take alimony, and now she's married again she doesn't need it anyway. But then, what would you do after dinner? You can't go to the movies every night in the week, and a man who works all day needs some relaxation.

When Evie and I were married, we used to go to all sorts of places—we even went to museums on Sundays and to those concerts they have way uptown. But there's not much point in doing that sort of thing by yourself. And if you start trotting a girl around, why, anybody knows how that finishes. You may not mean to get hooked up together at all, but some little thing happens and you're in for it, one way or the other. And if it's one way, you're bound to feel like a bum sooner or later, while if it's the other—well, I've been married to Evie, and once is enough. I'm not going to repeat at my age. This child is too wise.

Now, you can see as much of a girl as you like at Angelo's, and that's all right because you're both part of the crowd. You've got protection, if you see what I mean. And even if you should stop playing for matches, it wouldn't mean much to either of you. We're all pretty modern in the crowd and we understand about things like that. Of course, we've had some fairly wild birds at one time or another, and I don't say I agree with all the talk I hear. But there's no use being Victorian, like people were in 1910. You just have to be wise.

It's queer, though—you certainly couldn't call Evie Victorian. And yet she never genuinely fitted in with the crowd. She wasn't a gloom either, or a bluenose; she was really awfully pretty and the kind of girl that everybody likes right off. Why, Mr. Forman took a great shine to her and used to come over and sit at our table and tell her how he wished he had a daughter her age. But she just couldn't stand him. She said it was the look of his hands. Now, when anybody's been drinking for thirty semesters or so, like Mr. Forman, I think they're lucky if they have any hands at all. And if they do remind you of an alligator-skin bag, you ought to overlook it and be broad-minded. But Evie simply couldn't see it that way.

She was always wanting us to make friends with other young married people, even when they lived up by Grant's Tomb, where the climate's different. Well, that's all right, but once you go in for that sort of thing, you might as well stay in Waynesburg. That's that I kept telling her: "This is New York," I said, "this is New York." Let the Weather Bureau worry about the wide-open spaces. But all the same, after she was gone, I found a whole envelope full of real-estate ads—you know those mortgage manors with the built-in kiddie coops that all the Westchester cowboys come home to on the 5:49. Now, can you imagine that in a sensible girl?

So there it was, you see, and we didn't make a go of it. Well, it's no use crying over spilt giggle water, as they say, and a man has to take things like that in his stride. If he doesn't, he's lost in the shuffle in this man's hamlet. I can see it wasn't anybody's fault; I'm modern. Maybe if Evie had really liked the crowd—but there, I won't blame her. She's happy the way she is, I guess; and you can see the way I am. The only thing that ever hurts this little head is to think of Angelo's closing down, sardines or no sardines. But I'm sure he'll give me the eye, long enough ahead, if it does. He's always shot square with me.

Of course, occasionally you get sort of philosophic about this time in the evening, and wonder how things would have turned out if they'd been different. But I've almost quit doing that. There's no percentage in it.

I remember Mr. Forman, one of the first times Evie and I were here. She hadn't noticed his hands then, and when he got talking to us, we both thought he was a pretty quaint old character. I guess he took to us so because we both of us must have looked young and green. Anyhow, he started philosophizing. "Youth," he says. "Youth against the city; coming in every day—" Oh, he ought to have had it syndicated! "I've watched 'em come," says he, "and I've seen 'em go.

And some it makes, and some it breaks, and some just dry up gradually till the whitewing sweeps 'em away. Go back to your cornfields, young people," says he—as if Waynesburg didn't have car tracks!— "Go back and raise a family of nice little mortgages, because I'm a bad old man and you're breaking my heart"—and pretty soon he's crying into his glass.

We didn't pay any attention to him. We knew we were going to lick the world. But all the same, there's something in what he said. This town is a tough spot till you get wise to it—and it's too bad to see a fine man like Mr. Forman going to pieces the way he had these last two years. But then he's got what I call too much system in his drinking. You have to have just enough so it doesn't worry you.

Take me. If I'm stepping out a little more than usual tonight, it's just because of seeing Evie again. Of course it was bound to happen sometime, the way people come to New York; but a thing like that is apt to make you a little nervous just the same. It's easier, being modern the way we are. All the same, when I stepped out of the elevator and saw her waiting where she generally used to wait . . .

She hadn't come upstairs to the office, and that was decent of her. That girl at the front desk never could see me, and it's a laugh, your ex-wife ringing you up to pass the time of day or waiting out in the reception room. Though it wouldn't have been exactly a laugh to me.

I'd thought of all sorts of things to say to her when we did meet, but I didn't say any of them. I even forgot to take off my hat. I just said, "Hello, Evie. I didn't know you were in town," and she said, "Hello, Dick. I'm just here between trains"—and then we stared at each other.

I knew her right away, and yet I didn't know her, if you can get that. She was just as pretty as ever, but we weren't married any more. And then, her face was different. It didn't have that sort of quiet look on it when we were married. Of course, she'd let her hair grow too. She always had pretty hair. It had been five years. Well, there we were.

I must have looked like something, for, when we were out on the street she touched me on the arm.

"Don't worry, Dick," she said. "Everything's all right. I just thought, as long as I was in New York, it was silly not to see each other. Do you mind?"

"Not a bit," I said. . . . Well, you have to be polite, haven't you?

"How's Mr. Barris?" I said. . . . That's Evie's husband. It's a funny name.

"Oh, he's fine . . ." she said, "just fine."

"And the children?" I said. . . . I couldn't imagine them. "I suppose they're fine too?"

"Oh, they're fine," she said.

"Well, I'm glad to hear that, Evie," I said.

I don't know why it was so hard to talk; we ought to have been used to talking to each other.

She looked at me and laughed, quite the way she used to. "We can't stand here and gape at each other. Dick," she said.

"That's right," I said, so I flagged a taxi and told him Angelo's. Then I remembered she didn't like Angelo's. But she was decent and said that it was all right.

I'll hand it to Rocco. He knew who she was, all right, but he didn't even bat an eye—just took the order. We were the only people in the little room. She said she wanted some sherry; so that was that, with a double old-fashioned for me.

When he was gone, "Was that Rocco?" she said. "He didn't remember me."

"Well," said I, "you've been away a long time."

Then we looked at each other and knew we had nothing to say. She made rings with the bottom of the sherry glass.

"Oh, Dick," she said, "it's all so different from the way I thought it would be. Tell me about yourself."

"Oh, I'm still at the old stand," I said. "Same desk, as a matter of fact. Same salary, just about."

"How about the novel?"

"Oh," I said, "I'm working at it."

But she saw through me. "It's been five years," she said.

"A good idea's worth putting time on," said I, so she gave that up. Well, I wasn't going to cry on her.

"How about yourself?" said I. "Still living in Des Moines?"

"You know Mr. Barris lives in Cleveland," she said.

"I never can keep those two towns straight," I said. I felt better now, with that old-fashioned inside me, especially as Rocco was bringing another.

"Who came from Waynesburg?" she said, trying to kid me out of it.

"Me," I said. "But you'll have to admit I've come a long way."

I don't know why that made her look as if she wanted to cry. She hardly ever did cry—that was one thing about her.

"Oh, show me the snapshots!" I said. "I know you've got them." So she did. There was the house and the children and everything, including Mr. Barris in golf pants, and the family sedan. The little girl looks like Evie. That's a break for her. I don't know what our kids would have looked like. Terrible, I suppose.

I passed the pictures back. "They're nice," I said. "It's quite a house. I suppose you've even got a garbage incinerator."

"Of course," she said. "Why?"

"It looks like a house that would have a garbage incinerator," I said. "But you'd think Barris could afford a better car now he's a family man."

"Don't talk about George," she said.

"I'm through," I said. "So you're happy, Evie?"

She looked straight at me. "I am happy," she said—and that's the hell of it; I could see she was.

"Well," I said, "skoal!"—and that was the end of that old-fashioned. I was certainly coming back to normal in grand style. I could feel it creeping all over me. Then I heard her sort of talking to herself.

"It was a mistake," she was saying. "I ought to have known, but I couldn't help it. I thought—"

"Why say that?" I said. "It's always nice to revive old times. . . . Rocco! . . . Ah, there you are, sir. And in a minute some of the crowd may blow in."

She started putting on her gloves. "I suppose they're the same too," she said.

"Who?"

"Oh, the Parsons, and that man you called the Poached Egg, and—what was her name?—Ruth something . . . and—"

"Wait a minute," I said. "You're moving too fast for me. The Parsons broke up, and they say she's up at Saranac for her lungs. I don't know whatever did happen to the Poached Egg. As for that Ruth girl—well, after Ted Harrison popped himself—"

"Ted Harrison?" she said. "Who was Ted Harrison?"

Well, there we were. We just didn't have any point of contact at all. Of course, it wasn't her fault; she'd been away, and you do get quick action in this town. But she didn't even know who Ted Harrison had been.

"Oh, well," I said, "it doesn't signify. Just wait around a little. Some people I want you to meet will be coming in pretty soon. You'll like them; they're really awfully nice people."

"I don't think I can wait, Dick," she said. "I've got to get back to the hotel. I'm taking the night train."

"Back to Cleveland?" I said.

"Back to Cleveland," she said.

"Well," I said, "if you must, you must. And I won't tell Barris on you." I felt pretty cheery by now. She looked at me. "I'm sorry," I said.

"Oh, Dick, Dick!" she said. "Whatever are you going to do with your life? You had such a lot. I can't stand it."

"If you mean my hair," I said, "it's the barber's fault, not mine."

But she didn't pay any attention. "I didn't come back to show off," she said. "Really I didn't. I hoped—I really did—I'd come back and find you—"

"Clean and sober?" said I. "Well, I'm all of that."

"I—oh, what's the use?—I even thought you might be married."

"To some nice girl?" I said. "No, thanks. I've been."

"I held on as long as I could," she said.

"I'm not denying it," said I. "Let's leave it at that. No hard feelings."

She looked as if she wanted to say a whole lot more. Then she looked around the room and at Rocco coming in with the fresh supply. I don't know what she saw to make her look like that.

"No, it wouldn't have been," she said, sort of low to herself. "It couldn't have been. Good-by, Dick, and thank you."

"The pleasure is all mine," said I. "Only sorry you won't have another. Just a second and I'll get you a taxi."

But when I'd settled the bill and got my hat and coat, she was gone.

I went back to the little room and sat down again. I didn't feel like thinking, but I couldn't help it. For one thing, Evie's asking about all those people who had been in the crowd—why, they'd just disappeared. And I hadn't even realized it. Come to think of it, the only two left of that particular crowd who still came to Angelo's were Mr. Forman and myself. And what was that novel about that I'd been going to write?

"Rocco!" I called.

"Right with you, mister."

"You have the right idea," I said, but when he came in, I made him stay.

"Rocco," I said, "tell me something. How do I look today?"

"Oh, mister look ver' fine; seem ver' well."

That's the trouble with Rocco. He's always so damn pleasant.

"Don't two-time me, Rocco," I said. "Do you remember when I first started coming here?"

"Oh, yes: remember ver' well. Mister ver' good customer; ver' steady customer. Wish we had all like mister."

"Leave that outside," I said. "Just tell me one thing: Do I look a lot different?"

He spread out his hands. "Sure, mister look little different. Why not? Time pass. Rocco look different too."

"You're a liar," I said. "You haven't changed that Dago grin in twenty years. . . . All right, I look different, but how old do I look?"

He spread out his hands again. "Rocco don't know. Mister maybe forty, forty-one—mister in his prime."

"You low snake," I said. "I'm thirty-two." This was serious.

"Thirty-two? That's right. That's what Rocco mean"—and he grinned. But I didn't feel so funny.

"Tell me, Rocco," I said. "You've always been a friend of mine. Now be a friend. Tell me honestly. Do you think I drink too much?"

Gosh, you couldn't get anywhere with him! He just kept on grinning.

"Mister ver' good customer," he said; "ver' old, ver' steady customer. Mister carry what he drink ver' well."

"I know that!" I said. I was getting mad by now. "But is it too much? Be sensible, Rocco. I don't put away half what Mr. Forman does."

"Nobody drink so much as Mr. Forman. Some day Mr. Forman go pop. Rocco ver' sorry then, for Mr. Forman old customer."

"Well, that's a swell way of encouraging me. How about yourself, Rocco? How's your health?"

"Fine; thanks, mister. We have new bambino only other day."

"Well, I'm certainly glad to hear that. But look here, Rocco; you take a snifter—"

"Sure. Rocco drink wine—*strega*—ver' good. But Rocco have to work. Can't drink alla time."

"I get that. But I work too."

"Sure, mister work. But Rocco work alla time. Rocco have wife, tree bambini; have to work. Work to go back to Italy, buy *trattoria*, buy farm, have more bambini, be big man in town. That work for a man. Mister have another old-fashioned?"

He wouldn't talk any more. And the next one didn't go so well, because I'd started looking at myself in the mirror.

Oh, it just shows what a state I was in. And it shows you never ought to go back on your tracks. You know, for a while there I didn't like my face a bit.

That's why I say, modern or not, things like seeing Evie again don't do you any good. Because, when Mr. Forman came in and touched me on the shoulder, I jumped a mile. And just before I jumped I caught his face in the glass right over mine. I've apologized to him since, and I guess he's forgotten it. But they all must have thought I was crazy, running out like that and leaving the money on the table. And all that week I just got crazier and crazier, getting up and taking a cold shower in the mornings, and eating at tearooms and coming right back after dinner and hunting around to see if I could find whatever became of that novel. One good thing, I did get the room pretty well cleaned up. That woman who comes in never really cleans.

But what's the use of all that when you keep getting the fidgets? And getting the fidgets makes you think too much. Anyway, one evening it was nice and warm, and I thought, "I'll just take a walk. I can't sit here any more."

Well, I didn't have any particular direction in mind, but after a while, sure enough, there I was in front of Angelo's. Man, you should have seen the welcome they gave me. Angelo set up the drinks himself, and Rocco was grinning all over.

"Angelo think we lose our mos' steady customer," he said, "but mister come back. I know he come back."

And Mr. Forman never said a word about how I'd acted.

He wasn't a bit standoffish; in fact, Rocco had to ease him out at eleven that night.

Now, the only worry I've got is Angelo's retiring, as I say. But even if he does, maybe Rocco will keep the place on. Of course, even that would be a change, but I'd hardly mind. We've known each other a long while, and he knows I'm a good customer.

Too Early Spring

I'm writing this down because I don't ever want to forget the way it was. It doesn't seem as if I could, now, but they all tell you things change. And I guess they're right. Older people must have forgotten or they couldn't be the way they are. And that goes for even the best ones, like Dad and Mr. Grant. They try to understand but they don't seem to know how. And the others make you feel dirty or else they make you feel like a goof. Till, pretty soon, you begin to forget yourself—you begin to think, "Well, maybe they're right and it was that way." And that's the end of everything. So I've got to write this down. Because they smashed it forever—but it wasn't the way they said.

Mr. Grant always says in comp. class: "Begin at the beginning." Only I don't know quite where the beginning was. We had a good summer at Big Lake but it was just the same summer. I worked pretty hard at the practice basket I rigged up in the barn, and I learned how to do the back jackknife. I'll never dive like Kerry but you want to be as all-around as you can. And, when I took my measurements, at the end of the summer, I was 5 ft. 9¾ and I'd gained 12 lbs. 6 oz. That isn't bad for going on sixteen and the old chest expansion was O. K. You don't want to get too heavy, because basketball's a fast game, but the year before was the year when I got my height, and I was so skinny, I got tired. But this year, Kerry helped me practice, a couple of times, and he seemed to think I had a good chance for the team. So I felt pretty set up—they'd never had a Sophomore on it before. And Kerry's a natural athlete, so that means a lot from him. He's a pretty good brother too. Most Juniors at State wouldn't bother with a fellow in High.

It sounds as if I were trying to run away from what I have to write down, but I'm not. I want to remember that summer, too, because it's the last happy one I'll ever have. Oh, when I'm an old man—thirty or forty—things may be all right again. But that's a long time to wait and it won't be the same.

And yet, that summer was different, too, in a way. So it must have started then, though I didn't know it. I went around with the gang as usual and we had a good time. But, every now and then, it would strike me we were acting like awful kids. They thought I was getting the big head, but I wasn't. It just wasn't much fun—even going to the cave. It was like going on shooting marbles when you're in High.

I had sense enough not to try to tag after Kerry and his crowd. You can't do that. But when they all got out on the lake in canoes, warm evenings, and somebody brought a phonograph along, I used to go down to the Point, all by myself, and listen and listen. Maybe they'd be talking or maybe they'd be singing, but it all sounded mysterious across the water. I wasn't trying to hear what they said, you know. That's the kind of thing Tot Pickens does. I'd just listen, with my arms around my knees—and somehow it would hurt me to listen—and yet I'd rather do that than be with the gang.

I was sitting under the four pines, one night, right down by the edge of the water. There was a big moon and they were singing. It's funny how you can be unhappy and nobody know it but yourself.

I was thinking about Sheila Coe. She's Kerry's girl. They fight but they get along. She's awfully pretty and she can swim like a fool. Once Kerry sent me over with her tennis racket and we had quite a conversation. She was fine. And she didn't pull any of this big sister stuff, either, the way some girls will with a fellow's kid brother.

And when the canoe came along, by the edge of the lake, I thought for a moment it was her. I thought maybe she was looking for Kerry and maybe she'd stop and maybe she'd feel like talking to me again. I don't know why I thought that—I didn't have any reason. Then I saw it was just the Sharon kid, with a new kind of bob that made her look grown-up, and I felt sore. She didn't have any business out on the lake at her age. She was just a Sophomore in High, the same as me.

I chunked a stone in the water and it splashed right by the canoe, but she didn't squeal. She just said, "Fish," and chuckled. It struck me it was a kid's trick, trying to scare a kid.

"Hello, Helen," I said. "Where did you swipe the gunboat?"

"They don't know I've got it," she said. "Oh, hello, Chuck Peters. How's Big Lake?"

"All right," I said. "How was camp?"

"It was peachy," she said. "We had a peachy counselor, Miss Morgan. She was on the Wellesley field-hockey team."

"Well," I said, "we missed your society." Of course we hadn't, because they're across the lake and don't swim at our raft. But you ought to be polite.

"Thanks," she said. "Did you do the special reading for English? I thought it was dumb."

"It's always dumb," I said. "What canoe is that?"

"It's the old one," she said. "I'm not supposed to have it out at night. But you won't tell anybody, will you?"

"Be your age," I said. I felt generous. "I'll paddle a while, if you want," I said.

"All right," she said, so she brought it in and I got aboard. She went back in the bow and I took the paddle. I'm not strong on carting kids around, as a rule. But it was better than sitting there by myself.

"Where do you want to go?" I said.

"Oh, back towards the house," she said in a shy kind of voice. "I ought to, really. I just wanted to hear the singing."

"K. O.," I said. I didn't paddle fast, just let her slip. There was a lot of moon on the water. We kept around the edge so they wouldn't notice us. The singing sounded as if it came from a different country, a long way off.

She was a sensible kid, she didn't ask fool questions or giggle about nothing at all. Even when we went by Petters' Cove. That's where the lads from the bungalow colony go and it's pretty well populated on a warm night. You can hear them talking in low voices and now and then a laugh. Once Tot Pickens and a gang went over there with a flashlight, and a big Bohunk chased them for half a mile.

I felt funny, going by there with her. But I said, "Well, it's certainly Old Home Week"—in an offhand tone, because, after all, you've got to be sophisticated. And she said, "People are funny," in just the right sort of way. I took quite a shine to her after that and we talked. The Sharons have only been in town three years and somehow I'd never really noticed her before. Mrs. Sharon's awfully good-looking but she and Mr. Sharon fight. That's hard on a kid. And she was a quiet kid. She had a small kind of face and her eyes were sort of like a kitten's. You could see she got a great kick out of pretending to be grown-up—and yet it wasn't all pretending. A couple of times, I felt just as if I were talking to Sheila Coe. Only more comfortable, because, after all, we were the same age.

Do you know, after we put the canoe up, I walked all the way back home, around the lake? And most of the way, I ran. I felt swell too. I felt as if I could run forever and not stop. It was like finding something. I hadn't imagined anybody could ever feel the way I did about some things. And here was another person, even if it was a girl.

Kerry's door was open when I went by and he stuck his head out, and grinned.

"Well, kid," he said. "Stepping out?"

"Sure. With Greta Garbo," I said, and grinned back to show I didn't mean it. I felt sort of lightheaded, with the run and everything.

"Look here, kid—" he said, as if he was going to say something. Then he stopped. But there was a funny look on his face.

And yet I didn't see her again till we were both back in High. Mr. Sharon's uncle died, back East, and they closed the cottage suddenly. But all the rest of the time at Big Lake, I kept remembering that night and her little face. If I'd seen her in daylight, first, it might have been different. No, it wouldn't have been.

All the same, I wasn't even thinking of her when we bumped into each other, the first day of school. It was raining and she had on a green slicker and her hair was curly under her hat. We grinned and said hello and had to run. But something happened to us, I guess.

I'll say this now—it wasn't like Tot Pickens and Mabel Palmer. It wasn't like Junior David and Betty Page—though they've been going together ever since kindergarten. It wasn't like any of those things. We didn't get sticky and sloppy. It wasn't like going with a girl.

Gosh, there'd be days and days when we'd hardly see each other, except in class. I had basketball practice almost every afternoon and sometimes evenings and she was taking music lessons four times a week. But you don't have to be always twos-ing with a person, if you feel that way about them. You seem to know the way they're thinking and feeling, the way you know yourself.

Now let me describe her. She had that little face and the eyes like a kitten's. When it rained, her hair curled all over the back of her neck. Her hair was yellow. She wasn't a tall girl but she wasn't chunky—just light and well made and quick. She was awfully alive without being nervous—she never bit her fingernails or chewed the end of her pencil, but she'd answer quicker than anyone in the class. Nearly everybody liked her, but she wasn't best friends with any particular girl, the mushy way they get. The teachers all thought a lot of her, even Miss Eagles. Well, I had to spoil that.

If we'd been like Tot and Mabel, we could have had a lot more time together, I guess. But Helen isn't a liar and I'm not a snake. It wasn't easy, going over to her house, because Mr. and Mrs. Sharon would be polite to each other in front of you and yet there'd be something wrong. And she'd have to be fair to both of them and they were always pulling at her. But we'd look at each other across the table and then it would be all right.

I don't know when it was that we knew we'd get married to each other, some time. We just started talking about it, one day, as if we al-

ways had. We were sensible, we knew it couldn't happen right off.
We thought maybe when we were eighteen. That was two years but
we knew we had to be educated. You don't get as good a job, if you
aren't. Or that's what people say.

We weren't mushy either, like some people. We got to kissing each
other good-by, sometimes, because that's what you do when you're
in love. It was cool, the way she kissed you, it was like leaves. But
lots of the time we wouldn't even talk about getting married, we'd
just play checkers or go over the old Latin, or once in a while go to
the movies with the gang. It was really a wonderful winter. I played
every game after the first one and she'd sit in the gallery and watch
and I'd know she was there. You could see her little green hat or her
yellow hair. Those are the class colors, green and gold.

And it's a queer thing, but everybody seemed to be pleased. That's
what I can't get over. They liked to see us together. The grown people, I mean. Oh, of course, we got kidded too. And old Mrs. Withers
would ask me about "my little sweetheart," in that awful damp voice
of hers. But, mostly, they were all right. Even Mother was all right,
though she didn't like Mrs. Sharon. I did hear her say to Father, once,
"Really, George, how long is this going to last? Sometimes I feel as if
I just couldn't stand it."

Then Father chuckled and said to her, "Now, Mary, last year you
were worried about him because he didn't take any interest in girls
at all."

"Well," she said, "he still doesn't. Oh, Helen's a nice child—no
credit to Eva Sharon—and thank heaven she doesn't giggle. Well,
Charles is mature for *his* age too. But he acts so solemn about her. It
isn't natural."

"Oh, let Charlie alone," said Father. "The boy's all right. He's just
got a one-track mind."

But it wasn't so nice for us after the spring came.

In our part of the state, it comes pretty late, as a rule. But it was
early this year. The little kids were out with scooters when usually
they'd still be having snowfights and, all of a sudden, the radiators in
the classrooms smelt dry. You'd got used to that smell for months—
and then, there was a day when you hated it again and everybody
kept asking to open the windows. The monitors had a tough time,
that first week—they always do when spring starts—but this year it
was worse than ever because it came when you didn't expect it.

Usually, basketball's over by the time spring really breaks, but this
year it hit us while we still had three games to play. And it certainly

played hell with us as a team. After Bladesburg nearly licked us, Mr. Grant called off all practice till the day before the St. Matthew's game. He knew we were stale—and they've been state champions two years. They'd have walked all over us, the way we were going.

The first thing I did was telephone Helen. Because that meant there were six extra afternoons we could have, if she could get rid of her music lessons any way. Well, she said, wasn't it wonderful, her music teacher had a cold? And that seemed just like Fate.

Well, that was a great week and we were so happy. We went to the movies five times and once Mrs. Sharon let us take her little car. She knew I didn't have a driving license but of course I've driven ever since I was thirteen and she said it was all right. She was funny—sometimes she'd be awfully kind and friendly to you and sometimes she'd be like a piece of dry ice. She was that way with Mr. Sharon too. But it was a wonderful ride. We got stuff out of the kitchen—the cook's awfully sold on Helen—and drove way out in the country. And we found an old house, with the windows gone, on top of a hill, and parked the car and took the stuff up to the house and ate it there. There weren't any chairs or tables but we pretended there were.

We pretended it was our house, after we were married. I'll never forget that. She'd even brought paper napkins and paper plates and she set two places on the floor.

"Well, Charles," she said, sitting opposite me, with her feet tucked under, "I don't suppose you remember the days we were both in school."

"Sure," I said—she was always much quicker pretending things than I was—"I remember them all right. That was before Tot Pickens got to be President." And we both laughed.

"It seems very distant in the past to me—we've been married so long," she said, as if she really believed it. She looked at me.

"Would you mind turning off the radio, dear?" she said. "This modern music always gets on my nerves."

"Have we got a radio?" I said.

"Of course, Chuck."

"With television?"

"Of course, Chuck."

"Gee, I'm glad," I said. I went and turned it off.

"Of course, if you *want* to listen to the late market reports—" she said just like Mrs. Sharon.

"Nope," I said. "The market—uh—closed firm today. Up twenty-six points."

"That's quite a long way up, isn't it?"

"Well, the country's perfectly sound at heart, in spite of this damnfool Congress," I said, like Father.

She lowered her eyes a minute, just like her mother, and pushed away her plate.

"I'm not very hungry tonight," she said. "You won't mind if I go upstairs?"

"Aw, don't be like that," I said. It was too much like her mother.

"I was just seeing if I could," she said. "But I never will, Chuck."

"I'll never tell you you're nervous, either," I said. "I—oh, gosh!"

She grinned and it was all right. "Mr. Ashland and I have never had a serious dispute in our wedded lives," she said—and everybody knows who runs *that* family. "We just talk things over calmly and reach a satisfactory conclusion, usually mine."

"Say, what kind of house have we got?"

"It's a lovely house," she said. "We've got radios in every room and lots of servants. We've got a regular movie projector and a library full of good classics and there's always something in the icebox. I've got a shoe closet."

"A what?"

"A shoe closet. All my shoes are on tipped shelves, like Mother's. And all my dresses are on those padded hangers. And I say to the maid, 'Elsie, Madam will wear the new French model today.' "

"What are my clothes on?" I said. "Christmas trees?"

"Well," she said. "You've got lots of clothes and dogs. You smell of pipes and the open and something called Harrisburg tweed."

"I do not," I said. "I wish I had a dog. It's a long time since Jack."

"Oh, Chuck, I'm sorry," she said.

"Oh, that's all right," I said. "He was getting old and his ear was always bothering him. But he was a good pooch. Go ahead."

"Well," she said, "of course we give parties—"

"Cut the parties," I said.

"Chuck! They're grand ones!"

"I'm a homebody," I said. "Give me—er—my wife and my little family and—say, how many kids have we got, anyway?"

She counted on her fingers. "Seven."

"Good Lord," I said.

"Well, I always wanted seven. You can make it three, if you like."

"Oh, seven's all right, I suppose," I said. "But don't they get awfully in the way?"

"No," she said. "We have governesses and tutors and send them to boarding school."

"O. K.," I said. "But it's a strain on the old man's pocketbook, just the same."

"Chuck, will you ever talk like that? Chuck, this is when we're rich." Then suddenly, she looked sad. "Oh, Chuck, do you suppose we ever will?" she said.

"Why, sure," I said.

"I wouldn't mind if it was only a dump," she said. "I could cook for you. I keep asking Hilda how she makes things."

I felt awfully funny. I felt as if I were going to cry.

"We'll do it," I said. "Don't you worry."

"Oh, Chuck, you're a comfort," she said.

I held her for a while. It was like holding something awfully precious. It wasn't mushy or that way. I know what that's like too.

"It takes so long to get old," she said. "I wish I could grow up to-morrow. I wish we both could."

"Don't you worry," I said. "It's going to be all right."

We didn't say much, going back in the car, but we were happy enough. I thought we passed Miss Eagles at the turn. That worried me a little because of the driving license. But, after all, Mrs. Sharon had said we could take the car.

We wanted to go back again, after that, but it was too far to walk and that was the only time we had the car. Mrs. Sharon was awfully nice about it but she said, thinking it over, maybe we'd better wait till I got a license. Well, Father didn't want me to get one till I was seventeen but I thought he might come around. I didn't want to do anything that would get Helen in a jam with her family. That shows how careful I was of her. Or thought I was.

All the same, we decided we'd do something to celebrate if the team won the St. Matthew's game. We thought it would be fun if we could get a steak and cook supper out somewhere—something like that. Of course we could have done it easily enough with a gang, but we didn't want a gang. We wanted to be alone together, the way we'd been at the house. That was all we wanted. I don't see what's wrong about that. We even took home the paper plates, so as not to litter things up.

Boy, that was a game! We beat them 36-34 and it took an extra period and I thought it would never end. That two-goal lead they had looked as big as the Rocky Mountains all the first half. And they gave me the full school cheer with nine Peters when we tied them up. You don't forget things like that.

Afterwards, Mr. Grant had a kind of spread for the team at his house and a lot of people came in. Kerry had driven down from State to see the game and that made me feel pretty swell. And what made me feel better yet was his taking me aside and saying, "Listen, kid, I don't want you to get the swelled head, but you did a good job. Well, just remember this. Don't let anybody kid you out of going to State. You'll like it up there." And Mr. Grant heard him and laughed and said, "Well, Peters, I'm not proselytizing. But your brother might think about some of the Eastern colleges." It was all like the kind of dream you have when you can do anything. It was wonderful.

Only Helen wasn't there because the only girls were older girls. I'd seen her for a minute, right after the game, and she was fine, but it was only a minute. I wanted to tell her about that big St. Matthew's forward and—oh, everything. Well, you like to talk things over with your girl.

Father and Mother were swell but they had to go on to some big shindy at the country club. And Kerry was going there with Sheila Coe. But Mr. Grant said he'd run me back to the house in his car and he did. He's a great guy. He made jokes about my being the infant phenomenon of basketball, and they were good jokes too. I didn't mind them. But, all the same, when I'd said good night to him and gone into the house, I felt sort of let down.

I knew I'd be tired the next day but I didn't feel sleepy yet. I was too excited. I wanted to talk to somebody. I wandered around downstairs and wondered if Ida was still up. Well, she wasn't, but she'd left half a chocolate cake, covered over, on the kitchen table, and a note on top of it, "Congratulations to Mister Charles Peters." Well, that was awfully nice of her and I ate some. Then I turned the radio on and got the time signal—eleven—and some snappy music. But still I didn't feel like hitting the hay.

So I thought I'd call up Helen and then I thought—probably she's asleep and Hilda or Mrs. Sharon will answer the phone and be sore. And then I thought—well, anyhow, I could go over and walk around the block and look at her house. I'd get some fresh air out of it, anyway, and it would be a little like seeing her.

So I did—and it was a swell night—cool and a lot of stars—and I felt like a king, walking over. All the lower part of the Sharon house was dark but a window upstairs was lit. I knew it was her window. I went around back of the driveway and whistled once—the whistle we made up. I never expected her to hear.

But she did, and there she was at the window, smiling. She made motions that she'd come down to the side door.

Honestly, it took my breath away when I saw her. She had on a kind of yellow thing over her night clothes and she looked so pretty. Her feet were so pretty in those slippers. You almost expected her to be carrying one of those animals that kids like—she looked young enough. I know I oughtn't to have gone into the house. But we didn't think anything about it—we were just glad to see each other. We hadn't had any sort of chance to talk over the game.

We sat in front of the fire in the living room and she went out to the kitchen and got us cookies and milk. I wasn't really hungry, but it was like that time at the house, eating with her. Mr. and Mrs. Sharon were at the country club, too, so we weren't disturbing them or anything. We turned off the lights because there was plenty of light from the fire and Mr. Sharon's one of those people who can't stand having extra lights burning. Dad's that way about saving string.

It was quiet and lovely and the firelight made shadows on the ceiling. We talked a lot and then we just sat, each of us knowing the other was there. And the room got quieter and quieter and I'd told her about the game and I didn't feel excited or jumpy any more—just rested and happy. And then I knew by her breathing that she was asleep and I put my arm around her for just a minute. Because it was wonderful to hear that quiet breathing and know it was hers. I was going to wake her in a minute. I didn't realize how tired I was myself.

And then we were back in that house in the country and it was our home and we ought to have been happy. But something was wrong because there still wasn't any glass in the windows and a wind kept blowing through them and we tried to shut the doors but they wouldn't shut. It drove Helen distracted and we were both running through the house, trying to shut the doors, and we were cold and afraid. Then the sun rose outside the windows, burning and yellow and so big it covered the sky. And with the sun was a horrible, weeping voice. It was Mrs. Sharon's saying, "Oh, my God, oh my God."

I didn't know what had happened, for a minute, when I woke. And then I did and it was awful. Mrs. Sharon was saying "Oh, Helen—I trusted you . . ." and looking as if she were going to faint. And Mr. Sharon looked at her for a minute and his face was horrible and he said, "Bred in the bone," and she looked as if he'd hit her. Then he said to Helen—

I don't want to think of what they said. I don't want to think of any of the things they said. Mr. Sharon is a bad man. And she is a bad woman, even if she is Helen's mother. All the same, I could stand the things he said better than hers.

I don't want to think of any of it. And it is all spoiled now. Everything is spoiled. Miss Eagles saw us going to that house in the country and she said horrible things. They made Helen sick and she hasn't been back at school. There isn't any way I can see her. And if I could, it would be spoiled. We'd be thinking about the things they said.

I don't know how many of the people know, at school. But Tot Pickens passed me a note. And, that afternoon, I caught him behind his house. I'd have broken his nose if they hadn't pulled me off. I meant to. Mother cried when she heard about it and Dad took me into his room and talked to me. He said you can't lick the whole town. But I will anybody like Tot Pickens. Dad and Mother have been all right. But they say things about Helen and that's almost worse. They're for me because I'm their son. But they don't understand.

I thought I could talk to Kerry but I can't. He was nice but he looked at me such a funny way. I don't know—sort of impressed. It wasn't the way I wanted him to look. But he's been decent. He comes down almost every weekend and we play catch in the yard.

You see, I just go to school and back now. They want me to go with the gang, the way I did, but I can't do that. Not after Tot. Of course my marks are a lot better because I've got more time to study now. But it's lucky I haven't got Miss Eagles though Dad made her apologize. I couldn't recite to her.

I think Mr. Grant knows because he asked me to his house once and we had a conversation. Not about that, though I was terribly afraid he would. He showed me a lot of his old college things and the gold football he wears on his watch chain. He's got a lot of interesting things.

Then we got talking, somehow, about history and things like that and how times had changed. Why, there were kings and queens who got married younger than Helen and me. Only now we lived longer and had a lot more to learn. So it couldn't happen now. "It's civilization," he said. "And all civilization's against nature. But I suppose we've got to have it. Only sometimes it isn't easy." Well somehow or other, that made me feel less lonely. Before that I'd been feeling that I was the only person on earth who'd ever felt that way.

I'm going to Colorado, this summer, to a ranch, and next year, I'll go East to school. Mr. Grant says he thinks I can make the basketball team, if I work hard enough, though it isn't as big a game in the East as it is with us. Well, I'd like to show them something. It would be some satisfaction. He says not to be too fresh at first, but I won't be that.

It's a boys' school and there aren't even women teachers. And, maybe, afterwards, I could be a professional basketball player or something, where you don't have to see women at all. Kerry says I'll get over that; but I won't. They all sound like Mrs. Sharon to me now, when they laugh.

They're going to send Helen to a convent—I found out that. Maybe they'll let me see her before she goes. But, if we do, it will be all wrong and in front of people and everybody pretending. I sort of wish they don't—though I want to, terribly. When her mother took her upstairs that night—she wasn't the same Helen. She looked at me as if she was afraid of me. And no matter what they do for us now, they can't fix that.

The Three Fates

They said they were women, in the old days—and perhaps they were right about it. Not always right, of course, for Fate may be anything from an earthquake to a pebble you kick out of your path. But, at the moment, I am not thinking of that sort of accident—the missed train that would have carried you to glory, the road untaken that might have led you to a hangman's rope. I am thinking of the sort of people who are fate to others—and of my friend, John Tenterden. Because what happened to him began to happen at sixteen. And it certainly wasn't at his own volition. He didn't even fall in love—he was fallen in love with. And yet that was the first of the things that changed his life.

A quietish, dark-haired boy with a thin, pleasant face—up till then, he had jogged along the normal paths of adolescence in an average American suburb without particularly bothering himself as to the whys and wherefores of existence. His father was one of the suburb's four doctors, with a good, busy practice; his mother, the daughter of an economics professor at Cornell. They were vigorous, hard-working people with a great deal of common sense, and the five children—John was the third one—had an excellent time of it in the big wooden house with the untidy foundation-planting in the respectable though not very fashionable section of town where they lived.

It was the sort of family that believes in fresh air and cold baths and family jests and councils—they were all rather good at games and practical jokes, and a stranger in their midst was instantly made at home. That is to say, if he or she were "their sort"—if not, the Tenterdens agreed in private that the stranger was a stick or a queer duck, but redoubled their attentions, politely, nevertheless. If you looked at all old or frail, you were practically certain of having a knobby cushion put at your back by a hard-breathing young Tenterden and getting a coddled egg for breakfast whether you liked it or not. The anemic were given iron-tonic, the sturdy exercised, the despairing diverted and heartened by humorous stories in dialect and a common-sense philanthropy. It was a bracing atmosphere, and most people enjoyed it—the Tenterden house was popular, especially among the young. You could make as much noise as you pleased, for nobody minded noise there—there was always a screen door slamming somewhere, and a child or children running in, hot-faced, from a game, for a bath or a meal or a spare tennis-racket or a bandage.

Proverbially, in such a house the mistress is pale, overwrought and given to sick headaches—but Mrs. Tenterden was a wiry, brown-faced woman, much in demand for every sort of community activity from mixed doubles to charity-drives. She looked a little like an intelligent horse, just as Dr. Tenterden reminded you somewhat of a trusty, large-pawed dog—the kind of dog you forgive for barking because it does so with such a reasonable air. The combination was agreeable in the children—they inherited their father's fresh color and their mother's deep, equine eyes. The girls, indeed, might have been remarkably handsome, if they had ever taken the trouble—but taking that particular trouble is an art like any other. The Tenterdens were not very fond of art—they were well-informed and doughty at pencil-and-paper games, but art itself, art unaccredited by teachers and public opinion, they considered, quite sensibly, a little queer.

I was a nervous, rather sickly child, given to attacks of asthma, and I stayed for two weeks in their house, once, when my parents were away. It was very kind of them to do it—Dr. Tenterden was our family doctor, to be sure, but they took me in out of pure generosity. "We'll soon get the roses in his cheeks!" said Dr. Tenterden. The first few days of my stay, I enjoyed myself hugely—I thought I had never seen people who led so fine and tumultuous a life. After that, the glamor faded, insensibly but definitely. I do not think it was envy on my part for not being able to join in their games except feebly—after all, like most active people, they liked an audience and I was a most willing one. I missed something very much and did not know what it was.

I think now that they were two things: privacy and thought. There was no privacy at all in the Tenterden household; they were never happier than when all collected in one room doing different things at once; even in the bathroom, with the door locked, you somehow felt that the urge and surge of Tenterden life was waiting in the corridor and, at any moment, might rap brisk knuckles on the door. As for thought, that is probably a question of definition. The children always got excellent marks at school, and Mrs. Tenterden, as I say, was the daughter of an economics professor. No doubt Dr. Tenterden thought about his cases—I know he worked like a bulldog to keep certain people alive. But thought, genuine thought, demands a certain amount of quiet for its flowering—and quiet was the last thing the Tenterdens, as a family, liked or enjoyed. Perhaps I am exaggerating the effect of a sudden dip into the life of a large family on the temperament of a rather thin-skinned only child. But I know that when I returned to my own room, in my own house, at the end of the visit, I sank into its quiet as one sinks into a bed.

Such was the environment in which John Tenterden grew up. As I say, he was quietish, for a Tenterden, but otherwise unremarkable. He had the darkest eyes in the family and the sort of olive skin that must have harked back to some distant Latin ancestor. That made him rather an ugly baby, and once you started as anything in the annals of the Tenterdens, that thing you remained. Gwen was the beauty and Richard the scholar, and so it would always be. They were kindly and seldom twitted John about his looks, even when he became distinctly handsome—they simply saw no change.

As the third child, younger than Richard and Gwen but quite a bit older than Bob and Sally, he filled an inconspicuous though definite place in the family system. They would have missed and mourned him if he had been drowned in a pond, but he was neither a senior to be consulted, nor a junior to be disciplined and petted; he was merely John. It was also agreed in the family that John was rather lazy; perhaps because he had a naturally good temper and no apparent specialties, except a butterfly-collection. This showed a scientific interest, and the Tenterdens approved of it, though it was hard to keep any collection undamaged in the swoop of Tenterden existence. However, when John's specimens were accidentally destroyed, he never seemed to mind particularly. He merely collected others. As for what he was to become, Richard would naturally succeed to the practice, but John might very well be a doctor, too, unless he chose to be an economics professor like his grandfather. There was nothing queer about him, and Richard had hopes of him as a baseball-player, though, being an elder brother, he tried not to puff John up.

When I was staying with them, John Tenterden showed me his butterflies, at his mother's request. People wandered in and out as he did so, and, being three years younger, I asked quite a few silly questions. They did not seem to bother John. He showed me his butterflies politely but without apparent enthusiasm, though his eyes grew darker as he did so. They were arranged with scrupulous neatness; many were beautiful, especially the moths. I said, "That's a peachy one!" several times—each time he gave me a quick glance. I had already got into trouble with the use of the word "lovely" at the

Tenterdens and was trying to avoid it—they considered it slightly effeminate, except when applied to a sunset or a dish.

Finally he showed me an enormous silvery creature, so beautifully mounted that it still seemed alive, in spite of the pin. The great pale wings were full spread, it seemed as if it had settled on the cardboard for a moment, and in another it would rise and fly to the lamp. I was a child but a sensitive one. I said, in a voice of sincere conviction, "Oh, that's lovely, John!"

"Lunar moth—*neostera pallida*," he said, rather severely. "It's fairly common. Except for the size, of course—it's a fairly big one. They're quite easy to find." But I saw his finger go out to touch the spread wing very gently, and then draw back without touching it. He put it away, with careful carelessness.

"Come out, some time, and you can help me catch them," he said. "It's quite easy."

"Are they all as lovely as that?" I said, imprudently, for the second time.

He gave me an odd look. "Sure—they're all like that," he said. "I mean the lunar ones. They must have fun, flying at night, though they're silly about lamps. I like watching them, but you have to collect, of course. It's scientific."

His eyes altered, as Gwen and Richard came bounding into the room.

"Showing off your bugs, you old bug-hunter!" said Richard, heartily. "Well, get it over with—the Collison twins just came and we're going to 'nitiate them into the Ugliwugs. You can come too, if you like," he said graciously to me. "It's a terrible 'nitiation—we didn't give you half of it because Mother said you'd be scared and yell all night."

"All right," said John obediently. Something had clicked shut in his face, and he was all Tenterden. At the initiation, which I watched with sycophantic dread, it was he who thought of the glue. He didn't repeat the invitation to go moth-hunting, and I was too shy to ask him. Indeed, he rather bullied me after that—which I felt, obscurely, was a pity because I wanted to admire him. When my parents asked me, later, which one of the Tenterdens I had liked best, I said Robert, who was nearest my age. So they had Robert over to play with me several times, though it never worked very well.

As a matter of fact, I detested Robert—he was younger than I but much stronger and liked to hit me in the wind. I used to hope, secretly, that John would come sometime instead of Robert. I could see him coming up the steps with the lunar moth in his hand. But it never happened, of course. Then we moved into the city. I began to go to school regularly; and suburb and Tenterdens passed out of my mind.

So I wasn't there when the Fates began their game with John Tenterden, six years later. But nothing had changed very much in the Tenterden household. Dr. Tenterden was a trifle grayer and the youngest children made most of the basic noise. But Sunday night supper was even more of a bracing hullabaloo than ever, especially when Richard and Gwen were home from their respective colleges with their friends. They had many friends, all the right, healthy, fun-loving sort, yet serious-minded—young earnest giants who hit the line hard for their college and strapping girls who were as little afraid of a ten-mile hike as they were of a hard exam in Chemistry. Gwen was tentatively engaged to one of the young men, but on the most aseptic basis; their caresses seemed to consist in each pushing the other a good deal when they were in the same games. As for Richard, he knew that he could not honorably marry for at least five years, so he was not engaged. He did exercises with Indian clubs instead.

Now and then, John made harmless sport for the visitors—sixteen is always good sport to youth in the twenties. But not often, for, as they generally agreed, he was a good kid—well-liked at school and center-fielder on the baseball team. And yet, oddly enough, he had no intimates, or, if he did, he did not bring them home. Perhaps it was not so odd. If he had brought them home, he would have had no place to put them—the house was always so full. The Tenterdens noticed, vaguely, that when he came in, he did not bring a crowd whooping behind him. But life moved too fast for such details. And then the impossible thing happened—the first of the things that changed John Tenterden's life.

There was a girl named Mona Gregg in the class below him at school; a sallow, straight-haired, narrow-eyed little girl with very red lips and a nervous habit of chewing the ends of her pencils. Her father had been an unsuccessful vaudeville actor before he got a job as night desk-clerk at the Myrick Hotel, and she had many of the faults of the theatre and hotel child, the sharpness, the precocity, the pertness. Her classmates considered her queer and something of a sneak, though they envied her familiarity with elevators, railroad trains and different kinds of ice cream. And she fell in love with John Tenterden as devastatingly as if she were eighteen and he twenty-five.

At first, of course, he didn't notice it. Two years' difference in age is a yawning gulf, in the 'teens. Then he began to notice that he was always meeting her in the corridors of the school. He would say

"Hello, Mona"; she would say "Hello, John," and stare at him. He was popular enough, as I say, to be used to certain occasional looks of admiration. But this was different, from the first. He found himself noticing Mona more than he wanted to, without either interest or pleasure. She wore ugly plaid dresses in the winter—the collars were not quite clean. She did not try to fall into conversation with him, but somehow, he felt that she wanted to, and it affected him unpleasantly. Pretty soon he found that he breathed easier when he was in a classroom that she could not enter. But sometimes the grades were together in the same room. Then he would look up from his book and feel her eyes upon him—if he turned, he would see her, chewing her pencil with sharp small teeth and nervously looking away.

Such things are ridiculous, of course. I have often considered how ridiculous they are. Other times, other manners, and some of the Renaissance great ladies would still be in the schoolroom today. But there is no doubt as to the effect upon John Tenterden. He felt both furious and humiliated, and yet there was nothing he could do. You can kick an unattractive dog that fawns upon you—it is harder to kick a girl of fifteen, when you have been politely brought up. John Tenterden discovered that he was meeting Mona outside the school, in streets where she had no normal orbit. They would pass, he would say "Hello" politely, and she would meekly watch him depart. It got so that he went by the Myrick Hotel on the other side of the street, or kept away from it entirely. The look of the dingy entrance with its faded canopy reminded him inevitably of Mona, with her sallow face and red lips.

There was no one he could turn to for aid—for, if a grown man is a figure of ridicule in such circumstances, how much more so a growing boy. Once, she hung about in front of the Tenterden house for an hour and a half—fortunately, at a time when everyone else was out of it—and John, reverting to barbarism, had serious thoughts of peppering her with an air-gun from a window. But the Tenterden children had been taught how to behave with guns. Finally, when his patience was exhausted, she went away. Oh yes, it was very funny. It was not so funny, too.

It was a bad winter for colds and influenza, and Mona Gregg had always been a sniffling little girl. Nowadays, the people who dabble in amateur psychiatry might say that she developed pneumonia as a gesture of unrequited love. We were not so complicated, then. John Tenterden, when he heard that she was ill, had the entirely natural and boyish wish that she would die. But, unfortunately, he was too old to wish it without prickings of conscience. As the case went up and down—Dr. Tenterden always talked about his cases to his family in his bluff, hearty way—the stings of John Tenterden's conscience became acute. Only once or twice he dared ask a direct question; that would have shown too much interest. But, by all the circuitous means known to adolescence, he tried to keep up with the progress of Mona's illness.

Sometimes it was very easy—his father would say, without provocation, at breakfast, "Well, the little Gregg girl's coming along nicely." Or, "How I hate cases in hotels! That Gregg child would have a fifty per cent better chance in the hospital if we could only move her." In either case, John's heart would give a jump of relief. He made a pact with his conscience—if he heard about Mona before he went to school, he would not have to worry again till after dinner. But once, at the height of the influenza epidemic, he did not hear for almost two days, and his agony became intense.

I say "agony" with justification. By that time he had come to believe, you see, that if he could honestly wish for Mona's recovery, she would get well. And yet, if she did get well, he looked forward, with the bleak and limited gaze of boyhood, to a future perpetually haunted by Mona. Also, though the Tenterdens were hardly a prayerful family, he had heard, in the breezy Sunday school they all attended ("Doesn't do the children any harm to get a bit of religion") that God is not deceived by false prayers. It is the letter that killeth and the spirit that maketh alive. Suppose he prayed, and God knew he didn't mean it, and Mona died instead, just to show him. An abnormal problem? Look back in your own childhood and see what you see.

His life split in two. It says a good deal for his character that, at school and at home, he still made a fair show of being John Tenterden. But, within him, the struggle increased. School ceased to be a refuge—he remembered that when Pudge Perkins died, they had announced it at a special assembly just after noon recess. So now, when each period ended, he waited tensely—and, when work was resumed, he felt little relief. It hadn't happened this time but it might next.

One morning, he gathered from his father that the crisis of Mona's illness was at hand. The knowledge weighed on him, horribly, all day. The Tenterdens were not Catholics but, that evening, after supper, he slipped away to the Catholic church in the poorer part of the town. He felt shy and ill at ease in the district beyond the tracks—the small stores, still indecorously open, had a different air to them, and people wheeled perambulators, fought, lounged and gossiped along the sidewalks. A couple of boys jeered at him and he carefully paid no attention—no Tenterden could, with honor, decline a fight, but these were not normal conditions. When he finally got to the church, he walked around the block twice before he was able to go in.

It was an ugly church with a garish altar and puttyish stations of the Cross, but to John Tenterden there was something foreign, mysterious, and powerful in its dimness and strangeness. He could not approve of it, but it was obviously strong magic. He tried to remember what little Catholic boys had said about their religion. You had masses said and burned candles. He looked around for candles, but, to his horror, could not see any. Then he saw, in front of a plaster statue, what seemed like a lot of small night lights, each in a red glass. They were not his idea of candles, but they must do. He watched till he saw a woman light one to be quite sure.

Then he went over, himself. There was a money-box near the statue—yes, you paid for the candles, of course. Here and there, about the church, there were grown people, praying—the sight made him less shy and deepened his sense of magic. He lit a night light in front of the statue and sank on the prie-dieu before it, repeating, in a whisper, "Oh God, spare the life of Mona Gregg—don't let her die." After he had said this a sufficient number of times, he looked timidly at the light. It was still burning, and he felt better.

He then went to the next statue and repeated the process. Fortunately, he had money enough for all the statues. At first, he did not notice their names, then, as he began to feel more at home, he became more curious. He even thought for a moment of omitting St. Patrick—Mona Gregg had once called a classmate a dumb mick—then superstitiously decided that that would break the charm. When he had finished his round, he felt intensely relieved for the first time in many days. Even if the prayers were unacceptable, there were still the candles. The thing had been done professionally, and Mona Gregg must live.

He even felt a little proud of himself for having thought of the Catholic church—neither Richard nor Gwen would have thought of it. As he walked home through the crowded streets, past the flaringly lighted shops, they seemed no longer alien and disreputable but normal and friendly. Mona Gregg had been in a killing-bottle, like a ragged, sickly moth, but now she was going to get out.

So certain did he feel of the future that next morning he did not even bother to waylay his father at breakfast. He set out for school feeling oddly light-headed with relief—he had slept heavily and hotly. It might be a headache coming on—he had them, now and then, though he had never spoken of them to his family. By the middle of the morning, there was a band around his temples and a dryness in his throat, but he hardly noticed them. He was too busy tasting the exquisite pleasure of not having been a murderer, of not having killed Mona Gregg.

Everything seemed bright and vivid and in a high key. When recess came, he played basketball fiercely and swiftly, in spite of the headache. After recess, they rang the bells for a special assembly. John had been a monitor for years—he found himself marching his file in. After a pause, the Principal rose and the room hushed. The younger children rustled and squeaked—special assemblies were always exciting—the older ones looked serious. The Principal cleared his throat. He had not called them together just to chat with them. He had an important announcement to make—a saddening one—

At this point, there was an unusual noise in the room—a sharp, frightening crack that sounded like a pistol-shot in the stillness. It was John Tenterden's forehead, hitting the wood of the desk in front of him. He had fainted.

Dr. Tenterden felt a little irritated and self-conscious that he had not diagnosed the influenza before—as he would tell you, he rather fancied himself as a diagnostician. However, he made his family joke that evening about the shoemaker's child going barefoot, and the family laughed. He was more worried than his manner showed—for a day or two it seemed as though John were going to be seriously ill. Then the fever dropped and the case became normal. Some delirium was normal enough, too, with high fever—but it was different, when it was your own son. Dr. Tenterden was not an imaginative man. Nevertheless, at one point in the delirium, he had leaned forward and said in a steady, convincing voice, "Stop it, John! Mona Gregg is not dead. She is getting better. Do not worry about Mona Gregg."

It was an incident he tried to forget as soon as possible—he did not like to do such things. Nevertheless, he thought he had got through to the boy—and next day, the fever had begun to drop. He tried to shut out of his mind the harsh, adolescent voice, saying, "Mona Gregg's dead. I killed her," over and over from the bed. And then there was something about an announcement and the Principal. But John had not even heard the announcement the Principal was going to make—he had fainted before it was made, from all accounts— and the announcement had concerned a case of cheating in the Eighth Grade, with which John could not have been involved. Dr. Tenterden gave it up. He had heard religious old ladies swear like troopers under anesthesia—there was no use in a practical man's meddling with such things.

John's constitution was good—on the whole, he mended quickly. Still, as his father said, it had been a sharp bout—hang it all, the boy and his mother might go down to Atlantic City for a week, to the quiet hotel where Dr. Tenterden had sent a number of patients. John assented to this politely but without enthusiasm—he felt weak and depressed, as one usually does after influenza. Also, he couldn't remember if he had talked about Mona Gregg during his illness, and that worried him. But when his father remarked, in an overly casual voice, "Gregg's taking his family out to Arizona—I advised it, if possible. The child's lung is still spotty and it won't do her any harm to be in a dry climate for a year or so," he knew that he had.

John digested the information silently. His illness had set a gap between past and present—it now seemed absurd to him that he should ever have suffered so about Mona Gregg. He could not think of lighting the candles in the church without blushing. Everthing had turned out for the best, and Mona was not even coming back to school. And yet, he knew that he must see her before she left, though he did not know why.

He watched his time carefully and slipped out of the house when he was supposed to be resting. It was a raw Spring day with a biting wind, and he felt tired by the time he got to the hotel. The woman who opened the door of the small, stuffy suite looked surprised to see him—he had said "Mr. Tenterden calling" to the girl at the switchboard, and Mrs. Gregg must have expected his father. He explained, noting the resemblance to Mona as he did so—yes, Mona would pluck her eyebrows that way and wear that sort of a negligee with soiled feathers, when she grew up.

"Oh yes," said the woman, staring at him, "Mona's talked about you. She was always so interested in her little school friends—always a popular child—George," she called. A large man with tousled hair and a collarless shirt came out of the bathroom.

"George, this is the doctor's son—one of Mona's little school friends. He came to see how Mona was."

"Oh," said George, and stared at John Tenterden. "Well, your father's a good doctor. Don't know how we'll ever pay him, but he's good."

"Now, George!" said the woman. George yawned. "Sit down, Bud," he said. "Her mother'll see if Mona's awake."

John sat down on the edge of a couch that had been a bed and would be a bed again.

"We're a little crowded, here. Since Mona was sick," said George.

"Well, I sleep days, of course, so it hasn't been so bad. So you're John Tenterden. Mona's talked about you quite a lot."

He leaned forward, and his flabby face became suddenly the face of a snarling dog.

"If I thought you'd been up to anything with her," he said in a flat voice, "I'd break your damn neck. High school kid or no high school kid."

"Now, George," said the woman, coming back into the room. "Is that a nice way to talk? You can see what he's like, George. And you know what Mona's like."

"Oh, I know what Mona's like," said the man. "She's like you. She's romantic." He spoke wearily, but there was a trace of pride in his voice. "She can tell you the whole plot of a picture she's only seen once, and the way she keeps up with the film stars, sick as she is! Excuse me, Bud, I didn't mean anything."

"She's made the most beautiful album since she was sick," said the woman, proudly. "It's called 'My Friends in Movieland.' She's had a letter about it already from Mary Pickford. She told Mary how sick she was. Well, she says she'd be delighted to see you, young man."

John Tenterden got up and followed her into the other room. He had thought about Mona so much that he vaguely expected to find a different Mona, now—a remarkable one. But it was merely Mona Gregg. She was thin, she had on a red Japanese kimono, she was lying in bed, propped up with pillows. The small room smelt of sickness. On the medicine-table beside her was a sputum-cup.

"Hello, Mona," he said gruffly, extending the package he had carried in his hands till the paper had fingerprints on it. "I'm glad to hear you're better. I brought you some candy."

He exhaled heavily, having rid himself of his speech. He had meant to add, "I hope they're the kind you like," but he had forgotten at the last moment.

"Hello, John," said Mona, in a mincing voice. "It was nice of you to come. I'm not allowed to eat much candy, but thank you just the same. How's school?"

"Oh, school's all right, I guess," said John, sitting down. "I've been sick myself—influenza—so I don't know."

"Did you have to have oxygen?" said Mona. "I had to have oxygen and I guess it saved my life. It feels funny."

"No, I didn't have to have oxygen," said John. He cleared his throat. "You must have been pretty sick," he said.

"I was awfully sick," said Mona, with obvious pleasure. "I'm pretty sick still. That's why we're going to Arizona."

"Well, Arizona's a nice place to go," said John, carefully avoiding her eyes. "Your mother said you'd been making a—a scrapbook," he said.

"An album," said Mona. "I call it 'My Friends in Movieland.' It's all about the stars. I've got eleven autographed photographs already. Shall I show it to you?"

"Sure," said John. She showed it to him. It took quite a time. Mrs. Gregg went in and out. Now and then, she would look at Mona. When she did so, John averted his eyes, as from something naked. In the look there was fear and a possessive love, both undisciplined.

It took quite a time but at last it was done. John Tenterden got up. "Well, I've got to go, Mona," he said. "I probably won't see you again before I go away. But I'm glad you're better."

He stood looking at her. A curious, wrenching sob rose to his lips and died there. It surprised him very much. He was infinitely glad to be free of Mona Gregg. He was sorry and humiliated that she should love him. And yet, there was something else—a queer feeling he could never have explained to Richard or Gwen. It wasn't patronage but it was very like gratitude. He looked at Mona's thin, hungry face.

"Everybody at school's talking about you, Mona," he said. "They all wish they could go to Arizona, too. You ought to write some of us and tell us about it."

Mona's cheeks flushed with satisfaction.

"I don't suppose I'll have a chance to write ordinary letters much," she said carelessly. "With my album and everything. But I guess I could send postcards, anyway. You could pass them around the class."

"Gee, that'd be great!" said John, fervently. "Well, good-bye, Mona."

"Good-bye, John. And I hope," she said, with hauteur and from the distance of one who gets autographed photographs of stars, "that you have a good time, too."

John Tenterden had been able to slip out of his house without difficulty. Returning, he was not quite so fortunate. His brother, Richard, down for a week end, met him in the hall.

"Hello, kid," he said, "you look pretty well for a sick man. Where have you been, this windy day? Out paying a call on your girl?"

"No," said John.

"I believe he has," said Richard, with relish. "He's blushing." He laid a heavy, fraternal hand on John's shoulder. "Sometime I want to have a little talk with you, John, my boy," he said. "You're growing up, you know. And no kid brother of mine is going to make a fool of—oh, well, we won't go into that now. But that's a date."

He waited for some expression of gratitude from John. As none came, he tactfully changed the subject.

"By the way," he said, "I was looking around for my old bamboo rod, thought you might have swiped it. But there isn't any light in your closet and I'm afraid I smashed some truck of yours. Apologies, old man."

He pointed to the hall table. Upon it was a broken box and on the box a crushed lunar moth. The wings were off the body, and one wing had been torn in half.

"Tried to stick it together again but I'm not much good at that sort of thing," said Robert briskly. "Suppose we'd better throw it away—after all, a kid your age isn't interested in that sort of thing—"

"You had no business to touch it," said John, beginning to tremble.

"Hey?" said Richard.

"You had no business to touch it. It was mine. You had no business to come in my room," said John Tenterden. He paused. "You're a stupid fool," he said.

"Kid," said Richard, in a heavy voice, "you've been sick. If you hadn't been, you'd get a licking, here and now. Keep a civil tongue in your head or you'll get it anyway."

"I'm sorry, Dick," said John, in a confused voice, still staring at the moth.

"That's better," said Richard. He paused. Something glinted in his eyes. "And now, let's go back to what we were talking about," he said. "You weren't supposed to go out. Why did you go out?"

"I wanted some fresh air," said John sullenly. Richard regarded him.

"You're a bad liar, Johnno," said Richard. "A darn bad liar. I'm going to ask you once more. Why did you go out when you weren't supposed to go out?"

"And suppose I don't choose to tell you?" said John desperately, recognizing the gambit, a familiar one since childhood.

"Well, then," said Richard, judicially, "we'll have to take other measures, sick or not. Come on, Johnno, we haven't done this for a long time. But if you think I'm going to have any kid brother of mine fooling around with hotel-trash—oh, I've heard things about you, Johnno—"

He laid a hand on John's arm again. "Keep off me, you stupid fool," said John and hit him. It was a beautiful punch, well-timed. Richard went to the floor with a crash and came up raging.

It was, perhaps, fortunate for both of them that Mrs. Tenterden returned just then.

John apologized and was a very docile convalescent in Atlantic City. Nevertheless, John was changed. He had time to think many things over, in the bright sleepy air. He was not sorry for hitting Richard—Richard would never bully him again. He was not sorry, now, for having prayed in the church. There was a whole world beyond the Tenterden cosmos—a world where people died and fell in love. He had suspected its existence with his mind, before. But now, he knew.

The Blood of the Martyrs

The man who expected to be shot lay with his eyes open, staring at the upper left-hand corner of his cell. He was fairly well over his last beating, and they might come for him any time now. There was a yellow stain in the cell corner near the ceiling; he had liked it at first, then disliked it; now he was coming back to liking it again.

He could see it more clearly with his glasses on, but he only put on his glasses for special occasions now—the first thing in the morning, and when they brought the food in, and for interviews with the General. The lenses of the glasses had been cracked in a beating some months before, and it strained his eyes to wear them too long. Fortunately, in his present life he had very few occasions demanding clear vision. But, nevertheless, the accident to his glasses worried him, as it worries all near-sighted people. You put your glasses on the first thing in the morning and the world leaps into proportion; if it does not do so, something is wrong with the world.

The man did not believe greatly in symbols, but his chief nightmare, nowadays, was an endless one in which, suddenly and without warning, a large piece of glass would drop out of one of the lenses and he would grope around the cell, trying to find it. He would grope very carefully and gingerly, for hours of darkness, but the end was always the same—the small, unmistakable crunch of irreplaceable glass beneath his heel or his knee. Then he would wake up sweating, with his hands cold. This dream alternated with the one of being shot, but he found no great benefit in the change.

As he lay there, you could see that he had an intellectual head—the head of a thinker or a scholar, old and bald, with the big, domed brow. It was, as a matter of fact, a well-known head; it had often appeared in the columns of newspapers and journals, sometimes when the surrounding text was in a language Professor Malzius could not read. The body, though stooped and worn, was still a strong peasant body and capable of surviving a good deal of ill-treatment, as his captors had found out. He had fewer teeth than when he came to prison, and both the ribs and the knee had been badly set, but these were minor matters. It also occurred to him that his blood count was probably poor. However, if he could ever get out and to a first-class hospital, he was probably good for at least ten years more of work. But, of course, he would not get out. They would shoot him before that, and it would be over.

Sometimes he wished passionately that it would be over—tonight—this moment; at other times he was shaken by the mere blind fear of death. The latter he tried to treat as he would have treated an attack of malaria, knowing that it was an attack, but not always with success. He should have been able to face it better than most—he was Gregor Malzius, the scientist—but that did not always help. The fear of death persisted, even when one had noted and classified it as a purely physical reaction. When he was out of here, he would be able to write a very instructive little paper on the fear of death. He could even do it here, if he had writing materials, but there was no use asking for those. Once they had been given him and he had spent two days quite happily. But they had torn up the work and spat upon it in front of his face. It was a childish thing to do, but it discouraged a man from working.

It seemed odd that he had never seen anybody shot, but he never had. During the war, his reputation and his bad eyesight had exempted him from active service. He had been bombed a couple of times when his reserve battalion was guarding the railway bridge, but that was quite different. You were not tied to a stake, and the airplanes were not trying to kill you as an individual. He knew the place where it was done here, of course. But prisoners did not see the executions, they merely heard, if the wind was from the right quarter.

He had tried again and again to visualize how it would be, but it always kept mixing with an old steel engraving he had seen in boyhood—the execution of William Walker, the American filibuster, in Honduras. William Walker was a small man with a white semi-Napoleonic face. He was standing, very correctly dressed, in front of an open grave, and before him a ragged line of picturesque natives were raising their muskets. When he was shot he would instantly and tidily fall into the grave, like a man dropping through a trap door; as a boy, the extreme neatness of the arrangement had greatly impressed Gregor Malzius. Behind the wall there were palm trees, and, somewhere off to the right, blue and warm, the Caribbean Sea. It would not be like that at all, for his own execution; and yet, whenever he thought of it, he thought of it as being like that.

Well, it was his own fault. He could have accepted the new regime; some respectable people had done that. He could have fled the country; many honorable people had. A scientist should be concerned with the eternal, not with transient political phenomena; and a scientist should be able to live anywhere. But thirty years at the university were thirty years, and, after all, he was Malzius, one of the first biochemists in the world. To the last, he had not believed that they would touch him. Well, he had been wrong about that.

The truth, of course, was the truth. One taught it or one did not teach it. If one did not teach it, it hardly mattered what one did. But he had no quarrel with any established government; he was willing to run up a flag every Tuesday, as long as they let him alone. Most people were fools, and one government was as good as another for them—it had taken them twenty years to accept his theory of cell mutation. Now, if he'd been like his friend Bonnard—a fellow who signed protests, attended meetings for the cause of world peace, and generally played the fool in public—they'd have had some reason to complain. An excellent man in his field, Bonnard—none better—but outside of it, how deplorably like an actor, with his short gray beard, his pink cheeks and his impulsive enthusiasm! Any government could put a fellow like Bonnard in prison—though it would be an injury to science and, therefore, wrong. For that matter, he thought grimly, Bonnard would enjoy being a martyr. He'd walk gracefully to the execution post with a begged cigarette in his mouth, and some theatrical last quip. But Bonnard was safe in his own land—doubtless writing heated and generous articles on The Case of Professor Malzius—and he, Malzius, was the man who was going to be shot. He would like a cigarette, too, on his way to execution; he had not smoked in five months. But he certainly didn't intend to ask for one, and they wouldn't think of offering him any. That was the difference between him and Bonnard.

His mind went back with longing to the stuffy laboratory and stuffier lecture hall at the university; his feet yearned for the worn steps he had climbed ten thousand times, and his eyes for the long steady look through the truthful lens into worlds too tiny for the unaided eye. They had called him "The Bear" and "Old Prickly," but they had fought to work under him, the best of the young men. They said he would explain the Last Judgment in terms of cellular phenomena, but they had crowded to his lectures. It was Williams, the Englishman, who had made up the legend that he carried a chocolate éclair and a set of improper post cards in his battered brief case. Quite untrue, of course—chocolate always made him ill, and he had never looked at an improper post card in his life. And Williams would never know that he knew the legend, too; for Williams had been killed long ago in the war. For a moment, Professor Malzius felt blind hate at the thought of an excellent scientific machine like

Williams being smashed in a war. But blind hate was an improper emotion for a scientist, and he put it aside.

He smiled grimly again; they hadn't been able to break up his classes—lucky he was The Bear! He'd seen one colleague hooted from his desk by a band of determined young hoodlums—too bad, but if a man couldn't keep order in his own classroom, he'd better get out. They'd wrecked his own laboratory, but not while he was there.

It was so senseless, so silly. "In God's name," he said reasonably to no one, "what sort of conspirator do you think I would make? A man of my age and habits! I am interested in cellular phenomena!" And yet they were beating him because he would not tell about the boys. As if he had even paid attention to half the nonsense! There were certain passwords and greetings—a bar of music you whistled, entering a restaurant; the address of a firm that specialized, ostensibly, in vacuum cleaners. But they were not his own property. They belonged to the young men who had trusted The Bear. He did not know what half of them meant, and the one time he had gone to a meeting, he had felt like a fool. For they were fools and childish—playing the childish games of conspiracy that people like Bonnard enjoyed. Could they even make a better world than the present? He doubted it extremely. And yet, he could not betray them; they had come to him, looking over their shoulders, with darkness in their eyes.

A horrible, an appalling thing—to be trusted. He had no wish to be a guide and counselor of young men. He wanted to do his work. Suppose they were poor and ragged and oppressed; he had been a peasant himself, he had eaten black bread. It was by his own efforts that he was Professor Malzius. He did not wish the confidences of boys like Gregopolous and the others—for, after all, what was Gregopolous? An excellent and untiring laboratory assistant—and a laboratory assistant he would remain to the end of his days. He had pattered about the laboratory like a fox terrier, with a fox terrier's quick bright eyes. Like a devoted dog, he had made a god of Professor Malzius. "I don't want your problems, man. I don't want to know what you are doing outside the laboratory." But Gregopolous had brought his problems and his terrible trust none the less, humbly and proudly, like a fox terrier with a bone. After that—well, what was a man to do?

He hoped they would get it over with, and quickly. The world should be like a chemical formula, full of reason and logic. Instead, there were all these young men, and their eyes. They conspired, hopelessly and childishly, for what they called freedom against the new regime. They wore no overcoats in winter and were often hunted and killed. Even if they did not conspire, they had miserable little love affairs and ate the wrong food—yes, even before, at the university, they had been the same. Why the devil would they not accept? Then they could do their work. Of course, a great many of them would not be allowed to accept—they had the wrong ideas or the wrong politics—but then they could run away. If Malzius, at twenty, had had to run from his country, he would still have been a scientist. To talk of a free world was a delusion; men were not free in the world. Those who wished got a space of time to get their work done. That was all. And yet, he had not accepted—he did not know why.

Now he heard the sound of steps along the corridor. His body began to quiver and the places where he had been beaten hurt him. He noted it as an interesting reflex. Sometimes they merely flashed the light in the cell and passed by. On the other hand, it might be death. It was a hard question to decide.

The lock creaked, the door opened. "Get up, Malzius!" said the hard, bright voice of the guard. Gregor Malzius got up, a little stiffly, but quickly.

"Put on your glasses, you old fool!" said the guard, with a laugh. "You are going to the General."

Professor Malzius found the stone floors of the corridor uneven, though he knew them well enough. Once or twice the guard struck him, lightly and without malice, as one strikes an old horse with a whip. The blows were familiar and did not register on Professor Malzius' consciousness; he merely felt proud of not stumbling. He was apt to stumble; once he had hurt his knee.

He noticed, it seemed to him, an unusual tenseness and officiousness about his guard. Once, even, in a brightly lighted corridor the guard moved to strike him, but refrained. However, that, too, happened occasionally, with one guard or another, and Professor Malzius merely noted the fact. It was a small fact, but an important one in the economy in which he lived.

But there could be no doubt that something unusual was going on in the castle. There were more guards than usual, many of them strangers. He tried to think, carefully, as he walked, if it could be one of the new national holidays. It was hard to keep track of them all. The General might be in a good humor. Then they would merely have a cat-and-mouse conversation for half an hour and nothing really bad would happen. Once, even, there had been a cigar. Professor Malzius, the scientist, licked his lips at the thought.

Now he was being turned over to a squad of other guards, with salutings. This was really unusual; Professor Malzius bit his mouth, inconspicuously. He had the poignant distrust of a monk or an old prisoner at any break in routine. Old prisoners are your true conservatives; they only demand that the order around them remains exactly the same.

It alarmed him as well that the new guards did not laugh at him. New guards almost always laughed when they saw him for the first time. He was used to the laughter and missed it—his throat felt dry. He would have liked, just once, to eat at the university restaurant before he died. It was bad food, ill cooked and starchy, food good enough for poor students and professors, but he would have liked to be there, in the big smoky room that smelt of copper boilers and cabbage, with a small cup of bitter coffee before him and a cheap cigarette. He did not ask for his dog or his notebooks, the old photographs in his bedroom, his incomplete experiments or his freedom. Just to lunch once more at the university restaurant and have people point out The Bear. It seemed a small thing to ask, but of course it was quite impossible.

"Halt!" said a voice, and he halted. There were, for the third time, salutings. Then the door of the General's office opened and he was told to go in.

He stood, just inside the door, in the posture of attention, as he had been taught. The crack in the left lens of his glasses made a crack across the room, and his eyes were paining him already, but he paid no attention to that. There was the familiar figure of the General, with his air of a well-fed and extremely healthy tomcat, and there was another man, seated at the General's desk. He could not see the other man very well—the crack made him bulge and waver—but he did not like his being there.

"Well, professor," said the General, in an easy, purring voice.

Malzius' entire body jerked. He had made a fearful, an unpardonable omission. He must remedy it at once. "Long live the state," he shouted in a loud thick voice, and saluted. He knew, bitterly, that his salute was ridiculous and that he looked ridiculous, making it. But perhaps the General would laugh—he had done so before. Then everything would be all right, for it was not quite as easy to beat a man after you had laughed at him.

The General did not laugh. He made a half turn instead, toward the man at the desk. The gesture said, "You see, he is well trained." It was the gesture of a man of the world, accustomed to deal with unruly peasants and animals—the gesture of a man fitted to be General.

The man at the desk paid no attention to the General's gesture. He lifted his head, and Malzius saw him more clearly and with complete unbelief. It was not a man but a picture come alive. Professor Malzius had seen the picture a hundred times; they had made him salute and take off his hat in front of it, when he had had a hat. Indeed, the picture had presided over his beatings. The man himself was a little smaller, but the picture was a good picture. There were many dictators in the world, and this was one type. The face was white, beaky and semi-Napoleonic; the lean, military body sat squarely in its chair. The eyes dominated the face, and the mouth was rigid. I remember also a hypnotist, and a woman Charcot showed me, at his clinic in Paris, thought Professor Malzius. But there is also, obviously, an endocrine unbalance. Then his thoughts stopped.

"Tell the man to come closer," said the man at the desk. "Can he hear me? Is he deaf?"

"No, Your Excellency," said the General, with enormous, purring respect. "But he is a little old, though perfectly healthy. . . . Are you not, Professor Malzius?"

"Yes, I am perfectly healthy. I am very well treated here," said Professor Malzius, in his loud thick voice. They were not going to catch him with traps like that, not even by dressing up somebody as the Dictator. He fixed his eyes on the big old-fashioned inkwell on the General's desk—that, at least, was perfectly sane.

"Come closer," said the man at the desk to Professor Malzius, and the latter advanced till he could almost touch the inkwell with his fingers. Then he stopped with a jerk, hoping he had done right. The movement removed the man at the desk from the crack in his lenses, and Professor Malzius knew suddenly that it was true. This was, indeed, the Dictator, this man with the rigid mouth. He began to talk.

"I have been very well treated here and the General has acted with the greatest consideration," he said. "But I am Professor Gregor Malzius—professor of biochemistry. For thirty years I have lectured at the university; I am a fellow of the Royal Society, a corresponding member of the Academy of Sciences at Berlin, at Rome, at Boston, at Paris and Stockholm. I have received the Nottingham Medal, the Lamarck Medal, the Order of St. John of Portugal and the Nobel Prize. I think my blood count is low, but I have received a great many degrees and my experiments on the migratory cells are not finished. I do not wish to complain of my treatment, but I must continue my experiments."

He stopped, like a clock that has run down, surprised to hear the sound of his own voice. He noted, in one part of his mind, that the

General had made a move to silence him, but had himself been silenced by the Dictator.

"Yes, Professor Malzius," said the man at the desk, in a harsh, toneless voice. "There has been a regrettable error." The rigid face stared at Professor Malzius. Professor Malzius stared back. He did not say anything.

"In these days," said the Dictator, his voice rising, "the nation demands the submission of every citizen. Encircled by jealous foes, our reborn land yet steps forward toward her magnificent destiny." The words continued for some time, the voice rose and fell. Professor Malzius listened respectfully; he had heard the words many times before and they had ceased to have meaning to him. He was thinking of certain cells of the body that rebel against the intricate processes of Nature and set up their own bellicose state. Doubtless they, too, have a destiny, he thought, but in medicine it is called cancer.

"Jealous and spiteful tongues in other countries have declared that it is our purpose to wipe out learning and science," concluded the Dictator. "That is not our purpose. After the cleansing, the rebirth. We mean to move forward to the greatest science in the world—our own science, based on the enduring principles of our nationhood." He ceased abruptly, his eyes fell into their dream. Very like the girl Charcot showed me in my young days, thought Professor Malzius; there was first the ebullition, then the calm.

"I was part of the cleansing? You did not mean to hurt me?" he asked timidly.

"Yes, Professor Malzius," said the General, smiling, "you were part of the cleansing. Now that is over. His Excellency has spoken."

"I do not understand," said Professor Malzius, gazing at the fixed face of the man behind the desk.

"It is very simple," said the General. He spoke in a slow careful voice, as one speaks to a deaf man or a child. "You are a distinguished man of science—you have received the Nobel Prize. That was a service to the state. You became, however, infected by the wrong political ideas. That was treachery to the state. You had, therefore, as decreed by His Excellency, to pass through a certain period for probation and rehabilitation. But that, we believe, is finished."

"You do not wish to know the names of the young men any more?" said Professor Malzius. "You do not want the addresses?"

"That is no longer of importance," said the General patiently. "There is no longer opposition. The leaders were caught and executed three weeks ago."

"There is no longer opposition," repeated Professor Malzius.

"At the trial, you were not even involved."

"I was not even involved," said Professor Malzius. "Yes."

"Now," said the General, with a look at the Dictator, "we come to the future. I will be frank—the new state is frank with its citizens."

"It is so," said the Dictator, his eyes still sunk in his dream.

"There has been—let us say—a certain agitation in foreign countries regarding Professor Malzius," said the General, his eyes still fixed on the Dictator. "That means nothing, of course. Nevertheless, your acquaintance, Professor Bonnard, and others have meddled in matters that do not concern them."

"They asked after me?" said Professor Malzius, with surprise. "It is true, my experiments were reaching a point that——"

"No foreign influence could turn us from our firm purpose," said the Dictator. "But it is our firm purpose to show our nation first in science and culture as we have already shown her first in manliness and statehood. For that reason, you are here, Professor Malzius." He smiled.

Professor Malzius stared. His cheeks began to tremble.

"I do not understand," said Professor Malzius. "You will give me my laboratory back?"

"Yes," said the Dictator, and the General nodded as one nods to a stupid child.

Professor Malzius passed a hand across his brow.

"My post at the university?" he said. "My experiments?"

"It is the purpose of our regime to offer the fullest encouragement to our loyal sons of science," said the Dictator.

"First of all," said Professor Malzius, "I must go to a hospital. My blood count is poor. But that will not take long." His voice had become impatient and his eyes glowed. "Then—my notebooks were burned, I suppose. That was silly, but we can start in again. I have a very good memory, an excellent memory. The theories are in my head, you know," and he tapped it. "I must have assistants, of course; little Gregopolous was my best one——"

"The man Gregopolous has been executed," said the General, in a stern voice. "You had best forget him."

"Oh," said Professor Malzius. "Well, then, I must have someone else. You see, these are important experiments. There must be some young men—clever ones—they cannot all be dead. I will know them." He laughed a little, nervously. "The Bear always got the pick of the crop," he said. "They used to call me The Bear, you know." He stopped and looked at them for a moment with ghastly eyes. "You are not fooling me?" he said. He burst into tears.

When he recovered he was alone in the room with the General. The General was looking at him as he himself had looked once at strange forms of life under the microscope, with neither disgust nor attraction, but with great interest.

"His Excellency forgives your unworthy suggestion," he said. "He knows you are overwrought."

"Yes," said Professor Malzius. He sobbed once and dried his glasses.

"Come, come," said the General, with a certain bluff heartiness. "We mustn't have our new president of the National Academy crying. It would look badly in the photographs."

"President of the Academy?" said Professor Malzius quickly. "Oh, no; I mustn't be that. They make speeches; they have administrative work. But I am a scientist, a teacher."

"I'm afraid you can't very well avoid it," said the General, still heartily, though he looked at Professor Malzius. "Your induction will be quite a ceremony. His Excellency himself will preside. And you will speak on the new glories of our science. It will be a magnificent answer to the petty and jealous criticisms of our neighbors. Oh, you needn't worry about the speech," he added quickly. "It will be prepared; you will only have to read it. His Excellency thinks of everything."

"Very well," said Professor Malzius; "and then may I go back to my work?"

"Oh, don't worry about that," said the General, smiling. "I'm only a simple soldier; I don't know about those things. But you'll have plenty of work."

"The more the better," said Malzius eagerly. "I still have ten good years."

He opened his mouth to smile, and a shade of dismay crossed the General's face.

"Yes," he said, as if to himself. "The teeth must be attended to. At once. And a rest, undoubtedly, before the photographs are taken. Milk. You are feeling sufficiently well, Professor Malzius?"

"I am very happy," said Professor Malzius. "I have been very well treated and I come of peasant stock."

"Good," said the General. He paused for a moment, and spoke in a more official voice.

"Of course, it is understood, Professor Malzius——" he said.

"Yes?" said Professor Malzius. "I beg your pardon. I was thinking of something else."

"It is understood, Professor Malzius," repeated the General, "that your—er—rehabilitation in the service of the state is a permanent matter. Naturally, you will be under observation, but, even so, there must be no mistake."

"I am a scientist," said Professor Malzius impatiently. "What have I to do with politics? If you wish me to take oaths of loyalty, I will take as many as you wish."

"I am glad you take that attitude," said the General, though he looked at Professor Malzius curiously. "I may say that I regret the unpleasant side of our interviews. I trust you bear no ill will."

"Why should I be angry?" said Professor Malzius. "You were told to do one thing. Now you are told to do another. That is all."

"It is not quite so simple as that," said the General rather stiffly. He looked at Professor Malzius for a third time. "And I'd have sworn you were one of the stiff-necked ones," he said. "Well, well, every man has his breaking point, I suppose. In a few moments you will receive the final commands of His Excellency. Tonight you will go to the capitol and speak over the radio. You will have no difficulty there—the speech is written. But it will put a quietus on the activities of our friend Bonnard and the question that has been raised in the British Parliament. Then a few weeks of rest by the sea and the dental work, and then, my dear president of the National Academy, you will be ready to undertake your new duties. I congratulate you and hope we shall meet often under pleasant auspices." He bowed from the waist to Malzius, the bow of a man of the world, though there was still something feline in his moustaches. Then he stood to attention, and Malzius, too, for the Dictator had come into the room.

"It is settled?" said the Dictator. "Good, Gregor Malzius, I welcome you to the service of the new state. You have cast your errors aside and are part of our destiny."

"Yes," said Professor Malzius, "I will be able to do my work now."

The Dictator frowned a little.

"You will not only be able to continue your invaluable researches," he said, "but you will also be able—and it will be part of your duty—to further our national ideals. Our reborn nation must rule the world for the world's good. There is a fire within us that is not in other stocks. Our civilization must be extended everywhere. The future wills it. It will furnish the subject of your first discourse as president of the Academy."

"But," said Professor Malzius, in a low voice, "I am not a soldier. I am a biochemist. I have no experience in these matters you speak of."

The Dictator nodded. "You are a distinguished man of science," he said. "You will prove that our women must bear soldiers, our men abandon this nonsense of republics and democracies for trust in those born to rule them. You will prove by scientific law that certain races—our race in particular—are destined to rule the world. You will prove they are destined to rule by the virtues of war, and that war is part of our heritage."

"But," said Professor Malzius, "it is not like that. I mean," he said, "one looks and watches in the laboratory. One waits for a long time. It is a long process, very long. And then, if the theory is not proved, one discards the theory. That is the way it is done. I probably do not explain it well. But I am a biochemist; I do not know how to look for the virtues of one race against another, and I can prove nothing about war, except that it kills. If I said anything else, the whole world would laugh at me."

"Not one in this nation would laugh at you," said the Dictator.

"But if they do not laugh at me when I am wrong, there is no science," said Professor Malzius, knotting his brows. He paused. "Do not misunderstand me," he said earnestly. "I have ten years of good work left; I want to get back to my laboratory. But, you see, there are the young men—if I am to teach the young men."

He paused again, seeing their faces before him. There were many. There was Williams, the Englishman, who had died in the war, and little Gregopolous with the fox-terrier eyes. There were all who had passed through his classrooms, from the stupidest to the best. They had shot little Gregopolous for treason, but that did not alter the case. From all over the world they had come—he remembered the Indian student and the Chinese. They wore cheap overcoats, they were hungry for knowledge, they ate the bad, starchy food of the poor restaurants, they had miserable little love affairs and played childish games of politics, instead of doing their work. Nevertheless, a few were promising—all must be given the truth. It did not matter if they died, but they must be given the truth. Otherwise there could be no continuity and no science.

He looked at the Dictator before him—yes, it was a hysteric face. He would know how to deal with it in his classroom—but such faces should not rule countries or young men. One was willing to go through a great many meaningless ceremonies in order to do one's work—wear a uniform or salute or be president of the Academy. That did not matter; it was part of the due to Caesar. But not to tell lies to young men on one's own subject. After all, they had called him The Bear and said he carried improper post cards in his brief case.

They had given him their terrible confidence—not for love or kindness, but because they had found him honest. It was too late to change.

The Dictator looked sharply at the General. "I thought this had been explained to Professor Malzius," he said.

"Why, yes," said Professor Malzius. "I will sign any papers. I assure you I am not interested in politics—a man like myself, imagine! One state is as good as another. And I miss my tobacco—I have not smoked in five months. But, you see, one cannot be a scientist and tell lies."

He looked at the two men.

"What happens if I do not?" he said, in a low voice. But, looking at the Dictator, he had his answer. It was a fanatic face.

"Why, we shall resume our conversations, Professor Malzius," said the General, with a simper.

"Then I shall be beaten again," said Professor Malzius. He stated what he knew to be a fact.

"The process of rehabilitation is obviously not quite complete," said the General, "but perhaps, in time—"

"It will not be necessary," said Professor Malzius. "I cannot be beaten again." He stared wearily around the room. His shoulders straightened—it was so he had looked in the classroom when they had called him The Bear. "Call your other officers in," he said in a clear voice. "There are papers for me to sign. I should like them all to witness."

"Why——" said the General. "Why——" He looked doubtfully at the Dictator.

An expression of gratification appeared on the lean, semi-Napoleonic face. A white hand, curiously limp, touched the hand of Professor Malzius.

"You will feel so much better, Gregor," said the hoarse, tense voice. "I am so very glad you have given in."

"Why, of course, I give in," said Gregor Malzius. "Are you not the Dictator? And besides, if I do not, I shall be beaten again. And I cannot—you understand?—I cannot be beaten again."

He paused, breathing a little. But already the room was full of other faces. He knew them well, the hard faces of the new regime. But youthful some of them too.

The Dictator was saying something with regard to receiving the distinguished scientist, Professor Gregor Malzius, into the service of the state.

"Take the pen," said the General in an undertone. "The inkwell is there, Professor Malzius. Now you may sign."

Professor Malzius stood, his fingers gripping the big, old-fashioned inkwell. It was full of ink—the servants of the Dictator were very efficient. They could shoot small people with the eyes of fox terriers for treason, but their trains arrived on time and their inkwells did not run dry.

"The state," he said, breathing. "Yes. But science does not know about states. And you are a little man—a little, unimportant man."

Then, before the General could stop him, he had picked up the inkwell and thrown it in the Dictator's face. The next moment the General's fist caught him on the side of the head and he fell behind the desk to the floor. But lying there, through his cracked glasses, he could still see the grotesque splashes of ink on the Dictator's face and uniform, and the small cut above his eye where the blood was gathering. They had not fired; he had thought he would be too close to the Dictator for them to fire in time.

"Take that man out and shoot him. At once," said the Dictator in a dry voice. He did not move to wipe the stains from his uniform—and for that Professor Malzius admired him. They rushed then, each anxious to be first. But Professor Malzius made no resistance.

As he was being hustled along the corridors, he fell now and then. On the second fall, his glasses were broken completely, but that did not matter to him. They were in a great hurry, he thought, but all the better—one did not have to think while one could not see.

Now and then he heard his voice make sounds of discomfort, but his voice was detached from himself. There was little Gregopolous—he could see him very plainly—and Williams, with his fresh English coloring—and all the men whom he had taught.

He had given them nothing but work and the truth; they had given him their terrible trust. If he had been beaten again, he might have betrayed them. But he had avoided that.

He felt a last weakness—a wish that someone might know. They would not, of course; he would have died of typhoid in the castle and there would be regretful notices in the newspapers. And then he would be forgotten, except for his work, and that was as it should be. He had never thought much of martyrs—hysterical people in the main. Though he'd like Bonnard to have known about the ink; it was in the coarse vein of humor that Bonnard could not appreciate. But then, he was a peasant; Bonnard had often told him so.

They were coming out into an open courtyard now; he felt the fresh air of outdoors. "Gently," he said. "A little gently. What's the haste?" But already they were tying him to the post. Someone struck him in the face and his eyes watered. "A schoolboy covered with ink," he muttered through his lost teeth. "A hysterical schoolboy too. But you cannot kill truth."

They were not good last words, and he knew that they were not. He must try to think of better ones—not shame Bonnard. But now they had a gag in his mouth; just as well; it saved him the trouble.

His body ached, bound against the post, but his sight and his mind were clearer. He could make out the evening sky, gray with fog, the sky that belonged to no country, but to all the world.

He could make out the gray high buttress of the castle. They had made it a jail, but it would not always be a jail. Perhaps in time it would not even exist. But if a little bit of truth were gathered, that would always exist, while there were men to remember and redis-cover it. It was only the liars and the cruel who always failed.

Sixty years ago, he had been a little boy, eating black bread and thin cabbage soup in a poor house. It had been a bitter life, but he could not complain of it. He had had some good teachers and they had called him The Bear.

The gag hurt his mouth—they were getting ready now. There had been a girl called Anna once; he had almost forgotten her. And his rooms had smelt a certain way and he had had a dog. It did not mat-ter what they did with the medals. He raised his head and looked once more at the gray foggy sky. In a moment there would be no thought, but, while there was thought, one must remember and note. His pulse rate was lower than he would have expected and his breathing oddly even, but those were not the important things. The important thing was beyond, in the gray sky that had no country, in the stones of the earth and the feeble human spirit. The important thing was truth.

"Ready!" called the officer. "Aim! Fire!" But Professor Malzius did not hear the three commands of the officer. He was thinking about the young men.

Into Egypt

It had finally been decided to let them go and now, for three days, they had been passing. The dust on the road to the frontier had not settled for three days or nights. But the strictest orders had been given and there were very few incidents. There could easily have been more.

Even the concentration camps had been swept clean, for this thing was to be final. After it, the State could say "How fearless we are—we let even known conspirators depart." It is true that, in the case of those in the concentration camps, there had been a preliminary rectification—a weeding, so to speak. But the news of that would not be officially published for some time and the numbers could always be disputed. If you kill a few people, they remain persons with names and identities, but, if you kill in the hundreds, there is simply a number for most of those who read the newspapers. And, once you start arguing about numbers, you begin to wonder if the thing ever happened at all. This too had been foreseen.

In fact, everything had been foreseen—and with great acuteness. There had been the usual diplomatic tension, solved, finally, by the usual firm stand. At the last moment, the other Powers had decided to co-operate. They had done so unwillingly, grudgingly, and with many representations, but they had done so. It was another great victory. And everywhere the trains rolled and the dust rose on the roads, for, at last and at length, the Accursed People were going. Every one of them, man, woman and child, to the third and the fourth generation—every one of them with a drop of that blood in his veins. And this was the end of it all and, by sunset on the third day, the land would know them no more. It was another great victory—perhaps the greatest. There would be a week of celebration after it, with appropriate ceremonies and speeches, and the date would be marked in the new calendar, with the date of the founding of the State and other dates.

Nevertheless, and even with the noteworthy efficiency of which the State was so proud, any mass evacuation is bound to be a complicated and fatiguing affair. The lieutenant stationed at the crossroads found it so—he was young and in the best of health but the strain was beginning to tell on him, though he would never have admitted it. He had been a little nervous at first—a little nervous and exceedingly anxious that everything should go according to plan. After all, it was an important post, the last crossroads before the frontier. A minor road, of course—they'd be busier on the main highways and at the ports of embarkation—but a last crossroads, nevertheless. He couldn't flatter himself it was worth a decoration—the bigwigs would get those. But, all the same, he was expected to evacuate so many thousands—he knew the figures by heart. Easy enough to say one had only to follow the plan! That might do for civilians—an officer was an officer. Would he show himself enough of an officer, would he make a fool of himself in front of his men? Would he even, perhaps, by some horrible, unforeseen mischance, get his road clogged with fleeing humanity till they had to send somebody over from Staff to straighten the tangle out? The thought was appalling.

He could see it happening in his mind—as a boy, he had been imaginative. He could hear the staff officer's words while he stood at attention, eyes front. One's first real command and a black mark on one's record! Yes, even if it was only police work—that didn't matter—a citizen of the State, a member of the Party must be held to an unflinching standard. If one failed to meet that standard there was nothing left in life. His throat had been dry and his movements a little jerky as he made his last dispositions and saw the first black specks begin to straggle toward the crossroads.

He could afford to laugh at that now, if he had had time. He could even afford to remember old Franz, his orderly, trying to put the brandy in his coffee, that first morning. "It's a chilly morning, Lieutenant," but there had been a question in Franz's eyes. He'd refused the brandy, of course, and told Franz off properly, too. The new State did not depend on Dutch courage but on the racial valor of its citizens. And the telling-off had helped—it had made his own voice firmer and given a little fillip of anger to his pulse. But Franz was an old soldier and imperturbable. What was it he had said, later? "The lieutenant must not worry. Civilians are always sheep—it is merely a matter of herding them." An improper remark, of course, to one's lieutenant, but it had helped settle his mind and make it cooler. Yes, an orderly like Franz was worth something, once one learned the knack of keeping him in his place.

Then they had begun to come, slowly, stragglingly, not like soldiers. He couldn't remember who had been the first. It was strange but he could not—he had been sure that he would remember. Perhaps a plodding family, with the scared children looking at him—

perhaps one of the old men with long beards and burning eyes. But, after three days, they all mixed, the individual faces. As Franz had said, they became civilian sheep—sheep that one must herd and keep moving, keep always through day and night, moving on to the frontier. As they went, they wailed. When the wailing grew too loud, one took measures; but, sooner or later it always began again. It would break out down the road, die down as it came toward the post. It seemed to come out of their mouths without their knowledge—the sound of broken wood, of wheat ground between stones. He had tried to stop it completely at first, now he no longer bothered. And yet there were many—a great many—who did not wail.

At first, it had been interesting to see how many different types there were. He had not thought to find such variety among the Accursed People—one had one's own mental picture, reinforced by the pictures in the newspapers. But, seeing them was different. They were not at all like the picture. They were tall and short, plump and lean, black-haired, yellow-haired, red-haired. It was obvious, even under the film of dust, that some had been rich, others poor, some thoughtful, others active. Indeed, it was often hard to tell them, by the looks. But that was not his affair—his affair was to keep them moving. All the same, it gave you a shock, sometimes, at first.

Perhaps the queerest thing was that they all looked so ordinary, so much a part of everyday. That was because one had been used to seeing them—it could be no more than that. But, under the film of dust and heat, one would look at a face. And then one would think, unconsciously, "Why, what is that fellow doing, so far from where he lives? Why, for heaven's sake, is he straggling along this road? He doesn't look happy." Then the mind would resume control and one would remember. But the thought would come, now and then, without orders from the mind.

He had seen very few that he knew. That was natural—he came from the South. He had seen Willi Schneider, to be sure—that had been the second day and it was very dusty. When he was a little boy, very young, he had played in Willi's garden with Willi; in the summers, and, as they had played, there had come to them, through the open window, the ripple of a piano and the clear, rippling flow of Willi's mother's voice. It was not a great voice—not a Brunhild voice—but beautiful in *lieder* and beautifully sure. She had sung at their own house; that was odd to remember. Of course, her husband had not been one of them—a councilor, in fact. Needless to say, that had been long before the discovery that even the faintest trace of that blood tainted. As for Willi and himself, they had been friends—yes, even through the first year or so at school. Both of them had meant to run away and be cowboys, and they had had a secret password. Naturally, things had changed, later on.

For a horrible moment, he had thought that Willi would speak to him—recall the warm air of summer and the smell of linden and those young, unmanly days. But Willi did not. Their eyes met, for an instant, then both had looked away. Willi was helping an old woman along, an old woman who muttered fretfully as she walked, like a cat with sore paws. They were both of them covered with dust and the old woman went slowly. Willi's mother had walked with a quick step and her voice had not been cracked or fretful. After play, she had given them both cream buns, laughing and moving her hands, in a bright green dress. It was not permitted to think further of Willi Schneider.

That was the only real acquaintance but there were other, recognizable faces. There was the woman who had kept the newsstand, the brisk little waiter at the summer hotel, the taxi chauffeur with the squint and the heart specialist. Then there was the former scientist—one could still tell him from his pictures—and the actor one had often seen. That was all that one knew and not all on the same day. That was enough. He had not imagined the taxi chauffeur with a wife and children and that the youngest child should be lame. That had surprised him—surprised him almost as much as seeing the heart specialist walking along the road like any man. It had surprised him, also, to see the scientist led along between two others and to recognize the fact that he was mad.

But that also mixed with the dust—the endless, stifling cloud of the dust, the endless, moving current. The dust got in one's throat and one's eyes—it was hard to cut, even with brandy, from one's throat. It lay on the endless bundles people carried; queer bundles, bulging out at the ends, with here a ticking clock, and there a green bunch of carrots. It lay on the handcarts a few of them pushed—the handcarts bearing the sort of goods that one would snatch, haphazard, from a burning house. It rose and whirled and penetrated—it was never still. At night, slashed by the efficient searchlights that made the night bright as day, it was still a mist above the road. As for sleep—well, one slept when one could, for a couple of hours after midnight, when they too slept, ungracefully, in heaps and clumps by the road. But, except for the first night, he could not even remember Franz pulling his boots off.

His men had been excellent, admirable, indefatigable. That was, of course, due to the Leader and the State, but still, he would put it in his report. They had kept the stream moving, always. The attitude had been the newly prescribed one—not that of punishment, richly as that was deserved, but of complete aloofness, as if the Accursed People did not even exist. Naturally, now and then, the men had had their fun. One could not blame them for that—some of the incidents had been extremely comic. There had been the old woman with the hen—a comedy character. Of course, she had not been permitted to keep the hen. They should have taken it away from her at the inspection point. But she had looked very funny, holding on to the squawking chicken by the tail feathers, with the tears running down her face.

Yes, the attitude of the men would certainly go in his report. He would devote a special paragraph to the musicians also—they had been indefatigable. They had played the prescribed tunes continually, in spite of the dust and the heat. One would hope that those tunes would sink into the hearts of the Accursed People, to be forever a warning and a memory. Particularly if they happened to know the words. But one could never be sure about people like that.

Staff cars had come four times, the first morning, and once there had been a general. He had felt nervous, when they came, but there had been no complaint. After that, they had let him alone, except for an occasional visit—that must mean they thought him up to his work. Once, even, the road had been almost clear, for a few minutes—he was moving them along faster than they did at the inspection point. The thought had gone to his head for an instant, but he kept cool—and, soon enough, the road had been crowded again.

As regarded casualties—he could not keep the exact figure in his head, but it was a minor one. A couple of heart attacks—one of the man who had been a judge, or so the others said. Unpleasant but valuable to see the life drain out of a face like that. He had made himself watch it—one must harden oneself. They had wanted to remove the body—of course, that had not been allowed. The women taken in childbirth had been adequately dealt with—one could do nothing to assist. But he had insisted, for decency's sake, on a screen, and Franz had been very clever at rigging one up. Only two of those had died, the rest had gone on—they showed a remarkable tenacity. Then there were the five executions, including the man suddenly gone crazy, who had roared and foamed. A nasty moment, that—for a second the whole current had stopped flowing. But his men had jumped in at once—he himself had acted quickly. The others were merely incorrigible stragglers and of no account.

And now, it was almost over and soon the homeland would be free. Free as it never had been—for, without the Accursed People, it would be unlike any other country on earth. They were gone, with their books and their music, their false, delusive science and their quick way of thinking. They were gone, all the people like Willi Schneider and his mother, who had spent so much time in talking and being friendly. They were gone, the willful people, who clung close together and yet so willfully supported the new and the untried. The men who haggled over pennies, and the others who gave—the sweater, the mimic, the philosopher, the discoverer—all were gone. Yes, and with them went their slaves' religion, the religion of the weak and the humble, the religion that fought so bitterly and yet exalted the prophet above the armed man.

One could be a whole man, with them gone, without their doubts and their mockery and their bitter, self-accusing laughter, their melancholy, deep as a well, and their endless aspiration for something that could not be touched with the hand. One could be solid and virile and untroubled, virile and huge as the old, thunderous gods. It was so that the Leader had spoken, so it must be true. And the countries who weakly received them would be themselves corrupted into warm unmanliness and mockery, into a desire for peace and a search for things not tangible. But the homeland would stand still and listen to the beat of its own heart—not even listen, but stand like a proud fierce animal, a perfect, living machine. To get children, to conquer others, to die gloriously in battle—that was the end of man. It had been a long time forgotten, but the Leader had remembered it. And, naturally, one could not do that completely with them in the land, for they had other ideas.

He thought of these things dutifully because it was right to think of them. They had been repeated and repeated in his ears till they had occupied his mind. But, meanwhile, he was very tired and the dust still rose. They were coming by clumps and groups, now—the last stragglers—they were no longer a solid, flowing current. The afternoon had turned hot—unseasonably hot. He didn't want any more brandy—the thought of it sickened his stomach. He wanted a glass of beer—iced beer, cold and dark, with foam on it—and a chance to unbutton his collar. He wanted to have the thing done and sit down and have Franz pull off his boots. If it were only a little cooler, a little quieter—if even these last would not wail so, now and then—if only the dust would not rise! He found himself humming, for comfort, a Christmas hymn—it brought a little, frail coolness to his mind.

"Silent night, holy night,
All is calm, all is bright. . . ."

The old gods were virile and thunderous, but, down in the South, they would still deck the tree, in kindliness. Call it a custom—call it anything you like—it still came out of the heart. And it was a custom of the homeland—it could not be wrong. Oh, the beautiful, crisp snow of Christmas Day, the greetings between friends, the bright, lighted tree! Well, there'd be a Christmas to come. Perhaps he'd be married, by then—he had thought of it, often. If he were, they would have a tree—young couples were sentimental, in the South. A tree and a small manger beneath it, with the animals and the child. They carved the figures out of wood, in his country, with loving care—the thought of them was very peaceful and cool. In the old days, he had always given Willi Schneider part of his almond cake—one knew it was not Willi's festival but one was friendly, for all that. And that must be forgotten. He had had no right to give Willi part of his almond cake—it was the tree that mattered, the tree and the tiny candles, the smell of the fresh pine and the clear, frosty sweetness of the day. They would keep that, he and his wife, keep it with rejoicing, and Willi would not look in through the window, with his old face or his new face. He would not look in at all, ever any more. For now the homeland was released, after many years.

Now the dust was beginning to settle—the current in the road had dwindled to a straggling trickle. He was able to think, for the first time, of the land to which that trickle was going—a hungry land, the papers said, in spite of its boastful ways. The road led blankly into it, beyond the rise of ground—hard to tell what it was like. But they would be dispersed, not only here, but over many lands. Of course, the situation was not comparable—all the same, it must be a queer feeling. A queer feeling, yes, to start out anew, with nothing but the clothes on your back and what you could push in a handcart, if you had a handcart. For an instant the thought came, unbidden, "It must be a great people that can bear such things." But they were the Accursed People—the thought should not have come.

He sighed and turned back to his duty. It was really wonderful—even on the third day there was such order, such precision. It was something to be proud of—something to remember long. The Leader would speak of it, undoubtedly. The ones who came now were the very last stragglers, the weakest, but they were being moved along as promptly as if they were strong. The dust actually no longer rose in a cloud—it was settling, slowly but surely.

He did not quite remember when he had last eaten. It did not matter, for the sun was sinking fast, in a red warm glow. In a moment, in an hour, it would be done—he could rest and undo his collar, have some beer. There was nobody on the road now—nobody at all. He stood rigidly at his post—the picture of an officer, though somewhat dusty—but he knew that his eyes were closing. Nobody on the road—nobody for a whole five minutes . . . for eight . . . for ten.

He was roused by Franz's voice in his ear—he must have gone to sleep, standing up. He had heard of that happening to soldiers on the march—he felt rather proud that, now, it had happened to him. But there seemed to be a little trouble on the road—he walked forward to it, stiffly, trying to clear his throat.

It was a commonplace grouping—he had seen dozens like it in the course of the three days—an older man, a young woman, and, of course, the child that she held. No doubt about them, either—the man's features were strongly marked, the woman had the liquid eyes. As for the child, that was merely a wrapped bundle. They should have started before—stupid people—the man looked strong enough. Their belongings were done up like all poor people's belongings.

He stood in front of them, now, erect and a soldier. "Well," he said. "Don't you know the orders? No livestock to be taken. Didn't they examine you, down the road?" ("And a pretty fool I'll look like, reporting one confiscated donkey to Headquarters," he thought, with irritation. "We've been able to manage, with the chickens, but this is really too much! What can they be thinking of at the inspection point? Oh, well, they're tired too, I suppose, but it's my responsibility.")

He put a rasp in his voice—he had to, they looked at him so stupidly. "Well?" he said. "Answer me! Don't you know an officer when you see one?"

"We have come a long way," said the man, in a low voice. "We heard there was danger to the child. So we are going. May we pass?" The voice was civil enough, but the eyes were dark and large, the face tired and worn. He was resting one hand on his staff, in a peasant gesture. The woman said nothing at all and one felt that she would say nothing. She sat on the back of the gray donkey and the child in her arms, too, was silent, though it moved.

The lieutenant tried to think rapidly. After all, these were the last. But the thoughts buzzed around his head and would not come out of his mouth. That was fatigue. It should be easy enough for a lieutenant to give an order.

He found himself saying, conversationally, "There are just the three of you?"

"That is all," said the man and looked at him with great simplicity. "But we heard there was danger to the child. So we could not stay any more. We could not stay at all."

"Indeed," said the lieutenant and then said again, "indeed."

"Yes," said the man. "But we shall do well enough—we have been in exile before." He spoke patiently and yet with a certain authority. When the lieutenant did not answer, he laid his other hand on the rein of the gray donkey. It moved forward a step and with it, also, the child stirred and moved. The lieutenant, turning, saw the child's face now, and its hands, as it turned and moved its small hands to the glow of the sunset.

"If the lieutenant pleases—" said an eager voice, the voice of the Northern corporal.

"The lieutenant does not please," said the lieutenant. He nodded at the man. "You may proceed."

"But Lieutenant—" said the eager voice.

"Swine and dog," said the lieutenant, feeling something snap in his mind, "are we to hinder the Leader's plans because of one gray donkey? The order says—all out of the country by sunset. Let them go. You will report to me, Corporal, in the morning."

He turned on his heel and walked a straight line to the field hut, not looking back. When Franz, the orderly, came in a little later, he found him sitting in a chair.

"If the lieutenant would take some brandy—" he said, respectfully.

"The lieutenant has had enough brandy," said the lieutenant, in a hoarse, dusty voice. "Have my orders been obeyed?"

"Yes, Lieutenant."

"They are gone—the very last of them?"

"Yes, Lieutenant."

"They did not look back?"

"No, Lieutenant."

The lieutenant said nothing, for a while, and Franz busied himself with boots. After some time, he spoke.

"The lieutenant should try to sleep," he said. "We have carried out our orders. And now, they are gone."

"Yes," said the lieutenant, and, suddenly, he saw them again, the whole multitude, dispersed among every country—the ones who had walked his road, the ones at the points of embarkation. There were a great many of them, and that he had expected. But they were not dispersed as he had thought. They were not dispersed as he had thought, for, with each one went shame, like a visible burden. And the shame was not theirs, though they carried it—the shame belonged to the land that had driven them forth—his own land. He could see it growing and spreading like a black blot—the shame of his country spread over the whole earth.

"The lieutenant will have some brandy," he said. "Quickly, Franz."

When the brandy was brought, he stared at it for a moment, in the cup.

"Tell me, Franz," he said. "Did you know them well? Any of them? Before?"

"Oh yes, Lieutenant," said Franz, in his smooth, orderly's voice. "In the last war, I was billeted—well, the name of the town does not matter, but the woman was one of them. Of course that was before we knew about them," he said, respectfully. "That was more than twenty years ago. But she was very kind to me—I used to make toys for her children. I have often wondered what happened to her—she was very considerate and kind. Doubtless I was wrong, Lieutenant? But that was in another country."

"Yes, Franz," said the lieutenant. "There were children, you say?"

"Yes, Lieutenant."

"You saw the child today? The last one?"

"Yes, Lieutenant."

"Its hands had been hurt," said the lieutenant. "In the middle. Right through. I saw them. I wish I had not seen that. I wish I had not seen its hands."

By the Waters of Babylon

The north and the west and the south are good hunting ground, but it is forbidden to go east. It is forbidden to go to any of the Dead Places except to search for metal and then he who touches the metal must be a priest or the son of a priest. Afterwards, both the man and the metal must be purified. These are the rules and the laws; they are well made. It is forbidden to cross the great river and look upon the place that was the Place of the Gods—this is most strictly forbidden. We do not even say its name though we know its name. It is there that spirits live, and demons—it is there that there are the ashes of the Great Burning. These things are forbidden—they have been forbidden since the beginning of time.

My father is a priest; I am the son of a priest. I have been in the Dead Places near us, with my father—at first, I was afraid. When my father went into the house to search for the metal, I stood by the door and my heart felt small and weak. It was a dead man's house, a spirit house. It did not have the smell of man, though there were old bones in a corner. But it is not fitting that a priest's son should show fear. I looked at the bones in the shadow and kept my voice still.

Then my father came out with the metal—a good, strong piece. He looked at me with both eyes but I had not run away. He gave me the metal to hold—I took it and did not die. So he knew that I was truly his son and would be a priest in my time. That was when I was very young—nevertheless, my brothers would not have done it, though they are good hunters. After that, they gave me the good piece of meat and the warm corner by the fire. My father watched over me—he was glad that I should be a priest. But when I boasted or wept without a reason, he punished me more strictly than my brothers. That was right.

After a time, I myself was allowed to go into the dead houses and search for metal. So I learned the ways of those houses—and if I saw bones, I was no longer afraid. The bones are light and old—sometimes they will fall into dust if you touch them. But that is a great sin.

I was taught the chants and the spells—I was taught how to stop the running of blood from a wound and many secrets. A priest must know many secrets—that was what my father said. If the hunters think we do all things by chants and spells, they may believe so—it does not hurt them. I was taught how to read in the old books and how to make the old writings—that was hard and took a long time. My knowledge made me happy—it was like a fire in my heart. Most of all, I liked to hear of the Old Days and the stories of the gods. I asked myself many questions that I could not answer, but it was good to ask them. At night, I would lie awake and listen to the wind—it seemed to me that it was the voice of the gods as they flew through the air.

We are not ignorant like the Forest People—our women spin wool on the wheel, our priests wear a white robe. We do not eat grubs from the tree, we have not forgotten the old writings, although they are hard to understand. Nevertheless, my knowledge and my lack of knowledge burned in me—I wished to know more. When I was a man at last, I came to my father and said, "It is time for me to go on my journey. Give me your leave."

He looked at me for a long time, stroking his beard, then he said at last, "Yes. It is time." That night, in the house of the priesthood, I asked for and received purification. My body hurt but my spirit was a cool stone. It was my father himself who questioned me about my dreams.

He bade me look into the smoke of the fire and see—I saw and told what I saw. It was what I have always seen—a river, and, beyond it, a great Dead Place and in it the gods walking. I have always thought about that. His eyes were stern when I told him—he was no longer my father but a priest. He said, "This is a strong dream."

"It is mine," I said, while the smoke waved and my head felt light. They were singing the Star song in the outer chamber and it was like the buzzing of bees in my head.

He asked me how the gods were dressed and I told him how they were dressed. We know how they were dressed from the book, but I saw them as if they were before me. When I had finished, he threw the sticks three times and studied them as they fell.

"This is a very strong dream," he said. "It may eat you up."

"I am not afraid," I said and looked at him with both eyes. My voice sounded thin in my ears but that was because of the smoke.

He touched me on the breast and the forehead. He gave me the bow and the three arrows.

"Take them," he said. "It is forbidden to travel east. It is forbidden to cross the river. It is forbidden to go to the Place of the Gods. All these things are forbidden."

"All these things are forbidden," I said, but it was my voice that spoke and not my spirit. He looked at me again.

"My son," he said. "Once I had young dreams. If your dreams do not eat you up, you may be a great priest. If they eat you, you are still my son. Now go on your journey."

I went fasting, as is the law. My body hurt but not my heart. When the dawn came, I was out of sight of the village. I prayed and purified myself, waiting for a sign. The sign was an eagle. It flew east.

Sometimes signs are sent by bad spirits. I waited again on the flat rock, fasting, taking no food. I was very still—I could feel the sky above me and the earth beneath. I waited till the sun was beginning to sink. Then three deer passed in the valley, going east—they did not wind me or see me. There was a white fawn with them—a very great sign.

I followed them, at a distance, waiting for what would happen. My heart was troubled about going east, yet I knew that I must go. My head hummed with my fasting—I did not even see the panther spring upon the white fawn. But, before I knew it, the bow was in my hand. I shouted and the panther lifted his head from the fawn. It is not easy to kill a panther with one arrow but the arrow went through his eye and into his brain. He died as he tried to spring—he rolled over, tearing at the ground. Then I knew I was meant to go east—I knew that was my journey. When the night came, I made my fire and roasted meat.

It is eight suns' journey to the east and a man passes by many Dead Places. The Forest People are afraid of them but I am not. Once I made my fire on the edge of a Dead Place at night and, next morning, in the dead house, I found a good knife, little rusted. That was small to what came afterward but it made my heart feel big. Always when I looked for game, it was in front of my arrow, and twice I passed hunting parties of the Forest People without their knowing. So I knew my magic was strong and my journey clean, in spite of the law.

Toward the setting of the eighth sun, I came to the banks of the great river. It was half-a-day's journey after I had left the god-road—we do not use the god-roads now for they are falling apart into great blocks of stone, and the forest is safer going. A long way off, I had seen the water through trees but the trees were thick. At last, I came out upon an open place at the top of a cliff. There was the great river below, like a giant in the sun. It is very long, very wide. It could eat all the streams we know and still be thirsty. Its name is Ou-dis-sun, the Sacred, the Long. No man of my tribe had seen it, not even my father, the priest. It was magic and I prayed.

Then I raised my eyes and looked south. It was there, the Place of the Gods.

How can I tell what it was like—you do not know. It was there, in the red light, and they were too big to be houses. It was there with the red light upon it, mighty and ruined. I knew that in another moment the gods would see me. I covered my eyes with my hands and crept back into the forest.

Surely, that was enough to do, and live. Surely it was enough to spend the night upon the cliff. The Forest People themselves do not come near. Yet, all through the night, I knew that I should have to cross the river and walk in the places of the gods, although the gods ate me up. My magic did not help me at all and yet there was a fire in my bowels, a fire in my mind. When the sun rose, I thought, "My journey has been clean. Now I will go home from my journey." But, even as I thought so, I knew I could not. If I went to the Place of the Gods, I would surely die, but, if I did not go, I could never be at peace with my spirit again. It is better to lose one's life than one's spirit, if one is a priest and the son of a priest.

Nevertheless, as I made the raft, the tears ran out of my eyes. The Forest People could have killed me without fight, if they had come upon me then, but they did not come. When the raft was made, I said the sayings for the dead and painted myself for death. My heart was cold as a frog and my knees like water, but the burning in my mind would not let me have peace. As I pushed the raft from the shore, I began my death song—I had the right. It was a fine song.

"I am John, son of John," I sang. "My people are the Hill People.
    They are the men.
I go into the Dead Places but I am not slain.
I take the metal from the Dead Places but I am not blasted.
I travel upon the god-roads and am not afraid. E-yah! I have killed
    the panther, I have killed the fawn!
E-yah! I have come to the great river. No man has come there
    before.
It is forbidden to go east, but I have gone, forbidden to go on the
    great river, but I am there.
Open your hearts, you spirits, and hear my song.
    Now I go to the Place of the Gods, I shall not return.
My body is painted for death and my limbs weak, but my heart is
    big as I go to the Place of the Gods!"

All the same, when I came to the Place of the Gods, I was afraid, afraid. The current of the great river is very strong—it gripped my raft with its hands. That was magic, for the river itself is wide and calm. I could feel evil spirits about me, in the bright morning; I could feel their breath on my neck as I was swept down the stream. Never have I been so much alone—I tried to think of my knowledge, but it was a squirrel's heap of winter nuts. There was no strength in my knowledge any more and I felt small and naked as a new-hatched bird—alone upon the great river, the servant of the gods.

Yet, after a while, my eyes were opened and I saw. I saw both banks of the river—I saw that once there had been god-roads across it, though now they were broken and fallen like broken vines. Very great they were, and wonderful and broken—broken in the time of the Great Burning when the fire fell out of the sky. And always the current took me nearer to the Place of the Gods, and the huge ruins rose before my eyes.

I do not know the customs of rivers—we are the People of the Hills. I tried to guide my raft with the pole but it spun around. I thought the river meant to take me past the Place of the Gods and out into the Bitter Water of the legends. I grew angry then—my heart felt strong. I said aloud, "I am a priest and the son of a priest!" The gods heard me—they showed me how to paddle with the pole on one side of the raft. The current changed itself—I drew near to the Place of the Gods.

When I was very near, my raft struck and turned over. I can swim in our lakes—I swam to the shore. There was a great spike of rusted metal sticking out into the river—I hauled myself up upon it and sat there, panting. I had saved my bow and two arrows and the knife I found in the Dead Place but that was all. My raft went whirling downstream toward the Bitter Water. I looked after it, and thought if it had trod me under, at least I would be safely dead. Nevertheless, when I had dried my bowstring and re-strung it, I walked forward to the Place of the Gods.

It felt like ground underfoot; it did not burn me. It is not true what some of the tales say, that the ground there burns forever, for I have been there. Here and there were the marks and stains of the Great Burning, on the ruins, that is true. But they were old marks and old stains. It is not true either, what some of our priests say, that it is an island covered with fogs and enchantments. It is not. It is a great Dead Place—greater than any Dead Place we know. Everywhere in it there are god-roads, though most are cracked and broken. Everywhere there are the ruins of the high towers of the gods.

How shall I tell what I saw? I went carefully, my strung bow in my hand, my skin ready for danger. There should have been the wailings of spirits and the shrieks of demons, but there were not. It was very silent and sunny where I had landed—the wind and the rain and the birds that drop seeds had done their work—the grass grew in the cracks of the broken stone. It is a fair island—no wonder the gods built there. If I had come there, a god, I also would have built.

How shall I tell what I saw? The towers are not all broken—here and there one still stands, like a great tree in a forest, and the birds nest high. But the towers themselves look blind, for the gods are gone. I saw a fish-hawk, catching fish in the river. I saw a little dance of white butterflies over a great heap of broken stones and columns. I went there and looked about me—there was a carved stone with cut-letters, broken in half. I can read letters but I could not understand these. They said UBTREAS. There was also the shattered image of a man or a god. It had been made of white stone and he wore his hair tied back like a woman's. His name was ASHING, as I read on the cracked half of a stone. I thought it wise to pray to ASHING, though I do not know that god.

How shall I tell what I saw? There was no smell of man left, on stone or metal. Nor were there many trees in that wilderness of stone. There are many pigeons, nesting and dropping in the towers—the gods must have loved them, or, perhaps, they used them for sacrifices. There are wild cats that roam the god-roads, green-eyed, unafraid of man. At night they wail like demons but they are not demons. The wild dogs are more dangerous, for they hunt in a pack, but them I did not meet till later. Everywhere there are the carved stones, carved with magical numbers or words.

I went North—I did not try to hide myself. When a god or a demon saw me, then I would die, but meanwhile I was no longer afraid. My hunger for knowledge burned in me—there was so much that I could not understand. After awhile, I knew that my belly was hungry. I could have hunted for my meat, but I did not hunt. It is known that the gods did not hunt as we do—they got their food from enchanted boxes and jars. Sometimes these are still found in the Dead Places—once, when I was a child and foolish, I opened such a jar and tasted it and found the food sweet. But my father found out and punished me for it strictly, for, often, that food is death. Now, though, I had long gone past what was forbidden, and I entered the likeliest towers, looking for the food of the gods.

I found it at last in the ruins of a great temple in the mid-city. A mighty temple it must have been, for the roof was painted like the sky at night with its stars—that much I could see, though the colors were faint and dim. It went down into great caves and tunnels—perhaps they kept their slaves there. But when I started to climb down, I heard the squeaking of rats, so I did not go—rats are unclean, and there must have been many tribes of them, from the squeaking. But near there, I found food, in the heart of a ruin, behind a door that still opened. I ate only the fruits from the jars—they had a very sweet taste. There was drink, too, in bottles of glass—the drink of the gods was strong and made my head swim. After I had eaten and drunk, I slept on the top of a stone, my bow at my side.

When I woke, the sun was low. Looking down from where I lay, I saw a dog sitting on his haunches. His tongue was hanging out of his mouth; he looked as if he were laughing. He was a big dog, with a gray-brown coat, as big as a wolf. I sprang up and shouted at him but he did not move—he just sat there as if he were laughing. I did not like that. When I reached for a stone to throw, he moved swiftly out of the way of the stone. He was not afraid of me; he looked at me as if I were meat. No doubt I could have killed him with an arrow, but I did not know if there were others. Moreover, night was falling.

I looked about me—not far away there was a great, broken god-road, leading North. The towers were high enough, but not so high, and while many of the dead-houses were wrecked, there were some that stood. I went toward this god-road, keeping to the heights of the ruins, while the dog followed. When I had reached the god-road, I saw that there were others behind him. If I had slept later, they would have come upon me asleep and torn out my throat. As it was, they were sure enough of me; they did not hurry. When I went into the dead-house, they kept watch at the entrance—doubtless they thought they would have a fine hunt. But a dog cannot open a door and I knew, from the books, that the gods did not like to live on the ground but on high.

I had just found a door I could open when the dogs decided to rush. Ha! They were surprised when I shut the door in their faces—it was a good door, of strong metal. I could hear their foolish baying beyond it but I did not stop to answer them. I was in darkness—I found stairs and climbed. There were many stairs, turning around till my head was dizzy. At the top was another door—I found the knob and opened it. I was in a long small chamber—on one side of it was a bronze door that could not be opened, for it had no handle. Perhaps there was a magic word to open it but I did not have the word. I turned to the door in the opposite side of the wall. The lock of it was broken and I opened it and went it.

Within, there was a place of great riches. The god who lived there must have been a powerful god. The first room was a small ante-room—I waited there for some time, telling the spirits of the place that I came in peace and not as a robber. When it seemed to me that they had had time to hear me, I went on. Ah, what riches! Few, even, of the windows had been broken—it was all as it had been. The great windows that looked over the city had not been broken at all though they were dusty and streaked with many years. There were coverings on the floors, the colors not greatly faded, and the chairs were soft and deep. There were pictures upon the walls, very strange, very wonderful—I remember one of a bunch of flowers in a jar—if you came close to it, you could see nothing but bits of color, but if you stood away from it, the flowers might have been picked yesterday. It made my heart feel strange to look at this picture—and to look at the figure of a bird, in some hard clay, on a table and see it so like our birds. Everywhere there were books and writings, many in tongues that I could not read. The god who lived there must have been a wise god and full of knowledge. I felt I had right there, as I sought knowledge also.

Nevertheless, it was strange. There was a washing-place but no water—perhaps the gods washed in air. There was a cooking-place but no wood, and though there was a machine to cook food, there was no place to put fire in it. Nor were there candles or lamps—there were things that looked like lamps but they had neither oil nor wick. All these things were magic, but I touched them and lived—the magic had gone out of them. Let me tell one thing to show. In the washing-place, a thing said "Hot" but it was not hot to the touch—another thing said "Cold" but it was not cold. This must have been a strong magic but the magic was gone. I do not understand—they had ways—I wish that I knew.

It was close and dry and dusty in their house of the gods, I have said the magic was gone but that is not true—it had gone from the magic things but it had not gone from the place. I felt the spirits about me, weighing upon me. Nor had I ever slept in a Dead Place before—and yet, tonight, I must sleep there. When I thought of it, my tongue felt dry in my throat, in spite of my wish for knowledge. Almost I would have gone down again and faced the dogs, but I did not.

I had not gone through all the rooms when the darkness fell. When it fell, I went back to the big room looking over the city and made fire. There was a place to make fire and a box with wood in it, though I do not think they cooked there. I wrapped myself in a floor-covering and slept in front of the fire—I was very tired.

Now I tell what is very strong magic. I woke in the midst of the night. When I woke, the fire had gone out and I was cold. It seemed to me that all around me there were whisperings and voices. I closed my eyes to shut them out. Some will say that I slept again, but I do not think that I slept. I could feel the spirits drawing my spirit out of my body as a fish is drawn on a line.

Why should I lie about it? I am a priest and the son of a priest. If there are spirits, as they say, in the small Dead Places near us, what spirits must there not be in that great Place of the Gods? And would not they wish to speak? After such long years? I know that I felt myself drawn as a fish is drawn on a line. I had stepped out of my body—I could see my body asleep in front of the cold fire, but it was not I. I was drawn to look out upon the city of the gods.

It should have been dark, for it was night, but it was not dark. Everywhere there were lights—lines of light—circles and blurs of light—ten thousand torches would not have been the same. The sky itself was alight—you could barely see the stars for the glow in the sky. I thought to myself "This is strong magic" and trembled. There was a roaring in my ears like the rushing of rivers. Then my eyes grew used to the light and my ears to the sound. I knew that I was seeing the city as it had been when the gods were alive.

That was a sight indeed—yes, that was a sight: I could not have seen it in the body—my body would have died. Everywhere went the gods, on foot and in chariots—there were gods beyond number and counting and their chariots blocked the streets. They had turned night to day for their pleasure—they did not sleep with the sun. The noise of their coming and going was the noise of many waters. It was magic what they could do—it was magic what they did.

I looked out of another window—the great vines of their bridges were mended and the god-roads went East and West. Restless, restless, were the gods and always in motion! They burrowed tunnels under rivers—they flew in the air. With unbelievable tools they did giant works—no part of the earth was safe from them, for, if they wished for a thing, they summoned it from the other side of the world. And always, as they labored and rested, as they feasted and made love, there was a drum in their ears—the pulse of the giant city, beating and beating like a man's heart.

Were they happy? What is happiness to the gods? They were great, they were mighty, they were wonderful and terrible. As I looked upon them and their magic, I felt like a child—but a little more, it seemed to me, and they would pull down the moon from the sky. I saw them with wisdom beyond wisdom and knowledge beyond knowledge. And yet not all they did was well done—even I could see that—and yet their wisdom could not but grow until all was peace.

Then I saw their fate come upon them and that was terrible past speech. It came upon them as they walked the streets of their city. I have been in the fights with the Forest People—I have seen men die. But this was not like that. When gods war with gods, they use weapons we do not know. It was fire falling out of the sky and a mist that poisoned. It was the time of the Great Burning and the Destruction. They ran about like ants in the streets of their city—poor gods, poor gods! Then the towers began to fall. A few escaped—yes, a few. The legends tell it. But, even after the city had become a Dead Place, for many years the poison was still in the ground. I saw it happen, I saw the last of them die. It was darkness over the broken city and I wept.

All this, I saw. I saw it as I have told it, though not in the body. When I woke in the morning, I was hungry, but I did not think first of my hunger for my heart was perplexed and confused. I knew the reason for the Dead Places but I did not see why it had happened. It seemed to me it should not have happened, with all the magic they had. I went through the house looking for an answer. There was so much in the house I could not understand—and yet I am a priest and the son of a priest. It was like being on one side of the great river, at night, with no light to show the way.

Then I saw the dead god. He was sitting in his chair, by the window, in a room I had not entered before and, for the first moment, I thought that he was alive. Then I saw the skin on the back of his hand—it was like dry leather. The room was shut, hot and dry—no doubt that had kept him as he was. At first I was afraid to approach him—then the fear left me. He was sitting looking out over the city—he was dressed in the clothes of the gods. His age was neither young nor old—I could not tell his age. But there was wisdom in his face and great sadness. You could see that he would have not run away. He had sat at his window, watching his city die—then he himself had died. But it is better to lose one's life than one's spirit—and you could see from the face that his spirit had not been lost. I knew, that, if I touched him, he would fall into dust—and yet, there was something unconquered in the face.

That is all of my story, for then I knew he was a man—I knew then that they had been men, neither gods nor demons. It is a great knowledge, hard to tell and believe. They were men—they went a dark road, but they were men. I had no fear after that—I had no fear going home, though twice I fought off the dogs and once I was hunted for two days by the Forest People. When I saw my father again, I prayed and was purified. He touched my lips and my breast, he said, "You went away a boy. You come back a man and a priest." I said, "Father, they were men! I have been in the Place of the Gods and seen it! Now slay me, if it is the law—but still I know they were men."

He looked at me out of both eyes. He said, "The law is not always the same shape—you have done what you have done. I could not have done it my time, but you come after me. Tell!"

I told and he listened. After that, I wished to tell all the people but he showed me otherwise. He said, "Truth is a hard deer to hunt. If you eat too much truth at once, you may die of the truth. It was not idly that our fathers forbade the Dead Places." He was right—it is better the truth should come little by little. I have learned that, being a priest. Perhaps, in the old days, they ate knowledge too fast.

Nevertheless, we make a beginning. It is not for the metal alone we go to the Dead Places now—there are the books and the writings. They are hard to learn. And the magic tools are broken—but we can look at them and wonder. At least, we make a beginning. And, when I am chief priest we shall go beyond the great river. We shall go to the Place of the Gods—the place newyork—not one man but a company. We shall look for the images of the gods and find the god ASHING and the others—the gods Licoln and Biltmore and Moses. But they were men who built the city, not gods or demons. They were men. I remember the dead man's face. They were men who were here before us. We must build again.

POETRY

SELECTIONS FROM *JOHN BROWN'S BODY*

Readers interested in references in the poem should refer to John Brown's Body, *edited and annotated by Mabel A. Bessey (Farrar and Rinehart, 1941) and to* Stephen Vincent Benét: John Brown's Body, *with an Introduction and Notes by Jack L. Capps and C. Robert Kemble. Department of English, United States Military Academy (Holt, Rinehart and Winston, 1968). This edition is particularly useful because it lists the sources Benét used when writing* John Brown's Body. *The selections included here are "Invocation," Book Two about the Battle of Bull Run, a short part of Book Six which conveys a sense of the epic scope Benét sought in his poem, Book Seven about the Battle of Gettysburg, and the closing piece of the final Book Eight.*

The reader should understand that Benét interwove actual figures such as Robert E. Lee and Abraham Lincoln with invented characters such as Clay Wingate, Sally Dupré, Jake Diefer, Jack Ellyat, and others, whom he employed to flesh out the historical episodes of the Civil War.

INVOCATION

American muse, whose strong and diverse heart
So many men have tried to understand
But only made it smaller with their art,
Because you are as various as your land,

As mountainous-deep, as flowered with blue rivers,
Thirsty with deserts, buried under snows,
As native as the shape of Navajo quivers,
And native, too, as the sea-voyaged rose.

Swift runner, never captured or subdued,
Seven-branched elk beside the mountain stream,
That half a hundred hunters have pursued
But never matched their bullets with the dream,

Where the great huntsmen failed, I set my sorry
And mortal snare for your immortal quarry.

You are the buffalo-ghost, the broncho-ghost
With dollar-silver in your saddle-horn,
The cowboys riding in from Painted Post,
The Indian arrow in the Indian corn,

And you are the clipped velvet of the lawns
Where Shropshire grows from Massachusetts sods,
The grey Maine rocks—and the war-painted dawns
That break above the Garden of the Gods.

The prairie-schooners crawling toward the ore
And the cheap car, parked by the station-door.

When the skyscrapers lift their foggy plumes
Of stranded smoke out of a stony mouth
You are that high stone and its arrogant fumes,
And you are ruined gardens in the South

And bleak New England farms, so winter-white
Even their roofs look lonely, and the deep
The middle grainland where the wind of night
Is like all blind earth sighing in her sleep.

A friend, an enemy, a sacred hag
With two tied oceans in her medicine-bag.

They tried to fit you with an English song
And clip your speech into the English tale.
But, even from the first, the words went wrong,
The catbird pecked away the nightingale.

The homesick men begot high-cheekboned things
Whose wit was whittled with a different sound
And Thames and all the rivers of the kings
Ran into Mississippi and were drowned.

They planted England with a stubborn trust.
But the cleft dust was never English dust.

Stepchild of every exile from content
And all the disavouched, hard-bitten pack
Shipped overseas to steal a continent
With neither shirts nor honor to their back.

Pimping grandee and rump-faced regicide,
Apple-cheeked younkers from a windmill-square,
Puritans stubborn as the nails of Pride,
Rakes from Versailles and thieves from County Clare,

The black-robed priests who broke their hearts in vain
To make you God and France or God and Spain.

These were your lovers in your buckskin-youth.
And each one married with a dream so proud
He never knew it could not be the truth
And that he coupled with a girl of cloud.

And now to see you is more difficult yet
Except as an immensity of wheel
Made up of wheels, oiled with inhuman sweat
And glittering with the heat of ladled steel.

All these you are, and each is partly you,
And none is false, and none is wholly true.

So how to see you as you really are,
So how to suck the pure, distillate, stored
Essence of essence from the hidden star
And make it pierce like a riposting sword.

For, as we hunt you down, you must escape
And we pursue a shadow of our own
That can be caught in a magician's cape
But has the flatness of a painted stone.

Never the running stag, the gull at wing,
The pure elixir, the American thing.

And yet, at moments when the mind was hot
With something fierier than joy or grief,

When each known spot was an eternal spot
And every leaf was an immortal leaf,

I think that I have seen you, not as one,
But clad in diverse semblances and powers,
Always the same, as light falls from the sun,
And always different, as the differing hours.

Yet, through each altered garment that you wore
The naked body, shaking the heart's core.

All day the snow fell on that Eastern town
With its soft, pelting, little, endless sigh
Of infinite flakes that brought the tall sky down
Till I could put my hands in the white sky

And taste cold scraps of heaven on my tongue
And walk in such a changed and luminous light
As gods inhabit when the gods are young.
All day it fell. And when the gathered night

Was a blue shadow cast by a pale glow
I saw you then, snow-image, bird of the snow.

And I have seen and heard you in the dry
Close-huddled furnace of the city street
When the parched moon was planted in the sky
And the limp air hung dead against the heat.

I saw you rise, red as that rusty plant,
Dizzied with lights, half-mad with senseless sound,
Enormous metal, shaking to the chant
Of a triphammer striking iron ground.

Enormous power, ugly to the fool,
And beautiful as a well-handled tool.

These, and the memory of that windy day
On the bare hills, beyond the last barbed wire,
When all the orange poppies bloomed one way
As if a breath would blow them into fire,

I keep forever, like the sea-lion's tusk
The broken sailor brings away to land,
But when he touches it, he smells the musk,
And the whole sea lies hollow in his hand.

So, from a hundred visions, I make one,
And out of darkness build my mocking sun.

And should that task seem fruitless in the eyes
Of those a different magic sets apart
To see through the ice-crystal of the wise
No nation but the nation that is Art,

Their words are just. But when the birchbark-call
Is shaken with the sound that hunters make
The moose comes plunging through the forest-wall
Although the rifle waits beside the lake.

Art has no nations—but the mortal sky
Lingers like gold in immortality.

This flesh was seeded from no foreign grain
But Pennsylvania and Kentucky wheat,
And it has soaked in California rain
And five years tempered in New England sleet.

To strive at last, against an alien proof
And by the changes of an alien moon,
To build again that blue, American roof
Over a half-forgotten battle-tune

And call unsurely, from a haunted ground,
Armies of shadows and the shadow-sound.

In your Long House there is an attic-place
Full of dead epics and machines that rust,
And there, occasionally, with casual face,
You come awhile to stir the sleepy dust;

Neither in pride nor mercy, but in vast
Indifference at so many gifts unsought,

The yellowed satins, smelling of the past,
And all the loot the lucky pirates brought.

I only bring a cup of silver air,
Yet, in your casualness, receive it there.

Receive the dream too haughty for the breast,
Receive the words that should have walked as bold
As the storm walks along the mountain-crest
And are like beggars whining in the cold.

The maimed presumption, the unskilful skill,
The patchwork colors, fading from the first,
And all the fire that fretted at the will
With such a barren ecstasy of thirst.

Receive them all—and should you choose to touch them
With one slant ray of quick, American light,
Even the dust will have no power to smutch them,
Even the worst will glitter in the night.

If not—the dry bones littered by the way
May still point giants toward their golden prey.

BOOK TWO (THE BATTLE OF BULL RUN)

A smoke-stained Stars-and-Stripes droops from a broken tooth-pick and ninety tired men march out of fallen Sumter to their ships, drums rattling and colors flying.

Their faces are worn and angry, their bellies empty and cold, but the stubborn salute of a gun, fifty times repeated, keeps their backs straight as they march out, and answers something stubborn and mute in their flesh.

Beauregard, *beau sabreur*, hussar-sword with the gilded hilt, the gilded metal of the guard twisted into lovelocks and roses, vain as Murat, dashing as Murat, Pierre Gustave Toutant Beauregard is a pose of conquering courtesy under a palmetto-banner. The lugubrious little march goes grimly by his courtesy, he watches it unsmiling, a light half-real, half that of invisible footlights on his French, dark, handsome face.

The stone falls in the pool, the ripples spread.
The colt in the Long Meadow kicked up his heels.
"That was a fly," he thought, "It's early for flies."
But being alive, in April, was too fine
For flies or anything else to bother a colt.
He kicked up his heels again, this time in pure joy,
And started to run a race with the wind and his shadow.
After the stable stuffiness, the sun.
After the straw-littered boards, the squelch of the turf.
His little hoofs felt lighter than dancing-shoes,
He scared himself with a blue-jay, his heart was a leaf.
He was pure joy in action, he was the unvexed
Delight of all moving lightness and swift-footed pace,
The pride of the flesh, the young Spring neighing and
    rearing.
Sally Dupré called to him from the fence.
He came like a charge in a spatter of clean-cut clods,
Ears back, eyes wide and wild with folly and youth.
He drew up snorting.
                    She laughed and brushed at her skirt
Where the mud had splashed it.
                        "There, Star—there, silly boy!
Why won't you ever learn sense?"
                            But her eyes were hot,
Her hands were shaking as she offered the sugar
—Long-fingered, appleblossom-shadow hands—
Star blew at the sugar once, then mumbled it up.
She patted the pink nose. "There, silly Star!
That's for Fort Sumter, Star!" How hot her eyes were!
"Star, do you know you're a Confederate horse?
Do you know I'm going to call you Beauregard?"

Star whinnied, and asked for more sugar. She put her hand
On his neck for a moment that matched the new green
    leaves
And sticky buds of April.
                        You would have said
They were grace in quietness, seen so, woman and
    horse. . . .

The widened ripple breaks against a stone
The heavy noon walks over Chancellorsville

On brazen shoes, but where the squadron rode
Into the ambush, the blue flies are coming
To blow on the dead meat.

Carter, the telegraph-operator, sighed
And propped his eyes awake again.
                                            He was tired.
Dog-tired, stone-tired, body and mind burnt up
With too much poker last night and too little sleep.
He hated the Sunday trick. It was Riley's turn
To take it, but Riley's wife was having a child.
He cursed the child and the wife and Sunday and Riley,
Nothing ever happened at Stroudsburg Siding
And yet he had to be here and keep awake
With the flat, stale taste of too little sleep in his mouth
And wait for nothing to happen.
                                            His bulky body
Lusted for sleep with every muscle and nerve.
He'd rather have sleep than a woman or whiskey or
    money.
He'd give up the next three women that might occur
For ten minutes' sleep, he'd never play poker again,
He'd—battered face beginning to droop on his hands—
Sleep—women—whiskey—eyelids too heavy to lift—
"Yes, Ma, I said, " 'Now I lay me.' "—
                                            The sounder chattered
And his head snapped back with a sharp, neck-breaking
    jerk.
By God, he'd nearly—*chat—chitter-chatter-chat-chat*—
For a moment he took it in without understanding
And then the vein in his forehead began to swell
And his eyes bulged wide awake.
                                            "By Jesus!" he said,
And stared at the sounder as if it had turned to a snake.
"By Jesus!" he said, "By Jesus, they've done it!" he said.

The cruelty of cold trumpets wounds the air.
The ponderous princes draw their gauntlets on.
The captains fit their coal-black armor on.

Judah P. Benjamin, the dapper Jew,
Seal-sleek, black-eyed, lawyer and epicure,

Able, well-hated, face alive with life,
Looked round the council-chamber with the slight
Perpetual smile he held before himself
Continually like a silk-ribbed fan.
Behind the fan, his quick, shrewd, fluid mind
Weighed Gentiles in an old balance.
                                        There they were.
Toombs, the tall, laughing, restless Georgian,
As fine to look at as a yearling bull,
As hard to manage.
                        Stephens, sickly and pale,
Sweet-voiced, weak-bodied, ailingly austere,
The mind's thin steel wearing the body out,
The racked intelligence, the crippled charm.
Mallory—Reagan—Walker—at the head
Davis.

        The mind behind the silk-ribbed fan
Was a dark prince, clothed in an Eastern stuff,
Whose brown hands cupped about a crystal egg
That filmed with colored cloud. The eyes stared, searching.

"I am the Jew. What am I doing here?
The Jew is in my blood and in my hands,
The lonely, bitter and quicksilver drop,
The stain of myrrh that dyes no Gentile mind
With tinctures out of the East and the sad blare
Of the curled ramshorn on Atonement Day.
A river runs between these men and me,
A river of blood and time and liquid gold,
—Oh white rivers of Canaan, running the night!—
And we are colleagues. And we speak to each other
Across the roar of that river, but no more.
I hide myself behind a smiling fan.
They hide themselves behind a Gentile mask
And, if they fall, they will be lifted up,
Being the people, but if I once fall
I fall forever, like the rejected stone.
That is the Jew of it, my Gentile friends,
To see too far ahead and yet go on
And I can smile at it behind my fan
With a drowned mirth that you would find uncouth.
For here we are, the makeshift Cabinet

Of a new nation, gravely setting down
Rules, precedents and cautions, never once
Admitting aloud the cold, plain Franklin sense
That if we do not hang together now
We shall undoubtedly hang separately.
It is the Jew, to see too far ahead—

I wonder what they're doing in the North,
And how their Cabinet shapes, and, how they take
Their railsplitter, and if they waste their time
As we waste ours and Mr. Davis's.

Jefferson Davis, pride of Mississippi,
First President of the Confederate States,
What are you thinking now?
                              Your eyes look tired.
Your face looks more and more like John Calhoun.
And that is just, because you are his son
In everything but blood, the austere child
Of his ideas, the flower of states-rights.
I will not gird against you, Jefferson Davis.
I sent you a challenge once, but that's forgotten,
And though your blood runs differently from mine,
The Jew salutes you from behind his fan,
Because you are the South he fell in love with
When that young black-haired girl with the Gentile-eyes,
Proud, and a Catholic, and with honey-lips,
First dinted her French heels upon his heart. . . .
We have changed since, but the remembered Spring
Can change no more, even in the Autumn smokes.
We cannot help that havoc of the heart
But my changed mind remembers half the spring
And shall till winter falls.
                              No, Jefferson Davis,
You are not she—you are not the warm night
On the bayou, or the New Orleans lamps,
The white-wine bubbles in the crystal cup,
The almond blossoms, sleepy with the sun:
But, nevertheless, you are the South in word,
Deed, thought and temper, the cut cameo
Brittle but durable, refined but fine,
The hands well-shaped, not subtle, but not weak,

The mind set in tradition but not unjust,
The generous slaveholder, the gentleman
Who neither forces his gentility
Nor lets it be held lightly—
                    and yet, and yet
I think you look too much like John Calhoun,
I think your temper is too brittly-poised,
I think your hands too scholar-sensitive,
And though they say you mingle in your voice
The trumpet and the harp, I think it lacks
That gift of warming men which coarser voices
Draw from the common dirt you tread upon
But do not take in your hands. I think you are
All things except success, all honesty
Except the ultimate honesty of the earth,
All talents but the genius of the sun.
And yet I would not have you otherwise,
Although I see too clearly what you are.

Except—except—oh honeydropping Spring,
Oh black-haired woman with the Gentile eyes!
Tell me, you Gentiles, when your Gentile wives
Pray in the church for you and for the South,
How do they pray?—not in that lulling voice
Where some drowned bell of France makes undertones
To the warm river washing the levee.
You do not have so good a prayer as mine.
You cannot have so good a prayer as mine."

Lincoln, six feet one in his stocking feet,
The lank man, knotty and tough as a hickory rail,
Whose hands were always too big for white-kid gloves,
Whose wit was a coonskin sack of dry, tall tales,
Whose weathered face was homely as a plowed field—
Abraham Lincoln, who padded up and down
The sacred White House in nightshirt and carpet-
    slippers,
And yet could strike young hero-worshipping Hay
As dignified past any neat, balanced, fine
Plutarchan sentences carved in a Latin bronze;
The low clown out of the prairies, the ape-buffoon,

The small-town lawyer, the crude small-time politician,
State-character but comparative failure at forty
In spite of ambition enough for twenty Caesars,
Honesty rare as a man without self-pity,
Kindness as large and plain as a praire wind,
And a self-confidence like an iron bar:
This Lincoln, President now by the grace of luck,
Disunion, politics, Douglas and a few speeches
Which make the monumental booming of Webster
Sound empty as the belly of a burst drum,
Lincoln shambled in to the Cabinet meeting
And sat, ungainly and awkward. Seated so
He did not seem so tall nor quite so strange
Though he was strange enough. His new broadcloth suit
Felt tight and formal across his big shoulders still
And his new shiny top-hat was not yet battered
To the bulging shape of the old familiar hat
He'd worn at Springfield, stuffed with its hoard of papers.
He was pretty tired. All week the office-seekers
Had plagued him as the flies in fly-time plague
A gaunt-headed, patient horse. The children weren't well
And Mollie was worried about them so sharp with her
    tongue.
But he knew Mollie and tried to let it go by.
Men tracked dirt in the house and women liked carpets.
Each had a piece of the right, that was all most people
    could stand.

Look at his Cabinet here. There were Seward and Chase,
Both of them good men, couldn't afford to lose them,
But Chase hates Seward like poison and Seward hates
    Chase
And both of 'em think they ought to be President
Instead of me. When Seward wrote me that letter
The other day, he practically told me so.
I suppose a man who was touchy about his pride
Would send them both to the dickens when he
    found out,
But I can't do that as long as they do their work.
The Union's too big a horse to keep changing the saddle
Each time it pinches you. As long as you're sure

The saddle fits, you're bound to put up with the pinches
And not keep fussing the horse.

                     When I was a boy
I remember figuring out when I went to town
That if I had just one pumpkin to bump in a sack
It was hard to carry, but once you could get two
    pumpkins,
One in each end of the sack, it balanced things up.
Seward and Chase'll do for my pair of pumpkins.
And as for me—if anyone else comes by
Who shows me that he can manage this job of mine
Better than I can—well, he can have the job.
It's harder sweating than driving six cross mules,
But I haven't run into that other fellow yet
And till or supposing I meet him, the job's my job
And nobody else's.

                Seward and Chase don't know that.
They'll learn it, in time.

                  Wonder how Jefferson Davis
Feels, down there in Montgomery, about Sumter.
He must be thinking pretty hard and fast,
For he's an able man, no doubt of that.
We were born less than forty miles apart,
Less than a year apart—he got the start
Of me in age, and raising too, I guess,
In fact, from all you hear about the man,
If you set out to pick one of us two
For President, by birth and folks and schooling,
General raising, training up in office,
I guess you'd pick him, nine times out of ten
And yet, somehow, I've got to last him out.

These thoughts passed through the mind in a moment's
    flash.
Then that mind turned to business.

                      It was the calling
Of seventy-five thousand volunteers.

Shake out the long line of verse like a lanyard of woven
    steel

And let us praise while we can what things no praise can
  deface,
The corn that hurried so fast to be ground in an iron
  wheel
The obdurate, bloody dream that slept before it grew
  base.

Not the silk flag and the shouts, the catchword
  patrioteers,
The screaming noise of the press, the preachers who
  howled for blood,
But a certain and stubborn pith in the hearts of the
  cannoneers
Who hardly knew their guns before they died in the mud.
They came like a run of salmon where the ice-fed
  Kennebec flings
Its death at the arrow-silver of the packed and mounting
  host,
They came like the young deer trooping to the ford by
  Eutaw Springs,
Their new horns fuzzy with velvet, their coats still rough
  with the frost.

North and South they assembled, one cry and the
  other cry,
And both are ghosts to us now, old drums hung up on a
  wall,
But they were the first hot wave of youth too-ready
  to die,
And they went to war with an air, as if they went to a ball.

Dress-uniform boys who rubbed their buttons brighter
  than gold,
And gave them to girls for flowers and raspberry-
  lemonade,
Unused to the sick fatigue, the route-march made in the
  cold,
The stink of the fever camps, the tarnish rotting the blade.

We in our time have seen that impulse going to war
And how that impulse is dealt with. We have seen the
  circle complete.

The ripe wheat wasted like trash between the fool and
   the whore.
We cannot praise again that anger of the ripe wheat.

This we have seen as well, distorted and half-forgotten
In what came before and after, where the blind went
   leading the blind,
The first swift rising of youth before the symbols were
   rotten,
The price too much to pay, the payment haughty in kind.

So with these men and then. They were much like the
   men you know,
Under the beards and the strangeness of clothes with a
   different fit.
They wrote mush-notes to their girls and wondered how
   it would go,
Half-scared, half-fierce at the thought, but none yet
   ready to quit.

Georgia, New York, Virginia, Rhode Island, Florida,
   Maine,
Piney-woods squirrel-hunter and clerk with the brand-
   new gun,
Thus they were marshalled and drilled, while Spring
   turned Summer again,
Until they could stumble toward death at gartersnake-
   crooked Bull Run.

Wingate sat in his room at night
Between the moon and the candle-light,
Reading his Byron with knitted brows,
While his mind drank in the peace of his house,
It was long past twelve, and the night was deep
With moonlight and silence and wind and sleep,
And the small, dim noises, thousand-fold,
That all old houses and forests hold.
The boards that creak for nothing at all,
The leaf that rustles, the bough that sighs,
The nibble of mice in the wainscot-wall,
And the slow clock ticking the time that dies

All distilled in a single sound
Like a giant breathing underground,
A sound more sleepy than sleep itself.
Wingate put his book on the shelf
And went to the window. It was good
To walk in the ghost through a silver wood
And set one's mettle against the far
Bayonet-point of the fixed North Star.
He stood there a moment, wondering.
North Star, wasp with the silver sting
Blue-nosed star on the Yankee banners,
We are coming against you to teach you manners!
With crumbs of thunder and wreaths of myrtle
And cannon that dance to a Dixie chorus,
With a song that bites like a snapping-turtle
And the tiger-lily of Summer before us,
To pull you down like a torn bandanna,
And drown you deeper than the Savannah!

And still, while his arrogance made its cry,
He shivered a little, wondering why.

There was his uniform, grey as ash,
The boots that shone like a well-rubbed table,
The tassels of silk on the colored sash
And sleek Black Whistle down in the stable,
The housewife, stitched from a beauty's fan,
The pocket-Bible with Mother's writing,
The sabre never yet fleshed in man,
And all the crisp new toys of fighting.
He gloated at them with a boyish pride,
But still he wondered, Monmouth-eyed.
The Black Horse Troop was a cavalier
And gallant name for a lady's ear.
He liked the sound and the ringing brag
And the girls who stitched on the county flag,
The smell of horses and saddle-leather
And the feel of the squadron riding together,
From the loose-reined canter of colts at large,
To the crammed, tense second before the charge:
He liked it all with the young, keen zest
Of a hound unleashed and a hawk unjessed.

And yet—what happened to men in war?
Why were they all going out to war?

He brooded a moment. It wasn't slavery,
That stale red-herring of Yankee knavery
Nor even states-rights, at least not solely,
But something so dim that it must be holy.
A voice, a fragrance, a taste of wine,
A face half-seen in old candleshine,
A yellow river, a blowing dust,
Something beyond you that you must trust,
Something so shrouded it must be great,
The dead men building the living State
From 'simmon-seed on a sandy bottom,
The woman South in her rivers laving
That body whiter than new-blown cotton
And savage and sweet as wild-orange-blossom,
The dark hair streams on the barbarous bosom,
If there ever has been a land worth saving—
In Dixie land, I'll take my stand,
And live and die for Dixie! . . .

And yet—and yet—in some cold Northern room,
Does anyone else stare out the obdurate moon
With doubtful passion, seeing his toys of fighting
Scribbled all over with such silver writing
From such a heart of peace, they seem the stale
Cast properties of a dead and childish tale?
And does he see, too soon,
Over the horse, over the horse and rider,
The grey, soft swathing shadowness of the spider,
Spinning his quiet loom?
No—no other man is cursed
With such doubleness of eye,
They can hunger, they can thirst,
But they know for what and why.

I can drink the midnight out,
And rise empty, having dined.
For my courage and my doubt
Are a double strand of mind,
And too subtly intertwined.

They are my flesh, they are my bone,
My shame and my foundation-stone.
I was born alone, to live alone.

Sally Dupré, Sally Dupré,
Eyes that are neither black nor grey,
Why do you haunt me, night and day?

Sea-changing eyes, with the deep, drowned glimmer
Of bar-gold crumbling from sunken ships,
Where the sea-dwarfs creep through the streaked, green
    shimmer
To press the gold to their glass-cold lips.
They sculpture the gold for a precious ring,
In the caverns under the under-skies,
They would marry the sea to a sailor-king!
You have taken my heart from me, sea-born eyes.
You have taken it, yes, but I do not know.
There are too many roads where I must go.
There are too many beds where I have slept
For a night unweeping, to quit unwept,
And it needs a king to marry the sea.

Why have you taken my heart from me?
I am not justice nor loyalty.
I am the shape of the weathercock,
That all winds come to and all winds mock.
You are the image of sea-carved stone,
The silent thing that can suffer alone,
The little women are easier,
The easy women make lighter love,
I will not take your face to the war,
I will not carry your cast-off glove.

Sally Dupré, Sally Dupré,
Heart and body like sea-blown spray,
I cannot forget you, night or day.

So Wingate pondered in Wingate Hall,
And hated and loved in a single breath,
As he tried to unriddle the doubtful scrawl
Of war and courage and love and death,

And then was suddenly nothing but sleep—
And tomorrow they marched—to a two-months chasing
Of Yankees running away like sheep
And peace in time for the Macon racing.

He got in his bed. Where the moonlight poured,
It lay like frost on a sleeping sword.

It was stuffy at night in the cabins, stuffy but warm.
And smells are a matter of habit. So, if the air
Was thick as black butter with the commingled smells
Of greens and fried fat and field-sweat and heavy sleep,
The walls were well-chinked, the low roof kept out the
    rain.
Not like the tumble-down cabins at Zachary's place
Where the field-hands lived all year on hominy-grits
And a piece of spoiled pork at Christmas.
                                        But Zachary
Was a mean man out of the Bottoms, no quality to him.
Wingate was quality. Wingate cared for its own.
A Wingate cabin was better than most such cabins,
You might have called it a sty, had they set you there;
A Middle Age serf might have envied the well-chinked
    walls.
While as for its tenants then, being folk unversed
In any law but the law of the Wingate name,
They were glad to have it, glad for fire on the hearth,
A roof from the dark-veined wind.
                                        Their bellies were warm
And full of food. They were heavy in love with each
    other.
They liked their cabin and lying next to each other,
Long nights of winter when the slow-burning pine-knots
Danced ghosts and witches over the low, near ceiling,
Short nights of summer, after the work of the fields,
When the hot body aches with the ripened sweetness
And the children and the new tunes are begotten
    together.

"What you so wakeful for, black boy?"
                                        "Thinkin', woman."

"You got no call to be thinkin', little black boy,
Thinkin's a trouble, a h'ant lookin' over de shoulder,
Set yo' head on my breas' and forget about thinkin'."

"I got my head on yo' breas', and it's sof' dere, woman,
Sof' and sweet as a mournin' out of de Scriptures,
Sof' as two Solomon doves. But I can't help thinkin'."

"Ain't I good enough for you no more, black boy?
Don' you love me no more dat you mus' keep thinkin'?"

"You's better'n good to me and I loves you, woman,
Till I feels like Meshuck down in de fiery furnace,
Till I feels like God's own chile. But I keeps on thinkin',
Wonderin' what I'd feel like if I was free."

"Hush, black boy, hush for de Lord's sake!"
                                        "But listen, woman—"

"Hush yo'self, black boy, lean yo'self on my breas',
Talk like that and paterollers'll git you,
Swinge you all to bits with a blacksnake whip,
Squinch-owl carry yo' talk to de paterollers,
It ain't safe to talk like that."
                            "I got to, woman,
I got a feelin' in my heart."
                                        "Den you sot on dat feelin'!
Never heard you talk so in all my born days!
Ain't we got a good cabin here?"
                                        "Sho', we got a good cabin."
"Ain't we got good vitties, ain't old Mistis kind to us?"

"Sho' we got good vittles, and ole Mistis she's kind.
I'se mighty fond of ole Mistis."
                                        "Den what you talkin',
You brash fool-nigger?"
                                "I just got a feelin', woman.
Ole Marse Billy, he's goin' away tomorrow,
Marse Clay, he's goin' with him to fight de Yankees,
All of 'em goin', yes suh."
                                        "And what if dey is?"

"Well, sposin' de Yankees beats?"

                                "Ain't you got *no* sense,
  nigger?
Like to see any ole Yankees lick ole Marse Billy
And young Marse Clay!"

                        "Hi, woman, ain't dat de trufe!"
"Well, den—"

            "But I sees 'em all, jus' goin' and goin',
Goin' to war like Joshua, goin' like David,
And it makes me want to be free. Ain't you never
  thought
At all about bein' free?"

                    "Sho', co'se I thought of it.
I always reckoned when ole Marse Billy died,
Old Mistis mebbe gwine to set some of us free,
Mebbe she will."

                  "But we-uns gwine to be old den,
We won't be young and have the use of our hands,
We won't see our young 'uns growin' up free around us,
We won't have the strength to hoe our own co'n
  ourselves,
I want to be free, like me, while I got my strength."

"You might be a lot worse off and not be free,
What'd you do if ole man Zachary owned us?"

"Kill him, I reckon."

                "Hush, black boy, for God's sake hush!"

"I can't help it, woman. Dey ain't so many like him
But what dey is is too pizen-mean to live.
Can't you hear dat feelin' I got, woman? I ain't scared
Of talk and de paterollers, and I ain't mean.
I'se mighty fond of ole Mistis and ole Marse Billy,
I'se mighty fond of 'em all at de Big House,
I wouldn't be nobody else's nigger for nothin'.
But I hears 'em goin' away, all goin' away,
With horses and guns and things, all stompin' and
  wavin',
And I hears de chariot-wheels and de Jordan River,
Rollin' and rollin' and rollin' thu' my sleep,

And I wants to be free. I wants to see my chillun
Growin' up free, and all bust out of Egypt!
I wants to be free like an eagle in de air,
Like an eagle in de air."

Iron-filings scattered over a dusty
Map of crook-cornered States in yellow and blue.
Little, grouped male and female iron-filings,
Scattered over a patchwork-quilt whose patches
Are the red-earth stuff of Georgia, the pine-bough green
    of Vermont.
Here you are clustered as thick as a clump of bees
In swarming time. The clumps make cities and towns.
Here you are strewn at random, like single seeds
Lost out of the wind's pocket.
                   But now, but now,
The thunderstone has fallen on your map
And all the iron-filings shiver and move
Under the grippings of that blinded force,
The cold pull of the ash-and-cinder star.

The map is vexed with the long battle-worms
Of filings, clustered and moving.
                      If it is
An enemy of the sun who has so stolen
Power from a burnt star to do this work,
Let the bleak essence of the utter cold
Beyond the last gleam of the most outpost light
Freeze in his veins forever.
                  But if it is
A fault in the very metal of the heart,
We and our children must acquit that fault
With the old bloody wastage, or give up
Playing the father to it.
                O vexed and strange,
Salt-bitter, apple-sweet, strong-handed life!
Your million lovers cast themselves like sea
Against your mountainy breast, with a clashing noise
And a proud clamor—and like sea recoil,
Sucked down beneath the forefoot of the new

Advancing surf. They feed the battle-worms,
Not only War's, but in the second's pause
Between the assaulting and the broken wave,
The voices of the lovers can be heard,
The sea-gull cry.

Jake Diefer, the barrel-chested Pennsylvanian,
Hand like a ham and arms that could wrestle a bull,
A roast of a man, all solid meat and good fat,
A slow-thought-chewing Clydesdale horse of a man,
Roused out of his wife's arms. The dawn outside
Was ruddy as his big cheeks. He yawned and stretched
Gigantically, hawking and clearing his throat.
His wife, hair tousled around her like tousled corn,
Stared at him with sleep-blind eyes.

                              "Jake, it ain't come
    morning,
Already yet?"

                    He nodded and started to dress.
She burrowed deeper into the bed for a minute
And then threw off the covers.

                              They didn't say much
Then, or at breakfast. Eating was something serious.
But he looked around the big kitchen once or twice
In a puzzled way, as if trying hard to remember it.
She too, when she was busy with the first batch
Of pancakes, burnt one or two, because she was staring
At the "SALT" on the salt-box, for no particular reason.
The boy ate with them and didn't say a word,
Being too sleepy.

                    Afterwards, when the team
Was hitched up and waiting, with the boy on the seat,
Holding the reins till Jake was ready to take them,
Jake didn't take them at once.

                              The sun was up now,
The spilt-milk-mist of first morning lay on the farm,
Jake looked at it all with those same mildly-puzzled eyes,
The red barn, the fat rich fields just done with the winter,
Just beginning the work of another year.
The boy would have to do the rest of the planting.

He blew on his hands and stared at his wife dumbly.
He cleared his throat.
                              "Well, good-by, Minnie," he said,
"Don't you hire any feller for harvest without you
    write me,
And if any more of those lightning-rodders come
    around,
We don't want no more dum lightning-rods."
                                                    He tried
To think if there was anything else, but there wasn't.
She suddenly threw her big, red arms around his neck,
He kissed her with clumsy force.
                              Then he got on the wagon
And clucked to the horses as she started to cry.

Up in the mountains where the hogs are thin
And razorbacked, wild Indians of hogs,
The laurel's green in April—and if the nights
Are cold as the cold cloud of watersmoke
Above a mountain-spring, the midday sun
Has heat enough in it to make you sweat.

They are a curious and most native stock,
The lanky men, the lost, forgotten seeds
Spilled from the first great wave-march toward the West
And set to sprout by chance in the deep cracks
Of that hill-billy world of laurel-hells.
They keep the beechwood-fiddle and the salt
Old-fashioned ballad-English of our first
Rowdy, corn-liquor-drinking, ignorant youth;
Also the rifle and the frying-pan,
The old feud-temper and the old feud-way
Of thinking strangers better shot on sight
But treating strangers that one leaves unshot
With border-hospitality.
                              The girls
Have the brief-blooming, rhododendron-youth
Of pioneer women, and the black-toothed age.
And if you yearn to meet your pioneers,
You'll find them there, the same men, inbred sons
Of inbred sires perhaps, but still the same;

A pioneer-island in a world that has
No use for pioneers—the unsplit rock
Of Fundamentalism, calomel,
Clan-virtues, clannish vices, fiddle-tunes
And a hard God.
                    They are our last frontier.
They shot the railway-train when it first came,
And when the Fords first came, they shot the Fords.
It could not save them. They are dying now
Or being educated, which is the same.
One need not weep romantic tears for them,
But when the last moonshiner buys his radio,
And the last, lost, wild-rabbit of a girl
Is civilized with a mail-order dress,
Something will pass that was American
And all the movies will not bring it back.

They are misfit and strange in our new day,
In Sixty-One they were not quite so strange,
Before the Fords, before the day of the Fords . . .

Luke Breckinridge, his rifle on his shoulder,
Slipped through green forest alleys toward the town,
A gawky boy with smoldering eyes, whose feet
Whispered the crooked paths like moccasins.
He wasn't looking for trouble, going down,
But he was on guard, as always. When he stopped
To scoop some water in the palm of his hand
From a sweet trickle between moss-grown rocks,
You might have thought him careless for a minute,
But when the snapped stick cracked six feet behind him
He was all sudden rifle and hard eyes.
The pause endured a long death-quiet instant,
Then he knew who it was.
                        "Hi, Jim," he said,
Lowering his rifle. The green laurel-screen
Hardly had moved, but Jim was there beside him.
The cousins looked at each other. Their rifles seemed
To look as well, with much the same taut silentness.
"Goin' to town, Luke?"
                        "Uh-huh, goin' to town,
You goin'?"

     "Looks as if I was goin'."
                        "Looks
As if you was after squirrels."
                 "I might be.
You goin' after squirrels?" "I might be, too."
"Not so many squirrels near town."
                     "No, reckon there's not."

Jim hesitated. His gaunt hands caressed
The smooth guard of his rifle. His eyes were sharp.
"Might go along a piece together," he said.
Luke didn't move. Their eyes clashed for a moment,
Then Luke spoke, casually.
                 "I hear the Kelceys
Air goin' to fight in this here war," he said.
Jim nodded slowly, "Yuh, I heerd that too."
He watched Luke's trigger-hand.
                 "I might be goin'
Myself sometime," he said reflectively
Sliding his own hand down. Luke saw the movement.
"We-uns don't like the Kelceys much," he said
With his eyes down to pinpoints.
                Then Jim smiled.
"We-uns neither," he said.
               His hand slid back.

They went along together after that
But neither of them spoke for half-a-mile,
Then finally, Jim said, half-diffidently,
"You know who we air goin' to fight outside?
I heard it was the British. Air that so?"
"Hell, no," said Luke, with scorn. He puckered his
   brows.
"Dunno's I rightly know just who they air."
He admitted finally, "But 'tain't the British.
It's some trash-lot of furriners, that's shore.
They call 'em Yankees near as I kin make it,
But they ain't Injuns neither."
                "Well," said Jim
Soothingly, "Reckon it don't rightly matter
Long as the Kelceys take the other side."

It was noon when the company marched to the railroad-
    station.
The town was ready for them. The streets were packed.
There were flags and streamers and pictures of Lincoln
    and Hamlin.
The bad little boys climbed up on the trees and yelled,
The good little boys had clean paper-collars on,
And swung big-eyed on white-painted wicket-gates,
Wanting to yell, and feeling like Fourth of July.
Somebody fastened a tin can full of firecrackers
To a yellow dog's tail and sent him howling and
    racketing
The length of the street.
                    "There goes Jeff Davis!" said somebody,
And everybody laughed, and the little boys
Punched each other and squealed between fits of
    laughing
"There goes Jeff Davis—lookit ole yellow Jeff Davis!"
And then the laugh died and rose again in a strange
Half-shrill, half-strangled unexpected shout
As they heard the Hillsboro' Silver Cornet Band
Swinging "John Brown's Body" ahead of the soldiers.
I have heard that soul of crowd go out in the queer
Groan between laughter and tears that baffles the wise.
I have heard that whanging band.

"We'll hang Jeff Davis on a sour-apple tree."
Double-roll on the snare-drums, double squeal of the
    fife,
"We'll hang Jeff Davis on a sour-apple tree!"
Clash of the cymbals zinging, throaty blare of cornets,
"We'll hang Jeff Davis on a sour-apple tree!"
"On to Richmond! On to Richmond! On to Richmond!"
"Yeah! There they come! Yeah! Yeah!"
And they came, the bearskin drum-major leading the
    band,
Twirling his silver-balled baton with turkey-cock pomp,
The cornet-blowers, the ranks. The drum-major was
    fine,

But the little boys thought the captain was even finer,
He looked just like a captain out of a book
With his sword and his shoulder-straps and his
    discipline-face.
He wasn't just Henry Fairfield, he was a captain,
—Henry Fairfield worried about his sword,
Hoping to God that he wouldn't drop his sword,
And wondering hotly whether his discipline-face
Really looked disciplined or only peevish—
"*Yeah!* There they come! There's Jack! There's Charlie!
    Yeah! Yeah!"
The color-guard with the stiff, new flapping flag,
And the ranks and the ranks and the ranks, the amateur
Blue, wavering ranks, in their ill-fitting tight coats,
Shoulders galled already by their new guns,
—They were three-months' men, they had drilled in
    civilian clothes
Till a week ago—"There's Charlie! There's Hank, yeah,
    yeah!"
"On to Richmond, boys! Three cheers for Abe Lincoln!
Three cheers for the boys! Three groans for old Jeff
    Davis
And the dirty Rebs!"
"*We'll hang Jeff Davis on a sour-apple tree!*"

Jack Ellyat, marching, saw between blue shoulders
A blur of faces. They all were faces he knew,
Old Mrs. Cobb with her wart and her Paisley shawl,
Little George Freeman, the slim Tucker girls,
All of them cheering and shouting—and all of them
    strange
Suddenly, different, faces he'd never seen.
Faces somehow turned into one crowd-face.
His legs went marching along all right but they felt
Like somebody else's legs, his mind was sucked dry.
It was real, they were going away, the town was cheering
    them.
Henry Fairfield was marching ahead with his sword.
Just as he'd thought about it a thousand times,
These months—but it wasn't the way that he'd thought
    about it.

"On to Richmond! On to Richmond! On to Richmond!"
There were Mother and Father and Jane and the house.
Jane was waving a flag. He laughed and called to them.
But his voice was stiff in his throat, not like his real
    voice.
This, everything, it was too quick, too crowded, not
    Phaëton
Charging his snarling horses at a black sea,
But a numb, hurried minute with legs that marched
Mechanically, feeling nothing at all.
The white crowd-face—the sweat on the red seamed
    neck
Of the man ahead—"On to Richmond!"—blue shoulders
    bobbing—
Flags—cheering—somebody kissed him—Ellen Baker—
She was crying—wet mouth of tears—didn't want her to
    kiss him—
Why did she want to—the station—*halt*—Mother and
    Jane.
The engineer wore a flag in his coat lapel,
The engine had "On to Richmond!" chalked all over it.
Nothing to say now—Mother looks tired to death—
I wish I weren't going—no, I'm glad that I am—
The damn band's playing "John Brown's Body" again,
I wish they'd stop it!—I wish to God we could start—
There—*close up, men!*—oh my God, they've let Ned out!
I told them for God's sake to lock him up in the cellar,
But they've let him out—maybe he got out by himself—
He's got too much sense—"No, down, Ned! Down,
    good dog!
Down, I tell you!—"
                    "*Good-by, boys! Good-by! We'll
                    hang Jeff Davis!*"
The engine squealed, the packed train started to move.
Ned wanted to come, but they wouldn't let him come.
They had to kick him away, he couldn't see why.

In another column, footsore Curly Hatton
Groaned at the thought of marching any more.
His legs weren't built for marching and they knew it,

Butterball-legs under a butterball-body.
The plump good-tempered face with its round eyes
Blue and astonished as a china-doll's,
Stared at the road ahead and hated it
Because there was so much of it ahead
And all of it so dry.
                         He didn't mind
The rest so much. He didn't even mind
Being the one sure necessary joke
Of the whole regiment. He'd always been
A necessary joke—fat people were.
Fat babies always were supposed to laugh.
Fat little boys had fingers poked at them.
And, even with the road, and being fat,
You had a good time in this funny war,
Considering everything, and one thing most.

His mind slipped back two months. He saw himself
In the cool room at Weatherby's Retreat
Where all the girls were sewing the new star
In the new flag for the first volunteers.
He hadn't thought of fighting much before,
He was too easy-going. If Virginia
Wanted secession, that was her affair.
It seemed too bad to break the Union up
After some seventy years of housekeeping.
But he could understand the way you'd feel
If you were thin and angry at the Yanks.
He knew a lot of Yankees that he liked,
But then he liked most people, on the whole
Although most girls and women made him shy.
He loved the look of them and the way they walked,
He loved their voices and their little sweet mouths,
But something always seemed to hold him back,
When he was near them.
                         He was too fat, too friendly,
Too comfortable for dreams, too easy-shy.
The porcelain dolls stood on the mantelpiece,
Waiting such slim and arrant cavaliers
As porcelain dolls must have to make them proud,
They had no mercy for fat Cupidons,
Not even Lucy, all the years before,

And Lucy was the porcelain belle of the world!
And so when she said.

                       And he couldn't believe
At first
        But she was silver and fire and steel
That day of the new stars and the new flag,
Fire and bright steel for the invading horde
And silver for the men who drove them off,
And so she sewed him in her flag and heart:
Though even now, he couldn't believe she had
In spite of all the letters and the socks
And kissing him before he went away.
But it was so—the necessary joke
Made into a man at last, a man in love
And loved by the most porcelain belle of the world.
And he was ready to march to the world's end
And fight ten million Yanks to keep it so.

"Oh God, after we're married—the cool night
Over the garden—and Lucy sitting there
In her blue dress while the big stars come out."
His face was funny with love and footsore pride,
The man beside him saw it, gave a laugh,
"Curly's thinking it's time for a julep, boys!
Hot work for fat men, Curly!"

The crows fly over the Henry House, through the red
    sky of evening, cawing,
Judith Henry, bedridden, watches them through the
    clouded glass of old sight.
(July is hot in Virginia—a parched, sun-leathered farmer
    sawing
Dry sticks with a cicada-saw that creaks all the lukewarm
    night.)

But Judith Henry's hands are cool in spite of all
    midsummer's burning,
Cool, muted and frail with age like the smoothness of
    old yellow linen, the cool touch of old, dulled rings.
Her years go past her in bed like falling waters and the
    waters of a millwheel turning,

And she is not ill content to lie there, dozing and calm,
   remembering youth, to the gushing of those
   watersprings.

She has known Time like the cock of red dawn and Time
   like a tired clock slowing;
She has seen so many faces and bodies, young and then
   old, so much life, so many patterns of death and birth.
She knows that she must leave them soon. She is not
   afraid to flow with that river's flowing.
But the wrinkled earth still hangs at her sufficed breast
   like a weary child, she is unwilling to go while she still
   has milk for the earth.

She will go in her sleep, most likely, she has the sunk
   death-sleep of the old already,
(War-bugles by the Potomac, you cannot reach her ears
   with your brass lyric, piercing the crowded dark.)
It does not matter, the farm will go on, the farm and the
   children bury her in her best dress, the plow cut its
   furrow, steady,
(War-horses of the Shenandoah, why should you hurry
   so fast to tramp the last ashy fire from so feeble and
   retired a spark?)
There is nothing here but a creek and a house called the
   Henry House, a farm and a bedridden woman and
   people with country faces.
There is nothing for you here. And La Haye Sainte was a
   quiet farm and the mile by it a quiet mile.
And Lexington was a place to work in like any one of a
   dozen dull, little places.
And they raised good crops at Blenheim till the soldiers
   came and spoiled the crops for a while.

The red evening fades into twilight, the crows have gone
   to their trees, the slow, hot stars are emerging.
It is cooler now on the hill—and in the camps it is cooler,
   where the untried soldiers find their bivouac hard.
Where, from North and South, the blind wrestlers of
   armies converge on the forgotten house like the double
   pincers of an iron claw converging.

And Johnston hurries his tired brigades from the Valley,
   to bring them up in time before McDowell can fall on
   Beauregard.

The congressmen came out to see Bull Run,
The congressmen who like free shows and spectacles.
They brought their wives and carriages along,
They brought their speeches and their picnic-lunch,
Their black constituent-hats and their devotion:
Some even brought a little whiskey, too,
(A little whiskey is a comforting thing
For congressmen in the sun, in the heat of the sun.)
The bearded congressmen with orator's mouths,
The fine, clean-shaved, Websterian congressmen,
Come out to see the gladiator's show
Like Iliad gods, wrapped in the sacred cloud
Of Florida-water, wisdom and bay-rum,
Of free cigars, democracy and votes,
That lends such portliness to congressmen.
(The gates fly wide, the bronze troop marches out
Into the stripped and deadly circus-ring,
"Ave, Caesar!" the cry goes up, and shakes
The purple awning over Caesar's seat.)
"Ave, Caesar! Ave, O congressmen,
We who are about to die,
Salute you, congressmen!"
Eleven States,
New York, Rhode Island, Maine,
Connecticut, Michigan and the gathered West,
Salute you, congressmen!
The red-fezzed Fire-Zouaves, flamingo-bright,
Salute you, congressmen!
The raw boys still in their civilian clothes,
Salute you, congressmen!
The second Wisconsin in its homespun grey,
Salutes you, congressmen!
The Garibaldi Guards in cocksfeather hats,
Salute you, congressmen!
The Second Ohio with their Bedouin-caps,
Salutes you, congressmen!

Sherman's brigade, grey-headed Heintzelman,
Ricketts' and Griffin's doomed and valiant guns,
The tough, hard-bitten regulars of Sykes
Who covered the retreat with the Marines,
Burnside and Porter, Willcox and McDowell,
All the vast, unprepared, militia-mass
Of boys in red and yellow Zouave pants,
Who carried peach-preserves inside their kits
And dreamt of being generals overnight;
The straggling companies where every man
Was a sovereign and a voter—the slack regiments
Where every company marched a different step;
The clumsy and unwieldy-new brigades
Not yet distempered into battle-worms;
The whole, huge, innocent army, ready to fight
But only half-taught in the tricks of fighting,
Ready to die like picture-postcard boys
While fighting still had banners and a sword
And just as ready to run in blind mob-panic,
Salutes you with a vast and thunderous cry,
Ave, Caesar, ave, O congressmen,
Ave, O Iliad gods who forced the fight!
You bring your carriages and your picnic-lunch
To cheer us in our need.
                You come with speeches,
Your togas smell of heroism and bay-rum.
You are the people and the voice of the people
And, when the fight is done, your carriages
Will bear you safely, through the streaming rout
Of broken troops, throwing their guns away.
You come to see the gladiator's show,
But from a high place, as befits the wise:
You will not see the long windrows of men
Strewn like dead pears before the Henry House
Or the stone-wall of Jackson breathe its parched
Devouring breath upon the failing charge,
Ave, Caesar, ave, O congressmen,
Cigar-smoke wraps you in a godlike cloud,
And if you are not to depart from us
As easily and divinely as you came,
It hardly matters.
              Fighting Joe Hooker once

Said with that tart, unbridled tongue of his
That made so many needles enemies,
"Who ever saw a dead cavalryman?"
                              The phrase
Stings with a needle sharpness, just or not,
But even he was never heard to say,
"Who ever saw a dead congressman?"
And yet, he was a man with a sharp tongue.

The day broke, hot and calm. In the little farm-houses
That are scattered here and there in that rolling country
Of oak and rail-fence, crooked creeks and second-
   growth pine,
The early-risers stand looking out of the door
At the long dawn-shadows for a minute or two
—Shadows are always cool—but the blue-glass sky
Is fusing with heat even now, heat that prickles the
 hairs
On the back of your hand.
                    They sigh and turn back to the house.
"Looks like a scorcher today, boys!"
                              They think already
Of the cool jug of vinegar-water down by the hedge.

Judith Henry wakened with the first light,
She had the short sleep of age, and the long patience.
She waited for breakfast in vague, half-drowsy
   wonderment
At various things. Yesterday some men had gone by
And stopped for a drink of water. She'd heard they were
   soldiers.
She couldn't be sure. It had seemed to worry the folks
But it took more than soldiers and such to worry
   her now.
Young people always worried a lot too much.
No soldiers that had any sense would fight around here.
She'd had a good night. Today would be a good day.

A mile and a half away, before the Stone Bridge,
A Union gun opened fire.

Six miles away, McDowell had planned his battle
And planned it well, as far as such things can be
    planned—
A feint at one point, a flanking march at another
To circle Beauregard's left and crumple it up.
There were Johnston's eight thousand men to be
    reckoned with
But Patterson should be holding them, miles away,
And even if they slipped loose from Patterson's fingers
The thing might still be done.
                              If you take a flat map
And move wooden blocks upon it strategically,
The thing looks well, the blocks behave as they should.
The science of war is moving live men like blocks.
And getting the blocks into place at a fixed moment.
But it takes time to mold your men into blocks
And flat maps turn into country where creeks and gullies
Hamper your wooden squares. They stick in the brush,
They are tired and rest, they straggle after ripe
    blackberries,
And you cannot lift them up in your hand and move
    them.
—A string of blocks curling smoothly around the left
Of another string of blocks and crunching it up—
It is all so clear in the maps, so clear in the mind,
But the orders are slow, the men in the blocks are slow
To move, when they start they take too long on
    the way—
The General loses his stars and the block-men die
In unstrategic defiance of martial law
Because still used to just being men, not block-parts.
McDowell was neither a fool nor a fighting fool;
He knew his dice, he knew both armies unready,
But congressmen and nation wanted a battle
And he felt their hands on his shoulders, forcing his play.
He knew well enough when he played that he played for
    his head
As Beauregard and Johnston were playing for theirs,
So he played with the skill he had—and does not lie
Under a cupolaed gloom on Riverside Drive.

Put Grant in his place that day and with those same dice,
Grant might have done little better.
                                        Wherefore, now,
Irvin McDowell, half-forgotten general,
Who tried the game and found no luck in the game
And never got the chance to try it again
But did not backbite the gamblers who found more luck
    in it
Then or later in double-edged reminiscences;
If any laurel can grow in the sad-colored fields
Between Bull Run and Cub Run and Cat Hairpin Bend
You should have a share of it for your hardworking
    ghost
Because you played as you could with your cold, forced
    dice
And neither wasted your men like the fighting fools
Nor posed as an injured Napoleon twenty years later.
Meanwhile, McDowell watched his long flanking column
File by, on the Warrentown pike, in the first dawn-
    freshness.
"Gentlemen, that's a big force," he said to his staff.

A full rifled battery begins to talk spitefully to Evans' Carolinians.
The grey skirmish-line, thrown forward on the other side of Bull
Run, ducks its head involuntarily as a locomotive noise goes by
in the air above it, and waits for a flicker of blue in the scrub-oaks
ahead.

Beauregard, eager *sabreur*, whose heart was a French
Print of a sabretasche-War with "La Gloire" written
    under it,
Lovable, fiery, bizarre, picturesque as his name,
Galloped toward Mitchell's Ford with bald, quiet Joe
    Johnston,
The little precise Scotch-dominie of a general,
Stubborn as flint, in advance not always so lucky,
In retreat more dangerous than a running wolf—
Slant shadow, sniffing the traps and the poisoned meat,
And going on to pause and slash at the first
Unwary dogs before the hunters came up.

Grant said of him once,
"I was always anxious with Joe Johnston in front of me,
I was never half so anxious in front of Lee."
He kissed his friends in the Nelson-way we've forgotten,
He could make men cheer him after six-weeks retreating.
Another man said of him, after the war was done,
Still with that puzzled comparison we find
When Lee, the reticent sword, comes into the question,
"Yes, Lee was a great general, a good man;
But I never wanted to put my arms round his neck
As I used to want to with Johnston."
                              The two sayings
Make a good epitaph for so Scotch a ghost,
Or would if they were all.
                              They are not quite all,
He had to write his reminiscences, too,
And tell what he would have done if it had not been
For Davis and chance and a dozen turns of the wheel.
That was the thistle in him—the other strain—
But he was older then.
                              I'd like to have seen him
That day as he galloped along beside Beauregard,
Sabreur and dominie planning the battle-lines.
They'd ordered Jackson up to the threatened left
But Beauregard was sure that the main assault
Would come on the right. He'd planned it so—a good
    plan—
But once the blocks start moving, they keep on moving.

〜〜〜

The hands of the scuffed brown clock in the kitchen of
    the Henry House point to nine-forty-five.
Judith Henry does not hear the clock, she hears in the
    sky a vast dim roar like piles of heavy lumber
    crashingly falling.
They are carrying her in her bed to a ravine below the
    Sudley Road, maybe she will be safe there, maybe the
    battle will go by and leave her alive.
The crows have been scared from their nests by the
    strange crashing, they circle in the sky like a flight of
    blackened leaves, wheeling and calling.

Back at Centerville, there are three-months' men,
A Pennsylvania regiment, a New York Battery.
They hear the spent wave of the roar of the opening
    guns,
But they are three-months' men, their time is up today.
They would have fought yesterday or a week ago,
But then they were still enlisted—today they are not—
Their time is up, and there can't be much use or sense
In fighting longer than you've promised to fight.
They pack up their things and decide they'd better go
    home,
And quietly march away from that gathering roar.

Luke Breckinridge, crouched by the Warrentown pike,
Saw stuffed dolls in blue coats and baggy trousers
Go down like squirrels under the rifle-cracks.
His eyes glowed as a bullet ripped his sleeve
And he felt well. Armies weren't such a much,
Too damn many orders, too damn much saluting,
Too many damn officers you weren't allowed
To shoot when they talked mean to you because
They were your officers, which didn't make sense.
But this was something he could understand,
Except for those dirty stinkers of big guns,
It wasn't right to shoot you with big guns
But it was a good scrap except for that—
Carried a little high, then . . . change it . . . good . . .
Though men were hard to miss when you were used
To squirrels. His eyes were narrow. He hardly heard
The officer's voice. The woods in front of him
Were full of Kelceys he was going to kill,
Blue-coated Kelcey dolls in baggy trousers.
It was a beautiful and sufficing sight.

   The first blue wave of Burnside is beaten back from the pike to
stumble a little way and rally against Porter's fresh brigade.
   Bee and Bartow move down from the Henry House plateau—

grey and butternut lines trampling the bullet-cut oak-leaves, splashing across Young's Branch.

Tall, black-bearded Bee rides by on his strong horse, his long black hair fluttering.

Imboden's red-shirted gunners unlimber by the Henry House to answer the Parrotts and howitzers of Ricketts and Griffin.

The air is a sheet of iron, continually and dully shaken.

Shippy, the little man with the sharp rat-eyes,
Saw someone run in front of them waving a sword;
Then they were going along toward a whining sound
That ran like cold spring-water along his spine.
God, he was in for it now! His sharp rat-eyes
Flickered around and about him hopelessly.
If a fellow could only drop out, if a fellow could only
Pretend he was hurt a little and then drop out
Behind a big, safe oak-tree—no use—no use—
He was in for it, now. He couldn't get away.
*"Come on, boys—come on, men—clean them out with
   the bayonet!"*
He saw a rail-fence ahead, a quiet rail-fence,
But men were back of it—grey lumps—a million bees
Stinging the air—Oh Jesus, the corporal's got it—
He couldn't shoot, even—he was too scared to shoot—
His legs took him on—he couldn't stop his legs
Or the weak urine suddenly trickling down them.

Curly Hatton, toiling along the slow
Crest of the Henry Hill, over slippery ground,
Glanced at the still-blue sky that lay so deep
Above the little pines, so pooled, so calm.
He thought, with the slow drowsiness of fatigue,
Of Lucy feeding the white, greedy swans
On the blue pool by Weatherby's Retreat.
They stretched their necks, and clattered with their wings.
There was a fragrance sleeping in her hair.
"Close up, folks—don't straggle—we're going into action!"
His butterball-legs moved faster—Lucy—Lucy—

Bee and Bartow's brigades are broken in their turn—it is fight and
run away—fight and run away, all day—the day will go to whichever
of the untried wrestlers can bear the pain of the grips an instant
longer than the other.

Beauregard and Johnston hurry toward the firing—McDowell has
already gone—

The chessplayers have gone back to little pieces on the shaken
board—little pieces that cannot see the board as a whole.

The block-plan is lost—there is no plan any more—only the
bloodstained, fighting blocks, the bloodstained and blackened men.

Jack Ellyat heard the guns with a knock at his heart
When he first heard them. They were going to be in it,
    soon.
He wondered how it would feel. They would win, of
    course,
But how would it feel? He'd never killed anything much.
Ducks and rabbits, but ducks and rabbits weren't men.
He'd never even seen a man killed, a man die,
Except Uncle Amos, and Uncle Amos was old.
He saw a red sop spreading across the close
Feathers of a duck's breast—it had been all right,
But now it made him feel sick for a while, somehow.
Then they were down on the ground, and they were
    firing,
And that was all right—just fire as you fired at drill.
Was anyone firing at them? He couldn't tell.
There was a stone bridge. Were there rebels beyond the
    bridge?
The shot he was firing now might go and kill rebels
But it didn't feel like it.
                         A man down the line
Fell and rolled flat, with a minor coughing sound
And then was quiet. Ellyat felt the cough
In the pit of his stomach a minute.
But, after that, it was just like a man falling down.
It was all so calm except for their guns and the distant
Shake in the air of cannon. No more men were hit,
And, after a while, they all got up and marched on.
If Rebels had been by the bridge, the rebels were
    gone,

And they were going on somewhere, you couldn't say
    where,
Just marching along the way that they always did.
The only funny thing was, leaving the man
Who had made that cough, back there in the trampled
    grass
With the red stain sopping through the blue of his coat
Like the stain on a duck's breast. He hardly knew
    the man
But it felt funny to leave him just lying there.

The wreckage of Bee, Barrow and Evans' commands streams back into a shallow ravine below a little wood—broken blocks hammered into splinters by war—two thousand confused men reeling past their staggering flags and the hoarse curses and rallying cries of their officers, like sheep in a narrow run.

Bee tries to halt them furiously—he stands up in his stirrups, tree-tall, while the blue flood of the North trickles over the stream and pours on and on.

He waves his sword—the toyish glitter sparkles—he points to a grey dyke at the top of the ravine—a grey dyke of musket-holding Virginians, silent and ready.

"*Look, men, there's Jackson's brigade! It stands there like a stone wall. Rally behind the Virginians!*"

They rally behind them—Johnston and Beauregard are there—the Scotch dominie plucks a flag and carries it forward to rally the Fourth Alabama—the French hussar-sword rallies them with bursting rockets of oratory—his horse is shot under him, but he mounts again.

And the grey stone wall holds like a stiff dyke while the tired men get their breath behind it—and the odd, lemon-sucking, ex-professor of tactics who saw John Brown hung in his carpet-slippers and prayed a Presbyterian prayer for his damned soul, has a new name that will last as long as the face they cut for him on Stone Mountain, and has the same clang of rock against the chisel-blade.

Judith Henry, Judith Henry, they have moved you back at last, in doubt and confusion, to the little house where you know every knothole by heart.

It is not safe, but now there is no place safe, you are between the artillery and the artillery, and the incessant noise comes to your
dim ears like the sea-roar within a shell where you are lying.

The walls of the house are riddled, the brown clock in the kitchen
gouged by a bullet, a jar leaks red preserves on the cupboard
shelf where the shell-splinter came and tore the cupboard apart.

The casual guns do not look for you, Judith Henry, they find you in
passing merely and touch you only a little, but the touch is
enough to give your helpless body five sudden wounds and
leave you helplessly dying.

Wingate gentled Black Whistle's pawing
With hand and wisdom and horseman's play
And listened anew to the bulldogs gnawing
Their bone of iron, a mile away.
There was a wood that a bonfire crowned
With thick dark smoke without flame for neighbor,
And the dull, monotonous, heavy sound
Of a hill or a woman in too-long labor,
But that was all for the Black Horse Troop
And had been all since the day's beginning,
That stray boy beating his metal hoop
And the tight-lipped wonder if they were winning.
Wainscott Bristol, behind his eyes,
Was getting in bed with a sweet-toothed wench,
Huger Shepley felt for his dice
And Stuart Cazenove swore in French
"*Mille diables* and Yankee blood!
How long are we going to stick in the mud?"
While a Cotter hummed with a mocking sigh,
" 'If you want a good time, jine the cavalry!' "
"Stuart's in it, Wade Hampton's in it."
"The Yanks'll quit in another minute!"
"General Bean's just lost us!"
                                    "Steady!"
"And he won't find us until he's ready!"
"It must be two—we've been here since six."
"It's Virginia up to her old-time tricks!
They never did trust a Georgia man,
But Georgia'll fight while Virginia can!"

The restless talk was a simmering brew
That made the horses restless too;
They stamped and snuffled and pricked their ears—
There were cheers, off somewhere—but which side's cheers?
Had the Yankees whipped? Were the Yankees breaking?
The whole troop grumbled and wondered, aching
For fighting or fleeing or fornicating
Or anything else except this bored waiting.

An aide rode up on a sweating mare
And they glowered at him with hostile stare.
He had been in it and they had not.
He had smelt the powder and heard the shot,
And they hated his soul and his martial noise
With the envious hate of little boys.
Then "Yaaih! Yaaih!"
                    —and Wingate felt
The whole troop lift like a lifted dart
And loosened the sabre at his belt,
And felt his chest too small for his heart.

Curly Hatton was nothing any more
But a dry throat and a pair of burnt black hands
That held a hot gun he was always firing
Though he no longer remembered why he fired.
They ran up a cluttered hill and took hacked ground
And held it for a while and fired for a while,
And then the blue men came and they ran away,
To go back, after a while, when the blue men ran.
There was a riddled house and a crow in a tree,
There was uneven ground. It was hard to run.
The gun was heavy and hot. There once had been
A person named Lucy and a flag and a star
And a cane chair beside wistarias
Where a nigger brought you a drink. These had ceased to
    exist.
There was only very hot sun and being thirsty.
Yells—crashings—screams from black lips—a dead,
    tattered crow
In a tattered tree. There had once been a person named
    Lucy

Who had had an importance. There was none of
    her now.

Up the hill again. Damn tired of running up hill.
And then he found he couldn't run any more,
He had to fall down and be sick. Even that was hard,
Because somebody near kept making a squealing noise—
The dolefully nasty noise of a badly-hurt dog.
It got on his nerve and he tried to say something to it,
But it was he who made it, so he couldn't stop it.

Jack Ellyat, going toward the battle again,
Saw the other side of the hill where Curly was lying,
Saw, for a little while, the two battered houses,
The stuffed dead stretched in numb, disorderly postures,
And heard for a while again that whining sound
That made you want to duck, and feel queer if you did.

To him it was noise and smoke and the powder-taste
And, once and again, through the smoke, for a moment
    seen,
Small, monstrous pictures, gone through the brain like
    light,
And yet forever bitten into the brain;
A marsh, a monstrous arras of live and dead
Still shaking under the thrust of the weaver's hand,
The crowd of a deadly fair.
                          Then, orders again.
And they were going away from the smoke once more.

The books say "Keyes' brigade made a late and weak
Demonstration in front of the Robinson house
And then withdrew to the left, by flank, down Young's
    Branch,
Taking no further part in the day."
                          To Jack Ellyat
It was a deadly fair in a burning field
Where strange crowds rushed to and fro and strange
    drunkards lay
Sprawled in a stupor deeper than wine or sleep,
A whining noise you shrank from and wanted to duck at,

And one dead cough left behind them in the tall grass
With the slow blood sopping its clothes like the blood
  on a shot duck's breast.

    Imboden is wounded, Jackson is shot through the hand, the guns of Ricketts and Griffin, on the Henry House plateau, are taken and retaken; the gunners shot down at their guns while they hold their fire, thinking the advancing Thirty-Third Virginia is one of their own regiments, in the dimness of the battle-cloud.

    It is nearly three o'clock—the South gathers for a final charge—on the left, Elzey's brigade, new-come from the Shenandoah, defiles through the oaks near the Sudley Road to reinforce the grey wrestler—the blue wrestler staggers and goes back, on unsteady heels.

    The charge sweeps the plateau—Barrow is killed, black-haired Bee mortally wounded, but the charge goes on.

    For a moment, the Union line is a solid crescent again—a crescent with porcupine-pricks of steel—and then a crescent of sand—and then spilt sand, streaming away.

    There is no panic at first. There is merely a moment when men have borne enough and begin to go home. The panic comes later, when they start to jostle each other.

    Jefferson Davis, riding from Manassas, reaches the back-wash of the battle. A calm grey-bearded stranger tells him calmly that the battle is lost and the South defeated. But he keeps on, his weak eyes stung with the dust, a picture, perhaps, of a Plutarch death on a shield in his schooled mind—and is in time to see the last blue troops disappear beyond Bull Run, and hear the last sour grumble of their guns.

Judith Henry, Judith Henry, your body has born its ghost at last,
    there are no more pictures of peace or terror left in the broken
    machine of the brain that was such a cunning picture-maker:
Terrified ghost, so rudely dishoused by such casual violence, be at
    rest; there are others dishoused in this falling night, the falling
    night is a sack of darkness, indifferent as Saturn to wars or gen-
    erals, indifferent to shame or victory.
War is a while but peace is a while and soon enough the earth-colored
    hands of the earth-workers will scoop the last buried shells and
    the last clotted bullet-slag from the racked embittered acre,
And the rustling visitors drive out fair Sundays to look at the monu-

ment near the rebuilt house, buy picture postcards and wonder
dimly what you were like when you lived and what you thought
when you knew you were going to die.

Wingate felt a frog in his throat
As he patted Black Whistle's reeking coat
And reined him in for a minute's breath.
He was hot as the devil and tired to death,
And both were glad for the sum in the West
And a panting second of utter rest,
While Wingate's mind went patching together
Like a cobbler piecing out scraps of leather
The broken glimmers of what they'd done
Since the sun in the West was a rising sun,
The long, bored hours of shiftless waiting
And that single instant of pure, fierce hating
When the charge came down like a cataract
On a long blue beach of broken sand
And Thought was nothing but all was Act
And the sabre seemed to master the hand.
Wainscott Bristol, a raging terrier
Killing the Yankee that shot Phil Ferrier
With a cut that spattered the bloody brains
Over his saddle and bridle-reins,
One Cotter cursing, the other praying,
And both of them slashing like scythes of slaying,
Stuart Cazenove singing "Lord Randall"
And Howard Brooke as white as a candle,
While Father fought like a fiend in satin,
And killed as he quoted tag-ends of Latin,
The prisoners with their sick, dazed wonder
And the mouths of children caught in a blunder
And over it all, the guns, the thunder,
The pace, the being willing to die,
The stinging color of victory.

He remembered it all like a harsh, tense dream.
It had a color. It had a gleam.
But he had outridden and lost the rest
And he was alone with the bloody West
And a trampled road, and a black hill-crest.

The road and the bushes all about
Were cluttered with relics of Yankee rout,
Haversacks spilling their shirts and socks,
A burst canteen and a cartridge-box.
Rifles and cups trampled underfoot,
A woman's locket, a slashed black boot
Stained and oozing along the slash
And a ripe pear crushed to a yellow mash
Who had carried the locket and munched the pear,
And why was a dead cat lying there,
Stark and grinning, a furry sack,
With a red flannel tongue and a broken back?
You didn't fight wars with a tabby-cat. . . .
He found he was telling the Yankees that,
They couldn't hear him of course, but still . . .
He shut his eyes for a minute until
He felt less dizzy. There, that was better,
And the evening wind was chilly and keen—
—He'd have to write Mother some sort of letter—
—He'd promised Amanda a Yank canteen,
But he didn't feel like getting it here,
Where that dead cat snickered from ear to ear—

Back in the pinewoods, clear and far,
A bugle sang like a falling star.
He shivered, turned Black Whistle around
And galloped hastily toward the sound.

Curly Hatton opened his eyes again.
A minute ago he had been marching, marching,
Forever up and down enormous hills
While his throat scratched with thirst and something
    howled—
But then there was a clear minute—and he was lying
In a long, crowded, strangely-churchly gloom
Where lanterns bobbed like marshlights in a swamp
And there was a perpetual rustling noise
Of dry leaves stirred by a complaining wind.
No, they were only voices of wounded men.
"Water. Water. Water. Water. Water."
He heard the rain on the roof and sucked his lips.

"Water. Water. Water. Water. Water."
Oh, heavy sluices of dark, sweet, Summer rain,
Pour down on me and wash me free again,
Cleanse me of battles, make my flesh smell sweet,
I am so sick of thirst, so tired of pain,
So stale with wounds and the heat!
Somebody went by, a doctor with red sleeves;
He stared at the red sleeves and tried to speak
But when he spoke, he whispered. This was a church.
He could see a dim altar now and a shadow-pulpit.
He was wounded. They had put the wounded men in a
   church.
Lucy's face came to him a minute and then dissolved,
A drowned face, ebbing away with a smile on its mouth.
He had meant to marry that face in another church.
But he was dying instead. It was strange to die.

All night from the hour of three, the dead man's hour, the rain falls in
   heavy gusts, in black irresistible streams as if the whole sky were
      falling in one wet huddle.
All night, living and dead sleep under it, without moving, on the
   field; the surgeons work in the church; the wounded moan; the
      dissevered fragments of companies and regimens look for each
         other, trying to come together.
In the morning, when the burial-parties go out, the rain is still falling,
   damping the powder of the three rounds fired over the grave;
      before the grave is well-dug, the bottom of the grave is a puddle.
All day long the Southern armies bury their dead to the sodden
   drums of the rain; all day the bugle calls a hoarse-throated "Taps";
      the bugler lets the water run from his bugle-mouth and wipes it
         clean again and curses the rainy weather.

All night the Union army fled in retreat.
Like horses scared by a shadow—a stumbling flood
Of panicky men who had been brave for a while
And might be brave again on another day
But now were merely children chased by the night
And each man tainting his neighbor with the same
Blind fear
            When men or horses begin to run

Like that, they keep on running till they tire out
Unless a strong hand masters a bridle-rein.
Here there was no hand to master, no rein to clutch,
Where the riderless horses kicked their way through the
    crowd
And the congressmen's carriages choked Cat Hairpin
    Bend.
Sykes and the regulars covered the retreat,
And a few brigades were kept in some sort of order,
But the rest—They tried to stop them at Centerville.
McDowell and his tired staff held a haggard conference
But before the officers could order retreat
The men were walking away.
                                    They had fought and lost.
They were going to Washington, they were going back
To their tents and their cooking-fires and their letters
    from Susie.
They were going back home to Maine or Vermont or
    Ohio,
And they didn't care who knew it, and that was that.

Meanwhile, on the battlefield, Johnston and Beauregard,
Now joined by the dusty Davis, found themselves
As dazed by their victory as their foes by defeat.
They had beaten one armed mob with another
    armed mob
And Washington was theirs for the simple act
Of stretching a hand to the apple up on the bough,
If they had known. But they could not know it then.
They too saw spectres—unbroken Union reserves
Moving to cut their supply-line near Manassas.
They called back the pursuit, such scattered pursuit as
    it was.
Their men were tired and disordered. The chance
    went by
While only the stiff-necked Jackson saw it clear
As a fighting-psalm or a phrase in Napoleon's tactics.
He said to the surgeon who was binding his wound,
With a taciturn snap, "Give me ten thousand fresh troops
And I will be in Washington by tomorrow."
But they could not give him the troops while there yet
    was time.

He had three days' rations cooked for the Stonewall
　　Brigade
And dourly awaited the order that never came.
He had always been at God's orders, and God had
　　used him
As an instrument in winning a certain fight.
Now, if God saw fit to give him the men and guns,
He would take Washington for the glory of God.
If He didn't, it was God's will and not to be questioned.

Meanwhile he could while the hours of waiting away
By seeing the Stonewall Brigade was properly fed,
Endeavoring, with that rigid kindness of his
To show Imboden his error in using profanity
—In the heat of battle many things might be excused,
But nothing excused profanity, even then—
And writing his Pastor at Lexington a letter
Enclosing that check for the colored Sunday-school
Which he'd promised, and, being busy, had failed to
　　send.
There is not one word of Bull Run in all that letter
Except the mention of "a fatiguing day's service."
It would not have occurred to Jackson there might have
　　been.

Walt Whitman, unofficial observer to the cosmos, reads of the defeat in a Brooklyn room. The scene rises before him, more real than the paper he stares upon. He sees the defeated army pouring along Pennsylvania Avenue in the drizzling rain, a few regiments in good order, marching in silence, with lowering faces—the rest a drenched, hungry mob that plods along on blistered feet and falls asleep on the stoops of houses, in vacant lots, in basement-areas huddled, too tired to remember battle or be ashamed of flight.

Nothing said—no cries or cheers from the windows, no jeers from the secessionists in the watching crowd—half the crowd is secessionist at heart, even now, more than ever now.

Two old women, white-haired, stand all day in the rain, giving coffee and soup and bread to the passing men. The tears stream down their faces as they cut the bread and pour out the coffee.

Whitman sees it all in his mind's eye—the tears of the two women—the strange look on the men's faces, awake or asleep—the

dripping, smoke-colored rain. Perplexed and deep in his heart, something stirs and moves—he is each one of them in turn—the beaten
men, the tired women, the boy who sleeps there quietly with his
musket still clutched tightly to him. The long lines of a poem begin
to lash themselves against his mind, with the lashing surge and long
thunder of Montauk surf.

Horace Greeley has written Lincoln an hysterical letter—he has
not slept for seven nights—in New York, "on every brow sits sullen,
scorching, black despair."

He was trumpeting "On to Richmond!" two weeks ago. But then
the war was a thing for an editorial—a triumphal parade of Unionists
over rebels. Now there has been a battle and a defeat. He pleads for
an armistice—a national convention—anything on almost any terms
to end this war.

Many think as he does; many fine words ring hollow as the skull
of an orator, the skull of a maker of war. They have raised the Devil
with slogans and editorials, but where is the charm that will lay him?
Who will bind the Devil aroused?

Only Lincoln, awkwardly enduring, confused by a thousand
counsels, is neither overwhelmed nor touched to folly by the madness that runs along the streets like a dog in August scared of itself,
scaring everyone who crosses its path.

Defeat is a fact and victory can be a fact. If the idea is good, it will
survive defeat, it may even survive the victory.

His huge, patient, laborious hands start kneading the stuff of the
Union together again; he gathers up the scraps and puts them together; he sweeps the corners and the cracks and patches together the
lost courage and the rags of belief.

The dough didn't rise that time—maybe it will next time. God
must have tried and discarded a lot of experiment-worlds before he
got one even good enough to whirl for a minute—it is the same with
a belief, with a cause.

It is wrong to talk of Lincoln and a star together—that old rubbed
image is a scrap of tinsel, a scrap of dead poetry—it dries up and
blows away when it touches a man. And yet Lincoln had a star, if
you will have it so—and was haunted by a prairie-star.

Down in the South another man, most unlike him but as steadfast
is haunted by another star that has little to do with tinsel, and the
man they call "Evacuation" Lee begins to grow taller and to cast a
longer shadow.

FROM BOOK SIX

Now the earth begins to roll its wheel toward the sun,
The deep mud-gullies are drying.
                              The sluggish armies
That have slept the bear-months through in their winter-
    camps,
Begin to stir and be restless.
                          They're tired enough
Of leaky huts and the rain and punishment-drill.
They haven't forgotten what it was like last time,
But next time we'll lick 'em, next time it won't be so bad,
Somehow we won't get killed, we won't march so hard.
"These huts looked pretty good when we first hit camp
But they look sort of lousy now—we might as well git—
Fight the Rebs—and the Yanks—and finish it up."
So they think in the bored, skin-itching months
While the roads are dying. "We're sick of this crummy
    place,
We might as well git, it doesn't much matter where."
But when they git, they are cross at leaving the huts,
"We fixed up ours first rate. We had regular lamps.
We knew the girls at the Depot. It wasn't so bad.
Why the hell do we have to git when we just got fixed?
Oh, well, we might as well travel."
                              So they go on,
The huts drop behind, the dry road opens ahead. . . .

Fighting Joe Hooker feels good when he looks at
    his men.
A blue-eyed, uncomplex man with a gift for phrase.
"The finest army on the planet," he says.
The phrase is to turn against him with other phrases
When he is beaten—but now he is confident.
Tall, sandy, active, sentimental and tart,
His horseman's shoulder is not yet bowed by the weight
Of knowing the dice are his and the cast of them,
The weight of command, the weight of Lee's ghostly
    name.
He rides, preparing his fate.
                          In the other camps,
Lee writes letters, is glad to get buttermilk,

Wrings food and shoes and clothes from his
    commissariat,
Trusts in God and whets a knife on a stone.
Jackson plays with his new-born daughter, waiting for
    Spring,
His rare laugh clangs as he talks to his wife and child.
He is looking well. War always agrees with him,
And this, perhaps, is the happiest time of his life.
He has three months of it left.
                              By the swollen flood
Of the Mississippi, stumpy Grant is a mole
Gnawing at Vicksburg. He has been blocked four times
But he will carry that beaver-dam at last.
There is no brilliant lamp in that dogged mind
And no conceit of brilliance to shake the hand,
But hand and mind can use the tools that they get
This long way out of Galena.
                              Sherman is there
And Sherman loves him and finds him hard to make out,
In Sherman's impatient fashion—the quick, sharp man
Seeing ten thousand things where the slow sees one
And yet with a sort of younger brother awe
At the infinite persistence of that slow will
—They make a good pair of hunting dogs, Grant and
    Sherman,
The nervous, explosive, passionate, slashing hound
And the quiet, equable, deadly holder-on,
Faded-brown as a cinnamon-bear in Spring—
See them like that, the brown dog and the white dog,
Calling them back and forth through the scrubby woods
After the little white scut of Victory,
Or see them as elder brother and younger brother,
But remember this. In their time they were famous men
And yet they were not jealous, one of the other.
When the gold has peeled from the man on the gilded
    horse,
Ri ing Fifth Avenue, and the palm-girl's blind;
When the big round tomb gapes empty under the sky,
Vacant with summer air, when it's all forgotten,
When nobody reads the books, when the flags are moth-
    dust,

Write up that. You won't have to write it so often.
It will do as well as the railway-station tombs.

So with the troops and the leaders of the bear-armies,
The front-page-newspaper-things.
                                        Tall Lincoln reviews
Endless columns crunching across new snow.
They pass uncheering at the marching-salute.
Lincoln sits on his horse with his farmer's seat,
Watching the eyes go by and the eyes come on.
The gaunt, long body is dressed in its Sunday black,
The gaunt face, strange as an omen, sad and foreboding.
The eyes look at him, he looks back at the eyes;
They pass and pass. They go back to their camps at last.
"So that was him," they say. "So that's the old man.
I'm glad we saw him. He isn't so much on looks
But he looks like people you know. He looks sad all
     right,
I never saw nobody look quite as sad as that
Without it made you feel foolish. He don't do that.
He makes you feel—I dunno—I'm glad we could
     see him.
He was glad to see us but you could tell all the same
This war's plumb killin' him. You can tell by his face.
I never saw such a look on any man's face.
I guess it's tough for him. Well, we saw him, for once."

That day in Richmond, a mob of angry women
Swarm in the streets and riot for bread or peace.
They loot some shops, a few for the bread they need,
A few for thieving, most because they are moved
By discontent and hunger to do as the rest.
The troops are called out. The troops are about to fire,
But Davis gets on a wagon and calms the crowd
Before the tumbled bodies clutter the street.
He never did a better thing with his voice
And it should be told. Next day they riot again,
But this time the fire is weaker. They are dispersed,
A few arrested. Bread grows dearer than ever.
The housewives still go out with their market-baskets,
But coffee's four dollars a pound and tea eleven.

They come back with a scraping of this and a scrap of
    that
And try to remember old lazy, lagnappe days,
The slew-foot negro chanting his devilled crabs
Along the street, and the market-women piling
The wicker baskets with everything good and fresh;
Topping it off with a great green fist of parsley
That you used to pretty the sides of the serving-dish
And never bothered to eat.
                              They improvise dishes,
"Blockade pudding" . . . "Confederate fricassee,"
Serve hominy grits on the Royal Derby china
And laugh or weep in their cups of willow-bark tea.

Davis goes back from the riot, his shoulders stooped,
The glow of speech has left him and he feels cold.
He eats a scant meal quickly and turns to the endless
Papers piled on his desk, the squabbles and plans.
A haggard dictator, fretting the men he rules
And being fretted by them.
                              He dreams, perhaps,
Of old days, riding wild horses beside his wife
Back in his youth, on a Mississippi road.
That was a good time. It is past. He drowns in his papers.

The curtain is going up on that battlesmoked,
Crowded third act which is to decide this war
And yet not end it for years.
                              Turn your eyes away
From these chiefs and captains, put them back in their
    books.
Let the armies sleep like bears in a hollow cave.
War is an iron screen in front of a time,
With pictures smoked upon it in red and black,
Some gallant enough, some deadly, but all intense.
We look at the pictures, thinking we know the time,
We only know the screen.
                              Look behind it now
At the great parti-colored quilt of these patchwork States.
This part and that is vexed by a battle-worm,
But the ploughs go ahead, the factory chimneys smoke,
A new age curdles and boils in a hot steel caldron

And pours into rails and wheels and fingers of steel,
Steel is being born like a white-hot rose
In the dark smoke-cradle of Pittsburg—
                                   a man with a crude
Eye of metal and crystal looks at a smear
On a thin glass plate and wonders—
                                   a shawled old woman
Sits on a curbstone calling the evening news.
War, to her, is a good day when papers sell
Or a bad day when papers don't. War is fat black type.
Anything's realer than war.
                         By Omaha
The valleys and gorges are white with the covered
    wagons
Moving out toward the West and the new, free land.
All through the war they go on.
                              Five thousand teams
Pass Laramie in a month in the last war-year,
Draft-evaders, homesteaders, pioneers,
Old soldiers, Southern emigrants, sunburnt children. . . .
Men are founding colleges, finding gold,
Selling bad beef to the army and making fortunes,
Ploughing the stone-cropped field that their fathers
    ploughed.
(Anything's realer than war.)
                            A moth of a woman,
Shut in a garden, lives on scraps of Eternity
With a dog, a procession of sunsets and certain poems
She scribbles on bits of paper. Such poems may be
Ice-crystals, rubies cracked with refracted light,
Or all vast death like a wide field in ten short lines.
She writes to the rough, swart-minded Higginson
Minding his negro troops in a lost bayou,
"War feels to me like an oblique place."
                                       A man
Dreams of a sky machine that will match the birds
And another, dusting the shelves of a country store,
Saves his pennies until they turn into dimes.
(Anything's realer than war.)
                            A dozen men
Charter a railroad to go all across the Plains
And link two seas with a whistling iron horse.

A whiskered doctor stubbornly tries to find
The causes of childbed-fever—and, doing so,
Will save more lives than all these war-months have
   spent,
And never inhabit a railway-station tomb.
All this through the war, all this behind the flat screen. . . .

      I heard the song of breath
      Go up from city and country,
      The even breath of the sleeper,
      The tired breath of the sick,
      The dry cough in the throat
      Of the man with the death-sweat on him,
      And the quiet monotone
      We breathe but do not hear.

      The harsh gasp of the runner,
      The long sigh of power
      Heaving the weight aloft,
      The grey breath of the old.
      Men at the end of strength
      With their lungs turned lead and fire,
      Panting like thirsty dogs;
      A child's breath, blowing a flame.

      The breath that is the voice,
      The silver, the woodwinds speaking,
      The dear voice of your lover,
      The hard voice of your foe,
      And the vast breath of wind,
      Mysterious over mountains,
      Caught in pines like a bird
      Or filling all hammered heaven.

      I heard the song of breath,
      Like a great strand of music,
      Blown between void and void,
      Uncorporal as the light,
      The breath of nations asleep,
      And the piled hills they sleep in,
      The word that never was flesh
      And yet is nothing but life.

What are you, bodiless sibyl,
Unseen except as the frost-cloud
Puffed from a silver mouth
When the hard winter's cold?
We cannot live without breath,
And yet we breathe without knowledge,
And the vast strand of sound
Goes on, eternally sighing,
Without dimension or space,
Without beginning or end.

I heard the song of breath
And lost it in all sharp voices,
Even my own voice lost
Like a thread in that huge strand,
Lost like a skein of air,
And with it, continents lost
In the great throat of Death.
I trembled, asking in vain,
Whence come you, whither art gone?
The continents flow and melt
Like wax in the naked candle,
Burnt by the wick of time—
Where is the breath of the Chaldees,
The dark, Minoan breath?
I said to myself in hate,
Hearing that mighty rushing,
Though you raise a new Adam up
And blow fresh fire in his visage,
He has only a loan of air,
And gets but a breathing-space.
But then I was quieted.

I heard the song of breath,
The gulf hollow with voices,
Fused into one slow voice
That never paused or was faint.
Man, breathing his life,
And with him all life breathing,
The young horse and the snake,
Beetle, lion and dove,
Solemn harps of the fir,

Trumpets of sea and whirlwind
And the vast, tiny grass
Blown by a breath and speaking.
I heard these things. I heard
The multitudinous river.
When I came back to my life,
My voice was numb in my ears,
I wondered that I still breathed.

BOOK SEVEN (THE BATTLE OF GETTYSBURG)

They came on to fish-hook Gettysburg in this way, after
　this fashion.
Over hot pikes heavy with pollen, past fields where the
　wheat was high.
Peaches grew in the orchards; it was a fertile country,
Full of red barns and fresh springs and dun, deep-
　uddered kine.

A farmer lived with a clear stream that ran through his
　very house-room,
They cooled the butter in it and the milk, in their wide,
　stone jars;
A dusty Georgian came there, to eat and go on to battle;
They dipped the milk from the jars, it was cold and
　sweet in his mouth

He heard the clear stream's music as the German
　housewife served him,
Remembering the Shenandoah and a stream poured from
　a rock;
He ate and drank and went on to the gunwheels crushing
　the harvest.
It was a thing he remembered as long as any guns.

Country of broad-backed horses, stone houses and long,
　green meadows,
Where Getty came with his ox-team to found a steady
　town

And the little trains of my boyhood puffed solemnly up
    the Valley
Past the market-squares and the lindens and the Quaker
    meeting-house.

Penn stood under his oak with a painted sachem
    beside him,
The market-women sold scrapple when the first red
    maples turned;
When the buckeyes slipped from their sheaths, you
    could gather a pile of buckeyes,
Red-brown as old polished boots, good to touch and
    hold in the hand.

The ice-cream parlor was papered with scenes from *Paul
    and Virginia*,
The pigs were fat all year, you could stand a spoon in the
    cream
—Penn stood under his oak with a feathered pipe in his
    fingers,
His eyes were quiet with God, but his wits and his
    bargain sharp.

So I remember it all, and the light sound of buckeyes
    falling
On the worn rose-bricks of the pavement, herring-
    boned, trodden for years;
The great yellow shocks of wheat and the dust-white
    road through Summer,
And, in Fall, the green walnut shells, and the stain they
    left for a while.

So I remember you, ripe country of broad-backed
    horses,
Valley of cold, sweet springs and dairies with limestone-
    floors;
And so they found you that year, when they scared your
    cows with their cannon,
And the strange South moved against you, lean marchers
    lost in the corn.

Two months have passed since Jackson died in the woods
And they brought his body back to the Richmond State
   House
To lie there, heaped with flowers, while the bells tolled,
Two months of feints and waiting.
                        And now, at length,
The South goes north again in the second raid,
In the last cast for fortune.
                 A two-edged chance
And yet a chance that may burnish a failing star;
For now, on the wide expanse of the Western board,
Strong pieces that fought for the South have been swept
   away
Or penned up in hollow Vicksburg.
                     One cool Spring night
Porter's ironclads run the shore-batteries
Through a velvet stabbed with hot flashes.
                        Grant lands his men.
Drives the relieving force of Johnston away
And sits at last in front of the hollow town
Like a huge brown bear on its haunches, terribly
   waiting.
His guns begin to peck at the pillared porches,
The sleepy, sun-spattered streets. His siege has begun.
Forty-eight days that siege and those guns go on
Like a slow hand closing around a hungry throat,
Ever more hungry.
             The hunger of hollow towns,
The hunger of sieges, the hunger of lost hope.
As day goes by after day and the shells still whine
Till the town is a great mole-burrow of pits and caves
Where the thin women hide their children, where the
   tired men
Burrow away from the death that falls from the air
And the common sky turned hostile—and still no
   hope,
Still no sight in the sky when the morning breaks
But the brown bear there on his haunches, steadfastly
   waiting.
Waiting like Time for the honey-tree to fall.

The news creeps back to the watchers oversea.
They ponder on it, aloof and irresolute.
The balance they watch is dipping against the South.
It will take great strokes to redress that balance again.
There will be one more moment of shaken scales
When the Laird rams almost alter the scheme of things,
But it is distant.
                    The watchers stare at the board
Waiting a surer omen than Chancellorsville
Or any battle won on a Southern ground.

Lee sees that dip of the balance and so prepares
His cast for the surer omen and his last stroke
At the steel-bossed Northern shield. Once before he
    tried
That spear-rush North and was halted. It was a chance.
This is a chance. He weighs the chance in his hand
Like a stone, reflecting.
                        Four years from Harper's Ferry—
Two years since the First Manassas—and this last year
Stroke after stroke successful—but still no end.

He is a man with a knotty club in his hand
Beating off bulls from the breaks in a pasture fence
And he has beaten them back at each fresh assault,
McClellan—Burnside—Hooker at Chancellorsville—
Pope at the Second Manassas—Banks in the Valley—
But the pasture is trampled; his army needs new pasture.
An army moves like a locust, eating the grain,
And this grain is well-nigh eaten. He cannot mend
The breaks in his fence with famine or starving hands,
And if he waits the wheel of another year
The bulls will come back full-fed, shaking sharper horns
While he faces them empty, armed with a hunger-cracked
Unmagic stick.
                There is only this thing to do,
To strike at the shield with the strength that he still
    can use
Hoping to burst it asunder with one stiff blow
And carry the war up North, to the untouched fields
Where his tattered men can feed on the bulls' own grain,
Get shoes and clothes, take Washington if they can,

Hold the fighting-gauge in any event.
                                        He weighs
The chance in his hand. I think that he weighed it well
And felt a high tide risen up in his heart
And in his men a high tide.
                            They were veterans,
They had never been beaten wholly and blocked but
    once,
He had driven four Union armies within a year
And broken three blue commanders from their
    command.
Even now they were fresh from triumph.
                                        He cast his stone
Clanging at fortune, and set his fate on the odds.

Lincoln hears the rumor in Washington.
They are moving North.
                        The Pennsylvania cities
Hear it and shake, they are loose, they are moving
    North.
Call up your shotgun-militia, bury your silver,
Shoulder a gun or run away from the State,
They are loose, they are moving.
                                Fighting Joe Hooker has heard it.
He swings his army back across the Potomac,
Rapidly planning, while Lee still visions him South.
Stuart's horse should have brought the news of that
    move
But Stuart is off on a last and luckless raid
Far to the East, and the grey host moves without eyes
Through crucial days.
                        They are in the Cumberland now,
Taking minor towns, feeding fat for a little while,
Pressing horses and shoes, paying out Confederate bills
To slow Dutch storekeepers who groan at the money.
They are loose, they are in the North, they are here and
    there.
Halleck rubs his elbows and wonders where,
Lincoln is sleepless, the telegraph-sounders click
In the War Office day and night.
                                There are lies and rumors,

They are only a mile from Philadelphia now,
They are burning York—they are marching on
   Baltimore—

Meanwhile, Lee rides through the heart of the
   Cumberland.
A great hot sunset colors the marching men,
Colors the horse and the sword and the bearded face
But cannot change that face from its strong repose.
And—miles away—Joe Hooker, by telegraph
Calls for the garrison left at Harper's Ferry
To join him. Elbow-rubbing Halleck refuses.
Hooker resigns command—and fades from the East
To travel West, fight keenly at Lookout Mountain,
Follow Sherman's march as far as Atlanta,
Be ranked by Howard, and tartly resign once more
Before the end and the fame and the Grand Review,
To die a slow death, in bed, with his fire gone out,
A campfire quenched and forgotten.
                              He deserved
A better and brusquer end that marched with his
   nickname,
This disappointed, hot-tempered, most human man
Who had such faith in himself except for once,
And the once, being Chancellorsville, wiped out the rest.
He was often touchy and life was touchy with him,
But the last revenge was a trifle out of proportion.
Such things will happen—Jackson went in his strength,
Stuart was riding his horse when the bullet took him,
And Custer died to the trumpet—Dutch Longstreet lived
To quarrel and fight dead battles. Lee passed in silence.
McClellan talked on forever in word and print.
Grant lived to be President. Thomas died sick at heart.

So Hooker goes from our picture—and a spent aide
Reaches Meade's hut at three o'clock in the morning
To wake him with unexpected news of command.
The thin Pennsylvanian puts on his spectacles
To read the order. Tall, sad-faced and austere,
He has the sharp, long nose of a fighting-bird,
A prudent mouth and a cool, considering mind.
An iron-grey man with none of Hooker's panache,

But resolute and able, well skilled in war;
They call him "the damned old goggle-eyed snapping-
　　turtle"
At times, and he does not call out the idol-shout
When he rides his lines, but his prudence is a hard
　　prudence,
And can last out storms that break the men with
　　panache,
Though it summons no counter-storm when the storm is
　　done.

His sombre schoolmaster-eyes read the order well.
It is three days before the battle.
　　　　　　　　　　　　　　　He thinks at first
Of a grand review, gives it up, and begins to act.

That morning a spy brings news to Lee in his tent
That the Union army has moved and is on the march.
Lee calls back Ewell and Early from their forays
And summons his host together by the cross-roads
Where Getty came with his ox-cart.
　　　　　　　　　　　　　　　So now we see
These two crab-armies fumbling for each other,
As if through a fog of rumor and false report,
These last two days of sleepy, hay-harvest June.
Hot June lying asleep on a shock of wheat
Where the pollen-wind blows over the burnt-gold
　　stubble
And the thirsty men march past, stirring thick grey dust
From the trodden pikes—till at last, the crab-claws touch
At Getty's town, and clutch, and the peaches fall
Cut by the bullets, splashing under the trees.

That meeting was not willed by a human mind,
When we come to sift it.
　　　　　　　　　　　You say a fate rode a horse
Ahead of those lumbering hosts, and in either hand
He carried a skein of omen. And when, at last,
He came to a certain umbrella-copse of trees
That never had heard a cannon or seen dead men,
He knotted the skeins together and flung them down

With a sound like metal.

                Perhaps. It may have been so.
All that we know is—Meade intended to fight
Some fifteen miles away on the Pipe Creek Line
And where Lee meant to fight him, if forced to fight,
We do not know, but it was not there where they fought.
Yet the riding fate,
Blind and deaf and a doom on a lunging horse,
Threw down his skeins and gathered the battle there.

       The buttercup-meadows
       Are very yellow.
       A child comes there
       To fill her hands.
       The gold she gathers
       Is soft and precious
       As sweet new butter
       Fresh from the churn.

       She fills her frock
       With the yellow flowers,
       The butter she gathers
       Is smooth as gold,
       Little bright cups
       Of new-churned sunshine
       For a well-behaved
       Hoop-skirted doll.

       Her frock's full
       And her hands are mothy
       With yellow pollen
       But she keeps on.
       Down by the fence
       They are even thicker.
       She runs, bowed down with
       Buttercup-gold.

       She sees a road
       And she sees a rider.
       His face is grey

With a different dust.
He talks loud.
He rattles like tinware.
He has a long sword
To kill little girls.

He shouts at her now,
But she does not answer.
"Where is the town?"
But she will not hear.
There are other riders
Jangling behind him.
"We won't hurt you, youngster!"
But they have swords.

The buttercups fall
Like spilt butter.
She runs away.
She runs to her house.
She hides her face
In her mother's apron
And tries to tell her
How dreadful it was.

Buford came to Gettysburg late that night
Riding West with his brigades of blue horse,
While Pettigrew and his North Carolinians
Were moving East toward the town with a wagon-train,
Hoping to capture shoes.
                        The two came in touch.
Pettigrew halted and waited for men and orders.
Buford threw out his pickets beyond the town.

The next morning was July first. It was hot and calm.
On the grey side, Heth's division was ready to march
And drive the blue pickets in. There was still no thought
Of a planned and decisive battle on either side
Though Buford had seen the strength of those two
   hill-ridges
Soon enough to be famous, and marked one down
As a place to rally if he should be driven back.

He talks with his staff in front of a tavern now.
An officer rides up from the near First Corps.
"What are you doing here, sir?"

       The officer
Explains. He, too, has come there to look for shoes.
—Fabulous shoes of Gettysburg, dead men's shoes,
Did anyone ever wear you, when it was done,
When the men were gone, when the farms were spoiled
 with the bones,
What became of your nails and leather? The swords went
 home,
The swords went into museums and neat glass cases,
The swords look well there. They are clean from the war.
You wouldn't put old shoes in a neat glass case,
Still stuck with the mud of marching.

         And yet, a man
With a taste for such straws and fables, blown by the
 wind,
Might hide a pair in a labelled case sometime
Just to see how the leather looked, set down by the
 swords.

The officer is hardly through with his tale
When Buford orders him back to his command.
"Why, what is the matter, general?"

       As he speaks
The far-off hollow slam of a single gun
Breaks the warm stillness. The horses prick up their ears.
"That's the matter," says Buford and gallops away.

Jake Diefer, the barrel-chested Pennsylvanian,
Marched toward Getty's town past orderly fences,
Thinking of harvest.

      The boy was growing up strong
And the corn-haired woman was smart at managing
 things
But it was a shame what you had to pay hired men now
Though they'd had good crops last year and good prices
 too.
The crops looked pretty this summer.

        He stared at the long

Gold of the wheat reflectively, weighing it all,
Turning it into money and cows and taxes,
A new horse-reaper, some first-class paint for the barn,
Maybe a dress for the woman.
                         His thoughts were few,
But this one tasted rough and good in his mouth
Like a spear of rough, raw grain. He crunched at it now.
—And yet, that wasn't all, the paint and the cash,
They were the wheat but the wheat was—he didn't
    know—
But it made you feel good to see some good wheat again
And see it grown up proper.
                       He wasn't a man
To cut a slice of poetry from a farm.
He liked the kind of manure that he knew about
And seldom burst into tears when his horses died
Or found a beautiful thought in a bumble-bee,
But now, as he tramped along like a laden steer,
The tall wheat, rustling, filled his heart with its sound.

Look at that column well, as it passes by,
Remembering Bull Run and the cocksfeather hats,
The congressmen, the raw militia brigades
Who went to war with a flag and a haircloth trunk
In bright red pants and ideals and ignorance,
Ready to fight like picture-postcard boys
While fighting still had banners and a sword
And just as ready to run in blind mob-panic. . . .
These men were once those men. These men are the
    soldiers,
Good thieves, good fighters, excellent foragers,
The grumbling men who dislike to be killed in war
And yet will hold when the raw militia break
And live where the raw militia needlessly die,
Having been schooled to that end.
                       The school is not
A pretty school. They wear no cocksfeather hats.
Some men march in their drawers and their stocking feet.
They have handkerchiefs round their heads, they are
    footsore and chafed,
Their faces are sweaty leather.
                     And when they pass

The little towns where the people wish them godspeed,
A few are touched by the cheers and the crying women
But most have seen a number of crying women,
And heard a number of cheers.
                              The ruder yell back
To the sincere citizens cool in their own front yards,
"Aw, get a gun and fight for your home yourself!"
They grin and fall silent. Nevertheless they go on.
Jake Diefer, the barrel-chested Pennsylvanian,
The steer-thewed, fist-plank-splitter from Cumberland,
Came through the heat and the dust and the mounting
     roar
That could not drown the rustle of the tall wheat
Making its growing sound, its windrustled sound,
In his heart that sound, that brief and abiding sound,
To a fork and a road he knew.
                              And then he heard
That mixed, indocile noise of combat indeed
And as if it were strange to him when it was not strange.
—He never took much account of the roads they went,
They were always going somewhere and roads were
     roads.
But he knew this road.
                         He knew its turns and its hills,
And what ploughlands lay beyond it, beyond the town,
On the way to Chambersburg.
                              He saw with wild eyes
Not the road before him or anything real at all
But grey men in an unreal wheatfield, tramping it down,
Filling their tattered hats with the ripe, rough grain
While a shell burst over a barn.
                              "Grasshoppers!" he said
Through stiff dry lips to himself as he tried to gauge
That mounting roar and its distance.
                              "The Johnnies is there!
The Johnnies and us is fighting in Gettysburg,
There must be Johnnies back by the farm already,
By Jesus, those damn Johnnies is on my farm!"

That battle of the first day was a minor battle
As such are counted.

             That is, it killed many men.
Killed more than died at Bull Run, left thousands
   stricken
With wounds that time might heal for a little while
Or never heal till the breath was out of the flesh.
The First Corps lost half its number in killed and
   wounded.
The pale-faced women, huddled behind drawn blinds
Back in the town, or in apple-cellars, hiding,
Thought it the end of the world, no doubt.
                        And yet,
As the books remark, it was only a minor battle.
There were only two corps engaged on the Union side,
Longstreet had not yet come up, nor Ewell's whole
   force,
Hill's corps lacked a division till evening fell.
It was only a minor battle.
                When the first shot
Clanged out, it was fired from a clump of Union vedettes
Holding a farm in the woods beyond the town.
The farmer was there to hear it—and then to see
The troopers scramble back on their restless horses
And go off, firing, as a grey mass came on.

He must have been a peaceable man, that farmer.
It is said that he died of what he had heard and seen
In that one brief moment, although no bullet came near
   him
And the storm passed by and did not burst on his farm.
No doubt he was easily frightened. He should have
   reflected
That even minor battles are hardly the place
For peaceable men—but he died instead, it is said.
There were other deaths that day, as of Smiths and
   Clancys,
Otises, Boyds, Virginia and Pennsylvania,
New York, Carolina, Wisconsin, the gathered West,
The tattered Southern marchers dead on the wheat-
   shocks.
Among these deaths a few famous.
                    Reynolds is dead,
The model soldier, gallant and courteous,

Shot from his saddle in the first of the fight.
He was Doubleday's friend, but Doubleday has no time
To grieve him, the Union right being driven in
And Heth's Confederates pressing on toward the town.
He holds the onrush back till Howard comes up
And takes command for a while.

                                        The fighting is grim.
Meade has heard the news. He sends Hancock up to the
   field.
Hancock takes command in mid-combat. The grey
   comes on.
Five color-bearers are killed at one Union color,
The last man, dying, still holds up the sagging flag.
The pale-faced women creeping out of their houses,
Plead with retreating bluecoats, "Don't leave us boys,
Stay with us—hold the town." Their faces are thin,
Their words come tumbling out of a frightened mouth.
In a field, far off, a peaceable farmer puts
His hands to his ears, still hearing that one sharp shot
That he will hear and hear till he dies of it.
It is Hill and Ewell now against Hancock and Howard
And a confused, wild clamor—and the high keen
Of the Rebel yell—and the shrill-edged bullet song
Beating down men and grain, while the sweaty fighters
Grunt as they ram their charges with blackened hands.

Till Hancock and Howard are beaten away at last,
Outnumbered and outflanked, clean out of the town,
Retreating as best they can to a fish-hook ridge,
And the clamor dies and the sun is going down
And the tired men think about food.

                                        The dust-bitten staff
Of Ewell, riding along through the captured streets,
Hear the thud of a bullet striking their general.
Flesh or bone? Death-wound or rub of the game?
"The general's hurt!" They gasp and volley their
   questions.
Ewell turns his head like a bird, "No, I'm not hurt, sir,
But, supposing the ball had struck you, General Gordon,
We'd have the trouble of carrying you from the field.
You can see how much better fixed for a fight I am.
It don't hurt a mite to be shot in your wooden leg."

So it ends. Lee comes on the field in time to see
The village taken, the Union wave in retreat.
Meade will not reach the ground till one the next
    morning.

So it ends, this lesser battle of the first day,
Starkly disputed and piecemeal won and lost
By corps-commanders who carried no magic plans
Stowed in their sleeves, but fought and held as they
    could.
It is past. The board is staked for the greater game
Which is to follow—The beaten Union brigades
Recoil from the cross-roads town that they tried to hold.
And so recoiling, rest on a destined ground.
Who chose that ground?
                        There are claimants enough in the
                        books.
Howard thanked by Congress for choosing it
As doubtless, they would have thanked him as well had
    he
Chosen another, once the battle was won,
And there are a dozen ifs on the Southern side,
How, in that first day's evening, if one had known,
If Lee had been there in time, if Jackson had lived,
The heights that cost so much blood in the vain attempt
To take days later, could have been taken then.
And the ifs and the thanks and the rest are all true
    enough
But we can only say, when we look at the board,
"There it happened. There is the way of the land.
There was the fate, and there the blind swords were
    crossed."

You took a carriage to that battlefield.
Now, I suppose, you take a motor-bus,
But then, it was a carriage—and you ate
Fried chicken out of wrappings of waxed paper,
While the slow guide buzzed on about the war
And the enormous, curdled summer clouds

Piled up like giant cream puffs in the blue.
The carriage smelt of axle-grease and leather
And the old horse nodded a sleepy head
Adorned with a straw hat. His ears stuck through it.
It was the middle of hay-fever summer
And it was hot. And you could stand and look
All the way down from Cemetery Ridge,
Much as it was, except for monuments
And startling groups of monumental men
Bursting in bronze and marble from the ground,
And all the curious names upon the gravestones. . . .

So peaceable it was, so calm and hot,
So tidy and great-skied.

                    No men had fought
There but enormous, monumental men
Who bled neat streams of uncorrupting bronze,
Even at the Round Tops, even by Pickett's boulder,
Where the bronze, open book could still be read
By visitors and sparrows and the wind:
And the wind came, the wind moved in the grass,
Saying . . . while the long light . . . and all so
   calm . . .
     "Pickett came
       And the South came
       And the end came,
       And the grass comes
       And the wind blows
       On the bronze book
       On the bronze men
       On the grown grass,
       And the wind says
       'Long ago
       Long
       Ago.' "

Then it was time to buy a paperweight
With flags upon it in decalcomania
And hope you wouldn't break it, driving home.

Draw a clumsy fish-hook now on a piece of paper,
To the left of the shank, by the bend of the curving hook,
Draw a Maltese cross with the top block cut away.
The cross is the town. Nine roads star out from it
East, West, South, North.
                    And now, still more to the left
Of the lopped-off cross, on the other side of the town,
Draw a long, slightly-wavy line of ridges and hills
Roughly parallel to the fish-hook shank.
(The hook of the fish-hook is turned away from the cross
And the wavy line.)
            There your ground and your ridges lie.
The fish-hook is Cemetery Ridge and the North
Waiting to be assaulted—the wavy line
Seminary Ridge whence the Southern assault will come.

The valley between is more than a mile in breadth.
It is some three miles from the lowest jut of the cross
To the button at the far end of the fish-hook shank,
Big Round Top, with Little Round Top not far away.
Both ridges are strong and rocky, well made for war.
But the Northern one is the stronger shorter one.
Lee's army must spread out like an uncoiled snake
Lying along a fence-rail, while Meade's can coil
Or halfway coil, like a snake part clung to a stone.
Meade has the more men and the easier shifts to make,
Lee the old prestige of triumph and his tried skill.
His task is—to coil his snake round the other snake
Halfway clung to the stone, and shatter it so,
Or to break some point in the shank of the fish-hook
   line
And so cut the snake in two.
               Meade's task is to hold.

That is the chess and the scheme of the wooden blocks
Set down on the contour map.
               Having learned so much,
Forget it now, while the ripple-lines of the map
Arise into bouldered ridges, tree-grown, bird-visited,
Where the gnats buzz, and the wren builds a hollow nest
And the rocks are grey in the sun and black in the rain,

And the jacks-in-the-pulpit grow in the cool, damp
  hollows.
See no names of leaders painted upon the blocks
Such as "Hill," or "Hancock," or "Pender"—
                              but see instead
Three miles of living men—three long double miles
Of men and guns and horses and fires and wagons,
Teamsters, surgeons, generals, orderlies,
A hundred and sixty thousand living men
Asleep or eating or thinking or writing brief
Notes in the thought of death, shooting dice or swearing,
Groaning in hospital wagons, standing guard
While the slow stars walk through heaven in silver mail,
Hearing a stream or a joke or a horse cropping grass
Or hearing nothing, being too tired to hear.
All night till the round sun comes and the morning
  breaks,
Three double miles of live men.
Listen to them, their breath goes up through the night
In a great chord of life, in the sighing murmur
Of wind-stirred wheat.
                  A hundred and sixty thousand
Breathing men, at night, on two hostile ridges set down.

Jack Ellyat slept that night on the rocky ground
Of Cemetery Hill while the cold stars marched,
And if his bed was harder than Jacob's stone
Yet he could sleep on it now and be glad for sleep.

He had been through Chancellorsville and the whistling
  wood,
He had been through this last day. It is well to sleep
After such days.
             He had seen, in the last four months,
Many roads, much weather and death, and two men fey
Before they died with the prescience of death to come,
John Haberdeen and the corporal from Millerstown.
Such things are often remembered even in sleep.
He thought to himself, before he lay on the ground,
"We got it hot today in that red-brick town

But we'll get it hotter tomorrow."
                                        And when he woke
And saw the round sun risen in the clear sky.
He could feel that thought steam up from the rocky
    ground
And touch each man.
                            One man looked down from the hill,
"That must be their whole damn army," he said and
    whistled,
"It'll be a picnic today, boys. Yes, it'll be
A regular basket-picnic." He whistled again.

"Shut your trap about picnics, Ace," said another man,
"You make me too damn hungry!"
                                        He sighed out loud.
"We had enough of a picnic at Chancellorsville,"
He said. "I ain't felt right in my stummick since.
Can you make 'em out?"
                            "Sure," said Ace, "but they're
                            pretty far."

"Wonder who we'll get? That bunch we got yesterday
Was a mean-shootin' bunch."
                                        "Now don't you worry,"
                                        said Ace,
"We'll get plenty."
                        The other man sighed again.
"Did you see that darky woman selling hot pies,
Two days ago, on the road?" he said, licking his lips,
"Blackberry pies. The boys ahead got a lot
And Jake and me clubbed together for three. And then
Just as we were ready to make the sneak,
Who comes up with a roar but the provost-guard?
Did we get any pies? I guess you know if we did.
I couldn't spit for an hour, I felt so mad.
Next war I'm goin' to be provost-guard or bust."

A thin voice said abruptly, "They're moving—lookit—
They're moving. I tell you—lookit—"
                                        They all looked then.
A little crackling noise as of burning thornsticks
Began far away—ceased wholly—began again—

"We won't get it awhile," thought Ellyat. "They're trying
    the left.
We won't get it awhile, but we'll get it soon.
I feel funny today. I don't think I'm going to be killed
But I feel funny. That's their whole army all right.
I wonder if those other two felt like this,
John Haberdeen and the corporal from Millerstown?
What's it like to see your name on a bullet?
It must feel queer. This is going to be a big one.
The Johnnies know it. That house looks pretty down
    there.
Phaëton, charioteer in your drunken car,
What have you got for a man that carries my name?
We're a damn good company now, if we say it ourselves,
And the Old Man knows it—but this one's bound to be
    tough.
I wonder what they're feeling like over there.

Charioteer, you were driving yesterday,
No doubt, but I did not see you. I see you now.
What have you got today for a man with my name?"

The firing began that morning at nine o'clock,
But it was three before the attacks were launched.
There were two attacks, one a drive on the Union left
To take the Round Tops, the other one on the right.
Lee had planned them to strike together and, striking so,
Cut the Union snake in three pieces.
                            It did not happen.
On the left, Dutch Longstreet, slow, pugnacious and
    stubborn,
Hard to beat and just as hard to convince,
Has his own ideas of the battle and does not move
For hours after the hour that Lee had planned,
Though, when he does, he moves with pugnacious
    strength.
Facing him, in the valley before the Round Tops,
Sickles thrusts out blue troops in a weak right angle,
Some distance from the Ridge, by the Emmettsburg pike.
There is a peach orchard there, a field of ripe wheat
And other peaceable things soon not to be peaceful.

They say the bluecoats, marching through the ripe
    wheat,
Made a blue-and-yellow picture that men remember
Even now in their age, in their crack-voiced age.
They say the noise was incessant as the sound
Of all wolves howling, when that attack came on.
They say, when the guns all spoke, that the solid ground
Of the rocky ridges trembled like a sick child.
We have made the sick earth tremble with other shakings
In our time, in our time, in our time, but it has not
    taught us
To leave the grain in the field.
                                    So the storm came on
Yelling against the angle.
                            The men who fought there
Were the tried fighters, the hammered, the weather-
    beaten,
The very hard-dying men.
                            They came and died
And came again and died and stood there and died,
Till at last the angle was crumpled and broken in,
Sickles shot down, Willard, Barlow and Semmes shot
    down,
Wheatfield and orchard bloody and trampled and taken,
And Hood's tall Texans sweeping on toward the Round
    Tops
As Hood fell wounded.
                            On Little Round Top's height
Stands a lonely figure, seeing that rush come on—
Greek-mouthed Warren, Meade's chief of engineers.
—Sometimes, and in battle even, a moment comes
When a man with eyes can see a dip in the scales
And, so seeing, reverse a fortune. Warren has eyes
And such a moment comes to him now. He turns
—In a clear flash seeing the crests of the Round Tops
    taken,
The grey artillery there and the battle lost—
And rides off hell-for-leather to gather troops
And bring them up in the very nick of time,
While the grey rush still advances, keening its cry.
The crest is three times taken and then retaken
In fierce wolf-flurries of combat, in gasping Iliads

Too Rapid to note or remember, too obscure to freeze in
   a song.
But at last, when the round sun drops, when the nun-
   footed night,
Dark-veiled walker, holding the first weak stars
Like children against her breast, spreads her pure cloths
   there,
The Union still holds the Round Tops and the two hard
   keys of war.

Night falls. The blood drips in the rocks of the Devil's
   Den.
The murmur begins to rise from the thirsty ground
Where the twenty thousand dead and wounded lie.
Such was Longstreet's war, and such the Union defence,
The deaths and the woundings, the victory and defeat
At the end of the fish-hook shank.
                         And so Longstreet
                         failed
Ere Ewell and Early struck the fish-hook itself
At Culp's Hill and the Ridge and at Cemetery Hill,
With better fortune, though not with fortune enough
To plant hard triumph deep on the sharp-edged rocks
And break the scales of the snake.
                         When that last attack
Came, with its cry, Jack Ellyat saw it come on.

They had been waiting for hours on that hard hill,
Sometimes under fire, sometimes untroubled by shells.
A man chewed a stick of grass and hummed to himself.
Another played mumbledeypeg with a worn black knife.
Two men were talking girls till they got too mad
And the sergeant stopped them.
                       Then they waited again.

Jack Ellyat waited, hearing that other roar
Rise and fall, be distant and then approach.
Now and then he turned on his side and looked at
   the sky
As if to build a house of peace from that blue,
But could find no house of peace there.

                                        Only the roar,
The slow sun sinking, the fey touch at his mind. . . .

He was lying behind a tree and a chunk of rock
On thick, coarse grass. Farther down the slope of the hill
There were houses, a rough stone wall and blue loungy
    men
Behind them lay the batteries on the crest.

He wondered if there were people still in the houses.
One house had a long, slant roof. He followed the slant
Of the roof with his finger, idly, pleased with the line.

The shelling burst out from the Southern guns again.
Their own batteries answered behind them. He looked at
    his house
While the shells came down. I'd like to live in that house.
Now the shelling lessened.
                              The man with the old black
                              knife
Shut up the knife and began to baby his rifle.
They're coming, Jack thought. This is it.
                                        There was an abrupt
Slight stiffening in the bodies of other men,
A few chopped ends of words scattered back and forth,
Eyes looking, hands busy in swift, well-accustomed
    gestures.
This is it. He felt his own hands moving like theirs
Though he was not telling them to. This is it. He felt
The old familiar tightness around his chest.
The man with the grass chewed his stalk a little too hard
And then suddenly spat it out.
                              Jack Ellyat saw
Through the falling night, that slight, grey fringe that
    was war
Coming against them, not as it came in pictures
With a ruler-edge, but a crinkled and smudgy line
Like a child's vague scrawl in soft crayon, but moving on
But with its little red handkerchiefs of flags
Sagging up and down, here and there.
                                        It was still quite far,

It was still like a toy attack—it was swallowed now
By a wood and came out larger with larger flags.
Their own guns on the crest were trying to break it up
—Smoking sand thrown into an ant-legged line—
But it still kept on—one fringe and another fringe
And another and—

            He lost them all for a moment
In a dip of ground.

              This is it, he thought with a parched
Mind. It's a big one. They must be yelling all right
Though you can't hear them. They're going to do it this
   time.
Do it or bust—you can tell from the way they come—
I hope to Christ that the batteries do their job
When they get out of that dip.

               Hell, they've lost 'em now,
And they're still coming.

             He heard a thin gnat-shrieking
"Hold your fire till they're close enough, men!"

                   The new lieutenant.
The new lieutenant looked thin. "Aw, go home," he
   muttered,
"We're no militia—What do you think we are?"

Then suddenly, down by his house, the low stone wall
Flashed and was instantly huge with a wall of smoke.
He was yelling now. He saw a red battleflag
Push through smoke like a prow and be blotted out
By smoke and flash.

            His heart knocked hard in his chest.
"Do it or bust," he mumbled, holding his fire
While the rags of smoke blew off

               He heard a thick chunk
Beside him, turned his head for a flicker of time.
The man who had chewed on the grass was injuredly
   trying
To rise on his knees, his face annoyed by a smile.
Then the blood poured over the smile and he crumpled up.
Ellyat stretched out a hand to touch him and felt the
   hand
Rasped by a file.

He jerked back the hand and sucked it.
"Bastards," he said in a minor and even voice.

All this had occurred, it seemed, in no time at all,
But when he turned back, the smoky slope of the hill
Was grey—and a staggering red advancing flag
And those same shouting strangers he knew so well,
No longer ants—but there—and stumblingly running—
And that high, shrill, hated keen piercing all the flat
  thunder.

His lips went back. He felt something swell in his chest
Like a huge, indocile bubble.
                        "By God," he said,
Loading and firing, "You're not going to get this hill,
You're not going to get this hill. By God, but you're not!"
He saw one grey man spin like a crazy dancer
And another fall at his heels—but the hill kept growing
  them.
Something made him look toward his left.
                            A yellow-fanged face
Was aiming a pistol over a chunk of rock.
He fired and the face went down like a broken pipe
While something hit him sharply and took his breath.
"Get back, you suckers," he croaked, "Get back there,
  you suckers!"
He wouldn't have time to load now—they were too near.
He was up and screaming. He swung his gun like a club
Through a twilight full of bright stabbings, and felt it
  crash
On a thing that broke. He had no breath any more.
He had no thoughts. Then the blunt fist hit him again.

He was down in the grass and the black sheep of night
  ran over him . . .

∞

That day, Melora Vilas sat by the spring
With her child in her arms and felt the warm wind blow
Ruffling the little pool that had shown two faces

Apart and then clung together for a brief while
As if the mouths had been silver and so fused there. . . .

The wind blew at the child's shut fists but it could not
   open them.
The child slept well. The child was a strong, young child.

"Wind, you have blown the green leaf and the brown leaf
And in and out of my restless heart you blow,
Wakening me again.
              I had thought for a while
My heart was a child and could sleep like any child,
But now that the wind is warm, I remember my lover,
Must you blow all summer, warm wind?"

"Divide anew this once-divided flesh
Into twelve shares of mercy and on each
Bestow a fair and succourable child,
Yet, in full summer, when the ripened stalks
Bow in the wind like golden-headed men,
Under the sun, the shares will reunite
Into unmerciful and childless love."

She thought again, "No, it's not that, it's not that,
I love my child with an 'L' because he's little,
I love my child with an 'S' because he's strong.
With an 'M' because he's mine.
                    But I'm restless now.
We cut the heart on the tree but the bark's grown back
   there.
I've got my half of the dime but I want his.
The winter-sleep is over."

The shadows were longer now. The child waked and
   cried.
She rocked and hushed it, feeling the warm wind blow.
"I've got to find him," she said.

About that time, the men rode up to the house
From the other way. Their horses were rough and wild.

There were a dozen of them and they came fast.
Bent should have been out in the woods but he had come
    down
To mend a split wagon-wheel. He was caught in the
    barn.
They couldn't warn him in time, though John Vilas tried,
But they held John Vilas and started to search the place
While the younger children scuttled around like mice
Squeaking "It's drafters, Mom—it's the drafters again!"
Even then, if Bent had hidden under the hay
They might not have found him, being much pressed for
    time,
But perhaps he was tired of hiding.
                                        At any rate
When Melora reached the edge of the little clearing,
She saw them there and Bent there, up on a horse,
Her mother rigid as wood and her father dumb
And the head man saying, gently enough on the whole,
"Don't you worry, ma'am—he'll make a good soldier yet
If he acts proper."
                    That was how they got Bent.

On the crest of the hill, the sweaty cannoneers,
The blackened Pennsylvanians, picked up their rammers
And fought the charge with handspikes and clubs and
    stones,
Biting and howling. It is said that they cried
Wildly, "Death on the soil of our native state
Rather than lose our guns." A general says so.
He was not there. I do not know what they cried
But that they fought, there was witness—and that the
    grey
Wave that came on them fought, there was witness too.
For an instant that wheel of combat—and for an instant
A brief, hard-breathing hush.
                                Then came the hard sound
Of a column tramping—blue reinforcements at last,
A doomsday sound to the grey.
                                The hard column came
Over the battered crest and went in with a yell.

The grey charge bent and gave ground, the grey charge
   was broken.
The sweaty gunners fell to their guns again
And began to scatter the shells in the ebbing wave.

Thus ended the second day of the locked bull-horns
And the wounding or slaying of the twenty thousand.
And thus night came to cover it.
                      So the field
Was alive all night with whispers and words and sights,
So the slow blood dripped in the rocks of the Devil's
   Den.
Lincoln, back in his White House, asks for news.
The War Department has little. There are reports
Of heavy firing near Gettysburg—that is all.
Davis, in Richmond, knows as little as he.
In hollow Vicksburg, the shells come down and come
   down
And the end is but two days off.
                  On the field itself
Meade calls a council and considers retreat.
His left has held and the Round Tops still are his.
But his right has been shaken, his centre pierced for a
   time,
The enemy holds part of his works on Culp's Hill,
His losses have been most stark.
                    He thinks of these
                    things
And decides at last to fight it out where he stands.

Ellyat lay upon Cemetery Hill.
His wounds had begun to burn.
                    He was rising up
Through cold and vacant darknesses into faint light,
The yellow, watery light of a misty moon.
He stirred a little and groaned.
                  There was something cool
On his face and hands. It was dew. He lay on his back
And stared at a blowing cloud and a moist, dark sky.
"Old charioteer," he thought.

                              He remembered dully
The charge. The charge had come. They had beaten the
   charge.
Now it was moist dark sky and the dew and his pain.

He tried to get his canteen but he couldn't reach it.
That made him afraid.
                         "I want some water," he said.
He turned his head through stiff ages.
                                        Two feet away
A man was lying quietly, fast asleep,
A bearded man in an enemy uniform.
He had a canteen. Ellyat wet his lips with his tongue.
"Hey Johnnie, got some water?" he whispered weakly.
Then he saw that the Johnnie had only half a head,
And frowned because such men could not lend canteens.

He was half-delirious now, and it seemed to him
As if he had two bodies, one that was pain
And one that lay beyond pain, on a couch of dew,
And stared at the other with sober wondering eyes.
"Everyone's dead around here but me," he thought,
"And as long as I don't sing out, they'll think that I'm
   dead
And those stretcher-bearers won't find me—there goes
   their lantern
No, it's the moon—Sing out and tell 'em you're here."
The hot body cried and groaned. The cool watched it
   idly.
The yellow moon burst open like a ripe fruit
And from it rolled on a dark, streaked shelf of sky
A car and horses, bearing the brazen ball
Of the unbearable sun, that halted above him
In full rush forward, yet frozen, a motion congealed,
Heavy with light.
                    Toy death above Gettysburg.
He saw it so and cried out in a weak, thin voice
While something jagged fitted into his heart
And the cool body watched idly.
                                   And then it was
A lantern, bobbing along through the clumped dead men,

That halted now for an instant. He cried again.
A voice said, "Listen, Jerry, you're hearing things,
I've passed that feller twice and he's dead all right,
I'll bet you money."

                Ellyat heard himself piping,
"I'm alive, God damn you! Can't you hear I'm alive?"

Something laughed, quite close now.
                      "All right, Bub," said a cloud,
"We'll take your word for it. My, but the boy's got
   language!
Go ahead and cuss while we get you up on the
   stretcher—
It helps some—easy there, Joe."

                     Jack Ellyat fell
Out of his bodies into a whispering blackness
Through which, now and then, he could hear certain
   talking clouds
Cough or remark.
              One said. "That's two and a half
You owe me, Joe. You're pickin' 'em wrong tonight."
"Well, poor suckers," said Joseph. "But all the same,
If this one doesn't last till the dressing station
The bet's off—take it slower, Jerry—it hurts him."

Another clear dawn breaks over Gettysburg,
Promising heat and fair weather—and with the dawn
The guns are crashing again.
                It is the third day.
The morning wears with a stubborn fight at Culp's Hill
That ends at last in Confederate repulse
And that barb-end of the fish-hook cleared of the grey.

Lee has tried his strokes on the right and left of the line.
The centre remains—that centre yesterday pierced
For a brief, wild moment in Wilcox's attack,
But since then trenched, reinforced and alive with guns.
It is a chance. All war is a chance like that.
Lee considers the chance and the force he has left to
   spend

And states his will.
                                   Dutch Longstreet, the independent,
Demurs, as he has demurred since the fight began.
He had disapproved of this battle from the first
And that disapproval has added and is to add
Another weight in the balance against the grey.
It is not our task to try him for sense or folly,
Such men are the men they are—but an hour comes
Sometimes, to fix such men in most fateful parts,
As now with Longstreet who, if he had his orders
As they were given, neither obeyed them quite
Nor quite refused them, but acted as he thought best,
So did the half-thing, failed as he thought he would,
Felt justified and wrote all of his reasons down
Later in controversy.
                          We do not need
Such controversies to see that pugnacious man
Talking to Lee, a stubborn line in his brow
And that unseen fate between them.
                                       Lee hears him out
Unmoved, unchanging.
                          "The enemy is there
And I am going to strike him," says Lee, inflexibly.

          Wingate cursed with an equal stress
          The guns in the sky and his weariness,
          The nightmare riding of yesterday
          When they slept in the saddle by whole platoons
          And the Pennsylvania farmer's grey
          With hocks as puffy as toy balloons,
          A graceless horse, without gaits or speed,
          But all he had for his time of need.
          "I'd as soon be riding a Jersey cow."
          But the Black Horse Troop was piebald now
          And the Black Horse Troop was worn to the blade
          With the dull fatigue of this last, long raid.
          Huger Shepley rode in a tense
          Gloom of the spirit that found offence
          In all things under the summer skies
          And the recklessness in Bristol's eyes
          Had lost its color of merriment.

Horses and men, they were well-nigh spent.
Wingate grinned as he heard the "Mount,"
"Reckon we look sort of no-account,
But we're here at last for somebody's fight."
They rode toward the curve of the Union right.

At one o'clock the first signal-gun was fired
And the solid ground began to be sick anew.
For two hours then that sickness, the unhushed roar
Of two hundred and fifty cannon firing like one.

By Philadelphia, eighty-odd miles away,
An old man stooped and put his ear to the ground
And heard that roar, it is said, like the vague sea-clash
In a hollow conch-shell, there, in his flowerbeds.
He had planted trumpet-flowers for fifteen years
But now the flowers were blowing an iron noise
Through earth itself. He wiped his face on his sleeve
And tottered-back to his house with fear in his eyes.

The caissons began to blow up in the Union batteries. . . .

The cannonade fell still. All along the fish-hook line,
The tired men stared at the smoke and waited for it to
    clear;
The men in the centre waited, their rifles gripped in their
    hands,
By the trees of the riding fate, and the low stone wall,
    and the guns.

These were Hancock's men, the men of the Second
    Corps,
Eleven States were mixed there, where Minnesota stood
In battle-order with Maine, and Rhode Island beside
    New York,
The metals of all the North, cooled into an axe of war.

The strong sticks of the North, bound into a fasces-shape,
The hard winters of snow, the wind with the cutting
    edge,

And against them came that summer that does not die
   with the year,
Magnolia and honeysuckle and the blue Virginia flag.

Tall Pickett went up to Longstreet—his handsome face
   was drawn.
George Pickett, old friend of Lincoln's in days gone by
   with the blast,
When he was a courteous youth and Lincoln the strange
   shawled man
Who would talk in a Springfield street with a boy who
   dreamt of a sword.

Dreamt of a martial sword, as swords are martial in
   dreams,
And the courtesy to use it, in the old bright way of the
   tales.
Those days are gone with the blast. He has his sword in
   his hand.
And he will use it today, and remember that using long.

He came to Longstreet for orders, but Longstreet would
   not speak.
He saw Old Peter's mouth and the thought in Old
   Peter's mind.
He knew the task that was set and the men that he had to
   lead
And a pride came into his face while Longstreet stood
   there dumb.

"I shall go forward, sir," he said and turned to his men.
The commands went down the line. The grey ranks
   started to move.
Slowly at first, then faster, in order, stepping like deer,
The Virginians, the fifteen thousand, the seventh wave of
   the tide.

There was a death-torn mile of broken ground to cross,
And a low stone wall at the end, and behind it the
   Second Corps,
And behind that force another, fresh men who had not
   yet fought.

They started to cross that ground. The guns began to
    tear them.

From the hill they say that it seemed more like a sea than
    a wave,
A sea continually torn by stones flung out of the sky,
And yet, as it came, still closing, closing and rolling on,
As the moving sea closes over the flaws and rips of the
    tide.
You could mark the path that they took by the dead that
    they left behind,
Spilled from that deadly march as a cart spills meal on a
    road,
And yet they came on unceasing, the fifteen thousand no
    more,
And the blue Virginia flag did not fall, did not fall, did
    not fall.

They halted but once to fire as they came. Then the
    smoke closed down
And you could not see them, and then, as it cleared again
    for a breath,
They were coming still but divided, gnawed at by blue
    attacks,
One flank half-severed and halted, but the centre still
    like a tide.

Cushing ran down the last of his guns to the battle-line.
The rest had been smashed to scrap by Lee's artillery
    fire.
He held his guts in his hand as the charge came up the
    wall
And his gun spoke out for him once before he fell to the
    ground.

Armistead leapt the wall and laid his hand on the gun,
The last of the three brigadiers who ordered Pickett's
    brigades,
He waved his hat on his sword and "Give 'em the steel!"
    he cried,
A few men followed him over. The rest were beaten or
    dead.

A few men followed him over. There had been fifteen
   thousand
When that sea began its march toward the fish-hook
   ridge and the wall.
So they came on in strength, light-footed, stepping like
   deer,
So they died or were taken. So the iron entered their flesh.

Lee, a mile away, in the shade of a little wood,
Stared, with his mouth shut down, and saw them go and
   be slain,
And then saw for a single moment, the blue Virginia flag
Planted beyond the wall, by that other flag that
   he knew.

The two flags planted together, one instant, like hostile
   flowers.
Then the smoke wrapped both in a mantle—and when it
   had blown away,
Armistead lay in his blood, and the rest were dead or
   down,
And the valley grey with the fallen and the wreck of the
   broken wave.

Pickett gazed around him, the boy who had dreamt of a
   sword
And talked with a man named Lincoln. The sword was
   still in his hand.
He had gone out with fifteen thousand. He came back to
   his lines with five.
He fought well till the war was over, but a thing was
   cracked in his heart.

    Wingate, waiting the sultry sound
    That would pour the troop over hostile ground,
    Petted his grey like a loving son
    And wondered whether the brute would run
    When it came to fighting, or merely shy
    There was a look in the rolling eye
    That he knew too well to criticize

Having seen it sometimes in other eyes.
"Poor old Fatty," he said, "Don't fret,
It's tough, but it hasn't happened yet
And we may get through it if you behave,
Though it looks just now like a right close shave.
There's something funny about this fight—"

He thought of Lucy in candlelight,
White and gold as the evening star,
Giving bright ribbons to men at war.
But the face grew dimmer and ever dimmer,
The gold was there but the gold was fainter,
And a slow brush streaked it with something
    grimmer
Than the proper tint of a lady's painter
Till the shadow she cast was a ruddy shadow.
He rubbed his eyes and stared at the meadow. . . .

"There was a girl I used to go with,
    Long ago, when the skies were cooler,
There was a tree we used to grow with
    Marking our heights with a stolen ruler.

There was a cave where we hid and fought once.
    There was a pool where the wind kept writing.
There was a possum-child we caught once.
    Caged it awhile, for all its biting.

There was a gap in a fence to see there,
    Down where the sparrows were always
    wrangling.
There was a girl who used to be there,
    Dark and thin, with her long braids dangling.

Dark and thin in her scuffed brown slippers
    With a boy's sling stuck in her apron-pocket,
With a sting in her tongue like a gallinipper's
    And the eyes of a ghost in a silver locket.

White and gold, white and gold,
You cannot be cold as she was cold,

Cold of the air and the running stream
And cold of the ice-tempered dream.

Gold and white, gold and white,
You burn with the heat of candlelight.
But what if I set you down alone
Beside the burning meteor-stone?

Blow North, blow South, blow hot, blow cold,
My body is pledged to white and gold,
My honor given to kith and kin,
And my doom-clothes ready to wrap me in
For the shut heart and the open hand
As long as Wingate Hall shall stand
And the fire burn and the water cool
And a fool beget another fool—

But now, in the hour before this fight,
I have forgotten gold and white.
I will remember lost delight.
She has the Appleton mouth, it seems,
And the Appleton way of riding,
But if she quarrels or when she gleams,
Something comes out from hiding.

She can sew all day on an Appleton hem
And look like a saint in plaster,
But when the fiddles begin to play,
And her feet beat fast but her heart beats faster,
An alien grace is alive in them
And she looks like her father, the dancing-
master,
The scapegrace elegant, 'French Dupré.' "
Then the word came and the bugle sang
And he was part of the running clang,
The rush and the shock and the sabres licking
And the fallen horses screaming and kicking.
His grey was tired and his arm unsteady
And he whirled like a leaf in a shrieking eddy
Where every man was fighting his neighbor
And there was no room for the tricks of sabre
But only a wild and nightmare sickling.

His head felt burnt—there was something trickling
Into his eyes—then the new charge broke
The eddy apart like scattered smoke;
The cut on his head half made him blind.
If he had a mind, he had lost that mind.

He came to himself in a battered place,
Staring at Wainscott Bristol's face,
The dried blood made it a ferret's mask.

"What happened?" he croaked.
                         "Well, you can ask,"
Said Bristol, drawling, "But don't ask me,
For any facts of the jamboree.
I reckon we've been to an Irish wake
Or maybe cuttin' a johnny-cake
With most of the Union cavalry-corps.
I don't know yet, but it was a war.
Are you crazy still? You were for a piece.
You yelled you were Destiny's long-lost niece
And wanted to charge the whole Yank line
Because they'd stolen your valentine.
You fought like a fool but you talked right wild.
You got a bad bump, too."
                         Wingate smiled
"I reckon I did, but I don't know when.
Did we win or what?"
                     "And I say again,"
Said Bristol, heavily, "don't ask me.
Inquire of General Robert Lee.
I know we're in for a long night ride
And they say we got whipped on the other side.
What's left of the Troop are down by the road.
We lost John Leicester and Harry Spode
And the Lawley boys and Ballantyne.
The Major's all right—but there's Jim Divine
And Francis Carroll and Judson White—
I wish I had some liquor tonight."

Wingate touched the cut on his head.
It burned, but it no longer bled.
"I wish I could sleep ten years," he said.

The night of the third day falls. The battle is done.
Lee entrenches that night upon Seminary Ridge.
All next day the battered armies still face each other
Like enchanted beasts.
                     Lee thinks he may be attacked,
Hopes for it, perhaps, is not, and prepares his retreat.

Vicksburg has fallen, hollow Vicksburg has fallen,
The cavedwellers creep from their caves and blink at
    the sun.
The pan of the Southern balance goes down and down.
The cotton is withering.

Army of Northern Virginia, haggard and tattered,
Tramping back on the pikes, through the dust-white
    summer,
With your wounds still fresh, your burden of prisoners,
Your burden of sick and wounded,
"One long groan of human anguish six miles long."
You reach the swollen Potomac at long last,
A foe behind, a risen river in front,
And fording that swollen river, in the dim starlight,
In the yellow and early dawn,
Still have heart enough for the tall, long-striding soldiers
To mock the short, half swept away by the stream.
"Better change our name to Lee's Waders, boys!"
"Come on you shorty—get a ride on my back."
"Aw, it's just we ain't had a bath in seven years
And General Lee, he knows we need a good bath."

So you splash and slip through the water and come at last
Safe, to the Southern side, while Meade does not strike;
Safe to take other roads, safe to march upon roads you
    know
For two long years. And yet—each road that you take,
Each dusty road leads to Appomattox now.

CODA FROM BOOK EIGHT

John Brown's body lies a-mouldering in the grave.
Spread over it the bloodstained flag of his song,
For the sun to bleach, the wind and the birds to tear,
The snow to cover over with a pure fleece
And the New England cloud to work upon
With the grey absolution of its slow, most lilac-smelling
    rain,
Until there is nothing there
That ever knew a master or a slave
Or, brooding on the symbol of a wrong,
Threw down the irons in the field of peace.
John Brown is dead, he will not come again,
A stray ghost-walker with a ghostly gun.
Let the strong metal rust
In the enclosing dust
And the consuming coal
That was the furious soul
And still like iron groans,
Anointed with the earth,
Grow colder than the stones
While the white roots of grass and little weeds
Suck the last hollow wildfire from the singing bones.

Bury the South together with this man,
Bury the bygone South.
Bury the minstrel with the honey-mouth,
Bury the broadsword virtues of the clan,
Bury the unmachined, the planter's pride,
The courtesy and the bitter arrogance,
The pistol-hearted horsemen who could ride
Like jolly centaurs under the hot stars.
Bury the whip, bury the branding-bars,
Bury the unjust thing
That some tamed into mercy, being wise,
But could not starve the tiger from its eyes
Or make it feed where beasts of mercy feed.
Bury the fiddle-music and the dance,
The sick magnolias of the false romance
And all the chivalry that went to seed
Before its ripening.

And with these things, bury the purple dream
Of the America we have not been,
The tropic empire, seeking the warm sea,
The last foray of aristocracy
Based not on dollars or initiative
Or any blood for what that blood was worth
But on a certain code, a manner of birth,
A certain manner of knowing how to live,
The pastoral rebellion of the earth
Against machines, against the Age of Steam,
The Hamiltonian extremes against the Franklin mean,
The genius of the land
Against the metal hand,
The great, slave-driven bark,
Full-oared upon the dark,
With gilded figurehead,
With fetters for the crew
And spices for the few,
The passion that is dead,
The pomp we never knew,
Bury this, too.

Bury this destiny unmanifest,
This system broken underneath the test,
Beside John Brown and though he knows his enemy is
   there
He is too full of sleep at last to care.

He was a stone, this man who lies so still,
A stone flung from a sling against a wall,
A sacrificial instrument of kill,
A cold prayer hardened to a musket-ball:
And yet, he knew the uses of a hill,
And he must have his justice, after all.

He was a lover of certain pastoral things,
He had the shepherd's gift.
When he walked at peace, when he drank from the
   watersprings,
His eyes would lift
To see God, robed in a glory, but sometimes, too,
Merely the sky,

Untroubled by wrath or angels, vacant and blue,
Vacant and high.

He knew not only doom but the shape of the land,
Reaping and sowing.
He could take a lump of any earth in his hand
And feel the growing.

He was a farmer, he didn't think much of towns,
The wheels, the vastness.
He liked the wide fields, the yellows, the lonely browns,
The black ewe's fastness.

Out of his body grows revolving steel,
Out of his body grows the spinning wheel
Made up of wheels, the new, mechanic birth,
No longer bound by toil
To the unsparing soil
Or the old furrow-line,
The great, metallic beast
Expanding West and East,
His heart a spinning coil,
His juices burning oil,
His body serpentine.
Out of John Brown's strong sinews the tall skyscrapers
    grow,
Out of his heart the chanting buildings rise,
Rivet and girder, motor and dynamo,
Pillar of smoke by day and fire by night,
The steel-faced cities reaching at the skies,
The whole enormous and rotating cage
Hung with hard jewels of electric light,
Smoky with sorrow, black with splendor, dyed
Whiter than damask for a crystal bride
With metal suns, the engine-handed Age,
The genie we have raised to rule the earth,
Obsequious to our will
But servant-master still,
The tireless serf already half a god—

Touch the familiar sod
Once, then gaze at the air

And see the portent there,
With eyes for once washed clear
Of worship and of fear:
There is its hunger, there its living thirst,
There is the beating of the tremendous heart
You cannot read for omens.
                              Stand apart
From the loud crowd and look upon the flame
Alone and steadfast, without praise or blame.
This is the monster and the sleeping queen
And both have roots struck deep in your own mind,
This is reality that you have seen,
This is reality that made you blind.

So, when the crowd gives tongue
And prophets, old or young,
Bawl out their strange despair
Or fall in worship there,
Let them applaud the image or condemn
But keep your distance and your soul from them.
And, if the heart within your breast must burst
Like a cracked crucible and pour its steel
White-hot before the white heat of the wheel,
Strive to recast once more
That attar of the ore
In the strong mold of pain
Till it is whole again,
And while the prophets shudder or adore
Before the flame, hoping it will give ear,
If you at last must have a word to say,
Say neither, in their way,
"It is a deadly magic and accursed,"
Nor "It is blest," but only "It is here."

AMERICANS

THE BALLAD OF WILLIAM SYCAMORE
(1790–1871)

My father, he was a mountaineer,
His fist was a knotty hammer;
He was quick on his feet as a running deer,
And he spoke with a Yankee stammer.

My mother, she was merry and brave,
And so she came to her labor,
With a tall green fir for her doctor grave
And a stream for her comforting neighbor.

And some are wrapped in the linen fine,
And some like a godling's scion;
But I was cradled on twigs of pine
In the skin of a mountain lion.

And some remember a white, starched lap
And a ewer with silver handles;
But I remember a coonskin cap
And the smell of bayberry candles.

The cabin logs, with the bark still rough,
And my mother who laughed at trifles,
And the tall, lank visitors, brown as snuff,
With their long, straight squirrel-rifles.

I can hear them dance, like a foggy song,
Through the deepest one of my slumbers,
The fiddle squeaking the boots along
And my father calling the numbers.

The quick feet shaking the puncheon-floor,
And the fiddle squealing and squealing,
Till the dried herbs rattled above the door
And the dust went up to the ceiling.

There are children lucky from dawn till dusk,
But never a child so lucky!
For I cut my teeth on "Money Musk"
In the Bloody Ground of Kentucky!

When I grew tall as the Indian corn,
My father had little to lend me,
But he gave me his great, old powder-horn
And his woodsman's skill to befriend me.

With a leather shirt to cover my back,
And a redskin nose to unravel
Each forest sign, I carried my pack
As far as a scout could travel.

Till I lost my boyhood and found my wife,
A girl like a Salem clipper!
A woman straight as a hunting-knife
With eyes as bright as the Dipper!

We cleared our camp where the buffalo feed,
Unheard-of streams were our flagons;
And I sowed my sons like the apple-seed
On the trail of the Western wagons.

They were right, tight boys, never sulky or slow,
A fruitful, a goodly muster.
The eldest died at the Alamo.
The youngest fell with Custer.

The letter that told it burned my hand.
Yet we smiled and said, "So be it!"
But I could not live when they fenced the land,
For it broke my heart to see it.

I saddled a red, unbroken colt
And rode him into the day there;
And he threw me down like a thunderbolt
And rolled on me as I lay there.

The hunter's whistle hummed in my ear
As the city-men tried to move me,

And I died in my boots like a pioneer
With the whole wide sky above me.

Now I lie in the heart of the fat, black soil,
Like the seed of a prairie-thistle;
It has washed my bones with honey and oil
And picked them clean as a whistle.

And my youth returns, like the rains of Spring,
And my sons, like the wild-geese flying;
And I lie and hear the meadow-lark sing
And have much content in my dying.

Go play with the towns you have built of blocks,
The towns where you would have bound me!
I sleep in my earth like a tired fox,
And my buffalo have found me.

THE MOUNTAIN WHIPPOORWILL

OR, HOW HILL-BILLY JIM WON THE GREAT FIDDLERS' PRIZE

(*A Georgia Romance*)

Up in the mountains, it's lonesome all the time,
(Sof' win' slewin' thu' the sweet-potato vine).

Up in the mountains, it's lonesome for a child,
(Whippoorwills a-callin' when the sap runs wild).

Up in the mountains, mountains in the fog,
Everythin's as lazy as an old houn' dog.

Born in the mountains, never raised a pet,
Don't want nuthin' an' never got it yet.

Born in the mountains, lonesome-born,
Raised runnin' ragged thu' the cockleburrs and corn.

Never knew my pappy, mebbe never should.
Think he was a fiddle made of mountain laurel-wood.

Never had a mammy to teach me pretty-please.
Think she was a whippoorwill, a-skitin' thu' the trees.

Never had a brother ner a whole pair of pants,
But when I start to fiddle, why, yuh got to start to dance!

Listen to my fiddle—Kingdom Come—Kingdom Come!
Hear the frogs a-chunkin' "Jug o' rum, Jug o' rum!"
Hear that mountain-whippoorwill be lonesome in the air,
An' I'll tell yuh how I traveled to the Essex County Fair.

Essex County has a mighty pretty fair,
All the smarty fiddlers from the South come there.

Elbows flyin' as they rosin up the bow
For the First Prize Contest in the Georgia Fiddlers' Show.

Old Dan Wheeling, with his whiskers in his ears,
King-pin fiddler for nearly twenty years.

Big Tom Sargent, with his blue wall-eye,
An' Little Jimmy Weezer that can make a fiddle cry.

All sittin' roun', spittin' high an' struttin' proud,
(Listen, little whippoorwill, yuh better bug yore eyes!)
Tun-a-tun-a-tunin' while the jedges told the crowd
Them that got the mostest claps'd win the bestest prize.

Everybody waitin' for the first tweedle-dee,
When in comes a-stumblin'—hill-billy me!

Bowed right pretty to the jedges an' the rest,
Took a silver dollar from a hole inside my vest,

Plunked it on the table an' said, "There's my callin' card!
An' anyone that licks me—well, he's got to fiddle hard!"

Old Dan Wheeling, he was laughin' fit to holler,
Little Jimmy Weezer said, "There's one dead dollar!"

Big Tom Sargent had a yaller-toothy grin,
But I tucked my little whippoorwill spang underneath
    my chin,
An' petted it an' tuned it till the jedges said, "Begin!"

Big Tom Sargent was the first in line;
He could fiddle all the bugs off a sweet-potato vine.

He could fiddle down a possum from a mile-high tree.
He could fiddle up a whale from the bottom of the sea.

Yuh could hear hands spankin' till they spanked each
    other raw,
When he finished variations on "Turkey in the Straw."

Little Jimmy Weezer was the next to play;
He could fiddle all night, he could fiddle all day.

He could fiddle chills, he could fiddle fever,
He could make a fiddle rustle like a lowland river.

He could make a fiddle croon like a lovin' woman.
An' they clapped like thunder when he'd finished
    strummin'.

Then came the ruck of the bob-tailed fiddlers,
The let's go-easies, the fair-to-middlers.

They got their claps an' they lost their bicker,
An' settled back for some more corn-licker.

An' the crowd was tired of their no-count squealing,
When out in the center steps Old Dan Wheeling.

He fiddled high and he fiddled low,
(Listen, little whippoorwill; yuh got to spread yore
    wings!)
He fiddled with a cheerywood bow.
(Old Dan Wheeling's got bee-honey in his strings.)

He fiddled the wind by the lonesome moon,
He fiddled a most almighty tune.

He started fiddling like a ghost,
He ended fiddling like a host.

He fiddled north an' he fiddled south,
He fiddled the heart right out of yore mouth.

He fiddled here an' he fiddled there.
He fiddled salvation everywhere.

When he was finished, the crowd cut loose,
(Whippoorwill, they's rain on yore breast.)
An' I sat there wonderin', "What's the use?"
(Whippoorwill, fly home to yore nest.)

But I stood up pert an' I took my bow,
An' my fiddle went to my shoulder, so.

An'—they wasn't no crowd to get me fazed—
But I was alone where I was raised.

Up in the mountains, so still it makes yuh skeered.
Where God lies sleepin' in his big white beard.

An' I heard the sound of the squirrel in the pine,
An' I heard the earth a-breathin' thu' the long night-time.

They've fiddled the rose, an' they've fiddled the thorn,
But they haven't fiddled the mountain-corn.

They've fiddled sinful an' fiddled moral,
But they haven't fiddled the breshwood-laurel.

They've fiddled loud, an' they've fiddled still,
But they haven't fiddled the whippoorwill.

I started off with a *dump-diddle-dump,*
(Oh, hell's broke loose in Georgia!)
Skunk-cabbage growin' by the bee-gum stump,
(Whippoorwill, yo're singin' now!)

Oh, Georgia booze is mighty fine booze,
The best yuh ever poured yuh,
But it eats the soles right offen yore shoes,
For Hell's broke loose in Georgia.

My mother was a whippoorwill pert,
My father, he was lazy,
But I'm Hell broke loose in a new store shirt
To fiddle all Georgia crazy.

Swing yore partners—up an' down the middle!
Sashay now—oh, listen to that fiddle!
Flapjacks flippin' on a red-hot griddle,
An' hell broke loose,
Hell broke loose,
Fire on the mountains—snakes in the grass.
Satan's here a-bilin'—oh, Lordy, let him pass!
Go down Moses, set my people free,
Pop goes the weasel thu' the old Red Sea!
Jonah sittin' on a hickory-bough,
Up jumps a whale—an' where's yore prophet now?
Rabbit in the pea-patch, possum in the pot,
Try an' stop my fiddle, now my fiddle's gettin' hot!
Whippoorwill, singin' thu' the mountain hush,
Whippoorwill, shoutin' from the burnin' bush,
Whippoorwill, cryin' in the stable-door,
Sing to-night as yuh never sang before!
Hell's broke loose like a stompin' mountain-shoat,
Sing till yuh bust the gold in yore throat!
Hell's broke loose for forty miles aroun'
Bound to stop yore music if yuh don't sing it down.
Sing on the mountains, little whippoorwill,
Sing to the valleys, an' slap 'em with a hill,
For I'm struttin' high as an eagle's quill,
An' Hell's broke loose,
Hell's broke loose,
Hell's broke loose in Georgia!

They wasn't a sound when I stopped bowin',
(*Whippoorwill, yuh can sing no more.*)
But, somewhere or other, the dawn was growin',
(*Oh, mountain whippoorwill!*)

An' I thought, "I've fiddled all night an' lost.
Yo're a good hill-billy, but yuh've been bossed."

So I went to congratulate old man Dan,
—But he put his fiddle into my han'—
An' then the noise of the crowd began.

AMERICAN NAMES

I have fallen in love with American names,
The sharp names that never get fat,
The snakeskin-titles of mining-claims,
The plumed war-bonnet of Medicine Hat,
Tucson and Deadwood and Lost Mule Flat.

Scine and Piave are silver spoons,
But the spoonbowl-metal is thin and worn,
There are English counties like hunting-tunes
Played on the keys of a postboy's horn,
But I will remember where I was born.

I will remember Carquinez Straits,
Little French Lick and Lundy's Lane,
The Yankee ships and the Yankee dates
And the bullet-towns of Calamity Jane.
I will remember Skunktown Plain.

I will fall in love with a Salem tree
And a rawhide quirt from Santa Cruz,
I will get me a bottle of Boston sea
And a blue-gum nigger to sing me blues.
I am tired of loving a foreign muse.

Rue des Martyrs and Bleeding-Heart-Yard,
Senlis, Pisa, and Blindman's Oast,
It is a magic ghost you guard
But I am sick for a newer ghost,
Harrisburg, Spartanburg, Painted Post.

Henry and John were never so
And Henry and John were always right?
Granted, but when it was time to go
And the tea and the laurels had stood all night,
Did they never watch for Nantucket Light?

I shall not rest quiet in Montparnasse.
I shall not lie easy at Winchelsea.
You may bury my body in Sussex grass,
You may bury my tongue at Champmédy.
I shall not be there. I shall rise and pass.
Bury my heart at Wounded Knee.

From *A Book of Americans*

POCAHONTAS

1595?–1617

Princess Pocahontas,
Powhatan's daughter,
Stared at the white men
Come across the water.

She was like a wild deer
Or a bright, plumed bird,
Ready then to flash away
At one harsh word.

When the faces answered hers,
Paler yet, but smiling,
Pocahontas looked and looked,
Found them quite beguiling.

Liked the whites and trusted them,
Spite of kin and kith,
Fed and protected
Captain John Smith.

Pocahontas was revered
By each and every one.
She married John Rolfe
She had a Rolfe son.

She crossed the sea to London Town
And must have found it queer,
To be Lady Rebecca
And the toast of the year.

"La Belle Sauvage! La Belle sauvage!
Our nonpareil is she!"
But Princess Pocahontas
Gazed sadly toward the sea.

They gave her silks and furbelows.
She pined, as wild things do
And, when she died at Gravesend
She was only twenty-two.

Poor wild bird—
No one can be blamed.
But gentle Pocahontas
Was a wild thing tamed.

And everywhere the lesson runs,
All through the ages:
Wild things die
In the very finest cages.

PILGRIMS AND PURITANS

1620

The Pilgrims and the Puritans
Were English to the bone
But didn't like the English Church
And wished to have their own
And so, at last, they sailed away
To settle Massachusetts Bay.

And there they found New England rocks
And Indians with bows on
But didn't mind them half as much
(Though they were nearly frozen)
As being harried, mocked and spurned in
Old England for the faith they burned in.

The stony fields, the cruel sea
They met with resolution
And so developed, finally,
An iron constitution

And, as a punishment for sinners,
Invented boiled New England dinners.

They worked and traded, fished and farmed
And made New England mighty
On codfish, conscience, self-respect
And smuggled aqua-vitae.
They hated fun. They hated fools.
They liked plain manners and good schools.

They fought and suffered, starved and died
For their own way of thinking
But people who had different views
They popped, as quick as winking,
Within the roomy local jail
Or whipped through town at the cart's rail.

They didn't care for Quakers but
They loathed gay cavaliers
And what they thought of clowns and plays
Would simply burn your ears
While merry tunes and Christmas revels
They deemed contraptions of the Devil's.

THOMAS JEFFERSON

1743–1826

Thomas Jefferson,
What do you say
Under the gravestone
Hidden away?

"I was a giver,
I was a molder,
I was a builder
With a strong shoulder."

Six feet and over,
Large-boned and ruddy,
The eyes grey-hazel
But bright with study.

The big hands clever
With pen and fiddle
And ready, ever,
For any riddle.

From buying empires
To planting 'taters,
From Declarations
To trick dumb-waiters.

"I liked the people,
The sweat and crowd of them,
Trusted them always
And spoke aloud of them.

"I liked all learning
And wished to share it
A broad like pollen
For all who merit.

"I liked fine houses
With Greek pilasters,
And built them surely,
My touch a master's.

"I liked queer gadgets
And secret shelves,
And helping nations
To rule themselves.

"Jealous of others?
Not always candid?
But huge of vision
And open-handed.

"A wild-goose-chaser?
Now and again,
Build Monticello,
You little men!

"Design my plow, sirs,
They use it still,

Or found my college
At Charlottesville.

"And still go questing
New things and thinkers,
And keep as busy
As twenty-tinkers.

"While always guarding
The people's freedom—
You need more hands, sir?
I didn't need 'em.

"They call you rascal?
They called me worse.
You'd do grand things, sir,
But lack the purse?

"I got no riches.
I died a debtor.
I died free-hearted
And that was better.

"For life was freakish
But life was fervent,
And I was always
Life's willing servant.

"Life, life's too weighty?
Too long a haul, sir?
I lived past eighty.
I liked it all, sir."

DOLLY MADISON

1772–1849

Dolly Madison
(Dorothea Payne),
Married, was widowed
And married again.

Passing by other
More dashing names
To set her cap
For "the great little" James.

She loved fine clothes,
Though she was a Quaker.
She wore linen masks
So the sun wouldn't bake her.

Her eyes were large,
Her manners urban,
And she posed for her portrait
Wearing a turban.

She brushed her satins,
Tended her beauty,
Smoothed her laces,
Minded her duty.

But, though fine and grand
On her at-home day,
She could still take snuff
With Henry Clay.

When the British began
To cut more capers
And burned the White House,
She didn't have vapors.

The roofs fell in
And the cut-glass burst—
But she saved George Washington's
Portrait first.

She didn't talk much.
She eschewed all tears.
She went to a ball
At fourscore years.

But her very last words
Set us staring—for—

"There's nothing in this life
Worth caring for."

Said by a lady
Who loved her life
And, more than most,
Was a perfect wife,

Make us wonder a little,
Though with no stigma,
If Dolly could have been
An enigma.

DANIEL BOONE

1735–1820

When Daniel Boone goes by, at night,
The phantom deer arise
And all lost, wild America
Is burning in their eyes.

CRAZY HORSE

?–1877

The Indians of the Wild West
We found were hard to tame,
For they seemed really quite possessed
To keep their ways the same.

They liked to hunt, they liked to fight,
And (this I grieve to say)
They could not see the white man's right
To take their land away.

So there was fire upon the Plains,
And deeds of derring-do,
Where Sioux were bashing soldier's brains
And soldiers bashing Sioux'.

And here is bold Chief Crazy Horse,
A warrior, keen and tried,

Who fought with fortitude and force
—But on the losing side.

Where Custer fell, where Miles pursued,
He led his native sons,
And did his best, though it was crude
And lacked the Gatling guns.

It was his land. They were his men.
He cheered and led them on.
—The hunting ground is pasture, now.
The buffalo are gone.

NEGRO SPIRITUALS

We do not know who made them.
The lips that gave them birth
Are dust in the slaves' burying ground,
Anonymous as earth.

The poets, the musicians.
Were bondsmen bred and born.
They picked the master's cotton,
They hoed the master's corn.

The load was heavy on their backs,
The way was long and cold,
—But out of stolen Africa,
The singing river rolled,
And David's hands were dusky hands,
But David's harp was gold.

ODE TO WALT WHITMAN

(MAY 31, 1810–MARCH 26, 1892)

Now comes Fourth Month and the early buds on the
     trees.
By the roads of Long Island, the forsythia has flowered,
In the North, the cold will be breaking; even in Maine
The cold will be breaking soon; the young, bull-voiced
     freshets

Roar from green mountains, gorging the chilly brooks
With the brown, trout-feeding waters, the unlocked
    springs;
Now Mississippi stretches with the Spring rains. . . .

It is forty years and more,
The time of the ripeness and withering of a man,
Since you lay in the house in Camden and heard, at last,
The great, slow footstep, splashing the Third Month
    snow
In the little, commonplace street
—Town snow, already trampled and growing old,
Soot-flecked and dingy, patterned with passing feet,
The bullet-pocks of rain, the strong urine of horses,
The slashing, bright steel runners of small boys' sleds
Hitching on behind the fast cutters.
They dragged their sleds to the tops of the hills and
    yelled
The Indian yell of all boyhood, for pure joy
Of the cold and the last gold light and the swift rush
    down
Belly-flopping into darkness, into bedtime.
You saw them come home, late, hungry and burning-
    cheeked,
The boys and girls, the strong children,
Dusty with snow, their mittens wet with the silver drops
    of thawed snow.

All winter long, you had heard their sharp footsteps
    passing,
The skating crunch of their runners,
An old man, tied to a house, after many years,
An old man with his rivery, clean white hair,
His bright eyes, his majestic poverty,
His fresh pink skin like the first strawberry-bloom,
His innocent, large, easy old man's clothes
—Brown splotches on the hands of clean old men
At County Farms or sitting on warm park-benches
Like patient flies, talking of their good sons,
"Yes, my son's good to me"—
An old man, poor, without sons, waiting achingly

For spring to warm his lameness,
For spring to flourish,
And yet, when the eyes glowed, neither old nor tied.

All winter long there had been footsteps passing,
Steps of postmen and neighbors, quick steps of friends,
All winter long you had waited that great, snow-treading
    step,
The enemy, the vast comrade,
The step behind, in the wards, when the low lamp
    flickered
And the sick boy gasped for breath,
*"Lean on me! Lean upon my shoulder! By God, you shall
    not die!"*
The step ahead, on the long, wave-thundering beaches of
    Paumanok,
Invisible, printless, weighty,
The shape half-seen through the wet, sweet sea-fog of
    youth,
Night's angel and the dark Sea's,
The grand, remorseless treader,
Magnificent Death.

"Let me taste all, my flesh and my fat are sweet,
My body hardy as lilac, the strong flower.
I have tasted the calamus; I can taste the nightbane."

Always the water about you since you were born,
The endless lapping of water, the strong motion,
The gulls by the ferries knew you, and the wild
    sea-birds,
The sandpiper, printing the beach with delicate prints.
At last, old, wheeled to the wharf, you still watched the
    water,
The tanned boys, flat-bodied, diving, the passage of
    ships,
The proud port, distant, the people, the work of
    harbors. . . .

"I have picked out a bit of hill with a southern exposure.
I like to be near the trees. I like to be near
The water-sound of the trees."

Now, all was the same in the cluttered, three-windowed
   room,
Low-ceiled, getting the sun like a schooner's cabin,
The crowding photos hiding the ugly wall-paper.
The floor-litter, the strong chair, timbered like a ship,
The hairy black-and-silver of the old wolfskin;

In the back-yard, neither lilac nor pear yet bloomed
But the branch of the lilac swelling with first sap;
And there, in the house, the figures, the nurse, the woman,
The passing doctor, the friends, the little clan,
The disciple with the notebook who's always there.

All these and the pain and the water-bed to ease you
And you said it rustled of oceans and were glad
And the pain shut and relaxed and shut once more.

"Old body, counsellor, why do you thus torment me?
Have we not been friends from our youth?"

But now it came,
Slow, perceived by no others,
The splashing step through the grey, soft, Saturday rain,
Inexorable footstep of the huge friend.
"Are you there at last, fine enemy?
Ah, haste, friend, hasten, come closer!
Breathe upon me with your grave, your releasing lips!
I have heard and spoken; watched the bodies of boys
Flash in the copper sun and dive to green waters,
Seen the fine ships and the strong matrons and the tall
   axemen,
The young girls, free, athletic; the drunkard, retching
In his poor dream; the thief taken by officers;
The President, calm, grave, advising the nation;
The infant, with milk-wet lips in his bee-like slumber.
They are mine; all, all are mine; must I leave them, truly?
I have cherished them in my veins like milk and fruit.
I have warmed them at my bare breast like the eggs of
   pigeons.
The great plains of the buffalo are mine, the towns, the
   hills, the ship-bearing waters.
These States are my wandering sons.

I had them in my youth; I cannot desert them.
The green leaf of America is printed on my heart
     forever."

Now it entered the house, it marched upon the stair.
By the bedside the faces dimmed, the huge shoulder
     blotting them,
—It is so they die on the plains, the great, old buffalo,
The herd-leaders, the beasts with the kingly eyes,
Innocent, curly-browed,
They sink to the earth like mountains, hairy and silent,
And their tongues are cut by the hunter.
                              Oh, singing tongue!
Great tongue of bronze and salt and the free grasses,
Tongue of America, speaking for the first time,
Must the hunter have you at last?

Now, face to face, you saw him
And lifted the right arm once, as a pilot lifts it,
Signalling with the bell,
In the passage at night, on the river known yet unknown,
—Perhaps to touch his shoulder, perhaps in pain—
Then the rain fell on the roof and the twilight darkened
And they said that in death you looked like a marvelous
     old, wise child.

2

It is Fourth Month now and spring in another century,
Let us go to the hillside and ask; he will like to hear us;
"Is it good, the sleep?"

                    "It is good, the sleep and the
                         waking.
I have picked out a bit of hill where the south sun warms
     me.
I like to be near the trees."

Nay, let him ask, rather.
"Is it well with you, comrades?
The cities great, portentous, humming with action?

The bridges mightily spanning wide-breasted rivers?
The great plains growing the wheat, the old lilac hardy,
    well-budded?
Is it well with these States?"

"The cities are great, portentous, a world-marvel,
The bridges arched like the necks of beautiful horses.
We have made the dry land bloom and the dead land
    blossom."

"Is it well with these States?"

"The old wound of your war is healed and we are one
    nation.
We have linked the whole land with the steel and the
    hard highways.
We have fought new wars and won them. In the French
    field
There are bones of Texarkana and Little Falls,
Aliens, our own; in the low-lying Belgian ground;
In the cold sea of the English; in dark-faced islands.
Men speak of them well or ill; they themselves are
    silent."

"Is it well with these States?"

"We have made many, fine new toys.
We—
There is a rust on the land.
A rust and a creeping blight and a scaled evil,
For six years eating, yet deeper than those six years,
Men labor to master it but it is not mastered.
There is the soft, grey, foul tent of the hatching worm
Shrouding the elm, the chestnut, the Southern cypress.
There is shadow in the bright sun, there is shadow upon
    the streets.
They burn the grain in the furnace while men go hungry.
They pile the cloth of the looms while men go ragged.
We walk naked in our plenty."

"My tan-faced children?"

"These are your tan-faced children.
These skilled men, idle, with the holes in their shoes.
These drifters from State to State, these wolvish,
    bewildered boys
Who ride the blinds and the box-cars from jail to jail,
Burnt in their youth like cinders of hot smokestacks,
Learning the thief's crouch and the cadger's whine,
Dishonored, abandoned, disinherited.
These, dying in the bright sunlight they cannot eat,
Or the strong men, sitting at home, their hands clasping
    nothing,
Looking at their lost hands.
These are your tan-faced children, the parched young,
The old man rooting in waste-heaps, the family rotting
In the flat, before eviction,
With the toys of plenty about them,
The shiny toys making ice and music and light,
But no price for the shiny toys and the last can empty.
The sleepers in blind corners of the night.
The women with dry breasts and phantom eyes.
The walkers upon nothing, the four million.
These are your tan-faced children."

"But the land?"

"Over the great plains of the buffalo-land,
The dust-storm blows, the choking, sifting, small dust.
The skin of that land is ploughed by the dry, fierce wind
And blown away, like a torrent;
It drifts foot-high above the young sprouts of grain
And the water fouls, the horses stumble and sicken,
The wash-board cattle stagger and die of drought.
We tore the buffalo's pasture with the steel blade.
We made the waste land blossom and it has blossomed.
That was our fate; now that land takes its own revenge,
And the giant dust-flower blooms above five States."

"But the gains of the years, who got them?"

"Many, great gains.
Many, yet few; they robbed us in the broad daylight,
Saying, 'Give us this and that; we are kings and titans;
We know the ropes; we are solid; we are hard-headed;
We will build you cities and railroads.'—as if *they* built
    them!
They, the preying men, the men whose hearts were like
    engines,
Gouging the hills for gold, laying waste the timber,
The men like band-saws, moving over the land.
And, after them, the others,
Soft-bodied, lacking even the pirate's candor,
Men of paper, robbing by paper, with paper faces,
Rustling like frightened paper when the storm broke.
The men with the jaws of moth and aphis and beetle,
Boring the dusty, secret hole in the corn,
Fixed, sucking the land, with neither wish nor pride
But the wish to suck and continue.
They have been sprayed, a little.
But they say they will have the land back again, these
    men."

"There were many such in my time.
I have seen the rich arrogant and the poor oppressed.
I have seen democracy, also. I have seen
The good man slain, the knave and the fool in power,
The democratic vista botched by the people,
Yet not despaired, loving the giant land,
Though I prophesied to these States."

"Now they say we must have one tyranny or another
And a dark bell rings in our hearts."

"Was the blood spilt for nothing, then?"

3

Under dry winter
Arbutus grows.
It is careless of man.
It is careless of man.

Man can tear it,
Crush it, destroy it;
Uproot the trailers,
The thumb-shaped leafings.

A man in grey clothes
May come there also,
Lie all day there
In weak spring sunlight.

White, firm-muscled,
The flesh of his body;
Wind, sun, earth
In him, possessing him.

In his heart
A flock of birds crying.
In his belly
The new grass growing.

In his skull
Sunlight and silence,
Like a vast room
Full of sunlight and silence.

In the lines of his palms
The roads of America,
In the knots of his hands
The anger of America.

In the sweat of his flesh
The sorrows of America,
In the seed of his loins
The glory of America.

The sap of the birch-tree
Is in his pelt,
The maple, the red-bud
Are his nails and parings.

He grows through the earth and is part of it like the
    roots of new grass.

Little arbutus
Delicate, tinted,
Tiny, tender,
Fragile, immortal.

If you can grow,
A man can grow
Not like others
But like a man.

Man is a bull
But he has not slain you
And this man lies
Like a lover beside you.

Beside the arbutus,
The green-leaved Spring,
He lies like a lover
By his young bride,
In the white hour,
The white, first waking.

4

They say, they say, they say and let them say.
Call you a revolutionist—you were one—
A nationalist—you were one—a man of peace,
A man describing battles, an old fraud,
A Charlus, an adept self-advertiser,
A "good, grey poet"—oh, God save us all!
God save us from the memoirs and the memories!
And yet, they count. They have to. If they didn't
There'd be no Ph.Ds. And each disciple
Jealously guards his own particular store
Of acorns fallen from the oak's abundance
And spits and scratches at the other gatherers.
"I was there when he died!"
                              "He was not there when he died!"
"It was me he trusted, me! X got on his nerves!
He couldn't stand X in the room!"

"Y's well-intentioned
But a notorious liar—and, as for Z . . ."

So all disciples, always and forever.
—And the dire court at Longwood, those last years,
The skull of Sterne, grinning at the anatomists,
Poe's hospital-bed, the madness of the Dean,
The bright, coughing blood Keats wrote in to the girl,
The terrible corpse of France, shrunk, naked and
    solitary—
Oh, yes, you were spared some things.
Though why did Mrs. Davis sue the estate
And what did you mean when you said——
                                    And who cares?
You're still the giant lode we quarry
For gold, fools' gold and all the earthy metals,
The matchless mine.
Still the trail-breaker, still the rolling river.

You and your land, your turbulent, seeking land
Where anything can grow.

And they have wasted the pasture and the fresh valley,
Stunk the river, shot the ten thousand sky-darkening
    pigeons
To build sham castles for imitation Medici
And the rugged sons of the rugged sons of death.
The slum, the sharecropper's cabin, the senseless tower,
The factory town with the dirty stoops of twilight,
The yelling cheapness, the bitter want among plenty,
But never Monticello, never again.
And there are many years in the dust of America
And they are not ended yet.

Far north, far north are the sources of the great river,
The headwaters, the cold lakes,
By the little sweet-tasting brooks of the blond country,
The country of snow and wheat,
Or west among the black mountains, the glacial springs.
Far north and west they lie and few come to them, few
    taste them,
But, day and night, they flow south,

By the French grave and the Indian, steadily flowing,
By the forgotten camps of the broken heart,
By the countries of black earth, fertile, and yellow earth
    and red earth,
A growing, a swelling torrent:
Rivers meet it, and tiny rivulets,
Meet it, stain it,
Great rivers, rivers of pride, come bowing their watery
    heads
Like muddy gift-bearers, bringing their secret burdens,
Rivers from the high horse-plains and the deep, green
    Eastern pastures
Sink into it and are lost and rejoice and shout with it,
    shout within it,
They and their secret gifts,
A fleck of gold from Montana, a sliver of steel from
    Pittsburgh,
A wheat-grain from Minnesota, an apple-blossom from
    Tennessee,
Roiled, mixed with the mud and earth of the changing
    bottoms
In the vast, rending floods,
But rolling, rolling from Arkansas, Kansas, Iowa,
Rolling from Ohio, Wisconsin, Illinois,
Rolling and shouting:
Till, at last, it is Mississippi,
The Father of Waters; the matchless; the great flood
Dyed with the earth of States; with the dust and the sun
    and the seed of half the States;
The huge heart-vein, pulsing and pulsing; gigantic; ever
    broader, ever mightier;
It rolls past broken landings and camellia-smelling
    woods; strange birds fly over it;
It rolls through the tropic magic, the almost-jungle, the
    warm darkness breeding the warm, enormous stars;
It rolls to the blue Gulf; ocean; and the painted birds fly.
The grey moss mixes with it, the hawk's feather has
    fallen in it,
The cardinal feather, the feather of the small thrush
Singing spring to New England,
The apple-pip and the pepper-seed and the checkerberry,
And always the water flowing, earthy, majestic,

Fed with snow and heat, dew and moonlight.
Always the wide, sure water,
Over the rotted deer-horn
The gold, Spanish money,
The long-rusted iron of many undertakings,
Over De Soto's bones and Joliet's wonder,
And the long forest-years before them, the brief years
    after,
The broad flood, the eternal motion, the restless-hearted
Always, forever, Mississippi, the god.

                                    April, 1935.

YOUTH AND LOVE

PORTRAIT OF YOUNG LOVE

If you were with me—as you're not, of course,
I'd taste the elegant tortures of Despair
With a slow, languid, long-refining tongue;
Puzzle for days on one particular stare,
Or if you knew a word's peculiar force,
Or what you looked like when you were quite young.

You'd lift me heaven-high—till a word grated.
Dash me hell-deep—oh that luxurious Pit,
Fatly and well encushioned with self-pity,
Where Love's an epicure not quickly sated!
What mournful musics wander over it,
Faint-blown from some long-lost celestial city!

Such bitter joyousness I'd have, and action,
Were you here—be no more the fool who broods
On true Adventure till he wakes her scorning—
But we're too petty for such noble warning.
And I find just as perfect satisfaction
In analyzing these, and other moods!

THE GENERAL PUBLIC

"Ah, did you once see Shelley plain?"

—BROWNING

"Shelley? Oh, yes, I saw him often then,"
The old man said. A dry smile creased his face
With many wrinkles. "That's a great poem, now!
That one of Browning's! Shelley? Shelley plain?
The time that I remember best is this—

"A thin mire crept along the rutted ways,
And all the trees were harried by cold rain

That drove a moment fiercely and then ceased,
Falling so slow it hung like a grey mist
Over the school. The walks were like blurred glass.
The buildings reeked with vapor, black and harsh
Against the deepening darkness of the sky;
And each lamp was a hazy yellow moon,
Filling the space about with golden motes,
And making all things larger than they were.
One yellow halo hung above a door,
That gave on a black passage. Round about
Struggled a howling crowd of boys, pell-mell,
Pushing and jostling like a stormy sea,
With shouting faces, turned a pasty white
By the strange light, for foam. They all had clods,
Or slimy balls of mud. A few gripped stones.
And there, his back against the battered door,
His pile of books scattered about his feet,
Stood Shelley while two others held him fast,
And the clods beat upon him. 'Shelley! Shelley!'
The high shouts rang through all the corridors,
'Shelley! Mad Shelley! Come along and help!'
And all the crowd dug madly at the earth,
Scratching and clawing at the streaming mud,
And fouled each other and themselves. And still
Shelley stood up. His eyes were like a flame
Set in some white, still room; for all his face
Was white, a whiteness like no human color,
But white and dreadful as consuming fire.
His hands shook now and then, like slender cords
Which bear too heavy weights. He did not speak.
So I saw Shelley plain."
　　　　　　　　　"And you?" I said.

"I? I threw straighter than the most of them,
And had firm clods. I hit him—well, at least
Thrice in the face. He made good sport that night."

TO ROSEMARY

If you were gone afar,
And lost the pattern
Of all your delightful ways,

And the web undone,
How would one make you anew,
From what dew and flowers,
What burning and mingled atoms,
Under the sun?

Not from too-satin roses,
Or those rare blossoms,
Orchids, scentless and precious
As precious stone.
But out of lemon-verbena,
Rose-geranium,
These alone.

Not with running horses,
Or Spanish cannon,
Organs, voiced like a lion,
Clamor and speed.
But perhaps with old music-boxes,
Young, tawny kittens,
Wild-strawberry-seed.

Even so, it were more
Than a god could compass
To fashion the body merely,
The lovely shroud.
But then—ah, how to recapture
That evanescence,
The fire that cried in pure crystal
Out of its cloud!

DIFFERENCE

My mind's a map. A mad sea-captain drew it
Under a flowing moon until he knew it;
Winds with brass trumpets, puffy-cheeked as jugs,
And states bright-patterned like Arabian rugs.
"Here there be tygers." "Here we buried Jim."
Here is the strait where eyeless fishes swim
About their buried idol, drowned so cold
He weeps away his eyes in salt and gold.
A country like the dark side of the moon,

A cider-apple country, harsh and boon,
A country savage as a chestnut-rind,
A land of hungry sorcerers.
                              Your mind?

—Your mind is water through an April night,
A cherry-branch, plume-feathery with its white,
A lavender as fragrant as your words,
A room where Peace and Honor talk like birds,
Sewing bright coins upon the tragic cloth
Of heavy Fate, and Mockery, like a moth,
Flutters and beats about those lovely things.
You are the soul, enchanted with its wings,
The single voice that raises up the dead
To shake the pride of angels.
                              I have said.

A NONSENSE SONG

Rosemary, Rosemary, let down your hair!
The cow's in the hammock, the crow's in the chair!
I was making you songs out of sawdust and silk,
But they came in to call and they spilt them like milk.

The cat's in the coffee, the wind's in the east,
He screams like a peacock and whines like a priest
And the saw of his voice makes my blood turn to mice—
So let down your long hair and shut off his advice!

Pluck out the thin hairpins and let the waves stream,
Brown-gold as brook-waters that dance through a
    dream,
Gentle-curled as young cloudlings, sweet-fragrant as bay,
Till it takes all the fierceness of living away.

Oh, when you are with me, my heart is white steel.
But the bat's in the belfry, the mold's in the meal,
And I think I hear skeletons climbing the stair!
—Rosemary, Rosemary, let down your bright hair!

TO ROSEMARY, ON THE METHODS BY WHICH SHE MIGHT BECOME AN ANGEL

Nor where the sober sisters, grave as willows,
Walk like old twilights by the jasper sea,
Nor where the plump hunt of cherubs holly-hilloes
Chasing their ruddy fox, the sun, you'll be!

Not with the stained-glass prophets, bearded grimly,
Not with the fledgling saved, meek Wisdom's lot,
Kissing a silver book that glimmers dimly,
For acolytes are mild and you are not.

They'll give you a curled tuba, tall as Rumor,
They'll sit you on a puff of Autumn cloud,
Gilded-fantastic as your scorn and humor
And let you blow that tuba much too loud.

Against the unceasing chant to sinless Zion,
Three impudent seraph notes, three starry coals,
Sweet as wild grass and happy as a lion
—And all the saints will throw you aureoles.

ALL NIGHT LONG

WE WERE in bed by nine, but she did not hear the clock,
She lay in her quiet first sleep, soft-breathing, head by
  her arm,
And the rising, radiant moon spilled silver out of its
  crock
On her hair and forehead and eyes as we rested, gentle
  and warm.

All night long it remained, that calm, compassionate
  sheet,
All the long night it wrapped us in whiteness like
  ermine-fur,
I did not sleep all the night, but lay, with wings on my
  feet,
Still, the cool at my lips, seeing her, worshipping her.

Oh, the bright sparks of dawn when day broke, burning
  and wild!

Oh, the first waking glance from her sleepy, beautiful
  eyes!
With a heart and a mind newborn as a naked, young,
  golden child,
I took her into my arms. We saw the morning arise!

MEDITATIONS AND COMPLAINTS

JUDGMENT

"He'll let us off with fifty years!" one said.
And one, "I always knew that Bible lied!"
One who was philanthropic stood aside,
Patting his sniveling virtues on the head.
"Yes, there may be some—pain," another wheezed.
"One rending touch to fit the soul for bliss."
"A bare formality!" one seemed to hiss.
And everyone was pink and fed and pleased.

Then thunder came, and with an earthquake sound
Shook those fat corpses from their flabby languor.
The sky was furious with immortal anger,
We miserable sinners hugged the ground:
Seeing through all the torment, saying, "Yes,"
God's quiet face, serenely merciless.

THE LOST WIFE

In the daytime, maybe, your heart's not breaking,
For there's the sun and the sky and working
And the neighbors to give you a word or hear you,
But, ah, the long nights when the wind comes shaking
The cold, black curtain, pulling and jerking,
And no one there in the bed to be near you.

And worse than the clods on the coffin falling
Are the clothes in the closet that no one wears now
And the things like hairpins you're always finding.
And you wouldn't mind the ghost of her calling
As much as knowing that no one cares now
If the carpet fades when the sun gets blinding.

I look in the houses, when twilight narrows,
And in each a man comes back to a woman.
The thought of that coming has spurs to ride me.
—Death, you have taken the great like sparrows,

But she was so slight, so small, so human.
You might have left her to lie beside me.

SPARROW

Lord, may I be
A sparrow in a tree.

No ominous and splendid bird of prey
But something that is fearful every day
Yet keeps its small fresh flesh full of heat and lightness.
Pigeons are better dressed and robins stouter,
The white owl has all winter in his whiteness
And the blue heron is a kingly dream
At evening, by the pale stream,
But, even in the lion's cage, in Zoos,
You'll find a sparrow, picking up the crumbs
And taking life precisely as it comes
With the black, wary eye that marks the doubter;
Squabbling in crowds, dust-bathing in the sun,
Small, joyous, impudent, a gutter-child
In Lesbia's bosom or December's chill,
Full of impertinence and hard to kill
As Queen Anne's lace and poppies in the wheat—
I won't pretend the fellow has a Muse
But that he has advice, and good advice,
All lovers know who've walked the city's street
And wished the stones were bread.
Peacocks are handsomer and owls more wise.
(At least, by all repute.)
And parrots live on flattery and fruit,
Live to great age. The sparrow's none of these,
The sparrow is a humorist, and dies.
There are so many things that he is not.
He will not tear the stag nor sweep the seas
Nor fall, majestical, to a king's arrow.
Yet how he lives, and how he loves in living
Up to the dusty tip of every feather!
How he endures oppression and the weather
And asks for neither justice nor forgiving!
Lord, in your mercy, let me be a sparrow!

His rapid heart's so hot.
And some can sing—song-sparrows, so they say—
And, one thing, Lord—the times are iron, now.
Perhaps you have forgot.
They shoot the wise and brave on every bough,
But sparrows are the last things that get shot.

COMPLAINT OF BODY, THE ASS, AGAINST HIS RIDER, THE SOUL

BODY

Well, here we go!
I told you that the weather looked like snow.
Why couldn't we have stayed there at the inn?
There was good straw and barley in the bin
And a grey jenny with a melting eye,
Neat-hoofed and sly—I rather like them sly—
Master a trader and a man of sense.
He likes his life and dinner. So do I.
Sleeps warm and doesn't try to cross a pass
A mountain-goat would balk at in his prime,
Where the hail falls as big as Peter's Pence
And every stone you slip on rolls a mile!
But that's not you, of course—that's not our style—
We're far too dandipratted and sublime!
Which of us is the ass?

Good ground, beyond the snow?
I've heard that little song before, you know.
Past cliff and ragged mount
And the wind's skinning-knife,
Far and forever far,
The water of the fount,
The water that is life
And the bright star?
Give me my water from a decent trough,
Not dabs of ice licked out of freezing stone
And, as for stars, why, let the stars alone,
You'll have us both in glory soon enough!

Alas, alack!
I'm carrying an idiot on my back.
I'm carrying Mr. Who to God Knows Where.
Oh, do not fix me with that burning stare
Of beauteous disdain!
I'm not a colt. I know my ass's rights.
A stall and fodder and sound sleep of nights.
One can't expect to live on sugarcane
But what's the sense, when one grows old and stiff,
Of scrambling up this devil-haunted cliff
To play hot cockles with the Northern Lights?
I'll balk, that's what I'll do!
And all the worse for you!
Oh, lash me if you like—I know your way—
Rake my poor sides and leave the bloody weal
Beneath your spurring steel.
My lungs are fire and my limbs are lead.

Go on ahead? I can't go on ahead.
Desert you in your need? Nay, master, nay.

Nay, master, nay; I grumble as I must
And yet, as you perceive, I do go on,
Grudging, impenitent and full of fear
And knowing my own death.
You have no fear because you have no breath.
Your silver essence knows nor cold nor heat.
Your world's beyond. My only world is here.
(Oh, the sweet rollings in the summer dust,
The smell of hay and thistles and the street,
The quick life, done so soon!)
You'll have your guerdon when the journey's done.
You'll play the hero where the wine is poured,
You and the moon—but I
Who served you well and shall become a bone,
Why do I live when it must be to die?
Why should I serve—and still have no reward?

SOUL

Your plaint is sound, yet I must rule you still
With bridle, bit and will.

For, without me, you are the child unborn
And the infertile corn.
I am not cruelty but I am he,
Drowning in sea, who yet disdains the sea,
And you that sea, that shore
And the brave, laboring oar,
Little upon the main,
That drives on reefs I know not of but does not drive in
   vain.
For I'm your master but your scholar, too,
And learn great things of you.
And, though I shall forsake you, nothing loth,
To gumble with the clods,
To sleep into the stone,
I'll answer for us both
When I stand up alone.
For it is part as your ambassador
I go before
To tell the gods who sit above the show,
How, in this world they never stoop to know,
Under what skies, against what mortal odds,
The dust grows noble with desire and pain,
And that not once but every day anew.

[CRITICS]

From SVB to Philip Barry

When *Homo sapiens* raised his head
And walked erect in Eden's vale,
There was a critic there, who said
"I liked him better with a tail."

When people first began to hark
To stories of the fall of Troy,
There was a critic to remark
"Is this obscure? Oh boy, oh boy!"

When Hamlet shook his trammels off
And darkness fell upon the slain,
There was a critic there, to cough
"Why must he write about a Dane?"

"The tale's too old, the tale's too new,
The tale is one my uncle tells.
This, Mr. Keats, will never do.
He should have written something else."

Beauty and workmanship and fire,
All things that lift above the sod,
One works to make these things entire—
And then come critics.
                    O my God!

                    Respectfully submitted
                    [Signed] SVB

"FOR YOU WHO ARE TO COME . . ."

FOR CITY LOVERS

Do not desire to seek who once we were,
Or where we did, or what, or in whose name.
Those buildings have been torn down. When the first
   wreckers
Tore the house open like a pack of cards
And the sun came in all over, everywhere,
They found some old newspapers and a cork
And footprints on the very dusty floor
But neither mouse nor angel.
                       Then even these
Went, even the little marks of shabby shoes,
The one sharp impress of the naked heel.

You cannot call us up there any more.
The number has been changed. There was a card
Downstairs, with names and such, under the bell.
But that's long gone. Yes, and we, they and you
And telegrams and flowers and the years
Went up and down these stairs, day after day,
And kept the stair-rail polished with our hands.
But we have moved to other neighborhoods.

Do not arraign that doorsill with your eyes
Nor try to make your hardened mind recall
How the old windows looked when they were lit
Or who the woman was on the third floor.
There are no ghosts to raise. There is the blank
Face of the stone, the hard line of the street,
The boys crying through twilight. That is all.

Go buy yourself a drink and talk about it.
Carry a humming head home through the rain.
But do not wear rosemary, touch cold iron,
Or leave out food before you go to bed.
For there's no fear of ghosts. That boy and girl
Are dust the sparrows bathe in, under the sun:
Under the virgin rock their bones lie sunken

Past pave and conduit and hidden waters
Stifled like unborn children in the darkness,
Past light and speech, cable and rooted steel,
Under the caissons, under the foundation.

Peace, peace, for there are people with those names
Somewhere or elsewhere, and you must not vex
Strangers with words about an old address.
But, for those others, do not be afraid.
They are beyond you. They are too deep down
For steel to pierce, for engines to uncover.
Not all the desperate splitters of the earth,
Nitro or air-drill or the chewing shovel
Shall ever mouth them up from where they lie.

LITANY FOR DICTATORSHIPS

For all those beaten, for the broken heads,
The fosterless, the simple, the oppressed,
The ghosts in the burning city of our time . . .

For those taken in rapid cars to the house and beaten
By the skilful boys, the boys with the rubber fists,
—Held down and beaten, the table cutting their loins,
Or kicked in the groin and left, with the muscles jerking
Like a headless hen's on the floor of the slaughter-house
While they brought the next man in with his white eyes
    staring.
For those who still said "Red Front!" or "God Save the
    Crown!"
And for those who were not courageous
But were beaten nevertheless.
For those who spit out the bloody stumps of their teeth
Quietly in the hall,
Sleep well on stone or iron, watch for the time
And kill the guard in the privy before they die,
Those with the deep-socketed eyes and the lamp burning.

For those who carry the scars, who walk lame—for those
Whose nameless graves are made in the prison-yard
And the earth smoothed back before morning and the
    lime scattered.

For those slain at once. For those living through months
    and years
Enduring, watching, hoping, going each day
To the work or the queue for meat or the secret club,
Living meanwhile, begetting children, smuggling guns,
And found and killed at the end like rats in a drain.

For those escaping
Incredibly into exile and wandering there.
For those who live in the small rooms of foreign cities
And who yet think of the country, the long green grass,
The childhood voices, the language, the way wind smelt
    then,
The shape of rooms, the coffee drunk at the table,
The talk with friends, the loved city, the waiter's face,
The gravestones, with the name, where they will not lie
Nor in any of that earth. Their children are strangers.

For those who planned and were leaders and were beaten
And for those, humble and stupid, who had no plan
But were denounced, but grew angry, but told a joke,
But could not explain, but were sent away to the camp,
But had their bodies shipped back in the sealed coffins,
"Died of pneumonia." "Died trying to escape."

For those growers of wheat who were shot by their own
    wheat-stacks,
For those growers of bread who were sent to the ice-
    locked wastes,
And their flesh remembers their fields.

For those denounced by their song, horrible children
For a peppermint-star and the praise of the Perfect State,
For all those strangled or gelded or merely starved
To make perfect states; for the priest hanged in his cassock,
The Jew with his chest crushed in and his eyes dying,
The revolutionist lynched by the private guards
To make perfect states, in the names of the perfect states.

For those betrayed by the neighbors they shook hands
    with
And for the traitors, sitting in the hard chair

With the loose sweat crawling their hair and their fingers
    restless
As they tell the street and the house and the man's name.

And for those sitting at table in the house
With the lamp lit and the plates and the smell of food,
Talking so quietly; when they hear the cars
And the knock at the door, and they look at each other
    quickly
And the woman goes to the door with a stiff face,
Smoothing her dress.
                         "We are all good citizens here.
We believe in the Perfect State."
                                        And that was the last
Time Tony or Karl or Shorty came to the house
And the family was liquidated later.
It was the last time.
                        We heard the shots in the night
But nobody knew next day what the trouble was
And a man must go to his work. So I didn't see him
For three days, then, and me near out of my mind
And all the patrols on the streets with their dirty guns
And when he came back, he looked drunk, and the blood
    was on him.

For the women who mourn their dead in the secret night,
For the children taught to keep quiet, the old children,
The children spat-on at school.
                               For the wrecked laboratory,
The gutted house, the dunged picture, the pissed-in well,
The naked corpse of Knowledge flung in the square
And no man lifting a hand and no man speaking.

For the cold of the pistol-butt and the bullet's heat,
For the rope that chokes, the manacles that bind,
The huge voice, metal, that lies from a thousand tubes
And the stuttering machine-gun that answers all.

For the man crucified on the crossed machine-guns
Without name, without resurrection, without stars,
His dark head heavy with death and his flesh long sour

With the smell of his many prisons—John Smith, John Doe,
John Nobody—oh, crack your mind for his name!
Faceless as water, naked as the dust,
Dishonored as the earth the gas-shells poison
And barbarous with portent.
                              This is he.
This is the man they ate at the green table
Putting their gloves on ere they touched the meat.
This is the fruit of war, the fruit of peace,
The ripeness of invention, the new lamb,
The answer to the wisdom of the wise.
And still he hangs, and still he will not die,
And still, on the steel city of our years
The light fails and the terrible blood streams down.
We thought we were done with these things but we were
    wrong.
We thought, because we had power, we had wisdom.
We thought the long train would run to the end of Time.
We thought the light would increase.
Now the long train stands derailed and the bandits
    loot it.
Now the boar and the asp have power in our time.
Now the night rolls back on the West and the night is
    solid.
Our fathers and ourselves sowed dragon's teeth.
Our children know and suffer the armed men.

MINOR LITANY

This being a time confused and with few clear stars,
Either private ones or public,
Out of its darkness I make a litany
For the lost, for the half-lost, for the desperate,
For all of those who suffer, not in the flesh.
I will say their name, but not yet.
                              This is for those
Who talk to the bearded man in the quiet office,
Sensibly, calmly, explaining just how it was,
And suddenly burst into noisy, quacking tears;
For those who live through the party, wishing for death;
For those who take the sensible country walks,

Wondering if people stare;
For those who try to hook rugs in the big, bright room
And do it badly and are pleased with the praise;
For the night and the fear and the demons of the night;
For the lying back on the couch and the wincing talk.

This is for those who work and those who may not,
For those who suddenly come to a locked door,
And the work falls out of their hands;
For those who step off the pavement into hell,
Having not observed the red light and the warning
    signals
Because they were busy or ignorant or proud.

This is for those who are bound in the paper chains
That are stronger than links of iron; this is for those
Who each day heave the papier-mache rock
Up the huge and burning hill,
And there is no rock and no hill, but they do not
    know it.

This is for those who wait till six for the drink,
Till eleven for the tablet;
And for those who cannot wait but go to the darkness;
And for those who long for the darkness but do not go,
Who walk to the window and see the body falling,
Hear the thud of air in the ears,
And then turn back to the room and sit down again,
None having observed the occurrence but themselves.

Christ, have mercy upon us.
Freud, have mercy upon us.
Life, have mercy upon us.

This is for those
Who painfully haul the dark fish out of the dark,
The child's old nightmare, embalmed in its own pain,
And, after that, get well or do not get well,
But do not forget the sulphur in the mouth

Or the time when the world was different, not for a while.
And for those also, the veterans

Of another kind of war,
Who say "No thanks" to the cocktails, who say "No
    thanks.
Well, yes, give me Coca-Cola" with the trained smile,
Those who hid the bottles so cleverly in the trunk,
Who bribed the attendant, who promised to be good,
Who woke in the dirty bed in the unknown town.
They are cured, now, very much cured.
They are tanned and fine. Their eyes are their only scars.

This is for those with the light white scars on the wrists,
Who remember the smell of gas and the vomiting,
And it meant little and it is a well-known symptom
And they were always careful to phone, before.
Nevertheless, they remember.
                                    This is for those
Who heard the music suddenly get too loud,
Who could not alter the fancy when it came.

Chloral, have mercy upon us.
Amytal, have mercy upon us.
Nembutal, have mercy upon us.

This occurs more or less than it did in the past times.
There are statistics. There are no real statistics.
There is also no heroism. There is merely
Fatigue, pain, great confusion, sometimes recovery.

The name, as you know, is Legion.
What's your name, friend? Where are you from and how
    did you get here?
The name is Legion. It's Legion in the case history.
Friends, Romans, countrymen,
Mr. and Mrs. Legion is the name.

NIGHTMARE NUMBER THREE

We had expected everything but revolt
And I kind of wonder myself when they started
    thinking—
But there's no dice in that now.
                                    I've heard fellows say

They must have planned it for years and maybe they did.
Looking back, you can find little incidents here and there,
Like the concrete-mixer in Jersey eating the wop
Or the roto press that printed "Fiddle-dee-dee!"
In a three-color process all over Senator Sloop,
Just as he was making a speech. The thing about that
Was, how could it walk upstairs? But it was upstairs,
Clicking and mumbling in the Senate Chamber.
They had to knock out the wall to take it away
And the wrecking-crew said it grinned.

         It was only the best
Machines, of course, the superhuman machines,
The ones we'd built to be better than flesh and bone,
But the cars were in it, of course . . .

        and they hunted us
Like rabbits through the cramped streets on that Bloody
 Monday,
The Madison Avenue busses leading the charge.
The busses were pretty bad—but I'll not forget
The smash of glass when the Duesenberg left the show-
 room
And pinned three brokers to the Racquet Club steps
Or the long howl of the horns when they saw men run,
When they saw them looking for holes in the solid
 ground . . .

I guess they were tired of being ridden in
And stopped and started by pygmies for silly ends,
Of wrapping cheap cigarettes and bad chocolate bars
Collecting nickels and waving platinum hair
And letting six million people live in a town.
I guess it was that. I guess they got tired of us
And the whole smell of human hands.

         But it was a shock
To climb sixteen flights of stairs to Art Zuckow's office
(Nobody took the elevators twice)
And find him strangled to death in a nest of telephones,
The octopus-tendrils waving over his head,
And a sort of quiet humming filling the air. . . .
Do they eat? . . . There was red . . . But I did not stop to
 look.

I don't know yet how I got to the roof in time
And it's lonely, here on the roof.
                                        For a while, I thought
That window-cleaner would make it, and keep me
    company.
But they got him with his own hoist at the sixteenth floor
And dragged him in, with a squeal.
You see, they coöperate. Well, we taught them that
And it's fair enough, I suppose. You see, we built them.
We taught them to think for themselves.
It was bound to come. You can see it was bound to come.
And it won't be so bad, in the country. I hate to think
Of the reapers, running wild in the Kansas fields,
And the transport planes like hawks on a chickenyard,
But the horses might help. We might make a deal with
    the horses.
At least, you've more chance, out there.
                                        And they need us, too.
They're bound to realize that when they once calm down.
They'll need oil and spare parts and adjustments and
    tuning up.
Slaves? Well, in a way, you know, we were slaves before.
There won't be so much real difference—honest, there
    won't.
(I wish I hadn't looked into that beauty-parlor
And seen what was happening there.
But those are female machines and a bit high-strung.)
Oh, we'll settle down. We'll arrange it. We'll compromise.
It wouldn't make sense to wipe out the whole human
    race.
Why, I bet if I went to my old Plymouth now
(Of course you'd have to do it the tactful way)
And said, "Look here! Who got you the swell French
    horn?"
He wouldn't turn me over to those police cars;
At least I don't think he would.
                                        Oh, it's going to be jake.
There won't be so much real difference—honest, there
    won't—
And I'd go down in a minute and take my chance—
I'm a good American and I always liked them—

Except for one small detail that bothers me
And that's the food proposition. Because, you see,
The concrete-mixer may have made a mistake,
And it looks like just high spirits.
But, if it's got so they like the flavor . . . well . . .

1936

All night they marched, the infantrymen under pack,
But the hands gripping the rifles were naked bone
And the hollow pits of the eyes stared, vacant and black,
When the moonlight shone.

The gas mask lay like a blot on the empty chest,
The slanting helmets were spattered with rust and mold,
But they burrowed the hill for the machine-gun nest
As they had of old.

And the guns rolled, and the tanks, but there was no
    sound,
Never the gasp or rustle of living men
Where the skeletons strung their wire on disputed
    ground. . . .
I knew them, then.

"It is eighteen years," I cried. "You must come no more."
"We know your names. We know that you are the dead.
Must you march forever from France and the last, blind
    war?"
"Fool! From the next!" they said.

NIGHTMARE AT NOON

THERE are no trenches dug in the park, not yet.
There are no soldiers falling out of the sky.
It's a fine, clear day, in the park. It is bright and hot.
The trees are in full, green, summer-heavy leaf.
An airplane drones overhead but no one's afraid.
There's no reason to be afraid, in a fine, big city
That was not built for a war. There is time and time.

There was time in Norway and time, and the thing fell.
When they woke, they saw the planes with the black
   crosses.
When they woke, they heard the guns rolling in the
   street.
They could not believe, at first. It was hard to believe.
They had been friendly and thriving and inventive.
They had had good arts, decent living, peace for years.
Those were not enough, it seems.
There were people there who wrote books and painted
   pictures,
Worked, came home tired, liked to be let alone.
They made fun of the strut and the stamp and the
   strained salute,
They made fun of the would-be Caesars who howl and
   foam.
That was not enough, it seems. It was not enough.
When they woke, they saw the planes with the black
   crosses.

There is grass in the park. There are children on the long
   meadow
Watched by some hot, peaceful nuns. Where the ducks
   are fed
There are black children and white and the anxious
   teachers
Who keep counting them like chickens. It's quite a job
To take so many school-kids out to the park,
But when they've eaten their picnic, they'll go home.
(And they could have better homes, in a rich city.)
But they won't be sent to Kansas or Michigan
At twenty-four hours' notice,
Dazed, bewildered, clutching their broken toys,
Hundreds on hundreds filling the blacked-out trains.
Just to keep them safe, just so they may live not die.
Just so there's one chance that they may not die but live.
That does not enter our thoughts. There is plenty of time.

In Holland, one hears, some children were less lucky.
It was hard to send them anywhere in Holland.
It is a small country, you see. The thing happened quickly.

The bombs from the sky are quite indifferent to children.
The machine-gunners do not distinguish. In Rotterdam
One quarter of the city was blown to bits.
That included, naturally, ordinary buildings
With the usual furnishings, such as cats and children.
It was an old, peaceful city, Rotterdam,
Clean, tidy, full of flowers.
But that was not enough, it seems.
It was not enough to keep all the children safe.
It was ended in a week, and the freedom ended.

There is no air-raid siren yet, in the park.
All the glass still stands, in the windows around the park.
The man on the bench is reading a Yiddish paper.
He will not be shot because of that, oddly enough.
He will not even be beaten or imprisoned.
Not yet, not yet.
You can be a Finn or a Dane and an American.
You can be German or French and an American,
Jew, Bohunk, Nigger, Mick—all the dirty names
We call each other—and yet American.
We've stuck to that quite a while.
Go into Joe's Diner and try to tell the truckers
You belong to a Master Race and you'll get a laugh.
What's that, brother? Double-talk?
I'm a stranger here myself but it's a free country.
It's a free country . . .
Oh yes, I know the faults and the other side,
The lyncher's rope, the bought justice, the wasted land,
The scale on the leaf, the borers in the corn,
The finks with their clubs, the grey sky of relief,
All the long shame of our hearts and the long disunion.
I am merely remarking—as a country, we try.
As a country, I think we try.

They tried in Spain but the tanks and the planes won out.
They fought very well and long.
They fought to be free but it seems that was not enough.
They did not have the equipment. So they lost.
They tried in Finland. The resistance was shrewd,
Skilful, intelligent, waged by a free folk.

They tried in Greece, and they threw them back for a
  while
By the soul and spirit and passion of common men.
Call the roll of fourteen nations. Call the roll
Of the blacked-out lands, the lands that used to be free.

But do not call it loud. There is plenty of time.
There is plenty of time, while the bombs on London fall
And turn the world to wind and water and fire.
There is time to sleep while the fire-bombs fall on
  London.
They are stubborn people in London.

We are slow to wake, good-natured as a country.
(It is our fault and our virtue.) We like to raise
A man to the highest power and then throw bricks at him.
We don't like war and we like to speak our minds.
We're used to speaking our minds.
                                        There are certain words,
Our own and others', we're used to—words we've used,
Heard, had to recite, forgotten,
Rubbed shiny in the pocket, left home for keepsakes,
Inherited, stuck away in the back-drawer,
In the locked, trunk, at the back of the quiet mind.

Liberty, equality, fraternity.
To none will we sell, refuse or deny, right or justice.
We hold these truths to be self-evident.

I am merely saying—what if these words pass?
What if they pass and are gone and are no more,
Eviscerated, blotted out of the world?
We're used to them, so used that we half-forget,
The way you forget the looks of your own house
And yet you can walk around it, in the darkness.
You can't put a price on sunlight or the air,
You can't put a price on these, so they must be easy.
They were bought with belief and passion, at great cost.
They were bought with the bitter and anonymous blood
Of farmers, teachers, shoemakers and fools
Who broke the old rule and the pride of kings.

And some never saw the end and many were weary,
Some doubtful, many confused.
They were bought by the ragged boys at Valmy mill,
The yokels at Lexington with the long light guns
And the dry, New England faces,
The iron barons, writing a charter out
For their own iron advantage, not the people,
And yet the people got it into their hands
And marked it with their own sweat.
It took long to buy these words.
It took a long time to buy them and much pain.

Thenceforward and forever free.
Thenceforward and forever free.
No man may be bound or fined or slain till he has been
    judged by his peers.
To form a more perfect Union.

The others have their words too, and strong words,
Strong as the tanks, explosive as the bombs.

The State is all, worship the State!
The Leader is all, worship the Leader!
Strength is all, worship strength!
Worship, bow down or die!

I shall go back through the park to my safe house,
This is not London or Paris.
This is the high, bright city, the lucky place,
The place that always had time.
The boys in their shirtleeves here, the big, flowering
    girls,
The bicycle-riders, the kids with the model planes,
The lovers who lie on the grass, uncaring of eyes,
As if they lay on an island out of time,
The tough kids, squirting the water at the fountain,
Whistled at by the cop.
The dopes who write "Jimmy's a dope" on the tunnel
    walls.
These are all quite safe and nothing will happen to them.
Nothing will happen, of course.
Go tell Frank the Yanks aren't coming, in Union Square.

Go tell the new brokers' story about the President.
Whatever it is. That's going to help a lot.
There's time to drink your highball—plenty of time.
Go tell fire it only burns in another country,
Go tell the bombers this is the wrong address,
The hurricane to pass on the other side.
Go tell the earthquake it must not shake the ground.

The bell has rung in the night and the air quakes with it.

I shall not sleep tonight when I hear the plane.

                                                    1940.

TUESDAY, NOVEMBER 5th, 1940

We remember, F.D.R.
We remember the bitter faces of the apple-sellers
And their red cracked hands,
We remember the gray, cold wind of '32
When the job stopped, and the bank stopped,
And the merry-go-round broke down,
And, finally,
Everything seemed to stop.
The whole big works of America,
Bogged down with a creeping panic,
And nobody knew how to fix it, while the wise guys
    sold the country short,
Till one man said (and we listened)
"The one thing we have to fear is fear."
Well, it's quite a long while since then, and the wise guys
    may not remember.
But we do, F.D.R.

We remember some other things.
We remember the home saved and the crop saved and the
    courage put back in men's faces.
We remember you said from the start,
"I don't expect to make a hit every time I come to bat."
We remember that.
And sometimes you've struck out and we know it
But we know the batting average, too.

(Not we-the-Wall-Street-people but we the people.)
It's written in our lives, in our kids, growing up with a
    chance,
It's written in the faces of the old folks who don't have
    to go to the poorhouse
And the tanned faces of the boys from the CCC,
It's written in the water and earth of the Tennessee Valley
The contour-plowing that saves the dust-stricken land,
And the lights coming on for the first time, on lonely
    farms.

Now, there's another election.
And they say you went to Groton and Harvard.
And they say you don't know the people.
And they say you want to be a dictator
(The same bunch of dignified penguins who were yelling
    and howling for a dictator in '32,
And you gave them their self-respect back, instead, and
    they've never forgiven the gift)
The professional dispensers of snake-bite and poison ivy
In syndicated columns;
The air-conditioned boys from the big slicks, wrapped
    up in their latest serializations
(Yes, you can frequently tell them from the canned-soup
    advertisements.
They get illustrated differently)
These, and others, are Viewing with Alarm.
In fact, to tell you a secret, they say you're terrible.
And, if I may speak from the record, we know them,
    too.
And that's jake with us.

It's jake with us, because we know.
And we know you never were a Fuehrer and never will
    be,
Not a Fuehrer, just a guy in pitching for the bunch of us,
For all of us, the whole people.
A big guy pitching, with America in his heart.
A man who knows the tides and ways of the people
As Abe Lincoln knew the wind on the prairies,
And has never once stopped believing in them.
(The slow, tenacious memory of the people,

Somehow, holding on to the Lincolns, no matter who
   yelled against them . . .)

A country squire from Hyde Park with a Harvard
   accent,
Who never once failed the people
And whom the people won't fail.

SELECTIONS FROM *WESTERN STAR*

The selections included here are the "Invocation" and "Prelude" and the full text of what Benét originally intended to be Book One but withdrew before the poem was published. Two selections from the Book appeared in 1939: the section about Robert the Devil, published as "The Ballad of the Duke's Mercy," Atlantic, February 1939, pp. 169–174; and the section about Marco Polo, published as "The Ballad of Marco Polo," Atlantic, August 1939, pp. 191–193.

INVOCATION

Not for the great, not for the marvelous,
Not for the barren husbands of the gold;
Not for the arrowmakers of the soul,
Wasted with truth, the star-regarding wise;
Not even for the few
Who would not be the hunter nor the prey,
Who stood between the eater and the meat,
The wilderness saints, the guiltless, the absolved,
Born out of Time, the seekers of the balm
Where the green grass grows from the broken heart;
But for all these, the nameless, numberless
Seed of the field, the mortal wood and earth
Hewn for the clearing, trampled for the floor,
Uprooted and cast out upon the stone
From Jamestown to Benicia.
This is their song, this is their testament,
Carved to their likeness, speaking in their tongue
And branded with the iron of their star.
I say you shall remember them. I say
When night has fallen on your loneliness
And the deep wood beyond the ruined wall
Seems to step forward swiftly with the dusk,
You shall remember them. You shall not see
Water or wheat or axe-mark on the tree

And not remember them.
You shall not win without remembering them,
For they won every shadow of the moon,
All the vast shadows, and you shall not lose
Without a dark remembrance of their loss
For they lost all and none remembered them.

Hear the wind
Blow through the buffalo-grass,
Blow over wild-grape and brier.
This was frontier, and this,
And this, your house, was frontier.
There were footprints upon the hill
And men lie burned under,
Tamers of earth and rivers.
They died at the end of labor,
Forgotten is the name.

Now, in full summer, by the Eastern shore,
Between the seamark and the roads going West,
I call two oceans to remember them.
I fill the hollow darkness with their names.

PRELUDE

Americans are always moving on.
It's an old Spanish custom gone astray,
A sort of English fever, I believe,
Or just a mere desire to take French leave,
I couldn't say. I couldn't really say.
But, when the whistle blows, they go away.
Sometimes there never was a whistle blown,
But they don't care, for they can blow their own
Whistles of willow-stick and rabbit-bone,
Quail-calling through the rain
A dozen tunes but only one refrain,
"We don't know where we're going, but we're on
    our way!"
—Bird-whistles, sleepy with Virginia night,
Veery and oriole,
Calling the morning from the Chesapeake
To rise, in pomp, with redbud at her breast,

The whistles of the great trains going west,
Lonely, at night, through cold Nebraska towns,
The chunking of the bullfrogs in the creek
Where the forgotten wampum slowly drowns,
Cow-horn and turkey-call,
And last, purest of all,
The spell of peace, the rapture of the ear,
The water-music mounting into light,
The hermit thrush that is New England's soul—
These are the notes they hear.

Americans, what are Americans?
I went downtown as I had done before.
I took my girl to town
To buy a calico gown,
I traded in my pelts at Offut's store.
And then, when I came back, the folks were gone,
Warm ashes on the hearth, but nothing more.
And, if you ask me just what made them go,
And what they thought they'd find by going there,
Why, you can ask the horses, or the Ford,
Hauling its gipsy children through the mud,
With the wry klaxon croaking "Going on!"
And the tame rooster on the running-board.
But I don't know—I do not really know.
I think it must be something in the blood.
Perhaps it's only something in the air.

Oh, paint your wagons with "Pike's Peak or Bust!"
Pack up the fiddle, rosin up the bow,
Vamoose, skedaddle, mosey, hit the grit!
(We pick our words, like nuggets, for the shine,
And, where they didn't fit, we make them fit,
Whittling a language out of birch and pine.)
We're off for Californ-iay,
We're off down the wild O-hi-o!
And every girl on Natchez bluff
Will cry as we go by-o!
So, when the gospel train pulls out
And God calls "All aboard!"
Will you be there with the Lord, brother,

Will you be there with the Lord?
Yes, I'll be there,
Oh, I'll be there,
I'll have crossed that rolling river in the morning!

2

The stranger finds them easy to explain
(Americans, I said Americans,)
And tells them so in public and at length.
(It's an old Roman virtue to be frank,
A tattered Grecian parchment on the shelves,
Explaining the barbarians to themselves,
A lost, Egyptian prank.)
Here is the weakness. On the other hand,
Here is what really might be called the strength.
And then he makes a list.
Sometimes he thumps the table with his fist.
Sometimes, he's very bland.
O few, stiff-collared and unhappy men
Wilting in silence, to the cultured boom
Of the trained voice in the perspiring room!
O books, O endless, minatory books!
(Explaining the barbarians to themselves)
He came and went. He liked our women's looks.
Ate lunch and said the skyscrapers were high,
And then, in state, passed by,
To the next lecture, to the desolate tryst.
Sometimes to waken, in the narrow berth
When the green curtains swayed like giant leaves
In the dry, prairie-gust,
Wake, with an aching head, and taste the dust,
The floury wheat-dust, smelling of the sheaves,
And wonder, for a second of dismay,
If there was something that one might have missed,
Between the chicken salad and the train,
Between the ladies' luncheon and the station,
Something that might explain one's explanation
—But not for long—for nothing could be missed.
(We paid him well, so nothing could be missed.
We showed him all the sewers and the cars,

We gave him a degree at Convocation.)
He talked—and all outside, the prairie-day
Drowned into evening, and the shadows spread,
And, by the muddy river, miles away,
The outcast found the Indian arrowhead.

3

And I have listened also, in my youth,
And more than once or twice,
To the trained speech, the excellent advice,
The clear, dramatic statement of the sum,
And, after it was dumb,
Heard, like a spook, the curious echo come,
The echo of unkempt and drawling mirth
—The lounging mirth of cracker-barrel men,
Snowed in by winter, spitting at the fire,
And telling the disreputable truth
With the sad eye that marks the perfect liar—
And, by that laughter, was set free again.

So, when you ask about Americans,
I cannot tell their motives or their plans
Or make a neat design of what they are.
I only see the fortune and the bane,
The fortune of the breakers of the earth,
The doom arisen with the western star.

Oh yes, I know, the double trails have met,
The long traverse is done, the scent is cold,
The blaze dies out upon the fallen tree.
We have another hope to make us old,
Another, and a truceless enemy,
And, of the anguish and the bitter sweat,
Nothing remains but little words. And yet—

Star in the West, fool's silver of the sky,
Desolate lamp above the mountain-pass
Where the trail falters and the oxen die,
Spiked planet on the prairie of wild grass,
Flower of frost, flower of rock and ice,
Red flower over the blood sacrifice.

There is a wilderness we walk alone
However well-companioned, and a place
Where the dry wind blows over the dry bone
And sunlight is a devil in the face,
The sandstorm and the empty water-hole
And the dead body, driven by its soul.

But not the first illusion, the new earth,
The march upon the solitary fire,
The casting of the dice of death and birth
Against a giant, for a blind desire,
The stream uncrossed, the promise still untried,
The metal sleeping in the mountainside.

That sun-dance has been blotted from the map,
Call as you will, those dancers will not come
To tear their breasts upon the bloody strap,
Mute-visaged, to the passion of a drum,
For some strange empire, nor the painted ghosts
Speak from the smoke and summon up the hosts.

And, for the star that made the torment brave,
It should exist, if it exist at all,
But as the gleam of mica in the cave
Where the long train roars like a waterfall
And the steel shoes bite down upon the steel,
A spark ground out and dying on the wheel.

Star-rocket, bursting when the dawn was grey,
Will-o'-the-wisp that led the riflemen
Westward and westward, killing down the day,
Until, at last, they had to turn again,
Burnt out like their own powder in the quest
Because there was no longer any West.

Only the treeless ocean, and the shock
Of the long roller, breaking from Japan,
The black sea-lion, roaring on his rock,
But never a quarry for a rifleman
Until the windy night came down once more
And the sea rustled like a forest-floor.

Then it arose, beyond the last dark wave,
Mockingly near, unmercifully far,
Cold with enchantment, naked from the grave,
The free-born image, the outlier's star,
The loadstone of the iron in the breast,
Never to be forgotten or possessed.

Rose, glittered like an idol, and was gone,
Leaving its battered servants to their fate,
The land fenced in, the golden apple won,
Plow, saw and engine building up a State,
And certain men, discarded from their wars,
Too long deceived to follow other stars.

Old riders in the saddle of the past,
Old sergeants, carrying Apache lead,
Old signal-smokes, grown meaningless at last,
—Why should one voice play bondsman to the dead,
Or rake the ashes of the desert fire
For any token of that lost desire?

Why should one song go nosing like a hound
After a phantom in a hunting shirt,
Or mark again the dark and bloody ground
Where the enduring got their mortal hurt,
Where the knife flickered and the arrow sung
And the Spring wind was bitter on the tongue?

If that were all, there might be little worth
In diligence or custom or the bare
Lust of the mind to plow rebellious earth
Because its metal found resistance there
And nothing but the granite could retain
The hard line, cut in the unwilling grain.

But, where the ragged acres still resist
And nothing but the stoneboat gets a crop,
Where the black butte stands up like a clenched fist
Against the evening, and the signboards stop,
Something remains, obscure to understand,
But living, and a genius of the land.

Something the ponies know,
The last, rough-coated ponies of the plains,
Scraping their little forefeet in the snow
All winter long to find the buried grass,
In the high uplands, out beyond Cheyenne,
Rumps turned against the blizzard, patiently
Enduring all the outrage of the sky,
Waiting like gods for Spring to come again,
While their wise eyes remember the Spring rains
And the whole mountain blossomed overnight
Into a world of green, and tiny flowers,
Something surpassing any song of ours,
Something as casual as air and light,
Something that passes—and that does not pass.
It always has been so.

4

Out of your fever and your moving on,
(Americans, Americans, Americans,)
Out of your unassuaged and restless hearts,
Out of your conquest, out of your despair,
I make my song. I call
Straitly upon the Four,
Earth, Water, Fire, and Air,
Dark earth of exile, Earth, the Indian-giver,
Sun of the desert, Water of the great river,
And Air, that blows the painted leaves of Fall.
I blow my smoke the ceremonial ways.
I say the ways are open for the ghosts,
Open for rolling wagons and strong teams,
For the slow wheels of Conestoga carts,
Creaking like fate across the prairie days,
For wolf and owl and bear
And the long hunter, secret as them all,
Fed at their tables, nourished with their meat,
And robbing each for scraps of forest-lore,
For all the moccasined feet
That whispered by the solitary streams,
Red bead and white, sachem and renegade
And the poor Jew who followed for the trade

And lost his pack of trinkets with his hair,
The bound who would be freed,
The sowers of wild seed,
The runners through the storm,
The women who gave birth
Stretched on the naked earth
With an old beaver-pelt to keep them warm,
The broken, who were broken for the tales,
The lost, the eaters of the locoweed.

I call upon the sorrow of the forest,
I name the places where the blood was shed,
And, for the hours when the need was sorest,
The brokenhearted camps of no return
Where the wood smoldered and the water stank
And the forgotten wounds began to burn
As the sick men divided the last bread,
I set the token by the riverbank,
I scatter the cornmeal for the great dead.

5

O whistlers who could carry that lost air,
Americans, who whistle as you go!
(And, where it is you do not really know,
You do not really care.)
Lend me your music for a little while,
The vagrant music of ten thousand marches,
Common as dust, the gay, forsaken lilt
Twanged on a banjo and a frying pan
That bore the footsore on for one more mile,
The song that built its own triumphal arches
Of lath and plaster on a floor of silt
And never looked behind to see them fall,
Till I can see the fate, and see it all,
With something of the wonder and the awe
Those mutinous sailors saw,
Dogs of the sea and sweepings of the dock,
When the Italian devil drove them on
Past' all known land, into the utter seas,
Into the whirlpool, into nothingness,

And, after all the travail and the stress,
The mortal struggle and the mortal fear,
They tumbled up at dawn,
Sleepy and cursing, damning drink and bread,
To see before them there,
Neither the kraken nor the loadstone rock,
But, thin with distance, thin but dead ahead,
The line of unimaginable coasts.

[ORIGINAL BOOK ONE OF *WESTERN STAR*]

In the North are the graves of France, by the cold harbors
Or scattered in the long forest like drops of wine,
The hunters, tireless as wolves, the black-haired runners,
The men of the clear, gay language, supple as willow,
Hard as the brass of trumpets, exact as light.
They liked good sauces and laughter, though some were
    surly.
They brought thrift and their women with them and a
    white flag
With a king's gold lilies upon it. They ventured far.
Their paddles knew many lakes and many rivers.
They died in torture, breathing the Huron fire.
They were small in the endless wood but their axes sang.
They built towns on the grey rock. They endured great
    snows.
Their footsteps rang on the savageness of winter.
They made good soup of strange flesh and remembered
    the vines of
                        Beaune and the light, warm earth.
Their seignories are still marked. They left trail and
    trace.
The Spring and Fall of the year were their homesick
    seasons
For then the ships came and went. It was many years.
But at last their lost France forsook them and it was
    ended,
Ended upon the Plains of Abraham.
It is not ended, ever,
While the three-days snowfall whispers, while the red
    leaf falls on grey stone.

In the South, where the huge, slow river pours to the gulf
Are the graves of France. They worked iron with a light
   hand.
They named the city after the older city.
They died of the fever quickly in the white mist
That rose from the marsh at evening. Nevertheless
The tea-rose-women flowered, the earth was kind,
The dandies carried their sword-canes through narrow
   streets,
The black, clear coffee smelt of the lotos-leaf.
They were little beside the great marsh and the rolling river
But they spent their grace and their music against the night,
Echoing and diminishing in the forest
Alien and wild and pathless, dimming all candles,
Heavy with odors, the spectre waiting beyond,
While the lustres gleamed and the laughter chimed like
   the lustres
And the fever-cart moved on to the sandy graves.
At the last, the Corsican sold them and it was ended,
Ended with pen and cannon and sunken flag.
It is not ended, ever,
While the black mud sucks in the marshes, while the
   gardens bloom yearlong.

In the South and the West and the South are the graves of
   Spain,
The proud fantastics, the horsemen of the great saddles,
The iron-plated seekers of gold and youth.
They fought men in feather-armor. They survived
The dolorous might and conquered, They tore each other
For gold or gloomy honor and yet survived.
They cast grave, beautiful bells. They loved sun and
   scarlets.
Their bits were well-chased and cruel in the soft mouth.
The dark-eyed women aged early in the cool chambers
Where they were guarded like seed-corn from the white
   noon.
They danced and their dancing glittered with a dark fire.
They were male, their bodies were fluent as stretching
   lions.
There were many children in the house of the sun.
Their passion and their arrogance were carved

In olivewood, smoked by the flame of many candles.
Tomorrow was as good as today to them.
Proverbs were good and love like a burning wound
And horses and the punctilio of death.
And, always, at the back of the mind, they heard,
In peace or anger, the beating of the slow drops
On the dark, stained wood of the Cross, the old, ghostly
    sorrow,
Forever restless, never quite staunched or stilled.
These people made slaves and ground the meal in the
    stones
For God or treasure. Nevertheless, they were lords.
These people had much fate and met it with passion.
They were little among the high plains and the tall mountains
But they spent their hunger and passed. It is many years
Since the long rifles broke them. It has gone by.
It is lost like the cracked bells of forgotten missions.
It is drowned in the green where the sunken plate-ships lie.
It is not ended, ever,
While the yucca grows in the waste, while the changed
    blood runs in the heart.

There is no ground from the East Sea to the West
Where the men called English lie not. There is no ground
From the cold sea to the hot where they have not left
    their graves
And the four winds blow on the graves of dark Gael and
    ruddy Gael.

The wide North wheatfields know who served the rich
    land
Like frost-giants plowing, homesick for the far *saaters*.
They know what the blond women brought in their
    painted chests.
The red barns of Pennsylvania knew men like oxen,
The tulips of Hudson's valley remember men,
The smokes of that calm, long Fall are their pipe-smoke,
    blowing.
The Jew has been spilt on the city-stones like water . . .

Everywhere lies the land.
Everywhere walk the red spirits of the land.

Everywhere the land is still vast. There are trees uncut
   and waste fields.

Everywhere they came, from the settled, known
Dust oversea where the one grave crowds the other.
The sun marched West and they came. The sea ran West
   and they came.

It was for gold and gods and broken love and the smell
   of the sea in the nostrils,
For the furs, the deep-swimming fish, the good timber,
   the bride-earth waiting, alone,
To worship in peace; to escape; because they were
   damned; for bread; what would you?; there were many.

There was a shape in the mind and a word spoken; there
   was gull-talk as the crammed ship made heavy
   weather, going.

The shape, like a dancer poised, like a wide sail shaken
   out; the unknown shape beyond oceans; terribly
   asking.

They were not born in the land. They found plenty here
   and hunger. They found death walking the forest.
                              Living or dead, they remained.

(The graves of the red men are strewn like fallen leaves.
   They were the possessors.

They fought but they were the weaker. The shame is old.)

These are our ancients, these of the restless graves; if they
   were content, they came not.

Lift up your eyes to the naked, Westing sun; it was so
   they looked from the ship rail, long years gone.

Coward or rogue or valiant; many peoples; it was so, it
   was so that in the beginnings they came.

The horse, the forest, the greybeard sea,
The brandy come from the apple-tree,
These are the treasure of Normandy.

It is so today. It was even so
Nine centuries and a half ago
When Robert the Devil, son of war,
With squire and huntsman and servitor,
Rode at eve on the hard, packed sand
That lay like a piece of Noman's land
Between the forest and the white foam,
Bringing the spoils of his hunting home.
Four great herons of silver plume
Slain by his falcon, My Joyous Doom,
Osprey and mallard and one wild swan
And a poacher with ears already gone.
The raw stumps dripped as he ran along
Bound to a horse with a leather thong,
Three parts naked and smelling foul
With the wild, dazed stare of a netted owl,
But he did not trip and he did not fall
Though the Duke had judged him, once for all,
His breath came easy as he ran
And he seemed more otter or stag than man,
As the sea-mist wrapped them closer round.

Yet he was the first to hear the sound
That was neither hoofs nor the grumbling sea
As they rounded a headland suddenly,
The jetting scream of woman or hare
That wailed from a clump of figures there,
Snarling and fighting and vague to mark
By the broken planks of a viking bark,
And now closed in, like wolves on a doe.

"By God!" said Robert, " 'twas over so,
The best sport comes at the end of the day!
Advance Our honor and clear Our way!
Ware steel, 'ware falcon, so-ho, so-ho!"

He had not stricken one merry blow
To mark his bounty from ear to lip

And his hand still played with his riding-whip,
When he heard from the twilight the ancient cry
That summons the justice of Normandy
By forest and meadow and sea and shore,
"Haro! Haro! On me fait tort!"
And a woman snatched at his bridle-rein.
The whip swung high, but it came again
Wailing and harsh at his saddlebow,
"On me fait tort! Haro! Haro!
Son of Rollo, by earth and sea,
I cry on the justice of Normandy,
Having no man to cry for me
Who lies man-slain in your lands tonight!"

"Speak." said Robert "We give you right."

He looked at her now. She was tall and bold
And her colors once had been rose and gold
But the eyes in her head were judgment old
As she told her tale with the hurried breath
Of one just come from the claws of death,
While the falcon screamed and the chase went by
And Robert the Devil, cold of eye,
Beheld the doing of his commands
And the poacher bit at his fettered hands.

"Asker for justice, your name and sire?"

"Ghislaine, sole daughter of Odo the Fire,
Good with the hammer, a cunning smith
And the surly temper that goes therewith.
The hunting-knife that your father had
Will show if his work was good or bad."

"Daughter of Odo, how know you me?"

"By the look of the Dukes of Normandy,
The black dog carried on every back
Since the bargain made by Rollo the Black,
The hard hand and the sea-cold eye
And the justice the coward cannot buy."

"Norman woman, how falls it now
You come to your land in a viking prow?"

"I walked one eve by the edge of the sand
And my heart was heavy in my white hand
For my father was grim and my mother dead
And I had small joy of my maidenhead,
Knowing it destined for Jean the Lame.
—It was that eve that the raiders came."

"Were you thieved in stealth, were you won by strife?"

"I fought as I might with tooth and knife,
Fought as the cornered vixen can,
But at last the strength went out of me,
For his arms were the arms of a goodly man
And his lips had the taste of the naked sea."

"Was he lord or churl that took you to bed?"

"Men called him the son of Svend the Red.
He gave me honor and the white bread.
He gave me mercy and the raw gold.
But we might not go to his father's hold
For he had been outlaw since his youth.
It is my sorrow, it is my ruth
That at last I sickened of ship and wave
And the sea that was our childrens' grave
And wept on his breast till he promised me
To kneel to the Duke of Normandy,
Suing to be his faithful man
While the winds blew and the waters ran.
But, as we came hither, the storm-wind blew
And the hungry coast ate ship and crew
And the few strong swimmers the fishers slew.
They would not have slain him, sword in hand,
Had they come against him with half the land!
But naked and swimming he fought with them
And his blood is stiff on my kirtle-hem.
And now it is time that I should be slain,
But they shall not lie where he has lain
If there is justice in Normandy!
Haro, my lord! I have cried my cry."

"Nay" said Duke Robert "One word more.
Are you wife or leman or outlawed whore?"

"I am woman, my lord, and I go with child."

Robert the Devil barely smiled
And the flame began to leap in his eye.
"Now here is a riddle for Normandy!
Stolen daughter of Odo the Smith,
You have broken the bonds of kin and kith.
It is not well that our cousin the Dane
Should thieve our women and not be slain
And worse that our women condone the theft
While they have honor or dagger left.
Therefore I give my fishers right
For this manslaying in your despite.
They shall not pay for the foeman dead.
They shall not lose either hand or head.
But, since they were fishers, and slew a knight
Who came to serve us in this our need,
They shall be whipped till their bodies bleed.
Is it just?"
                    "It is just." said tall Ghislaine.
"Show me the place where I may be slain."

"Now softly, softly," came Robert's word,
"You have cried Haro to your liege-lord,
But she who mates with the outlaw sea
Is neither Denmark nor Normandy,
And who shall pay the price of your head,
Now Odo the Smith is a long time dead?
Neither leman nor wife nor maid,
Naked of husband and law and lord,
Outcast trull, are you not afraid?"

"Nay," said the woman, "Show me the sword."

Robert slapped his hand on his thigh.
"By god, it is pity that you should die!
For I think you would bear no craven sons,
And the bold were ever the fruitful ones.
Now is there any of my meinie

Who will claim this woman for Normandy?
If there be such, let him stand forth!"

There was bitter silence, South and North.

"And yet" said Robert. "I deem you men.
And you have the name.
                              Now I say again
If any man here have soul and pith
To claim this daughter of Odo the Smith,
He shall have honor and she her life
For I deem she will make no common wife."

The poacher lifted his wounded head.
"I claim the woman, dread lord," he said
And his voice was the sea and the marsh at eve
And the track in the reeds that the herons leave
And the rustle of the fallen leaf.
"I claim this woman for joy or grief."

"So," quoth Robert, smiling awry,
"There is one man left in Normandy.
Woman, how like you this son of clay?"

They stared at each other like deer at bay,
Silent and breathing and watchful-eyed
Where the sunlight dapples the riverside
And the wild herb feeds the wilder heart.
They stared, and their glances did not part.

He snapped the leash of the bitten thong.
"I am foul" he said "But my hands are strong.
They cut my ears for snaring the geese
But the hair will grow and the wound have peace.
They call me Fulke of the Secret Oar.
I thought all women were hares, before.
The child shall not find me over-rough."

She said "This man is punished enough.
I can twist his heart if he thinks I can.
I find no other fault in this man."

"Now" said Duke Robert, "Let none deny
The mercy and justice of Normandy.
Man and woman, I set you free.
Fulke of the Snares, you are thief no more
But Fulke of the Herons by sea and shore
For I make you my warden of all that flies
Where the reeds grow thick and the marshland lies,
Swan and sandpiper, great and small,
And the royal heron, the duke of all.
You shall kill for meat, whenever you will,
But you shall see to it no others kill
Excepting the Master of Normandy
When he flies his hawks by the narrow sea.
And, without money and without price,
He shall grant you a badge with his device,
With three broad pence and a fishing-spear
And a cask of cider, every year.
And, every year, he may ask of you,
Four king herons of silver hue,
And such other game as may offer sport
To three good hawks of the choicer sort
—And the first-born son that your wife shall breed
To fight for his banner, if he have need.
Is it well?" he said.
                    "It is well," they said.
He summoned a priest with a shaven head,
The hunting-priest that rode by his side.
"See that this couple are groom and bride!"
"Nay, first," said the woman, "I bury my dead.
Is it well?" she said.
                    "It is well," they said.

It is long ago since these were wed,
It is long ago since these were dead.
Their dust is little, their seeking done.

It is long since the sea-rover's son
Ran in the marshes, a stripling youth,
And tested all matters with knife and tooth
While his mother sang an outland song.
When he came to his growth, he was tall and strong.
They called him Odo Le Haraine.

He was wolf's bane and otter's bane.
His heart was an unquiet fire.
He served hard masters for little hire
To follow the Bastard of Normandy
When he set prows on a narrow sea
For William's fortune and England's woe.

In the beginning, these things were so.

In the beginning, the sea said, "I take and whelm."

There was a bark out of Cyprus, with a headstrong
    skipper, red-bearded.
He was running away from some emperor, some god,
    some fate—how do I know?—it was long ago, very
    long.
He had a stolen woman with him, white as a moonbeam,
    when she moved the thick, gold bracelets rang on her
    arm.
They spread an awning on deck, a scarlet awning. They
    ate figs and drank wine in the shade while the overseer
    cursed the rowers.
At night they had love, on the narrow couch, spread
    with skin of a wolf he had killed and the silks of a
    king's treasury.
All day they lounged under the awning and had love and
    the look of the eyes.
But he was a careful skipper, a mighty thief, a great
    pirate, crafty and foreseeing, knowing every line of his
    ship as a huntsman knows hound and spear.
It did my heart good to see him put forth on me. It did
    my soul pleasure to see his craft and his strength.
The fleets of the world could not catch him, but I caught
    him; he knew every eddy of Middle Sea like the lines
    in his palm; he could smell a lee shore through fog;
    but me he did not know.
The first ten days I gave him fair weather and constant
    winds; he had his fill of love; his heart grew with it;
    they shone on deck, he and she; it was nothing, it was
    little enough to grant such a man.
Then I sent my storm, not a great one but sudden.

When half the rowers were dead and the overseer had
  been pierced to death in the darkness by the chained
  hands,
When sail and mast had gone overboard and the awning
  was a red rag and the last slaves howled with broken
  mouths as they wrenched at the splintered oars,
I watched him through the blind darkness: he did not
  pray or supplicate: he bared his teeth in the wind and
  worked every inch from his ship.
The woman was lashed beside him at the last: once or
  twice they looked at each other, but they said nothing.
He was a master of craft and she knew him a master,
  even then: she did not speak of the silks the water had
  spoiled, nor of love nor fate: she looked, merely: she
  was a great woman.
I saw them go down together, through the green glooms
  into the sunken, but I could not draw his lips together
  in submission: even at the last his teeth were bared: she
  did not call out or remember another year.
The rowers—who counts rowers?—their souls were
  made of water and ran to grey water again—but that
  one was a prize to drown.
There was a Phoenician—how long ago?—who came,
  seeking tin, and, when he had it, thought he would
  seek further islands.
He was two-handed also, but his bark was cranker: it did
  not take so long.
They lie very deep down, they lie past count or
  reckoning, they blackened with third in the calms,
  they were driven beyond all land, they carried treasure
  and courage, they lie deep down.
Some cursed and some were afraid: a few bared their
  teeth: some died in sleep or ignorance: it is all one
  now: it is very long ago.
There was a galley from Carthage. There were ships out
  of Tyre and Egypt.
It is long ago. It is long. It is an old wave.
Come forth again, you small, mighty men: come forth
  and try grips with me!"

Leif was blown from Norway with a crew of thirty-five,
His head still buzzing with a waif word that spoke of a
    new land,
The yellow cub of the old sea-bear who sat in Ericstead,
Nursing his gout and his heathen gods, remembering
    voyages.

All Eric's sons were sailors. When the child was yet
    unweaned
They bore it down in a hollow shield to wet its lips with
    the foam.
The boys played viking on the beach and screamed like
    gulls in the cold.
The grey fog clung to the women's hair, the grey drops
    sprinkled the shield.

Leif was the eldest of them, a strong oar, bitted with
    bronze,
A longship marked for strange landfalls, a lucky skipper
    to serve,
He had Christ's sign on his forehead but his heart was
    the gannet's heart
That faces the Northwester.
                                So he and his men set sail.
Set sail for the rocks of Greenland, but the blind storm
    fell on them
And for days that had no number they drove where the
    tempest willed,
Westward and always Westward, till earth was an idle
    dream
And the days of it unremembered, but the ship like a live
    thing still.

They had no magic shut in a box to show them North
    and South
Nor any course to follow, for the whole world lay
    behind,
There was only sea and the pole-star, and the sea was
    very great.
When the fog came down, they drifted, a nutshell steered
    by a wraith.

A nutshell lost in waste billows and blown by a warlock
     wind,
For these were not Christian waters, where the green
     berg chilled the heart,
And, down in the sea-trolls' cavern, the shapeless hosts
     of the deep
Sat mumbling the bones of heroes forgotten by Christ
     and Thor.

It was all one to Leif's shipmen. If the storm came, they
     rode the storm,
If the warlock rose from the ocean, they would drive a
     spear at his side.
They slept on the bare oar-benches, when they had time
     to sleep,
And dreamt of grass and sweet water and roasted meat in
     the fire.

It is not told who sighted the first, faint smudge of
     land,
Like an oar drifting the waters, like an elm-branch
     drowned in the wave,
That hail is lost in the darkness, they took no record
     of it.
They knew they had come a journey. That was enough
     for the fame.

The new land drifted toward them, they could smell the
     land by now.
The bearded men stared Westward with blue, sea-weary
     eyes.
A harsh coast and a barren, with fields of ice inland
And the stretch between sea and glacier one naked and
     lifeless stone.

The second land they came to was a better land to see,
Th white sands gleamed in the sunlight, the trees grew
     thick and strong,
A man might raise a hearth there and live forgotten of
     Time.
Leif called it Markland the Wooded and put to sea once
     more.

So, after two days sailing, they touched at a grassy isle
And tasted the sweet dew of the grass with lips where
   the salt still lay,
So they passed into shallow waters where the ship itself
   took ground
And did not wait for the next high tide but ran ashore
   with a cry.

I see them tasting that dew-sweet grass. I see them
   running ashore
Through the little pools of the ebb-tide and crying out as
   they run,
One man took a stone and skipped it, like a child
   released from a task,
Another strove with his shipmate like two cub-wolves in
   the sun.

Beyond them the virgin forest lay as it had lain from the
   first,
A forest of game and weather, a pure and savage domain,
No foot had ever trod it but the skin-shod foot of the
   wild
And the stag might die in his age there and never hear
   arrow fly.

The earth was a purse of bounty, the salmon leaped in
   the streams,
The grass withered but little for there was no frost in the
   year.
They built a house by the forest and lived there, caught
   in a dream,
For the day and the night were changed there and the
   sun shone winterlong.

They found green vines in the forest, they found wild
   grapes on the vine,
They loaded the ship with timber and brought the cargo
   home.
But the wealth was not in the cargo, the wealth was the
   trodden wave
And the star tracked down past sunset till the forest rose
   from the sea.

They made their sagas of it when Leif was a grey
    old man
Fed out of a bowl by children, with hands too shaken to
    hold
The sword-hilt or the wine-cup or the rudder of the
    ship,
When Thorvald mouldered in Vineland, the arrow that
    slew him dust.

The voice rang from the ale-bench, the magic sang from
    the harp,
"Lieth a land to Westward—a star that our fathers
    found—
Vineland the Good they named it—it was thus that the
    ship set forth—
They spoke thus and they did thus—we tell the tale as it
    fell."

The harp uttered its music but the words were brief and
    plain.
The song was a skein of sea-dyed yarn that passed from
    hand to hand.
I make my saga of it, with short words out of the North
And dye it with earth and water and the cones of the
    forest-pine.

There was a land called Vineland. It was thus they came
    to its shore
And lived there like men enchanted, for a year of Indian
    grace—
A phantom walks on the sea-beach, a man with a winged
    helm—
The ghost of a ship puts Eastward, with sun-dried grapes
    in its hold—

After came Thorvald and Thorfinn and Freydis, slayer of
    men,
There was trading and war and murder and a white child
    born in the wild.
The Skraelings cast down sable-furs in barter for scarlet
    cloth

And when Karlsefni's bullock roared the Skraelings ran
    away.

There was a fort they lived in and a clearing made with
    their hands,
A stream where the women washed their gear, a fire
    where the men told tales
And always there was the forest that listened and said no
    word.
The ships went back to Greenland. The wind in the
    forest blew.

It blew from Time, it blew upon Time, and the palisade
    sank down,
The grass grew-over the booths of Leif and over the fire-
    scorched stone.
Already the crosses tottered, where Thorvald lay in his
    grave.
The thick moss covered them, fallen; the seasons levelled
    the mound.

For awhile there was still a clearing, for awhile there was
    trace and sign,
A scrap of red cloth, sun-faded, in a skin-clad woman's
    hair,
The broken blade of a war-axe, long rusted with many
    rains.
Then the rune blurred out altogether. The land had
    mastered the rune.

The new growth covered the clearing. The wood came
    down to the sea.
The grape might grow for an age there and never be
    pressed to wine.
The gold and the iron lay hidden like spirits under the
    ground
And the fame slept and the evil until Columbus came.

Now watch, while darkness covers the shape again
From Labrador to Horn,

And, from the thrice-barred gate, not even dreams come
    forth.
Watch, while the hard eyes of seafaring men
Still looking West, see only storm and scud,
And think of it like darkness in the blood,
An omen and a portent and a doom,
Playground of monsters, limbo of lost ships,
Where the sea sickens and the kraken grips
And even the cold mermaids of the gloom
Carry a heathen and a golden comb
And have the blood of sailors on their lips;
While Greenland withers and the knowledge fails
Into a story, into an old song,
Till even that grows dim,
And the great sea-adventure of the North,
The long wave of that saga of the strong,
Rushing to break beyond the ocean-rim
And sprinkle utter West with Northern foam,
Rolls back, and there is sunset on the sails
And the grey fingers of the spinning Norn
Knot up the pattern for the rune come home.

Watch, watch and turn the glass,
Seeing the seasons and the decades pass
While the blind harper sings St. Brandan's isle,
Where the sea-saints lie in a blessed sleep
No surf can waken, it has grown so deep,
No evil of the deep can change that blessed, sleepy
    smile
—Fortunate islands, islands of the blest,
Hid in the West, oh, somewhere in the West!
We spoke them, white as sleeping swans, but then the
    tempest came,
We smelt the spices in the offshore breeze,

We saw the golden fruit upon the trees
But might not lay our hands upon the same.
It is as well, for we are mortal men,
And they who touch upon those haunting shores,
The few, the siren-driven,
Once they have anchored in that silent port

And seen the fashion of that harbourage
Where the bronze slaves of Solomon drowse at their
   brazen oars,
Rest there for aye, forgetting earth and heaven.

Turn the sands and let them run
Widdershins against the sun
Turn them for another age,
Harold of Norway's thread is spun,
Harold of England's fights are done,
William the Bastard's work begun,
What his eye desired, his right hand took
And he kept the tally in Domesday Book
Of Norman cider and Saxon mead
—And the seed of the seed of our very seed,
The ghost-forerunners, the clay and marl
Who suffered alike under count and jarl
But would not abate, for good or bad,
One jot of the custom their fathers had.
"The king is the king and the sun the sun,
But it is not custom that this be done.
You may ride to hounds through the standing corn
For that was the custom when we were born,
But you shall not trample except to hunt
Or you shall see if our bills be blunt.
You may chasten the noble and slay the serf
And stuff your gullets with English turf,
That is in reason, now and then,
And the sons of our sons shall say amen.
You may hang the abbot and burn the reeve,
But, touch on the folk with a by-your-leave,
For the oxen answer the proper yoke
But we plow by the custom of the folk,
It is all unwritten of brush or pen
But it is the custom of Englishmen
And it is not broken, except with strife."
Say Hodge the plowman and Cis, his wife,
Say Martin the yeoman and Cob the carter
And they swear it is true by St. Peter Martyr,
And the seas have washed over the ancient troth
But we know the nature of this their oath

By charter and patent, by bill and deed,
And the marsh that lies by Runnymede,
By Tyler and Hampden, by Cade and Ball
And the cracked bell silent in Faneuil Hall,
By the names of color and trade and town,
Smith and Lincoln, Standish and Brown,
By the acorn grown from an old wives' saw
To the deep oak-forest of English law
And the oak-leaf carried oversea,
It is an old and stubborn tree.
It is an old and stubborn thing.
And the king who irks it shall not be king.

For it is the rede of English Jack
Who carried the fardels on his back,
Who hunted the rat that ate the malt
And swinked in the sun for his bread and salt,
Who built the house and cozened the priest
And drank at his grandson's wedding-feast,
Grey as a badger, old Surlytongue,
With his strength unspent and his thews unwrung,
For they made him of oak and English weather
And hand-forged iron, all together,
With the appleblossom to give him mirth
And the heart in his bosom of fertile earth,
That, though he were buried, he yet should quicken
And the seed of his body arise and thicken,
A green herb growing, a dog-rose blowing,
A seed flung out on the wind for sowing,
Tougher than witchgrass against distress
And a Ribstone pippin for hardiness,
The strange, the various English stock
Where the blackthorn marries the lady smock
And old man's beard and love-in-a-mist,
Cowslip, nettle and honesty
Are all ground up in the selfsame grist
By the insolence of the wild bee,
In spite of Scotch thistle and Irish clover
And the yellow broom that the French brought over,
To make—though the metaphor may seen odd,
A sod-cake reserved for an English God,
No canting prophet of milk and honey

But a solid protector of honest money.
For it was Jack's habit, long ago,
To breed the rapid and trust the slow,
To suffer the leaven but like the lump
And sober the shrill at the village pump,
To muddle through at needles and pins
While the clever men were breaking their shins,
And do it, not only by beef and brawn
And the ancient furrow going on,
But thanks to the few fantasticoes
Who wore their honor like a red rose,
Who tossed their hats ahead of the ships
And died with the verses on their lips,
The few, the arrant, the disavowed,
The wildfire of the Wessex cloud,
Richard and Francis and the rest,
True children of the cuckoo's nest.

Nevertheless, he mainly held
To the ancient maxim his fathers spelled
And kept it down to the last black letter,
"Brag's a good dog, but hold fast better."
He was no man to meet in the dark
For he would bite before he would bark.
His hates were enduring, his friendships slow,
And his trust and liking took time to grow,
But once he had given and found it good,
He loved the fellow like his own blood.
It was good to look on at a proper hanging
And good to listen to lark and throstle,
But a milksop was good for nothing but banging,
Cruel and merry, earth's true apostle,
With his ashplant gripped in his big right hand
And his feet set firmly on his own land,
The beanstalk-climber, the giant-killer,
Dusty with pollen as moth or miller,
Who could cudgel his son and beat his wife
And wrestle with death for a sick ewe's life
All night long in the lambing-shed
With Job's own patience—old Stubbornhead,
Old Surlytongue, old Weatherwise,
With the blue Ocean in his eyes.

There is bone of his bone within us still,
And the roots of his orchards are hard to kill,
Though Jackson built another house
And roofed it over with greener boughs,
He came to the wilderness, tattered and torn,
When the hands of the shearers had left his shorn,
With three red kernels of English corn,
To marry a maiden all forlorn,
To clear the ground and suffer the bane
And die remembering Sussex rain,
But not till he saw with his own eyes
That his firstborn child was otherwise,
And, out of that grain, our wheatfields rise
And, out of that changeling, we were born,
Although our ghosts are other ghosts,
And we return, as strangers now,
To Jack's house, and the magic cow,
The cow that had the crumpled horn,
And shall be strangers evermore.

Turn, turn the glass, and let the sands
Run South and East to other lands,
Where Venice floats upon the sea,
The galley of the golden oar
And all the length of Italy
Brickles with light and life and sun,
The sleep is over, the dark sleep
That lay like lead upon the wise,
The almond-blossom Spring begun.
The mind is growing its new wings.
The brown sea-captains walk like kings.
The ships put forth upon the deep.
The merchants seek far merchandise.

∞

Marco Polo, curious man,
What drove you to seek for Kublai Khan?

"Perhaps it was youth, for I was young,
Perhaps it was my father's tongue,
The desert-hawk I had never seen
Till the years of my age were turned fifteen,

For I was not born when he went away
To trade beyond the rim of the day,
And, when he returned, we were strange and shy,
Meeting each other, he and I,
For a lost bride's eyes looked out at him,
My mother's, who died in bearing me,
And the lines in his visage were great and grim
And I knew he had been to Tartary.

Marco Polo, how did it fall
That at last you followed him, after all!

When the world shut in with candlelight,
They would talk to each other, night on night,
While the water lapped at the landing-stair
And they hardly knew that I was there
Except as a shadow the candle threw
When the wind before the morning blew
And the great house creaked like a ship of stone,
Maffeo and Nicolo,
Talking of marvels past reknown,
Talking of wonders still to do—
Their talk was honey and wine and snow,
How could I help but drink it down?
How could I help but thirst and burn,
When they opened the bag of camel's hair
And looked at the marvel hidden there
And said "It is time and we must return."?

Marco Polo, what did you see
When at length you came to Tartary?

I know I have been where I have been,
But how can I tell you what I have seen?
I knew the desert of the dry tree
Whose branches bear eternity
And the hot sickness of the noon.
I drank the mare's-milk of the tents,
I saw the musk-ox gape at me,
I have had gold and frankincense
And silks that glitter like the moon.
But what can I tell that will make you see!

Marco Polo, wandering sword,
What manner of man did you call lord?

I have been the pope's and the doge's man,
But I never knew master like Kublai Khan.
The songs of his body sit ten by ten
At buffets of precious napery,
When he hunts, he hunts with ten thousand men
And his gerfalcons darken the sky,
He has jewels uncounted and golden plate
Whence even his meanest slaves may eat
And he sits and numbers the hairs of Fate,
With a great, tame lion couched at his feet
And his mercy as fair as a white ram's fleece,
Mighty in battle and just in peace,
Star of the city of Kanbalu,
Khan of Khans and Great of the Great
Whose bounty falls like the evening dew—
Since Adam delved and Eve span
Who ever saw prince like Kublai Khan?

Marco Polo, tell me how
Your Venice talks of your travels now.

They call me braggard, they call me liar,
They gawk at me like an eater of fire!
"Millions" Polo, the fable-monger,
Who dines on a lizard to stay his hunger,
Such being his custom in Cathay.
But they laughed with their mouths another way,
When we came back in '95
Like ghosts returned to a world alive,
With our gear still smelling of musk and civet
And my father's beard grown whiter than privet,
Two old men and a younger one
Who had looked in the eye of Eastern sun
And lived—and lived to tell the tale
That I tell to the shadows in this my jail.
Why my very cousins did not own us,
And the jeering crowd was ready to stone us
Till we ripped the rubies out of our rags
And proved we were Polos—by moneybags!

Let them laugh as long as they like today,
I have seen Cathay, I have seen Cathay!
I have seen Quinsai, the city of bridges,
Twelve thousand bridges of fair, cut stone,
And I count their talk the buzzing of midges,
When I think of the wonders my eyes have known.
Their little Europe, their dwarfish West,
Their doge with his ring and his marriage-fee!
I have taken the eggs from the phoenix-nest
And walked by the shores of the Ocean-Sea,
The earth-encircler, the Asian main,
And, if Kublai lived, I would go again,
For what is their quarrel of gimcrack lords,
Their toy-fleets sailing a herry-pond,
By the might that mastered the Tartar hordes?
There are worlds beyond, there are worlds beyond!
Worlds to be conquered, worlds to be found,
By river and desert and burning ground,
Even, perchance, by the Ocean-Sea,
If a man has courage enough to dare,
And I know that others will follow me,
And I mark the roads that will take them there,
The roads of the golden caravan,
The riches that Europe never knew,
For—there was a prince named Kublai Khan—
And the sons of his sons will welcome you.

The glass turns, the maps are drawn,
The working of the fate goes on,
It has been roused. It will have men.
Nothing will make it sleep again.
It is like water underground
That no man sees and few men hear,
But, now and then, there is an ear
To catch the solitary sound
And spend all life in vain essay
To bring those waters to the day.
It is the long, sea-beaten cave,
Where blind men bring to utter gloom
The chance-found spills of wind and wave,
Unknowing that they serve a doom.

The time ticks on, the time is long,
But it can wait, for it is strong
As air and water, earth and fire,
And patient with its deep desire.
For it is that Knowledge grows,
In glacial patience, like the floes
That take an age to move a rod,
The patience of the mills of God.
And it is so that Knowledge grows,
Like sudden blossoms on the rose,
When, for no reason that we know,
The time is ripe to blossom so.

So let us scan two hundred years
Before the destined man appears,
The son of chance, the Genoese,
What blossoms on the branch are these?

There is a compass for the ships,
There is a tale on seamen's lips,
There is a memory of Crusade
And—always—there is honest trade,
The prize and peace of every war,
The thing men die, and bargain, for.

"The Crescent grows stronger, day by day,
The Knights Hospitallers fight and pray,
But who is our buckler now but they?
We have trafficked for years with far Cathay,
But now the Paynims drive us away,
They have slaughtered our bishops and slain our
    priests
And served them quartered at heathen feasts,
And I cannot get silk or musk or spice,
Though I offer for them at any price,
For Polo's road is shut with a sword,
And there is no comfort but in the Lord!
They have taken Acre, they swarm in Spain,
The Sepulchre lies in their hands again,
And, as I am a Christian, I groan in pain,
For they plundered my cousin's argosy
In broad daylight on the open sea,

And the price of his ransom will ruin me!
If I traffic with Egypt for dates and limes,
I must bribe some pirate a dozen times,
And the risk on the coasting-trade alone
Is enough to wring the blood from a stone.
We are all poor sinners, as God knows well,
But even poor sinners must buy and sell,
And whence will your amber and sugar come,
Your swords of temper, your robes of feasts,
When these devils have taken Byzantium
And shut us utterly from the East?

Seamen and voyagers, show us a way,
We have lost Cathay, we must find Cathay,
We have money and we will pay,
Show us a sea-road to Cathay!"
And the kings say "Fighting is Christian work
And we burn to be rid of this heathen Turk,
But even God's knights have bellies to fill
And—it takes money to pay the bill.
For, we honor the dead for the True Belief
But we know who inherits the vacant fief,
Cousin Bide-Quiet and Brother Knavery,
As John did Richard's, for all his bravery.
Nevertheless, since times are evil,
We must seek new ways of cheating the devil
And they say Cipango is built of gold
And the wealth of the Indies is wealth untold.
We have had a taste, we have had a smack
Of the riches that lie at the world's back,
The Asian glory of khan and king,
And it leaves us empty and hungering.
For a sceptre is nought but a stinging nettle
If the hand that holds it lacks yellow metal
And it's cold, Lear sitting on bankrupt thrones,
So, by God's Five Wounds and our father's bones,
We swear, that if anyone comes to say
He can show us the best and the cheapest way
To loot the treasure of dim Cathay,
We may even adventure a ship or two
And find some felons to be his crew,
Should no weightier matter be on hand

Such as filching a slice of our neighbor's land.
For our hearts have been touched by the sorry
    plight
of the poor souls dwelling in heathen night
With no comforting knowledge of sin or hell
—Wherever it is they are said to dwell—
And we yearn to bring them into the fold,
If it can be done, and they have the gold."

The scholars say and the learned men,
"Knowledge is growing her wings again.
We seek and question, we delve and find,
We test all things by the questing mind,
And the dry branch burgeons with lilied bloom
Where we raise dead Science out of the tomb
And loosen the cerecloths of the years
Till the marble gleams and the shape appears,
The Greek, the sibyl of the vows,
With Wisdom's fillet on her brows.

We may lack for gold, we may faint for bread,
But we walk with gods when we wake the dead
And make them tell us the thing they hid
When the earth was fresh on the coffin-lid
And the worms and Plato held debate,
For Life is little but Wisdom great.
So question us and we will reply,
These are the stars you must voyage by,
Aristotle and Ptolemy
Give us a clew to the Western sea,
Seneca hath a prophecy,
And the words are Greek, but the truth is plain,
If you sail due West from the ports of Spain
You must strike on Cipango, transmarine,
For nothing but Ocean lies between,
Witness the writings that bear our name"
Toscanelli and Martin Behaim,
Who charted the known and the unknown lands,
Sans dragon or marvel but clear and fair
—A round world spinning in silver air—
And went a hemisphere astray

Though you were the best of all your day,
Nevertheless, you had seeing eyes,
And even your error helped make men wise.

What says Henry the Navigator,
Shut in his tower as night grows later,
The great stargazer of the seas,
The beacon of the Portuguese?

"I keep the hidden granary
Of the wild harvest of the sea
And find life short and labor nought
Beside the patience of my thought
That creeps on farther, day by day,
By splintered ship and drowning man
And shall creep on, till I can lay
My cords upon Leviathan
And see him wallow in the net
His might has always broken through,
And tame him for a servant yet
And christen him for Christ anew.

For this I weary brain and hand
On this last outpost of the land,
Sagres the stony, known of old,
Where, even in the churchyard mold,
The dead still hear the beating wave.
And, when they come to dig my grave,
Let it be here, above the surf,
An oar's-length of sea-beaten turf,
And lay the maps of South and West
Like ghostly jewels on my breast,
The charts of the uncharted shores,
The finger laid on the Azores.

For this I summon and confer
With pilot and geographer
And school my seamen to the stark
Encounter with the outmost dark.
They perish in the Guinea sun,
They drink the hemlock of the sea,

But, though they die, the map goes on,
And still a few come back to me.

It took ten years to round one cape,
And still I see the sultry shape
Bojador, rising on my sleep,
If I had tears, I would weep
For all the cost in death and fame
To give the chart that single name.
But I have given all my tears
To ransom men of after years
From the blind perils mine endure,
That even fools may sail secure
With sleepy helm and idle mind,
By landmarks captains died to find.

I keep the salt-encrusted key
Of grey Atlantic's treasury
And, every day, at flood and ebb,
The moon and I spin out our web
Stronger than steel and cobweb-thin
To gather all sea-knowledge in,
For, while I live, my word is still
"Strive to do well" though all go ill,
The motto of the arms I chose
Bearing the Cross against God's foes
At fierce Ceuta, in my youth.
But now I know a deeper truth.
The work must pass, the man must die,
The cunning of the brain go by
And darkness master us once more
If skill have no inheritor.
Therefore I fish in every sea
To bring the stout of heart to me,
Breed them and foster them and slay them,
By workings of the deep dismay them,
But never loose them from my grip
Once they have proved their seamanship.
For they shall find when I am dead,
And I shall hear them, through the gale,
As they fling out the sounding-lead
Where no man ever thought to sail."

Now it is time and now the hour breaks,
Now, as the fifteenth century turns old,
Now the great board is ready for the stakes
And the great gamesmen burning for the gold
Which shall redeem the souls they gave away
To the four winds and famine and the sea,
The broken hopes, the bywords of defeat,
The insolence of landsmen in the street
And all the slow starvation of delay
That comes to those who wait
In the lean antechambers of the great,
Twiddling their battered caps with tarry thumbs
While the page snickers and the lackey comes
To say that great men are not seen today.
"This is the hour when the great men dine,
This is the hour when the king's at prayer,
Go home to your black bread and sour wine,
Or dine on very air
You are no pimp or Excellence or priest
To break upon His Majesty at feast
Or bawl your tidings in Her Grace's ear
When she has two new monkeys and a fool
And sits to the court-painter of the year.
Yes, yes, the Adelant has had your plea.
(I saw it in his secretary's fire.)
What, will the man still hang on me? I tire!
Go home, I say, and save your breath to cool
Your porridge, for I do not like the stare
You fix upon me with those hollow Oes
Burnt in your head by fever and the South
As you would eat me up and wipe your mouth
Now sailors breed like vermin everywhere,
And when I scent you—faugh!—I hold my nose.
Go, wash your beard and learn to be less odd,
And, if you have a God,
As even sailors must have, I suppose,
Thank Him you were not cudgelled down the stair!"

But now, at last, the drum
Beats, and the fate is ready, and they come,
Spaniard, Venetian, Saxton, Portuguese,

Some with gold chains and some in tattered frieze.
Sons of poor fortune, beggars of reknown,
Cast out, like water-dogs, to swim or drown.
Once they had teeth to bite and mouths to fill
And with the sea's own devil in them still,
The cold, unique persistence of the wave,
Ruffler and Christian, vagabond and knave,
Planters of crosses, scourges of the slave,
Lean as their ration, weathered like their decks
With little toys and medals at their necks,
Black-eyed and walking with the sailer's roll,
Muscled like cats and Latin to the soul,
Faces of teak and olive, deeply tanned,
The lips shut in the habit of command,
The big nose raking like an Arab mast,
The passionate heart untempered to the last
But schooled in the obedience of the sea
And constant as its own inconstancy,
Needles of iron, pointing to the mark,
Driftwood and dyewood, flaring in the dark,
Lights on the wave from Guinea to Fayal,
Gomez and Cadamosto and Cabral
And all the Neptunes of that horoscope,
Cam of the Congo, Diaz of Good Hope,
Cabot, who raised the genie from the jar
In Mecca, underneath an Arab star,
And young Da Gama, beardless as a girl,
Dreaming his first wild dream of Indian pearl.

Beat the long roll for them as they stand up
To drink illusion in a parting cup
And pledge their souls and bodies in the game,
Some to get money, some to lie with fame,
Some to be knights but few to die ashore
Or keep the treasure that they suffered for,
Flower of Portugal, flower of Spain,
Of Genoa and Venice and the main,
They pass, like spirits, arrogantly-eyed.
Cloaking their hunger with their sombre pride.

O masked and hooded watcher, turn the glass!
And let the last few sands

Filter like coins of price between your hands,
For, even as they pass,
A shape arises and a figure stands
With its hand raised to knock on a king's door
And change the shape of Ocean evermore.
He cannot enter here. The Queen's at mass.
The king is making ready for the war.
The Duke's abed—abed and nobly drunk
As is his custom, Tuesdays. By the Faith,
I'll not arouse him now for any wraith!
Yet—it were ill to turn a dog away
Into the sun, on such a broiling day,
And then—how dull we are here, afternoons
Since the good Queen put down the merry tunes!—
And even talking makes the time pass by.
He looks too tall and ruddy for a spy.
Too active for a clerk, too aquiline
For a mere trader in Canary wine
Though he has been a seaman by his walk,
Grey-eyed, clean-shaved, an accent in his talk,
I took him first for a Franciscan monk,
He wears the grey robe and the knotted cord
And yet, that hand looks fitter for a sword
Than rosary or scourging discipline,
But where and how and why
Got he those trenches on his countenance
As if he fought a private war with Chance
And they were scars that never could be healed
Though God himself came down to win the field?
In God's name, then, who let the fellow in?
Are all my wits asleep?
Has Saint Iago's self disdained to keep
The royal gates of Leon and Castile
That strangers with a voice of honeymeal
And a most damnably persistent tongue
Should lure me from my constant vigilance
And make me open doors against my will?
There's magic in the air!
                              His back was straight
When he and I stood chatting at the gate,
But now, he walks around like ten grandees,
As much at home with everything he sees

As if he were returned to his own hall,
After some absence, to look over all,
Change this and that, make idleness repent
But, on the whole, be measurably content
With the poor privilege of royalty!
I'll wager he's a taskmaster to flee!
I think he must be made of hemp and steel.
Watch his eyes now—why, if he gripped my hand,
He'd break the bones of it and think no more
Than he would think of breaking down that door
Had I refused him way. There's danger here!
Let others sift the matter. I'll stand clear.
Your papers? You have papers? Those and these?
And the Queen's seal! Most strange. Yet they seem true.
There is the private mark she grants to few.
I do not understand, but—follow me.
Your name and rank again, sir, if you please?
(I had forgot it, looking at the man.)
"Christobal Colon, seaman, Genoese."
He sailed from Palos on Redemption Day
In Nomine Jesu Christi, with fair wind.
The low, white houses of the double street,
Under the hill, along the waterfront,
Began to shrink to the enchanted town
Children can build on rainy afternoons
With a brown cloth humped into rounded hills
For background, an old mirror for the sea
And, in between, a little cardboard port
Where dolls stand in low doorways evermore
And a brown, china dog lies in the square
Forever scratching one perpetual flea
With one stiff leg. The roofs are flat and square.
The green-sponge trees will never shed a leaf.
There is no weed on the cigar-box quay
And the three pea-pods on the glass are still.

So build it then, but, if you have the luck,
Scatter white dust along the double street
And plant the ways with green verbena sprigs
So there may be some fragrance of the South
To haunt your voyagers, as they go down,
Bundle on back, to the detested ships,

Lurching or sober, through the milk-warm night,
Remembering, with anger or despair,
The beds they left, the flesh they lay upon,
The candle they set burning in the church.
The hot fish, frying in the rancid oil
For the last meal, in the ramshackle hut
And the long, dolorous weeping in the dark.

It is begun. There is no turning back.
You, with the supple fingers of the thief,
Are fresh from jail and half regretting it
As the bronzed bully-drunkard by your side
Withers your very liver with his tales
Of phantom ships and demon-ridden seas.
He wears a tinkling keepsake on a cord
Round his bull-throat, a tarnished copper heart,
And you can see where "Maria" was gouged
From one side and "Dolores" haggled in.
He smells of sweat and garlic and red wine
And the hot bodies of big servant-girls
And he will die on La Natividad
After immortal hardships overcome
The best man of the forty left behind.

You are another kind of voyager,
You bustling little skipjack of a man,
Plump as a duck with scurvy merry eyes,
You should have lived and prospered on the land,
Selling bad scent to blowsy chambermaids
And buying stolen ribbons for a song,
But you were just a whit too clever once
And pulled the whiskers of the sleepy law
Till it awoke and yawned and sought for you
But may not lay you by the tripping heels
Till you return, such being the king's word.
So you embark, humming the bawdy tune
Which, with your tales, will yet lift up the hearts
Of the despairing and the desolate
When hope is dead and all land left behind.

And what are you, tall spectre, with the dark
Cheek and the darker cloud upon your brow?

Juan called the Silent, good at sheet and oar
But known as the Unlucky through the town,
Since all goes crisscross with you, soon or late.
You have a wife and children you must feed,
And, if you go, folk may be merciful,
For it's a kindly place when all is said,
And, if you go, they say there may be gold
And every seaman may fill up his cap
With naked gold and buy his children bread.
And, if you die, folk may be pitiful.
Pass, Juan the Silent.
                              Here's a sturdy three,
Pressed men, their arms about each others' necks,
Bawling a stumbling ditty as they go.
They are sworn brothers now—will be at knives
Before the voyage is even well begun,
And then again be brothers—one to die
In a grass hut, watching the lizards crawl,
One to be hanged in Hispaniola fort,
And one, the weakest, to snuff out in bed,
With every one of his companions gone,
A mumbling, old, forgotten miracle
With even children wearied of his tales.

Here's Pedro the sea-lawyer, who can sign
A sprawling P on the ship's articles
Where Juan the Silent breathes and makes his mark,
Stickler for rules, breeder of mutiny,
Sharp-faced, thin-nosed, scolding as a jay,
Licking his lips and arguing to himself
As his quick eyes begin to single out
The grumblers he can count on in the crew.

These dozen here are neither pressed nor forced,
They are the bolts and planking of the ships,
The ropes and spars that last foul weather out.
You'll find their like on any caravel,
Breaking their teeth on lumps of flinty bread,
Rationed on stinking water in the calms
When the tar creeps and bubbles with heat
And strength fails and the scurvy comes aboard.
They have forgotten why they went to sea

Or what they thought to find upon it once
Save the great toil and the exhausted sleep,
The storm, the shipmate fallen from the spar,
The boots of mates, the captain's iron fist,
The sick man chattering in the other bunk,
The breathing in the foc'sle after dark
And the long trick till dawn, under the stars.

The years pass over them like wave and wave
And they do not remember time by years
But by ill skippers and good passages,
Names of lost ships, names of forgotten girls
Hungrily met and drunkenly possessed
In one port or the next, but all the same
For every port has liquor and the girls,
Crimp, cheat and landshark, eating up the pay,
And the one seamen's chapel by the quays
Whose poor priest rubs the Virgin with his sleeve
When no one's looking, to wipe off the damp
That tarnishes the glitter of her crown.
And next time, next time, next time (so they swear)
I'll steal an oar and shoulder it and go
Inland and inland, over hill and dale,
Until some orange-sucker looks at me
And asks me what the lousy oar is for,
And then I'll know I've come ashore at last.
I'll buy a chicken farm and milk a cow.
I'll marry a rich widow with a squint.
By God, I'll hire a snotty little boy
(When I'm the keeper of my father's inn)
To yell "All hands on deck! Arise and shine!"
Cold mornings, when the wind blows half a gale,
Just to get up and throw a boot at him
And then slip back to bed and sleep and sleep.
You'll see. You'll hear about me. You'll be told.
So they drone on to each new cabin-boy.
So they make land. So they go back to sea,
O, we shall see them gape with wasted mouths
Under king's windows for the pay denied,
The little hire they starved for; we shall hear
Their voices crying on the Admiral's fame
Feeble and bodiless and menacing

Like the long whisper of an ebbing tide
And we shall see their fever-shaken hands
Point to their yellow faces hatefully
In mockery of his Indies and the gold.
But this is distant now.
They go aboard to stow their traps and sleep
As they have done a dozen times before,
And when they sleep, they do not even dream.

Who else to make the ninety? Now they pass
Like fog itself, anonymous and swift,
Talking the lingua-franca of the seas,
Brown face and Latin hand,
Sheath-knife and dagger, venturer and rogue,
Rag, tag and bobtail closing up the pack . . .
You'd have them more seductive gentlemen,
On fire for glory, chaste with sacrifices,
Great hearts, prophetic virtues, noble minds?
So, doubtless, would the Admiral they serve,
But, being man, he takes what he can get
And, being what he is, will not retract
One inch from his set plan, for all their pain.
He'll squeeze them like an orange in his hands
With coax and threat and monumental lie,
Until the very pips cry out at him
And the spoilt juices rankle in the sun,
And cast them so, unbending to the last,
On barren shores of immortality
They never sought and somehow died to gain.
Suppose you call for volunteers to sail
Westward from San Francisco into hell
(In times when every man believes in hell)
Some may be saints, and broken gallants some
But it will be the random and the curst
Who man the ropes and work the vessel out
Past buoy and beacon into the unknown,
For they gave up salvation long ago
And are so well acquainted with despair
They barely turn their eyes to look at him
When he is there and he is never far
But silently admit him elbow-room
Like an old, tedious, familiar hound

Who comes to beg among them, every day,
The scraps and broken victual of their hearts.

Perhaps these passers-by will please you more.
Here is a doctor and a notary
(So, an we reach the courts of Prester John
We'll do it with due warrant of the law
And have a Christian clyster in our store
To soothe the bowels of barbaric kings)
And, if our doctor cannot find a purge
Searching enough to mend a broken head
Or bleed the sick till they are—sick no more—
Why, here's our barber-surgeon who shall set
His burning irons to the mangled flesh
And cauterize you till you faint with pain.
He'll draw your teeth so expeditiously,
You'll rub your gums and find them sorer still
And crack a dozen grisly little jests
Upon you, as your shipmates hold you down,
For he's a wit.
                    Laugh, laugh, I'd have you laugh!
It is so merry, leaving all behind,
Drink, victual, hearthstone, woman, safety, life,
To follow mad Italians to the gulf
Where the sea changes to a sea of flame
And fritter there through all eternity,
Blackened and burning, like forgotten sin;
To struggle with the last and drowning wave,
Clay-cold, stone-cold, obliterated, dark,
Under a starless heaven, and go down.
It is the greatest jest was ever jested.
All Palos rings with it. O crack your sides,
Whoop and thump ribs and chew it over well!
It is not often Chance will offer you
Such hangdog knaves to jeer at as they pass
From you spoilt friar of an Admiral
(How cozened he the King to dub him so?)
To the historian he gravely takes
To write each byword of his folly down.
God pity the poor devil and his pen
For his cracked master is so sure of wealth
He's even shipped an assayer of ores

To test the sea-foam in his empty pans
And weigh the phantom gold of the world's end.
Oh, he's forehanded!—by this aching mirth
That snatches me and will not let me go!
Of course, if you've a brother or a son,
Who sails tomorrow, I can understand
And sympathize in all sobriety.
Tch, tch—one really shouldn't laugh at all.
It is too piteous—poor souls, poor souls.
But we—he, he—we'll have a cousin there.
He's always been my plague. I'll whisper it.
You know those striplings with the hungry eyes,
Sit by the fire and—when the cat's away,
The mice, you know—well, well, we trust our wives,
But there's no harm in prudence, after all,
Safe bind, safe find and—I can see it still,
How eagerly he swallowed down the bait!
"Sail to the Indies! Make your fortune sure!"
Of course, of course—and who's to fit him out
But his good cousin? So we're rid of him,
Blessedly rid of him for good and all,
And he's a hero and a noble youth
But "Husband, it was yours, the generous heart!"
Tra la—tra lirra la—it pays, it pays!
As I could tell you certain tales to prove,
But I'm a modest man.
                          Draw closer yet!
See, see—t's he! 'tis he!—oh, the sheep's eyes
He casts behind him!—hoping some last sign,
Flutter of handkerchief or wave of hand
She'll never give if there is faith in locks
And good mamas who like their sons-in-law—
Oh, how it feeds my heart! that downcast mouth!
Those long legs, none so jaunty, by the Mass,
As they were wont to be by Cousin's fire!
He's gone!—he's gone!—and I can toddle back
To chat with good mama and take my ease
Yawn at the last and find the night grows late.
Time for the candle climbing up the stairs,
Time for mamma to bid us both good-night
And whisper just one word in daughter's ear
I am too courteous to listen to,

As we stand blinking at our chamber-door,
While, on his narrow plank, he twists and turns
And feels the first hot torment of the fleas
He is too proud to scratch for, blister him!
(There's but one point I boggle over, still,
How came the Pinzons to be led astray,
In this unchancy voyage to Noman'sland,
For they are skilful pilots and sane men?
Tush, tush—and have no honest men been fooled
By knaves before in this deceitful world?
It must be so. They should have come to me.
Yet, I could wish they did not go themselves,
For that's the test.)
                          Return? Return? How can he return?
Suppose, since we're supposing miracles,
They do return—five years from Easter Day,
Surely 'twill be no sooner!—even suppose,
The few survivors strut in cloth of gold—
Are there no storms and perils of the deep,
No dog-faced men, no land and water fiends,
No heathen arrows, no expedient pest
To blot one gangling youngster from the list?
Often coughs hollow—has his chest of lath
And dainty in his feeding as a prince
For all his lean voracity of eye—
Yes, yes indeed—there's solid comfort there
And God protects the honest, after all!
O jest, o priceless and sufficing jest,
O men and wives and cousins! O my ribs!
They'll ache tomorrow. Cousin, fare you, well?

So they go by, brown face and Latin hand,
And, with them, go three strange and alien ghosts.
Luis de Torres, the converted Jew,
The liquid-eyed interpreter of tongues
Who found his Greek and Coptic little aid
When he was set to question naked chiefs
In a green jungle, drenched with yellow sun.
"*Where is the gold mine?*" Now he tries again,
in Latin, and the savage nods and smiles,
Offering food and flowers. He shakes his head.
"*Where is the gold mine?*" in Armenian.

"Where is the gold? Do you believe in God?"
The voice dies out. The jungle swallows it.
The parrots screen about his dazzled head.

And you, what freak of fortune brings you here,
You, with the ruddy color of the North,
Who clench your fists before you draw your knife
And freckle with the sun before you tan?
What Bristol cog or London merchantman,
"Lion" or "Fortune" or "Deliverance"
Left you marooned upon a Spanish quay,
Biting your thumbs at fortune? Was it dice
Woman or shipwreck, luck or promises
Or the mere accidents of daily bread
That cast you out like flotsam on the tide?
Who struck you with a rod of almondwood
And changed the very letters of your name
Out of their grating Saxon to the slow
Ripple of Spanish waters on the stone?
What shepfolds do you dream of in your dreams,
Tallarte de Lajes, native of England?
And do you ever jog your memory
For phrases of a half-forgotten past
Out of a tongue now foreign, to disturb
One other exile with a distant year
When he was not Guilelmio Ires
But knew the blossom on the Galway thorn
And the black rocks of Aran out at sea?
Pass by—pass by—we question you in vain.
You are two men. If you were Arthur Lake
And William Rice or William Irishman
Once, in a dream, it shall not profit
Now that the ships are ready for the sea.

It is for this—the birth in the unknown year,
The shabby house in the sea-port, crowded and small,
The bowl of pasta under the evening-lamp
And the five children around it.
                           We know the names.
We must know the house, since the tablet stares from the
   wall,

For it has been fixed there for more than forty years
And tablets never tell lies, once the mayor has come
To pull the string he unveils them, after the speech.
There are letters of gilt on marble. There is a crowd
And photographs are taken. The paper says
Next morning, in three columns, how all went well,
Including the toots of the regimental band
Who played appropriate airs. The weather was fine.
The descendant of the hero was simply dressed
But seemed much moved by the tribute.

                                    There was a time
When heroes walked the street in the angry flesh,
Felt heat and cold, ate onions and went to bed
And never had enough money—but that is done.
We have made all safe for you, now. The hero is tame.
You can copy the long inscription on the wall
With a fountain pen in your diary and never once
Remember he came from two bodies. There is his pen.
There is his chair, his table, his uncles's hat
And a chamberpot of the time. It is all quite safe.
The stairs are stairs. The windows open and shut.
The crack in the ceiling is an actual crack.
The woodwork has been restored on the best advice.
We can show you all of the hero except the hero.

And yet it was, though we cannot find it again
In chairs or tables or portraits painted to please
The fame, from the words of others, when death had
     stripped
The body of its strong muscles and stubborn flesh
And cleansed the skull of the coiled, pulsating brain;
Though there is neither life-mask nor death-mask cut
To show how the eyes looked out and the lips were
     curved
And the years marked cheek and forehead but not the
     will.
Tall man, grey-eyed as Odin, striding Italian,
Blond in your youth as the straw of Italian wheat
But early grey, the forehead arched like a dome,
The face rather full than meagre, the color high,
Big-boned, mighty-limbed, strong-handed, hard to
     wear out,

Though later plagued by the gout and the waking swoons
That left you for hours speechless—
                                        I turn my eyes
To the faces shown in the portraits you never saw.
This is a saint and this is a dreaming lion.
This smooth, sly cleric might share with Machiavel
The chestnuts of his exile and find them sweet.
This decked hidalgo never laid hand to rope.
This last smacks more of the sailor, but who can tell?

I see a boy's hand, stripping on iron comb
Through greasy wool—I hear the thud of the loom,
And with it, mixing, the noises of port and quay,
The wind blowing past the harbor, the nameless smell,
The lingua-franca, blent of a dozen tongues
That the sailors talk to each other, the lying, lame

Disrated bo'sun, telling the streetboys tales.
There were three brothers, one that we do not know
And two that you put your trust in.
                                        "Remember, sons,"
You say in your will to the sons of the two dim women,
Felipa, the wife that you left in Portugal
And Beatriz, who lies heavy on your soul,
"Remember sons, remember to be friends.
I have known no better friends than my two brothers."
There was a sister married a cheesemonger
And doubtless thrived, a mother who lived and died,
A father, weaver of wool, who got into debt
And out again, to die leaving debts unpaid,
Domenico Colombo. It was a name
Common as wool or ships for the time and place.
And the gods should father a hero with godlike seed
If he is to prove immortal.
Yet one man turned to his wife in the aching night
Neither in youth nor rapture, but with the mere
Desire of the simple, after the long day done,
And the tired, familiar embrace was mortal enough.

It is for this—the first vague landfall made
By the boy of fourteen, all elbows and feet and hands,

Big for his years, no doubt, but new to his ship
And cursed when his long legs stumbled.

                                  "O nameless brat,
Whose aunts are known for women of public shame,
Whose father was a bachelor till he died,
Descendant of a blue ghost and a sick sardine,
Who taught you to spit to windward?"

                                  It is for this,
The lean years of the apprentice, the obscure
And needy ballad of youth that the man forgets,
Thrusts down in his mind or alters to suit the fame,
The small shames, the petty triumphs, the fight to rise.
Always the bleak, unending fight to rise.

There may have been a time of study and toil
At Pavis—and a boy who listened awhile
To learned doctors, talking cosmography,
And then went back to the loom or the naked sea—
But we are not certain of it, despite his word.
We know the big fist, hardened by helm and rope,
Was clever at maps and sketches and penmanship,
We know there were books and knowledge sought in the
   books
And men sucked dry of their knowledge to quench a thirst
That grew by the draughts it sought for, as if they were
No torrents of earth it drank of, but the salt
Mid-ocean wave, the elixir of the sea.
We know there were many journeys and many ports.
(It is for this, the buffets in the dark,
The counters lost and won and lost again
In the long game of rising, in the long
Roving beneath the still unlucky stars.)
And Portugal at the last.

                            Now the man is still
Not old in years but the hair had begun to grey.
It is time to marry, time to settle and thrive
In Lisbon or Port Santos like other men
Who wed with sea-captains' daughters and sail the seas
For the pay that buys bed and cradle and christening-fee
And keeps the house snug in winter.

                                You have risen.

You are a skilful seaman, you draw shrewd maps,
You should not lack for employment.

                                        What drives you forth
To the last rocks of Port Santos, to stare and stare
Westward, at utter ocean, with clouded eyes?
Why do you sit at nights by a guttered flame
To read in a dead man's log-books? His daughter's here
To teach you more kindly knowledge. Is she not fair?
Has she not borne you a son? Go, look at the child,
Forget these dreams, these broken sailors you ply
With wine and talk till they wrangle like drunken gulls,
Screaming of undiscovered, unholy shores,
These tales you gather from every living lip
Of nuts and seeds and carved timbers, come from the
    west,
Strange corpses, cast on far islands, of men unknown,
Forget this Toscanelli the Florentine
You write to for further knowledge. Forget the king.
No king will listen to you, talk as you may.
You are risen to some small credit. Let it suffice.

It is for this—the sleights and the strategems,
The cards reshuffled, the wearisome hand replayed
Again and again and again and each time lost.
The shoes worn out in the anterooms of the great.
The voice grown husky, dinning at the deaf ear.
The legerdemain with eggs and parables
To tickle the fool to listen, the promise staled,
The endless journeys, the endless interviews,
The patronage of dukes, the bounty of priests,
The bone tossed to the beggar to shut his mouth
But never halting an instant, for good or ill,
The dread, loquacious persistence of tongue and pen,
Or bating a single jot of the arrogance
That claimed like a king from kings when it spoke of pay,
The false alarms of hope, the cup snatched away
Just as the hand had raised it to the dry lips—
(Meanwhile we have fled, with our son, from Portugal.
That king played false with our project. We give him up.
We will send our brother, Bartholomew, to try
If the English king may serve us. It matters not

What toil he spends to gain the mind of the king.
He is our brother and trusty.
                              We are for Spain.
True, they war with the Moors, they will be stubborn to
    move.
But what are years to our project? What is time
But days gone by like the wave? We begin again?
Well then, we begin again. We will pray a little
To God whose pledged and acknowledged servant we are,
Buy a mule and start on our travels with a calm heart.
Our wife may live or die, but we take our son.
He is ours and shall live to aid us.
                              And, in this Spain,
Exile, adventurer, grim and unwearied ghost,
With life half over and with nothing gained
But the repeating of a single tale
Till it has grown so much a part of us
It whispers in the beating of our blood,
Sleeps with our sleep, wakes with our wakening,
Constant as hunger, true as poverty,
Inseparable as the hope deferred,
We yet, in some brief passage out of Time,
Shall, for a little, lose account of it,
Kissing the ghostly lips of Beatriz
Whose name shall lie so heavy on our soul.)

It is for this, the gaining of friend and patron,
The councils held, the talking, the verdict lost,
The instant appeal, the endless, intricate chess
Played with a woman for fortune.
                              I see that board
Like a seaman's card between them. The red-haired queen
Stares at the stationed pieces with cool, blue eyes.
She has known since youth that she was a match for men
But it has not made her reckless, though she can dare
More greatly then her husband, with the exact
Sure daring of river-tempered, Toledo steel.
She is fair, as gold-lettered steel, she is shrewd and
    prudent
As a precise, fine instrument of steel
And her heart will give, if you strike it unhandily,

The steely ring of the bigot, for all the grace
Of look and gesture, the open largeness of mind
That draws the skilful to serve her.
                                        Do not think
She sits like a frozen angel, stiff in her chair,
No, the eyes are alert and candid, the grave lips smile,
That mask that all queens must wear is a pleasing mask.
Here is a man with a project. My wise men say
He is daft, yet let us consider. We should know men.
It is our business to know them. (The firm, plump hand
Moves a golden bishop forward to spy the land.)
Daft, daft—yet he draws us, somehow. We do not think
A daft man could gain our interest as this man does
And we should be too busied with holy wars
To have much patience with weaklings.
                                        (Now what will he play?
His pieces are made of the driftwood of the five seas
But he has dyed them with something thicker than paint
And it is the skill we strive with that keeps us here.)
He wears monk's robes, but we see no madness in that.
Nay, virtue, rather. Let us deal with him so.
He rallies his broken pawns for a new attempt?
Here's stubborness! We might wish that some of our lord's
Fine gentlemen had an equal stubbornness.
It would not illy become them. Yes, we might wish
That burning singleness of mind and will
For many gentlemen—
                        (Check—and countercheck—
And the mate forced, so. What now? He would play again?
Well, let him play, in the name of the mercy of queens
Though he plays long games, by conscience!)
                                        If it be true—
And the man seems no mere liar—if he could find
A sea-road into the Indies—We drive the Moors,
We thrust the Jews from our nation, we admit
The Holy Inquisition to guard our faith.
There are three strokes for God in a troublous time—
But if we could plant the Cross on the golden sands
Of far Cipango—there are our merchants, too—
And to bring Christ's word to far nations—They give us gold
But we give them mercies immortal—
                                        Ha, what is this?

He presses us too closely to suit our mind.
Must queens decide in a moment? It has been years?
Let him wait some trifle longer.
                              We hide the queen
So, in another battle. Aha, well-played!
He seeks her still. He will not be put off or checked.
His driftwood pieces circle her very throne.
He will not doff one atom of his pretence.
Now, by saints and angels, our liking goes out to him
And should we decide to aid him, we'll find the gold
Though we pledge our jewels for it!
                              You smile, my lord?
There will be no need for such gestures? Perchance,
    perchance,
But is it common and matter of every day
That Isabella should speak so?
                              Yet let him wait
A little still, while we con the matter again,
And bate some portion of these mighty rewards
He claims from us, should he prosper.
                              What, what, he's gone?
Gone from our court—set off for our neighbor France
To give his golden Indies to sleek King Charles?
Who let him 'scape like this? How are we served
By all of you, to let such prizes slip
Out of our hands and break our promises?
Come, you waste time in these apologies.
Search for him instantly! We are the Queen.
He shall have every tittle of his terms,
Caravels, crows, tenth-portion of the gold,
Don's title, regent's power, high admiralty,
All that he asks but hasten—bring him back!

So the game is won. So the hoofs of a dusty horse
Ring upon Pinos Bridge and a messenger
Hales back a white-haired man on his way to France.
One would like to know what they thought when they
    spoke again,
The red-haired queen and the sailor risen at last,
For both were uncommon creatures.
                              I do not know.
But I see him taking the letters for the Great Khan

With a firm hand.
　　　　　　　　They believed. He had beaten his stars.
There were other moments to come but not that moment.
If he slept that night, he slept well.
　　　　　　　　　　　　　If he waked and saw
The dawn rise over the roofs of Santa Fe,
He found it a princely omen.
　　　　　　　　　　Such men are not
The stern-lipped heroes we cherish in schoolboy-tales.
Their sternness is other sternness.
　　　　　　　　　　　And such as he
Come, weeping and laughing, out of that fertile earth
Which, in one span of time,
Nourished Savanarola and Lorenzo,
The saints, the poisons, the traitors, the great art,
Warm as the sun on Simonetta's flesh
And cold as Simonetta in the grave,
Lamb-earth and wolf-earth, earth of the extremes,
The double earth that feeds the double spirit

It was the grey half-hour before dawn
When they cast off. The sails began to fill.
There had been prayers before, no doubt. There were
Jokes, cries, farewells, a tedium of waiting
For the grey blur of watchers, who had come
Heartsick or curious or half-asleep
To see the last of them.
All ships have always sailed to those farewells.
You cannot turn away till the ship sails
And not feel empty, though the morning's cold
And you used up your triteness long ago.
A man blew on his fingers. A woman moaned.
An emissary fidgeted and stared,
Impatient to be gone from his bad inn.
The ships lay black and vague on the grey river.
Nothing would ever stir them.
　　　　　　　　　　Then, all at once,
The thin wail rose, the watchers came alive,
Calling and jostling, suddenly united
In outcry, for an instant not to last
As the first vessel slowly moved downstream.

They saw it from the corners of their eyes.
(The crews, the rope and timber of the ships.)
They heard the thin wail rise and die away,
Mixed with the bo'sun's shout.
They were too busy with their hands to strike
Befitting postures or philosophize
But, when the sails leaned forward, they knew this.
That string of houses, pulled away from them
By wind and current, had been Palos once
But now, and suddenly, it was the land
And they were going out.
                           The river ran.
The first taste of the spray came, salt and sharp.
The sun was risen with heat, now.
Back in the port, the watchers straggled home,
Ate, or wiped off the tears, or prayed to God
For miracles of rescue.
                           They were gone.
Now the long billow of Atlantic met them.
And, when night fell again, they were out at sea.

"*Ay de mi, ay de mi,*
We are alone on the grey sea!"

"Whereas, most Christian, noble, excellent
And powerful princes, King and Queen of Spain,
Lords of the islands of the sea, our sovereigns,
In this the year of 1492
I saw your royal banners placed by arms
Upon Alhambra's towers and beheld
The Moorish king come forth to kiss your hands . . ."

"*Ay de mi, ay de mi,*
We lived on the land most wantonly
But we are punished, being at sea."

"Immediately then, in consequence
Of information given your Highnesses
By me, concerning India and the Grand
Khan, which is, in our language, King of Kings;

How that he often had entreated Rome
To send him doctors of our holy faith
But was not so provided; for which lack
Numberless souls were lost and still are lost
Therefore your Highnesses, as Catholic Christians,
Determined to send ME, CHRISTOBAL COLON,
To the said parts of India, to view
The said princes and peoples and their lands
And find how best convert them . . ."

"Ay de mi, ay de mi,
We are bound for the devil and may not flee.
For all around is the cruel sea!"

". . . Ordering that I should not go by land
Eastward, as is the custom, but by sea,
Voyaging West, by which course, till this year
We do not know that anyone hath passed,
And, for that purpose, heaped great favors on me,
Ennobling me. . . . ."

"Tell tell Pilar she need not grieve
Ay de mi!
There will be other fools to thieve.
Ay de mi!
Tell her her longing goes to waste.
The sea has made her lover chaste,
It was but water she embraced.
Ay de mi, ay de mi!"

". . . High Admiral of the Ocean Sea,
Perpetual Viceroy and governor
Of all the islands and the continents
By me discovered or to be discovered
Within the confines of the Western Main,
These titles passing to my oldest son
And so to his, forever and forever . . ."

"Tell all our kin the thieving's past.
Ay de mi!
And we are honest men at last.

Ay de mi!
Tell them they may dress in black
And beg the sea for what they lack.
Honest men do not come back.
Ay de mi!"

".... Departed therefore
To Palos, where I armed three ships and sailed
For the Canary islands of your Highnesses
To steer my course thence and to navigate
Until I should arrive at India
And so deliver your high embassy ..."

"Tell all the brats we leave behind,
Ay de mi!
Their daddy was the Western wind.
Ay de mi!
They need not know what stranger came
To stake us in a devil's game.
They should not even know his name.
Ay de mi!"

"... Also, my sovereign Princes, I propose
Not only to set down here every night
Each happening of the day, and every day
To mark all navigation of the night
But also to draw up and make a chart
Showing all lands and waters of these seas
And, further, to compose
A book and illustrate the whole in picture,
By latitude and longitude.
                              Wherefore
It will be necessary to forget
The need of sleep and watch each mile of sea
Closely and shrewdly to do all these things,
Which will be a great labor. ..."

"O kings and princes, who are ye?
Ay de mi!
That send us on this drowning sea?
Ay de mi!

Curst be the wind and curst the wave,
And curst of all this white-haired knave
Who leads us to our living grave!
Ay de mi, ay de mi!"

They touched at the Canaries to refit
After but six days sail. He had not thought
To spend three weeks there, eating out his heart
With more delays, but he was used by now
To the black bread of patience, and it must be.
The Pinta's rudder had broken the second day
And Martin Pinzon brought her into port
Limping and yawing like a crippled quail.
It might be accident. He was not sure.
He knew the owners men of little faith
In voyage or Indies or monk-admiral
But he thought Pinzon trusty.

                         Let it pass
For chance, at need. There must be other ships
To take the Pinta's place—

                     What not one bark?
Well, patch her then, patch her as best you may
And see you change the Nina's lateen sails
To square ones, for she lags too far behind,
Rigged as she is. The men are not content?
They will be less content a month from now.
My foot is on the path and yet I halt,
Tethered by spiderwebs to these smooth isles.
When will I see my Indies?

                      Yet he spared
Nor time nor labor to make all secure
In the three cockleshells that were his fleet,
Topheavy beanpods, high at bow and stern,
Square-sailed, broad-waisted, squatting on the seas
Like ugly ducklings.

                   Only one was decked,
The Santa Maria, known for her dull sailing,
But chosen as the flagship of the fleet
Since she was sixty-three feet over all
And had a kennel where an admiral

Might stow his chest and break his shins on it
When he turned in, at dawn.
                              You could have stowed her
With all sail spread in a cathedral aisle
And never touched the transept with her prow
Or shadowed the side-chapels with her sails
But she seemed big to them.
                              She had a deck.
They cursed her for a sluggard but were proud.
Juan de la Cosa owned her.
                              For the rest,
The crews lived as crews lived, in dirt and wet,
Huddled in the high poops for rest and sleep
And grateful for the blessed noisomeness
That made the sea-drenched gear begin to steam
From the mere heat of packed and stifling flesh,
Sleeping spoon-fashion in the crawling dark.
The pilots had the quarters of their rank.
Quarters an oiler on a Biscay tramp
Would turn his nose at—but they found them meet,
Skilled men and grave, knowing their dignity
And making others know it, with the slow
Stare that such pilots turn upon the fool,
The tired stare of the long-remembering eyes.
You'll find them in another incarnation,
Dressed in their broadcloth, Mississippi kings,
Reading the river like a muddy book,
Gods of the freckled boys of river-towns
From Hannibal to Natchez and the sea,
But, sea or river, steam or painted sail,
They're always pilots.
                              For the other folk,
Assayer, notary, historian,
It is not written how they were bestowed
Nor in what hole or corner of his ship
Luis de Torres, the converted Jew
Interpreted the misery of his flesh
To an uncomprehending cabin-wall,
Dreaming, perhaps, in the last ghostly qualm
And faintness of exhuastion, that he heard
Out of great waters an immortal voice

And quaked, because the God of Abraham
Had found him out in his apostasy.

We know they sailed through channels of green isles,
Stowed water and provision, mended gear,
And saw the lofty cone of Teneriffe
Smoke like a demon dancing in a flame,
They saw the flames, they heard the mountain groan.
They crossed themselves and muttered. It was ill.
It was an ill beginning. The admiral's voice
Talked of volcanoes. Let him talk his fill.
He was the admiral but they were seamen
And knew bad luck from good.
                                        The muttering died
But Pedro, the sea-lawyer, fed on it
And had a bale of devils for their ears
That very eve that left them sick at heart.
Now, for three days, they loitered near the land
That lingered like a tantalizing ghost
Just within sight, desirable and green
While the breeze failed to such exhausted airs
As barely stirred the Admiral's white hair.

He tramped the deck, watched every hopeful cloud,
Wrote in his journal, wore the time away
As such men do who are not easy men
Nor patient by their natures, but have learned
To look like patience through extremity,
Taut as a bowstring underneath their calm
And vexed by all the bitterness of dreams.
Their hearts beat to another time than ours
And they're not grateful to their miracles
For they've expected them since they were born.
They will survive the deep and mortal wound
And bleed at every needle-prick of chance,
Never quite absent from the narrow cell
Wherein they hold unending colloquy
With the unswerving God they know they serve
But do not know they alter, day by day,
Until He is their likeness, only crowned.

Now, in the glassy mirror of the sea,
He saw himself stand up before the Khan
And take the water from the golden dish
For the baptizing.
                    Now he heaped the gold
Before the dazzled eyes of Ferdinand
And the crowd clamored and the Queen said "Rise!"
Now he had gained his audience with the pope
And was embarked upon that last Crusade
Which should not fail, because it was his own.
Now, on his entry of Jerusalem,
After the crushing of the Moslem host
At the place called Armageddon—
                              The scene dissolved.
He was the master of three leaky ships
Becalmed, by the Canaries. That was all.
Viceroy and governor of emptiness,
High Admiral of Nothing, don of Nowhere,
The titles passing to his eldest son
Forever and forever.
                    The glassy mirror
Ruffled a little, smoothed, ruffled again.
The breeze came with the sunset. God was true.

Down in the waist, an unrepentant thief
Groaned to his comrade, and a stripling wept.

The morning came.
The three specks crawled upon an endless blue,
Empty as space, alone, a gradual curve
Of blue that ended where it touched the sky
And the faint line divided blue from blue.
It was the middle of eternity
And they died in it. They could watch the wake
And know they moved. They saw the petty white
Spend into blue and die away in it.
But, when they looked beyond,
They knew they stood as still as the fixed stars,
Hung in a void of nothing beyond nothing
Away, away to the horizon-line
And nothing there except small, stuffless cloud;

Crawling the gradual and solid curve
Of palpable, blue nothing,
Interminably, with a moveless speed,
The phantom haste of runners in a dream.

The sun rose. The sun sank. It was a day.
The stars came out. The wind blew all the night
Westward and Westward. There was no more land.

Now, knowing that he could not trust his crew,
(He says) he kept a secret reckoning
Of the true distance traversed night and day
But gave them out a tale of fewer leagues
That they might think themselves the nearer home
And not lose heart, in eyeshot of the goal;
There was no log. He judged the speed they made
By weed and bubbles and the drifting scum
Seen from the poop. He had an hour glass
To mark the time, but men forgot to turn it
And he was wroth.
                    For other admiral's gear
There was a compass, a crude astrolabe,
Good for the time, some manner of a chart
Three-quarters guess however it was drawn
And showing sea from Spain to India,
These, and a guess of seven hundred leagues
From Ferro to Cipango, which was wrong.
These, and the eyes, these and the seamanship,
These and the will that knew it could not yield.

The second day from the Canaries, fair
With following winds. The distance from known land
Reckoned at best some hundred fifty leagues.
This day, there floated by
Stump of a broken mast from some wrecked ship,
Now waterlogged, so from no recent wreck
But evident as such. No other trace
Of flotsam that might tell of wreck or ship,
Though, from the mast, we judge her to have been
Larger than our own flagship.
                    Third day fair.

Fourth day continued fair and nought to mark
Save that our compass-needle seems to veer
From its fixed steadfastness to the North Star,
Straying Northwest a little every league,
Which is unheard-of. Keep it from the crew.
Fifth day, a heron and a junco seen,
And it is known they cannot keep the air
More than a score of leagues away from land
So they must be good omens. Speak of them.
Sixth night, beheld a mighty flame of fire
Fall, suddenly, out of a cloudless sky
Into the calm and star-reflecting deep
But four or five leagues distant—very strange
And aweful, so to see it hiss and fall
And the crew muttering it was from God.
All flames, all powers, all ruins are from God,
But we will do Him the humility
To think, if He desired to chasten us,
He would not loose a judgment from His hand
And overshoot us by five leagues of sea,
Especially when He has granted us
Such signal favors and clear promises
In the still nighttime, after the long fast,
When all the limbs grow light and something wakes;
In the hot blinding of the dizzy sun
When the Queen had not listened and the glare
Beat stunningly from the white marketplace;
And in the cool, the refuging dim gloom,
Praying before the candles, hour on hour,
Until they turned to little pins of flame;
The still voice speaking, low and confident,
"Christopher, my good servant,"
How can this rabble of the dockside know?

The seventh day, fair, mild and temperate,
Showing God's will.
                    Our pilots much dismayed
To see the compass vary more and more
And now so greatly it could not be hid
From knowledge of the crew, who took it ill,
Seeing the very eyesight of the ships,
The one pathfinder of the trackless wave

Now play them false.
                              (*"What are these seas we sail?*
Mary above, what are these seas we sail
That can corrupt cold iron with their breath?
It is another world, another world!")

The Admiral, who had secretly considered
This difficult matter, hoping it might pass,
Now was at sundry pains to prove to them
That it could be, at worst, no devilwork
But a mere shifting of the bleak North Star.
True, this hath never been observed before
But all stars have their courses, as we know,
And what could make the iron turn aside
Unless the star moved also?
                              Thus instructed,
They quieted and did not mutiny.

Saw herb and floating weed and in the weed
Found a live crab and kept it for a sign.
And now they passed
Into the keeping of the great, calm Trades
Who rule the ocean of those latitudes
In temperate, serene magnificence,
Law-giving kings, whose thrones are summer cloud,
Whose barbless tridents never knew the storm,
Robed in unsullied waters, seamen's friends,
Steadily blowing West and ever West
With grave and unremitting majesty.

He drank the morning. It was bland and pure
As Andalusian Aprils, and as sweet.
The knotted cords about his heart and brain
Slackened a little, He was sure of God
But now he did not have to pray to Him
For this was peace, this was cool-bodied peace
Touching his burning forehead with her hand
And gentle as a spirit with his pain.
He had great gifts, but few were happy ones
And none made others happy, soon or late,
And yet I think that he was happy then,
For a few rare and unreturning days,

Happy and curious as a busy child,
Half won to a forgotten innocence
Almost an hour, breathlessly alive
To every sight and smell and taste and sound,
Stretching his hands to all, washed clean of care
By an unasked and ample and slow magic,
By the unhurried, ever-blowing wind.

They sailed so well. The mornings were so cool.
The steady bronze blew West and always West.
For many days they did not shift a sail.

The men themselves were glad enough of ease
And the gay weather. Notary and Jew
And every other oddity aboard
Crawled from their cupboards like drenched dragonflies
To buzz and look about with landsmen's eyes
And dry their rumpled wings in the bright sun.
They felt that they had suffered. They felt brave.
They thought how they would tell the dangerous tale
When they were home. One could be calm and think
Of pleasant horrors now,
With nothing but a shiver of the mind,
A just sufficient tingling in the skin,
Not the true knife, the frozen stab of fear.
One could look out at sea and almost yawn.

And then the whispering began to run
From one man to another, in the dark
As day succeeded day and the Trades blew
And the blue magic of the weather held,
Whispering that the breeze could never change
Nor they return against it, but must drive
Westward and Westward till the end of Time
And die marooned upon some heathen isle,
Grey prisoners of an unchanging wind,
Offered like sacrifices on the sea.

So, though all fortune seemed to smile at them,
They scared themselves with phantoms but made haste,
Crowding all canvas on. Land must be near.
There was a flight of birds, a flight of clouds,

And masses like low islands in the north.
Press on, press on!
                    The morning broke. No land.

They sounded with two-hundred-fathom line
For bottom, but could find none. Drizzling rain
Began to fall. That might betoken land.
But the day passed and the night followed it
And now they floated upon weedy seas
And, with the evening, came three singing birds
That circled round the ships like choristers,
Reminding every man of the dear land
With their sweet jargon and their pretty song,
Singing of the long pasture, loved of man,
The earth of his true harvests, the tree-shaded
And murmuring, fresh streams that succor him,
The fires that keep the winter from his heart,
And, at the last, they sang of how he lies,
Image of earth, to earth returned and sleeps
In comfortable earth, not far from home,
And, when the morning came, they flew away.

And all next day, the longing vessels lay
Becalmed or barely moving to light airs,
Amidst a mocking image of their dream,
An endless meadow of green, floating weed,
Tangled and salt and stretching everywhere.

Now the wind veered, and so one terror passed,
The dread of being blown beyond return
By an East wind unending.
                          Now they feared
The tireless drifting of the matted weed,
That seemed to close around them more and more
As if it had a will and plucked at them
With an infinity of tiny hands
To draw them in, at last,
To that old, fabled hell of derelicts,
The dead, stagnated center of all calms
Where the strong ships lie mastered by the weed
And every cockboat has its skeletons
But even the last rats are dead and gone.

Next day they came into more open water
And, for two days, they glided sluggishly
Upon a sea as placid as a pool.
Too calm, they thought, too calm. They watched the wind
They had distrusted with as anxious care
As if it were their child and sickened fast.
If it should fail, no other wind might rise
For years to vex the stillness of these mild
And lakish waters, barely slipping past
With the dry lisp of wind rather than water.
They sounded with the line. No bottom still.

This was the day they saw Leviathan,
The fish of the great waters, the king whale
Sporting himself with ocean for his bath
And marvelled at him—and were grieved with him,
Because he was no island but a beast,
Because he need not wait upon the wind,
Because he knew where there was rest and land.
And now began the season of false hopes
And growing clamor, the embittered time
Of fraying nerve, wild rumor, and distrust.
Each day the Admiral dangled in their eyes
Some toy or trinket, promising release,
Some reason why they must be near the goal,
And every night still found them far at sea.
And every night, alone,
Tireless and cunning and unmerciful,
He bent above the fragments of the day
And out of its base metal forged anew
The chiming bauble of another dream,
Good for the morrow, transient as the wave,
But serving, with the ceaseless, silvery tongue
To coax the ships a little farther still.

Sometimes, he says, God aided, as when now
After two days of barely furrowing
Long lifeless waves, a sudden swell arose
Unheralded by wind, and broke the spell
That lay like a dead water on their hearts.
Saying it mounted like the Red Sea wave
And was as great a providence of God.

And, next day, Martin Pinzon saw the land
Lying Southwest, near sunset, in the red
Stream of the sunset, like a floating cloud,
And they all knelt and sang the *Gloria*
Strongly and gleefully, and drove for it,
Changing their course to reach it with the dawn
And, in the morning, it had passed away.
The seven days that followed were the same,
The sky scanned with the hunger of the eyes,
The birds, the weed, the signal given again
By flag and bombard of approaching land,
The exultation, the waiting, the despair.
And, on the evening of the seventh day,
They still drove on, almost two months from Spain,
And one and thirty days from their last land,
And there was nothing anywhere but sea.

It was that evening that they changed their course
Southwest once more, to follow certain birds,
And so lost more than westing, and the fate
That might have broken them upon Cape Fear
Or, at its pleasure, haled them into port
To name the Carolinas with the slow
Grave names of Spanish angels.
                                    It might have been.
It was not in the omens.
                          Now, night and day,
He scanned his reckonings. Land must be near
Or he was mad and all he trusted vain.
They had traversed the seven hundred leagues
He counted to Cipango, days ago.
Three thousand miles of sea,
And still the wind blew and the water ran
And the huge ocean ended with the sky
But with no nearer bound.
                            They had set sail
In Summer. Now the year turned toward its Fall.
Where would the winter find them.
                                  Yet he was sure,
Sure of the land as if he walked on it
And all was fair and glowing and desired
As his fantastic spirit joyed in all,

The cloudless sky, the flotsam on the sea
(It must be land-weed, now.)
And the good breeze that blew them West and West
Fragrant as May and morning in Seville
—All but the fearful and the weary men
Who looked on all and felt their spirits die.

He swears the Indies are not far.
Ay de mi!
No farther than the Western star!
Ay de mi!
Will nothing cure him of the sea
But the bare steel of mutiny?
Must we slay him to be free?
Ay de mi, Ay de mi!

It was the breaking-point. They cried "Return!"
They shook their fists and railed. He promised them
Reward upon reward, but they were sick
Of stale, deceptive, endless, promises
And the rewards of bladderweed and spray.
"Return, return! We suffer here no more!
Return or we are damned eternally!"
Yet, in the end, he lashed them with his tongue
And drove them to the ropes again, unwilling.
—Magellan saying they could eat the leather
From the ship's spars before he would return
And Hudson lowered to his last command,
Sick and a captain, by the mutinous hands
That set him drifting in an open boat
To pay him for they suffering they had.
Cover the greatness with the wreaths of fame
And yet, remember these.
Thinking of greatness, still remember these.—
Knowing he so could drive another time,
Perhaps another still, and then the end.
He turned the hour-glass with steady hands,
The seaman having forgotten. The sands run slowly
But, fast or slow, they are run out at last.

All Thursday the eleventh of October
Sailed West Southwest, upon a mounting sea,

Higher than hitherto, and, as he sailed
Saw floating pardelas and a green rush,
The men upon the Pinta saw a reed
And fished a little stick out of the waves
Once marked or cut by iron. From the Nina
Came message of a dog-rose-covered bough,
So breathed more freely. Sunset of that day
They had run twenty-seven leagues.

        At dark,
The Admiral sailed his first course to the West
And, at the hour of ten o'clock at night,
Standing upon the castle of the poop,
Beheld a light.

     At first, so indistinct
He did not dare affirm that it was land
Being so faint, and like the feeble gleam
Of some wax-candle, moving up and down
As if in signal. Nevertheless, he called
Pedro Gutierrez, a king's chamberlain,
Who also thought he saw it. Summoned then
Rodrigo Sanchez de Segovia
Who said that he saw nothing.

       Nevertheless
The Admiral was sure, and when they sang
The *Salve,* which they used to sing each eve,
The Admiral admonished every man
To keep the sharpest lookout for the land
And promised a silk doublet in reward
Besides the pension offered by the King,
Ten thousand maravedis every year.
They then continued on their Western course,
The Pinta leading, as she sailed the best,
Till two hours after midnight.

       Then a gun
Fired from the Pinta told that land was found.
Rodrigo de Triana saw it first
But the reward and pension were adjudged
The Admiral's, since he had seen the light.
The land seemed two leagues off. They took in sail
And lay all night there under storm-square sails
Waiting for dawn.

      And, when the dawn had broken,

A savage, waking out of a green sleep,
Going to wash his body in the sea,
Looked seaward idly, looked again and stared
And thought "Great birds" and then thought "Magic birds"
And trembled and fell down upon the sand.

And, when the same dawn broke upon the ships
After the endless night, the fevered men
Beheld a level and a pleasant shore
Green as an orchard, full of leaves and trees
And brown specks running from them to the white
Sands of a beach and crowding—naked people,
Indians.

The Admiral and the Pinzons went ashore
In the armed boat, all armed, complete with steel,
Complete with Spanish honor and bright steel,
The monk's robe doffed for unaccustomed steel
And, over it, a floating, scarlet cloak,
Long treasured, hardly spotted by the sea.

He bore the Royal Standard, and the rest
The banners of their voyage, the Green Cross
Where the crowned letters played at King and Queen.
It was a heavy boatload with its steel
And yet the armor on their backs seemed light
As the last ripple washed upon the sand
And the prodigious stiffly stepped ashore,
Carrying God and banners and the steel.

They stared a moment, drinking with their eyes.
They heard the sound of a sweet, noisy stream
In the green wood. They saw the parrots fly.
There was strange, gallant fruit upon the trees,
Fruit of the sun and sleep, untasted peace.
It was a new, fair land.

The Admiral, once the standards were set up,
Instantly summoned the fleet's notary
And, in his presence, and the presences
Of captains, parrots, sand and a king's groom,
Called all as witnesses to certify

That he took full possession of this earth
In the high names of Leon and Castile,
Which, being attested, was at once reduced
To writing, in due form and proper phrase
And fitting depositions signed and sealed,
Rodrigo Descovedo, notary.

The brown, strange people crowded nearer now,
Naked and awestruck, wondering and milk,
To touch the steel of these descended gods
Propitiatingly, with soft, warm hands
And marvel at the beards upon their cheeks
And the uncanny whiteness of their flesh
Where the sun had not tanned it—to receive
The beads of glass, the caps of scarlet cloth,
The first, heavenly gifts.
Later, to cut their fingers on the swords
Which, too, were gifts, after a godlike sense,
Though, in their ignorance, they knew it not,
Since they were naked, without iron or shame.

They seemed poor creatures but they were well-informed
And civil-mannered, swimming to the ships
To bring us fruit and balls of cotton thread,
Parrots and spears. We gave them little bells
Which they delighted in. But they will give
All that they own for scraps of broken glass
If offered, being very uninformed,
Which trading we forbade and ordered none
To buy their cotton save at our command
To take it for your Royal Highnesses.

They have coarse hair and many paint themselves
In diverse fashions. All we saw were men
Save one young girl. Their eyes are beautiful.
The only arms they use are wooden canes
But a few carried little tags of gold
Worn in their noses, so they know of it
And, questioning them by signs, I understood
There is a richer land, some distance south,
Ruled by a mighty king and stuffed with gold.
We strove to win them more by love than fear

And they will make good servants, being mild
And easy to win over to the Faith
Since they have neither weapons nor a God.
If it please God, I will take six of them
When we depart, to show your Highnesses
That they may learn our language and return
Or otherwise be dealth with, as you choose.
Fifty good men could conquer the whole island
And keep all in subjection, as we deem,
And it is very fair and very green
And surely, to the Southward, there is gold.

ON WRITING AND OTHER MATTERS

The purpose of including these selections is to demonstrate Benét's acute insights into his life, his own and others' work, and his sense of humor. I have included here a typescript version of "The Most Unforgettable Character I've Met." A shorter version appeared in Reader's Digest, 37 (Oct. 1940), 113–116. *As far as can be ascertained, the letter to Bloomingdale's has never been published. The letter to John Farrar about "Children's Poems" is without doubt a critique of a manuscript John Farrar had sent him.*

The Most Unforgettable Character I've Met

Some years ago, I went to a dinner that concerned itself with modern education. There were prominent and able speakers and they talked well. True, on some points they disagreed—even educators do that. But on one point they united in severity—the sort of education that produces what they called "the military mind." It so happened that there were no professional soldiers in the audience—nor had any of the speakers, apparently, ever talked to so curious a creature. But they were able to describe him with some exactitude—at least as be existed in the U.S.A. It was a horrific portrait—this man with neither tastes nor interests outside of parades and red tape. But then, as they pointed out, what else could you expect? No sensitive or intelligent man would enter the army in the first place—if he did so, four years of West Point would most certainly indoctrinate him with blood and iron—and the deadening routine of Army peacetime life would take care of the rest. I listened with great interest but, unfortunately, under a handicap. I had been brought up among the men they were talking about and knew something of what they were like. And that, as one of the best of them would have pointed out to me, is always a disadvantage, in a general argument. He taught semantics without ever using the word—he distrusted the large, empty phrase, the snap judgment, the ringing platitude—he loved to take them apart and show you their emptiness. If you came to him mouthing some second-hand opinion, he refused to be satisfied with it—he wanted you to think for yourself. In fact, he would make you think for yourself, whether you liked it or not. He had the most independent and one of the most comprehensive minds I have ever known. By profession, he was an officer in the Ordnance Department of the United States Regular Army.

I was lucky enough to be his son and he taught me a great many things. For one thing, by example, precept and demonstration, he taught me most of what I know about the actual technique of English verse. He could do so because he knew it—and I do not mean by that that he had a gentlemanly acquaintance with the better-known poems of Tennyson and Browning. He knew it from Chaucer to Mary Anne O'Byrne, the Washerwoman poet of Watervliet, N.Y. and his knowledge was extensive and catholic. He introduced us to Beddoes and Stephen Crane, to the early poems of Robinson and the ballads of Father Prout. He could write any fixed form of verse with deftness, precision and tang. And if you came to him with a lame rhyme, a limping meter, an inchoate idea, he could show you, with the precision of a surgeon, just what was wrong. He praised infrequently, but, when he did praise, you knew that you had met a standard, and tingled. I think I worked harder for that praise than for any other—I know no other has meant quite so much to me. That was not because he was my father but because he knew. I do not know where he got his gift of creative criticism—if he had been at the dinner I speak of, he would probably have ascribed it politely to the deadening routine of Army life.

For he knew about that sort of thing and it amused him. He was fond of referring to himself as a member of the brutal and licentious soldiery, with that sidewise glance that hesitated for just one instant to see if you understood what he was talking about and, if you didn't, passed on. That was the way of his mind. It did not endear him to the pompous and the self-important and there were times when it did not endear him to the War Department. During the years that he was stationed in California, several Japanese war-scares blew up and calmed down. They never had any particular result—but they would produce long cipher telegrams from Washington. I remember one particular one when, in lengthy and urgent terms, the Department asked him for an immediate and official report on the "proposed defences" of Benicia Arsenal. My father wired back, tersely, "Benicia Arsenal completely indefensible from any point of view." After that, they let him alone, for a while.

And, as he was a shock to the Department, so, at times, he was a shock to his subordinate officers. He believed in giving them their heads—sometimes they had not been used to that. If a man came to him with some unimportant problem that should have been solved on the man's own responsibility, my father would listen patiently and then say, "Well, Jones, what would you do if I were dead? Consider me dead."

"But Colonel, I—"

"Consider me dead."

So, very soon, they came to trust him and work for him, for they found he had none of the small jealousies of command. He detested efficiency-experts, root and branch—but his work moved smoothly and he got the most out of his men. I asked him about that, once, and he said, with the sidewise glance, "My son, congenital laziness is a very great gift. If you're lazy enough, you will always be able to get people to do your work for you. Now, our family are naturally lazy. Always remember that."

That was not entirely accurate, of course. During the first World War, he commanded the only training camp for Ordnance officers in this country. He was proud of certain things about that command—and that he had a right to be proud of them, the record shows. It had an excellent health record, for one thing—not a minor matter, in a training camp. He protected and fought for his men and their well-being against inefficient cooks, conflicting orders and red tape. He got them trained and sent them out. He was also proud of his one conscientious objector, with whom he would engage in long, philosophic arguments, when he had the time. The objector was an honest man and had come expecting to be martyrized. My father merely argued with him. Having argued with my father myself on abstract problems, I am not quite sure whether the objector might not have preferred the rifle-butts of tradition.

For argument with my father was apt to be a little unsettling for the tender-minded. He would take any side of an argument for the pure joy of controversy. Also, he loved a fool and he loved to draw a fool out till all his candid beauties stood revealed. He did not do it unkindly but the laughing spirit was there. I remember his demonstrating to a rather Y.M.C.A.-minded young officer that every human action, even mother-love, is dictated by the purest selfishness. The demonstration had something of the beauty of an abstract equation. It shook the young man to the core and was completely irrefutable—till my father blew it away with one breath.

"My son, you will find human nature full of curious and interesting peculiarities." That was one of his sayings, and that was his great gift. He loved the human spectacle, and its incongruities. He was never tired of observing it and watching it. He had, for himself, a very high and inflexible sense of honor—but, as an observer, his interest was in seeing how the material behaved. That gave him a curious tolerance, sometimes misconstrued. For he did not fool himself. I remember his saying when we heard of the death of so-and-so, "Yes, X was a thoroughly bad man in a good many ways and I was very fond of him. There are a number of men of great virtue I would rather see dead than X."

It is difficult to explain my own feelings about him, except to say this. I knew, from the time that I was a small boy, that he understood the way I worked. He might not and sometimes did not approve of what I had done—but he knew why I had done it. Now, when you are growing up, even with the most delightful of parents, that does not always happen. It did with me. The comment that came upon my actions was often unexpected, sometimes drastic but never uncomprehending. At the age of sixteen, I became a Jack London socialist. For some time after that my father took considerable pleasure in writing me letters in red ink, concerned with violent plots for the overthrow of capitalism and signed "Yours For The Revolution." I wonder what the War Department would have made of them, if they had ever come to its attention.

His usual letters were signed, "Your respectable father"—a phrase he had taken from a flowery Southern tombstone. It didn't much matter what they were written about—they had a complete flavor of personality. The small domestic events of daily life turned over and laughed beneath his pen. In his letters, in the private diary he kept for many years, he could sketch with the satiric terseness of Jane Austen. Unfortunately, when he sat down at last to write the memoirs he never finished, he grew a little pen-shy. He hadn't the confessing temperament, and, while they are wise, they are more formal than he was.

I don't remember any "good advice" as such—I don't remember any "trying to be a pal"—that most wretched of attempts to bridge the gap between two generations. He never talked "straight from the shoulder," thank the Lord—he never sentimentalized anything. No, I don't remember any of those things that are talked about in articles. I remember a life, a personality, and an example he never tried to show or make anyone else live up to.

In person he was tall and slight—straight but not ramrod straight. There was the stamp of the Army upon him and yet there wasn't—he could be extremely dignified, officially, but, when reading he liked to sprawl, with one leg over the arm of a chair. I remember endless long walks and many games of tennis. His tennis was entirely characteristic—he served underhand, cut every ball and could place the ball on a dime. It infuriated stalwart people who struck great strokes and fell. It infuriated one I remember—an athletic Colonel—who after losing the first set to my father at 6-3 complained that an underhand serve was not in the rule books. My father did not argue the matter—that was not his style. He served overhand for the next two sets—something he had not done in a dozen years—and beat the gentleman 6-1, 6-0. That sort of thing, if remembered, is apt to teach a boy something.

In youth, he must have been a romantic-looking young officer—dark hair, dark eyes and side-whiskers. When my mother first met him he was calling himself Bunthorne and had a sunflower worked on his buttonhole—it was the heyday of "Patience." They married young and happily and, wherever they went, made friends. My mother's warm gift for life made that inevitable. Fortunately, they both loved traveling, and each new post brought new experiences. These included, almost invariably, unusual and delightful people. It could have been otherwise, no doubt—if I gave a list of the posts, you might not be impressed by the names. But names never greatly impressed my mother and father.

They were deeply united, and very different. My mother loved people warmly—my father was interested in the way they behaved. Groups, associations, societies and clubs, especially for worthy purposes, left him entirely indifferent—in these, as in matters of religion, he remained an agnostic and an individualist. Once, when my mother and he were walking along a street in San Francisco, she grew excited and clutched his arm.

"Jack!" she said, "Jack! Do you see that man ahead of us? Why, his pocket's on fire."

"Yes," said my father, tolerantly, "It does seem to be on fire. I've noticed it for some time."

"Noticed it for some time!" said my mother. "Then why didn't you do something about it?"

"Why, I didn't want to disturb him," said my father. "He may be the kind of man who likes to have his pocket on fire."

He liked good manners and hated sloppy thinking. There was nothing of the pedant about him but he had collected, informally and for his own amusement, through the widest sort of reading, a great store of extraordinary, entertaining and, as he said, useless information. I have stated what he knew about the structure of English verse—he knew quite as much about the history of the Byzantine Empire. Curious, apperceptive and making its own judgments, his mind reached out in all directions. A well-meaning lady once asked him if he wouldn't "be lonely" and "need a hobby" when he retired from the army. "Oh, I have one," he said, with his characteristic courtesy, "I intend to collect stuffed whales."

A pity he didn't enter some other career? I wonder if I think so. He could have been a teacher, a lawyer, a critic—with a little luck, the best critic of his time, for he had the discovering eye. But he never was the least bit interested in making money and the ups and downs of a literary life would have worried him. The Army gave him what books cannot—an active life and the handling of men. He never got to be Chief of Ordnance as his father had—he was constitutionally unable to push himself and frequently afflicted by a sense of humor in regard to his official superiors. Still, when the War ended, they were going to make him a brigadier and give him thirty thousand men. They could not very well avoid it for his work had been well done. There are many such men in the Army—men who do their work without quarreling about the reward. Sometimes it is large work too—really quite as important work as running a tobacco-factory or writing a best-seller though, naturally, not so well-paid. There was a classmate of my father's named George W. Goethals. Perhaps he too had what my educators call "the military mind." Yet he did a fairly good job on the Panama Canal.

And yet I have not caught the personality—the warm, living, breathing, thinking man, fastidious, ironic, reticent of his deepest emotions (and yet one knew!)—the fatalist without pose, the gentleman without pretense. He was not a saint and didn't like saints—he made mistakes and had prejudices. He loved to roll the worst verse over his tongue as he loved to savor the best. He had, on those who knew him, an extraordinary and unsought influence. In a world where most human beings are quite content to take their opinions ready-made, he was and remained his own man. He had humor and tolerance but these came from the deep roots of honor. He looked at the world and smiled—a smile of his own. It was interesting, petty, beautiful, hideous, but always interesting. That was where he differed from the pessimist and the reformer, both of whom get violently angry at human nature and want to change it into something else. It interested my father, per se. He had not an unduly high opinion of it, in the mass; but he thought it tried.

So that is what I remember most—the voice could be dry but was never cold beginning some acute remark or preposterous hypothesis with "Well, my son—" while the sidewise glance went by. And whenever I have succumbed to the temptation of being a stuffed shirt I hear its amused and definite comment.

He died twelve years ago and I was not there. But I have been told that, in death, he looked like a Roman senator. And that, too, is very easy for me to believe.

Letter to Bloomingdale's:—

24 Main Street, Stonington, Conn.

On Thursday July 3, I purchased from you, for cash, one number 73 chaisette, grade D1 60326 B1. It arrived this morning and I am writing to tell you how much we are enjoying it. We haven't had so much fun in the family since the gas-heater blew up.

It arrived, of course, in its component parts, according to the good old assumption of department-stores that each customer is also a trained engineer. Usually I do not mind this—it flatters my vanity. I have assembled beds and put together dog-houses. But chaisette number 73 is something else again. I am not blaming the salesman who sold it to me—but when he said that you could put the contraption together in half an hour or so, I think he was hopeful. A crew of skilled mechanics from the River Rouge, working from an adequate blueprint, might be able to do so in the course of an eight-hour day. Without blueprint or directions, and with amateur labor, things are going to take a little longer. By the end of the week, we may be able to get chaisette number 73 so that you can sit upon one portion of it without the rest of it collapsing. At least that is our goal, though sometimes when I look at chaisette number 73, I wonder if it will ever be achieved.

I am not going to ask you if any parts are missing. I am not going to ask you why holes are bored in certain parts of the framework when there seems to be nothing to go in those holes. I am not going to ask you how the little springs on the mattress hook on, or where. I am not going to ask you if the entire thing was designed by Joe Cook.

Though I will make one or two remarks on the quality of the paint wherewith the chaisette is painted. It is nice white paint—nice soft white paint that comes off on the face and the hands and the clothes and the surrounding landscape. Already enough has come off to paint a reasonably-sized shed, but there seems to be plenty left. Was this just an added touch of humor—using gooey paint? Or what?

I am curious to find out, of course, how the handles work—those charming little blue handles that give you a choice of three different positions for the chaisette. Well, perhaps we will know, some day. At present, when you press the handles, either nothing happens at all, or else you are abruptly offered a choice of 73 different positions, most of them landing you on the back of your neck. It is funny, of course. But is it kind? Is it kind of the Bloomingdale Brothers? I didn't ask them for a ball-bearing man-trap—I just wanted something to sit on, to lie on and dream, in the sun.

Please understand, this is not a complaint—merely a record of personal experience with chaisette number 73. It may be of value to you in your dealings with other customers—I do not know. There are others of us who are not trained engineers. Of course, if I could have a photograph or a drawing of what chaisette number 73 is supposed to look like when I get it together—that might be a help. But what I would really like to know is the name of the man whose brain conceived and designed this rubber-tired monstrosity. I would like to know because I should like to fry him, in deep fat.

Very sincerely yours,

Letters to the Guggenheim Foundation

I PLAN FOR STUDY

[SUBMITTED TO THE JOHN SIMON GUGGENHEIM
MEMORIAL FOUNDATION]

[PENCILLED DATE DEC. 11, '25, NOT IN SVB'S HAND]

As regards the plan of study, I shall try to outline my aims as clearly and succinctly as possible, realizing, however, that any plan which deals with unaccomplished creative work cannot be charted quite as definitely as if it dealt with research.

For the past ten years, my chief interest has been the writing of poetry and I feel that I have now reached a point in the development of my work where, if I were financially able, I should devote myself exclusively to that one task for a period of some years. It is, however, practically impossible for an author, under present-day conditions of writing and publishing, to support himself solely by the writing of verse. At least I know that it is impossible for me. This means that the work which I do best and to which I should like to give all the time and energy possible, must instead be done in spare-hours, with what energy is left after doing other and more lucrative work, and seldom except under a feeling of financial strain. This is not a complaint—it is merely a statement of fact. I know that if I could count on even a few free months out of a year, relieved from economic pressure and the necessity of writing hack short-stories for a living, I could do more work in my chosen field and of a better quality than I am doing now. And I feel, with some conviction, that the next few years may be of particular importance to me in the development of my craft, if it is to develop at all.

As for the projected work itself—I have three subjects for long poems under consideration, and have had for some time. All three would require labor, time and experimentation which it would be difficult for me to give under present conditions—and all three would need, besides, a certain leisure and freshness of mind which, at present, I doubt if I should be able to give at all. One is a long narrative poem on an American historical subject for which I have collected material over a considerable period— one a modern narrative laid in New York City—and one a somewhat erratic romance in a vein I have not tried before. I should also like to round out with four or five additional poems the series of American ballads begun in *Tiger Joy*. I have other projects in mind—but those are the most important. There is, in addition, for instance, a historical novel, to be called "The Singing Sword," the greater part of which is laid in Europe—and it would be of the greatest value to me to visit some of the places I wish to deal with—but doing so would not interrupt the main course of my work, once I felt free to pursue that work without having to think too constantly of a definite financial reward.

If awarded a scholarship, I should go to France to carry out my plans and probably live either in or near Paris, or in some small place in the provinces, depending on circumstance. I have lived in France before (1920–1921 and 1921–1922, returning to America for the summer of 1921)—I am familiar with the life—the atmosphere is congenial to me—and I know that I can work there under the most favorable conditions. My wife finished her education at the Government Ecole Normale at Sèvres, having received one of the French Government fellowships awarded by the Committee of Collegiate Alumnae (1919–1920), and we would not find the slightest difficulty in living abroad on a minimum amount of funds. The scale of living there, for Americans, with the present exchange on the dollar, would more than compensate for any actual diminution in income incurred by my giving up the greater part of my present hack-work, and I would be able to do what I want to do in comparative peace of mind. At the same time, living within reaching distance of Paris, I would be in touch with adequate facilities for any needed research and with those sources of artistic stimulation by contact with other arts than those of the writer which are of such service to any worker in the field of letters.

I cannot promise accomplishment—no writer with a degree of honesty can. I can promise work, and I think I can promise, with some definiteness, better work and a greater amount of it, under such conditions, than it seems likely I shall be able to produce without them. I should intend to finish at least one book of narrative poems at the end of the year—with, possibly, other work mapped out or in train—that is all that I can say. I realize that to do that, in the way I should wish to do it, would take more energy and harder labor than I have yet expended on any single object—but I should be more than grateful for the opportunity. My ultimate purpose in study, or, for that matter, in existence, is to attempt to write good poetry, and, given the opportunity, I shall do the best I can to further that purpose.

I should therefore like to apply for a fellowship on the John Simon Guggenheim Memorial Foundation for the one year period beginning January 1, 1926.

In case the above information does not fully cover the requirements of the questionnaire, I should be glad to furnish any additional information that may be necessary.

Very sincerely, STEPHEN VINCENT BENÉT

II

February 1st 1927   89 Avenue de Neuilly
                                     Neuilly-sur-Seine, Seine, France.

Dear Mr. Moe:—

I am taking the liberty of applying for a six months' renewal of my fellowship, should the Foundation see fit to grant it, and enclosing a preliminary report and a formal application herewith. The poem is getting along very well, but I've had to do such a lot of preliminary reading for it, among other things, that I won't be able to finish it in the time. I was hoping some private windfall would happen along, so I could finish it on my own funds, and so delayed, but nothing seems to be in sight, and I don't want to hold the poem back or break it off to write short stories if I can help it, which is what I'll have to do without luck or a renewal. This is a nice quiet place here, near the Bois which is good for the children, and with a separate room for me to work in. So all goes well in spite of the decline of the dollar.

With all best wishes
Sincerely, STEPHEN VINCENT BENÉT

III

February 1st, 1927   89 Avenue de Neuilly,
                                     Neuilly-sur-Seine, France

John Simon Guggenheim Memorial Foundation
Dear Sirs:—

I wish to submit my formal application for a six months' renewal of the John Simon Guggenheim Memorial Fellowship awarded me for 1926–1927, the renewal to run six months from July 15th 1927 when the present fellowship expires.

My reasons for wishing a renewal of this fellowship are stated in the attached preliminary report covering work already done to February 1st 1927.

Very sincerely, STEPHEN VINCENT BENÉT

IV   PRELIMINARY REPORT

Stephen Vincent Benét
89 Avenue de Neuilly,
Neuilly-sur-Seine,
Seine, France.

I reached France on August first. 1926, sailing from New York July 22nd, and went immediately to Paris. Until January first, 1927, I lived in Paris itself at 14 bis Rue Jadin, XVII. Since then I have been living at 89 Avenue de Neuilly, Neuilly, a ten minutes' walk from one of the gates of the city, and a place where I find working-conditions even more favorable than in the city itself.

My work has progressed favorably and in spite of the fall of the dollar in regard to the franc and the consequent rise in the price of living for Americans drawing their income in dollars, I find it possible for myself and my family to live perfectly comfortably for something like a half to two-thirds of what we were paying in New York. I have a separate room to work in—one of the servant's rooms at the top of the building—and the American Library has been most kind in helping me with the research I have had to do.

When I first applied for a Guggenheim fellowship, I stated in the plan submitted, that what I hoped to do was to complete in the given year at least one long poem or volume of poems, with such incidental work as might naturally arise.

I had, at that time, several projects for a long poem upon an American theme. One was to deal with De Soto, or to deal in general with some of the Spanish explorers, and the curious color and flare of the Spanish adventure in the New World. It was for that reason that I thought tentatively of going to Spain, and making certain historical researches there. But there were other projects—in particular a project for a long poem dealing with the Civil War, which I had then thought about for almost a year—and it is upon this last that I am working now.

As regards the poem itself. I have planned it in a prologue, eight books or sections, and an epilogue. The working-title I have for it at present is "The Horses of Anger," but I am not entirely satisfied with it and may change it before publication. Each section or book will run to between thirty and forty pages of typewritten manuscript. The prologue runs to five. There is an average of about fifty lines of verse to a page. The completed book should make between 280 and 300 pages of my manuscript or between 14,000 and 15,000 lines.

Except for the prologue and epilogue, the action of the poem is a continuous action, beginning shortly before the John Brown raid and ending shortly after the surrender at Appomattox. But, naturally, it does not follow history in the strict sense—that is to say I have not described and do not mean to describe every battle, every fluctuation of fortune, every event. I have spent a good deal of space on various men and incidents relatively unimportant to history and dealt scantly or not at all with others of greater text-book importance. That is to say—it is a poem, an attempt at an interpretation, not a history or a recital of events.

Concerning Children's Poems

Dear John [Farrar]:—

With the best will in the world, I cannot do very much for these.

Some of the ideas are interesting and one or two of them novel.
The two on the use of words, toward the end of the mss. for instance,
and the one about "crowds accumulate, armies unite" etc. which, if
well done would be a useful mnemonic rhyme. But the technique
throughout is so uniformally amateurish that the ideas don't get
through. It is as if the author lacked any ear for rhyme and meter.
"Mary Jones," for instance, starts out in one meter in the first verse.
The second verse is in an entirely different one and the last verse is
practically unscannable. And the same defects persist through most
of the verses. It's hard to find a really musical one in the lot.

Now the whole point about verse for children is that it should be
easy to remember because of its strongly marked beat. It should be
something a child can chant or sing, practically. It can be very simple.
God knows Mother Goose is simple. But all the famous Mother
Goose rhymes go to a very strong beat. You dam well can't mis-say
them—the beat is too strong—it's in the words. A Child's Garden of
Verses is simple. But simple as those verses are they were written by
an expert craftsman. And the Milne things are done by as expert a
writer of light verse, from the technical standpoint, as exists today.

The trouble with these is that the author simply hasn't learned his
craft. He is writing, apparently, without ear and without any real
knowledge of versification. He'll rhyme tedious and invidious, gew-
gaws and jack-straws etc etc and it doesn't seem to make any difference to him if one line is a foot too short and the next line two feet
too long. It's very curious to see anybody lack the feel and sense of
rhythm so completely.

Now versification, of course, is something that can be learned, as
playing a musical instrument can be learned. If you start without a
natural aptitude, of course you start under a handicap. Nevertheless,
as in all writing, practice is the thing. If the gent. really wants to write
verse, he ought to try grounding himself in the simplest regular
forms—see, for instance if he can write ten successive lines in heroic
couplet each one of which will scan properly—write a dozen limer-

icks and see that they're technically perfect—write 3 additional verses to "Bobby Shaftoe" and see they stick to the original meter and rhyme as they should. In other words, he'll have to do his five-finger exercises. He hasn't done 'em yet and this work shows it. Let him study the Bab Ballads or Lewis Carroll or anybody good, and see how neat and expert they are on the technical side.

I am sorry to turn in such a bad report on this but in all honesty I could do no other. It seems to me unpublishable as it stands.

As ever

FOREWORD TO MURIEL RUKEYSER'S
THEORY OF FLIGHT

Some people are born with their craft already in their hand, and, from her first book, Miss Rukeyser seems to be one of these. There is little of the uncertainty, the fumbling, the innocently direct imitation of admirations which one unconsciously associates with a first book of verse. It is, some of it, work in a method, but the method is handled maturely and the occasional uncertainties are rather from experimentation than any technical insufficiency. Moreover, there is a great deal of power—a remarkable power for twenty-one. I don't know quite what Miss Rukeyser will do with the future but she certainly will be a writer. It sticks out all over the book.

Politically, she is a Left Winger and a revolutionary. She speaks for her part of the generation born "in Prinzip's year" that found the world they grew up in too bitterly tainted by that year to accept.

> "We focus on our times, destroying you, fathers
> in the long ground—you have given strange birth
> to us who turn against you in our blood,"

she says in "The Blood Is Justified" and again

> "I do not say : Forgive, to my kindred dead,
> only : Understand my treason, See I betray you kissing,
> I overthrow your milestones weeping among your tombs."

I do not intend to add, in this preface, to the dreary and unreal discussion about unconscious fascists, conscious proletarians, and other figures of straw which has afflicted recent criticism with head noises and small specks in front of the eyes. But I will remark that when Miss Rukeyser speaks her politics—and she speaks with sincerity and fire—she does so like a poet, not like a slightly worn phonograph record, and she does so in poetic terms. For evidence, I offer the section "The Lynchings of Jesus" in the long poem "Theory of Flight"; the short "shot" of the coal-mine in the elegy for Ruth Lehman and the poem "The Blood Is Justified," among others. They are worth reading, to see what a young and talented person thinks of certain contemporary things—and how a poet of talent can make poetry out of them.

I use the word "shot" advisedly—for the mind behind these poems is an urban and a modern one. It has fed on the quick jerk of the news-reel, the hard lights in the sky, the long deserted night-street, the take-off of the plane from the ground. It knows nature as well—the look of landscape, the quietness of hills. But its experience has been largely an urban experience, and it is interesting to see the poetry of youth so based. When Miss Rukeyser thinks of energy, she thinks of a dynamo rather than a river, an electric spark rather than a trampling hoof—and that is interesting, too.

Perhaps that makes her verse sound like verse of the "Oh, Grandmother Dynamo, what great big wheels you have!" school—and that, most decidedly, it is not. Witness "Song for Dead Children," "Breathing Landscape," and the beautiful and original "Thousands of Days," with its serene and successful assonance. She can write powerfully; she can also write delicately, to a new and light-footed pattern. Her technique is sure, and is developing in original directions. Her long poem, "Theory of Flight," is a rather unusual achievement for a girl in her twenties. It has passages of confusion and journalistic passages, it also has passages that remind one of structural steel. There is a largeness of attempt about it which is one of the surest signs of genuine ability. Her later lyrics, particularly the ones I have mentioned, are more successfully and surely integrated. But only an original mind could have accomplished both.

Miss Rukeyser is twenty-one. She was born and brought up in New York City and has attended Vassar, the Columbia Summer School, and the Roosevelt School of the Air (the latter to gather material for "Theory of Flight"). At present, she is on the staff of "New Theatre." I think we may expect a good deal from her in the future. And it would seem to me that in this first book she displays an accomplishment which ranks her among the most interesting and individual of our younger poets.

FROM THE FOREWORD TO JOY DAVIDMAN, *LETTERS TO A COMRADE*, YALE UNIVERSITY PRESS, 1938:

If I have stressed Miss Davidman's social and contemporary poems, it is not because they are the only poems in the book. But a good many social and poems succeed in being merely social and contemporary. They have admirable intentions but no execution. But

Miss Davidman is able to say things so they stick in the mind. And in "Twentieth-Century Americanism"—to mention a single poem—she has done a very interesting thing. She has given the point of view of the city-bred toward America—the America that does not come from the grass-roots but from the long blocks of apartments under the electric light. (page 6)

FROM THE FOREWORD TO NORMAN ROSTEN, *RETURN AGAIN, TRAVELER*, YALE UNIVERSITY PRESS, 1940:

The American idea has been full of brag and self-depreciation ever since it first started. From "Yankee Doodle" to "Ballad for Americans" it has been able to believe in something and laugh at itself at the same time in a way that confuses educated visitors. "O 'er the hills in legions, boys!" and "I'm starving to death on my government claim" are two sides of the same silver dollar—if all of us had ever believed in one to the exclusion of the other, we would be a very different country. It is this double aspect of the American past and the American present—the lustiness and the mockery, the affirmation and the questioning—that forms the theme of Mr. Norman Rosten's *Return Again, Traveler.* (page 9)

FROM THE FOREWORD TO MARGARET WALKER, *FOR MY PEOPLE*, YALE UNIVERSITY PRESS, 1942:

Straight forwardness, directness, reality are good things to find in a young poet. It is rarer to find them combined with a controlled intensity of emotion and a language that, at times, even when it is most modern, has something of the surge of biblical poetry. And it is obvious that Miss Walker uses that language because it comes naturally to her and is part of her inheritance. A contemporary writer, living in a contemporary world, when she speaks of and for her people older voices are mixed with hers—the voices of Methodist forebears and preachers who preached the Word, the anonymous voices of many who lived and were forgotten and yet out of bondage and hope made a lasting music. Miss Walker is not merely a sounding board for these voices—I do not mean that. Nor do I mean that this is interesting and moving poetry because it was written by a Negro. It is too late in the day for that sort of meaningless patronage—and poetry must exist in its own right. These poems keep on talking to you after the book is shut because, out of deep feeling, Miss Walker has made living and passionate speech.

"We Have Been Believers," "Delta," "Southern Song," "For My People"—they are full of the rain and the sun that fall upon the faces and shoulders of her people, full of the bitter questioning and the answers not yet found, the pride and the disillusion and the reality. It is difficult for me to read these poems unmoved—I think it will be difficult for others. Yet it is not only the larger problems of her "playmates in the clay and dust" that interest Margaret Walker—she is interested in people wherever they are. In the second section of her book you will find ballads and portraits—figures of legend, like John Henry and Stagolee and the uncanny Molly Means—figures of realism like Poppa Chicken and Teacher and Gus, the Lineman, who couldn't die—figures "of Old Man River, round New Orleans, with her gumbo, rice, and good red beans." They are set for voice and the blues, they could be sung as easily as spoken. And, first and last, they are a part of our earth.

Miss Walker can write formal verse as well; she can write her own kind of sonnet. But, in whatever medium she is working, the note is true and unforced. There is a deep sincerity in all these poems—a sincerity at times disquieting. For this is what one American has found and seen—this is the song of her people, of her part of America. You cannot deny its honesty, you cannot deny its candor. And this is not far away or long ago—this is part of our nation, speaking.

I do not know what work Miss Walker will do in the future, though I should be very much surprised if this book were all she had to give. But I do know that, in this book, she has spoken of her people so that all may listen. I think that is something for any poet to have done. (pages 7–9)

Two Letters to Pauli Murray

215 East 68th Street
New York, N.Y.
October [25] 1939

Dear Miss Murray:—

Of course you didn't talk too much. You couldn't. I was in the room.

On the work you send me—"The Negro Worker Joins the CIO" is the better of the two pieces and the more developed. At least to me. From a purely technical point of view, I wouldn't mix free verse and rhyme—each ought to stand on its own feet. I mean, I think the four lines where you rhyme "bigger" and "nigger" would be better (a) if you put everything you had to say in rhyme or (b) if you took the rhyme out. It seems like a piece of another poem, with another beat, put in this one.

The sketch of your family, with the "rich Fitzgeralds" and "the poor Fitzgeralds," is perfectly fascinating material. It makes me wonder again, and not for the first time, why nobody has really tried to handle this sort of subject. As of course you know yourself, it's just material, in its present form. It is the nubbin, the germ from which a remarkable novel or a remarkable story might come. . . .

I don't know that you should try doing such a novel yet; you probably should practice more and write more first. Because that is the way—and the only way—with occasional criticism—that one learns writing. But this occurs to me—which might be good practice work. Take any one of the three sisters you mention and write 2500 words about her. Let's see the character, what she looks like, what she does, any little mannerisms, any ways of speech. Take your childhood's home or childhood's town—I think you said you were brought up in the South—write 2500 words about it and try to make it come alive—as Tom Wolfe makes Asheville come alive in his books. Take your first arrival in New York and write how it struck you. And make me (I'm using "me" for convenience, I mean the reader) see, hear, taste, feel, smell, be shocked or pleased, as you did and were shocked or pleased or both. There have been some rather good pieces in the *New Yorker* recently, about New York childhoods, from different points of view, by different people. Take a look at them, if they happen to come your way—see what details make the childhood seem vivid to you, what details don't. Try to see, think, hear, feel, reproduce as clearly and as intensely as possible.

It is a long road—it always is.

I don't know any short cuts—I don't know any easy way. But, if you are bound and determined to be a writer, you frequently get there. You are more fortunate than most of us in having, in your background, and your own life, a fascinating, rich mine of material. I am not fooling about that, or trying to be courteous. It is merely true. For all art comes out of life and out of human beings, and the richer, more varied the life and the human beings, the greater chance for the artist. . . .

Meanwhile I shall always be interested to see anything you send me.

With all good wishes,
Stephen Vincent Benét

TO PAULI MURRAY, IN ANSWER TO HER LETTER OF APRIL 17, 1940.
SVB'S LETTER UNDATED).

215 East 68th St.
Dear Miss Murray:—

You know that I'm always glad to see your work, and I think you're getting ahead with it. You seem to be—well, loosening up a little is the way I'd put it—writing with more fluency and more free-dom, with fewer places where the verse lets down with a bump, and with more individuality. It's a job to be done, like any job—it's a pro-fession to be learned, like any profession—it isn't learned in a month or a year—it takes time and practise. But it can be learned.

I'll make some criticisms, and, as you know, I make frank ones. First of all on the Spring Morning In North Carolina.

This is well observed—it is the material for a poem, rather than a poem itself. It is the material for a poem because you have put in something like 20 characteristic details of Spring, but you've put them in so they're all about the same size. The material isn't fused—there isn't any real progression toward a finale. The tomcat could fol-low the cardinals or the blue jay after the pear-leaves without much change in the verse. Now, in a great poem, let's say, that wouldn't be so. I see so many details here that I don't get a general picture—and yet a general picture is what I want. I want something that *is* Spring—the essence of North Carolina spring, too. What's the difference between a Southern Spring and a Northern Spring? Suppose you were doing a poem on Spring In Connecticut—what would be the essence that would make it different? Do you see what I mean? I don't mean this in harsh criticism—it is very valuable practise to write a description of something in front of your eyes, see how closely and truly you can come to it. But realism, by itself, isn't quite enough. Try it over, some time—try seeing, feeling, getting toward the way you feel about Spring in North Carolina, the way it's different from any other Spring, what makes it so. You can do it.

And incidentally, watch expressions like "Shy violets". There are certain words and expressions, "rosy-fingered dawn" "Swan of Avon" etc etc that were wonderful discoveries when they were first made. But by use and re-use they have become rubber stamps. When you're tempted to put one in—don't. I don't mean that you should deliberately go to the other extreme and allude to 'noisy violets' which wouldn't be true. But I want the violets as you see 'em—not as several hundred poets have seen 'em. The same applies to "The cheewinks carol a gladsome tune". Do they? But any bird does that. If you want to introduce the cheewinks—well, what does their song suggest to you that makes it different from any other song? On the other hand "The pear leaves shiver with delight" is good—I have seen leaves shiver, it brings up the scene. If you'd said "The pear tree is in beauty clad today" for instance—I wouldn't have seen anything—it would have just been general conversation.

I don't mean to make such an exhaustive criticism of a few small points. But I'm doing it because that sort of thing is a fault that beginning writers are apt to fall into in verse, to substitute a generalized vagueness for a real description.

"You Are the Earth" I like. "The Wanderer" I like, particularly "The Answer". It is good, it is moving, it has a sort of biblical feeling in it which is genuine and powerful. You have what, to me, is a bad metaphor in "The Question" where you say "Spring hides beneath my armpits". That is the reverse of the "shy violets" thing—an image so excessive that it isn't convincing. Because armpits, to most of us advertisement-conditioned people suggest smell. Can you have Spring hide somewhere else?

Now the prose piece. The material is swell. It moved me, shocked me and made me think of a particular problem I hadn't thought much of before—the Jim Crow bus thing. Which is what it was meant to do. But it has, as a piece of writing, certain faults.

You start well—I'm interested. You're a Southerner going back to the South—a Southerner who happens to be of a certain color. You tell why you like the South and why you hate it. Good, I'm all ready, as a reader, to go along with you on your journey.

Then on the first paragraph of page 2, you change from the direct I to "we". You give me some general information about the difficulties of Negroes in reserving front seats in busses. It's good information. But you have switched from the particular to the general, from one person, whom I know, to a lot of people. I want, as a reader, in my mind, to keep on seeing *you*—seeing you trying to reserve a front seat, being unable to do it, knowing from long experience that you will be unable to do it. I want, perhaps, a little dialog at the bus office—this friend of yours asking you "Can't we get front seats?"— you telling her from bitter experience why not. Because you are my pair of eyes that I see the scene through. And the situation must come out through what you see and hear, not through general statements.

Now in page 4, you have a very nice description of the country you're passing through—excellently done. You then introduce your friend. I've never seen her before. I didn't know she was with you. A single line might characterize the kind of person she is—get me interested in her—but you don't give it to me. She has a pain in her side but I don't know why, except for the jolting of the bus. I'd feel a lot more sympathetic about her if I knew what she was like. If I read in the paper that John Smith has died of pneumonia, I think 'Too bad' and forget it. If I read in the paper that a friend of mine has died of pneumonia, I feel shocked and sorry. It's the writer's business to get the reader interested in his characters—so the reader cares what happens to them.

The same applies to the other people in the bus. The whites sit silent with shame. That's interesting—that's a good point. But what do they look like, what kind of people are they? I've lived in the South—I can, by an effort of will, populate the bus, if I have to. But it's by an effort of will. Give me one or two people at least—what they look like—the kind of folks they are. The same applies to the other Negro occupants. When the police come in you say "the Negro passengers alternate between consoling us . . . and giving vent to their resentment through boisterous, hysterical remarks." All right— give me a couple of the remarks—let's hear them. Give me a line on the police. Show me the bus-driver's face. Let me see the people in the bus—oh—as you'd see em on the screen. Let me see their various reactions when this incident occurs. And keep to yourself as a pair of eyes. You're telling me a story—this happened to you. If you were telling it in conversation, you'd tell about some of the people. You wouldn't give page-length description of them but you'd tell enough about them so I could see them. Do it here—and, in this particular piece, don't switch too much between "I" and "we". "I" has to come first, Your experience is important because it's a typical experience. But I can only *see* its being typical through *you*.

Now all this isn't to say that it isn't an interesting piece as it stands. It is. But you can make it a dozen times more effective by working on it. I am also not quite sure of your last two sentences.

The point is—the effective point—the contrast between the Easter season and what has happened to you and your friend. It might be better writing just to leave it at that. I'm not sure. But it might. Because, if you make your point directly, and then proceed to editorialize about it—it often blurs the effect.

It seems to me, if you rewrote it, knit it together and reworked it, the kind of piece that a magazine like "The Atlantic" might possibly be interested in. I don't know. But it might be worth a try. "Common Sense" also sometimes runs good things—sometimes runs good verse, too. You might try some work on them. Use my name in any way you like with either magazine and say, if you want to, that you're doing it at my suggestion.

Now the actual writing of "Disorderly Conduct" is for the most part, good, direct and simple. It seems to me better, as writing, than the previous prose you showed me and I think you're improving. Keep up the good work. And, as you know, none of the criticisms I make are intended in a harsh or depreciatory spirit. They merely concern the technique of writing, that we all have to learn, that we spend our lives learning, that, even after long practice, we must still try to improve and improve—to see more clearly, hear more faithfully—if we wish to be writers at all. And you have so much to write about. You have such rich material, once you have learned to smelt it out of the ore. And I think you are learning.

With every good wish

Stephen Vincent Benét

If This Should Change

If this should change, remember the tree and the brook,
The long day's summer, the voices clever and kind,
The true verse that burned on the page of the book,
The true love, body and mind.

Remember the tulip in the pinched backyard
And how it asked for nothing except to grow
And that was enough to do. Remember the hard
Country earth, under snow.

All tastes of food and water, of salt and grass,
A bird flying, a cat asleep in the sun,
The hard-paved street where the faces pass and pass
And never get done.

Huge-flowing Mississippi, under full moon,
The giant landscape where the great rivers crawl
And the shabby apartment and the last year's tune,
Remember, remember all.

They all made something, from the wine drunk with friends
In gaiety, without care, without hurt or shame,
To the faces of the dead that a strangeness attends,
The same, not the same.

They all made something. They made eyes and ears,
A country, a time, work, all that is hard to say,
And behind them were many bodies and many years
And night and day.

There was the sight from sea of the straight-backed town
And the old graves, deep in the grass, where the grass is wet.
Though the wind blow and the stones of the walls fall down,
Remember, do not forget.

Though the sky crack and the heart crack under the sky,
There was all we knew. It is not to be finished yet.
There was good bread, well eaten, in company.
Remember, maintain, remember, never forget.

Not in the great inscriptions, but in the blood.
Not in the able words, but under the hat.
These things were freedom. That is why they were good.
Remember that.

FOR THE BEST IN PAPERBACKS, LOOK FOR THE

In every corner of the world, on every subject under the sun, Penguin represents quality and variety—the very best in publishing today.

For complete information about books available from Penguin—including Puffins, Penguin Classics, and Arkana—and how to order them, write to us at the appropriate address below. Please note that for copyright reasons the selection of books varies from country to country.

In the United Kingdom: Please write to *Dept. EP, Penguin Books Ltd, Bath Road, Harmondsworth, West Drayton, Middlesex UB7 0DA.*

In the United States: Please write to *Penguin Putnam Inc., P.O. Box 12289 Dept. B, Newark, New Jersey 07101-5289* or call 1-800-788-6262.

In Canada: Please write to *Penguin Books Canada Ltd, 10 Alcorn Avenue, Suite 300, Toronto, Ontario M4V 3B2.*

In Australia: Please write to *Penguin Books Australia Ltd, P.O. Box 257, Ringwood, Victoria 3134.*

In New Zealand: Please write to *Penguin Books (NZ) Ltd, Private Bag 102902, North Shore Mail Centre, Auckland 10.*

In India: Please write to *Penguin Books India Pvt Ltd, 11 Panchsheel Shopping Centre, Panchsheel Park, New Delhi 110 017.*

In the Netherlands: Please write to *Penguin Books Netherlands bv, Postbus 3507, NL-1001 AH Amsterdam.*

In Germany: Please write to *Penguin Books Deutschland GmbH, Metzlerstrasse 26, 60594 Frankfurt am Main.*

In Spain: Please write to *Penguin Books S. A., Bravo Murillo 19, 1° B, 28015 Madrid.*

In Italy: Please write to *Penguin Italia s.r.l., Via Benedetto Croce 2, 20094 Corsico, Milano.*

In France: Please write to *Penguin France, Le Carré Wilson, 62 rue Benjamin Baillaud, 31500 Toulouse.*

In Japan: Please write to *Penguin Books Japan Ltd, Kaneko Building, 2-3-25 Koraku, Bunkyo-Ku, Tokyo 112.*

In South Africa: Please write to *Penguin Books South Africa (Pty) Ltd, Private Bag X14, Parkview, 2122 Johannesburg.*